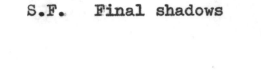

S.F.   Final shadows

Mynderse Library
31 Fall Street
Seneca Falls, NY 13148

Final Shadows

Final Shadows

Edited by
CHARLES L. GRANT

A FOUNDATION BOOK
DOUBLEDAY
New York   London   Toronto   Sydney   Auckland

A FOUNDATION BOOK
Published by Doubleday
a division of Bantam Doubleday Dell Publishing Group, Inc.
666 Fifth Avenue, New York, New York 10103

FOUNDATION, DOUBLEDAY, and the portrayal of the
letter F are trademarks of Doubleday, a division of
Bantam Doubleday Dell Publishing Group, Inc.

Library of Congress Cataloging-in-Publication Data

Final shadows/edited by Charles L. Grant.
    p. cm.
   "A Foundation book."
   1. Horror tales, American. 2. Horror tales, English. I. Grant,
Charles L.
PS648.H6F56 1991
813'.0873808—dc20 91-8274
CIP

ISBN 0-385-24732-x
ISBN 0-385-24646-3 (pbk.)
All Rights Reserved
Printed in the United States of America
September 1991
First Edition

ACKNOWLEDGMENTS

Final Shadows is dedicated, with a lifetime of love,
to Minerva Grant, who never lost her faith,
even when I tried her sorely

CONTENTS

Contents

Introduction

This is the final *Shadows*.

After a dozen years, it's time to pack it in.

The stories assembled here are no different from those in previous volumes: there are writers appearing in print for the first time, writers who have been in *Shadows* before, writers experimenting, writers manipulating the traditional, writers who only occasionally try a hand at Dark Fantasy. The only difference is, there are more of them this last time around. And at least half of them are from the U.K., writers whose idea of a *Shadows* story is often quite different from that of their North American counterparts.

In addition, the plan was, as I'd envisioned it some time ago, to use this final introduction to make some sort of closing statement about the field as it now stands; then to let the stories speak for themselves while

I just close the book and walk away; and finally, to remain objective about this whole business of putting to rest a series that has been, quite literally, my life for probably far too long.

But Dark Fantasy is out there anyway, and you can make your own judgments about where it's going, where it's been, and who its stars are and will be;

the stories, as always, will speak for themselves no matter what I say, and so don't, this time, look for introductions to each piece;

and as for remaining objective?

Impossible.

So I guess I really don't have a choice but just to close the book and walk away.

Sleep well.
Pleasant dreams.
This is the *Final Shadows*.

Charles L. Grant
Newton, N.J., 1990

The Boarder

A drop of vegetable soup lingered on the corner of her wrinkled lower lip, then found a crease alongside her mouth. A thin, greasy line formed as the drop followed the circuitous route to her chin, hung suspended for a moment, then dropped onto the imported silk dress she wore for the evening. "Dear, dear, *dear*. Where are my manners?" She dabbed at the dress with a linen napkin, smearing the soup even more, and threw up her arms helplessly.

Jack Sampson felt a flush of red color his cheeks at his inability to help. It didn't matter. Bridgett was out of the kitchen and by the old woman's side before he could have done anything anyway.

"It'll be fine, Mrs. Hatteras. Good as new." She dabbed the spot with a towel that appeared from under her apron, and cooed at the old lady. "I'll take a hand to it tonight while you sleep, and it'll be fresh as if from the store by tomorrow. Mark my words."

Jack doubted it. The dress must have been a good forty years old. Something pulled from a trunk with only a shadow of its previous finery. He fingered the linen napkin for something to do, dabbed at his own lips, and felt his index finger push through the frail material. Even the napkins were old. Past their point of usefulness, if anyone asked him. But these two didn't. And he would never voice his opinion. Not while he was living here. And certainly not on the first night of what he hoped would be a lengthy stay in the only accommodations that matched his wallet.

"Oh, Bridgett." The old woman burst into tears, choking out the words. "Where is he?"

Bridgett ran a slim hand through her graying hair and shot a quick look over toward Jack before returning her attention to the old woman.

"He hasn't been to dinner in so long, I've almost forgotten what he looks like," the old woman said. "It isn't like him not to call."

"He's just tied up in a meeting, Mrs. Hatteras. You know how absentminded he can be." Bridgett stroked the woman's hair, held her close. "Feeling a bit better? There now, you'll be fine."

The old woman sat bolt upright, straightened her lace collar. "The next course, Bridgett. And be quick about it. We have guests, you know."

"Yes, ma'am." Bridgett turned on her heel for the swinging door that led to the kitchen, and glanced back at Jack before she pushed through.

Mrs. Hatteras smiled at her young guest. The despair of minutes ago vanished as if an eraser had been taken to her face. She looked long and hard, seemed to relish the idea of a man at her table, and one uncomfortable with her overt stare at that.

He rubbed a hand over his stubbly face, and wished he had shaved before dinner, then immediately questioned the absurdity of his own thought. Clearly this was a woman who had once had means. Bridgett had implied that when he answered the ad for the room to rent. Somehow over the course of time, things changed. Became old, worn, in need of extensive repair.

He looked at the hole in his napkin, the wrinkled face that hid a broken mind.

Things had become frail. Tenuous.
Bridgett had implied that as well.

"Dinner is at eight—every night. You will be there unless I've been told in advance otherwise." The thin, wiry housekeeper had held herself like a coiled spring as she talked to him across the great kitchen table that morning. "The bedroom has a fireplace. There is some wood out back. Of course you will chop it yourself." There had been no offer of coffee. No smell of bread baking in the massive ovens. A large padlock protected the walk-in freezer from intruders looking for midnight snacks.

"The bathroom down the hall will be yours, and yours alone. I'll show it to you shortly. No women, Mr. Sampson. No visitors of any kind. Safety for Mrs. Hatteras, you understand." She paused as if to take a breath, took none. "The doors are locked. Every night. Inside and out. I alone have the keys. For Mrs. Hatteras's safety. I trust you know what I mean. And that's agreeable to you?"

"I have no women friends. Here anyway. And there is no family to keep tabs on—you know that from my letters inquiring about the house. You might say I'm trying to find myself, and looking for a little isolation to do it in. I dabble in writing mostly, a novel, that kind of thing. So I'm looking for a little quiet, some time to myself. But you know that too." He was explaining himself again. Always explaining, or was it excusing?

"We have plenty of that. Quiet. More of that than anything. Nothing else."

"You've been here a long time, haven't you?"

"I take care of Mrs. Hatteras, as she did for me once. That's all you need to know. One month's rent. Cash. In advance."

Jack reached for his wallet, then pulled the bills out one at a time. He knew she would count it for herself anyway. In the privacy of her kitchen. In her time. "I believe it's all there. It's about all I have right now. I can get more when it's time. You know, an odd job here and there." He looked up, saw that her eyes never left his.

"Dinner at eight. Every night. It's quite important to her. Dinnertime."

He paused, bills poised in his outstretched hand. When she made no move to take them, he let the stack drop neatly to the table and stood up. "The few things I own are on the steps out front. I can bring them in now?"

A barely discernible nod.

He turned to the kitchen door that led outside.

"Always the front door, Mr. Sampson. The back door is for Mr. Hatteras only. Mrs. Hatteras's wishes. I have the key. Dinner at eight, Mr. Sampson. Always at eight."

"So, young man . . . you are young, aren't you?" Mrs. Hatteras stared at him now across the hand-carved dining table laden with burning, handmade candles and bowls of half-eaten soup. "Young. Like Alford was. When we were young, of course. When we met. So young. So full of hope. Dreams. He was a handsome man, still is, of course. A little older, but handsome. Like you. I like handsome men." She leaned heavily into the table toward him. "I like you. Yes, I can see that now. I do like you." She looked down at her wrinkled hands, then back at him, mischief in her eye. "And you like me. No"—she raised a hand toward him—"you needn't say a thing. I can see it in your face." Her voice dropped as if imparting a secret. "Your face tells me everything I need to know. A handsome face, yours. Young. Like Alford."

"Alford is your husband?" Jack felt the strain in his own voice. Heard the pitch higher than it should have been, and the discomfort the sound carried. She didn't need to answer, he knew it for himself. Guessed who he was from the look on her face. A flicker of anger? Confusion?

The old woman shrieked, gentility in her face displaced by a sneer, teeth bared. "Bridgett. Where are you, you little fool? I have hungry guests and they will not wait another minute."

"Here, ma'am. By your side."

Jack jumped at the sight of the housekeeper appearing from the deep corner shadows of the dining room. How long had she been standing there? And how much of the bizarre conversation had she witnessed before she decided to intercede, and on whose behalf?

"Salad, dear?" she asked Mrs. Hatteras.

"Yes, Bridgett, I believe so. And some for my guest. Alford's friend."

"I'm not Alford's friend, Mrs. Hatteras. I've never laid eyes on him." He caught Bridgett's warning look, the brief question on Mrs. Hatteras's face. "Although I do hope to meet him one day. Maybe soon. Tonight?" He hoped so. Some semblance of sanity was needed at this table, in this house. And the sooner the better. Although it was becoming crystal clear why Alford would stay away in the first place, it was murky as to why he would return. The plate, barely sprinkled with lettuce and a hint of radish, was laid before him.

"Eat up, my dear. We always clean our plates in this house. Don't we, Bridgett?"

"Indeed we do, ma'am."

"Waste not, want not. That's what my Alford always says." She speared a lettuce leaf with her fork, then pointed it at Jack. "Alford was right, you know. Always right. Said to just ask him, he'd tell you himself." She laughed suddenly, uproariously, then dropped her fork onto the plate and knocked the plate to the floor. She held her sides then, as if the sheer act of merriment would split her in two.

Jack cringed at the sound, tried to block out the piercing sound that poured from the woman at the head of the table and filled every corner of the room.

The raucous laughter stopped as suddenly as it started.

"Clean up this mess, Bridgett. And be quick about it. I wouldn't want Alford's friend to think we live like animals. You don't think that, do you? Of course you don't." The tone in her voice changed to one of accusation. "But then you wouldn't say it if you did, would you?"

"Look." Jack dropped his napkin down by the side of the uneaten salad, and pushed his chair back. He cleared his throat, felt his mouth dry to dust. "I don't know what's going on here, but . . . well, I . . . I think I've lost my appetite. Excuse me."

Bridgett moved around the table from her mistress to Jack's side, placed a firm hand on his shoulder, and replaced the napkin in his lap. "You haven't finished your dinner yet, Mr. Sampson. It isn't polite to leave before coffee is served."

Mrs. Hatteras clasped her hands together repeating the phrase in a childlike singsong. "It isn't polite to leave—it isn't polite to leave—it isn't polite to leave."

Bridgett took the opportunity to whisper in Jack's ear. "Please. She has little else. No friends come around anymore. There is no family. She has barely enough money to keep the house. You get used to it after a while. It's not so bad, really. Not so bad."

"What about her husband, Alford? He's family. He'll be here soon, won't he? Surely that will help."

"Soon enough, Mr. Sampson. Eat your salad."

"It isn't polite to leave." Mrs. Hatteras yawned, then closed her eyes. Her head fell back and her mouth opened in sudden sleep.

"There, Mr. Sampson. You see. She's quiet. Sleeping like a baby. I'll bring you your dinner now." Bridgett patted the sleeping woman on the shoulder as she passed and slipped into the kitchen.

"Here, first room on the right," Bridgett had said. "Your room overlooks the garden. The bathroom is there, down the hall."

Jack had dropped his one bag on the floor, opened the solid door to the bedroom, and stepped in. The room was expansive. A double bed by most standards, but smaller, revealing its age. Matching heavy drapes covered the wide windows and surrounded the headboard. A faded Oriental rug covered the hardwood floor in front of the spotlessly clean fireplace. He smiled at the small desk near the window. A perfect place to get a little writing done, and stare out at the garden for occasional distractions. He walked across the room for a closer look at his workplace, rubbed a hand over the fine grain of the wood, and decided it was just right. Typewriter here, pencils and pens here, paper over there—he glanced out the window and stopped. The garden was an unkempt disaster of weeds and overgrown vines. It had been years since a hand had pruned the shrubs or fertilized the roses. Maybe decades.

He turned back to the room in disappointment, and stared at the walls holding grim-faced portraits of unidentified people that seemed to focus on him from any point in the room. "Relatives of Mrs. Hatteras?" He looked to the doorway for an answer, found it empty, and turned his attention back to the pictures. He wondered if Mrs. Hatteras carried any of their mirthless traits, and hoped not. There would be little time for coffee and small talk if he launched himself as fully into his work as he planned. Still, it would be nice to know that the owner of the house had a sense of humor, if not a green thumb. Wherever she was. He had only seen the housekeeper, heard only the sounds of their footsteps walking up the wide, marred staircase to the first room on the right. He had noticed little else to fill him in on the mystery of the unseen owner, or the reason for the house being in this state. Or, he realized suddenly, what occupied all the rooms in the hallway behind closed doors. Maybe other transients, like himself? The thought seemed hopeful, almost wishful.

He turned the flat switch to the bedside lamp. A weak, yellow glow barely filled the corner of the room. He spied something sticking out from under the bed and nudged it with his foot. An ashtray, three cigarettes smoked to inch-long butts. He reached down for the ashtray, and brought it to his nose for a quick sniff. Stale smoke mingled with a more recent smell. One cigarette, at least, had been smoked in the past day or two.

"There. At the end of the hall." Jack jumped at her voice. "The open door. It's the bathroom, Mr. Sampson. Towels in the closet. Hot water only in the morning."

He brushed his hand through his hair, took a breath. "You startled me. You shouldn't scare people like that," he said, pointing a finger at her in mock disapproval.

Her eyes stayed as empty of emotion as her voice. "You will not be disturbed by me or anyone else, Mr. Sampson."

"I was just joking." Her face remained unchanged. "And I take showers in the morning, so no problem with the water. By the way, is there anyone else staying here? Any other boarders like myself?"

"No one."

"Not anyone? Even lately?"

"No. Only you. You wanted 'space,' I believe your letter said. 'An out of the way place.' "

"Yes. But I haven't even met my hostess yet. Seems like she'd want to know who was staying in her house."

"She knows. I've told her we have a guest. She'll meet you at dinner."

"Can I see her now? Maybe talk a bit?"

"There's no need, Mr. Sampson. I run the house. The way she wants me to. The way I always have. You'll meet her soon enough." Bridgett backed away, to leave him alone, he knew.

"It seems odd, that's all."

She stopped at the comment. "Mr. Sampson." He turned to her at the tone in her voice. "Mrs. Hatteras is not completely well. Age has played tricks with her mind. There are moments when she is quite lucid, but other times . . ."

He felt the hair rise on his neck, his back stiffen at her words. "Why are you telling me this now? You should have mentioned something earlier."

"She's really quite harmless, I assure you. But she's lonely, living for the day when the house will be filled with guests, as it once was. Now we take the few that come here for its isolation, its quiet. Like you."

"What else haven't you told me?"

"That's all you need to know. There is nothing else. Eight, Mr. Sampson. The main dining room." She left without looking back, no sound from her footsteps on the wood floors.

He rubbed some warmth into his arms, wondered if it was the chill of the room or of the odd housekeeper. Still, this place, for the most part, was just what he was after. For a little while anyway. And he was getting hungry. He glanced at his watch, saw that he had time to write a bit, and get settled before dinner.

A bowl of meat and vegetables, a stew of some kind, was laid before him. He tried a half smile at Bridgett for the offering, but knew it was unsuccessful. She carefully slid a second bowl from the heavy serving tray in front of the sleeping Mrs. Hatteras, and walked back into the shadows of the room to wait.

He pushed a large chunk of potato around the bowl, watched it disappear and reappear from the murky depths of the gravy, and turned his attention to the carrot. A minuscule amount of meat followed in their eddies. Things were tough for them, harder than he had realized. The small portions, the admonitions to eat everything on the plate, all of it was a means of preserving what once was, even when there was little left. Preserving to a point of guarding, at least on Bridgett's part. And just what was Bridgett guarding? A crazy old woman? A house that was better left to a historical society? Or was there more? No, some questions were better left unasked. He was here to get some work done, not pry into the sad lives of two aging women and one as yet mythical man. Still, it was nice to know that his stay would help them out somehow. That it was a little money in their empty pockets, a bit of company in a lonely house. That maybe he could mean something to someone. He stole a glance at the head of the table. If only the old woman wasn't so odd, if only she didn't take so many twists in and out of lucidity. He would never get used to her, but maybe he could learn tolerance.

Mrs. Hatteras coughed, rolled her head, and sat up fixing him with a solid stare and a toothy smile. "There you are. I knew you'd come back." She looked back over her shoulder into the dark shadows of the housekeeper's corner, and waved. "Bridgett. Alford has finally arrived. Bring him his dinner, will you? Oh, I see that he has it. Eat up, my dear. You must keep your strength. There are things to do. Guests arriving."

Jack dropped his fork into the bowl, sending droplets of gravy across the tablecloth.

"Why, Alford. Where are your manners, my dear? Bridgett, do something."

"Yes, ma'am." Bridgett appeared at his side, tray underarm, dabbed at the tablecloth, then wrapped his hand around the fork as if he were incapable of doing it by himself. She forced his hand to push the tines into a carrot, and brought the vegetable to his mouth.

"What are you doing?" He wrenched his hand free from hers, and slammed the fork and carrot down onto the table. "I am not an invalid, and further, I'm not Alford. Enough is enough." He glared at Bridgett.

"Bridgett. It's happening again. And I thought he would be better after the stay. They said he would. The doctors promised." Mrs. Hatteras covered her face with her hands and peered out between spread fingers.

"He'll be fine. You'll see. Won't you now?"

"I will not be fine. Geez, what am I saying?" He scraped his chair back, and stood. "Look. "Let's just call it a mistake all around. I'll just get my things and be heading out."

Mrs. Hatteras screamed. "Stop him, Bridgett. Don't let him go."

"He's not going anywhere."

Jack stopped midstride as if hit. He turned to Bridgett, saw cold anger in her eyes, her jaw set in grim determination. Terror gripped his middle at the sight of her, the realization. His spine turned to icy steel, froze him in place.

Bridgett's voice was calm, hard. "He won't leave me again. Not this time. Not ever." She pulled the heavy tray out from under her arm, took a step toward him.

Mrs. Hatteras screamed. "Don't let him go." She kicked out from under the table and brought him to his knees with the unexpected blow. Bridgett was on him then, slamming the tray into the side of his head. Once, twice, three times until he lay on the floor, staring at them with glazed eyes.

"No," he mumbled. Spittle accumulated at the corner of his mouth, stretched in a sticky stream to the floor. He tried to pull his lips together, but felt his thickened tongue in the way. Their conversation seemed distant, as if whispered through a tunnel.

"You killed him, didn't you?" Mrs. Hatteras said. "It was his temper again. Always his temper." A pointed shoe nudged him in the ribs. He smelled oily polish. "A nasty man. Always was. I could see it in his eyes."

"Shut up." The housekeeper leaned in close—he felt her breath hot on his cheek. "He's not dead. Just dazed."

"Make it quick this time, Bridgett. I hate to see him suffer. Although he deserves it."

"More than deserves it. He left us once, but not again." She paused as if a sudden thought had struck, a plan forming. "At least not for a while. I'll take care of him. You'll see."

"Like you've done before?"

A glimmer in her eyes. An eyebrow barely raised. "Eventually."

"What if he tries to leave? What if—?"

"Enough from you, old woman. I've taken care of you, haven't I? Made sure you've had clean clothes, enough to eat." Jack tried to raise his head. His vision blurred. He strained, focused on Bridgett hoisting him up from under his arms, saw his vision blur again. The housekeeper grunted with the effort, then pulled. A tug, a drag of his dead weight back into the chair with a strength disguised by her frame. "He'll keep for a while. For you, then for both of us. Until something else comes along."

Jack squinted with pain, twisted weakly in her grasp, and felt a thick stream of sticky liquid roll down the side of his face and into his open mouth. His head lolled to one side. A holiday tablecloth was wrapped two, then three times around his chest and pulled tight, forcing him to sit up in the chair. He heard their words echo dully in his mind as breath was squeezed from his bound chest.

"Alford dear, you always did like that particular tablecloth the best. It's so . . . festive. Isn't it Bridgett? Bright and colorful." She grabbed his hands that lay useless in his lap, gripped them as if with a vise.

He felt a dull pressure at her touch and looked at the source. Arthritic joints swollen and red, clasped tightly around young fingers fully fleshed, a hint of uneven edges from a boyhood nail-biting habit. Fragments of thought clustered and scattered away. His vision clouded, played tricks. Something . . . he squinted, blinked, looked closer . . . something . . . no. He gasped, felt the material bind with the effort.

Hands. Her hands. Arthritic joints swollen and red, clasped tightly around fingers perfectly manicured in wrinkled old-man skin.

His hands.

"We have so much to talk about, Alford. So many, many things."

"Now clean your plates. Both of you." Bridgett pushed the bowl toward him. "We don't waste anything here. Nothing."

The cigarette, recently smoked. Someone had been in the house, had stayed for a shorter visit than planned. Had dinner.

The locked freezer.

"Yes, Bridgett. As you wish. Waste not, want not. Right, Alford? That's what you always said. That's what he always says, Bridgett." The old woman released his hands, resumed her place at the head of the table and giggled in total delight. Merriment turned to immediate distrust. "He has a mean temper, you know."

"I know."

"But he's back where he belongs. With me. Forever with me."

Bridgett tucked the silver tray under her arm, stroked his hair out of his eyes. "For now."

It wasn't the money they wanted, it was something more. And when he wasn't needed for the company . . . His eyes widened in disbelief, shock He mouthed soundless words, pleading. A silent scream filled with sticky wetness.

He saw Bridgett then. Saw her look through him with years' worth of anger and a shattered mind. But her vision was clear now, as it had been how many times? And through how many visits by strangers, at least at first?

She shifted her weight against him, propped him up a little farther in the chair, and smiled. "Coffee?"

STEPHEN GALLAGHER

Magpie

Mr. McClure looked us over from the head of the classroom and said, "Who's running in the school cross-country on Wednesday? Let's have some hands in the air, here."

Let me tell you the worst thing about being a fat kid.

It has nothing to do with how you feel or how you look in the mirror; you feel okay and you see exactly what you want to see, so no problems there. The worst of it lies in those little incidents and throwaway remarks that stick in your memory and become an unwelcome part of your life for good. Real pieces of nothing, like a breezy *Hello, fatty* from the last Irishman in a passing road gang, forgotten by him a few strides later, for me a memory that rattles down a quarter of a century like a coin in a bottomless tin cup. Or the time that the French teacher got three of us standing in class to demonstrate the meanings of *petit, grand* and *gros*—and guess who got the ear-burning worst of *that* shabby little sequence.

Because the picture that I carried around in my head wasn't the same as the one the rest of the world seemed to see, I'd fall for trouble every time. So there we were one day, about thirty-five of us in Latin class, and Mr. McClure the Latin teacher was asking us which of the boys were going to be running in the school's annual cross-country race. This was a once-a-year three-mile slog across the local golf course and along muddy woodland tracks, and I had about as much chance of making it around the circuit as I had of levitating.

The girls nudged each other and all sixteen of the boys stared back with a kind of bovine stupidity, and so he changed his tack and asked who *wouldn't* be running.

And me, like a fool, I stuck my hand up.

He asked me why not and I told him that I had a dentist's appointment, and everybody roared. I sat there bewildered, because it happened to be true. The loudest of the barnyard sounds come from Colin Kelly and his cronies at the back of the room where they regularly shoved their four desks together and whiled away the hours defacing things. I suppose you'd have called Kelly the form's athlete; he had a collection of those little gilt cups and medals that the school bought cheaply out of a catalogue and handed out once a year on sports day. He was long-limbed and bony and he could dodge like a mongoose; and as far as the contents of his head were concerned, analysis would probably have yielded a teaspoonful of brains and a cupful of snot and a smattering of earwax, end of story.

McClure walked down the room toward them, and as they hushed and looked sheepish I could feel the heat moving away from me. McClure said, "What's the matter with you, Kelly?" and Kelly, surreptitiously trying to cover his exercise book with his elbow, said, "Nothing, sir."

"Are you running tomorrow?"

"Yes, sir."

"Don't mumble, Kelly."

"*Yes*, sir."

"Think you might win?"

"Yes, sir."

To be honest, this wasn't necessarily vanity on Kelly's part. He was probably fast enough to run on water without getting wet. McClure moved around to stand behind him and Kelly, beginning to sweat a little, fiddled with his pen as if trying to make out that he hadn't been using it for anything at all.

McClure said, "I know you've been training. What about the school record?"

"I'll get it easy," Kelly said.

"The word is *easily*, Kelly," McClure said, and he reached down and yanked the ineptly hidden exercise book by its protruding corner from under Kelly's forearm. Kelly's elbow hit the woodwork with a loud clunk and McClure said to the class in general, "Does anybody here doubt Kelly's chances?"

Not a hand went up. McClure held the book in front of him to study the result of Kelly's efforts; knowing Kelly, it was probably something obscene. "So we all know that Kelly can run," he said. "And we all know that Thomas can draw and tell stories, and that Kelly couldn't wield a pen to save his life." And then there was more laughter as McClure tore the page from the book before walloping Kelly over the head with it and dropping it back onto the desk before him.

He screwed up the page and put it into the pocket of his tweed jacket as he moved back up the room at that slow, patroling pace known only to schoolteachers and drill sergeants.

"We've all got something we're good at," he said. "It's putting the same kind of effort into everything else that's the real test of character. Wouldn't you say so, Kelly?"

"Yes, sir," Kelly mumbled, in a tone that was both dull and dark. I looked back and he was staring down at the desk with a face that looked like a sky just before a really bad rain.

As he drew level with me, McClure stopped and lowered his voice. "Who's your dentist, Thomas?" he said. "Is it Norman Hope?"

I said that it was. Norman Hope was an old boy of the school with a surgery in one of the big old houses at the head of the golf course. He picked up most of his custom among the kids and couldn't even see a tooth without drilling and filling it. He was cheerful and friendly and milking the system for all it was worth.

"I'll phone him for you this afternoon," McClure said.

"Thank you, sir," I said hollowly.

The lesson went on. But I was too miserable to take much of anything in.

I suppose that McClure must have been one of the old-school generation who believed in all that stuff about sport being some kind of metaphor for life. He'd been decorated in the war and he'd taught for more than twenty years, so you'd think he'd have known better. It was tough enough being a kid at the best of times, without having to fall victim to someone else's philosophy; but he was decent enough in his way, and in that country of memory where I so often go stalking with machine gun and machete he tends to die less lingeringly than most.

The prospect of having to put on the kit and run was making my heart sink like a stone into deep, dark water. But even then an alternative strategy was starting to shape up in the back of my mind, and it wasn't the biggest of my worries; that was reserved for Colin Kelly, a more immediate and less predictable concern. McClure had done me no favors by using my name to bring him down a peg or so; Kelly wasn't likely to take it with good grace. He could move like a cat, but he had the mental acuity of a paperweight. You don't ask the Colin Kellys of this world to take a broad view of anything. You just throw in their bananas and slam the cage door, fast.

The lesson dragged on, the incident apparently forgotten.

The four of them were waiting for me when school let out for the afternoon.

"Well, fuck me," Kelly said. "It's Thomas the Tank Engine."

I stopped in my tracks, mostly because three of them had spread to block my way and I could hear the fourth moving around behind me.

"Yeah," I said pleasantly, and with a confidence that I didn't feel. "Just steaming back to the old engine shed."

I'd emerged from the asphalt yard into the street only seconds before. Why couldn't I have taken another exit, just for today? Behind me was the main building of one of the last of the old-style grammar schools, a redbrick structure of motheaten charm with a gaggle of prefabricated overspill classrooms gathered around her skirts like bastard children. There had to be about twenty different ways in and out of the site; about five of these were official, the rest would have been impossible to cover.

But it was the end of the day. There was a hint of thunder in the air. I was toting along the great overstuffed briefcase that I always carried, everything that I could possibly need in one place because I could never rely on my memory to turn up with the right books for the right classes. And I was no great planner of battles, just an averagely bright kid who read a lot and didn't move around much and whose physique nature had adjusted accordingly. All I'd had in mind was getting home.

Kelly made a kind of frowning squint at my remark and said, "You being funny?"

"You started it," I said.

"He thinks I was joking," he said to the others, and they made a noise like a chorus of cows. Damned if I can remember much about any of them today; their names and something about the way that one or two of them may have looked, but that's about all. They were just the crud that stuck around Kelly.

As they lowed and snickered, Kelly said to me, "You want to try watching yourself sometime."

"For what?"

"Fucking entertainment, that's for what. You know what you are, don't you? You're a queer. You know what a queer is?"

"No," I said.

Apparently neither did Kelly for sure, because all he could say was, "It's what you are. Get his bag, Richard."

The one from behind me had a hold on my briefcase before I could get it up to hug it protectively to my chest, and he dug his nails into the flesh of my fingers to make me let go of the handle. We were right out in the middle of a dead-end street, but I knew better than to hope for any help from behind the windows of the houses.

Just kids playing. Ignore them, they'll go away.

They tossed my bag from one to another and I made a few half-hearted lunges to get it back but I knew that I was wasting my time and in the end I just watched them, resigned, until they began to get bored. I knew how it would go, I'd been here before.

"It weighs a ton," Richard complained, so then they stopped and Kelly opened it up to take a look inside.

"No wonder," he said. "Look at all the crap in here."

What they were doing now was terrifically personal to me, and they knew it. When Kelly turned my bag upside down and emptied everything out onto the ground, that sudden shower of trinkets and books that flapped like birds was like the slamming of a door on some inner happiness. Nothing from the bag would ever be quite the same for me again.

He looked down at where my felt-tip pens had scattered. It was a bundle of about two dozen of them, a range of colours brighter than any rainbow, and the bundle had split so that they lay in a heap like a half-finished skyscraper at the end of a Godzilla movie.

"Thinks he can draw," Kelly said, and he hawked up snot with a sound like Norman Hope's suction tube; and then he spat right into the middle of the tangle of pens, and it landed in a slug with a sound like a chunk of meat propelled from a catapult.

"Draw with that," he said.

The others followed suit. One of them, a plug-ugly kid called Doug, managed to spit down his chin and onto his own trousers.

When they'd gone I picked up all of the books, but I left the pens where they were. It didn't much matter, they were cheap and I had others.

But they were the ones that I'd always remember.

That night, around seven, Keith came over to my house.

We'd fixed this the day before. Keith was another of the regular gang of freaks who could be found shivering in their games kit around the goalmouth while the real play was all taking place downfield during the football season. His aversion to the track was as powerful as my own, and he'd asked me for some specialized help. He was short and skinny and pigeon-chested, and when stripped for the showers he looked like a long-legged duck. He was so nervous when he said hello to my mother that I had to bundle him upstairs before he could give the game away.

Keith said he was impressed by my bedroom, so he passed the test. This was my true home, the one place where the person that I was and the person that I wanted to be were merged into one. I had my drawings on the walls, my model aircraft suspended from the ceiling on cotton lines so that you could half close your eyes and imagine them in flight, my stacks of Sexton Blake and Tarzan paperbacks from the local market bookstall (where, in truly philistine manner, they clipped off the corners of the covers to mark a new price in the space; I'd spend hours with card and watercolors restoring the copies that I'd rescued), an old Dansette record player under the bed with a stack of well-worn ex-jukebox singles and only one middle between all of them, some much-prized copies of *Famous Monsters of Filmland*, which made me hunger for a film called *Metropolis* that I'd never even seen, more models, more books . . .

And, in what to the untrained eye would look like a disorganized mess on the chipped blue desk, my stories.

Keith said, "I brought some paper."

"What about the handwriting?"

"This is all I could get."

It was a note to the milkman, hastily written on a sheet torn from a cheap lined pad. Keith's mother's writing had the look of the hand of someone faintly retarded. Keith said, "Will it be enough?" and I said, "It'll have to do."

So then I settled down with a pad of Basildon Bond and the *Family Book of Health* for reference, and started to compose. Keith peered over my shoulder for a while, but then his interest started to wane. I hadn't minded him watching just as long as he didn't start making suggestions, but now he wandered off and looked out of the window.

"It's starting to rain," he said.

I didn't say anything. I wasn't the one who was going to have to walk home in it later.

"If it rains tomorrow," Keith said, "they'll have to call off the run."

"Don't bet on it," I said.

The signature was the easiest part. You wouldn't think so, but it was. I'd worked out a technique which involved placing the two sheets against the shade of my bedside lamp and making a rough trace of the original lines in pencil. With this as a guide it was simple to do a quick, straightforward signature in ink, and then remove the pencil lines with a soft eraser when the ink was completely dry. The final forgery wasn't going to be exact, because I'd felt it necessary to tidy up the original a little—what schoolteacher was going to believe in the authenticity of a note from a woman who couldn't even spell the days of the week? But the overall effect was just about right.

Keith had discovered the stories by now.

"Don't mess them up," I warned him. This was a time when I'd already laid down my belief that there was a special circle in hell reserved for the abusers of books, somewhere midway between the cat poisoners and the child molesters. Keith said that he wouldn't and then sat there hamfistedly turning the pages, and I winced every time like I'd just taken a slap on a bad sunburn. The second note, which would be my own, took me almost twice as long as the first because of this.

As I was finishing, he held up the pages stapled to imitate a magazine and said, "What's this one about?"

"You just read it, didn't you?"

"I was only looking at the pictures."

I went over and took it from him, and began to turn the pages with rather more care. "It's about a man who loses his dog and goes to the dogs' home looking for it. When he gets there he finds they've sold it to this professor who's used it in experiments, so he goes to the professor's house and kidnaps one of his children and does all the same things to it, so when the professor finds out the next morning he goes mad."

Great, subtle stuff. I paused at my favourite page in the entire story, the one showing the professor tearing his hair out at the city dump as he confronted a great mountain of trash bags from the medical school that were just in the process of going under the bulldozer. Most of the bags had split and there were dead dogs and monkeys hanging out, and from somewhere in the middle of the charnel heap a plaintive voice was crying *Dad-ee! Dad-ee!* in a shivery-edged balloon.

"What's happening in this bit, here?" Keith said as I turned to the next page, and I said, "That's afterwards. The dog comes back."

"Isn't it dead?"

"No, it was all a mistake. It was another dog that looked just the same."

Keith made a sick-face, and shuddered. He'd actually gone a shade paler.

"Got any more like that one?" he said.

So I took him through some of the others, me curious to see if I could scare him enough to make him ask me to stop, and him grappling with his awe as if he'd found some streak of the spirit that he'd never even sensed before. I showed him the one about the solitary morgue attendant getting drunk on New Year's Eve as all the lonely suicides were brought in, and his reaction at midnight when they all rose up and started to party. I showed him the one about the slaughterhouse worker who built up such a terrific charge of bad karma during working hours that disasters happened to everyone around him as he unwittingly discharged it like static, but this one wasn't too effective—Keith didn't understand the concept of karma and, to be honest, I was a little shaky on its details myself. So then I showed him the one about a man who set a trap for a rat and instead caught some miniature, blind armadillolike creature that bit him as he released it, and who started to pee tiny worms the next morning.

"Yuk," Keith said, and crossed his legs and squirmed.

And then I showed him the one called "Magpie."

This was my magnum opus. It concerned a man who trapped eight magpies and kept them in a cage in his darkened attic so they'd make his wishes come true in accordance with the old children's chanted rhyme that began *One for sorrow, Two for joy* and went on up to *Eight for a wish.* The story turned on the fact that he was cruel and neglected them, so that his wishes came true but all went bad in the end. Finally he repented of his wicked ways and returned to the attic for one last wish that would get him out of the big trouble that he'd brought upon himself, only to find that seven of the birds had starved to death and that only one—one, for sorrow—remained alive. And then there was this heavy knock on the attic door . . .

Keith didn't get this one, either. He said he'd never heard the rhyme, which I could hardly believe, and then he started arguing that it wasn't eight for a wish anyway, which was a pretty difficult line to pursue in view of what he'd just told me, and in the end it came down to me demanding, "Who's telling this story?" And then finally it was time for Keith to go home, and I was so peeved at him I almost didn't hand over the note that I'd done for him.

Afterwards, when it was a couple of hours later and I was on my way to bed, I took another look at the note that I'd drafted for myself. It read *Please excuse William Thomas from the cross-country run as he has a touch of sciatica,* and it was signed—although she'd never know it —by my mother. It was a less certain strategy than the dental appointment ploy and slightly compromised in that I'd already promised something similar for Keith when my other plan had fallen through, but still it looked pretty good to me.

I opened my wardrobe door and cleared back the shirts on the rail. "Magpie."

I put the note in the chalk circle on the floor of the wardrobe. Pinned to the back boards, in a line, were eight identical bird pictures. I touched each in turn, and then I touched the note, and then I closed the door.

Eight, for a wish. Did I dare to wish for something bad to happen to Colin Kelly? Did I have that much of a nerve?

I already knew the answer to that one.

But the note came first. I'd leave it in there until morning, and then I'd present it without the slightest doubt that it would be accepted and believed. Keith would just have to take his chances. I'd done something different for him, of course . . . different paper, a different wording, and a different disease from the *Family Book of Health.*

I didn't know what leukemia was, exactly, but something so tough to spell ought surely to be enough to keep a kid out of games for a week.

Wilson, the gym teacher, read the notes and made no comment. I took this as a tribute to my skill instead of seeing the truth of the situation—that to Wilson we were flyspecks almost beneath notice, and that whereas under normal circumstances he'd simply have bawled us out and sent us to get our kit and given us some added humiliation as a penance for our effrontery, today he had more important things on his mind. He was a hatchet-faced Scot, always in a tracksuit and a hurry, and the gym-teacher god had seen fit to eliminate every trace of humor and sense of justice from his nature. He spent nearly all of his time and energy on those kids who needed him least, and maybe they saw a different aspect of him. All I know is that he made kids like me feel like human ballast.

He told us that we were going to be race marshals, which I thought sounded great. The reality of it would be that we'd have to stand at some cold, wet spot in the woods where the track turned, waving the runners through and noting their names and times. But what the hell, it would be better than having to be one of them.

He kept us hanging around the tackle room for half an hour before giving us flags and a clipboard to carry and leading us out to the distant spot on the circuit where we'd have to stand. There was no conversation as Keith and I trooped in his wake toward the golf course. He didn't even look back at us, apart from when we were crossing the road. Without him along it would have been perfect because the school world seemed to fade out behind us as we pressed on into this different territory of birdsong and tree shadows and wide acres of grass just the other side of the pathway rail. The day was clear and cold. Rain had continued through the night, becoming so hard and fierce around one in the morning that it had sounded as if the roof above my bedroom had been stretched like a drumskin, but by dawn it had stopped to leave the sky washed out and clean.

Walking was no problem for me. I could walk forever. But on that circuit or anywhere else, I could run maybe two hundred yards before slowing to a plod like a gyroscope with a busted wheel.

"You'll wait here," Wilson said. We'd followed a muddy track, rutted and stony, that had led us to a spot in the woods where a stile marked the point where the pathway and the dirt track separated.

Digging in the pocket of his tracksuit pants he said, "If anyone's not certain of the way, you wave them on over the stile. You don't leave until I come back and say you can go. Do you hear?"

We said we heard.

"You note the name and the time of every boy who goes through. You note them in these columns on this page, and I want to be able to read every one of them. Do you understand?"

We said we understood.

He'd taken out a small felt bag, from which he took what I'll always think of as an old man's watch. "This comes back to me in perfect condition. Anything happens to it and I guarantee, your feet will not touch the ground."

By which I took it to mean that he'd probably knock us around so badly that we'd have to be carted home in a wheelbarrow. I looked at the watch and saw that it was a cheap Timex, probably cheaper than the one I'd been given for Christmas and that I was wearing.

But I didn't say so.

Wilson's retreating presence was like a thumbscrew being released. We were out of the race and we were no longer under supervision. We began to breathe the clean air of a couple of free-lancers.

Keith said, "Got any more stories?"

"I might," I said.

And then, to pass the time until the first of the runners should appear, I broke a rule and told him a story that I'd dreamed up but hadn't yet put onto paper. Keith's wide-eyed awe made him a great audience in many ways, although his regular failure to grasp the most central detail in a narrative tended to throw me a little. But it didn't seem to bother him, so I didn't let it bother me.

The story was about a struggling writer who couldn't get his book published and who finally in desperation went to the Devil to try to work out some kind of deal for the book to become a best-seller. In my story, the Devil had a shopfront office with the windows painted black and the word £oans in flowing gold script on the outside of the glass. There was such a place, right on the busiest road in the old town about ten minutes' walk from where my grandmother lived, and it had spooked me ever since infancy. I think it was that black glass and the overheard phrase loan shark that did it. Sometimes an image can get into your mind early and rearrange the furniture to make itself at home, so that even when the light has been let in and the demons turn out to be just shadows you find that you're stuck with the new floorplan for life. The writer haggled with the Devil for most of an afternoon, but they couldn't come up with a deal that suited them both until finally the Devil suggested taking one year from the very end of the writer's life in exchange for huge sales and a Hollywood deal, and the writer said okay. Who'd miss just one year, he thought, when by the time that it comes you'll be too old to enjoy it anyway? So he left his manuscript with the Devil and walked out into the street, and was promptly dropped by a massive heart attack as soon as he hit the pavement.

"What was his book about?" Keith said.

"That doesn't matter."

"Well, how come he dies?"

"Because he only has another year to live anyway," I explained patiently. "Only, he doesn't know it."

Keith contemplated the abyss of unexpected mortality for a while. Somewhere farther along the dirt road on which we stood were the faint sounds of an approaching van or tractor.

Keith said, "You want to try selling some of those."

"The world's not ready for me yet," I said modestly.

The tractor, when it came into view about a minute later, proved to be that of the course greensman. It jarred and splashed through the ruts in the track, the greensman peering forward over the raised front shovel that had been loaded with fencing posts and about half a dozen rolls of new barbed wire. I don't know which was the more ancient, the man or the vehicle, and he had a skinny grey dog of similar antiquity that rode along on the platform behind the saddle. Keith and I backed off nervously to let them pass, even though there was plenty of room on the track. I'd never seen or heard him speak directly to anyone before, apart from a shout of *Git off of there!* heard from about a quarter mile distance, and that fairly frequently.

But he pulled up level, and throttled back, and raised his voice over the sound of the hammering old engine. "What's all this about?" he called down to us.

"It's the school cross-country run," I said. "It happens every year."

"Not this year, it won't," he said. "Not through here. Who's organized it?"

"Mr. Wilson," I said.

"And has he bothered to check on his route this morning?"

"I wouldn't know."

The greensman glanced heavenward, and my heart leapt happily at the thought of Wilson the Terrible being cast as a buffoon in some other adult's drama. "Well," he said, "you can tell your Mr. Wilson that the rain's washed out the path and if he'd bothered to consult with me, I'd have told him so. You'd better not let anybody down there."

"It's too late," Keith chipped in. "They'll have started by now."

"Well, you turn them when they get here. That path drops away so sudden, you wouldn't see it coming. Send 'em around the outside of the wood and tell them to keep off the greens or I'll have 'em strung up like Nellie's bloomers." And then he slammed the tractor into gear against its noisy protests, and said, "Bloody Wilson again. I wouldn't pay the man in bottletops." And then the tractor lurched forward and the skinny dog, which had hopped down to mooch around and piss on something, hastily wound up business and galloped after.

When he'd gone, Keith looked at me.

"I'd better go and see what it's like," I said.

I climbed over the stile and followed the path for some way into the woodland before I reached the spot, and then I came upon it so suddenly that I almost lost my footing though I wasn't even taking it at a run. The path was cut into a steep gradient with a streambed below, and it was just beyond where this stony yard-wide shelf went out and around a big old tree that the washout had occurred. The land above had come down in a great wave of earth and simply erased the path, and an old retaining fence from somewhere up above had been dragged down out of line and across. Because of the way that the big tree screened it, the whole arrangement was as neat and unexpected as any prepared deadfall. From where I stood I could look down and see the broken wire of the fence tangled into a rusty skein and half hidden by raw earth and roots and leaves. The birds sang unconcerned and the stream bubbled in the middle distance and I was struck by a sudden and awesome thought, a realization that seeped in as slow and as warm as a pee in the pants . . .

Colin Kelly would undoubtedly be the front-runner in the field.

It was like a door opening out into a dark and inviting land, and I slammed it as quickly as I could.

I was back at the stile a couple of minutes later.

"What are we going to do?" Keith said.

"We'll just have to send everyone around."

"That means messing up all the timings. Wilson'll kill us."

"He'll be just the same whatever we do," I said, taking the marker flags and trying to stick them in some kind of crossed arrangement in front of the stile. "And somebody could *really* get killed back there."

"Is it as bad as that?"

"You want to see it."

I was still messing with the flags, trying to get them to stay in some arrangement that had a look of warning about it, when Colin Kelly came pounding into view venting steam like a train.

As predicted, there wasn't another runner within sight of him. Loose-limbed and sullen, bottom lip hanging to show his teeth as he sucked air, he looked as if he'd been put together out of coat hangers. He knew the route, and all he could see as he came up the dirt track was a familiar fat kid blocking it.

"Fucking get out of the way," he screeched as he bore down on me.

I stood my ground. "You can't use the path, Kelly."

"Says who?"

"It's all washed away. There's no way through the woods, you'll have to go around."

"Fuck off," Kelly said. He'd had to break his stride because I hadn't moved, and now he swung his arm to knock me aside; I ducked, and felt it pass through the air close to my head like a bony club. He ran into me and I pushed back at him, hard, and he stumbled and then recovered himself with an expression of rage and disbelief.

"I'm telling you to go around, Kelly," I tried to say in the brief half second that was available to me, but he was beyond listening; from that day to this I've never seen a sight uglier than his twisted face thrust up against my own or heard a sound more vicious than his scream of *"Shift!"* delivered at maximum decibels as he grabbed hold of me and threw me down into the dirt with a yank that jerked my shirt entirely out of my pants.

By the time that I'd struggled to my knees, grazed and winded but barely aware of either fact, he'd hurdled the stile and was gone.

Keith was standing pale and scared, his mouth hanging open in a dark little O.

"You'd better go back and tell Wilson what he did," I said, only my voice came out as barely a whisper. I sat heavily on the step-up part of the stile.

"Me?" Keith squeaked.

"Tell him everything that Kelly said to me and that I said to Kelly."

"Can't you do it?"

"No," I said. "Think about it, and you'll see why. I'll stay here and stop the others. I think the race is over."

So he went, and I stayed, and about four minutes later the rest of the field started to arrive.

Three weeks after that, during school time, I went around to Colin Kelly's house. It was midmorning, and I was lucky; I caught his parents just as they were getting ready to go out.

Mr. Kelly answered my ring at the door. It was a pleasant house on a road that had some trees along it, a few rungs upmarket from the place where I lived; there was a paved drive out front to park a car, instead of just the street. And the car looked nearly new.

"Yes?" Mr. Kelly said, squinting down at me as if his mind was running just a few steps behind his senses, and I said, "I'm from Colin's class. I've brought something for him. Is that all right?"

"Oh," he said, making an effort, and he smiled a forced and hollow smile. "Come in, won't you?"

I went into the hallway. Mr. Kelly was in a suit and tie and the atmosphere of the house seemed to be like that of the preparations on the morning of a funeral. The door to the kitchen was open and I could see all the way through to the back of the house, but I didn't see any Mrs. Kelly.

I said, "We had a sponsored swim last week and I volunteered to get the present and the card. We all signed it." And I held up the carrier bag for Mr. Kelly to take. As he took it, there was a sound from upstairs; I couldn't even have identified it, let alone understood it, but Mr. Kelly raised his voice to carry and said, "It's one of Colin's friends from school." And then he looked at me. "I'm sorry, er . . . ?"

"William. William Thomas."

"I'm sorry, William. We were just getting ready to go back to the hospital. I suppose you'll have to hear about this sometime. Colin lost the infected leg last night."

"I'm really sorry," I said.

"You can imagine, we're very upset."

"I wish I'd come another time."

"No. It's a very nice thought and a very nice gesture. I'm sure Colin will appreciate it. Let's have a look, here."

He seemed to have trouble telling one end of the carrier bag from the other, but finally he found his way in and partway drew out the item that I'd spent half the morning searching for.

"Trains," he said, looking at the picture on the front and trying to come up with something to say about it. "Colin likes trains."

"It's a Thomas the Tank Engine drawing pad," I explained. "It's a bit young, but it's the biggest one they did. Do you think he'll like it?"

"I'm sure he will."

"There are some felt-tip pens in there as well, all different colours. And I drew the card myself."

"Yes," he said. "A bird. How nice. We'll have to be going soon . . ."

"William. William Thomas."

"Can we give you a lift anywhere, William?"

I politely declined, even though they'd be passing the school. I was out on license and I had no plans to hurry back . . . and I didn't much take to the idea of sharing a car with the so far unseen Mrs. Kelly.

I glimpsed her, briefly, as the car passed me farther down the road; she was just an anonymous woman, yet another kid's mother in a world that was full of them, and her head was bent as if in prayer. Or perhaps she was reading the card, signed by all of the form and with the bird that I'd drawn on the front.

A dark bird.

Just the one.

One, for sorrow.

I burned the magpies shortly after that.

It wasn't that I'd ceased to believe in them. My faith was undiminished; it was like a child's touching faith in the baby Jesus, only darker and more ritualized and somehow more personal. It was as if I saw the outlines of forces unseen by others, the shapes of those great somber machines that worked under the surface of reality to keep the show seamless and complete and which, if you knew just the right place to push, might occasionally yield to persuasion. I think the truth of it was that I felt scorched by their primitive heat. They saw through me too clearly for comfort, and I was unnerved by their ability to spit out the twisted progeny of my unformed wishes and appalled by my own willingness to offer a secret embrace to such malevolent offspring.

And then time passed by, and even that conviction faded.

When I reached sixteen, the excess weight abruptly burned away as if a hoop of fire had been passed over me. When you start thinking about sex for roughly eighteen hours a day, I suppose the energy has to come from somewhere.

Colin Kelly didn't return to the school. His parents moved him out to a bungalow somewhere out on the coast, and by all accounts started to smother and to treat him like he was five years old again. He got one of those legs that looks like something made out of Airfix and Meccano. I've no idea what happened to Keith. Wilson quietly left the school at the end of the year but I don't know what happened to him, either.

Make of it what you like. Maybe it was chance, it all just happened. Maybe there's a callous God with a sick streak of humor who's fond of setting up these little ironies every now and again. Maybe there *was* some power locked up in those bird pictures that only someone cut deep enough could release.

Or maybe it was the dogshit that I found and smeared all over the barbed wire in the deadfall before I returned to the stile. Who can ever say?

JULIE R. GOOD

Fastening

The road led north, where it was cool and clean and there were blue mountains in the distance. I decided I would find a small town in those mountains and stop there for the night. But that was hours away, and now the black road poured itself for me, pulling me forward through towns, riverbanks, trees, and hills. These changing scenes, and the possibility of further change, delighted me.

With one moist arm I brushed my hair from my eyes. A warm wind had reached through my open car window to tease my ponytail from its restraining band. The same breeze curled around my toes, gluing my feet to my sandals.

Ahead of me, I noticed a small car pulled over to the side of the road. An old woman leaned against the hood, her wrinkled hands covering her face. I meant to keep on, but when I glanced in the rearview mirror, I saw that the wind had caught her black dress and was tugging it away from her thin white legs. Dust was blowing over her black leather shoes.

I pulled over and walked back to where she stood. At the sound of my steps she looked up, and wiped at the tears clinging to her cheeks. "Oh, my dear, thank you so much for stopping. I knew someone would, but it has taken such a long time, and I was beginning to lose hope."

"What's the trouble?"

She flipped her hand at the offending vehicle. "This car! It just stopped—made a funny noise and stopped. I don't know what's wrong with it—I'm certainly no mechanic—I just know it won't go. And it must! I'm going to stay with friends, and they'll be so worried if I don't arrive soon. I don't like to worry anyone. Do you?" She peered at me through blowing strands of silver hair.

I laughed. "No, of course not. But what can I do to help you?"

The wind was still playing havoc with her hair, and it obscured her eyes. "My friends live in the next town up the road. It's not very far, and if you're going that way anyway . . ."

Was this to be my adventure? I thought, disappointed. I glanced at the cars rushing by, but not one slowed, and their occupants would not meet my eyes.

Well, no matter. I'd drop her at her friends' and be on my way in half an hour.

"All right," I said, and began moving back to my car. She clung to my hand, murmuring her gratitude.

In the car she recovered soon enough—smoothing her hair, straightening her dress, sweeping the dust from her shoes onto the floor mat, and then wiping her dirty hands on the seat.

"Now then," she said in a bright voice. "We should probably introduce ourselves. My name is Mrs. Fast." She extended her hand across the space between us. I shook it, one hand on the steering wheel, eyes on the road, and told her my name. She asked me where I lived and what I did there. Before I could ask her the same, she put a hand to her throat, and said, "I am so very glad to have met you, believe me. This is the worst thing that has happened to me on my travels, and when I think of all the things that could have happened while my late husband, Holden, and I were jaunting about the world, I tell you, I breathe a sigh of relief." And she did sigh before going on. "You have made everything so much easier, my dear, by being so kind. It quite surprises me, your willingness to help. Why, most people your age would never give me a second glance, let alone a ride in their car. But young people today are so strange, don't you think? When I think of myself when I was young . . ."

I let her rattle on, refraining from pointing out that many people her own age had passed her by on the highway. Her voice, irritating at first, soon lulled me into a kind of driving trance, where there was only the road before me and the sound of her voice, words unimportant and unheeded, droning on above the humming of the tires.

In a short time we arrived at the next town, a quiet little place, and she directed me to her friends' house. I pulled to a stop before a neat lawn of sun-parched grass and she got out. "No car in the driveway," she said through the open window. "I hope you'll just wait a minute while I check . . ."

Her sentence trailed off. I watched as she knocked on the door several times, and then peered through the curtained windows. She turned and shrugged, a helpless smile pasted on her lips.

"I don't understand," she said, putting her head back through the car window. "We arranged everything over the phone weeks ago. I can't imagine why they wouldn't be here."

"Now what?" I said.

She looked at me with tearful eyes. "I know it's a lot to ask, after all that you've done for me already, but there's a little diner a few streets away, and I could just wait there until my friends come back, if you wouldn't mind?"

"Get in." I sighed and pushed the door open for her.

The diner down the street was pastel pink, as was the fat woman behind the counter, who looked on without expression as Mrs. Fast realized she had left her purse in her stranded car.

She turned to me, eyes and hands empty.

"I'll take you back to your car," I said through gritted teeth.

As we drove away, I chided myself for being ungracious. But then, I reasoned, I had set off to have an adventure, not to become an elderly woman's chauffeur.

She spent the trip back to her car apologizing for the inconvenience I was suffering, and praising me for my patience, while I tried to smile.

The smile disappeared when we discovered that her car had been broken into, and her purse and luggage stolen.

We drove back into town to call the police and a tow truck. She made the calls in a trembling voice, her hand at her throat. I couldn't help feeling sorry for her as she slumped without a word into the car seat.

I drove back to her friends' house, but it was still empty.

At that point my mind was a blank, but my mouth, without warning, spouted words that amazed me. "It's too late for me to continue my trip now. I may as well stay here for the night. Why don't you let me lend you the money for a room, and you can repay me when you get your money back?"

She agreed to that, after a mild protest, and we drove to a motel down the street from the pink diner. I walked Mrs. Fast to her room, and was turning to go to a late dinner, when I heard her faint voice through the closing door. "That's all right, my dear. You go get something to eat. Don't worry about me. I'm sure I'll be fine until tomorrow."

After our dinner I took a quick shower, slipped into my nightgown, and sat in bed watching TV for a while, just as though I were at home.

I called the garage in the morning, and was told that Mrs. Fast's car would be done early in the afternoon. We had breakfast together, watched game shows on TV, and then had lunch. Mrs. Fast expressed, in great detail, her indebtedness to me, and we drove to the garage.

I paid the bill—only a minor repair had been needed—without comment. I wanted to get unstuck from this situation as soon as possible.

Mrs. Fast thanked me, smiled, and followed the mechanic to her car. I chose to remain in the office with my self-pity. I was thinking that I had no more energy for any kind of adventure. All I wanted was to get back to my own empty apartment and my own empty life.

The mechanic returned to the office, trailing dust. "May I help you?"

I stared at him. "I'm sorry?"

He frowned. "Is there anything I can help you with?"

"You are helping me," I said with a laugh. I pointed out to the parking lot. "You were showing"—I paused, then shrugged—"my friend where her car is."

More dust settled into the puzzled lines of his face. "But I did show her. She left."

I collapsed onto the green vinyl couch, dust and hysterical laughter erupting in a cloud around me.

. . . .

I should have gotten her address earlier, but it hadn't occurred to me, and now . . . Well, I had no idea of where she lived, or even what her full name was. She was gone, and so was my money—for good, I thought.

When I returned home the next day, everyone wanted to know what sort of adventures I had had. I told them, exaggerating her fluttering hands, her gasping endearments. They laughed, and sympathized. Some of them suggested I call the police, but I decided my ego had been injured much worse than my wallet. Being ripped off by an old lady was not the highlight of my life, but for a while it was the highlight of office gossip.

Everything went on as it always had. I worked—typing, filing, brewing coffee; I watched TV. The heat abated, and summer crawled toward fall.

The empty house next to mine was sold. I had no particular interest as to who was moving in—I seldom spoke to my neighbors—until I saw the car parked in the street.

Of course, I didn't believe it at first. There were a lot of cars like that one. There was no reason to think that it could be her car.

But then I saw her. Black shoes, black dress, silver hair.

I approached her as she was unlocking her front door. She turned, started, and smiled. "My dear, how wonderful to see you! I was hoping I would run into you soon. I wanted to thank you for directing me to your wonderful city, and what a coincidence that the house next to yours should be for sale. Aren't you excited? When we became such friends on our little adventure, I never thought we would become neighbors, but I am so glad it turned out that way, aren't you?"

"Do you have my money?" I said, as soon as she gave me a chance.

She squinted at me. "I'm sorry, dear, I don't understand."

"The money you owe me for the hotel room, your meals, the repairs on your car."

She laughed, her hand on her breast. "But you must have forgotten. Of course I paid you back, when I got my car back." She squeezed my arm. "And I only got my car back because of all your help."

"I haven't forgotten anything about our little adventure. I know you didn't pay me. If you expect me to forget that, I think I can expect not to be seeing very much of you. I would appreciate it if you would keep your distance." And I turned and walked away, without waiting to see what her reaction would be.

For a while Mrs. Fast stayed away from me. I watched her chatting with the neighbors, who appeared to be charmed to death. I saw her wearing pink and flowered dresses, as well as the black one I had come to associate with her, but always she wore the creased black leather shoes.

I tried not to think about her too much, but that was difficult with her living right next door.

She made it even more difficult the day she knocked on my door and asked to borrow a cup of sugar.

"Of course, I know you didn't mean what you said before," she said, the words bubbling out of her in a sticky-sweet stream. "I wanted to give you a little time, but now I'm sure we'll be friends again. Do you have the sugar?"

I was so amazed I couldn't speak. I shook my head and closed the door.

Undaunted, she returned a week later to borrow something else. Again I refused. Still she kept returning, always bright-faced and smiling, always expectant of receiving what she asked for.

The fall wore on, grinding my nerves to a sharp edge.

They had forgotten about Mrs. Fast at work, and I didn't mention her. It embarrassed me that she had become my neighbor. I felt as though I were coming out of the bathroom with a piece of damp paper clinging to my shoe, and I didn't want anyone to notice it. But I knew I had to talk to someone. Beth was my closest friend among the other secretaries, so I invited her over one evening and told her everything.

"I can't believe it!" she said. "Are you going to call the police now?"

"I don't think I want to do that," I said, thinking it over as I spoke. "I don't want to put her in jail, or get her into any kind of trouble. I just want her to leave me alone." I looked at Beth. "I know it's asking a lot, but will you talk to her?"

"What do you want me to say?"

I shrugged. "Ask her to stop bothering me."

I could see that she didn't want to do it, but Beth was my friend. She didn't know how to say no to me. She sighed and walked over to the house next door.

And came back smiling.

"What a delight she is! Honestly, I don't know why you want to avoid her. She likes you—you should hear the nice things she says about you! I didn't have the heart to tell her what you told me to." She gave me a disapproving frown and went home.

I was stunned by Beth's betrayal. How could she have sided with Mrs. Fast?

Or was I overreacting? Mrs. Fast was an old woman. Could she have forgotten about the money?

I decided to think about it for a while, which I did by not thinking at all.

I came home from work one day beneath a sullen sky. Wind whipped my hair in my face, and sent leaves scudding onto my boots, where many of them stuck.

I turned the key in the lock, opened the front door, and stood rooted to the spot.

Someone was humming and moving around in the kitchen.

"Hello, dear!" she said with a laugh. "You're home from work early. I knew you wouldn't mind if I helped myself to some peanut butter."

"How did you get in?"

"Why, the front door was open."

"The front door was locked. I always lock it." I held up the key I still held in my hand. "I had to use this to let myself in."

She looked thoughtful for a moment, and then shook her head. "Your lock must be broken, or stuck. You really should have that taken care of. Oh, and by the way, thank you so much for sending your friend Beth over to see me the other day. It was so thoughtful of you to think of me."

She flashed that bright smile, waved her hand, and went out through the back door.

I checked the lock, and found that it worked fine. I tried to remember if I had locked it that morning, but my mind was blank, or perhaps numb.

For several days nothing happened, and then everything came unglued.

I came home from work, followed my usual routine, and went to bed.

It was windy that night, and for a long time I lay listening to the dead leaves dancing in the trees, and the windows shivering in their frames. It made me shiver, too, beneath my heap of blankets, and shivering, I slept.

It was the smallest of sounds that awoke me.

The refrigerator door had shut, and light footsteps crossed the kitchen floor.

I clenched my fists beneath the blankets, and swore into the darkness.

Downstairs, there was the clatter of stainless steel on a plate.

I pictured myself tearing down the stairs, ripping the plate from her hands, and slapping her across the face. That is what should have happened, but I could not make myself move. I was paralyzed by anger, and by something else I was finally forced to admit—fear.

The bedroom window rattled, and plates rattled in the sink under running water.

Footsteps came from the kitchen into the hallway, and stopped at the bottom of the stairs.

Beneath the blankets I clenched and unclenched my fists, over and over.

The footsteps came up the stairs and moved down the hallway.

The bedroom door opened, and the figure that stood there was outlined by the moonlight that poured through the trembling window.

I wanted to scream, but felt as though dry cotton filled my mouth.

She crossed the room, black shoes, black dress, and silver hair.

The bed squeaked as she sat on its edge.

There was a brief pause, during which the window and I held still, and only the moonlight moved across the floor.

The she lay down, squirming to get beneath the covers, sighing and wiggling in contentment once she had.

I felt her leather shoe brush against my naked leg.

And suddenly the cotton was pulled from my mouth, the paralysis fell from my body. My heart gave a great leap in my chest, and my voice followed it, springing from my lungs to my lips, and crying out in the cold stillness of that moonlit room.

I did not look back as I jumped from the bed and fled the room, running from the house in a nightgown and bare feet.

The street was ice beneath my feet, the wind more ice, pouring down my unprotected back, but I was not cold. I had left coldness behind, lying alone in my bed.

• • • •

I stayed the night with Beth. She asked countless excited questions, but I had no answers for her.

I went home the next day in borrowed clothing.

The bedroom was silent and empty, the bed made with tidy precision. I dressed in my own clothes, and packed a small bag.

At work I asked my boss to lunch. He was surprised, but willing. Some of my tension must have shown in my face, because he asked if I were in some sort of trouble.

"Yes," I said.

He was taken aback by my bluntness, but he offered to help if he could.

"You can," I said, "if you can find me a job in another city, or better yet, another state."

He lifted his eyebrows. "Is it some sort of legal trouble?"

"Certainly not!"

He smiled, as if amused, and promised to see what he could do.

I went to a hotel after work, and wore the same clothes to work the next day. During my lunch hour I went back to the house, and found it deserted, the sun shining through the dusty windows. I packed everything I could, and took it to the hotel.

Nothing ever happened there, but I spent each night feeling as though something could, and so I slept very little.

I was relieved when my boss told me he had found a job for me, in a sister company in a distant city.

I had not noticed, in my distracted state, but winter had passed while I was in hiding, and as I drove out of town I felt a cool spring breeze pressing against my face. I laughed aloud, and drove a little faster.

As I approached the outskirts of my intended destination, I felt a strange vibration move through the car. There was a terrible grinding noise as I pulled to the side of the road and stopped. I could not get the engine started again.

I stepped out of the car and looked up and down the highway. There were few cars in sight, and none of these seemed inclined to stop. I slid down the car until my back rested against the tire and my legs stuck out straight in front of me.

Having nothing else to do, I waited.

After a time, a car slowed down as it passed, and then pulled over. A young man got out and walked back down the road to where I was sitting.

"What's the trouble?" he said.

I opened my mouth to answer, and stopped. I had caught a glimpse of the shoes I was wearing. Black leather, and covered with dust from the road.

I covered my face with my hands and wept.

They were not my shoes, but they belonged to me now.

BRIAN HODGE

Past Tense

To say that our friendship was based on drinking would be, at best, a grave error. Sober or not, Kristen and I liked each other without reservation. But it seemed, nevertheless, that whenever we got together for a heart-to-heart session, the first crisis was what brand to order. And who shelled out for the lead-off round.

This evening it was stout on tap, and she drew first cash.

We had chosen this fern-infested Rush Street mecca because it was mutually inconvenient to both our workplaces. Comfortably full of furnishings as trendy as its clientele. At its epicenter sat a hollow rectangular bar, all mellow oak and brass; its overhead racks sprouted rows of wineglasses hanging from their stems, like crystal stalactites. Satelliting the bar were tables and booths, abundantly packed with festive groups, quiet pairs, and lone strays trying to hide their hunger to become part of one or the other.

Kristen and I were fringe dwellers, as far removed from the mainstream as we could get. Nestled into a brick corner at a table little bigger than a TV tray. Intimacy was a cardinal mandate.

When our drinks arrived, I held mine up to the light, which was unable to shine through the heavy brew. I ruminated about this, and after disposing of a foam mustache with a flick of her tongue, Kristen accused me of stalling. She was right, of course.

"You probably already know what I'm stalling about," I said.

She nodded, wisdom in her eyes, coupled with bemused patience. "Oh sure. You've lived with Lisa for, what, six months now?"

"Seven and a half."

"Wow, you *are* overdue. I knew it was coming."

"Another live-in love bites the dust," I said softly.

"Poor Lisa. I liked her, I really did." Her voice was light, without reproach. Only a slightly detectable seasoning of concern, as always. I think I might have preferred reproach this time, variety being the spice of life and all. "Have you told her yet?"

I made a muscle with one arm and perched the glass of stout above it. "I was hoping to get psyched up for it first."

Kristen gazed sadly out over the rest of the troops in the bar, as if to set eyes on the next eligible young lovely to set foot through the revolving door of my home and bed. Then she gave me a gray smile, perhaps wondering why her stability couldn't be contagious.

Lisa and I had met in mid-December, an encounter of pure chance when I was reduced by emergency Porsche trouble to relying on the wonders of public transportation. A bus, in this case.

Maybe her tenure in my life was longer than the norm because we met differently. She wasn't another in the parade of models and aspiring starlets I directed in TV commercials on Michigan Avenue.

It had been the peak of the Christmas shopping season, and a three-hundred-pound man bulled into her in his haste not to miss his stop. Sacks and gift-wrapped packages, behind which she had been effectively fortressed, went avalanching to a floor lubed with grimy slush. I helped her pick them up, no ulterior motive. Being on internal slowcook over my car, I hadn't even noticed her looks until after help was offered and underway.

Her looks, her *colors*. Delicately pale porcelain face and rose cheeks, with shoulder-length wisps of hair, shinier and blacker than a raven's wing. Altogether enchanting.

We talked, had coffee. Later that week, lunch, followed by dinners and excursions to the theater. It wasn't until I was already gold-medaling in the head-over-heels Olympics that I learned she was a million-airess-to-be, a department store heiress who kept an extremely low profile because she thought of all that money and its accompanying headaches made her nervous.

And so, by New Year's Eve, she was ready to move in and play at the domestic scene with a frustrated filmmaker who had sold out his dreams of substance and instead cranked out short-shorts in Chicago's megabucks advertising milieu.

While I figured it would probably be wise to first ask her predecessor, Meridy, to move out.

Kristen and I decided to switch to pitchers after the first round. Simpler, more economical. And the unspoken alarm had gone off to signify that, this evening, we were in for a long haul.

"Have you met someone else?" she asked. "Is somebody new going to be moving in?"

I twitched my head no. "Not this time. It just seems better off terminated, that's all. More fair, or something."

"Well, listen. You may be a hopeless satyr," she said, reaching across the table to lightly punch my shoulder, "but I admire your integrity. Most guys'd hang on to Lisa because of the money factor."

"Oh yeah." I polished an imaginary crown. "I'm a real prince."

We veered off course awhile, a normal staple of our serious talks. Cover relevant ground until reaching a good breakaway point for trivia, until one or the other would steer us back on track. In the interim, we'd cover books, music, movies, cabbages and kings.

We paused to watch a guy leave the bar, drink in hand, and maintain a dignified totter to approach a couple of secretarial types near our table. Head in the clouds; drifting smoke, actually. It's a cruel world. They shot him down in fifteen seconds, and he tottered back to the bar to wage war on his liver. Sad.

"I think I've settled on a diagnosis for your condition," she said once the floor show was over. Kristen always looked bright, healthy. With loose, uncomplicated dark blond hair and an outdoorsy complexion, she looked as if she belonged on Colorado ski slopes. And now she was utterly radiant.

"Doctor," I said. "Give it to me straight."

"You, Derek, are subject to what we barroom philosophers refer to as 'serial monogamy.' " She flexed long fingers, then studiously laced them together. "I mean, with a couple of exceptions, you're not a habitual cheater. You're a generally faithful guy . . . just faithful in a never-ending succession. There's always that greener pasture ahead for you, isn't there?"

I pointed down into my lap. "I always figured, to be honest, I'd have to admit I was led around by *that*."

"Mmmm . . . maybe. But you're still not the average male pull toy." She paused to refill our glasses. Kristen was the one female friend I had found who could keep pace with me all evening. This was important, not to be lost. "And you know why that is? You honestly fall in love. You get shot through the heart every single time."

I sent up that peculiar semaphore code for another pitcher. "Yeah, you're right on that. Sometimes I go into each new relationship with all the enthusiasm of a kamikaze pilot gunning for the S.S. *Saratoga*. Feels pretty glorious at the time, but it's ultimately bad for your health."

And I wondered, fleetingly, though not for the first time . . . Would things be different with Kristen? Would duration finally be achieved? I found it paradoxical that a large part of her appeal was precisely the same thing that kept us safe from one another. She was off-limits, in the gonadian sense of things. Her long-term love was a guy named Mark, a good friend of mine from the decade-past Dark Ages of college. But . . . no wedding, no ring, and no such plans so far. There still existed that remote chance of Kristen and me pairing off, slipping beyond the usual bounds of friendship. That one night we might drink just enough to erode the constraints and stoke the libidinal flames, and, so sorry, Mark, but nature has taken its irrevocable course. Hope you understand.

"Don't even think it," she said. But with a smile. One sharp observer, she was. There were times when I thought she could read my face through a ski mask at fifty paces. "I love you too much as a friend to end up hating you as an ex-lover. And we *would* be ex-lovers after a while, you know that. We would."

I looked up from the table, a semiguilty glance, then nodded slowly. We both did, a strange sort of reaffirmation. A residual melancholy rode the crest of the moment, and I think it came from both sides. I'm sure she had entertained the same notions, at least once or twice.

Looked at options, risks, probable outcomes. And decided it just wasn't worth it.

"I have this dream, sometimes," I told her. "I'm living alone, for a change. And one morning I wake up and every woman I've loved and messed up with and hurt . . . they're all there waiting for me. It's like there's dozens of them, you know. All there at once. And they form two lines, facing each other, and I have to run the gauntlet. So I run between the rows and I duck and cover my head, but it doesn't do much good, because there's so many of them. They slug me in the face, and kick me in the balls . . . just beat the living hell out of me. Except when I get to the end, see that latest love's face and think it's all over, there are even more of them. Women I don't know, future women, and it just never ever ends."

If anything, that would be poetic justice, but Kristen didn't let on if she felt that way. Her face screwed up, subtly, as if the dream had wormed its way beneath her skin, left a trace of the venom it routinely discharged into me on those mornings after.

The evening wore on, became night. Nothing was resolved, but then, nothing ever was. That was beyond even her capabilities. So we drank up, mutually voted down the idea of another pitcher. Walked out to the street together, where we hugged and swapped the briefest of platonic kisses, then went our opposite ways. As always. As expected. Safe and unentangled for another night.

I headed for my Porsche, mentally gearing up to go home and get into that terribly inevitable task of housecleaning. One more time.

The trip home was rife with memories, mental newsreels of past loves, loves that had withered and died after reaching the same temporal hallmark at which other couples were just hitting their stride. And I remembered one in particular, brought to mind by an otherwise throwaway comment Kristen had made earlier in the evening.

Steffy. Just one of the many whose ties to my life and heart existed solely in the past tense. She was another of the models I seemed to have such a proclivity for. Steffy of the throaty voice, the legs to inspire traffic accidents, and the pathological need to shop that rivaled Tammy Faye Bakker's. I knew from day one it wouldn't last.

But that was okay. Because everything we did was done for laughs. The drinking. The parties. The designer drugs. The sex. The marathon gold card sprees. The weekend morning hangovers and their attempted cures. Everything, one four-month chucklefest. Larry, Moe, and Curly should have had it so good.

Except for the omega day I asked her to move out. Steffy was hurt and furious in equal measures. Somehow I managed to convince her that I'd not met anyone else; I'd had neither time nor energy for that. I just thought it was time for us both to get on with trying to be adults. Or at least as close as *we* could come.

"You know what your problem is?" she said. "You can't handle sticking around after things settle down and get a little more normal. You always need that thrill of something new. You're a junkie for discovery."

In that moment, Steffy displayed more depth than she had during the entire four months. More, in fact, than I had suspected was even there. It was a turn-on; depths unplumbed, uncharted territories. I was ready to change my mind and ask her to please please stay, but knew it was too late. One more bridge was raging in flames.

"And I'm sorry you don't think my waters run deep enough." She heaped on so much sarcasm I wasn't sure if she truly meant that or not. But it didn't matter, not when she was out the door ten minutes later.

I sat down then and wondered. What's worse to do to someone? What's more painful? Leaving them because you've met somebody new . . . or leaving them even though you haven't?

Another of life's great imponderables.

Where are Plato and Socrates now that they're needed most?

I didn't waste much time after I got home, getting the unpleasantries over with. Repetition breeds efficiency, if not exactly anesthesia. I was just used to the pain. Every time the ax fell, by my own hand, it lopped a chunk out of me, too. Amputations may be quick, but they're never painless, never neat. So much emotional blood had been spilled in my home, the walls must have been sodden. An abattoir of the soul.

Lisa sat in stunned silence until she reached back inside to find her voice. The scene was messy, ugly, with plenty of tears to go around. But I loved her, this was certain. Maybe that was the problem. I loved her —all of them—too much.

At least too much to stand idly by while those initial flames of passion at the beginning of any relationship started to sputter and dwindle into embers of banality. As I often did, I wondered: Why can't every day be like day one?

And damn my overstimulated soul for being dissatisfied with any-thing less than that.

For the cost, the cost. So high, as the sodden walls could so well attest.

Lisa packed a few things to get her through the night and the next day or two. She made a phone call. And then my department store heiress and her eventual millions went weeping out the door, toward a friend with a vacant couch and an extraabsorbent shoulder. The rest of· her belongings could wait until I was elsewhere.

It always takes some getting used to, when they leave. Readjusting to an apartment whose occupancy has just been halved. A loft apartment with seemingly acres of open space, and bohemian brick walls and burnished wood floors, with endearing nooks and crannies and sky-lights. Doesn't take much of a push for it to feel very big and very empty, and in a hurry.

I settled onto the pit group that made up my sofa, and used the television remote to conjure forth company. Shutting down the higher cranial functions and filling dead time.

Blank, numb. Wretched until the coming dawn, too long away.

But such is the price paid by those who have perfected the artful crime of the sexual hit-and-run.

Lisa was officially past tense. As expected, as was the norm, she still had her key and used it a couple of days later to let herself in while I was away directing my micromasterpieces. She cleansed the loft of her belongings, an orderly exorcism of self.

Occasionally the wounded lady has wanted to enact a little revenge. Symbolic vandalism, sometimes. Twice I had come home to discover large electrical toys missing, a TV or stereo swiped out of anger. One of the especially clever ones rigged my phone to continually redial a re-corded message in Zurich, and so it did for the whole of one workday. These I endured without much complaint. If it helps them purge the bile from their systems, it's worth it. No festering *Fatal Attraction* psychopaths waiting in my wings, if I can help it.

Lisa, to my surprise, gravitated toward vengeance.

But for her to have instead left something behind . . . now *there* was a new twist.

At first I wondered where she had gotten them all. Because there were so incredibly many, no two alike. But then I realized that a department store heiress could pull this off with ease. She would have the connections. The resources. The money.

I had just never expected anyone to come up with such a graphic reaction to the situation, such a vivid editorial comment on what I was inside.

And Lisa was, after I'd had a chance to consider it, so damnably on target.

It must have been a week later when Kristen dropped by to check up on me. Wondering how the latest amputation had gone. Wondering about the fresh psychic scar tissue. Wondering, I suppose, why she just hadn't heard from me.

"I've been kind of preoccupied," I said quietly, standing in the doorway and blocking much of any view of the inside of the loft. "You know. Busy."

Her cheeks glowed with the climb up the stairs and general good health. A wide-brimmed thrift shop hat perched jauntily atop her head. "You don't look so hot, Derek. You feeling okay?"

I nodded, shuffled my feet. I wore jeans, a T-shirt, socks. Nothing else. Oh, a five-day beard, if that counts.

"Can I come in?" Her voice was starting to get that edge it honed when she was creeping toward vague unpleasant truths as if they were land mines angled to spray shrapnel into her face.

Should I let her in? I asked myself. Let her in, the first visitor to this brand-new environment and fellowship in which I lived? Would jealousy rear its hideous head? *Oh go on,* I decided. We were, after all, friends.

"Come on in. I'm sorry." I stepped out of the way, let her by.

Two steps in, she stopped frozen in her tracks. I barely had room enough behind her to swing the door shut again.

"Derek?" she said. "Is this . . . from one of your commercials?"

"No," I said. "They're all mine. Or at least, they are now. A special delivery from Lisa. She has a certain sense of style, don't you think?"

Kristen could not answer, but stood gamely trying to take it all in. She was as vacant-eyed and slate-wiped as I'd been upon first walking in a week before and trying to fathom such an extravagant display of angry pain. And while Kristen gave it her best shot, I walked farther in and took a seat on the floor in the midst of my latest soulmates.

She didn't get it, I could tell by her eyes. But then, she hadn't had my week of introspection. And you must admit, the sight of someone's home populated by dozens of mannequins takes some time to grow accustomed to.

But there they were, in perfect frozen poise, staring with their unblinking painted eyes. All different, with long wigs and short wigs, blondes and brunettes and redheads, wearing business clothing and formal wear and swimsuits and lingerie and casual wear of all styles and trends. Standing with motionless grace. Reposing on the pit group. Seated at the kitchen table.

All unique . . . on the outside. And yet identical on the inside, for they were all so very hollow. In her own one-of-a-kind way, I think what Lisa was saying was that I was just as plastic as they.

She wasn't far wrong.

Still, that wasn't the worst of it.

"Oh Derek," Kristen said, her voice slow and faraway. "Why didn't you get rid of them?"

I smiled and spread my arms wide, bumped into one of the still-life legs. The mannequin wobbled, an eternally slender blonde with blue eyes and thin pink lips that never lost their smile. I had named her Livvy. I steadied her, absently traced a finger down one hard thigh.

"I can't. They're what I always needed. I think Lisa recognized that even before I did."

Kristen still didn't get it. What I think she *was* starting to get was worried.

"Whatever I'm in the mood for, there's one here who fits the bill. I just have to look. And there aren't any hurt feelings, anywhere. It's a smorgasbord, and I don't have to pretend anymore."

Kristen's look, I knew that look. *He's finally snapped*, that's what it said. With it, I felt a curious liberation in my tongue, in what I could continue to divulge. A little more wouldn't hurt.

"They say that faith can move mountains," I told her, my voice dropping like that of some bewildered prophet. "Love and laughter? Doctors say those release chemicals in your body that add years to your life. Stress eats ulcers into you. Some people get caught up in such religious ecstasy that stigmata open in their hands and feet. But did you ever wonder about hate, and pain, and betrayal, just how much *they* can do? Because you've got to admit, they're the most intense of all."

I then held my hands out to indicate the walls, the ceiling, the floor. The mannequins. Hoping she would *see*.

Kristen wanted to come farther in, I honestly believe she did. But it was as if this plastic battalion held her at bay and turned her back and repelled her out the door, by simple virtue of its presence. This quiet menagerie of variable perfection. They're formidable at first glance, all right.

But perhaps, in time, Kristen would understand. Understand that they were teaching me, and I had no choice but to bend to their imparted lessons, lessons I so desperately needed to learn. And I made a receptive pupil.

I had to be. I was so vastly outnumbered.

I had been an emotional parasite. Taking, and taking, and taking, but giving only what I could easily spare at the moment. I soaked up love and pissed out indifference in return.

I hadn't counted them, didn't want to. But something in me, a new breed of instinct, perhaps, told me that there would be exactly one mannequin for every woman I had ever wronged, ever hurt, for all the wrong reasons. The number would come out a perfect match.

Just as I was a perfect match for *them*.

I live with the mannequins easily enough, now that I'm used to them being around. They're quiet. They make no unreasonable demands. They have no needs. They ask for no commitments. And I've long since dismissed neuroses and psychoses as the cause for when I look at one, and notice the perceptible change in the tilt of a head, the bend of an arm, the stance of a leg, the depth in an eye.

It's ideal.

Except . . .

At night, when I lie awake in the darkness, the skylights admitting just enough of the moon to turn my home into a garden of shadows, I listen. And hear the most minute of shuffling footsteps. And I can hear them conspiring in whispered plastic voices, a message passed along from one to another to the next, like solitary inmates tapping Morse code onto adjoining prison cell walls.

Those sounds . . . They're the stuff of midnight paralysis, of breath uselessly vapor-locked in the throat. Of sweaty palms and stained sheets. And the only thing that frightens me more is the thought of what they might do should I try—one at a time—to remove them from the premises. Or vacate it myself.

They will not be denied their due.

And I know that some morning, come first light, I will awaken to discover that they have formed that inevitable gauntlet I have long since learned to expect.

LORI NEGRIDGE ALLEN

Under
the Boardwalk

I didn't dig her up or tell anybody because maybe, just maybe she was a dummy, not a dead lady, okay?

Anyway, that would've been squealing, and in our neighborhood only rats squealed; if you were a good guy, you kept your trap shut.

Or maybe it had something to do with the old fur coat I'd found sticking out of a garbage pail a couple of weeks before that turned out to be a dead dog with half-eaten eyes and a mouth all stuffed with fat gray worms.

I shouldn't've looked.

'Cause that night I had this dream where it was *my* mouth the worms were in and when I tried to spit them out I couldn't 'cause the biggest worm of all was my tongue.

"Mom!" I screamed. "Mom! Mo-o-o-o-m!"

I'd never been so scared in my life.

Or so alone.

The next morning, Mom tightened the belt of her kimono, squeezed the big pink flowers on it into narrow strings, squeezed her eyes half shut so I couldn't see how bloodshot they were, said, "You've got to get it through that thick head of yours that you're a big girl now. The thing about nightmares is, the less attention you pay to them, the sooner they go away."

Oh yeah?

A couple of nights later, I found out the thing about nightmares is, if you scream and scream and nobody comes, the next night you scream even more *because* nobody'll come, and the next night after that the nightmare gets mad and won't let you scream at all. Your tongue's a worm and your teeth are worms all soft that crawl in and out the holes of your face and eat your face . . .

The way not to have nightmares is, you stop looking at scary things.

So when the waves at Coney Island uncovered the dummy's or the dead lady's finger, I left it alone. And I made my kid brother Joey the Pest leave it alone too.

The finger was pinky yellow. The nail'd been painted to show the half moon.

My nails had hardly any half moons. Yet.

The waves washed away more sand. The next finger was greenish, swollen around a ring.

Once I got a ring from a box of Cracker Jacks. My finger turned green too.

Not for anything was I gonna see the rest of that hand.

I held the money Mom gave me for french fries in my hand. Pretty soon my hand was gonna smell like money, and when I got the french fries they'd smell like money too. They'd even taste like money, old money that'd been held in my hand too long . . . my hand like that lady's under the sand.

I used to love Coney Island french fries, the thickness of them, the way they were cut in waves with a special knife my mom didn't know where to buy, the fat salt they let you put on extra if you wanted, the ketchup that was a little redder here than anywhere else. I used to love the way they were tough, so you had to chew them a long time, and the taste stayed in your mouth forever. I even used to love the way they looked in the bag, like great big fat Diamond kitchen matches, like little tan sticks with red paint (that was the ketchup) . . .

. . . like a bag of fingers with nail polish on them.

I shoulda told, I shoulda told, I shoulda told.

"Hey, wait up! Where's the fire?" Joey the Pest called. I'd accidentally on purpose forgotten that no matter where I went, Joey the Pest was sure to go. *Joey* wouldn't mind if french fries reminded him of a dead lady's fingers. Joey'd *prefer* them that way.

Get your fresh french fried fingers right here.

Nothing's real under the boardwalk. The sun never quite shines, the shade never quite falls, spaces between the planks above let in narrow lines of moving light that never quite dry out the sand. It's lower there than anywhere else, and once we got down and walked a few steps we couldn't see the beach at all, just a blue ribbon of sky, and pretty soon not even that.

The blanket people moved under their covers, not knowing or caring about us, and we pretended not to know or care about them. I knew more or less what they were doing. It had something to do with the white balloons we kept finding and weren't supposed to touch. It had nothing to do with me, not yet, not ever, but I still felt a little sorry for them, always under the boardwalk, with neither ceiling nor sky for protection. I needed either ceiling or sky, one or the other, or there was nothing for me to hang on to, nothing to keep me right. Like I needed to be either grown up or little. Being in between meant I was nowhere, like the lady was nowhere, because no one could find her, because I hadn't told.

All I wanted to do was get Mom her french fries and get back to the beach.

Joey the Pest had other ideas.

I called him Joey the Pest because he was six. Which meant you could never say to him, "Later." Later was Tomorrow, Tomorrow was When you grow up, When you grow up was Never, so everything had to be *Right now.*

Right now he ran up to the man in the raw clams booth and said straight out, "Guess what? Me and my sister found a dead lady in the waves and nobody but us knows where she is!"

I shoulda known. I could make him shut up for just so long, but I couldn't make him not tell anybody ever. Only he'd been holding it back so hard it came out all at once, like a story he'd just made up.

The clam man leaned forward on his splintered counter, waved his curved clam knife back and forth. "Kid, I think I got your number. You ain't got no money, right? And if you did, you wouldn't want one of these, right?" He shoved a plate of raw clams under Joey's nose, touched the tip of his knife to the foot of one so it pulled into the clam's body. "See that? That means it's alive! Can't get no fresher than live, no sirree!" He slurped the clam from its shell. "Dee-licious. Here kid, try one. Put some hair on your chest."

Joey backed away while the clam man cackled, but it didn't slow the Pest down much. He turned right around and went to the next booth where they sold corn on the cob, and he said to the corn lady, just as cheerfully as he had to the clam man (six-year-olds never learn), "Guess what? Me and my sister found a dead body in the sand and nobody but us knows where it is!"

The corn lady was kind of plump, maybe from licking butter off her hands all day, and her face was shiny with grease. She had a nice smile, like she knew a good joke when she heard it. "Guess what me and *my* sister found on the beach! We found *three* dead bodies, and would you believe not one of them had any noses? So what we figured was . . . Hold it right there, kid, it's been a slow day." Her phone was ringing. She waddled to the back of the shop to answer it. "No kidding! Anybody we know? The cops there yet? This I gotta see!" Then, looking down at Joey, "Sorry, kid, maybe we can swap stories some other time."

She rolled down her storefront and went off in the direction of the beach.

We heard lots of ringing phones and rolling storefronts.

We saw blanket people gather up their stuff and move off to some place where there was less commotion.

We found ourselves alone.

Except for him.

He was so skinny that his ribs stook out, but he had a moon face, like his head had rotted swollen. He was maggot white except for two squirmy blue lines on his forehead. He moved like he'd been put together wrong, with rubber bands maybe, and the rubber was too stretchy.

He'd come out of nowhere. Or maybe he'd been one of the blanket people. Or maybe he was the man in your nightmares you never quite see, but the corners of your eyes feel him, and the back of your head, and that place between your shoulders you can never quite reach. You never see him 'cause you're a kid and can scream and make him go away. But he comes back. When you're big and your mouth's plugged up with worms he comes back, and from that time on he's always there. You can't tell anybody about him because you're a grownup and maybe by now you're a mother too so who can you tell, your kids? He's your own personal someone you don't want to see, and if you fall asleep you're sure to see him, so you sit at your kitchen table all night in your kimono with the flowers on it, make believe it's coffee in your cup, take a big gulp every time your daughter screams. Everybody has to grow up. Why should you be the only one?

"Carol?" Joey whispered too loud, clutched my hand like he always said he was too big to do, "Carol, what if that's the guy that killed the lady? And we're the only ones who know where she is? And he's gonna get us?"

What could I say? No, Joey, it's not the killer, it's just the boogeyman? And what if we were both right? What if nightmare people crossed over into the real world, or the real world into the world that wasn't? And was I absolutely sure this wasn't some dream that would go away as soon as I screamed . . . *if* I could scream?

Yes. That's one thing I was sure of.

"Run, Joey," I said.

"Big boys don't run away," he answered, with his feet apart, his arms crossed in front of his chest for protection.

"Right, and neither do big girls. But *you're* still a little kid. Besides, didn't Mom say you better mind me or else? It's or else time, you hear? Now get going!"

"You're sure?"

"Move!"

"I'll get Mom," he said, and ran like the devil was after him. Which he wasn't. He was right here with me. Or something very much like him.

The man didn't seem to mind that Joey'd left. He'd hardly even looked at Joey. Just at me.

"Got any hair down there yet? Or under those pretty little arms of yours?" he asked in a voice like he was talking through glue.

Only under my right arm, four of them, but I wouldn't let him see. I pressed my elbows hard against my body. Nobody'd ever asked me anything like that before. Nobody'd ever looked at me like that before, and I didn't like it. I didn't like the way he was sweating either. It was cool under the boardwalk; he shouldn't't've felt that hot.

"Let's have a look," he said, and jerked my arms up hard.

"No, please . . ."

He let my arms go and laughed, a laugh that said I was old enough to be scared but too young to know what to be scared of, a laugh that said he could get me easy.

"I won't tell," I promised, not knowing if I was talking about the lady or me, or if it made any difference.

All around us bars of light kept moving or bars of dark kept moving or maybe the sands themselves kept moving. I couldn't be sure.

"I know you won't tell, Carol," he said softly.

"You know my name?"

"I know everything about you, Carol. I know the kind of school you go to, the garbage in your streets, the color of your mother's hair. Blond like yours, isn't it? I know that right now you're a very scared little girl. But you shouldn't be scared. Even if I was going to hurt you, which I'm not, my knife's so sharp you wouldn't feel a thing." He pressed the button, made the blade shoot out.

I shoulda run right then. I shoulda kicked him where it hurt and run like hell. I was the best runner on Sixth Street the East River side of Avenue B, and nobody, but nobody could catch me. But I couldn't. I don't know why. Maybe Joey was right. Maybe big boys and girls weren't supposed to run *or* scream, and my feet'd grown up before the rest of me. Or maybe it had something to do with the sand holding me down. Or maybe I didn't run then because I didn't run before . . . because we never run. Some of us are always here.

Some of us? No, there was still only me, dumb Carol, the one who didn't tell.

I put out my hands to shield my face. The money I was holding dropped to the sand, got buried in the sand, got lost. I put out my hands to push him away, to hold him back. I put out my hands so he couldn't come any closer. I could hear him breathing now, I could smell him. I put out my hands so I couldn't see him, but I *had* to see him, had to see what he was doing. So I put out my hands, spread my fingers, and peeked through them. Finger bars, bars of fingers in the air, moving fingers of bars . . .

No more bars.

One move of his knife and there were no more bars. My fingers were gone, fallen into the sand, sucked under the sand as though they'd never been.

He looked surprised, like he didn't know his knife was *that* sharp, or my fingers were that soft, or he was that strong.

I wasn't surprised. It kind of evened things out. I hadn't told anybody about the dead lady's fingers, so she'd taken mine. It was only fair. And he'd told the truth. It didn't hurt, I didn't feel a thing, only a coolness where the blood welled up and hit the air.

"Carol! Caarrrooolll!"

It was a lady's voice. My mom's? Coming closer.

"Damn it," the man said.

And he was gone.

I didn't know where—into one of the shops, into the subway, into a deep hole that only he knew about. I didn't know and I didn't care. My mom was coming. At least it sounded like my mom.

No it didn't. It didn't sound like her at all.

It didn't look like her either, not this pale lady under the boardwalk. She was almost as pale as *him*. The shifting light made shadows on her face that shouldn't've been there. She wasn't my mom, not really, not the mom I used to have. The mom I used to have would've found me in time, hugged me, kissed me, made it all better. This lady wasn't going to hug away my nightmares, wasn't going to hug me at all, she was afraid my blood'd get on her. She wasn't going to even *try* to make it all better, probably wouldn't be able even to *find* my fingers, much less glue them back on, so how could she be my mom? None of us have mothers, we're born alone, die alone, cut our own cords, dig our own graves in the sand, and if somebody pretends to care for a while, she doesn't, not really. Why should she? Nobody ever cared for her.

"Carol! Caaarrrooollll! Can't you hear me?"

I heard, but I never answered, so she couldn't find me. Why should she find me, this lady who never had a daughter?

"Carol!"

I heard.

I hear.

I hear the boardwalk change heavy storms into soft rains.

I hear the seasons come and go.

I hear the clatter of rickshaws overhead.

I hear the sand settling down, ever down, pulling me always under.

I hear the lost mothers calling to their children.

And the sand pulls me down.

I hear the lovers under their blankets whisper words they do not mean, and the mothers cry prayers they do not mean, and the pale men shout curses they do mean.

And the sand pulls me down.

I hear the lap-lap roar of the waves, the whistle-howl screech of the wind, the splash.

I hear the buried lady calling to me. I hear both ladies calling to me, "Carol, Carol . . ."

And the sand pulls me down, and the sand pulls me down.

BRIAN LUMLEY

The Picnickers

This story comes from a long time ago. I was a boy, so that shows how long ago it was. Part of it is from memory, and the rest is a reconstruction built up over the years through times when I've given it a lot of thought, filling in the gaps; for I wasn't privy to everything that happened that time, which is perhaps as well. But I do know that I'm prone to nightmares, and I believe that this is where they have their roots, so maybe getting it down on paper is my rite of exorcism. I hope so.

The summers were good and hot in those days, and no use anyone telling me that that's just an old man speaking, who only remembers the good things; they *were* better summers! I could, and did, go down to the beach at Harden every day. I'd get burned black by the time school came around again at the end of the holidays. The only black you'd get on that beach these days would be from the coal dust. In fact there isn't a beach anymore, just a sloping moonscape of slag from the pits, scarred by deep gulleys where polluted water gurgles down to a scummy, foaming black sea.

But at that time . . . men used to crab on the rocks when the tide was out, and cast for cod right off the sandbar where the small waves broke. And the receding sea would leave blue pools where we could swim in safety. Well, there's probably still sand down there, but it's ten foot deep under the strewn black guts of the mines, and the only pools now are pools of slurry.

It was summer when the gypsies came, the days were long and hot, and the beach was still a great drift of aching white sand.

Gypsies. They've changed, too, over the years. Now they travel in packs, motorized, in vehicles that shouldn't even be on the roads: furtive and scruffy, long-haired thieves who nobody wants and who don't much try to be wanted. Or perhaps I'm prejudiced. Anyway, they're not the real thing anymore. But in those days they were. Most of them, anyway . . .

Usually they'd come in packets of three or four families, small communities plodding the roads in their intricately painted, hand-carved horse-drawn caravans, some with canvas roofs and some wooden; all brass and black leather, varnished wood and lacquered chimney stacks, wrinkled brown faces and shiny brown eyes; with clothespegs and various gewgaws, hammered trinkets and rings that would turn your fingers green, strange songs sung for halfpennies and fortunes told from the lines in your hand. And occasionally a curse if someone was bad to them and theirs.

My uncle was the local doctor. He'd lost his wife in the Great War and had never remarried. She'd been a nurse and died somewhere on a battlefield in France. After the war he'd traveled a lot in Europe and beyond, spent years on the move, not wanting to settle. And when she was out of his system (not that she ever was, not really; her photographs were all over the house), then he had come home again to England, to the northeast where he'd been born. In the summers my parents would go down from Edinburgh to see him, and leave me there with him for company through the holidays.

This summer in question would be one of the last—of that sort, anyway—for the next war was already looming; of course, we didn't know that then.

"Gypsies, Sandy!" he said that day, just home from the mine where there'd been an accident. He was smudged with coal dust, which turned his sweat black where it dripped off him, with a pale band across his eyes and a white dome to his balding head from the protection of a miner's helmet.

"Gypsies?" I said, all eager. "Where?"

"Over in Slater's Copse. Seen 'em as I came over the viaduct. One caravan at least. Maybe there'll be more later."

That was it: I was supposed to run now, over the fields to the copse, to see the gypsies. That way I wouldn't ask questions about the accident in the mine. Uncle Zachary didn't much like to talk about his work, especially if the details were unpleasant or the resolution an unhappy one. But I wanted to know anyway. "Was it bad, down the mine?"

He nodded, the smile slipping from his grimy face as he saw that I'd seen through his ruse. "A bad one, aye," he said. "A man's lost his legs and probably his life. I did what I could." Following which he hadn't wanted to say any more. And so I went off to see the gypsies.

Before I actually left the house, though, I ran upstairs to my attic room. From there, through the binoculars Uncle Zachary had given me for my birthday, I could see a long, long way. And I could even see if he'd been telling the truth about the gypsies, or just pulling my leg as he sometimes did, a simple way of distracting my attention from the accident. I used to sit for hours up there, using those binoculars through my dormer window, scanning the land all about.

To the south lay the colliery: "Harden Pit," as the locals called it. Its chimneys were like long, thin guns aimed at the sky; its skeletal towers with their huge spoked wheels turning, lifting or lowering the cages; and at night its angry red coke ovens roaring, discharging their yellow- and white-blazing tonnage to be hosed down into mounds of foul-steaming coke.

Harden Pit lay beyond the viaduct with its twin lines of tracks glinting in the sunlight, shimmering in a heat haze. From here, on the knoll where Uncle Zachary's house stood—especially from my attic window —I could actually look down on the viaduct a little, see the shining tracks receding toward the colliery. The massive brick structure that supported them had been built when the collieries first opened up, to provide transport for the black gold, one viaduct out of many spanning the becks and streams of the northeast where they ran to the sea.

"Black gold," they'd called coal even then, when it cost only a few shillings per hundredweight!

This side of the viaduct and toward the sea cliffs, there stood Slater's Copse, a close-grown stand of oaks, rowans, hawthorns and hazelnuts. Old Slater was a farmer who had sold up to the coal industry, but he'd kept back small pockets of land for his and his family's enjoyment, and for the enjoyment of everyone else in the colliery communities. Long after this whole area was laid to waste, Slater's patches of green would still be here, shady oases in the grey and black desert.

And in the trees of Slater's Copse . . . Uncle Zachary hadn't been telling stories after all! I could glimpse the varnished wood, the young shire horse between his shafts, the curve of a spoked wheel behind a fence.

And so I left the house, ran down the shrub-grown slope of the knoll and along the front of the cemetery wall, then straight through the graveyard itself and the gate on the far side, and so into the fields with their paths leading to the new coast road on the one side and the viaduct on the other. Forsaking the paths, I forged through long grasses laden with pollen, leaving a smoky trail in my wake as I made for Slater's Copse and the gypsies.

Now, you might wonder why I was so taken with gypsies and gypsy urchins. The truth is that even old Zachary in his rambling house wasn't nearly so lonely as me. He had his work, calls to make every day, and his surgery in Essingham five nights a week. But I had no one. With my "posh" Edinburgh accent, I didn't hit it off with the colliery boys. Them with their hard, swaggering ways, and their harsh north-eastern twang. They called themselves "Geordies," though they weren't from Newcastle at all; and me, I was an outsider. Oh, I could look after myself. But why fight them when I could avoid them? And so the gypsies and I had something in common: we didn't belong here. I'd played with the gypsies before.

But not with this lot.

Approaching the copse, I saw a boy my own age and a woman, probably his mother, taking water from a spring. They heard me coming, even though the slight summer breeze off the sea favored me, and looked up. I waved . . . but their faces were pale under their dark cloth hats, where their eyes were like blots on old parchment. They didn't seem like my kind of gypsies at all. Or maybe they'd had trouble recently, or were perhaps expecting trouble. There was only one caravan and so they were one family on its own.

Then, out of the trees at the edge of the copse, the head of the family appeared. He was tall and thin, wore the same wide-brimmed cloth hat, looked out at me from its shade with eyes like golden triangular lamps. It could only have been a sunbeam, catching him where he stood with the top half of his body shaded; paradoxically, at the same time the sun had seemed to fade a little in the sky. But it was strange and I stopped moving forward, and he stood motionless, just looking. Behind him stood a girl, a shadow in the trees; and in the dappled gloom her eyes, too, were like candlelit turnip eyes in October.

"Hello!" I called from only fifty yards away. But they made no answer, turned their backs on me and melted back into the copse. So much for "playing" with the gypsies! With this bunch, anyway. But . . . I could always try again later. When they'd settled in down here.

I went to the viaduct instead.

The viaduct both fascinated and frightened me at one and the same time. Originally constructed solely to accommodate the railway, with the addition of a wooden walkway it also provided miners who lived in one village but worked in the other with a shortcut to their respective collieries. On this side, a mile to the north, stood Essingham; on the other, lying beyond the colliery itself and inland a half mile or so toward the metaled so-called coast road, Harden. The viaduct fascinated me because of the trains, shuddering and rumbling over its three towering arches, and scared me because of its vertiginous walkway.

The walkway had been built on the ocean-facing side of the viaduct, level with the railway tracks but separated from them by the viaduct's wall. It was of wooden planks protected on the otherwise open side by a fence of staves five feet high. Upward-curving iron arms fixed in brackets underneath held the walkway aloft, alone sustaining it against gravity's unending exertions. But they always looked dreadfully thin and rusty to me, those metal supports, and the vertical distance between them and the valley's floor seemed a terribly great one. In fact it was about one hundred and fifty feet. Not a *terrific* height, really, but it only takes a fifth of that to kill or maim a man if he falls.

I had an ambition: to walk across it from one end to the other. So far my best attempt had taken me a quarter-way across before being forced back. The trouble was the trains. The whistle of a distant train was always sufficient to send me flying, heart hammering, racing to get off the walkway before the train got onto the viaduct! But this time I didn't even make it that far. A miner, hurrying toward me from the other side, recognized me and called, "Here, lad! Are you the young 'un stayin' with Zach Gardner?"

"Yes, sir," I answered as he stamped closer. He was in his "pit black", streaked with sweat, his boots clattering on the wooden boards.

"Here," he said again, groping in a grimy pocket. "A threepenny bit!" He pressed the coin into my hand. "Now *run!* God knows you can go faster than me! Tell your uncle he's to come at once to Joe Anderson's. The ambulance men won't move him. Joe won't let them! He's delirious but he's hangin' on. We diven't think for long, though."

"The accident man?"

"Aye, that's him. Joe's at home. He says he can feel his legs but not the rest of his body. It'd be reet funny, that, if it wasn't so tragic. Bloody cages! He'll not be the last they trap! Now scramble, lad, d'you hear?"

I scrambled, glad of any excuse to turn away yet again from the challenge of the walkway.

Nowadays . . . a simple telephone call. And in those days, too, we had the phone; some of us. But Zachary Gardner hated them. Likewise cars, though he did keep a motorcycle and sidecar for making his rounds. Across the fields and by the copse I sped, aware of faces in the trees but not wasting time looking at them, and through the graveyard and up the cobbled track to the flat crest of the knoll, to where my uncle stood in the doorway in his shirtsleeves, all scrubbed clean again. And I gasped out my message.

Without a word, nodding, he went to the lean-to and started up the bike, and I climbed slowly and dizzily to my attic room, panting my lungs out. I took up my binoculars and watched the shining ribbon of road to the west, until Uncle Zachary's bike and sidecar came spurting into view, the banging of its pistons unheard at this distance; and I continued to watch him until he disappeared out of sight toward Harden, where a lone spire stood up, half hidden by a low hill. He came home again at dusk, very quiet, and we heard the next day how Joe Anderson had died that night.

The funeral was five days later at two in the afternoon; I watched for a while, but the bowed heads and the slim, sagging frame of the miner's widow distressed me and made me feel like a voyeur. So I watched the gypsies picnicking instead.

They were in the field next to the graveyard, but separated from it by
a high stone wall. The field had lain fallow for several years and was
deep in grasses, thick with clover and wildflowers. And up in my attic
room, I was the only one who knew the gypsies were there at all. They
had arrived as the ceremony was finishing and the first handful of dirt
went into the new grave. They sat on their colored blanket in the
bright sunlight, faces shaded by their huge hats, and I thought: *how
odd!* For while they had picnic baskets with them, they didn't appear to
be eating. Maybe they were saying some sort of gypsy grace first. Long,
silent prayers for the provision of their food. Their bowed heads told
me that must be it. Anyway, their inactivity was such that I quickly
grew bored and turned my attention elsewhere . . .

The shock came (not to me, you understand, for I was only on the
periphery of the thing, a child, to be seen and not heard) only three
days later. The first shock of several, it came first to Harden village, but
like a pebble dropped in a still pond its ripples began spreading almost
at once.

It was this: the recently widowed Muriel Anderson had committed
suicide, drowning herself in the beck under the viaduct. Unable to bear
the emptiness, still stunned by her husband's absence, she had thought
to follow him. But she'd retained sufficient of her senses to leave a
note: a simple plea that they lay her coffin next to his, in a single grave.
There were no children, no relatives; the funeral should be simple, with
as few people as possible. The sooner she could be with Joe again the
better, and she didn't want their reunion complicated by crowds of
mourners. Well, things were easier in those days. Her grief quickly
became the grief of the entire village, which almost as quickly dis-
persed, but her wishes were respected.

From my attic room I watched the gravediggers at work on Joe
Anderson's plot, shifting soil which hadn't quite settled yet, widening
the hole to accommodate two coffins. And later that afternoon I
watched them climb out of the hole, and saw the way they scratched
their heads. Then they separated and went off, one toward Harden on a
bicycle, heading for the viaduct shortcut, and the other coming my
way, toward the knoll, coming no doubt to speak with my Uncle Zachary. Idly, I looked for the gypsies then, but they weren't picnicking that
day and I couldn't find them around their caravan. And so, having

heard the gravedigger's cautious knock at the door of the house, and my uncle letting him in, I went downstairs to the study.

As I reached the study door I heard voices: my uncle's soft tones and the harsher, local dialect of the gravedigger, but both used so low that the conversation was little more than a series of whispers. I've worked out what was said since then, as indeed I've worked most things out, and so am able to reconstruct it here:

"*Holes,* you say?" That was my uncle.

"Aye!" said the other, with conviction. "In the side of the box. Drilled there, like. Fower of them."

"Wormholes?"

"Bloody big warms, gaffer!" "Big as half crowns, man, those holes! And anyhow, he's only been doon a fortneet."

There was a pause. Then: "And Billy's gone for the undertaker, you say?"

"Gone for Mr. Forster, aye. I told him, be as quick as you can."

"Well, John"—my uncle sighed—"while we're waiting, I suppose I'd better come and see what it is that's so worried you . . ."

I ducked back then, into the shadows of the stairwell. It wasn't that I was a snoop, and I certainly didn't feel like one, but it was as well to be discreet. They left the house and I followed on, at a respectful distance, to the graveyard. And I sat on the wall at the entrance, dangling my long skinny legs and waiting for them, sunbathing in the early evening glow. By the time they were finished in there, Mr. Forster had arrived in his big, shiny hearse.

"Come and see this," said my uncle quietly, his face quite pale, as Mr. Forster and Billy got out of the car. Mr. Forster was a thin man, which perhaps befitted his calling, but he was sweating anyway, and complaining that the car was like a furnace.

"That coffin"—his words were stiff, indignant—"is of the finest oak. Holes? Ridiculous! I never heard anything like it! Damage, more like," and he glowered at Billy and John. "*Spade* damage!" They all trooped back into the graveyard, and I went to follow them. But my uncle spotted me and waved me back.

"You'll be all right where you are, Sandy my lad," he said. So I shrugged and went back to the house. But as I turned away I did hear him say to Mr. Forster: "Sam, it's not spade damage. And these lads are quite right. Holes they said, and holes they are—four of them—all very neat and tidy, drilled right through the side of the box and the chips still lying there in the soil. Well, you screwed the lid down, and though I'll admit I don't like it, still I reckon we'd be wise to have it open again. Just to see what's what. Joe wouldn't mind, I'm sure, and there's only the handful of us to know about it. I reckon it was clever of these two lads to think to come for you and me."

"You because you're the doctor, and because you were closest," said Forster grudgingly, "and me because they've damaged my coffin!"

"No," John Lane spoke up, "because you built it—you're cousin, anyhow—and it's got holes in it!"

And off they went, beyond my range of hearing. But not beyond viewing. I ran as quickly as I could.

Back in my attic room I was in time to see Mr. Forster climb out of the hole and scratch his head as the others had done before him. Then he went back to his car and returned with a tool kit. Back down into the hole he went, my uncle with him. The two gravediggers stood at the side, looking down, hands stuffed in their trouser pockets. From the way they crowded close, jostling for a better position, I assumed that the men in the hole were opening the box. But then Billy and John seemed to stiffen a little. Their heads craned forward and down, and their hands slowly came out of their pockets.

They backed away from the open grave, well away until they came up against a row of leaning headstones, then stopped and looked at each other. My uncle and Mr. Forster came out of the grave, hurriedly and a little undignified, I thought. They, too, backed away; and both of them were brushing the dirt from their clothes, sort of crouched down into themselves.

In a little while they straightened up, and then my uncle gave himself a shake. He moved forward again, got down once more into the grave. He left Mr. Forster standing there ringing his hands, in company with Billy and John. My binoculars were good ones and I could actually see the sweat shining on Mr. Forster's thin face. None of the three took a pace forward until my uncle stood up and beckoned for assistance.

Then the two gravediggers went to him and hauled him out. And silent, they all piled into Mr. Forster's car, which he started up and headed toward the house. And of course I would have liked to know what this was all about, though I guessed I wouldn't be told. Which meant I'd have to eavesdrop again.

This time in the study the voices weren't so hushed; agitated, fearful, even outraged, but not hushed. There were four of them and they knew each other well, and it was broad daylight. If you see what I mean.

"Creatures? Creatures?" Mr. Forster was saying as I crept to the door. "Something in the ground, you say?"

"Like rats, d'you mean?" (John, the senior gravedigger.)

"I really don't know," said my uncle, but there was that in his voice which told me that he had his suspicions. "No, not rats," he finally said; and now he sounded determined, firm, as if he'd come to a decision. "Now look, you two, you've done your job and done it well, but this thing mustn't go any further. There's a guinea for each of you— from me, my promise—but you can't say anything about what you've seen today. Do you hear?"

"Whatever you say, gaffer," said John, gratefully. "But what'll you do about arl this? I mean—"

"Leave it to me." My uncle cut him off. "And mum's the word, hear?"

I heard the scraping of chairs and ducked back out of sight. Uncle Zachary ushered the gravediggers out of the house and quickly returned to his study. "Sam," he said, his voice coming to me very clear now, for he'd left the door ajar, "I don't think it's rats. I'm sure it isn't. Neither is it worms of any sort, nor anything else of that nature."

"Well, it's certainly nothing to do with me!" The other was still indignant, but more shocked than outraged, I thought.

"It's something to do with all of us, Sam," said my uncle. "I mean, how long do you think your business will last if this gets out, eh? No, it has nothing to do with you or the quality of workmanship," he continued, very quickly. "There's nothing personal in it at all. Oh, people will still die here, of course they will—but you can bet your boots they'll not want to be *buried* here!"

"But what on earth *is* it?" Forster's indignation or shock had evaporated; his voice was now very quiet and awed.

"I was in Bulgaria once," said my uncle. "I was staying at a small village, very tranquil if a little backward, on the border. Which is to say, the Danube. There was a flood and the riverbank got washed away, and part of the local graveyard with it. Something like this came to light, and the local people went very quiet and sullen. At the place I was staying, they told me there must be an 'obour' in the village. What's more, they knew how to find it."

"An obour?" said Forster. "Some kind of animal?"

My uncle's voice contained a shudder when he answered: "The worst possible sort of animal, yes." Then his chair scraped and he began pacing, and for a moment I lost track of his low-uttered words. But obviously Mr. Forster heard them clearly enough.

"*What?* Man, that's madness! And you a doctor!"

My uncle was ever slow to take offense. But I suspected that by now he'd be simmering. "They went looking for the obour with lanterns in the dark—woke up everyone in the village, in the dead of night, to see what they looked like by lantern light. For the eyes of the obour are yellow—and triangular!"

"Madness!" Forster gasped again.

And now my uncle *was* angry. "Oh, and do you have a better suggestion? So you tell me, Sam Forster, what *you* think can tunnel through packed earth and do . . . that?"

"But I—"

"Look at this book," my uncle snapped. And I heard him go to a bookshelf, then his footsteps crossing the room to his guest.

After a while Forster said, "Russian?"

"Romanian—but don't concern yourself with the text, look at the pictures!"

Again a pause. "But . . . this is too . . ."

"Yes, I know it is," said my uncle, before Forster could find the words he sought. "And I certainly hope I'm wrong, and that it is something ordinary. But tell me, can *anything* of this sort be ordinary?"

"What will we do?" Forster was quieter now. "The police?"

"What?" my uncle snorted. "Sergeant Bert Coggins and his three flat-foot constables? A more down-to-earth lot you couldn't ask for! Good Lord, no! The point is, if this really is something of the sort I've mentioned, it mustn't be frightened off. I mean, we don't know how long it's been here, and we certainly can't allow it to go somewhere else. No, it must be dealt with here and now."

"How?"

"I've an idea. It may be feasible, and it may not. But it certainly couldn't be considered outside the law, and it has to be worth a try. We have to work fast, though, for Muriel Anderson goes down the day after tomorrow, and it will have to be ready by then. Come on, let's go and speak to your cousin."

Mr. Forster's cousin, Jack Boulter, made his coffins for him; so I later discovered.

"Wait," said Forster, as I once more began backing away from the door. "Did they find this . . . this *creature*, these Bulgarian peasants of yours?"

"Oh, yes," my uncle answered. "They tied him in a net and drowned him in the river. And they burned his house down to the ground."

When they left the house and drove away I went into the study. On my uncle's desk lay the book he'd shown to Mr. Forster. It was open, lying facedown. Curiosity isn't confined to cats: small girls and boys also suffer from it. Or if they don't, then there's something wrong with them. I turned the book over and looked at the pictures. They were woodcuts, going from top to bottom of the two pages in long, narrow panels two to a page. Four pictures in all, with accompanying legends printed underneath. The book was old, the ink faded and the pictures poorly impressed; the text, of course, was completely alien to me.

The first picture showed a man, naked, with his arms raised to form a cross. He had what looked to be a thick rope coiled about his waist. His eyes were three-cornered, with radiating lines simulating a shining effect. The second picture showed the man with the rope uncoiled, dangling down loosely from his waist and looped around his feet. The end of the rope seemed frayed and there was some detail, but obscured by age and poor reproduction. I studied this picture carefully but was unable to understand it; the rope appeared to be fastened to the man's body just above his left hip. The third picture showed the man in an attitude of prayer, hands steepled before him, with the rope dangling as before, but crossing over at knee height into the fourth frame. There it coiled upward and was connected to the loosely clad body of a skeletally thin woman, whose flesh was mostly sloughed away to show the bones sticking through.

Now, if I tell my reader that these pictures made little or no sense to me, I know that he will be at pains to understand my ignorance. Well, let me say that it was not ignorance but innocence. I was a boy. None of these things which I have described made any great impression on me *at that time.* They were all incidents—mainly unconnected in my mind, or only loosely connected—occurring during the days I spent at my uncle's house; and as such they were very small pieces in the much larger jigsaw of my world, which was far more occupied with beaches, rock pools, crabs and eels, bathing in the sea, the simple but satisfying meals my uncle prepared for us, and so on. It is only in the years passed in between, and in certain dreams I have dreamed, that I have made the connections. In short, I was not investigative but merely curious.

Curious enough, at least, to scribble on a scrap of my uncle's notepaper the following words:

> Uncle Zachary,
> Is the man in these pictures a gypsy?

For the one connection I *had* made was the thing about the eyes. And I inserted the note into the book and closed it, and left it where I had found it—and then promptly forgot all about it, for there were other, more important things to do.

It would be, I think, a little before seven in the evening when I left the house. There would be another two hours of daylight, then an hour when the dusk turned to darkness, but I would need only a third of that total time to complete my projected walk. For it was my intention to cross the fields to the viaduct, then to cross the viaduct itself (!) and so proceed into Harden. I would return by the coast road, and back down the half-metaled dene path to the knoll and so home.

I took my binoculars with me, and as I passed midway between Slater's Copse and the viaduct, trained them upon the trees and the gleams of varnished woodwork and black, tarred roof hidden in them. I could see no movement about the caravan, but even as I stared so a figure rose up into view and came into focus. It was the head of the family, and he was looking back at me. He must have been sitting in the grass by the fence, or perhaps upon a tree stump, and had stood up as I focused my glasses. But it was curious that he should be looking at me as I was looking at him.

His face was in the shade of his hat, but I remember thinking, I wonder what is going on behind those queer, three-cornered eyes of his? And the thought also crossed my mind, I wonder what he must think of me, spying on him so rudely like this!

I immediately turned and ran, not out of any sort of fear but more from shame, and soon came to the viaduct. Out onto its walkway I proceeded, but at a slow walk now, not looking down through the stave fence on my left but straight ahead, and yet still aware that the side of the valley was now descending steeply underfoot, and that my physical height above solid ground was increasing with each pace I took. Almost to the middle I went, before thinking to hear in the still, warm evening air the haunting, as yet distant whistle of a train. A train! And I pictured the clattering, shuddering, rumbling agitation it would impart to the viaduct and its walkway!

I turned, made to fly back the way I had come . . . and there was the gypsy. He stood motionless, at the far end of the walkway, a tall, thin figure with his face in the shade of his hat, looking in my direction —looking, I knew, at me. Well, I wasn't going back *that* way! And now there *was* something of fear in my flight, but mainly I suspect fear of the approaching train. Whichever, the gypsy had supplied all the inspiration I needed to see the job through to the end, to answer the viaduct's challenge. And again I ran.

I reached the far side well in advance of the train, and looked back to see if the gypsy was still there. But he wasn't. Then, safe where the walkway met the rising slope once more, I waited until the train had passed, and thrilled to the thought that I had actually done it, crossed the viaduct's walkway! It would never frighten me again. As to the gypsy: I didn't give him another thought. It wasn't him I'd been afraid of but the viaduct, obviously . . .

The next morning I was up early, knocked awake by my uncle's banging at my door. "Sandy?" he called. "Are you up? I'm off into Harden, to see Mr. Boulter the joiner. Can you see to your own breakfast?"

"Yes," I called back, "and I'll make some sandwiches to take to the beach."

"Good! Then I'll see you when I see you. Mind how you go. You know where the key is." And off he went.

I spent the entire day on the beach. I swam in the tidal pools, caught small crabs for the fishermen to use as bait, fell asleep on the white sand and woke up itchy, with my sunburn already peeling. But it was only one more layer of skin to join many gone the same way, and I wasn't much concerned. It was late afternoon by then, my sandwiches eaten long ago and the sun beginning to slip; I felt small pangs of hunger starting up, changed out of my bathing costume and headed for home again.

My uncle had left a note for me pinned to the door of his study where it stood ajar:

Sandy,

I'm going back to the village, to Mr. Boulter's yard and then to the Vicarage. I'll be in about 9:00 p.m.—maybe. See you then, or if you're tired just tumble straight into bed.

—Zach

P.S. There are fresh sandwiches in the kitchen!

I went to the kitchen and returned munching on a beef sandwich, then ventured into the study. My uncle had drawn the curtains (something I had never before known him to do during daylight hours) and had left his reading lamp on. Upon his desk stood a funny contraption that caught my eye immediately. It was a small frame of rough, half-inch timber off-cuts, nailed together to form an oblong shape maybe eight inches long, five wide and three deep—like a box without top or bottom. It was fitted where the top would go with four small bolts at the corners; these held in position twin cutter blades (from some woodworking machine, I imagined), each seven inches long, which were slotted into grooves that ran down the corners from top edge to bottom edge. Small magnets were set central of the ends of the box, level with the top, and connected up to wires which passed through an entirely separate piece of electrical apparatus and then to a square three-pin plug. An extension cable lay on the study floor beside the desk, but it had been disconnected from the mains supply. My last observation was this: that a three-quarters-inch hole had been drilled through the wooden frame on one side.

Well, I looked at the whole setup from various angles but could make neither head nor tail of it. It did strike me, however, that if a cigar were to be inserted through the hole in the side of the box, and the bolts on that side released, the cigar's end would be neatly severed! But my uncle didn't smoke . . .

I experimented anyway, and when I drew back two of the tiny bolts toward the magnets, the cutter on that side at once slid down its grooves like a toy guillotine, thumping onto the top of the desk! For a moment I was alarmed that I had damaged the desk's finish . . . until I saw that it was already badly scored by a good many scratches and gouges, where apparently my uncle had amused himself doing much the same thing—except that he had probably drawn the bolts mechanically, by means of the electrical apparatus.

Anyway, I knew I shouldn't be in his study fooling about, and so I put the contraption back the way I had found it and returned to the kitchen for the rest of the sandwiches. I took them upstairs and ate them, then listened to my wireless until about nine o'clock—and still Uncle Zachary wasn't home. So I washed and got into my pajamas, which was when he chose to return—with Harden's vicar (the Reverend Fawcett) and Mr. Forster, and Forster's cousin, the joiner Jack Boulter, all in tow. As they entered the house I hurried to show myself on the landing.

"Sandy," my uncle called up to me, looking a little flustered. "Look, I'm sorry, nephew, but I've been very, *very* busy today. It's not fair, I know, but—"

"It's all right," I said. "I had a smashing day! And I'm tired." Which was the truth. "I'm going to read for a while before I sleep."

Then the conversation faded a little, or perhaps I was falling asleep. But I do remember Jack Boulter's voice saying, "Me, ah'll wark at it arl neet, if necessary. An' divven worry, it'll look no different from any other coffin. Just be sure you get them wires set up, that's arl, before two o'clock."

And my uncle answering him, "It will be done, Jack, no fear about that . . ."

The rest won't take long to tell.

I was up late, brought blindingly awake by the sun, already high in the sky, striking slantingly in through my window. Brushing the sleep from my eyes, I went and looked out. Down in the cemetery the gravediggers John and Billy were already at work, tidying the edges of the great hole and decorating it with flowers, but also filling in a small trench only inches deep, that led out of the graveyard and into the bracken at the foot of the knoll. John was mainly responsible for the latter, and I focused my glasses on him. There was something furtive about him: the way he kept looking this way and that, as if to be sure he wasn't observed, and whistling cheerily to himself as he filled in the small trench and disguised his work with chippings. It seemed to me that he was burying a cable of some sort.

I aimed my glasses at Slater's Copse next, but the curtains were drawn in the caravan's window and it seemed the gypsies weren't up and about yet. Well, no doubt they'd come picnicking later.

I washed and dressed, went downstairs and breakfasted on cereal with milk, then sought out my uncle—or would have, except that for the first time in my life I found his study door locked. I could hear voices from inside, however, and so I knocked.

"That'll be Sandy," came my uncle's voice, and a moment later the key turned in the lock. But instead of letting me in, he merely held the door open a crack. I could see Jack Boulter in there, working busily at some sort of apparatus on my uncle's desk—a device with a switch, and a small coloured light bulb—but that was all.

"Sandy, Sandy!" my uncle sighed, throwing up his hands in despair.

"I know," I said with a smile. "You're busy. It's all right, uncle, for I only came down to tell you I'll be staying up in my room."

That caused him to smile the first smile I'd seen on his face for some time. "Well, there's a bit of Irish for you," he said. But then he quickly sobered. "I'm sorry, nephew," he told me, "but what I'm about really is most important." He opened the door a little more. "You see how busy we are?"

I looked in and Jack Boulter nodded at me, then continued to screw down his apparatus onto my uncle's desk. Wires led from it through the curtains and out of the window, where they were trapped and prevented from slipping or being disturbed by the lowered sash. I looked at my uncle to see if there was any explanation.

"The, er—the wiring!" he finally blurted. "We're testing the wiring in the house, that's all. We shouldn't want the old place to burn down through faulty wiring, now should we?"

"No, indeed not," I answered, and went back upstairs.

I read, listened to the wireless, observed the land all about through my binoculars. In fact I had intended to go to the beach again, but there was something in the air: a hidden excitement, a muted air of expectancy, a sort of quiet tension. And so I stayed in my room, just waiting for something to happen. Which eventually it did.

And it was summoned by the bells, Harden's old church bells, pealing out their slow, doleful toll for Muriel Anderson.

But those bells changed everything. I can hear them even now, see and *feel* the changes that occurred. Before, there had been couples out walking: just odd pairs here and there, on the old dene lane, in the fields and on the paths. And yet by the time those bells were only halfway done the people had gone, disappeared, don't ask me where. Down in the graveyard, John and Billy had been putting the finishing touches to their handiwork, preparing the place, as it were, for this latest increase in the Great Majority; but now they speeded up, ran to the tiled lean-to in one tree-shaded corner of the graveyard and changed into clothes a little more fitting, before hurrying to the gate and waiting there for Mr. Forster's hearse. For the bells had told everyone that the ceremony at Harden church was over, and that the smallest possible cortege was now on its way. One and a half miles at fifteen miles per hour, which meant a journey of just six minutes.

Who else had been advised by the bells, I wondered?

I aimed my binoculars at Slater's Copse, and . . . they were there, all four, pale figures in the trees, their shaded faces turned toward the near-distant spire across the valley, half hidden by the low hill. And as they left the cover of the trees and headed for the field adjacent to the cemetery, I saw that indeed they had their picnic baskets with them: a large one which the man and woman carried between them, and a smaller one shared by their children. As usual.

The hearse arrived, containing only the coffin and its occupant, a great many wreaths and garlands, and of course the Reverend Fawcett and Mr. Forster, who with John and Billy formed the team of pallbearers. Precise and practiced, they carried Muriel Anderson to her grave where the only additional mourner was Jack Boulter, who had gone down from the house to join them. He got down into the flower-decked hole (to assist in the lowering of the coffin, of course) and after the casket had gone down in its loops of silken rope finally climbed out again, assisted by John and Billy. There followed the final service, and the first handful of soil went into the grave.

Through all of this activity my attention had been riveted on the graveyard; now that things were proceeding toward an end, however, I once again turned my glasses on the picnickers. And there they sat cross-legged on their blanket in the long grass outside the cemetery wall, with their picnic baskets between them. But *motionless* as always, with their heads bowed in a sort of grace. They sat there—as they had sat for Joe Anderson, and Mrs. Jones the greengrocer lady, and old George Carter the retired miner, whose soot-clogged lungs had finally collapsed on him—offering up their silent prayers or doing whatever they did.

Meanwhile, in the graveyard the ceremony was over at last, and John and Billy set to with their spades while the Reverend Fawcett, Jack Boulter, and Mr. Forster climbed the knoll to the house, where my uncle met them at the door. I heard him greet them, and the vicar's high-pitched, measured answer:

"Zach, Sam here tells me you have a certain book—with pictures? I should like to see it, if you don't mind. And then of course there's the matter of a roster. For now that we've initiated this thing I suppose we must see it through, and certainly I can see a good many long, lonely nights stretching ahead."

"Come in, come in," my uncle answered. "The book? It's in my study. By all means come through."

I *heard* this conversation, as I say, but nothing registered—not for a minute or two, anyway. Until—

There came a gasping and a frantic clattering as my uncle, with the Reverend Fawcett hot on his heels, came flying up the stairs to the landing, then up the short stairs to my room. They burst in, quite literally hurling the door wide, and my uncle was upon me in three great strides.

"Sandy," he gasped then, "what's all this about gypsies?" I put my glasses aside and looked at him, and saw that he was holding the sheet of notepaper with my scribbled query. He gripped my shoulder. "Why do you ask if the man in these pictures is a gypsy?"

Finally I knew what he was talking about. "Why, because of their eyes!" I answered. "Their three-cornered eyes." And as I picked up my binoculars and again trained them on the picnickers, I added: "But you can't see their faces from up here, because of their great hats . . ."

My uncle glanced out of the window and his jaw dropped. "Good Lord!" he whispered, eyes bulging in his suddenly white face. He almost snatched the glasses from me, and his huge hands shook as he put them to his eyes. After a moment he said, "My God, my God!" Simply that; and then he thrust the glasses at the Reverend Fawcett.

The Reverend was no less affected; he said, "Dear Jesus! Oh, my dear sweet Jesus! In broad daylight! Good heavens, Zach—*in broad daylight!*"

Then my uncle straightened up, towered huge, and his voice was steady again as he said, "Their shirts—look at their shirts!"

The vicar looked, and grimly nodded. "Their shirts, yes."

From the foot of the stairs came Jack Boulter's sudden query: "Zach, Reverend, are you up there? Zach, why man ar'm sorry, but there must be a fault. Damn the thing, but ar'm getna red light!"

"Fault?" cried my uncle, charging for the door and the stairs, with the vicar right behind him. "There's no fault, Jack! Press the button, man—*press the button!*"

Left alone again and not a little astonished, I looked at the gypsies in the field. Their shirts? But they had simply pulled them out of their trousers, so that they fell like small, personal tents to the grass where they sat. Which I imagined must keep them quite cool in the heat of the afternoon. And anyway, they always wore their shirts like that, when they picnicked.

But what was this? To complement the sudden uproar in the house, now there came this additional confusion outside! What could have startled the gypsies like this? What on earth was wrong with them? I threw open the window and leaned out, and without knowing why found my tongue cleaving to the roof of my mouth as once more, for the last time, I trained my glasses on the picnickers. And how to explain what I saw then? I saw it, but only briefly, in the moments before my uncle was there behind me, clapping his hand over my eyes, snatching the window and curtains shut, prising the glasses from my half-frozen fingers. Saw *and* heard it!

The gypsies straining to their feet and trying to run, overturning their picnic baskets in their sudden frenzy, seeming anchored to the ground by fat white ropes which lengthened behind them as they stumbled outward from their blanket. The agony of their dance there in the long grass, and the way they dragged on their ropes to haul them out of the ground, like strangely hopping blackbirds teasing worms; their terrified faces and shrieking mouths as their hats went flying; their shirts and dresses billowing, and their unbelievable screams. All four of them, screaming as one, but shrill as a keening wind, hissing like steam from a nest of kettles, or lobsters dropped live into boiling water, and yet cold and alien as the sweat on a dead fish!

And then the man's rope, incredibly long and taut as a bowstring, suddenly coming free of the ground—and likewise, one after another, the ropes of his family—and all of them *living things* that writhed like snakes and sprayed crimson from their raw red ends!

But all glimpsed so briefly, before my uncle intervened, and so little of it registering upon a mind which really couldn't accept it—not then. I had been aware, though, of the villagers advancing inexorably across the field, armed with the picks and shovels of their trade. (What? Ask John and Billy to keep mum about such as this? Even for a guinea?) And of the gypsies spinning like dervishes, coiling up those awful appendages about their waists, then wheeling more slowly and gradually crumpling exhausted to the earth; and of their picnic baskets scattered on the grass, all tumbled and . . . empty.

I've since discovered that in certain foreign parts "obour" means "night demon" or "ghost" or "vampire," while in others it means simply "ghoul." As for the gypsies: I know their caravan was burned out that same night, and that their bones were discovered in the ashes. It hardly worried me then and it doesn't now, and I'm glad that you don't see nearly so many of them around these days; but of course I'm prejudiced.

As they say in the northeast, a burden shared is a burden halved. But really, my dreams have been a terrible burden, and I can't see why I should continue to bear it alone.

This then has been my rite of exorcism. At least I hope so . . .

MELANIE TEM

Fry Day

My daughter Rachel always loved carnivals, and she'd have been delighted by this one. A seedy, smelly, gaudy, two-truck affair, it set up last Saturday in the little park near our house. I'm sure they don't have a permit. I'm sure they're violating all kinds of ordinances, not to mention the boundaries of good taste. Rachel would have been charmed by all that.

There are more people here than I expected. A lot of people I know —neighbors, the day clerk from the 7-Eleven, the relief mail carrier. I don't know many of their names anymore, but I remember their faces and most of their stories. This one's husband was killed in a car accident. That one is dying of cancer of the prostate, liver, bowel. I hardly believe in their sorrow, and it angers me to have it presented as though it mattered, as though it gives us something in common. None of them lost Rachel.

That one, passing now in front of me, has never had anything bad happen in her life, a story that seems far more plausible to me than the others, easier to accept. I smile at her and raise a hand in greeting. She waves back. Her bouquet of balloons both obscures and magnifies her face.

Unlike many children, Rachel never was afraid of clowns or barkers, the Ferris wheel or the tilt-a-whirl or the roller coaster, speed or height or centrifugal force or things that are not what they seem. The world for her was a good place, and only going to get better.

Which is why, thirteen and a half years ago at the age of twenty-one, she died. Brian James Dempsey killed her.

Killed *and* raped her, I remind myself diligently; it seems especially important to be precise tonight. Killed *and* raped *and* mutilated her. Along with, depending on which theory you subscribe to, fourteen or thirty-seven or a hundred other pretty young women with long dark hair.

A clown skips by. The orange yarn of his wig is raveling and he's lost the middle button of his polka-dot blouse, so that you can see the gray hair and the gray sweatshirt underneath. He bows elaborately to me and I bow back, laughing a little, a little bit scared.

Unless there's another stay, which at this point doesn't seem likely, Brian Dempsey will die in the Florida electric chair at five o'clock tomorrow morning, our time, for the only murder they've been able to convict him of. Not Rachel's.

At the end booth is a fortune-teller. She's dressed, of course, like a cartoon gypsy—bangles on her wrists and ankles, a black lace shawl over her head. Maybe she really is a gypsy. Maybe she really is a fortune-teller, come to this. She's reading the palm of Mrs. McCutheon, who used to baby-sit for me when Rachel was a baby. Foolishly, I wonder if the gypsy could have foretold Rachel's death, or the death of Mrs. McCutheon's daughter Libby, a grown woman with a husband and children, of a heart attack two years ago. I wonder if now she can see whether Brian Dempsey really will die tomorrow morning, and how it is that I could have lived after my daughter's death, and how I will go on living after her murderer's execution.

When Mrs. McCutheon gets up from the fortune-teller's table, she is crying. Her tears offend me, whether they're for me or for herself.

She doesn't know me at first; we haven't seen each other in a long time, and I've changed. When she realizes who I am, she gasps, "Oh, hello, dear," and looks at me as if she thinks she should say more. But I don't encourage her. Especially tonight, my grief is too good to share. Finally, Mrs. McCutheon just shakes her head and goes off down the midway.

The gypsy mistakes my hesitation for interest. "Come and see into your fu-tah!" she cries in a hoarse, heavy accent. "Fortunes one dollah only!"

"I can already see into my future," I tell her. "Thanks anyway." She shrugs and turns to another, likelier prospect. I went to a medium once, in those first desperate weeks after Rachel died, but I knew before I went that the woman would be a fake.

When the execution date was finally set, I called the governor's office to ask if I could come and watch. Be a witness to Brian Dempsey's extermination. Bear witness to what he did to my daughter, what he did to me. But Florida allows only official visitors at its executions. The woman on the phone sounded very young, younger than Rachel would be now, and she hardly gave me the time of day.

I couldn't stay home alone tonight, counting the hours. I tried to find out what his last meal would be, but they won't release that information till tomorrow, so I fixed for myself what I thought he might have: a hamburger, french fries, baked beans. He'll talk to his mother tonight. He'll dream. I couldn't stay home alone, trying to imagine all that, so I walked over here. It seems a fitting place for a vigil. Rachel loved carnivals, and this tacky little traveling sideshow will stay open all night.

"Hey, lady, win a dancing bear!" calls a barker in a dirty red-and-white-striped shirt from under a tattered red awning. "Flip the switch and it dances, just like Brian Dempsey!"

The plywood counter in front of him is crowded with the chintzy gadgets. The midway lights make him and them—and me, I suppose—look ghoulish. The toys are about the size of my clenched fists, and they make a tinny whirring sound when you turn them on. Actually, they look more like slightly melted human beings than like bears. All around me people are clapping, hooting, laughing appreciatively. I appreciate the gag, too. I laugh, too.

"Three chances to win for just one dollar, lady! Take home a souvenir of this great day in history to your kids and grandkids!"

Rachel was my only child, so all my grandchildren died with her. A few years afterward, when there were still no real suspects in her murder but serial killer Brian Dempsey had just started making the news, a young man I'd never heard of called me one afternoon from California. His voice breaking, he told me he'd been in love with my daughter and planned to marry her. Now he was married to someone else and his wife was expecting their first baby. If it was a girl, they wanted to name her Rachel.

I don't know why he called me. For my blessing, maybe; my permission, at least. I had none to give. I have no interest since Rachel died in other people's happiness, or in their pain.

I wait in the short line to pay the man my dollar. He takes it with a practiced gesture much like palming, and he doesn't look at my face or react to the condition of my hand. Probably he's seen worse. He offers me the bucket of multicolored balls and I take three. It doesn't matter which three, and it doesn't matter how I throw them, since the game is of course rigged.

I come close on two of my throws but don't hit anything. I've lost most of my dexterity and grip; my thumbs scarcely appose anymore. The tall kid next to me wins. I can't remember his name, but he's been living in foster homes since his mother shot his father and then herself when he was five or six. I wonder what he's doing here, how he dares be seen in public. His bear writhes and hops in his hands. Someone in the crowd yells, "Hey, Brian, it won't be long now!" and, briefly, I feel as if I've won something after all.

Over and over I've imagined what must have happened. At first I could hardly stand it, but I told myself I owed it to her; if she could go through it, the least I could do was think about it. So I've read everything that's ever been written about him, watched the TV movie four times, seen interviews, studied psychological theories about sociopaths. For a long time now, imagining in detail what must have happened to my daughter Rachel has been a daily habit; those are the first thoughts in my head when I wake up, if I've been able to sleep, and they give me energy and reason to face the day.

Speed and height and centrifugal force, and things that aren't what they seem. He'd have been quick—quick-thinking, quick with his hands and his words—though probably not quick, the experts have said, with his killing. Quick with his handsome smile. Even after all these years on death row, he has a quick and handsome smile. His approach to her that early, snowy morning thirteen and a half years ago —his offer of a ride to the bus stop, his thermos of steaming coffee— would have seemed to her an innocuous little adventure in a thoroughly adventurous world.

While he drove her into the mountains, he'd have kept up his patter, his pleasant jokes, his intelligent observations. Once she realized she was in terrible danger, she'd have thought of me. I was on my way to work by then, worried about a committee report that wasn't done. Things are not what they seem; she was already dead before I even knew she was missing.

That isn't going to happen to me this time. I'm going to know the exact moment Brian James Dempsey dies. I'm going to be wide awake and cheering. Then, I don't know what I'll do.

He didn't take her very far into the mountains. The roads were snow-packed, and he wouldn't have wanted to risk an accident. He dumped her nude body into the shaft of an abandoned silver mine just outside Idaho Springs; they didn't find it until nine weeks later. Most of his other victims, the ones he killed in summer, he buried; I suppose the ground was too frozen for him to bury Rachel, or maybe he'd forgotten his gloves.

The crowd is thinning. I'm approaching the end of this improvised midway; beyond it is the rest of the park, and the darkened houses of people with their own tragedies. Here's a guy swallowing fire. I watch him for a while and can't see the trick. His throat and lungs and chest must burn, like mine. I have a fleeting image of him setting all those houses on fire, one by one by one.

I check my watch, wind it. If the guy who flips the switch isn't late to work or the governor's heart doesn't start bleeding again at the last minute, Brian James Dempsey will be dead in five hours and ten minutes. Noticing a vague pain, I raise chilled fingers to loosen my lower lip from under my canine teeth. There's blood, but not much; I wipe it on my jacket, and nobody will notice.

This booth sells cotton candy. I'm one of a handful of customers. The kid behind the counter has an enormous "Fryin' Brian" button pinned to the bill of his cap, and an empty sleeve. As he hands me a large cone and, then, change, his glance inadvertently cuts across my face, and he does an obvious double take. But this is a traveling sideshow, after all, and it's nearly midnight; he probably sees all manner of strange and deformed creatures.

"Where'd you get the pin?" I ask him. It's one I don't have.

He doesn't hear me because he's already saying very loudly, not exactly to me but to the whole little crowd of us, "Hey, didja hear that Brian Dempsey didn't know tomorrow was Tuesday?"

One of the teenage girls behind me, who have been blatantly flirting with him, yells back as if this were a rehearsed routine, "No! Why?"

"Because he thought it was *Fry Day!*"

The girls shriek with laughter. I laugh, too, and wave the gaudy blue cotton candy as if it were a pompom. As I turn away from the counter toward the end of the midway, I think deliberately about those three pretty girls and the young man behind the counter, and I imagine in quick detail how he might lure them away from the carnival tonight, kill and rape and mutilate them. The fantasy calms me a little. The cotton candy sticks like clots of hair to my teeth.

There's even a freak show. I thought freak shows were illegal. I walk slowly past the tents and cages lined up across the end of the midway, staring at everything.

Siamese twin girls joined at the top of the head. Both of them stare back at me and give little shrieks, as if I frighten them. I stand in front of their tent for a long time, probably longer than my quarter entitles me to, savoring their distress and my own.

A boy with fur all over his body. WOLF BOY, one sign declares. DOG BOY, says another. He's sitting in an armchair reading *Time* magazine by the display light over his head, taking no notice at all of me. I long to be in there with him, to have my arms around his hairy neck, my teeth at his throat. I'd make him notice. I'd make us both a display. I'd make the world acknowledge this awful thing that has ruined my life. But others must have had the same impulse, because bars and mesh make a cage around the Wolf/Dog Boy, protecting him from me.

A Two-Headed Calf, asleep in its straw, all four eyes closed. A Fat Lady whose flesh oozes toward me as if it had a life and a purpose of its own. A woman with six fingers on each hand; since otherwise she looks quite ordinary, she makes sure you notice her deformity by leaning far forward on her stool and pressing her hands against the screen that shields her from anything other than the stares and words of the audience. The palms and all twelve fingers have hatch marks on them from the screen.

Rachel would have hated this part of the carnival. People being unkind to each other; people exploiting their own misfortunes. Thinking of her disapproval, I start to turn away.

Then fury at her propels me back. Rachel is *dead*. She let herself be killed, raped, mutilated. She brought this horror into my life and will make it stay forever. I owe her nothing.

But there's nothing more to see. I've come to the end of the freak show already. It must be hard to staff these days, when people accept so much. Reluctantly, I move away from the almost silent row of tents and cages toward the carousel on the other side of the midway.

The carousel is unstable. I watch it make a couple of rotations, remembering Rachel in pigtails on a pink horse, and the platform is noticeably lopsided and rickety. The same two or three bars of its tune are endlessly repeating, as if the tape is stuck. The old man who apparently runs the ride is asleep on his bench, legs stretched out in front of him, arms folded crookedly across his belly. At first I think he might be dead, but then I hear him snoring. The painted animals go around and around, up and down, without anybody on them.

I step over the old man's feet and duck under the rope. When my chance comes, I leap up onto the merry-go-round. It creaks and tilts under my weight.

I prowl among the animals. There are no pets here, no horses or noble Saint Bernards, only lions with teeth-lined gaping mouths, giant cats perpetually stiff-tailed and ready to pounce, snakes with coils piled higher than my waist and fangs dripping venom as peeling yellow paint.

The three variations—lion, tiger, snake—are repeated to fill up the little merry-go-round with perhaps a dozen wooden animals to ride. I've seen them all. I sit down near the edge of the platform and, with curved upraised arms and crossed legs, make another place where somebody could ride. A child, maybe. A pretty little girl. Her parents would let her on this ride because, unlike the teetering Ferris wheel at the other end of the midway or the roller coaster whose scaffolding is obviously listing, it would not seem dangerous. She would spot me right away and curious about what sort of animal I was supposed to be, she would come and sit in my lap. After a few rotations, a few stuck bars of the music, I would tighten my arms and legs around her until neither of us could breathe, and I'd never let her go.

"Fifty cents for the ride, lady," comes the stern, cracked voice.

Dirty hands on gaunt hips, the old man glares at me as his carousel takes me slowly past him, but he doesn't stop it. Maybe the control is stuck, so that it will only stop if it's dismantled. I get awkwardly to my knee, leaning into the turning motion, fish in my hip pocket, and on my next trip around hand him an assortment of nickels and dimes.

"See here," he says, and with unsettling agility leaps up beside me. "You missed the best one."

I can feel my nostrils flare at his odors: coffee, cigarettes, alcohol, dirt, and cold sweat. Under the ragged jacket, his new-looking bright blue sweatshirt reads BURN BRIAN BURN.

He takes my forearm in his horny fingers and leads me toward the center pole, which is unevenly striped and nowhere near vertical. With his other hand, he points. "There now, ain't she a beauty? Made her myself." Seeing at once what it is, I catch my breath.

A heavy wooden chair, tall as my head and wide as my shoulders, sturdy and polished, its surfaces reflecting the carnival lights. Leather straps across the back, seat, arms; shiny metal buckles. On the plank between the front legs, two inverted metal cones: electrodes. The cord, snaking so cleverly away that you have to look closely to see that it isn't plugged in. I prefer to pretend that it is.

"Gettin' a lot of business this week," the old man says with satisfaction. "Just like I thought."

Thrilled, I'm almost afraid to ask, "May I try it?"

He squints at me in a caricature of shrewdness. "Fifty cents extra."

I pay him without argument and take my place in the chair. The old man straps me in—one thong too tight across my breasts, another too low across my abdomen. He's just finished fastening the sharp buckles at my wrists when I notice that his jacket pockets are stuffed with trinkets, tiny replicas of this chair. "Wait," I say breathlessly. "Those are wonderful."

He chuckles and extracts a glittering handful. "Special shipment direct from Florida. Quarter apiece."

"I'll take them all."

He peers at me. I can tell that this is the first time he's noticed my face, but he doesn't seem particularly interested. "All? Must be a couple hundred here. Wasn't such a hot item as I thought. Might be some market for 'em tomorrow, *after*—"

"He killed my daughter." Killed *and* raped *and* . . .

There is a pause. We've made a complete rotation together, although here near the center it's harder to feel the motion. The magician across the way is still trying to get his frayed scarves untangled. "Well," the old man says, "I guess you're entitled."

"Yes."

"Let's say twenty cents apiece since it's quantity. Forty bucks."

"The money's in my back pocket." I manage to lift my hip off the seat of the electric chair long enough for him to slide his hand in and out of my pocket. I have no idea how much he takes. It doesn't matter. He empties his pockets of all the little electric chairs and piles them on the platform at my feet.

"Enjoy the ride," he tells me. He's leaning close over me, and my head is secured so that I can't avoid his rancid breath. He could avoid mine, as most people do, but he doesn't seem to mind. He's grinning. So am I. "Not much business this late, so you can stay on as long as you like."

Absurdly grateful, I try to nod my thanks, forgetting for the moment that my head won't move. He hasn't shaved my head, of course, but I can easily imagine that for myself. When I try to speak, my voice cracks and growls. He waves a twisted hand at me as if he knows what I want to say. Then he makes his way expertly among the silent and forever raging beasts and off the carousel, out of my restricted line of vision.

I'm alone. I can't see my watch anymore, but it must be nearing one o'clock. Brian Dempsey will die in a chair like this in four hours. The carousel keeps turning; before long, even its jerks and bumps have melded into a somnolent pattern.

I'm in my house, in my back yard filled with flowers. Rachel loved flowers. Under the rose arbor is a chair, so polished it glows, so sturdy I know it has rooted to my garden. In it is tied a handsome young man. He's crying. They're going to execute him. I go to him, kneel, smell the roses, put my arms around him. His body stiffens as if he would pull away from me if he could; I look at his face and see that he's afraid of me, and I know that he has reason to be. I hold him. I can feel his heartbeat, the pulse in his temple. The executioner is approaching, from the back door of my house, a whole parade of executioners each wearing a party hat and swallowing fire. They're going to kill him. I'm not trying to stop it. I just want to comfort him. I hold him close and am suffused with sorrow for us all.

I wake up enraged. I've been betrayed by my own dreams.

It's still pitch dark. I'm aware of a steady rotation, and of music that

is scarcely music anymore, and of lights, and of hands at my wrists and
under my arms. "Wake up, lady," says the voice of the old man, not, I
think, for the first time. "It's time."

"Oh, God, what time is it?"

"It's five o'clock."

Then from all up and down the midway comes a ragged cheer, and
the triumphant cry of "Brian Dempsey is dead!" I imagine the Siamese
twins saying it to each other, the Wolf Boy snarling it through bared
teeth, the fire swallower spitting it up. I say it, too: "Brian Dempsey is
dead!" Saying those words makes me tremble as though an electric
shock has gone through me, although I don't recognize them coming
out of my mouth and I hardly know what it means.

The old man is staring at me. He's not frightened, and he's certainly
not surprised, but he can't seem quite to take in what he's seeing. I
raise my hands to my face, but neither my face nor my hands are there
anymore in any recognizable form.

He lifts me out of the chair. I can hardly walk; I stumble over the
scattered trinkets as if they are bits of bone. My spine has bent at a
sharp angle; my feet hurt too much to bear my weight.

The old man picks me up in his arms, finds places finally to hold on
to my body. He steps off the still-turning platform of the carousel, and
without effort takes me the short distance to the end of the midway to
the row of tents and cages that make up the freak show.

Next to the Two-Headed Calf, on the very edge of the carnival
where the park leads to other people's houses, a cage is empty, except
for a chair like the one I dreamed in. The old man drops me into it but
doesn't bother to strap me down. He leaves, clangs the door shut behind him but doesn't lock it.

An early-morning line of watchers and revelers, celebrating the execution, is already starting to form outside my cage. They've come to see
what I've turned into, what Brian Dempsey has made me, what they all
can turn into if they try.

For the first time since my daughter Rachel was killed and raped and
mutilated, maybe for the first time in my life, I am at peace.

BILL PRONZINI

Out Behind
the Shed

There was a dead guy behind the parts shed.

I went out there to get a Ford oil pan for Barney and I saw him lying on his back in the weedy grass. He didn't have a face. There was blood and bone and pulp and black scorch marks where his face used to be. I couldn't even guess if he was anybody I knew.

I stood there shivering. It was cold . . . Jesus, it was cold for late March. The sky was all glary, like the sun coming off a sheet-metal roof. Only there wasn't any sun. Just a shiny silver overcast, so cold-hot bright it hurt your eyes to look at it. The wind was big and gusty, the kind that burns right through clothing and puts a rash like frostbite on your skin. No matter what I'd done all day I couldn't seem to get warm.

I'd known right off, as soon as I got out of bed, that it was going to be a bad day. The cold and the funny bright sky was one thing. Another was Madge. She'd started in on me about money again even before she made the coffee. How we were barely making ends meet and couldn't even afford to get the TV fixed, and why couldn't I find a better-paying job or let her go to work part-time or at least take a second job myself, nights, to bring in a little extra. The same old song and dance. The only old tune she hadn't played was the one about how much she ached for another kid before she got too old, as if two wasn't enough. Then I came in here to work and Barney was in a grumpy mood on account of a head cold and the fact that we hadn't had three new repair jobs in a week. Maybe he'd have to do some retrenching if things didn't pick up pretty soon, he said. That was the word he used, retrenching. Laying me off was what he meant. I'd been working for him five years, steady, never missed a day sick, never screwed up on a single job, and he was thinking about firing me. What would I do then? Thirty-six years old, wife and two kids, house mortgaged to the hilt, no skills except auto mechanic and nobody hiring mechanics right now. What the hell would I do?

Oh, it was a bad day, all right. I hadn't thought it could get much worse, but now I knew that it could.

Now there was this dead guy out here behind the shed.

I ran back inside the shop. Barney was still banging away under old Mrs. Cassell's Ford, with his legs sticking out over the end of the roller cart. I yelled at him to slide out. He did and I said, "Barney . . . Barney, there's a dead guy out by the parts shed."

He said, "You trying to be funny?"

"No," I said. "No kidding and no lie. He's out there in the grass behind the shed."

"Another of them derelicts come in on the freights, I suppose. You sure he's dead? Maybe he's just passed out."

"*Dead,* Barney. I know a dead guy when I see one."

He hauled up on his feet. He was a big Swede, five inches and fifty pounds bigger than me, and he had a way of looming over you that made you feel even smaller. He looked down into my face and then scowled and said in a different voice, "Froze to death?"

"No," I said. "He hasn't got a face anymore. His face is all blown away."

"Jesus. Somebody killed him, you mean?"

"Somebody must of. Who'd do a thing like that, Barney? Out behind our shed?"

He shook his head and cracked one of his big gnarly knuckles. The sound echoed like a gunshot in the cold garage. Then, without saying anything else, he swung around and fast-walked out through the rear door.

I didn't go with him. I went over and stood in front of the wall heater. But I still couldn't get warm. My shoulders kept hunching up and down inside my overalls and I couldn't feel my nose or ears or the tips of my fingers, as if they weren't there anymore. When I looked at my hands they were all red and chapped, like Madge's hands after she's been washing clothes or dishes. They twitched a little, too; the tendons were like worms wiggling under a handkerchief.

Pretty soon Barney came back. He had a funny look on his moon face but it wasn't the same kind he'd had when he went out. He said, "What the hell, Joe? I got no time for games and neither do you."

"Games?"

"There's nobody behind the shed," he said.

I stared at him. Then I said, "In the grass, not ten feet past the far corner."

"I looked in the grass," Barney said. His nose was running from the cold. He wiped it off on the sleeve of his overalls. "I looked all over. There's no dead guy. There's nobody."

"But I saw him. I swear to God."

"Well, he's not there now."

"Somebody must of come and dragged him off, then."

"Who'd do that?"

"Same one who killed him."

"There's no blood or nothing," Barney said. He was back to being grumpy. His voice had that hard edge and his eyes had a squeezed look. "None of the grass is even flattened down. You been seeing things, Joe."

"I tell you, it was the real thing."

"And I tell *you*, it wasn't. Go out and take another look, see for yourself. Then get that oil pan out of the shed and your ass back to work. I promised old lady Cassell we'd have her car ready by five-thirty."

I went outside again. The wind had picked up a couple of notches, turned even colder; it was like fire against my bare skin. The hills east of town were all shimmery with haze, like in one of those desert mirages. There was a tree smell in the air but it wasn't the usual good pine-and-spruce kind. It was a eucalyptus smell, even though there weren't any eucalyptus trees within two miles of here. It made me think of cat piss.

I put my head down and walked slow over to the parts shed. And stopped just as I reached it to draw in a long breath. And then went on to where I could see past the far corner.

The dead guy was there in the grass. Lying right where I'd seen him before, laid out on his back with one leg drawn up and his face blown away.

The wind gusted just then, and when it did it made sounds like howls and moans. I wanted to cover my ears. Cover my eyes, too, to keep from seeing what was in the grass. But I didn't do either one. All I did was stand there shivering with my eyes wide open, trying to blink away some of the shimmery haze that seemed to have crawled in behind them. Nothing much was clear now, inside or out—nothing except the dead guy.

"Joe!"

Barney, somewhere behind me. I didn't turn around but I did back up a couple of steps. Then I backed up some more, until I was past the corner and couldn't see the dead guy anymore. Then I swung around and ran to where Barney was in the shop doorway.

"He's there, Barney, he's there, he's there—"

He gave me a hard crack on the shoulder. It didn't hurt; only the cold hurt where it touched my face and hands. He said, "Get hold of yourself, man."

"I *swear* it," I said, "right where I saw him before."

"All right, take it easy."

"I don't know how you missed seeing him," I said. I pulled at his arm. "I'll show you, come on."

I kept tugging on him and finally he came along, grumbling. I led the way out behind the shed. The dead guy was still there, all right. I blew out the breath I'd been holding and said, "Didn't I tell you? Didn't I?"

Barney stared down at the dead guy. Then he stared at me with his mouth open a little and his nose dripping snot. He said, "I don't see anything."

"You don't . . . what?"

"Grass, just grass."

"What's the matter with you? You're looking right at him!"

"The hell I am. The only two people out here are you and me."

I blinked and blinked and shook my head and blinked some more but the dead guy didn't go away. He was *there.* I started to bend over and touch him, to make absolutely sure, but I couldn't do it. He'd be cold, as cold as the wind—colder. I couldn't stand to touch anything that cold and dead.

"I've had enough of this," Barney said.

I made myself look at him instead of the dead guy. The cat-piss smell had gotten so strong I felt like gagging.

"He's there," I said, pleading. "Oh God, Barney, can't you see him?"

"There's nobody there. How many times do I have to say it? You better go on inside, Joe. Both of us better. It's freezing out here." He put a hand on my arm but I shook it off. That made him mad. "All right," he said, "if that's the way you want it. How about if I call Madge? Or maybe Doc Kiley?"

"No," I said.

"Then quit acting like a damn fool. Get a grip on yourself, get back to work. I mean it, Joe. Any more of this crap and you'll regret it."

"No," I said again. "You're lying to me. That's it, isn't it? You're lying to me."

"Why would I lie to you?"

"I don't know, but that's what you're doing. Why don't you want me to believe he's there?"

"Goddamn it, *there's nobody there!*"

Things just kept happening today—bad things one right after another, things that made no sense. The cold, Madge, Barney, the dead guy, the haze, the cat-piss smell, Barney again—and now a cold wind chilling me inside as well as out, as if icy gusts had blown right in through my flesh and were howling and prowling around my heart. I'd never felt like this before. I'd never been this cold or this scared or this frantic.

I pulled away from Barney and ran back into the shop and into the office and unlocked the closet and took out the duck gun he lets me keep in there because Madge don't like guns in the house. When I got back to the shed, Barney was just coming out with a Ford oil pan in his gnarly hands. His mouth pinched up tight and his eyes got squinty when he saw me.

He said, "What the hell's the idea bringing that shotgun out here?"

"Something's going on," I said, "something crazy. You see that dead guy there or don't you?"

"You're the one who's crazy, Joe. Give me that thing before somebody gets hurt."

He took a step toward me. I backed up and leveled the duck gun at him. "Tell me the truth," I said, desperate now, "tell me you see him lying there!"

He didn't tell me. Instead he gave a sudden lunge and got one hand on the barrel and tried to yank the gun away and oh Jesus him pulling on it like that made me jerk the trigger. The load of birdshot hit him full on and he screamed and the wind screamed with him and then he stopped but the wind didn't. Inside and out, the wind kept right on screaming.

I stood looking down at him lying in the grass with one leg drawn up and his face blown away. I could see him clear, even through that shimmery haze. Just him down there. Nobody else.

Just Barney.

PETER TREMAYNE

Fear a' Ghorta

"Bless me, Father, for I have sinned."

Father Ignatius had heard the words a million times or more. He could not begin to recall the times he had sat in the dark oak womb of the confessional box, oppressed by the odor of polished wood, the musty smell of the velvet curtains and the camphor-scented candles, while he sat on the hassock which served as a cushion but which did not ease the hardness of the wooden bench on which the priest was supposed to sit. He could not begin to recall the times he had heard the opening line of the confessional formula echoing from the successive shadowy forms beyond the small fretwork grille. Father Ignatius had served both as curate and priest in the Church of the Most Holy Redeemer, on New York's West Third Street, for twenty years. Twenty years of confessions. He reckoned that he was now as broad-minded as anyone could be; nothing could shock him after listening to twenty years of sins from countless individuals. He had heard the opening line of the confessional ritual spoken in many tones—truculent, fearful, bored . . .

"Bless me, Father, for I have sinned."

Yet the hoarse whisper of the voice which came through the lattice held a timbre which made Father Ignatius stir uneasily. The emphasis on the words gave them an immediacy and a terrible urgency that the priest had never heard before. Father Ignatius frowned into the gloom at the shadow beyond the grille.

"How long has it been since your last confession, my son?" he asked.

There was a pause and then the hoarse whisper came: "Twenty-five years, Father."

"Twenty-five years?" A priest was not supposed to sound so condemnatory, but the words were wrenched from Father Ignatius in an accusing tone.

"I last made a confession on the first day of August, 1848."

The priest made a rapid calculation.

"Indeed," he confirmed. "Twenty-five years lacking four weeks. Why do you come to make confession now? Why, after all this time?"

"It is a long story, Father."

Father Ignatius turned, drew aside the velvet curtain and peered into the church. It was deserted. The man had obviously waited until last before coming to the box, waited until the last of the evening penitents had departed.

"We have plenty of time, my son," he said, bringing his attention back to the shadow beyond the grille.

"Then perhaps, Father, I could tell my story without interruption? In that way I will confess all and you will be able to understand why it is that I have been so long in coming back to the sanctuary of Holy Mother Church."

Father Ignatius listened to the cadences of the voice and then observed, "You are Irish, aren't you? I can tell by your accent."

The shadow gave a rueful laugh.

"Strange, after twenty-five years in New York I fondly thought that I had lost my accent. Is it so obvious that I am not a native of this city?"

"What is native, my son?" said Father Ignatius with a smile. "We are all immigrants here."

"But you are not Irish, Father," observed the voice.

"I was born in Austria. My parents brought me here when I was small." The priest hesitated. He had heard of the clannishness of the Irish. "Would you prefer an Irish priest to hear your confession? Father Flannery is in the Presbytery and I am sure . . ."

The voice was firm. "No. It does not matter who hears my confession. A priest is a priest, isn't this so, Father?"

"We are merely the link to God, my son. Very well. Perhaps you had best begin."

My name . . . ah, perhaps that does not matter. When I had friends they called me Pilib Rua, Foxy Pilib on account of my red hair. Among the Irish here I am called Fear a' Ghorta which, in the Irish language, means the Man of Hunger. Why I have been given this name will become obvious as I proceed.

My home was in the province of Connacht, in the west of Ireland, where I was weaned and educated for life. I was sixteen summers in my youth when I ran away from the drudgery of life on my father's croft. It was a terrible existence. We worked on the estate of Colonel Chetwynd, the English landlord who owned our part of the country. And a poor land it was. It was a place filled with poverty, where cold clung to your marrow and the rain was a constant and relentless downpour. There was no hope of improvement in our life for the poor sod which we worked was not ours to enjoy. We could work it but had to pay tithes and tribute to Colonel Chetwynd, and if our poor land did not give us sufficient to pay the rent then the Colonel's bailiffs would evict us, throwing us off the land in which our fathers and our forefathers had dwelt for centuries. To prevent those evicted crawling back to their homes for shelter the Colonel's men would burn the thatch from the roofs. Our small corner of Ireland was no different from any other corner of our poor conquered land. That was why I could not bear to face a future there. So I ran away to sea. I joined the Royal Navy as a means of escaping from the drudgery of my life and voyaged abroad for five years until, falling from a rigging, I suffered an injury which drew me back to my native land.

It was the period which we Irish call *na blianta ochreacha*—the hungry years or, more simply, *An Ocras Mhór*—The Great Hunger. Within the space of a few years, between 1845 and 1848, the population of our small ravaged land fell by two and a half million. Think of it, Father! Those that perished from starvation and its accompanying diseases in those few years numbered a million and a half. A further million vanished on the immigrant ships, many of them dying on the journey. And to die of what? Not the hunger they brought out of Ireland but a disease caught on the ships. The Irish immigrants were pressed into the holds of the timber ships—and the disease lived in the sawdust and timber residue. Healthy people would board the ships at Queenstown or Dublin only to be smitten on the voyage or when they reached sight of the new land.

And the famine itself? The famine was caused by a potato blight. The potato crop in Ireland was affected and potatoes melted into slimy decaying pulps. And yet, Father, there was enough food in the land to feed not only our eight million population but eighteen millions of people. Oh yes, there was grain enough, wheat enough, oats enough and meat in Ireland to feed three times our population.

Why, you ask, why did so many perish then? Why did the Irish starve to death in their tens of thousands?

Ah, I shall come to that.

I landed in the city of Galway in August of 1848 when the famine was in its fourth year and the dead lay unburied on the roads and lanes of my dear green province of Connacht. Homeless beggars roamed the streets of the city, while others gathered on the quays trying to find a place in the emigrant ships. The worst sight of all was the children . . . mere animated skeletons, some screaming for food, while many were past crying. They sat or lay, emaciated bundles of bone with scarcely any flesh, with only their eyes . . . large, round eyes, staring beseechingly in muted suffering.

I had heard of the extent of the famine in my voyaging. Indeed, I had heard it said that nearly a third of the population of the province of Connacht had already perished from the land by the time I set foot at Galway. Yet it had been impossible to visualize such suffering. As well as the suffering children there were those who had the famine dropsy, as we called it, with bodies swollen to twice their natural size, the gums spongy so that the teeth fell out, the joints enlarged, the skin red where the blood vessels had burst, and the legs turned black. They peopled Galway City like wraiths.

Among this swarm of figures from hell rode the well-fed English cavalry troopers and the administrators. Truly, after the centuries of struggle, it could be said that in those years of famine the English had finally conquered, conquered our spirit and our will.

I walked from Galway north along the shores of Loch Corrib until I turned west and came by easy stages to my village. It nestled at the foot of some gaunt hills facing the brooding Atlantic sea. The people scarcely recognised me in their plight. Many had died. Indeed, 'twas to a cold and empty croft that I returned. My father, mother, and two young brothers had been dead a year since.

"Why did you come back, Pilib Rua?" demanded Dangan Cutteen, who always acted as spokesman for the villagers. "Weren't you better off sailing the seas than returning to this bleak place."

I told him my story and how the Royal Navy had put me ashore because I had fallen from a rigging and was no longer any use to them.

Dangan Cutteen had scowled. "And what are you here but another mouth to go hungry?"

I was surprised at the bitterness in his voice. He was a man of fierce primeval passions but of equally fierce attachments. He was as hard and gaunt as the granite rocks and withal as protective to those he cared for as the bleak surrounding hills. From Dangan Cutteen I had learned seacraft by going out with him since I was a sprogeen, scarcely walking from my cradle. Many is the hour we spent in his curragh while he would teach me not only the way the fish ran but also the old ranns and proverbs of our native tongue. In his rich baritone, which droned like the wind, he would sing the wild traditional songs of our forefathers as we fought the currents and the tides of that restless coast.

Seeing the hurt in my eyes, Dangan Cutteen gripped me by the shoulders. "Yerrah, boy, let there be forgiveness at me. I am half insane with fear for our people. Nearly half the village has perished and I am helpless to aid them. The men grow desperate as they watch the old, the sick and the young grow wizened and frail before their eyes. God! God! What a fearsome sight it is to see the old and the young neither crying nor complaining but crawling over the potato ridges, turning sods of earth in the hope that a good potato might remain in the ground."

"But why are the people starving?" I demanded. "It is only the potato crops that have failed, and the oats, grain and barley yield in abundance. Why, coming into Galway, for every famine relief ship I saw entering port, I saw six ships loaded with grain and livestock and wool and flax sailing for England."

Dangan Cutteen gave out a bitter laugh. "The people starve because the grain and livestock belong to the England landlords who own the land of Ireland. And we . . . we Irish are but a poor, crushed and conquered people. We do not have the backbone to rise up and take what is ours that we might live. The English landlords threaten us with eviction if we do not pay our rents and whole families die of starvation so that the lords of the land have their due."

"Surely the politicians . . . ?"

Dangan Cutteen spat. "A curse on their dead ones! There is devastation in the land and what do the lickspittle representatives say? John O'Connell, the son of Daniel O'Connell whom the people hailed as "the Liberator," rose in the English Parliament and said, "I thank God I live among a people who would rather die than defraud the landlord of rent." Aye, they die, they die the Irish in their tens of thousands to feed the English landlords."

I heard hatred in Dangan Cutteen's voice. It was a hatred I came to share. Yes, I'll admit that. *An Ocras Mhór* left hatred behind it. Between Ireland and England the memory of what was done has endured and will endure like a sword probing a wound. There have been other famines in Ireland and doubtless there will be other famines to come but the days of the Great Hunger will never be forgotten nor forgiven.

During the first few days I stayed in my village, I joined with Dangan Cutteen and the others in putting out to sea in the curraghs in search of fish. Yet even the fish had apparently deserted their normal feeding grounds along the coast, perhaps sensing the presence of the terrible specter of hunger which stalked the land. Several of the women of the village protested at their menfolk putting to sea, for they felt that in their weak, starving condition the men would not have the strength to fight its contrary moods. But Dangan told them that there was only death before them anyway, so was it not better to look for death on the water rather than passively wait for it on the bleak land?

Came the day when Dangan Cutteen ordered the people of the village to gather together. He had decided to make a final appeal to the lord of the land, Colonel Chetwynd, to release some of the produce and livestock he was keeping in his barns. The people walked slowly in a body up the steep road to the great white-walled mansion which was the seat of Colonel Chetwynd's estate. It lay about a mile east of the village. With the afternoon sun slanting its golden rays across it, it looked a beautiful and peaceful place. It seemed a place at odds with the terror that was oppressing the land.

Colonel Chetwynd was obviously warned of our coming and, as we approached the big house, we saw him standing at the top of the great stairs that led to the main doors. At his side was the weasel-faced overseer of the estate, a man named Brashford. I recall him well. He had been brought over from England to manage the estate for the colonel twenty years before. Brashford made no pretense at hiding the fact that he carried a revolver in his pocket. I was sure that a corresponding bulge in the colonel's pocket concealed a similar weapon. Also, posted about the estate, there were half a dozen English soldiers sent up from the Galway garrison in case of trouble.

The soldiers were there not specifically for us but because there were rumors of a rising against the English throughout the country. I have never known a time when there were not such rumors, although I was too young to remember the uprisings of 1798 and 1803. It seemed that the Young Irelanders were determined to make another attempt to establish a republic in Ireland before the year was out and English troops were flooding into the country in preparation.

As we approached Colonel Chetwynd I saw there was a disdainful look on his fat, bloated features. It was at least six years since I had previously seen the man who was the sole arbiter of our lives and fortunes. He had not changed except that he appeared to me more dissolute, more debauched than before. There was no hunger or want about his replete figure.

"What do you want here?" His voice was nasal and he called in English.

We halted, unsure of ourselves. Then Dangan Cutteen moved forward. He was unused to speaking English and his voice was slow, soft and considered.

"Why, your honor, we want food."

"Food?" Colonel Chetwynd gave a sharp bark of laughter, abruptly like the bark of a fox at night.

"Your honor, we work on your estate. We know you have enough livestock—hogs, cattle, and sheep—and enough grain to keep us from harm. Yet we starve and sicken and die. We are in desperate need, your honor."

Colonel Chetwynd grimaced, his mouth ugly. "Am I to be a philanthropist, issuing alms out of altruism?"

"I have no understanding of those words, your honor," replied Dangan. "Is there not an abundance of food on your estate?"

"No business of yours," snapped the colonel. "It is my property and on it depends my income. Do I have to explain the principles of business with the likes of you?"

"You do not, your honor, for we are not discussing the principles of business but the principles of humanity. Our people are dying almost daily from *An Ocras Mhór*. Our potatoes, on which we rely, are blighted, our own pigs and fowls are long since dead, and now our old folk, the wee ones and the frail and sick, are dying. Yet in your barns is food aplenty."

It was then that the overseer, Brashford, whose face was almost apoplectic with rage, interrupted.

"I know this man, Colonel. Dangan Cutteen by name. A troublemaker if ever there was one. Let me drive these swine from the estate."

Colonel Chetwynd smiled thinly.

"No, Brashford. No. Mister Cutteen has a good argument here. He seems to be stating the law of supply and demand. He and his people want food. We have food."

For a moment we stood silently, not one of us sure that we had heard the colonel aright. Few of us had the subtle English and we thought that our interpretation might be at fault. Dangan took a pace frowning.

"Are you willing to give us the food, your honor?" he asked hesitantly.

Colonel Chetwynd threw back his head and guffawed loudly. "By the pox, no! I am willing to sell you the food. You must pay the price that I would get were I to ship it to England."

It was then that we realized the bitter humor of the man and a murmur of suppressed rage ran through us.

Dangan Cutteen did not lose his temper. "Your honor, you know that we have no money. We work on your estate to earn the rents and tithes you claim for our poor hovels. We have to provide our labor to you in order to remain on the land which was our forefathers' land long before you and yours came to it. For this we must be grateful, but the only extra money we have, in a good year, is when we can sell any abundance and surplus of our own produce at the market. There has been no surplus from our small potato plots since the start of the famine. We have no money."

Colonel Chetwynd was smiling evilly now and nodding his head. "Then we have no business to discuss, Mister Cutteen."

He made to turn away and Dangan Cutteen spoke sharply at last: "God forgive you, your honor!"

Colonel Chetwynd glanced back. "The question is settled, Cutteen. Business is business. You have no money. I am not a charity. My produce goes to England."

"And we are simply to starve to death?"

"Are there no fish left in the sea?" Brashford interrupted again.

"None that we can take," replied Dangan.

"Then eat grass," replied the overseer. "Didn't His Highness, the son of our Gracious Sovereign, Queen Victoria, suggest that the Irish nation could save itself by eating grass, for aren't the Irish capable of eating anything?"

The weasel-faced overseer laughed uproariously at his sally and the red-coated soldiers joined in his mirth.

Dangan Cutteen stood there a moment more, his face twisted in a scarcely controlled rage.

"But, Colonel . . ." he began slowly.

Colonel Chetwynd turned on him angrily. "Have I not made myself plain, Cutteen? There is no more to talk about. I don't care a damn about your people. Eat the bodies of your dead for all I care!"

He turned and stormed into his great, rich house leaving us standing there. Had Dangan told us to charge it and set it afire, I don't doubt that we would have met our end there and then. Brashford and the soldiers seemed to sense what was running through our minds for they lined up their revolvers and rifles and stood waiting. But Dangan Cutteen turned away and we followed him back to the village.

That afternoon lots were drawn as to who should crew a three-man curragh and go to sea in search of fish. Dangan wanted to go and I likewise, for we were still fairly healthy. But the lot fell to others and these were proud men, these men of the West, and none would change their seats in the boat. No sooner had the black dart of the curragh vanished beyond the headland than a wind came up, whistling and crying like the banshees of hell. The curragh did not return home. By dusk we gathered on the foreshore, silent and ghastly, and we waited; waited until dusk gave way to night. The gray murderous sea was empty of any craft.

It was in the gray light of the morning that a man from the neighboring village of Raheenduff came to us to tell us that a curragh had been washed ashore there upside down.

"They are all away," the man said of the crew, which is a way of saying in the West that all had perished.

A strange look come upon the features of Dangan Cutteen then. He gave a long sigh.

"Ní chuimhníonn cú gortach ar a coileán," he said softly. I thought it a strange time to utter the old saying which means "A hungry hound does not remember its whelp," which is to say that necessity knows no law. Dangan beckoned to Seán and Iolar, who were his brothers and closer to him than anyone. "We have work to do," he told them and he left without a backward glance to any of us.

That night I sat in my cabin trying to keep the specter of hunger away by boiling the edible carrageen seaweed, which grows along the shoreline, into a soup. I had decided that I must leave the village while I was still healthy and perhaps find a berth on a merchantman bound for the New World. It was true that I felt more remorse this time than when I had first run away to sea years before . . . for was I not leaving my fellow villagers and comrades to their deaths?

It was then that there came a sharp rap on the door and opening it I beheld Iolar in the gloom.

"Dangan has sent me," he said. "If you want to eat, there is food to be had."

"What?" I cried. "From where is the food come?"

Iolar raised a finger to his lips and shrugged.

"Follow me, Pilib Rua, and you shall see."

I was surprised when he led me through the darkened village and up the steep path to the old caves in the hills above the village. Few knew of the existence of these caves, for this was where the villagers had sheltered during the devastations of Cromwell, when the English could take the head off any Irish man, woman or child and receive a five-pound reward for doing so; a time when the English soldiers could ride down on villages and take off the young men and girls to ship them as slaves to the Barbados. The caves had been our secret shelter in those days.

I was startled to see the entire remnants of the village gathered in the caves when Iolar led me in. Everyone stood in silent wonder around a great roaring fire. I, too, stared in bewilderment at the great roasting spits that were turning over the flames, while on them were cuts of meat which crackled and sizzled as their natural greases dripped onto the fires which cooked them. And the smell . . . ah, the sweet smell of roasting pork!

And Dangan Cutteen was there, grim-faced and silent as he supervised the roasting.

What miracle had he wrought to bring us such a plentiful supply of meat?

Each person was given meat and everybody ate their fill without stinting. Not a word was spoken while we sat and made ourselves replete with the feast.

Only when the people began to move drowsily back toward the village, did I seek out Dangan and ask, "Where did the food come from? Did you steal it from the estate of Colonel Chetwynd? If so, we will be in trouble from the English soldiers on the morrow."

Dangan Cutteen glanced at me without a change of expression on his grim features. "The meat came with the courtesy of Colonel Chetwynd," he said softly.

Then he turned away after the villagers, leaving me alone in the cave staring at the dying embers of the fire, staring at the smoldering bones which lay behind.

It was the bones that first raised some tiny pricking in my mind . . . bones which belonged to no pig that I knew of. A chill began to run down my spine and sent my stomach heaving.

Some instinct made me turn toward the back of the cave, seizing a piece of wood from the fire to act as a torch. I held it aloft and moved forward.

I did not have to look far.

There, in a heap at the back of the cave, were the blood-stained but easily recognizable clothes that I had last seen worn by Colonel Chetwynd. And by them lay a torn and stained coat that Brashford had been wearing. I stood like a statue not wishing to believe what I now knew to be true. When Colonel Chetwynd had said to Dangan Cutteen, "I don't give a damn about your people. Eat the bodies of your dead for all I care!" he had sealed his own fate. He had pronounced his own sentence for his crimes against us.

We had been eating the flesh of Colonel Chetwynd and his overseer!

Such was the horror that overcame me that I fled crying with terror from the cave and did not stop at the village but went on to Galway. At Galway I persuaded the captain of a merchantman to give me a berth, working my passage here to New York.

· · · ·

The hoarse whisper from the shadow beyond the grille halted a moment and Father Ignatius heard the sound of an emotional swallow.

"I have not been able to tell this story for twenty-five years, Father. Please . . . please . . . I must have absolution."

Father Ignatius hesitated. It was a grim story. A horrendous story, but God must be the judge. He was merely the instrument and he was moved to pity for the owner of the hoarse voice; pity, in spite of the terrible tale for the fault lay clearly not with the man but those conditions which had forced the man into his grotesque sin.

"Please, Father!"

The pleading tone of the man's voice tugged at his soul.

Father Ignatius stirred himself.

"I will absolve you, my son," he said slowly, "even though the sin you have committed is beyond anything that I have ever heard in my years as a priest. I will absolve you because your story has moved deep compassion in my soul. Before you leave this church you must recite five decades of the rosary and make an offering . . . that I shall leave to your conscience and God."

The figure behind the screen let forth a deep shuddering sigh.

"God bless you, Father, for you have charity of mind and spirit."

"It is God's will to move me to compassion, my son," replied Father Ignatius, "and I am but an instrument of His infinite goodness and His compassion. Make a good Act of Contrition, my son."

The figure beyond the lattice bent its head.

"Oh my God, I am heartily sorry for having offended Thee. I beg pardon for all my sins. I detest them above all things because they offend Thy infinite goodness who are so deserving of all my love and I am firmly resolved by the help of Thy grace never to offend Thee again and carefully to avoid the occasion of my sin."

The ritual Act of Contrition was recited mechanically as Father Ignatius had often heard it recited. Yet it fell strangely on his ears for what had gone before had prepared him to hear some more emotional declaration of intent. But he shrugged. The Act of Contrition was said and was meant.

"*Absolvo te ab omnibus peccatis tuis in nomine Patris et Filii et Spiritus Sancti . . . Amen!*"

He genuflected.

The figure behind the grille sat with its head bowed for a moment and then came the long, drawn-out sigh again. "Am I truly absolved in the eyes of God and the Church for what I have done, Father?"

Father Ignatius frowned. "Do you doubt the rituals of the Church, my son?" His voice rose sharply.

"No, Father. Yet it seems that I have shouldered the burden of this guilt for so long that it is strange that it should be cast from me in a single moment."

"God, in His infinite wisdom, so ordained His priesthood to forgive sins however great," responded Father Ignatius with pursed lips. "From this moment on your sins do no longer exist. You are reborn into the world in the eyes of God as innocent as if you were a newly born child."

There was a silence behind the grille. Then the voice came, sounding almost triumphant. "Then I am reborn as pure as if the last twenty-five years had never existed?"

"Of course, my son."

"It is a wonderful feeling, Father."

Father Ignatius smiled and was about to gently dismiss the strange penitent when the fretwork grille that divided the confessional box splintered into fragments. A thick, hairy arm thrust through toward the priest, the squat, dirty fingers grasping the startled man's throat and choking off his cry of alarm.

Father Ignatius was aware of the grotesque face in the shadows, the wild staring eyes, blood-veined and burning like the coals of hell. He was aware, too, of the large twisted mouth, the blood-red lips drawn back to show pink gums from which sharp white teeth ground against each other.

The voice was clearly triumphant now. "I am innocent again! But your confessional has not dismissed the craving . . . You see, Father, the horror I felt when I ran wildly from that cave, twenty-five years ago, was not at the fact that I had eaten human flesh. It was at the realization that I had *enjoyed* it. Enjoyed it in spite of the knowledge of what it was. I am innocent again; therefore I must sin again. There will be others to hear my future confession but now . . . now I must have meat again . . . succulent human meat . . . I cannot live without it!"

NANCY HOLDER

The Sweetest Rain

"My darling, my princess," Mark whispered as he tenderly daubed Anne's brow. Her face was smooth and pasty as sculptor's clay, moist from the struggle to shape itself into her death mask.

"Annie." He looked at the monitors over the bed, beside it, at the foot of it. So many machines. The wheezing of the pump that made her lungs inflate, deflate. Her chest seemed motionless to him. He didn't trust the machines; he had begun to suspect she was gone, and that the doctors and nurses maintained a charade of hope for his benefit. For he knew he swayed atop another sort of verge, and they knew it too: the violent trembling he could not control, the numbness, the hours when he couldn't speak. Grief is death postponed, and no one, not even doctors, can control death.

Sunlight streamed yellow scars across her fragile, inert body, gleamed knifesharp off the aluminum sides of the bed. Her hands glowed white and yellow, dying daisies. Her wedding ring was in his fist, in his mouth. He gritted his teeth around it, furious with the sunshine. It should be raining, and dark, and the world freezing and miserable. The skies cracking open, and wailing because—

because—

Dear God, please, God, please.

Her chest rose. Did not fall.

Oh, dear God. Oh, dear God.

Fell.

Tears fell, new onto old; the thighs of his pants were mottled with weeping.

Her chest rose.

He flailed for purchase; he was slipping, falling, tumbling end over end. No sights, no sounds—

and then—

The machine exhaled for her.

The sunlight. The sound of his crying, his shoe toe knocking the leg of the bed.

"Sorry, darling, sorry." Hastily he daubed her brow again, put his other fingers around the drinking cup with the straw, in case she should awaken and ask for water.

She had not awakened for six months.

His precious girl. His darling. He caressed the air above her cornsilk hair, the gaunt dip of her cheek. Beneath her lids, eyes the color of midnight slept. Slept, nothing more. Rested from the travails of life, which he had tried so hard to shield her from.

From the travails . . .

And then the room eddied dark, pitch-frigid, and he felt nothing, saw nothing. He moved through black frozen ice; a hand pressed his shoulder, and someone murmured, "Daddy, Daddy, come away now. It's time now." And hands reached, many, as he slid away, away, away, with Anne.

When he awakened, his son and daughters ranged around the bed, staring down at him. He lay on his back; no machines, no monitors.

Sunlight in bars across the window. He squinted at it. Bars across the window.

Death cannot be controlled.

"Oh." Beth, the youngest, fell into a frightened, bright smile. She grabbed his hand. "Daddy. Daddy."

"Where is she?" he asked, and the two older children traded glances as Beth let go of him and covered a choking sob.

"Daddy, you know," murmured Toni, his oldest.

He shut his eyes.

"Dad." His son spoke firmly, almost harshly.

"Brian." Toni sat on her orange plastic chair—Beth scooted behind it—and took both of Mark's hands in one of hers. Crow's-feet lined her eyes, eyes of midnight blue, and scarred a little, turned-up mouth set in a straight, unhappy line.

"Dad, Mom's gone. Do you remember? She's gone."

He turned his head and drifted away.

"Daddy."

"I can't believe it." He studied the faces of each of his children. Anne's children and his. From her body. From their union.

"There was no one to come to a . . . service, Daddy," Toni said. "Gramma Lee is sick, and the family . . ." She licked her lips. "Well, you know we've lost contact through the years." There was an edge to her voice, almost an accusation.

"I want to see her grave." He glared at her. At them all. "Surely you did that much? Laid her to rest?"

Toni pursed her lips. Beth tore at bleeding cuticles, nails chewed to the quick. Something flared across Brian's face, vanished. "Are you sure you're ready, Dad?" he asked. His voice was flat and emotionless. Careful. They were treading cautiously, Anne's three babies. As well they should. As well they should.

"I want to see her grave." He hoisted himself out of his chair and looked out the window.

It was raining.

The headstone read:

ANNE BARTLETT ANDERSON
BELOVED WIFE AND MOTHER

There could be nothing else, nothing of her gentleness, her shyness, her femininity. His angel, his sweet love. He held his arms toward the gravestone in a posture of supplication.

How could one know which of the many dangers thrusting through the universe would impale one's heart? How could one be certain that all precautions had been taken, all contingencies planned for? Perhaps it was hubris to imagine it could be done—

—a foolish fall off a ladder, hanging a picture. Striking her head against the fireplace.

"You should have been there!" he'd railed at his children in the hospital waiting room, after the screaming ambulance, after the screaming beside the ladder. Their eyes blinked stupidly at him; he slapped the face of the one nearest, who happened to be little Beth.

Toni had enfolded the weeping child in her arms and said, "There, there," and the expression on her face shocked Mark.

Why, she *hated* him.

Anne, sweet Anne. The headstone should say that. She walked in beauty. Where she was, there was Eden. She was never fit for Earth; it was too monstrous, too base, for such a creature as she.

"Heavens, I won't break," she'd said, laughing, when he hesitated to embrace her the first time she told him she was pregnant.

But she had broken. "A fall like that, well, it's odd it should've caused such extensive damage," the doctors admitted. They were baffled, utterly.

But Mark was not. She was always dainty, always in need of care and protection.

"Lord, you act like a Victorian husband," Gramma Lee snapped at him soon after their wedding. "Will you give my daughter some breathing room, for heaven's sake? She's about to strangle."

No one had understood. Not even Anne, at least at first. "But I want to do things for myself," she insisted. "For heaven's sake, Mark, nothing's going to happen to me."

But something had. No matter that she hadn't driven the car, nor mingled with strangers, nor worked around the house. He wished they had been Victorians, that they'd had scores of servants to attend to her every need, that the fact of her fragility was not a shameful thing, something to be denied at every turn. He wanted sable furs for her lap, a rabbit muff to warm her hands, and oranges in winter, and a fleet of footmen carrying umbrellas to shelter her from the rain.

Now the downpour splattered on the granite, smacking the letters of her name like slaps.

Or a hail of bullets.

Or a crushing ton of fireplace bricks.

Mark wept, in the rain.

"Daddy, come away now," Toni said, taking his arm. She picked up his umbrella, which had gathered rainwater like a bowl, sighed and folded it, and held her own over his bowed head. "Come away now."

"I'll come back tomorrow," he whispered to the gravestone. He bent down and centered his bouquet of red roses—blood red, long-stemmed, her favorites—into the green plastic cone embedded in the grass.

And was there the faintest whisper in reply? He stopped rising and stared hard through the raindrops at the grave.

The softest, saddest, call to him?

Yes.

He burst into tears. "Oh, Annie, Annie." He covered his face with his hands. "Annie, are you really there?"

Yes.

He went back to the cemetery alone. When he returned, flushed, his children said nothing, only shared their private glances, their looks. Toni said, "Mom didn't . . . she would've wanted . . ." and shut her mouth. He didn't ask her what she wished to say. His thoughts were at the grave, replaying the first syllables between them, the long, unendurable silence over.

"Are you there, my darling, my treasure, my bride?"

Yes. Yes. I'm here. Oh, thank God, thank God, you can hear me. It's been . . . oh, thank you. Oh, I have needed you so. Needed you, my love.

Later, while Toni was washing the supper dishes, he stumbled into the kitchen to look at the calendar on the refrigerator. He paused. Seven months. She had been . . . there for seven months. But now, it was different. Now, he could be a husband again, be her confidant, her friend, her— Toni slammed down a glass and said, "Goddamnit, Dad, Beth's upstairs crying her eyes out. Talk to her!"

He looked at her dreamily, watched with fascination as her mouth moved. Vaguely he thought of Beth, their "surprise." He'd worried about Anne, having a child later in life like that. Toni was twelve years older than Beth. He'd wanted to hire a nurse, or a nanny, or whatever. Annie had insisted no, acquiesced to the cleaning lady and the diaper service.

"You treat me like a queen," she'd said, with a funny smile.

Yes, oh, yes. Like a princess. A spun-sugar princess.

Melting in the rain.

"Are you still here, Annie?" he whispered the next gray, sad morning. The sound of a lawn mower hummed in his ears. Mark was distraught: the gardener would mow right over Annie's grave without a thought for her rest, for the disturbance he was causing. There was something to be said for tall weeds and wildflowers covering her bed.

Yes. I'm here.

The gardener drew closer. The hum became a roar. Mark shifted, fingering the petals of the roses in his arms.

"I'll come back later," he said loudly, so she could hear him over the noise. "After he's gone."

No! Please. So lonely.

He groaned. "Oh, Annie, can't I do anything to ease your pain?" He touched the mound of grass. "Annie, Annie, when I'm home, all I do is think of you. My life is the hours I spend here, with you."

Lonely. So lonely. You can't imagine what it's like.

Tears streamed down his face. All the months he hadn't been there for her. The agony she must have endured, the terror, the helplessness.

The gardener approached slowly. Mark saw him in his peripheral vision, waiting respectfully, but waiting nevertheless.

"I'll come back later," Mark said, gathering up the roses, and pressed his lips against the frigid granite.

The gardener looked away as Mark passed him.

That night, Mark woke up in a sweat. It had just occurred to him, in a waking dream, that he had been mistaken: death could be controlled.

They could be buried in the same grave. Entwined throughout eternity, together, and he was all she needed; and she, him. For wasn't she the only necessity life deprived him of?

Death, controlled. Unlike the rain, or tears—

Muffled crying at the foot of his bed.

"Annie? Annie?" he said eagerly, switching on the light.

It was Beth, heaped with a teddy bear in her arms. She turned pleading eyes on her father and his face fell. His mind raced—*the hunting rifle downstairs, over the fireplace. Never shot it, but I could buy bullets—*

He patted his daughter absently and said, "There, there. Go back to bed."

No, Annie said. *It might not work.*

Mark frowned. "But I don't see why not. Once I'm buried—"

No. Not everyone stays behind. There are very few left in here. Very few.

He was surprised. She'd never mentioned that before. But then, they hadn't talked much about the cemetery. He knew only that it was cold, and dark, and very lonely. He thought his presence—his literal, physical presence—might ease that.

Don't do it, she pleaded.

"But you need me. It's worth a chance."

There was no answer. For a moment he thought she had faded. Terror clutched at him and then she said, *Perhaps there is another way.*

Three days later, as he bent to place the roses atop her grave, he saw something small and white glinting on the newly mown grass. Lying clean and delicate and—

—bone. A finger bone.

He recoiled. And then he realized what it was, and picked it up and clutched it against his heart in a state of ecstasy, a pilgrim worshiping a holy relic.

I will come to you, she said.

Months and months, up through the earth, buried treasures of ivory. Days and months, and he helped when he could, with grave dirt beneath his fingernails, grave mud, and his heart light with joy. Sunshine in rain, and no thunderclouds in a dulled, grey sky. And he took her home, and put her in a lovely cedar chest, her hope chest that she had packed with needlepoint pillows and washcloths while a young girl, dreaming of a husband. He put her there, lining the interior with white satin cut from her bridal gown. The corsages of their proms, her going-away wrist spray of red roses; fresh roses every day.

And when she was completely back, he gathered her up and laid her on the bed every night, and they talked, and laughed, and loved.

They loved. And she lay on the bed, small, inert, fragile and helpless, his princess of spun sugar.

"Daddy? Daddy?" Toni's voice sounded through the door.

"Go away," he said angrily, and buried his head against Annie's, wishing he could melt into her.

Love you. She did not move, not even when she spoke.

"Yes."

Need you.

"Yes."

Beth ran away from home. Toni called the police. Mark came to the door ten minutes after the officers arrived, because he had to hide Annie away in her cedar chest. She didn't mind, she sweetly assured him. It was far preferable to the loneliness, the chill of that other box. He was so good to think of secreting her away; so thoughtful and dear.

She didn't ask about her daughter. She never asked about any of the children.

A year passed. Beth never came back. Brian left. Toni held on, left the next year. Mark barely realized they were gone. He quit his job and did phone solicitation work out of his—of their—bedroom, so that he would never have to leave her side.

Bliss, unimaginable and ceaseless. He knew he had dreamed those months at her bedside in the hospital, her dying. He knew he had dreamed three children.

Love you.

"Yes."

Need you.

"Yes, yes, always."

And then the cemetery called. After five years, they called. A terrible mistake, they explained. Here they had planned a funeral, and looked at the plans, and well, it was all very embarrassing. The man responsible had been discharged and ah, if they could offer some sort of compensation . . .

The room collapsed as he put down the phone. The world shattered as he turned and faced her.

She knew. She knew he knew.

I needed you.

"You . . ." He couldn't speak.

She was gone. I swear to you. There was a hesitation, and then she spoke again. *She said, "I'm free. Finally, free," and then she left.*

"You liar!" he raged. With both his hands, he scattered her all over the room. She fell down like a rain, like a keening, weeping rain.

I needed, she begged. *I needed someone so badly. I was so afraid.*

*And you, you needed. We had each other. You thought she was there,
and I let you think that. I couldn't see the harm.*

The harm. He sat heavily on the bed. He clasped his hands together.
He had never visited Annie's grave. He had never left flowers for
her.

Never talked to her.

Never been there for her.

He sat until the shadows grew against the wall. Until the dark closed
in. All that time, *she* wept. He could feel her fear. What was there left
to do, but abandon her? Hate her for her deception?

Please. Please.

He would get his car keys, drive to the cemetery, demand to be
shown where his wife was buried. Goddamn that bitch, that other.
Lying, lying, when all along she knew, all the time, she wasn't—

She was unhappy with you.

He snapped his head up. "What?"

*Yes. She said you never let her do anything, go anywhere. She said if
she hadn't died by accident she probably would have either left you or
killed herself. She said you never loved the children. You were so
wrapped up in her—*

She stopped.

Oh, God. Oh, please, God, I'm sorry. I didn't mean it. I'm so sorry.

Lurching, he stood. The air punched from his lungs. Blood roared in
his brain.

*Mark, my love. Mark. You must have known, somewhere in your
heart. She was only dead seven months. But I, I was there for sixty years.
Sixty, alone. I need, I need, I need—*

He stumbled out of the room, arms outstretched like a blind man's.

He fell outside the house and stopped, raising his face to the sky. He
stood, sobbing, the rain of the streetlights coursing down on him, flooding him with cold, gray light, harsh light. Like a drunk, he wove down
the center of the streets. He stopped beside a mailbox and vomited out
his heart.

Not Anne. Lies. All lies. Not Anne.

You're going to strangle my daughter.

*Mark, sweetheart, I'm not retarded. I'm not infirm. Nothing's going to
happen to me.*

Lies. All lies.

He staggered past darkened houses. A dog ruffed once, grew still.

He had refused pets for the children. No flea bites for his princess, no dog hair to contend with.

Our house looks like a museum, Mark.

She'd said she wanted to join a book discussion group. Or go to an adult school class.

Please, honey. I need some outside interests.

Leave him. Kill herself. But she had never said she was unhappy. Not once had she intimated that things were not the way she wanted.

He walked. Hours passed. His lifetime passed.

Oh, God, I'm sorry.

And as he stood beneath the moon, he realized *her* desperation had made her say those things about Anne. Those hateful things. She was so frightened she would do anything, say anything, rather than let him leave her. None of it was true. None of it. He doubted the two of them had ever . . . spoken.

The streetlights shot their yellow rain down on him, needlesharp razor cuts.

The moon rounded the trees, dipped. More dogs barked. The streetlights cascaded through the fog.

Poor thing, poor terrified girl. Sixty years.

So sweet, so submissive. More so, actually, than Anne.

The moon ran into a pool of silvergrey light. A pool of water. Of tears. Of rain.

Perhaps Anne *had* been a little resentful.

The moon. The lights. The fog.

And if Anne *were* there?

His heart moved as he stood by the woods at the edge of town. Crickets sang. To lie there, in the dark, yearning for a word, for an end to the loneliness.

She was unhappy. She said if she hadn't died—

He remembered now, after such a very long time, that she'd been hanging the picture against his wishes. It was a landscape in oils someone (who?) had painted for her, a view of the Cornish countryside. She'd wanted to travel, but they never did.

Who? Who had painted that picture?

Midnight mists gathered in the trees lining the walk. He watched them undulate, rising on drafts toward the moon. Leaves of gold and brown jerked themselves from the maples and skimmed the cold air toward the storm drains.

Perhaps he had known the ladder was wobbly. Perhaps he hadn't gotten around to fixing it.

Perhaps he had broken it himself. Accidentally.

More leaves fell, autumn's brilliant downpour. He thought of Anne six years before, standing beside a burning heap of leaves with a rake in her hand, and of his sudden fear that she was going to jump into the fire, simply leap right in. How he had crossed his arms and backed away, afraid he might upset her equilibrium as she raked the leaves into the flames.

And he thought of the *other*, now. What heaven he had provided for her, in his house, in his room, in his bed. What refuge from the shroud, and the mower, and the void.

The moon thinned, washed him with a sigh. The grass shimmered, flooded with dew; droplets trickled off the eaves of the houses and made tiny ponds at the ends of spouts. A grey cat sauntered by, swimming through the wet night like a fish.

And hadn't he asked himself a dozen times why she seemed sweeter now? More loving and tender, more gentle and giving? Soaking in his thoughtfulness? Didn't something grow between them, something new and more intense that had nothing to do with death and everything to do with the two of them?

Two tender tears blossomed from his eyes like roses. Perhaps he had known. Somewhere in his being, somehow. Perhaps he understood.

Perhaps he forgave.

He turned around. The mists rose up, up, midnight blue with corn-silk tails. Up, drying up, a parched Cornish countryside. He recalled thinking how brown the painting was, how thirsty. No green. Nothing lush or verdant, the way he thought England must be, with all its rain. The painter had known nothing.

Nothing.

"Okay," he murmured, touching the thighs of his soaked trousers. "All right."

He walked in a straight line, on the sidewalk, one foot ahead of the other. He would ask her her real name. And he would make her a new box. Her own: a finer one, with padded satin. He would buy new bedclothes, of silk and lace. He would give her fancy underthings, all in white.

Yes. He wiped his face, lifted it to the blue mists that rose and steamed, escaping.

Rain needs something to fall upon:

He would go home now, home to his spun-sugar princess,

and pour himself upon her in a torrent.

NORMAN PARTRIDGE

Wrong Side
of the Road

She remembered this much: her name was Helen and he'd picked her up in a Reno bar in 1946. It was autumn—maybe October or maybe November—but autumn for sure because he'd said that her strawberry blond hair reminded him of the changing colors in the mountains.

Autumn, 1946. Reno, Nevada. About that much she was sure. And her name was Helen . . .

In 1946, Helen was employed as a cocktail waitress at the Prima Donna Casino. She made fairly decent money there, thanks to an excellent memory that allowed her to sell more drinks than the other girls, but she'd been looking for an excuse to quit because her backside was a lot better-looking than her front and her tips weren't exactly the greatest. Besides, working in spike heels was hell on her feet.

Helen was waiting for a girlfriend in a downtown bar when she spotted him. His name was Roy, and he was a war hero. He had a nice smile and a thick head of black hair just like Tyrone Power's, and Helen didn't mind too much that what he didn't have was a pair of legs.

"I'm just passin' through," he said in answer to her unspoken question. "I'm on my way to Hollywood. But I got time for dinner."

It wasn't like Helen, but she forgot all about her friend and accepted Roy's invitation. Over Bloody Marys and rare steaks at the Riverside, he told her about a best-seller-to-be he'd written about his wartime experiences, a book so hot that it had been picked up by Universal Studios after an eager producer had seen the galleys.

"That's great," said Helen. "Y'know, I was heading for Hollywood when I left Milwaukee, but I was stupid enough to think that I could beat the slots, and I lost my traveling money. That's the only reason I ended up staying in Reno. I think that's how a lot of people end up here."

"Coulda been worse. You coulda been stranded in Salt Lake City."

Helen laughed. "You're right about that. But Reno isn't really so bad —it's better than Milwaukee—and I don't think that I would have made it as an actress, anyway."

So it wasn't just the lure of the movies that drew Helen to Roy; she had outgrown her Hollywood dreams. And it wasn't the tragic war hero bit or the way he smiled, either, though Helen admitted that she found both qualities attractive. No, more important than the romantic stuff was Roy's genuine interest in her. Helen could tell that his attentiveness wasn't a con—she'd been around Reno long enough to recognize the kind of phony compassion that covered up sick wants and needs that she didn't want *or* need.

No, if anything, Roy was too sincere. There was something unusual about the way he asked questions; he had a voracious hunger for even the most minor details of her past. Helen answered him automatically, patiently, abandoning the defensive shield that came from dealing with one drunken gambler after another.

After a while Helen's voice started to crack, and she realized with a start that she'd spilled her life story in the time it took to drink a few Bloody Marys and eat a charbroiled Kansas City strip. She told Roy that her voice was going to give out if she kept gabbing, but he only smiled and flagged down their waiter. The little man returned momentarily with two ice cream sundaes and a bottle of Remy Martin, a combination that promised to be the perfect balm for Helen's throat.

"God, you've got a fantastic memory," Roy said, and then he asked her one final question.

Suddenly speechless, she nodded her reply.

Hours later, when the morning sun climbed into the sky above the Biggest Little City in the World, Helen found herself lying with Roy in a honeymoon suite, smelling the Lucky Tiger in his hair and running her fingers over his muscular chest, and letting his big hands travel where they wanted because no one knew her like her new husband did.

That day was all room-service champagne and tender kisses. And that night, as Helen loaded her belongings into Roy's specially modified Hudson, she realized that everything was going to be wonderful because Roy already knew all her secrets. He said that he understood about the abortion. He knew that she had left Milwaukee in disgrace, couldn't ever go back home, and wasn't exactly proud of everything she'd done since.

"Honey, I'm so happy," she said.

A cool wind had whispered off the mountains, leaving the Reno sky icy blue, perfect blue. Roy said that the moon was the color of rum, and Helen started singing "Rum and Coca-Cola." She hadn't thought it strange when he'd pulled up to a pawnshop on North Virginia and bought a tenor saxophone that was hanging in the window. But back then, on the day after her wedding, she hadn't known about Don Bragonier.

"I didn't know that you played the sax," she'd said.

"I don't." Roy had laughed. "But I'm gonna start learnin'."

Helen slid the battered alligator-skin case into the back seat, wedging the sax between two boxes filled with winter clothes. Suddenly she realized how little she knew about Roy. She stood on the grimy sidewalk, tottering in her spike heels, wondering if she should get into the same car with the man who was now her husband.

"C'mon," Roy shouted. "Hey, we got us a life to live."

Helen fingered her new diamond ring. She smiled. And then, blowing a final kiss at the Prima Donna, she kicked her uncomfortable heels into the gutter and hopped into the roomy Hudson.

•   •   •   •

Helen's feeling of unease didn't last long. Pulling into the mountains, Roy took a deep breath and said, "Now, let me tell you about myself."

Roy talked about the New York City gyms he'd frequented as a teenager, gray places where he'd spent countless hours sparring with kids who weren't half as talented as he was. He told Helen about the boxers he'd defeated at Madison Square Garden, and while she was sure that they were all famous men—contenders, Roy called them— she admitted that she hadn't heard of them. Helen *had* heard of Sugar Ray Robinson, though, and she was disappointed to learn that Sugar Ray had kayoed Roy in three rounds on a hot August evening in 1943.

Helen blushed, realizing that her embarrassment for Roy could never match his own. "After the Robinson fight, I was too ashamed to go back to the neighborhood," he said. "I enlisted in the Marine Corps as soon as I healed up—Jesus, Ray's jab made a mess outta my eyes. Anyway, a few months later I was in the Pacific."

Roy described the savagery he'd seen at Bougainville and Iwo Jima, horrors that had never been printed in the newspapers. And when Helen gasped and said that war made good men into madmen, Roy explained that madness was the nature of war. He admitted that he had gone battle-crazy on Iwo, where he'd used his well-honed seven-inch K-bar to dig gold teeth out of the mouths of Japanese corpses.

Roy wasn't proud of that. Helen forgave him, her voice full of compassion, and for the first time she realized that her new husband needed her as much as she needed him.

The talk turned to happier subjects. Roy shared his wartime buddies with Helen, telling stories about Rod Markam, Sal Harbeck, Vinny Tocolli, Gary Van Bellen, and a dozen other guys. Helen could almost picture their young faces, and crossing into California she got the weird feeling that there were several extra passengers wedged between the tenor sax and the moving boxes in the back seat.

A chill scraped up her spine. It was a strange feeling, the same one she got when she heard the squeaking door on "Inner Sanctum."

"Most of 'em are dead, of course. Never made it home." Roy brushed Helen's skirt away from her thigh, his fingers stroking her smooth, nyloned flesh. "I used to think they were lucky, but now my opinion's changed."

· · · ·

In Hollywood, Helen began to notice confusing variations in Roy's often told stories—especially his Iwo stories—variations that were more than simple exaggerations. The changes worried her.

Not that Roy was lying. Helen was sure that he wouldn't lie. Not to her, anyway. Not after he'd accepted so much truth from her lips.

But if not lies, then what?

Maybe boxing had made Roy a little punchy. That happened to fighters, didn't it? Or maybe Roy's forgetfulness was a way of dealing with the awful things that he had seen in the Pacific. Helen could understand that. She knew that the truth could be a painful thing.

Helen's mind had played tricks on her after the abortion. Night after night she had awakened sweaty and cold, thinking that she heard a baby crying. Each time she'd search her apartment, sure that in the next room, around the next corner, she'd find a screaming infant that was indeed her own.

Weird, remembering that.

But in the months to come, Helen decided that Roy's memory was exactly like the strange, waking dreams she'd had after the abortion, only he didn't seem to notice the changes. Some days it took Robinson six rounds to knock him out. Some days the fight went to a decision. And some days—usually rainy days when they were cooped up together in the cramped bungalow—Roy talked about Rod Markam, Sal Harbeck, Vinny Tocolli, and Gary Van Bellen as if they were still alive.

On days like that, Roy got out the tenor sax and told stories about Don Bragonier, a crazy guy he'd known on Iwo. Bragonier had been a jazz musician before the war, and he was the only guy in Roy's outfit who never talked about his hometown. He wouldn't even admit having one. "Man, I *move*. I'm from everywhere, like a gypsy." That was how Bragonier had put it.

After taking a burst of machine-gun fire in his legs, Roy found himself on the same hospital plane as Don. He had watched Don die from head wound complications (most of the time Don died on the plane, but occasionally he died in a Marianas hospital).

Roy always ended his Don Bragonier story by repeating his vow to master the sax in Bragonier's honor, but the awful squeals and squawks that came from the horn during the practice sessions that followed were enough to drive Helen out into the rain.

"Babe, I hope you don't believe in ghosts," Roy would say, not noticing that the very mention of ghosts made Helen cringe. " 'Cause my blowing could wake the dead."

Things didn't go so well in Hollywood. At first the producers kept Roy busy, arranging speaking dates for him, but soon it became apparent that the studio brass were hesitating. The producers told Roy not to worry. They promised that everything would change once his book came out.

Roy enjoyed himself while he waited. He drank a prodigious amount of rum and Coca-Cola. He took Helen to fancy parties. Occasionally he played poker with Errol Flynn and his cronies, and he brought home famous people who behaved like old friends.

The publisher named Roy's book *Marching Home.* The reviews were good; the sales weren't. The conventional wisdom ran this way: too many people had lost sons and brothers in the Pacific, and no one really wanted to know what kind of hell the front-line grunts had faced.

The studio brass dropped the movie, and then a month later they dropped Roy. They claimed that *Marching Home* was too grim. Someone mentioned nihilism, but Roy wasn't even sure what that meant.

"You've got a great yarn," one producer admitted. "Maybe we can pick it up down the road. But there isn't a whole lot of compassion in the book . . . I'm not blaming you or anything, and it's not that we want to phony things up with a load of happy-ending crap. But maybe you left that compassion back on Iwo Jima. Maybe you had to, just to survive."

What the producer didn't say, what he was afraid to say, was this: "Roy, maybe the war stole more than your legs. Maybe it stole your soul."

"I can get it back, Helen. You know I can."

Roy was getting worse. He talked about "getting it back" a lot lately. The producer's words haunted him; he wrote them down in a notebook and spent his mornings drinking coffee and staring at them. In the afternoon he sat in the backyard, rereading *Marching Home.* Helen watched Roy from the kitchenette window, shaking a little when he threw the book across the lawn, for that was how his reading sessions always ended.

One day when Roy was out playing poker, Helen sneaked a look at the book. She was shocked to discover that whole paragraphs had been crossed out and that the margins were full of tiny notes: *Not the way this happened . . . Bragonier died in hospital, not on plane . . . Vinny killed at Bougainville, not Iwo . . . Rod is still alive and living in Laramie. His wife just had a baby . . . Rod is dead, died in hand-to-hand combat near Motoyama Village on February 28, 1945 . . .*

"Oh, babe, I can get it back."

Helen looked at Roy. He was the only good thing in her life. But he didn't smile anymore and—

"They lied. Those goddamn book people in New York. That goddamn ghostwriter that the editor brought in, 'just to tidy things up,' he said. See, I've been reading my book over and over, and you ain't gonna believe this, but the things they printed ain't the things that happened. That's why the movie fell through. That damned ghostwriter changed everything, and then the publisher still had the balls to put my name on the cover and my picture on the back . . ."

Roy wheeled toward her. His big hands closed around her fingers, which were slick with dishwashing soap. He unintentionally twisted her wedding ring, and the diamond bit into her middle finger.

Helen winced.

Roy's voice quavered. "Believe me, Helen. I know we can work it out. It's just kinda mixed up in my head right now, but I know how to fix it. I need you to help me; your memory's so good. And mine, well, I don't think I can trust it anymore. But I can trust you, can't I?"

At least he was admitting his problem. Helen was glad of that. She nodded automatically, and then felt her face go crimson because she wasn't sure that she could be trusted at all. Lately she'd been talking to a doctor at the VA hospital, a sincere young man who said that he'd helped other veterans like Roy.

Roy didn't notice her blush. "Good. I knew I could count on you, doll. I'll tell you everything, 'cause you won't get mixed up, and you can write it all down. Then we can go from there to get it back. You can keep track of all the things we find out. And when we're done I'll show these Hollywood bastards. I'll have my own book." He tapped the well-worn copy of *Marching Home* with a stubby finger. "Not like this load of crap. I'll have *it*. Written down in my wife's own hand."

Helen massaged her sore finger, twisting the ring that joined her to Roy. She wanted to understand, but Roy's words were hard to follow. She wanted to ask him what *it* was (his compassion? his faith?), but she was afraid that he might break down if she admitted that she didn't know what he was talking about.

"It'll be hard gettin' back to Iwo. It'll be even harder to find the guys. God, we dug so many graves. But there's gotta be a way that we can do it."

Helen leaned against the counter. *No, Roy. Oh God, no.*

Roy smiled. "That's my pretty girl. I knew you'd be on my side." He wheeled himself to the back door, a look of pure contentment on his face. "Lately, I've been hearing a lot from the guys. They *want* to give it back to me. They know they took it, and they know how bad we need it back. Even the guys who died on Iwo know that." His hands curled into fists. "God love 'em. Y'know, I think that those poor souls want to help us worst of all."

That night, Helen gave Roy some medication to help him sleep. Then she went next door and used the neighbor's telephone.

Three men from the VA hospital came for Roy the following morning.

In 1955, after seven years as a maid at the Chateau Marmont in West Hollywood, Helen was appointed chief housekeeper. Her days off were Tuesday and Wednesday, and she spent them with Roy at the hospital.

That year, the doctors decided that Roy was ready to be released. Helen was against it, but there was no use arguing with the bureaucracy.

At first Roy seemed okay. He took the Hudson out of storage and overhauled the engine himself. He even got a bit part as a disabled vet in an Audie Murphy movie.

One day Helen came home from work and found Roy on the front porch, reading the afternoon paper. He looked up at her and said, "They're comin' home, Helen. The boys are comin' home."

Helen shivered as she read the article.

"Helen, if you put me back in the hospital I'll kill myself."

Helen dropped the paper. A hot wind carried it across the front lawn and it tumbled past the open, gaping hood of the Hudson.

She realized that she was too tired to fight Roy this time.

In 1955, the dead of Iwo Jima were exhumed and returned to American soil.

· · · ·

The first time they did it, on a cold October night in a Nebraska churchyard, Helen had no idea what to expect. She wheeled Roy across a frosty lawn, searching for Gary Van Bellen's headstone. Roy was shivering, and her first thought was that he needed another blanket, but just then Roy spotted Van Bellen's grave, and his half-suppressed cry of joy convinced her that he'd been shivering with anticipation.

"Dig it up," Roy said, his fingers scratching the leather armrests of his wheelchair.

Helen almost refused. For one horrible moment she was afraid that Roy wanted her to rip open Gary Van Bellen's coffin and chop off the dead man's legs. She imagined Roy screaming, "He stole them, Helen. Stole my legs! And now I want them back!"

That's how it would have happened on "Inner Sanctum." And that would have been the end of it. The cops would have arrived, stopped Roy, comforted Helen. But no cops arrived, and what might have been the end was only the beginning.

The digging wasn't bad. Helen had thought that coffins were buried six feet under, but that wasn't the case. Two feet down she hit the wooden cover of a coffin vault, which she pried open with a jack-handle. A few feet below, in a shadowy hole that smelled like earth-worms and dead flowers, lay Gary Van Bellen's coffin.

Roy handed Helen a crowbar, and she opened the pine box.

She didn't look down. Her mind warned her against that. But she smelled the rotten smell, and her mouth went instantly dry.

"Take it!" Roy insisted. She opened her eyes and looked up at him. His black hair was smeared sweatily across his forehead, and his once-tanned face was as pasty as moonlight.

Roy shoved an ear of sweet corn at Helen. Her fingers drifted over the wispy, tickling corn silk and closed around the yellow ribbon that Roy had tied around the husk.

"Okay. Now put it in his hands."

Eyes closed, Helen bent down and let her fingers do the seeing.

"Gary," Roy whispered. "It's like a trade, see? Now you got to give me something back."

Helen's hands drifted over a tattered uniform.

"I know you don't need it anymore, Gary. I gotta have it again."

Helen's fingers brushed a cold metal bracelet and then found Gary Van Bellen's hands. Thin, shrunken fingers. So stiff. So dry.

"It's an offering, Gary. To show you that I remember. You told me all about the farm. It's to show you that I listened." Roy raised his lantern with one hand and flipped through a yellow notebook with the other. "See, here's your story. Helen wrote it down for me. All about your family. I'll read it to you."

Small hands. So cold. Helen raised them, just slightly, and something cracked as she slipped the ear of corn underneath.

An offering. That's what Roy had called it. And when they were safely back in the Hudson, heading for the Wyoming border, Helen was sure that Roy had made his peace and everything was going to be okay again.

Roy parked in the shadow of an abandoned farmhouse. He taped an old newspaper over the car windows, but even with the morning light blacked out he was too keyed up to sleep. Helen lay in the back seat, staring at a page of comic strips, listening to her husband talk. "Honey, I can feel it coming back. Gary really helped me. He always did come through, and this time wasn't any different. I told you that he didn't need it anymore. I knew he'd understand. God, he wanted to give it back so bad."

They crossed into Wyoming at dusk. Roy hadn't said anything about going home, but Helen just naturally assumed that they were heading for California since they were traveling west.

False assumption.

"God, I feel good. It's almost like gettin' my legs back. Like gettin' something back that's been missing so long you forget what it's like to have it." Roy's hand brushed Helen's muddy slacks, patting the smooth curve of her inner thigh. "That Gary. I knew he'd help me. I just hope Rod will understand too. It shouldn't take us long to get to Laramie."

Roy told Helen to get out another yellow notebook, and he repeated the same old stories, the stories he said he'd heard from Gary Van Bellen's dead lips. Stories about Bougainville and Iwo Jima and the night he battled Sugar Ray Robinson.

Soon the notebook was full.

They stopped to sleep for a few hours, and then crossed into Albany County at sunrise. "Not far to Laramie," Roy said. "God, I'll bet it'll look just like Rod said it would."

Roy never said as much, but it seemed fairly obvious to Helen that the offerings were tokens of memory, something tangible that could tie

Roy to each man's past. Gary Van Bellen's was easy to figure: an ear of corn for a corn farmer. Rod Markham's—a bouquet of Indian paintbrush, columbine, and forget-me-nots—was almost conventional. Except this bouquet was wrapped in rusty barbed wire, probably because Rod had spent his teenage years riding fence for a Wyoming rancher.

Helen didn't try to understand some of the offerings. In the Chicago grave of Vinny Tocolli, she buried a dented canteen filled with the gold teeth that Roy had taken from Japanese corpses on Iwo. In a sandy grave on the Northern California coast, she covered Sal Harbeck's corpse with four gleaming hubcaps stolen off a new Cadillac, and then watched Roy pour a bottle of champagne into the grave, listening to the bubbly liquid splatter over the drumlike metal disks. Moist, salty air clung to her lips that night, ruining the taste of the champagne that she downed just to get through the ordeal.

Most of Roy's buddies came from small towns, so finding their graves was as easy as finding the local cemetery. Searches were harder in the big cities—some had a dozen or more cemeteries—but Roy wouldn't let Helen contact the VA or Marine Corps for help. He didn't trust the government. He used the phone book instead, contacting relatives of the deceased. Sometimes he would visit their homes and sit down to dinner like a favorite uncle.

They drove across the country, then back again, never traveling in a pattern that made any sense. Roy would cruise from New York to Miami and then decide that he had missed a stop in Virginia. After the first month Helen stopped looking at the odometer, because the enormous number she saw growing there frightened her.

In Santa Fe they buried a kite with a tail made from a prostitute's nylons. In Seattle they interred a set of cards backed with pictures of Gypsy Rose Lee. And in a grave in the middle of a dusty Texas boneyard, they placed a Bible, a shotgun shell, and a hickory switch.

After every stop, Roy dictated the same old stories, sure that he was finally setting the record straight. Helen didn't have the heart to tell him that his memory was as inconsistent as ever. She began to hope that someone would catch them and bring Roy's twisted pilgrimage to an end.

Roy said it over and over. "God, if we could only find Don Bragonier. I got so much back from the other guys, but I gave the most to Don. He's the one I really need. If we don't find him . . . Well, we just gotta keep looking."

Between cemeteries, they lived hand to mouth. Roy had an uncanny knack for finding back-room poker games in which he usually did quite well. He'd learned a few tricks in Hollywood, and he cheated brazenly because he believed that no one would accuse a cripple of cheating, especially a cripple who told such great stories about boxing and war and Hollywood.

On a warm July night in the back room of an upstate New York roadhouse, Roy met a gambler who had grown up with Don Bragonier.

And on the same night, kneeling on the oily pavement outside the Hudson, Helen prayed that their ordeal would finally be over.

The little old lady smiled warmly. "More coffee, Roy?"

Roy swallowed a bite of cherry pie. "Sure, Mrs. Bragonier. And thanks."

Mrs. Bragonier nodded at Helen, who waved a hand over her cup, refusing the silent offer. Helen asked, "Can I help you with the dishes?"

"No, dear," said Mrs. Bragonier, disappearing into the kitchen. "Guests aren't allowed to do dishes in this house."

They had arrived three hours earlier, three hours late according to Roy, who had become hopelessly lost in a maze of twisting Vermont roadways. He had insisted on contacting Don's family directly because that was the fastest way to find Don's grave, and although they hadn't phoned ahead, Mrs. Bragonier had welcomed them with open arms. The old woman recognized Roy from a wartime photo that her son had included in one of his many letters, and she seemed genuinely happy to have some company on a Fourth of July holiday that she would otherwise have spent alone. "Donald was my only child," she had explained. "And now that his father's gone, it's pretty lonely around here."

Helen had smiled through it all, but underneath she'd felt terribly out of place. After two years in the Hudson, she couldn't accustom herself to chatting in Mrs. Bragonier's dining room. The elegant Victorian furniture, the smell of freshly cut lilacs, and the seeming vastness of the room itself made Helen feel insignificant.

Mrs. Bragonier filled Roy's coffee cup and then sliced another piece of pie for him. Helen wished that he would get on with it, just find out where Don Bragonier was buried so they could leave the old woman's enormous house. But Roy was hesitating, she could tell, and she didn't know why.

Helen twisted her wedding ring. Had Roy realized that Don Bragonier was the last man on his list? Was he afraid that, after all his searching, the fabled Don Bragonier wouldn't be able to help him either?

Roy patted Helen's knee and she tightened instantly. Her hands drifted beneath the table and her fingers curled into the linen tablecloth.

"Donald mentioned you in his letters," said Mrs. Bragonier. "I know that you two were especially close, and I want to thank you for visiting."

It was a goodbye, but Helen could tell that Roy wasn't getting the message. A confused grin crossed his lips. "Donald? Oh, yeah—Don Bragonier. A great guy." Roy stared at Mrs. Bragonier and recognized something of Don in her face. "Ma'am, I don't mean to be rude, but when is Don going to get home? I really have to talk to him."

For a moment Helen expected Don Bragonier to come banging through the front door, a big, smiling hello on his lips. But then she saw Mrs. Bragonier redden, and she was out of her chair, trailing the old woman as she fled to the kitchen.

Helen caught Mrs. Bragonier's thin wrist. "I'm sorry. He forgets—"

Mrs. Bragonier whirled, but not in anger. She drew Helen into a warm embrace. "I understand," she whispered. "Donald's father was the same way. After the war ended, a day didn't go by without him asking when Donald was coming home. You see, he could never accept Donald's death. And your Roy, he's seen so much misery. He's suffered so. Believe me, I understand how it must be."

Helen smiled at that, and she wished, hugging Mrs. Bragonier, that the little old woman could truly understand.

Helen pushed Roy down a mossy gravel path, eager to find the grave. The soft glow of Roy's lantern revealed crooked headstones near the iron gate and then shone on straight, polished markers as they entered the newer section of the cemetery.

Donald Bragonier was buried near a birch grove. Helen slipped on a pair of leather gloves and set about her task.

A dull ache pulsed in her wrists as she worked the shovel into the hard soil. Her ragged breathing mixed with the summer wind, and she shuddered when she thought, for just an instant, that she heard a baby crying in the birches beyond the cemetery fence.

Helen ignored the sounds and opened the coffin. The familiar smell of rot and velvet poured over her.

"Take it. Take it."

Helen took the sax from Roy. Eyes shut, she eased the golden instrument into the coffin, heard its thin bamboo reed scrape the velvet lining.

She had no trouble closing the lid. There was plenty of room in the coffin for the sax, because there wasn't much left of Donald Bragonier.

"Don, you're my last chance. C'mon, buddy."

Sweat poured down Helen's forehead. A familiar shiver scraped up her spine.

"C'mon, Don. I know that there's more. You're forgettin' something."

Helen's head came up. She stared at Roy, a big man weeping in a sagging wheelchair. He looked down and his hands closed over her reaching fingers.

"It ain't no use, Helen. It just ain't no use."

Helen crawled out of the grave. This was how it would end. All the traveling. All the horror and misery. And it would end the same way that it had begun.

Roy's arms curled around her waist and she kissed him. She made to wipe his tears away but was surprised to find that they were already gone.

Roy's eyes were alive again. Helen remembered a night in Reno, long ago, the way his eyes had sparkled at her, and she smiled.

Roy tugged the glove off Helen's left hand. "God, Helen. I know how to find the rest of it. It's been in front of me all along and I just didn't see . . ."

How long ago had it been? Helen shook her head. Funny to forget your own anniversary.

Roy slid the wedding ring off her sweaty finger. "Thanks, doll. It helps. I think I almost got it back now." He let her hand slip free of his grip.

Helen stared down at the pale skin circling her tanned ring finger. Something slipped away. Roy was talking again, but she couldn't quite hear him. The wind was whispering through the trees. A baby was crying in the woods.

"I knew I gave it to them," Roy whispered. "Me, I mean. I gave a lot of *me* to those guys in the war. But I forgot that I gave so much of me to you."

Helen's fingers were slivers of ice. She turned away from the sad man in the wheelchair, picked up the shovel, and began to fill the open grave with hard clumps of soil.

Something exploded in the distance; the night sky flushed red and pink. Fireworks. The Fourth of July. Helen stared up from her work and watched sparks shower over a lake that was miles away.

Roy's voice was almost lost in a booming explosion. "Just wait here, Helen. I'll be back. There's gotta be a way. Maybe I can get Don's letters from his mother. Maybe they'll fill in the blanks."

Helen watched as flowers bloomed in the icy blue sky—Indian paintbrush, columbine, and forget-me-nots. The colors melted away, and a faint glow spread over the woods surrounding the cemetery.

Something small and white crawled through the birch grove. Helen dropped the shovel. She turned away from the crawling thing and saw the man in the wheelchair shoving a battered alligator-skin case into the trunk of his car.

Why was he doing that? Why had he locked her baby inside that tiny black suitcase?

The Hudson roared alive. Roy backed out of the cemetery and headed down the wrong side of the road. The Hudson's Drive-Master transmission rattled noisily as the big car accelerated.

"Wait," Helen cried. "Don't go. I gave something to you, too, and you've got to give it back."

Something rattled in the distance. Helen recognized the sound: gold teeth rattling inside a dented canteen.

The crying thing curled around the base of a tree. Helen ran to the cemetery fence. Her baby was going to catch its death.

Her baby. Roy's baby.

Helen wanted to yell at her child. Her mouth opened. She swallowed. Her hands closed around iron spikes and she laughed.

Strange not to remember her own baby's name.

Scarlet sparks erupted in the sky, silhouetting the treetops, and then darkness closed over the woods.

No wind. No crying. Silence.

Helen dropped to her knees. The grass was wet, shiny in the rum-colored moonlight. This odd place, with all its granite headstones. This was the place where her husband was buried.

But what was his name?

She hurried down the mossy path, reading headstones by the light of her lantern, but none of the chiseled names seemed familiar.

Skyrockets exploded overhead. People were cheering in the distance.

She closed her eyes. She remembered. Her name was Helen. He'd picked her up in a Reno bar in 1946. They'd moved to Hollywood and had the kid a year later. About that much she was sure.

No.

She tried again. Her name was Helen. He'd picked her up in a Reno bar in 1946. He'd taken her to the withered old abortionist. The butcher's sharp, rusty knives had made him laugh, and after it was over he'd poured Lucky Tiger on her wounds. About that much she was sure.

No.

Again. Her name was Helen. He'd picked her up in a Reno bar in 1946 . . .

SAMANTHA LEE

Island
of the Seals

It had been an unproductive day, to say the least. The constant singing of the seals out in the bay had made her strangely restless, distracting her from the task in hand. Crumpled and discarded sheets of paper overflowed the wastepaper basket onto the surrounding carpet. She hadn't written one cohesive paragraph since morning.

Eventually, near dusk, she gave up all pretense of concentration and, crossing to the window, watched the sleek gray bodies dipping and weaving far out in the still water. Like the legendary mermen of old, their tails and fins flashed in the gradually fading daylight. Mesmerized, she stared until the crescent moon began to rise and the vaporous tendrils of the sea mist obscured them at their love play. When they were completely out of sight she turned away, carrying with her into the newly darkened room the sound of their shrill and melancholy keening.

The night air had brought with it a sudden chill and she shivered involuntarily, pulling her shawl around her. The isolation was beginning to get her down. She craved company, the stimulation of human conversation. She shrugged, pulling herself back from the edge of depression and, setting the kettle on the small hob, began to prepare her solitary evening meal. Perhaps she would feel more "inspired" when she had eaten.

She had just finished lighting the ancient and rather temperamental oil lamp when the knock sounded lightly on the door. In the silence of the Hebridean evening it was like an atomic explosion and she froze in momentary shock.

At last, pulling herself together, she lifted the lamp high and moved across the small room to the half door, a trail of grotesque, lengthening shadows draping themselves in folds of chiaroscuro like a train behind her.

She undid the latch with her left hand and opened the top section of the door to waist level, swinging it in toward her and peering, as she did so, out into the garden.

Silhouetted in the picture-frame shape stood a young man. About his head the swiftly rising "ha," as the Islanders call the treacherous sea fog, swirled like a horse's breath on a frosty day. Behind him the shingle path which led down to the beach lay shrouded in secrecy.

She judged that he was about twenty-four years old, tall and tanned, with thick brown hair, sleek and shining as though damp from the sea. His eyes were brown too and fringed by dark lashes. But his most noticeable feature was the ears. Small for a man, they lay curled like fine pink shells, flat to his head.

He spoke, greeting her in the lilting tones of the Gaelic, with a voice that was at once soft and hypnotic. He wished her health and many blessings. He said he had seen her standing by the window and had been reminded how long it was since he had heard a human voice. And she, remembering that custom in the Islands demanded that hospitality be offered to anyone, friend or stranger, whom chance might bring to the door, bade him enter and sit awhile.

She gave him milk and oatcakes and they talked long into the night of many things. He knew much of the folklore of the outer isles, stories she had never heard before. The curious, soporific quality of his voice as he recounted to her magical tales of love and death lulled her into a semicoma of contentment. Sitting opposite him in the flickering firelight seemed the most natural thing in the world, as though her whole life she had been expecting his arrival, as though for the first time in her drab existence she had found something worthwhile.

He reached forward to touch her hand and to her surprise she did not draw it away but curled her fingers around his and put her other hand up to stroke the thick dark hair and fondle the small, strange ears.

He looked at her long and deep, his eyes as dark and unfathomable as the rock-pools in the bay. She felt the blood rush to her face and her limbs took on a strange lightness as she read in his gaze the promise of an end and a beginning. She stood up, stumbling in her agitation, and he placed his hand on her arm to steady her. His grip sent a surge of feeling through her body which left her incapable of resistance as he led her gently through the open door into the tiny bedroom.

Next morning, when she woke to the sound of the soft, insistent chanting of the seals among the rocks, he had gone. Only the mark of his head on the pillow remained to assure her that he had been there at all.

She waited for evening in a fine fury of apprehension, wishing the warm spring day away. Unable to concentrate on her writing she paced the room, hugging herself as the memories of the night flooded back in waves of emotion that made her head whirl.

By the time the sun had set, what remained of her pride was in shreds and when at last his light tap echoed on the half door, she flung herself at him, crying in relief. And it was as though he had never been gone, for he stilled her fears with his kisses, holding her in the circle of his arms until she fell asleep against his strong, dark body.

And so it continued all through the late spring and early summer, her love deepening and growing while in the background the ever present seal colony thrived in the ripening sun.

In the beginning she questioned him about his daily absences but he only smiled and changed the subject, until eventually she began to accept his reticence as a fact of their life together and ceased her inquiries.

Every morning he had disappeared as usual and her days were her own. She had given up all pretense of writing now. Her sense of unreality in the daylight hours increased as the months went by. Her love had become an obsession and she lived only for the nights; existed simply for the return of her solitary, secret lover and their hours together.

To pass the time between sunrise and sunset she would take long walks along the beach where the seal community had their home. She watched the small, furry pups growing under their mothers' constant care, the great bulls fighting to retain their territory, the young males trying out their growing strength in mock battles. She had an affinity with the seals that she had never had with her own kind. She had always been the outsider, a loner, considered slightly odd because she had no interest in the grasping opportunism that had overtaken humanity. It was one of the reasons she had begun to write. It gave her an excuse, a reason to enjoy her solitude unharassed by the predatory gossip that had hounded her schooldays and teens.

Now on the Island she had found the perfect balance. By day the seals gave her friendship without intrusion and by night she loved and was loved in return. True, she wasn't doing any work, but there would be plenty of time for that afterward. And she didn't want to think of afterward just yet. Even though she knew in her heart of hearts that somewhere, sometime, the magic summer would end.

It was the first week in September that the boat arrived, a powerful boat from the mainland carrying four powerful men. She watched them from the window as they landed and made camp among the rocks, covering the virgin shingle with a disorderly pile of accoutrements: tarpaulins and lengths of rope, a battered kettle, a primus stove.

They brewed some tea and sat in a circle drinking it and laughing together. Their harsh, mainland accents mingled with the intoxicating scent of the newly blooming gorse to drift in through the open cottage window.

The tallest of the men stood up and bent over the fire to refill his cup. As he straightened the sun glinted briefly on the knife in his belt and behind her curtain she felt her skin turn cold with the realization of why they had come.

It was time for the "culling."

Somewhere, far away on the mainland, the "authorities" had decided that the number of seals must be kept strictly in check. Faceless men, who had never seen the colony, had condemned half of it to death. And the four "conservationists" before her would have paid well for the privilege of butchering hundreds of helpless, trusting mammals.

For seal skins are valuable and the license to "cull" would be priced accordingly.

Then they wiped their hands, rolled up their sleeves and systematically began to kill.

In the grip of a horrible fascination she watched as they skinned the half-grown pups and the young males. They worked methodically, their long-handled clubs rising and falling rhythmically, careful only to strike the head so that the pelt should not be damaged. Some they killed: the lucky ones. Some they skinned while they were only half dead or stunned.

For two hours she gazed, ashen-faced, unable to tear her eyes away from the carnage. And all the time the pile of bloody skins mounted.

At last the "head man" raised an arm elbow-deep in gore to call a halt. As though nothing had happened the evening sunlight continued to illuminate a beach littered with blood and viscera, like the aftermath of a great battle.

In the shadow of a large outcropping of rock a seal mother bent whimpering over what was left of her offspring. Nudging it gently with her flippers she tried to push the pathetic scrap of exposed muscle and sinew toward the safety of the sea.

The "cullers" rinsed their carmine-stained hands and began to prepare an evening meal. They ate ravenously, totally oblivious of the devastation around them.

She turned from the window and lay down on the bed, her body weak with anguish and disgust. From outside she could hear the plaintive bleating of the seals punctuated by the coarse laughter of the men. And she wept with shame for humanity. For its needless cruelty and senseless greed. Wept until she had no more tears, turning her face to the wall.

Gradually the sky darkened and the autumn evening closed around her. Exhausted by her distress, her eyelids began to droop over eyes ravaged by the afternoon's atrocities, and she drifted thankfully into oblivion.

She woke to total darkness. Total darkness and deafening silence. A pang of terror gripped her, followed by an overpowering sense of foreboding. For she was alone. Tonight when she needed his strength as never before, he hadn't come. Feeling her way haltingly in the darkness she crossed to the window. The crescent moon hung almost obscured by the sea mist. It was a night like that first night had been. The only difference was that now and then the warning light of the alien boat blinked on and off, a pinpoint of scarlet through the silvery tendrils.

A primitive urge, stronger than she could contain, compelled her toward the beach. Lifting her shawl from where she had flung it earlier, she threw it around her thin shoulders and stumbled out into the mist. The fog came and went in dense clumps as she picked her way down the shingle path. She trudged on, completely losing her sense of direction, tripping on rocks, slipping on seaweed, only saved from occasionally walking into the sea by the cyclopean winking of the seal-cullers' light.

And with each step the feeling grew stronger. Terror and grief intermingled, guiding her toward some nameless destination in the fog-wrapped shroud of the night.

The compulsion had been leading her on in this aimless, semiblind state for almost an hour when a huge rock loomed out of the mist in front of her. And there, in the lee of its overhang, she finally found him.

His naked shoulder, as she bent to touch it, felt cold and oddly sticky. Nauseated by the sensation she drew back her hand. It was covered in blood. She leaned over to look more closely.

The back of his head had been battered to a pulp.

Controlling her repulsion with great effort she knelt down beside him and gently turned him over onto his back. The sudden shock of what she saw made her clamp her blood-soaked hand to her mouth in an attempt to still the hysterical screams which bubbled up in her throat threatening to engulf what was left of her sanity.

There wasn't an inch of skin left on him. Skin or hair. He'd been completely scalped and his ears had been cut off. The dark eyes that had looked at her with such love now stared up at her, glazed and unseeing in death.

The first wave of horror was superseded by an unimaginable grief. So deep and intense was the agony that she felt as though her body was being physically torn in two.

Gathering his flayed corpse to her chest she began to keen, a high continuous crooning moan. As her wailing mounted in pitch she started to rock, backward and forward, like a mother trying to soothe a fractious child to sleep. The tempo of her rocking increased and her tone took on a higher, whining quality as she pressed her face to what was left of his, heedless of the blood which stained her clothing and coagulated in her hair.

And as she wailed she began to hear, like an echo swirling through the mists over the still waters of the bay, soft voices raised to join in her lament. Comforting voices, whispering to her of the cool, green depths of the bottomless channel where the seals forever glide among the swaying seaweed forests. Beckoning her to where the dark, limpet-encrusted rock caverns know no sound but the singing of a seal-maiden to her sleek, gray love. Calling her away from a world grown too terrible to bear. Welcoming her home.

She raised her head and ceased to rock, sniffing the air like a dog that has scented his prey.

Then her clouded eyes cleared and she smiled.

"Wait for me," she called.

Then, bending tenderly to kiss the broken skull for the last time, she gently eased the tattered remains of her lost love onto the sand.

As she rose unsteadily to her feet, the red light from the boat winked on and her blood-stained mouth glistened momentarily in the dark. Absentmindedly, she pushed her disheveled hair away from her face and, clutching her shawl about her narrow body, she walked slowly and deliberately into the black, mist-enshrouded waters.

MICHAEL BISHOP

Thirteen Lies
About Hummingbirds

Her name was Memory Yang. She had just come aboard as a junior marketing researcher at Kyser, Godwin & Kale. What I first noticed about her—once past the nifty frisson of her name—was the way her Amerasian looks wouldn't be pigeonholed. From some angles, she had the gaunt pallor of a film-noir heroine; from others, the innocent sultriness of a geisha.

I was smitten again. Really snowed.

One night about a month after she came, I stayed late, working on the secondary accounts that were my burden at Kyser. Leaving, Memory and I met at the fourteenth-floor elevators, then rode down together in a glass-faced capsule.

It was spring. Streetlights shone on the eerie white plumes of the dogwoods in a pocket park across from our building. From my briefcase, I pulled three tissue-wrapped, long-stemmed red roses. One would have been too showily modest, a dozen too vulgarly smug.

"Pretty," said Memory Yang. "And they smell nice."

"They're for you."

Memory lowered her head. Maidenly embarrassment? If so, she was embarrassed not because she had attracted my attention and my unexpected gift. She was embarrassed *for me*.

"Corny?" I said. *"Too* corny?"

Head still down, she looked aside.

"Memory?" No answer. *"Miss Yang?"*

"Mr. Jurusik—"

"Peter. Pete."

"Mr. Jurusik, I hope what I tell you won't endanger my job."

That made me angry. "I'm not your boss, Memory."

"Mr. Jurusik, the problem is this: You're one of our hottest hotshots in copy-and-layout, right?"

I gave her raised eyebrows, noncommittal.

"And your idea of a brilliantly rad come-on is . . . roses?"

"Three roses."

She lifted her eyes to me. I saw then that Memory was no kid. She was a woman at least as old as I: a woman of some experience, a late career-starter. Any advantage earned by my rep at KG&K or my man-about-town sophistication went away like windshield fog under a roaring defroster.

"I thought it was the thought that counts," I said.

We were down. Foyer ferns, a vast slab of water-smooth marble flooring, and a uniformed security guard slid into view.

"The thought *does* count," Memory said. Side by side, we walked out to the hedge-fenced parking lot.

"What's the trouble, then? Do you doubt the sincerity of my thought?" I clamped my briefcase against my side and waved the rejected flowers.

"Not the sincerity—the quality."

"The quality? Then what would do it for you? The keys to my Audi? An airline ticket to Acapulco?"

Memory stopped walking. She took my lapel between a thumb and forefinger. "I'm not talking money." She tweezered my lapel in a vaguely threatening way. "Not necessarily, at least. I'm talking . . . imagination."

"Imagination?"

Under the greenish-yellow arc lamps, Memory peered into my eyes without really seeing me. To get her back, I had to twist free of her gently pinching fingers.

"Roses are better than a gold-plated zodiac charm," she finally said. "But not much. For the charm, you'd've at least had to find out my birthday."

"All right. Give me some suggestions."

For a moment, I thought she was going to climb into her car—a Volkswagen beetle, recently repainted—and drive off, leaving me to stew in my chagrin. But she didn't. Almost defiantly, she started lobbing examples: "A baseball signed by Hank Aaron. A full-color poster of the National Palace Museum in Taipei. A novel by García Márquez."

"Great. Go on."

"A shark's tooth. A ginkgo leaf. A geode."

What was this? The shopping list of a granola-eating nature lover? "Fine. Anything else?"

"A hummingbird." And then she did climb into her bug and putt-putt airily away.

A hummingbird? Had Memory given me her real wish-list or just a scaffold to build on? It would be easy to get Hank Aaron's John Hancock on a National League baseball—a friend of mine worked in public relations for the Braves. Travel posters weren't hard to find. And every bookstore in town had *Love in the Time of Cholera* stacked up so high that it looked as if García Márquez was putting a move on Stephen King's floor space.

The hard part of making use of Memory's examples, I saw, would come in figuring out beforehand what she'd go for. How could I have known that she liked baseball, Taiwanese art, Latin American novelists? Or hummingbirds?

So I played detective. I found out that Memory's birthday was less than a week away; that her ex-hubby was doing time for a drug conviction in Macon's Central Correctional Institute; that, as a result of wounds sustained during a holdup at his health spa two years ago, her father, an immigrant from Taiwan, was now disabled; that, late in Carter's presidency, her mother had suffered a fatal stroke; that her

only brother, Tom, lived in Connecticut; and that her favorite poet was
Wallace Stevens.

I did *not* go out and buy her a first edition of *Harmonium*. Not only
would that have been nearly impossible, it would have been—in
Memory's eyes—show-offy and obvious.

Instead, I had the jeweler wife of a copywriter friend make a three-
inch-long (that is, life-size) hummingbird out of semiprecious gem-
stones, gold wire, and lacquered cellophane. I lowered it into Memory's
cubicle on a thread. A hand-lettered card accompanied my gift.

The card said, *"Happy Birthday, Memory. There are at least thirteen
lies I can tell you about rubythroats. This is the first one:* 'I am a hummingbird.' *The remaining lies will follow in turn."*

I signed it—almost sincerely—*"Love, Peter."*

Memory, true to her name, remembered our less-than-zippy first
meeting. She caught the nod to Stevens's "Thirteen Ways of Looking
at a Blackbird." She agreed to go out with me.

We began carefully. No pushing. Movies, not art films. Ball games,
not museums. Del Taco's, not Nikolai's Roof. And when our easy
shoptalk began to give way to heart-to-hearts, I cooled down a little and
strategically backed off.

Three days into this new adventure, I was riding one of KG&K's
interior elevators down to the cafeteria. I had it to myself. I was thinking about Memory. Her body, mostly—the weird, hawklike softness of
her face, and the way her arms and legs coming out of her girlish
sundresses or her expensive tailored suits looked so tasty. I was absentmindedly combing my hair in the metal mirror on the rear wall, really
not so much for vanity as for something to do while the car purred
down-shaft.

I didn't even notice that the car had stopped until its doors had
opened and Heather Ligotti—an Italian blonde, a *real* Italian blonde—
was staring at me in the rippled aluminum of the mirror. I must have
started. Heather laughed. I was trying to put my comb away when she
caught my wrist.

"Sort of touching you still have it, Peter."

She meant the hand comb. It was jade green, with a handle. A
delicate thing, maybe a little too la-di-da for a man, but Heather had
given it to me during our fling, and I've never believed a guy has to
return every memento of a relationship just because things don't pan

out. If that's the way it worked, think of all the junk he'd have to take back himself.

"Relax, Peter. A month ago I'd've shot you. Not now. It's too late for the old 'in the heat of passion' defense."

"Very funny."

"Who's joking?" She deliberately bumped by hand. The teeth of my comb pricked me in the throat.

"Ow! Damn you!"

"The same to you. Doubled."

I looked at the comb. A perfect little bead of blood stood on one of its teeth. The aluminum mirror showed me another bead just like it, on the flesh under my chin. To keep from ruining my shirt collar, I put a thumb to the spot and pressed.

"And now you've got a yen for Miss Yang."

"That's none of your business."

Which hacked her off. But she held it in and said, "It is when you make everything so all-fired *public*, Peter."

"You want us to hide?"

"I just want you to know that Memory can take care of herself."

"I never doubted it."

"You always doubt it. And you're right so often, you begin to think that's the way it'll always go. One lie after another until the truth—with a capital T—can't be squelched any longer and the whole thing goes blooie."

"Heather, you're just—"

"—human, Peter. I'm human. And I'm getting off." She was pushing buttons right and left, and finally, when the car stopped on the next floor down, she did get off.

Stupid. She'd probably been going to the cafeteria, too. I rode the rest of the way down, proud of myself for usually picking someone on another floor, or in another building, or even in another town to get it on with. If you don't do that—which, this time, I wasn't—the results can be really messy.

I got out my handkerchief and dabbed at the scarlet prick among the rash-surrounded shaving stubble on my throat. I stuck the comb back in my pocket with my car keys.

Meanwhile, Memory and I were doing great. Five *good* days, full of subsurface sexual tension. It was the first time in my life I enjoyed seeing Dale Murphy fan in four out of five at-bats. Or Sly Stallone do anything at all.

On our sixth day, I decided to tell her Falsehood No. 2. After work, Memory and I drove to an old-fashioned tea room in Madison, Georgia, three counties away. We ordered spinach salad, creamed corn, and lemon chicken. Later, our white-jacketed waiter came out and set a dessert plate in front of Memory.

"Your fortune cookie, ma'am."

Memory eyed it suspiciously. Then she cracked the cookie open, took the fortune slip out, and read it.

As I already knew, it said, *"The blood spot on the gorget of the male is an outward sign of its passion."*

My tie was crimson silk. I waggled it at Memory—my randy Oliver Hardy impersonation.

"Two down." Memory smiled, then added, "Female rubythroats don't have red gorgets, Peter."

"According to Mr. Audubon, no, they don't."

Memory read the tiny scroll again. "So does this"—holding the fortune aloft—"imply that the females lack passion?"

I took the scroll from her and used a ballpoint to write on its unprinted side. "Here. A corollary to Lie Number Two." I passed the slip back to Memory.

She read its message: *"The female suppresses her blood spot from an inborn sense of propriety."*

Another smile. "You wish," she said, and I didn't know whether she meant that females actually did lack passion or that my attempt to unleash hers was a transparent botch.

Hopefully, I returned her smile.

Memory didn't lack passion. Even though the following day was a workday, she agreed to an interlude. At a bed-and-breakfast in a remodeled antebellum house, we spent most of that night playing out the feverish impulses of our blood.

In the morning, we made separate long-distance calls to KG&K to tell our bosses that we were sick and wouldn't be in.

"This is something I don't do," she said.

Ratling-naked next to her, I had to laugh.

"Lie about being sick," she said sharply. "We can't do this again, Peter."

My stomach lurched as if I *did* have a virus. "Memory—!"

"During the week, I mean. It's unprofessional."

We argued, but Memory had made up her mind. I thought that later, sensibly horny again, she'd change her mind, but she never did. In fact, Memory went back to work that afternoon, claiming that her attack of flu had been a feeble one. I stayed out the entire day, angry and resentful. After all, she had sabotaged the perfect pleasure jaunt.

The next weekend, I took Memory to my friend Robert Taggart's hunting and fishing cabin in the mountains of Pickens County. This was no rustic, ramshackle hideaway, but a well-appointed bachelor's lair featuring a music-and-video center, a wet bar, and a series of erotic lithographs at those spots on the walls where most good old boys would have hung deer heads, shotguns, or stolen animated beer signs.

Memory called the lithographs "tacky." Fortunately, the cabin had something that she liked: the hummingbird feeder hanging from a shingled eave of Robert's tool shed. A picture window in the loft bedroom allowed us to wallow leg over leg on Saturday afternoon watching the birds. Most were white-throated females. They would pop into sight at the feeder's phony scarlet blossoms, hover there siphoning the sugar water that Memory boiled for them, and flit off into . . . maybe another dimension. One territorial female feinted and attacked repeatedly, driving off all the others trying to drink from the feeder.

"The little bitch," Memory said.

Then that green-jacketed harridan disappeared, too, and for a long time the air was birdless—spookily so. I used this interlude to tell Memory my third premeditated lie:

" 'Hummingbirds do not fly; they matter-transmit.' "

She considered this, then kissed me on the temple and pointed at a spot between the king-size bed and the picture window.

"You're right," she said. "There's one . . . *now!*"

I blinked. So emphatic was Memory's suggestion, I thought a male rubythroat had materialized in the loft. The sound of its whirring wings, the ebony syringe of its beak, and the pulsing fire of its gorget burned into my retinas as if a flashbulb had popped. Then the mirage was gone, and all I could hear, clutching Memory's warm, supple body, was laughter.

The laughter of a sorceress.

"Another," she demanded.

We wrestled. Memory kept laughing. As she laughed, she dared me over and over to make up a fourth fantastic lie.

" *'Sex for hummingbirds is an exquisite agony.'* " I finally said, pinning her down. " *'To imagine it, stick your finger into the blur of an electric beater.'* "

She liked that. "Very good, Peter. Nine to go."

Yet more laughter, followed by a spontaneous binge of inventive sex —none of it, its exquisiteness aside, the least agonizing.

The next present I gave Memory was a circular aquarium containing a dozen flamboyantly colored tropical fish, several muck-eating snails, and an underwater forest of seaweed and waving ferns. I installed the aquarium in her apartment on a Friday afternoon while Memory was still at the office. When she arrived home, she found the glowing tank, the beautiful angel wings and clownfish, and, in a near-invisible Lucite cube suspended at the aquarium's heart, one iridescent hummingbird.

"Peter!" she said, approaching the radiant tank.

The hummingbird wasn't real. It was the same one I'd lowered to her desk as spectacular proof of my interest. Distorted by the fish-peopled water, though, it *looked* real. I kissed her on the forehead and slipped out the door, allowing her to find and read for herself the lie on the accompanying card:

"Eventually, a hummingbird in a tank of oxygenated sugar water will sip its way to freedom."

A major Atlanta soft-drink firm employing Kyser, Godwin & Kale decided to create, name, and test-market an energy-boosting drink in direct competition with Gatorade. Logan Metasavage gave the account to me and told me to have my entire campaign worked out in brilliant detail yesterday. I got to it.

I named this drink—some sort of citrus-flavored, sugar-laden, cherry-colored, additive-doped swill—NRG-Assist, and I designed a bottle resembling a hummingbird feeder, a label on which a pair of cartoon rubythroats are prominent, and a series of animated TV ads featuring the energetic hummers as product spokescreatures. The makers of NRG-Assist really liked it; they gave us a handsome bonus for executing the campaign so quickly. Thus did I back up—that week, anyway— my reputation as a company hotshot.

On Sunday, Memory and I went to a free symphonic concert on the grass in Chastain Park. Between sets, a light plane buzzed the crowd, trailing an advertising banner. This banner was the medium of my sixth falsehood, a public falsehood for which the company and I were generously reimbursed:

"Hummingbirds prefer NRG-Assist."

As an additional reward, KG&K gave me a twelve-day vacation in Palm Springs, Florida. Memory couldn't go, but that was okay: I knew a feisty little lady down there, anyway, and I stayed in touch with Memory via postcard and Southern Bell.

In the seventh week of our itemhood, Memory had a pregnancy scare. It was only a scare, but it fell between us like a sword; and the lie I handed her on a postcard purchased during my getaway to Florida—a card showing a red-gilled lizard on a palm tree—did nothing to ease her mind, even though I'd meant it lightly:

"The first hummingbirds were the get of an oversexed chameleon and a bewildered dragonfly."

What eased her mind was the arrival, about two weeks late, of her period. Its coming took care of some of my midnight sweats, too. Some. Not all.

Two nights after Memory told me that she was all right, I had a psychedelic nightmare. A horde of hummingbirds swept up from South America and cycloned into Atlanta in a whirring cloud of invisible wings and chittering, batlike squeaks—a cloud so dense, gemlike, and swift that the sun was blotted out; traffic disappeared behind a series of shifting emerald scrims; and hummingbird guano began to fall like wet caulking on sidewalks, gutter guards, window ledges, awnings, rooftops.

This vile bombardment went on and on. If you stuck your head outdoors, the backwash from a million beating wings would knock you down. Rays of sunlight struggling to penetrate the metallic cloud sparked blinding flashes off it. City people who weren't cowering in parked cars, or in the revolving doors of department stores, or in bus shelters, were lying on the pavement with their hands over their heads, like actors in mid-1950s Civil Defense films about the Soviet nuclear threat.

I woke up sweating. Is a plague of hummingbirds what I'd have sired on my Oriental dragonfly if Memory had really been pregnant? A noisy litter of rubythroats out of my lover's womb?

A tape recorder lay on the end table next to my bed. I kept it there in case midnight inspiration seized me during my efforts to devise a full-bore ad campaign for one of our clients. I picked it up, found its built-in microphone, and spoke my lie:

" '*One plague in Egypt was of hummingbirds: Pharaoh's people died with emerald plumage in their mouths.*' "

An evening later, when I played this back for Memory, she said, "There aren't any hummingbirds in the Old World, Peter. And there never have been."

"Don't be so literal-minded."

Memory wanted me to meet her daddy, to see that she had strong family ties here in Atlanta. So, in her VW beetle, we drove to her father's clapboard house in Decatur.

Mr. Yang, wearing a pair of smoky sunglasses, sat in a lawn chair watering his parched grass. The hose lay in a narrow trench next to the driveway, eeled up through some weedy Bermuda at his sneakered feet, and, pretty much hidden, spilled its contents into all the lower reaches of the yard, which the hose had flooded to a state of perilous squishiness.

"Howdy," the old man said, tilting his head like a dog.

He had on a Day-Glo orange jumpsuit and a paint-freckled Braves cap. At seventy-plus, he looked only about five years older than I did. Memory had told me that the bullet wounds responsible for his retirement included a blasted-away calf muscle, a shattered elbow, and a mangled hand. Only when he stood to greet us, though, did I notice his injuries.

"Daddy, there's a water shortage. You could be fined."

"Only if they catch me." Limping, he herded us up the walk to his air-conditioned house.

In the tiny living room, Mr. Yang felt his way into a low-slung easy chair. Next to this chair lay the corpse of an aged, silvery, lion-maned chow, the handiwork of a taxidermist.

"That's Chiang Kai-shek," Memory explained. "Daddy's last and longest-surviving seeing-eye dog."

She said that her father had been a masseur in Taipei, Taiwan (blind persons have a monopoly on that profession over there), and that he had founded a thriving, wholly upright massage parlor in Atlanta soon after coming to Georgia in the early 1950s. As Memory spoke, her father absentmindedly scratched Chiang's muzzle.

A shiver helixed my spine: I wasn't much comforted to hear that Mr. Yang had had Chiang Kai-shek stuffed because the faithful chow had given its life for him in the same brutal robbery attempt that had forced his retirement.

While Memory was in the kitchen, Mr. Yang informed me that his daughter loved me. Moreover, I was the first man for whom she had felt such tenderness since her divorce.

"Memory tells me you lie to her, Peter."

That knocked me back. I didn't know what to say.

"Lies about hummingbirds," he specified, smiling. "As a way of wooing her."

"I guess that's so," I said, only a little relieved.

"It can be hard, coming up with clever lies." Mr. Yang tilted his blind head. "Would you like to borrow one?"

"I guess so."

"Okay. Here. It's a steal from Stevens, but it's a 'lie' you must keep in mind if Memory really loves you."

My hands were clammy. My irritation was building.

Mr. Yang stared through his silver lenses at me: " 'A man and a woman are one. A man and a woman and a hummingbird are one.' "

A coldness unrelated to the air-conditioning hit me, for this "lie," echoing some lines in Stevens's blackbird poem, was a subtle threat. Mr. Yang wanted me to understand that my intentions toward Memory had better be honorable.

"Lie Number Nine, Peter," Mr. Yang said. "Feel free to tell it to Memory when you leave here this evening."

"I will," I said. "Thanks. Thanks a lot."

"I don't think her ex-husband—the two-timing no-account doing time in Macon—ever saw the truth in that lie."

"He didn't?"

"No, he didn't. He was a tail-chaser. When the feds arrested him for dealing coke, I told Memory to speak up about it. She did, too. In court."

"Good. Good for her."

"You're tense, young man. I can tell from your voice. Let me give you a massage."

This offer frightened me. The simple thought of the old man's touch set goosebumps sprouting. "But your hand . . ."

"With one hand, I'm better than most sighted people who have a healthy pair. If I didn't tire so fast, I'd still be working."

For some reason, I submitted. In a back bedroom, I lay naked on an aluminum table. The old man kneaded the flesh at my nape, my shoulder blades, the small of my back, my upper buttocks. It was as if he wanted to turn them into wholly different shapes—hills of loamy soil, maybe, or the body parts of a weird, two-legged alien. So my muscles stayed as taut as clock springs.

"Try to loosen up, Peter."

"I can't." My face lay on a stiff folded towel.

"Maybe it's because you've been mixing Memory and desire." He chuckled, not kindly. "Do you suppose?"

"Mmmmf." I had no memory. I had no desire.

"I can feel it in my fingers. There's something cruel in you, young man. Something dark and selfish."

He told me my birthday. He gave me the names of the last four women I had dated "seriously." He alluded to my parents' divorce and told me where my father was buried. He informed me that I had never been a baseball fan and that I had no more interest in poetry than I had in hummingbirds. Never fear, though—he wouldn't tell. Memory was a big girl and could find out these unremarkable secrets for herself —probably by a method akin to the tactile one that he was using now. In fact, it was entirely possible that she knew my secrets already.

I wanted to escape, but the old man's good hand held me to the table. Neither his massaging technique nor his menacing patter was likely to freshen or relax me.

Twenty minutes into this delicate sadism, he said, "Know why I named my daughter Memory?"

"No, sir."

"Memory is a form of knowledge." Mr. Yang leaned the heel of his hand onto my spine. "What one remembers, one knows. Memory— Mnemosyne, as the Greeks say—was the feminine source of all human creativity. I hoped our daughter would please her mother and me as happy memories do. Also, I trusted that memory—our daughter's, I mean—would serve her as a shield. See?"

"I don't know. Yes, sir. I think so."

"What you remember—really remember—you keep. I named Memory years before computers came along, but, in terms of memory storage, Memory's my computer. Some days, *I* hardly know my own name. But if I want to hear about my late wife, Memory taps into her memory and gives them to me so that my blindness doesn't matter—stories, songs, poems. You follow, young man?"

"Yes, sir." But I didn't. I just didn't want to give Mr. Yang an excuse to shatter a vertebra.

"I may forget, but my Memory won't. When she tells me what she knows, I always remind her . . . not to forget it."

Eventually, he released me. Eventually, the three of us—the old man slumped in his chair with a plate on his lap and Chiang Kai-shek beside him—ate what Memory had prepared for us.

I don't recall what that was, nor do I wish to.

Later, standing in the lobby of the Fox Theater on Peachtree, I told Memory her father's lie: " '*A man and a woman are one. A man and a woman and a hummingbird are one.*' "

"Nice," Memory said. "But I hope it isn't a lie."

"It's not *my* lie, Memory."

"I tell Daddy everything, Peter."

"You tell him everything," I said numbly. Suddenly, I had an unsettling suspicion.

"In that robbery your dad got shot up in . . ."

"What about it?"

"Were the holdup men caught?"

"Chaing Kai-shek tore one of them up. That gave Daddy time to shoot the other. In fact, he crippled the second creep even worse than those cowardly bastards did for him."

"Not bad for an old guy shooting blind."

"No," Memory said. "It wasn't."

On Friday afternoon, I went up to Robert's cabin by myself. I wanted to be alone. I filled the hummingbird feeder and watched until dusk as a pair of females flew aerial dogfights around each other—a battle for exclusive sipping rights.

When no birds appeared the next morning, though, I hurried to check out the feeder. Small red ants paraded up the wall of the shed, under the eave, along the feeder's drop line, and down the sticky glass bottle to the four plastic blossoms dispensing sugar water. Although a few ants had drowned in the clear syrup inside the cylinder, most hadn't—they swarmed like coolies all over the bottle. No wonder my hummingbirds hadn't returned.

I found a garden hose, leveled a cleansing spray on the feeder and the ants crawling over the shed, and tried to find a better spot for the feeder. Where? No place seemed absolutely safe from ant attack—so, finally, I dumped the bottle's gluey contents on an anthill next to the shed and went back inside.

Later, lying on Robert's bed, a fresh lie came marching into my mind—like a train of ants. Each ant carried one syllable of the conceit: *"Anteaters sometimes impersonate hummingbirds in order to gorge on the ants that have overrun their feeders."*

Ha ha, I thought bitterly. Very amusing.

I had a disturbing picture of Memory playfully straddling me, her glossy hair hanging down around my temples, her nipples moving over me like the pink felt nubs of Magic Markers. What was her eidolon doing? Tracing on my chest the words she was whispering to me inside the veil of her imaginary tresses:

"Often, Peter, some of these imposters—anteaters pretending to be hummingbirds—have trouble staying aloft."

Memory's smart-ass corollary to Falsehood No. 10. Even after her naked phantom had vanished, there was no doubt in my mind that she was calling me—subtly, of course—an imposter.

By dint of real effort, I sidestepped her for a whole week. I took lunch an hour earlier or later than she did, I stayed well out of her territories in the KG&K building, I stopped telephoning her in the evenings, and I let my answering machine reply to every call to my apartment, even when I was there to pick up. To Memory's credit, or maybe as a sample of her shrewdness, she called me only once that week, and her voice among my messages sounded neither desperate nor sad:

"My father enjoyed talking with you last week, Peter. He wants to stand us to dinner. Let me hear from you. Love ya. Bye."

I ignored the call, which came on a Tuesday evening. In fact, I made it until Thursday afternoon without Memory's spotting me on the fourteenth floor or chasing me down in the parking lot. As it was, she cornered me right after an unscheduled marketing meeting called by her boss, Vivian DuPriest, to which Logan Metasavage, my boss, had sent me as his proxy.

Throughout this meeting, at which I learned that my NGR-Assist hummingbird ads would debut that night on Channel 17, Memory acted as if nothing were wrong. When she buttonholed me after the meeting, she showed a possessiveness—fingering my tie, patting my pocket handkerchief—that made me blush.

"You *must* be busy, Peter. Well, Vi's kept me running, too, and it won't hurt Daddy to wait a while to see you again."

"Ah." (That old Jurusik wit in action.)

"Which reminds me. It's time for a hummingbird lie, Peter."

Criminy. The woman was insatiable.

"Don't get uptight. I know you've been busy. I have, too, but I still decided it was time for *me* to do one."

I just stared, feeling my blush fade.

"You should like it. It's about advertising. Ready?"

I had swallowed my tongue.

Memory laughed and kissed me on the forehead. " *'Hummingbirds regard the imperceptible eyeflashes of subliminal TV ads as heavy reading.' "*

I heard the words, but they were only words. Memory smiled and repeated them.

"Number Eleven," she said. "'The last two are yours, but if you just want to drop the whole game, fine. We'll find a less phony way to interact. You're too bright a guy for this crap, Peter."

That night, I drove straight to my apartment, locked myself in, and heated my dinner in the microwave. Peter, I thought, switching on the TV, review your situation.

Just then, one of my NRG-Assist spots came on. Two animated hummingbirds flew around a cartoony bottle of the stuff, chittering such lies as *"For instant energy replenishment"* and *"Fly with the fleetest when you NRG-Assist."*

But I noted something weird about the ad—a blur at the bottom of the screen, twin streaks of characters that came and went so fast it was hard to tell if they were real. During the regular program, I shoved my tray aside and looked around for my Polaroid. Then, camera in hand, I waited for the next commercial.

A repeat of my NRG-Assist spot was squeezed between a Toyota ad and a brokerage-firm come-on. During this rerun, I took four shots of the screen. One of them, developed, showed the illegal eyeflash message I'd suspected was there.

Computer-printed letters. It said: *"A hummingbird's minuscule heart can beat up to thirteen weeks after the bird has died. How long do you think yours will beat?"*

Lie No. 12. Truly heavy reading.

How had that ominous message appeared in my ad? Well, at least one version of the spot must have gone to our client's offices from KG&K that way. I had a hunch that Memory was the marketing rep who had fed the doctored clip to our client—who, in turn, had passed it on to the TV people for broadcasting. Her doctoring was clumsy and obvious, but when it was discovered, as it eventually would be, *I* was the ad exec who'd catch the flak.

That night, I packed. On Friday, I went to work as if nothing were wrong. I kept avoiding Memory, whom I once saw staring into copywriting-and-layout from the edge of her research-and-marketing warren. Later, pleading a queasy stomach (the truth, the honest-to-Jesus truth), I left about three hours early.

I drove to my bank, withdrew every penny in my savings account, and got on I-20 West out of Atlanta, to Birmingham and whatever unknown spots farther west the evil designs of Memory Yang might yet force me to flee. I cruised for hours. I didn't stop cruising until the air had an unfamiliar, high-altitude sting.

For the past ten or twelve days, I have been writing on motel stationery in a variety of motels in the Rockies and the Pacific Northwest: Econolodge, Day's Inn, Motel 6, you-name-it.

I jump every time I see a Volkswagen, and yesterday morning my heart nearly burst when I entered a mom-and-pop grocery in Klamath Falls, where I'd been holed up for two days, and saw a hummingbird brooch on the floral-print blouse of the female owner.

"Where did you get that?" I said.

"Pretty lady handed it to me yesterday right after you'd bought something from us. Said, if I didn't mind, to let you have it the next time you came in."

She shouted something after me as I fled, but I had no time to waste and beat it back to the motel to gather up my belongings and hit the road again. I drove south, into California, and continued treading asphalt long after night had fallen.

Two nights ago, in a ramshackle boardinghouse in Bakersfield, I dreamed that a wrinkled, gnomish old man was sitting astride my hams pulling my spinal cord, knob by Tinker Toy knob, through a hole he had punctured at the base of my neck. He reeled it out (even flat on my belly, I could see the wet column emerging from between my shoulder blades) like a man drawing a knotted rope out of a well.

On each knob—or knot—was a small photo-booth portrait of a young woman I had known. The gnome on my back touched the blood-smeared face on each photograph with a crooked thumb, grunted his pitying recognition, and continued extracting my spine. At last, finished, he got down from the bed and stumped out onto the landing using my flaccid backbone as a walking stick.

Later, something wakened me: a dog, furiously barking.

Face down on the daybed, I was unable to move. It took an hour—at least—to scrunch myself upright and hobble to the door. The moon was still up. Standing on the sidewalk across the street from the boardinghouse was a lion-maned dog. It barked at me, violently snapping its chops.

I slammed the door, grabbed my gear, and hustled down the back steps to the eucalyptus-ringed yard sheltering my Audi.

I have just returned to my second-floor room in a motel outside Socorro, New Mexico. I wasn't gone long, just long enough to buy some Kentucky Fried Chicken and a new set of fingernail clippers. The first thing I saw when I came back in—a shock worse than those given me by Memory's hummingbird pin and the resurrected seeing-eye dog —was a small hardcover book lying open on my bed.

A tiny creature rested in the crease between the book's yellow pages. I went across the room and lifted it squeamishly by a tail feather. I don't know whether this bird is male or female, for the blood spot at its throat is real blood—as if whoever brought it to me sliced its throat with a razor blade. Some of its blood stains the poetry in the volume, a first edition of *Harmonium*.

My phone line has been cut. When I peeked through the curtains a few minutes ago, a shadowy figure stood on the landing across the courtyard from my room. And the silhouette of a lion-maned dog was visible in the gloom beneath the landing.

The dead telephone rings.

"Hello," says the party calling me, a young woman. I already know who she is.

"This is your imagination speaking," she goes on, but actually it's Memory. "And you've a good one, Peter—better than I'd have ever guessed. Forgive me for doubting you."

"What do you want?"

"That first lie you told me: *'I am a hummingbird.'* "

I grip the dead phone, resolutely saying nothing.

"It wasn't a lie. That makes it the truth. Which, given the game we were playing, makes it a lie again. See?"

"I'm finished," I say. "I'm finished playing."

"Close your eyes, Peter."

I try to resist this command, but I can't. Memory's powers of coercion, even through the cut line, are irresistible.

"You're not finished until the last lie is spoken, Peter. But even though you started the game—then broke your promise to play it through to the end—I'll let you off the hook. *I'll* be Official Finisher, okay?"

I start to open my eyes.

"Don't!" Memory shouts through the handset. Both she and her blind daddy can access—can see—what I'm doing.

I keep my eyes closed.

"Here," Memory says. "Our thirteenth lie. *'A dead hummingbird symbolizes unspeakable grief.'* "

Does she mean me? Is her lie, as was Mr. Yang's, some kind of subtle physical threat? I'm not sure.

But my eyes open anyway, and when I look at the bed, I see that the first edition of *Harmonium* is really a Socorro phone book and that the butchered hummingbird in the crease between its pages has turned into my jade green hand comb.

Suddenly, there is a low hum in my ear—an abrupt dial tone—and I'm all alone in a shabby little room somewhere not too far from either the White Sands nuclear testing grounds or the treacherous Jornada del Muerto.

Doesn't Memory understand—didn't she ever know?—that hummingbirds don't pair-bond? That's the truth, perhaps the first truth I ever learned about myself.

A knock at my motel room's door: several insistent raps.

"Who is it?"

An old man's cagy voice says, "Your masseur, Mr. Jurusik. Let me in." And the knocking goes on and on . . .

COLIN GREENLAND

The Stone Face

The train went only as far as Dinton Fairway, so after that they had to take the bus. It was an old one, with dusty maroon seats and battered springs. Neil and Gwen sat up in front. Apart from a beaky woman with a toddler on her lap, they were the only passengers.

While the bus jolted them up hills and down again, Neil looked around for the sea. This would be better than last year's holiday, he reckoned; better than tramping around all those youth hostels. At the seaside, you could really relax. It would do them both good.

Gwen rested her chin on her fist and looked out of the window. "I thought it stayed summer longer down here," she said.

She put her hair behind her ears and got a cigarette out of her handbag.

"You're not supposed to smoke up the front." Neil reminded her. "You have to sit up the back."

"They won't mind here," said Gwen. She lit up.

Neil kept expecting the driver to say something to her, but he didn't.

The bus took them to the village, and stopped in the village square. They got directions from a man in a mac sitting at a stall selling brightly-colored tin buckets and spades and shrimping nets. He didn't look as if he'd been doing much business.

The guest house turned out to be farther on, up on the cliffs. It was quite warm walking up the road, despite the cold wind. At the top there was a row of four houses facing out to sea, all painted the same blue. Mrs. Wilberforce's was the second. Neil banged on the knocker.

"Bags I the bath," said Gwen.

Mrs. Wilberforce was a little grey woman in a pink headscarf and a pale blue nylon overall. Her face was all wrinkled and yellow, but her eyes were sharp. "Mr. and Mrs. Humphreys?" she said.

"That's us," said Neil. He saw her look straight at Gwen's hand, looking for the ring. Old bat, he thought.

"You're in the upstairs front," said Mrs. Wilberforce. She sounded like a toucan. "It's a lovely view," she said. She put her hands together and looked at their cases.

"We can manage," said Gwen brightly.

Neil reached out to help her, but she pushed past him and went in, carrying her case in front of her with both hands.

Upstairs there were three doors. The first had a transfer of angel fish on. "Bathroom," said Neil.

They glanced in. The ceiling was low, the walls were covered in thick tiles the color of old piano keys. There was a narrow bath, a basin with a mirror over it, a tiny Ascot for hot water, and a toilet. The air smelled violently of air freshener.

"Nice," said Gwen.

She put her case down on the landing and reached for the knob of the second door.

"That's hers," said Neil, whispering. He pointed to the other one. "Upstairs front," he said.

Upstairs front was a big bed in a small room. They had to squeeze past a wardrobe to get in. On the other side of the bed was an upright chair and a fireplace with a plywood screen in front. The screen was covered in seashells, glued all over it.

There was a big window, at the foot of the bed. Gwen stood looking out over the cliff.

Neil dumped his case on the bed and opened the catches.

"This is all right," he said.

He pressed down with both hands, testing the mattress. It didn't give much.

Gwen sat down. "This is hard."

"It's better for you," said Neil immediately.

"I suppose," said Gwen, gazing down at the sea again.

He looked. "It's a lovely view," he squawked, imitating Mrs. Wilberforce.

"Neil," said Gwen, punching him.

Well, it was. There was nothing much out there, though, at the moment. A couple of ships, a long way off, and a lot of cloud coming in.

"Are you going for your bath?" he asked.

"No."

"What's the matter?"

"That bathroom."

"It's all right," he said.

"Looks as if someone died in there."

He didn't see what she meant. Not that it mattered. "Must have some sort of a wash, Gwen." He took his sponge bag out of his case. "Back in a jiffy," he said, and leaned over the bed to kiss her cheek.

There was nothing wrong with the bathroom, even if it wasn't a room you'd want to hang about in. Neil sponged himself over quickly. He looked at himself in the mirror: curly brown hair, getting a bit long, actually, but that didn't matter on holiday; soft brown eyes; a broad flat nose that looked as if somebody had squashed it, and a big mouth. Gwen had used to tell him he had lovely lips, when they'd first been going out together. He gave himself a big smile, then put his shirt on and went downstairs.

Gwen was in the kitchen, wiping up. She'd tied her hair back, which meant she was making a special effort. Her hair was fairer than his, and straight and very fine, so it would never stay when she put it behind her ears. Her ears were very small for her face, which was long, and not what you'd call pretty, he supposed, though she had nice eyes, brown with a fleck of green to them, and heavy eyelids that made her look distant and dreamy. While she worked, Gwen was chatting to Mrs. Wilberforce. Mrs. Wilberforce was smoking a cigarette.

"I feel better for that," Neil said. "Let's go and look at the sea."

"Mrs. Wilberforce has got the tea on," said Gwen.

Mrs. Wilberforce prodded something in a saucepan. "I've got the tea on now," she said.

So they had their tea. While they were eating it started to rain, so they stayed in, the first evening. They sat in the parlor. Neil watched the telly with Mrs. Wilberforce, and Gwen read the paper.

They went to bed early.

Neil had been looking forward to this.

"Come here," he said, reaching for her under the covers.

She let him draw her over. She put her arm around his neck. Then when he went to kiss her, she buried her face in his shoulder.

"What's the matter?" he said.

"Nothing." Her voice was muffled in the pillows.

He felt her lying across him, like a dead weight. "What?" he said again. He hugged her, stroking her bottom through her nightie. "Come on. What is it?"

She twisted away from his hand. "She's listening," she said.

He had to think for a moment, who she meant.

"Mrs. Wilberforce? She's not," he said. "Come on, Gwen."

But it was no use.

He lay there with his hands under his head. Gwen rolled off him and lay on her side of the bed, with her back to him. Soon her breathing sounded slow and even.

A distant foghorn mooed. He could just about hear the sea, whispering back and forth through the rain.

Next day it had stopped raining, though it was still overcast, with a chilly breeze. At breakfast Mrs. Wilberforce told them they should walk along the beach to Bourne Bay, and back over the cliffs.

"It's a nice walk," she said.

Neil wondered when was the last time she had walked anywhere.

"There's a café at Bourne Bay where you can get your dinner," said Mrs. Wilberforce. She showed them on the map.

They went down into the village. Everywhere was very quiet. They passed the post office and general stores, where an old man was chatting to the postmistress while she slowly sliced a side of bacon. There was a pub called the Lobster Pot, which wasn't open yet. Just beyond was a line of wooden beach chalets, their paint peeling. None of them seemed to be occupied. A black cat was nosing at an old gym shoe someone had left behind. Gwen tried to call it, but it ran away.

The beach was just stones, no sand, and it was quite steep. To the west, it curved away around a headland out of sight. The tide was in. The sea looked pretty choppy. The rain had stirred it up until it was a murky gray-brown color, like washing-up water.

Gwen walked along with her head down and her hands in her pockets. Neil went down to the edge of the sea and threw stones. He tried to make them skip, but he couldn't get it right. He looked around for some more. He saw a face, looking up at him.

It was a stone. He picked it up.

"Look at that," he said.

Gwen was some way ahead. He called her. "Gwen!"

She turned, frowning, the wind blowing her hair into her eyes. "What?"

"Look at this!"

He ran to catch up with her. He showed her the stone.

"What about it?" she said.

"The face."

"Oh," she said.

The stone was flat and sort of kite-shaped. It was mottled, pink and brown and tan, with black bits. It was pitted and scarred, as if it had been bashing around for a long time. There were two big dents, one a bit bigger than the other, where a bone-white layer showed through from inside. And it had a little grinning mouth.

"See?"

"Oh yes," said Gwen. "It does look a bit like a face."

She couldn't see it. He could tell.

"I'm cold," she said. "Come on."

He put his arm around her, but she shrugged him off. She said, "It's difficult enough walking on these stones, in this wind."

They went around the headland into Bourne Bay and up the beach to the Merry Time Café.

It was an ordinary sort of café, with ice cream transfers on the windows and Formica tables inside. There was a huge enormous woman behind the counter reading a magazine and dipping pickled onions out of a great big jar. At the table in the corner nearest her was a blind man with little round black glasses and a white stick. He was eating egg and chips. There was egg yolk on his chin, and on his tie.

At the big table by the window was a young family on holiday: a bloke with ginger hair and rolled-up shirtsleeves, and his wife and three kids. The oldest couldn't have been more than five. They were all drinking Kia-Ora.

"How do," said Neil.

The ginger bloke smiled at him uncertainly. Nobody spoke.

Gwen sat down at a table just inside the door.

Neil looked at the menu on the wall above the counter. "I'm having sausage, chips, tomato and peas," he said. "What are you having, Gwen?"

"I'm not hungry," she said.

"You must have your dinner, Gwen."

"I'm not hungry, Neil," she said.

He went to the counter and ordered. He got them both a cup of tea. He took out the stone he'd found and put it on the table next to his cup, to look at while he was eating his meal.

Neil had this thing about the fronts of houses and cars, and tape recorders and things. He could make a face out of anything; and once he'd seen it, he couldn't not see it anymore. But the face of the stone was different. It was more definitely there, though you could see it was just a stone, it hadn't been carved or painted.

It looked like a little monkey. There was a bulgy forehead, a bit lopsided; then under it the two dents. The large white one was exactly the right shape for an eye socket. The other one was brown, with just a bit of white: that was an eye winking. Under the eyes, in the middle of the stone, were two nicks in a broad V shape, like a pair of brown-stained nostrils. Then under them was a broad lip and another nick, a curved one that made a perfect, tight little smile.

He held the stone out to Gwen. It just fitted nicely in the palm of his hand.

"Look," he said. "There's two eyes, there and there."

"Neil," she said.

He sat back in his chair. "Can you really not see that? It's a face, a really evil little face."

"Of course I can see it," she said. "I'm just not interested, that's all."

He was sure she couldn't see it.

Gwen opened her handbag and began to rummage around in it. "Have we got any cigarettes left?"

"You've got them," he said.

"Well, they're not in here," she said.

"I gave them to you."

"Did you? When?"

"On the train. When you wanted another one, and I said you might as well carry them. You had one on the bus. Don't you remember?"

Gwen had given up the search.

"Get us some more, Neil, there's a love."

"They're in your handbag," he insisted. "I saw you put them in your handbag."

She smiled sweetly.

He got up and went to the counter. The eyes of the children followed him solemnly. They still hadn't finished their orange soda. Their parents were talking, very quietly, as if they were in church.

Neil bought twenty Rothman's, two more cups of tea and a packet of custard creams. He carried them to the table, balancing the fags and the biscuits in the saucers, and sat down.

The blind man got up. He said cheerio to the woman at the counter. He came past Neil and Gwen's table, tapping his stick against the legs of the furniture. Then somehow he got confused by the door. He couldn't find his way out. Neil saw him swing his stick left and right and left again, and turn around three-quarters of a circle.

The blind man opened his mouth and began to bray. It was a horrible noise, like a trapped animal, moaning; like a creature in a slaughter-house.

The father of the little family got up in a hurry. His chair scraped on the lino. He took the blind man's arm confidently and reorientated him. "There you go, old chap."

"You could have helped that man, Neil," Gwen said, when the other man was back in his seat.

"I was going to," he said. "I was just going to." And he had been, on the point of getting up and going to help him, until he'd started making that horrible mad noise. You didn't know what to do when somebody suddenly did something like that. It caught you unawares.

"Anyway, so could you," he said.

Her eyes opened wide. "Not so easily," she said firmly. She began to fiddle with the cellophane from the custard creams. "It must be horrible to be like that," she said. "Not that he's missing much," she added, looking out at the gray clouds and the dull brown sea.

One of the children began to blow bubbles in his Kia-Ora, making the others giggle. He got told off.

Neil and Gwen went back over the cliffs.

"Did you have a nice walk?" called Mrs. Wilberforce from the kitchen.

"Lovely, thanks!" said Gwen.

After tea Gwen wanted to go down to the pub in the village, but Neil said they'd done enough walking for one day, so they stayed in the second evening too. There was nothing much on telly, so Neil read the paper while Gwen had a bath. His mind kept wandering to her in the bath, lying there in nothing but her bath-cap, soaping herself all over. He always wanted to come in when she was in the bath, to look at her, but she'd never let him.

So he waited until he heard her let the water out, then he waited a bit longer for her to get dry, and then he said goodnight to Mrs. Wilberforce and went upstairs.

Gwen was in bed, but he'd waited too long, because she was already asleep.

Neil went to the window and lifted the curtain. The sun had set, and the color had faded from the day. Below the cliffs the sea looked like lead; above, the sky was full of a strange pale light.

Sitting down on the end of the hard bed, he felt something beneath him: the stone, still in his trouser pocket. He took it out.

In the light from the window he could see tiny ragged teeth under the lip of the stone face. It looked less like a monkey now, more like a wizened little person, a goblin.

He wondered if it was just the shadow, the way this funny light was falling on it. He turned the stone around in his hand.

Now he could only just see the face. But he knew it was there.

He fell asleep and dreamed the stone he'd found had turned into a baby. It was only a tiny thing, but it could run. It ran away from him. Gwen wasn't there. He had to chase the baby along the beach, and then through the corridors of a huge old building, like a school or a hospital, that was half falling down. Behind the doors of the rooms he could hear children laughing.

He woke up suddenly, feeling stifled. The blankets his side had come untucked. Gwen was a dark mass of hair on the pillow beside him.

He sat up. It was twenty-five past two. The shells on the fire screen were glowing palely. For a moment he thought they were snails, a horde of snails, crawling all over it.

He needed to go to the toilet. He got out of bed. He stole along the landing in his bare feet, wishing the boards didn't creak so much. He looked at the door of Mrs. Wilberforce's room, willing her not to wake up, then opened the door to the bathroom.

Mrs. Wilberforce was sitting on the toilet.

She hadn't put the light on, but there was a weak light from the bathroom window. Neil saw everything in an instant.

She was still dressed. Her overall and her dress were rucked up to her waist, her tights were around her ankles. Her face was slack and staring; her crotch a black mystery.

He gulped an apology and pulled the door shut.

Mrs. Wilberforce hadn't moved. She hadn't even made a sound.

Horrified, Neil heard himself give a squeak of laughter. He rushed back into the bedroom and stood quivering behind the door.

Gwen murmured, "Wh . . . ?"

"Shh!" said Neil.

"What's the matter?"

"Mrs. Wilberforce," he hissed. "On the toilet! I burst right in!"

Gwen grunted. She rolled over and sat up, scratching her head crossly.

"I didn't mean to wake you up," he told her.

"What time is it?" she asked drowsily.

"Half-past two."

He stood listening at the door.

"What are you doing, Neil?" demanded Gwen, effortfully, as if she hadn't understood anything he'd said.

"Waiting," he told her. "For the toilet."

There was no sound from Mrs. Wilberforce in the bathroom. He wondered whether she was asleep sitting up. Her eyes had been open, though, he was sure of it.

Gwen got out of bed and pulled on her dressing gown. She came to the door.

"Where are you going?" he whispered.

"Where do you think?"

"Mrs. *Wilberforce,*" he insisted.

She pulled a face at him and went out of the room.

He was horrified. He watched around the edge of the door.

Gwen went to the door of the bathroom. She opened it. She reached her hand inside and turned on the light.

Neil watched her go in and close the door behind her.

Faintly, he heard the toilet seat shift. He didn't know what was happening. He hesitated in the bedroom doorway, unable to move, through or back.

He thought he could hear the sound of someone peeing.

Agonized, he tiptoed rapidly across the landing. He put his ear to the bathroom door.

The cistern flushed. The door opened. Gwen stood there, looking at him, her hand on the light switch.

"Neil," she said reproachfully.

Neil went into the bathroom. There was no one in there. He looked in the bath. Gwen went back to bed.

Neil bolted the bathroom door.

Mrs. Wilberforce's toilet was called "the Dreadnought." It was caked with brown lime scale. It had a mat in front of it with a picture of a sailing ship on.

She couldn't have got out of the bathroom and gone back to her room without him hearing her. She couldn't have.

Neil finished. He closed the lid of the Dreadnought and pulled the chain. Feeling very silly, he took a quick look at the ceiling.

The monkey sprang at him.

He recoiled. The mat slipped under his foot and he fell over backward, hitting his head on the pedestal as he went down. The creature was in his face, clinging to his hair and throttling him with its legs. It stank. It was warm and hairy in his face.

He struggled with it, trying to prise it away, knocking over the toilet brush holder with his elbow. The monkey clung on, sprawled across his eyes. It was snarling, like a little dog.

He tried to shout, but it had a knee in his throat and his voice came out as a hoarse gurgle. He twisted his head away, and shoved the thing aside with his arm.

"Gwen!" he shouted.

The creature swarmed up his arm and breathed hotly in his face.

He screamed.

It had the face of Mrs. Wilberforce.

It had the body of a monkey, a tailless monkey, and the head of Mrs. Wilberforce.

Her face glared into his. Her head was about the size of a grapefruit. She bared her teeth at him.

Gibbering, Neil banged his right arm into her face and came up into a crouch. He grabbed the thing by a shoulder and a haunch, keeping his elbow high, and flung it sprawling into the bath, then scrambled out of the room.

He heard its claws scrabbling on Mrs. Wilberforce's enamel. He fled into the bedroom.

"Don't make so much *noise,*" Gwen said from the bed.

All Neil could say was "A monster!" and "Mrs. Wilberforce!"

"Neil, you are an idiot," she said.

She got out of bed, and came toward him around the room. She looked annoyed. She was obviously going to open the door.

"Don't! Don't! No! There's—"

"Come on, Neil, out of the way."

"All right," he said. "All right." And went and stood on the other side of the wardrobe.

Tiredly she opened the door and looked outside. He watched. There was nothing out there. Everything was dark and still.

She stepped out onto the landing.

Neil was sure the thing was on the ceiling again. It would jump on her any minute.

But Gwen turned around and came back into the bedroom.

"There's nothing there," she said. "You were dreaming."

"I wasn't! There's—"

"Neil," said Gwen. She climbed into bed, and held the covers open for him to climb in after.

"All right," he said. "All right."

He got back into bed.

The thing would get fed up of hanging there. It would jump down, and Gwen would hear it. Then he'd like to see her set foot outside that door.

Minutes went by.

Nothing happened.

The next he knew, it was broad day. The curtains were open. The door was open too. Gwen was gone.

From below came the sounds of a radio playing accordion music, and bacon sizzling in a pan.

He got out of bed. He felt confused, as if he'd just had a really nasty dream but couldn't remember anything about it. He'd put on his slippers and dressing gown and was going out of the room before he remembered.

There was nothing on the ceiling.

He pushed the bathroom door open with his foot and looked carefully inside before going in.

Nothing there either.

He looked at himself in the mirror, and thought he looked a bit pale. He wondered if he was ill. He didn't feel ill. But he didn't normally have dreams like that, not as lifelike as that. He went downstairs.

It was Gwen in the kitchen, frying bacon and eggs. She was wearing Mrs. Wilberforce's nylon overall. Her calves and her feet were bare.

"What are you doing?" Neil asked, amazed, still half stupid from the dream.

"Conducting the Royal Philharmonic," she said. "What's it look like?"

"You've got her thing on," he said.

"Neil," said Gwen. She looked in the frying pan. "Oh. Oh dear," she said. "Your egg's broken."

The table was laid with breakfast for two. Mrs. Wilberforce wasn't around. Neil sat down, not knowing what was going on. He put sugar and milk on his corn flakes.

"Did she say you could do breakfast?" he asked tentatively.

"Who?" said Gwen, though it was obvious who he meant. She splashed fat over the eggs.

"Mrs. Wilberforce," he said emphatically but not too loudly.

"Well say so, then," said Gwen. "Don't just say 'she.' "

She took two plates of toast out of the oven, put eggs and bacon on them, and brought them to the table.

" 'She' is the cat's mother," said Gwen. "That's what my dad always says."

She sat down and poured tea.

"She's gone out," she said.

"Who's 'she'?" said Neil, mimicking her.

Gwen pulled a face.

"She couldn't be bothered waiting around for you to get up on a beautiful day like this."

And it was a beautiful day. The kitchen was full of sunshine, twinkling on the pots and pans. The sky outside the window was a bright, innocent blue, as if it had never been anything else.

"I had a horrible dream," he said.

"I noticed," Gwen said coolly.

"Did I wake you?" He thought that had been part of the dream.

"I like that," said Gwen. "You keep me up half the night, then you don't even have the decency to remember it."

He felt a bit embarrassed. He must have been making a proper fool of himself. But it had seemed so real. He concentrated on his breakfast.

Gwen, who always ate fast, had already finished hers. She reached in the pocket of the overall, just as if it was her own overall, and pulled out a packet of Player's. She lit one at the cooker.

"She'll kill you," Neil said.

Gwen took the cigarette out of her mouth, as if she was going to say something. Then she put it back and took another puff instead. "Hurry up and finish your breakfast, Neil."

"D'you want to go for a walk?" he said.

"Yes," said Gwen slowly. "But first I thought we might—"

She looked down at the table, then up at him.

Neil was astonished and delighted. He gobbled the rest of his breakfast, drank a cup of tea, then took her upstairs.

"Shouldn't you leave that down there, in case she comes home?" he said on the landing, pointing at the overall.

She shook her head. She had a funny look on her face, as if she had a secret.

Neil went toward the bedroom, but Gwen tugged his hand.

"What?"

She indicated the back room.

"*What?*" he said. "That's her room!"

She nodded, and pulled him toward it.

"She might be home any minute!" he said.

"No she won't," said Gwen. She sounded absolutely sure.

They went into Mrs. Wilberforce's room.

She had a big old bed with wooden boards at the head and the foot and a ruffle affair hanging down all the way round. She hadn't made her bed before she went out. Neil was surprised.

There were photos crammed on the mantelpiece, and roses on the curtains, but Neil didn't look anywhere else. Gwen was sitting on the bed, bouncing slightly. "This is better," she said. She started to unbutton the overall. She had nothing on under it.

"This is crazy. We can't do this. Not here," Neil said. Then he took off his dressing gown and pajamas, and got on top of her.

Then it was like it had been, years ago, right at the beginning. He could hardly believe it. He'd forgotten how good it could be. He'd forgotten how hot she could be. Being in the old woman's room, trespassing, it really turned her on, obviously. She had him doing all sorts of things, things she wouldn't normally let him do. "Like this," she kept saying. "Like this."

He couldn't keep it up for long. It was too much. When he came, she was disappointed, he could tell. But they never went on after that. He couldn't.

She used the bathroom first, then he did. He grinned to himself as he squeezed out his sponge. He couldn't remember the last time they'd done it in the morning, not gone back to bed and done it.

He hurried back into the room to collect his pajamas. Gwen was sitting on the bed with nothing on.

"When's she due back?" he asked. He looked at Mrs. Wilberforce's bedside clock. It said twenty-five past two. It must have stopped in the night. There was a stone lying beside it: his stone, the stone with the face.

"Just a minute," he said. He picked up the stone. It was sticky. "What's this doing here?"

"Don't look at me," said Gwen. She got off the bed.

But he wasn't, he was looking at his fingers. "Blood," he said. "Look. There's blood on it." He held up the stone. "How did this get in here?"

"Don't ask me," Gwen said. "It's your precious stone."

She left the room, the overall folded on her arm.

He stood there, looking at the stone face, and the bloody back of its head. There was blood on the bedside cabinet where it had lain.

"Gwen?"

He heard her going downstairs.

He went after her. It was incredible. She was going downstairs, in broad daylight, without a stitch on.

"Gwen!"

She stopped, turned and looked calmly up at him.

He brandished the stone at her.

"What about this?" he said. "You know. I know you know."

"It wasn't me," she said.

"Come back here," said Neil. "You can't go down like that."

Gwen went downstairs.

Neil went back into Mrs. Wilberforce's room and swept aside the frills below the bed. Mrs. Wilberforce stared out at him.

He heard himself make a horrible gasping, gagging sound.

Her eyes were rolled right up and her mouth was open. Her skin looked peculiar, pale and dingy.

He seized Mrs. Wilberforce by the arm and tried to drag her out from under the bed. She wouldn't move. She was heavy. It was amazing how heavy she was.

He groped around on her wrist, wondering how you took a pulse, knowing it was no good. It was as if some part of himself was standing over him as he crouched beside Mrs. Wilberforce's bed, trying to pull Mrs. Wilberforce out from under it, standing there watching and telling him it was no good.

He got up and pulled again on her right arm, and she slid sideways out on her back. Then her right foot caught on the leg of the bed and she swiveled.

He dropped her arm and went down on one knee, trying to lift her with his hands under her armpits, trying to make her sit up.

There was sticky black blood on the lino, and more caked in the hair on the back of the woman's head. Her eyes were rolled up so far she looked as if she was trying to see right over the top of her head, trying to see the wound.

She was dead as a beached fish.

Neil laid her down on the floor again. Her head lolled.

The monkey stone lay on the rug beside her. She seemed to be gaping at it.

He picked it up and went downstairs.

Gwen was in the kitchen, washing up. She had put the overall on again.

"Gwen."

"What."

She didn't look at him. She took a drag from a cigarette that she'd balanced on the edge of the sink.

"She's under the bed," he said. "You knew she was there. You knew."

He felt cold all over, but he felt as if he was burning too, as if a gigantic flame was drawing everything out of him. The only time he'd ever felt like that before was when he was a kid, when he'd touched a live lamp socket, for a dare. Shock, he thought. A state of shock. As if he was reading it, printed out somewhere.

"You put her there," he said.

"What else was I supposed to do?" asked Gwen. She smoked her cigarette.

"What happened? What did you do?"

"I put her under the bed."

She dipped a plate into the froth.

"But we just—you—"

"Come off it, Neil."

"But she's dead!"

"It's all *right*, Neil," said Gwen impatiently. "No one knows."

"But—but—"

"But," she said, imitating him.

"The neighbors!"

"Oh Neil, for goodness' sake."

"Yes, Gwen, goodness!" said Neil. He felt suddenly defiant. "What do you know about goodness, eh?"

He strode along the hall and out of the front door.

He stood in the road in his dressing gown, looking along the row of houses. It was spitting with rain. There was no sign of life in any of them.

Neil went up and down the row. In every house a small, faded card had been tucked in a corner of the front window. The same card in every one. NO VACANCIES, it said.

Gwen was standing at the front door in Mrs. Wilberforce's overall, watching him.

"Come on, Neil," she said.

She threw her cigarette end into a clump of dank grass and went back inside.

He followed.

She stood at the foot of the stairs, facing him with her hands on her hips.

"Shut the door, Neil."

He shut it.

She was unbuttoning the overall again.

She was cracked. That was it. She was never like this, never had been, never in a million years. She'd gone mad and killed Mrs. Wilberforce. No wonder he'd had that weird dream.

She slid the overall off her shoulders. She put her head back and ran her fingers through her hair. She opened her mouth and poked her tongue out a bit.

"Neil," she said.

"Gwen, there's a dead woman upstairs," he said. "She's dead. Dead, do you understand?"

"Mmm." She undid the sash of his dressing gown and kissed him on the throat.

Perhaps it wouldn't make any difference. Probably it wouldn't.

They left the dressing gown and the overall lying in the hall and went upstairs.

Gwen wanted to go in Mrs. Wilberforce's room again.

"No, Gwen!"

She went in anyway.

He stayed outside. The door swung to in his face.

"Gwen," he complained.

There was no sound from the room.

He waited a moment. Then he pushed the door open.

Gwen was lying on the bed with her arms behind her head. She had pushed the body back under the bed and rearranged the ruffles so you couldn't see it. The room looked normal again.

She reached out for him.

"Not in here, Gwen," he said. "It's not right."

"Stop fussing, Neil," she said. "Come here."

He went to the bed and lay down beside her.

She leaned over him, her hair brushing his skin. She kissed him, a line of kisses, from his lips down to his groin. She coaxed him up with her tongue. She'd never, never done that before. If he thought about Mrs. Wilberforce he'd wilt, so he made himself not think about Mrs. Wilberforce.

"You were the one complaining about her listening all the time," she said after a while. "We can do what we like now."

And later she murmured in his ear: "We can drop her off the cliff. No one'll ever know."

Neil, inside her, wondered if he was still in shock. He wondered if you could be an accessory to murder, if you could be found responsible, if you were in shock the whole time.

Gwen crooned. She laughed, deep in her throat.

When he woke up, he sat up straight away. Gwen was fast asleep beside him, naked and uncovered on Mrs. Wilberforce's sheets. He looked at the photos on the mantelpiece. All those people. Someone would know. Someone would find out.

He had to tell someone.

He got off the bed without waking Gwen and went into their own room. It felt as if he had been away for a long time, months even, maybe. The sea was sparkling in the sunlight.

He pulled his clothes. He put on his shoes and his jacket. He crept along the creaky landing and down the stairs without disturbing Gwen, and let himself out of the front door.

There was a gusty breeze blowing, and gulls crying overhead. Being out of doors made him feel more awake, more alive. The sun shone on his face.

In the village he saw two women standing with their shopping baskets, chatting. He went up and asked them where the nearest police station was. Dinton, they told him.

"Don't you have a policeman here?" he asked. "In the village?"

Both the women wore headscarves. One of them looked a bit like a crow. She had a black fringe and a big nose, and glasses as thick as the bottoms of beer bottles. "No policemen here, my dear," she said. "Not here in the village."

Neil suddenly thought she was the woman who'd been on the bus when they'd arrived, the one with the toddler. He decided not to say any more. He could phone from the post office, they told him; but then no, the post office was closed for the day: Mrs. Walters was off at her sister's.

He sat in the square and waited for the bus to Dinton. The village kids came out and looked at him. He thought he should reach in his jacket pocket and give them barley sugar or pennies or something. He supposed that was what the summer visitors did. He didn't have any barley sugar. Anyway, what he had to do was far too important to take any notice of them.

The bus came. It was about half full. Neil took a seat on the shady side. He dozed off on the journey and was confused for a minute, when he woke up, not to find Gwen beside him.

In Dinton he got directions to the police station. His way lay past the railway station.

They probably wouldn't be much good in a little out-of-the-way place like this, he thought: not the police, or the doctors either. He might as well get the next train back as waste time here. He'd sort it all out as soon as he got home. It probably wasn't actually safe for him to stay around Gwen, the way she was carrying on. It was only making her worse. He'd be better off out of it. In fact, there was no reason for them to know he'd been down here at all, if he was careful what he said.

There was a train already in. He just had time to buy a paper and hop on before it pulled out. He sat down in a seat by the window with his paper on his knee, feeling a great sense of relief. He was sure he'd made the right decision.

He was halfway through the cricket scores before he felt the stone give a little jump in his pocket.

KIM ANTIEAU

Medusa's Child

I found her on the steps of my apartment building. She was shivering, though the day was warm. Her light brown hair hung in strands about her face. Her cheekbones stretched her pale skin. I almost walked by her. I thought she was just another of the bag ladies who frequented my area. Then she looked up at me.

She had extraordinary eyes. They were black—two black lightless pupils. I had to paint those eyes. I had to paint her.

I am not certain how I got her to come up to my apartment. I know I promised food. Whatever I said, she followed me into the building and to my apartment.

Once inside, I asked her her name. She did not answer. I told her to make herself at home while I started dinner. I had spaghetti sauce from the day before, so I put it on the stove and started water to boil for noodles.

She stood in the middle of my living room which doubled as my studio because of the huge picture windows. I had several paintings on easels and two leaned against the wall. She walked over to them and touched the edges of each one with the tips of her fingers. She did it almost reverently.

"An artist," she whispered.

"Yes," I said. I glanced at her. Although her body was bent and her face lined, I guessed she was not even thirty years old.

She turned and looked at me with those huge black eyes.

"An artist," she said again.

I wondered then if I had latched on to some very strange person. She could utter only two words: *An artist.* Maybe she had been in love with a painter once and he had killed himself because she left him—or something equally as dramatic.

She came and stood close to me while I cooked and watched me stir sauce and break noodles into the boiling water. Once she reached out tentatively and touched my arm with one finger. Poor girl, I thought, she hasn't eaten in days and she's grateful to me.

"Leila," she said.

At first I did not know what she was saying, and then I realized she was answering my first question.

"I'm Matthew McClean. Matthew means 'Gift of God,' " I said, as I pulled two plates from the cupboard. "I was the sixth child after five girls. You can see why they thought I was a godsend." I laughed. She did not even smile.

"Leila means dark as night."

That was all she said. No story behind it. Was she born on a stormy night? Was her grandmother's name Leila? She's not much of a conversationalist, I thought, but that was all right. I hated chatterbox models.

I told her to sit down and we ate our first meal together. Neither of us said much. I was curious about her, but I did not want to pry and scare her away. I was getting more and more excited about the prospect of painting her: the mysterious woman lost in strands of greasy hair and ragged clothes.

She was more animated by the end of the meal. Color returned to her cheeks. She pushed her hair behind her ears, and I saw she was not unattractive. When she had finished her meal (she didn't eat much), she looked over at me. She smiled and said, "Well, Matthew, you want to paint me, don't you?"

I nodded.

"What will I get in return?" she asked.

I impulsively looked toward the door, wondering where the cowering waif was who had walked into the room a mere hour ago.

"I can pay you my standard rate for models."

She shook her head. "I don't want money. I need other things." She gazed at me. "How long have you been an artist?"

I was a little annoyed by her tone. First I had practically scraped her off my steps and put food into her starving body and now she was asking for my qualifications.

"I have been an artist all of my life," I said. "I have been commercially successful the last five." I was proud of that. Pretty good for only being thirty years old.

She nodded. "Young," she said. She sat quietly for a moment, looking around the room, and then she rested her fingers lightly on my arm. The hair on my arms stood up, as if drawn to her fingertips. Her touch was cool and pleasant.

"I want to stay here."

"Here? Don't you have a place to stay?"

"No."

Normally I would have tossed her out then and there. Several women had wanted to move in with me at different times and I had always said no, except once, and that had been a terrible mistake. I hardly painted at all until she moved out.

"Please, Matthew, I won't be any trouble. Just for a while, until you finish painting me." Suddenly she was the waif again.

I smiled and said, "Okay."

I made a sketch of her that night. She sat on my couch with her hands folded demurely in her lap. The sun was setting. The walls of the room turned gold and red. The gold touched Leila's head. For a moment her hair was flaxen, Rapunzel reincarnate. And then the red tinged her skin and she was like some fiery goddess, her hair gold snakes snapping at dust particles in the air.

The next morning I found her padding around the kitchen in a pair of my jeans and a T-shirt.

"I lifted them while you slept," she said. "I took a shower and washed my clothes. I'm baking an omelet for us."

She appeared taller than she had the night before, probably because she had bathed, eaten, and had a good night's sleep. My sofa bed was more comfortable than my own bed. Her eyes were bright and her cheeks rosy. She looked like a well-scrubbed college kid.

"Thanks," I said. "I am hungry."

I sat at the table and rubbed my eyes sleepily. What had possessed me to let this woman stay with me? I glanced up at her as she put the omelet in front of me. It's those damn eyes, I reminded myself.

She was a good model. She sat very still and looked off into some place within herself. The natural light from the overhead windows flattered her. Work went slowly. It was hard to capture the quality in her that had first attracted me. I could not get the eyes. They were too black. On canvas, they looked like huge holes in her face: she looked like a zombie, or as if she did not have a soul, something queer like that.

"What do you do when you aren't hanging around apartment buildings?" I asked while we ate lunch.

"I do things."

She continued eating, apparently not interested in answering my questions. I glanced out the window. Clouds had covered the sun and it looked like a summer storm was approaching.

"There goes the day's painting," I said.

"That's all right," she said. "We can spend the day getting to know each other."

I was surprised she wanted to talk, but when she got up and went to the couch, I followed and sat beside her. I began talking about myself. She held my hand loosely in hers and listened while I told her about my life, my crowded but happy childhood filled with dreams of becoming a famous artist, my time spent traveling before college, my successful years as an artist. For some reason I poured out my life to her as if it were some kind of liquid she could drink. It frightened me a little, letting someone know so much about me. She probed me for details— gently squeezing my hand when I was not sure what I wanted to say. As the storm washed against the windows, Leila seemed to grow more beautiful. Her voice became stronger, more assured. She was no longer the trembling bag lady I had met yesterday. I was amazed at the difference and chalked it up to my company and good food.

We talked the afternoon away (or rather I talked; she mostly listened). When we got hungry, she suggested a pizza. We ran outside into the rain, laughing and splashing in puddles as we made our way to the neighborhood pizza joint. I forgot she was a bit strange, forgot she was a hobo, and realized I had found a new friend: someone who liked to listen. My artist friends were not big on listening; they liked to talk and talk, mostly about their own work. Leila wanted to know more about me and I loved it. I sat with her in the pizza place, sipping a malt and pushing strings of cheese into my mouth, and I wondered why I had not found someone like her before.

When we got back to my apartment, Leila stood in the middle of the living room and began undressing. I sat on the couch and watched her. My stomach tingled. Soon she stood before me naked. She was beautiful. How could I have thought she was ugly? She came to me and I put my arms around her and pulled her toward me. My clothes slipped away and we were side by side on the couch.

"Imagine anything you like," she whispered. "I can be anyone or anything you want. Let yourself go."

For that moment, Leila was all I wanted. Her movements were gentle at first and then she was astride me, pushing herself down hard on me. She bent to bite my chest. She kissed my ear, her tongue darting in and out. "Imagine," she whispered, and she loomed up before me, her golden hair clinging to her breasts like hundreds of tiny fingers.

The next day I tried the portrait again. The work was frustratingly poor. I finally threw my paintbrushes down in a mock fit and cried, "You are impossible to paint!"

She laughed and put her arms around me and kissed the top of my head.

"Why don't you try something else?" she suggested.

"You don't want me to finish your portrait because you think I'll make you leave," I said, turning around to hug her.

"I hope you won't make me leave," she said quietly. I glanced up at her. She was staring at something I could not see, somewhere in her mind, and it made me uncomfortable. I knew so little about her.

In the days and weeks to follow I came to love Leila with an intensity I had never known. We did everything together. I wanted her with me all of the time. Nights we made love and then sat up for hours, talking about my current project. During the day, I often looked up from a difficult piece to see Leila dancing around the living room, swirling her skirts like some exotic dancer.

I learned little about her past. Sometimes she gazed out the window toward the heart of the city. She looked frightened. Her eyes paled, as if the life were slipping from them. When I went to her, she clung to me, seeming to draw life from my presence.

"What's out there?" I asked her.

"Nothing," she answered, turning to me. "All those people who don't know or care about me."

We stayed to ourselves most of the time. Leila wanted to meet my friends, but I always found an excuse not to call anyone. I liked having her all to myself.

A few weeks after I first met Leila, I went into a painting slump. And then Leila began to wane. That is the only word I can use. As my paintings grew worse, she changed. I urged her to go out while I tried to paint, but she would not. She stayed on the couch, sometimes biting her fingernails, sometimes looking out the window. When I asked her what was wrong, she just shook her head.

One day she said, "Leave me alone, Matthew. It's you, don't you understand? You've changed." She went to the bedroom and closed the door.

I stared at her unfinished portrait and wondered what I could have done. What was happening to us—to her? She had been such a vivacious person. Now she was withering away.

I stopped dreaming.

Leila and I grew further apart. Though we still slept together, she spent most nights hugging her side of the bed and would not let me near her. Those were the worst times. I felt so alone. Other nights she turned and made love to me furiously. No longer the golden goddess. A fury. Or a gorgon. Medusa's child.

Things worsened, and I was afraid she would leave me. I still loved her. I sat down and tried to figure out why. We never talked; she only listened. I never learned anything new from her. She was beautiful. Or was she? Had she ever stood tall? Was her hair golden? Had she danced for me?

"I need to meet new people," she told me one afternoon. "I feel like a prisoner here."

I sat at my easel turning one of my dark blobs of paint into a spider. Tracing a line here. Putting meat on it there.

"All right," I said. "We'll have a party Sunday."

She chewed her fingernails. How tired she looked. Was it really my fault? Was I somehow draining her of energy?

. . . .

For the party, Leila wore a black floor-length V-neck gown. I had bought it for her weeks earlier. I remembered the pleasure I had gotten seeing it on her then—and later off her. The silk had clung to her body, moving as she moved. Now the black dress hung unattractively on her, barely touching her skin anywhere.

Poets, artists, writers, and dilettantes filled the apartment. Ice hit the sides of glasses and twirled madly in baths of gin, vodka or rum. I passed around hors d'oeuvres, shrugging when anyone asked how the work went.

Leila was everywhere. Touching. Listening. The color returned to her face. She was animated, laughing, touching, listening.

Something was not right.

"I've met her before." A fellow artist, Pete Dobson, was tapping my arm.

"Really?" I turned to him.

"She looks a bit different, but it's her."

Leila was striding to another group. Tall and lithesome. Her golden hair shone and caught the light . . .

"Do you remember Franc de Winter?" Pete was talking to me again.

"Yeah, I think so. Isn't he in California?"

"He was." He sipped his drink and watched Leila. Her fingers lightly stroked the bare skin in the V of her dress.

"Leila used to live with him," Pete said. "Saw her at a party there. I'm pretty sure it was her."

Her eyes were dark holes, bright with life.

"What happened to him?" I asked.

"Don't you remember? He stopped working. Artist's block or something. She sort of disappeared right before he died—he killed himself."

Everything stopped. The people. The smoke. Time. For a split second, only Leila and I were in the room. She turned those horrible eyes on me and she knew I knew.

The terror and repulsion was with me all evening. I felt as if I were sinking into a quagmire and no one would help me out. I drank too much; someone gave me a pill and I swallowed it. Somehow I got through the evening. I kept wondering how she could have done it. She pretended to love me and had taken away all that made me me.

Leila was putting her things together before the last guest left. In fact, one man sat in my living room. A poet I barely knew.

"Where are you going?" I demanded.

"With Henry." Henry? The poet.

"So you can do to him what you did to me?"

She stared at me. I turned away. I could not look at those eyes.

"What have I done to you?" she asked. I was silent. She shrugged. Her indifference infuriated me. I wanted to smash my fists into her eyes.

She shut the suitcase and clicked the locks. "I'm leaving."

I grabbed the suitcase—it was mine, after all—and hurled it against the wall.

"Are you all right, Leila?" A voice came from the other room.

Didn't the little twit know she would ruin him? I charged into the living room. Before the man had a chance to react I had him up against a wall. I was not prone to violence, but Leila had bled me, and I was not going to let her off easily.

"Get out of here, you creep," I said.

"Leila?" he asked, his voice suddenly very high.

"It's all right, Henry," Leila said as she came out of the bedroom. "I'll catch up with you later."

The door slammed. She looked at me. "This is silly, Matthew."

There was no emotion in her voice. She had used me; now it was time to let me go. Suddenly I felt tired, worn. How long can a person live without dreams?

"Will I ever get it back?" I asked. "Or will I end up like Franc de Winter?"

"Get what back?" she asked. "Who's Franc de Winter?" She went to the window and looked out.

"You just take, don't you?" I said. "You find people like me and you drain them of their imagination, their creativity."

She laughed harshly. "Is that what you want to believe? First I was your muse and then I became some kind of monster sucking away your life? Believe what you want! When you took me into your apartment that first night you were going to paint me, make a masterpiece, use *me*, and then send me away with a cheese sandwich, weren't you? Woman does not live on bread alone." She laughed again. The sound was horrible.

"You disgust me," I said.

"I wasn't always this way," she said. "There was a time when I could take care of myself. You artists and your pomposity. You think you are the best dreamers? The most creative? My first love was an artist, too. I was a child. All he did was take from me, cage me with his love, keep me to himself. I had to do something to save myself. I learned to please him." She turned and stared at me. "I gave you what you wanted, didn't I? And when you couldn't paint anymore, you blamed me."

She looked back at the city.

"I lived the longest with an old Mexican woman. Five years," she said. "She could build an entire world around a worm hole."

"And you took that from her, didn't you?"

She shook her head. "No, Matthew, she gave herself to me freely."

She went back into the bedroom and returned with the suitcase.

"You can't leave, Leila." Maybe she could give it back to me; I didn't know for sure, but I could not let her go.

She sighed. "You will tire of this, Matthew. There is nothing left between us."

She tried to leave several times, but I threw her back. The hours turned into days. I locked her in the bedroom at night and only let her out after I slept. I spent the days pleading with her to give back what she had taken.

"I can't live without dreams, without my art," I told her.

"I don't care," she said.

I was without reason, I believe, during those days. I did not let her eat very much. I wandered around my apartment looking at my painting. I thought of Franc de Winter, I thought of the Leila I had loved. Everything was crumbling around me. The woman in the apartment was not the Leila I had known. With each hour she grew more sullen and ugly and nervous.

"I'm begging you! Please let me go," she said. Her eyes were dead, her hair straggly, her mouth cruel. "I'm dying." She stared out the window.

"I don't care," I said.

I realized then why the city frightened her. All those mindless people going to their mindless jobs. They were so frightened, so dazed; many of them thought of how to get home at night and little else. They had no imagination. Leila would die in that city.

"If I could help you paint again I would," she said on the fifth day, "but I can't."

On the tenth day I was tired and I believed her. She had emptied my soul and no humanity remained. I took her out of the building and led her into the heart of the city. She did not have the energy to struggle; she let herself be pulled along.

We walked down the stairway and into the subway station where hundreds of people waited to board the morning trains. I pushed Leila into the crowd. The people paid no attention to us. They stood on the gray floor in their gray suits waiting for the train.

Leila stumbled and almost fell into a man reading the paper. He sighed and moved out of her way. She touched his arm and peered into his eyes. "Help me," she whispered. "This man is crazy." She veered from him and into another person. I stood apart from them. Leila's face crinkled in pain again as a woman pulled her arm away. She bumped into one person after another. They ignored her or pulled away. Lines of pain ran down Leila's face and into her body. The emptiness of the place was devouring her. She began sobbing. "Someone help me, please," I heard her cry. She touched another person and he pushed her. She fell against the wall and crumbled to the concrete floor. Her head bobbed. Her mouth slackened. Saliva dribbled over her lip and down her chin. Her eyes were black stones. People kept a neat distance from her, either pretending she did not exist, or else not caring.

I did not care either. Not anymore. She had taken that from me. Foul air rushed around me as the train approached.

I climbed the stairs as the train pulled in. I heard people shuffle to get aboard, heard the doors swish closed. I stepped out onto the streets and walked toward home.

My dreams returned. Rather I should say: I dream now. Just one dream. I close my eyes and sleep comes and with it Leila. The dream is always the same. Leila sits on the cold concrete floor of the subway, lifeless, people walking around her. Saliva drips from her mouth, slowly at first, and then more rapidly, and suddenly the clear liquid is red, it is blood, and the blood pours from her mouth until the whole subway station is filled and though I am on the steps, the blood follows me, envelops me, and finally fills my lungs and drowns me.

When I awaken from this nightmare, alone in the dark, I am terrified for a few moments, wondering if I could have been wrong. And then I close my eyes and dream again.

JESSICA PALMER

The Tape

Delores Perry crested another hill. The panorama was breathtaking, a picture-postcard vision of New England. The world and all God's beauty, it appeared, were before her. To her right, a radiant white church stood, steeple reaching toward the heavens. It too seemed subdued by the splendor.

The deciduous trees—in a final celebration of life before winter's deathlike trance—were painted in flaming crimson, brilliant gold, flaring orange, while the pines still bore summer's laughing green. The bay and further out the Atlantic sparkled under the deep blue autumn sky, clear except for a few cotton-candy clouds.

The view was lost on her. Two months ago, it would have stopped her dead in her tracks. More than once she had, arrested by the scenery, found herself drifting into oncoming traffic only to veer off seconds before impact. It had happened often enough that she stopped counting the number of near collisions.

Today she didn't see it. She only had eyes for the narrow ribbon of concrete. Her hands operated the steering wheel, the stick—her feet, the clutch, the gas—on autopilot. She was only aware of driving as she was peripherally aware of her surroundings.

A cigarette dangled from her lips as she shifted into fifth. It bobbed up and down as her jaws worked constantly, clenching and unclenching. Her eyes darted following an unseen drama on her mind's screen. A tape played on, and on, and on, and on—like her life which seemed so many repeat performances—the mental tape of shrieking witch-parent messages.

You're no good. You couldn't find your ass with both hands and a road map, it said. *It'll never work. You're cursed*, it said. She tried to silence it when she fled her house with the dog, Arf. The age-old tape, the screaming mother's voice, even the walls seemed to speak to her. She left to go out into the sunshine, but the tape played on in metronome regularity. It played in the rhythm of the tires on blacktop and the tick of the turn signal. *You're cursed, cursed, cursed, cursed*, it whispered.

And indeed it seemed that she was. When she thought about it, she felt the rage begin to surface, the choking bile brought on by frustration. Again Delores tried to remind herself how many things had gone right. She wanted to feel pride at what she had accomplished.

As she did so, Maine came into focus and she remembered where she was and what she was doing. She was going to Deer Island. She was playing tourist-for-the-day, going out to explore her new home. It hadn't been on her agenda that day, but so far nothing had gone as planned. Fury caught her by the throat, and she pushed harder on the gas as she reached one of Highway One's many obscure twists and turns.

She leaned with car the to remain upright as she screeched around the curve. The dog placed its chin on her shoulder, whimpering, frightened by the savagery of her driving. She pushed him away. It only served to compound her bad feelings. First the bad day, the computer, then the tape, the helpless rage which she knew would soon be followed by depression. She drove to escape, but she hadn't escaped, and now she could add a feeling of guilt for picking on the poor dog.

Delores went into another turn at too high a speed, and it took all her strength to keep the car on the road. The little compact fishtailed, and Arf fell clumsily to his haunches. Shakily she forced herself to slow down and then pulled off the side of the road.

She sat for a few minutes, willing herself to a calm she didn't feel, and turned to pet Arf. He nuzzled her. The damn computer, the goddamn computer. It had been bad enough when her old system was destroyed in the move, but she had replaced it easily enough. She'd spent weeks trying to re-create the old software. Today would have been the last day. Tomorrow, she could have opened up shop. *Fucking systems crash.*

Her move here had been no half-baked scheme no matter how it appeared to family and friends. It was part of well-developed plan. When Delores decided to get away from the city, she searched carefully for a spot where her skills as a programmer, consultant and systems analyst would be useful.

After her divorce, she had saved her half of the settlement and planned. She scrimped for two years, knowing that eventually she would quit her job and strike out on her own. She had found the ideal location, not too far from her Boston home, a place where she had little competition. Maine was a market waiting to be discovered. Technicians, she had learned in her travels here, were nil, almost nonexistent. Programmers were even scarcer. She'd jumped every hurdle, from the protests of her friends and her ex to the financial hazards. She found a home and moved.

An RV rumbled past, and Delores eased the car back into traffic. *Deer Island.* She should have looked at the map. She was damn sick of Highway One with its waddling recreational vehicles and its tourists looking for the next available restaurant. As though in answer to her prayers, a highway sign announced "Deer Island, Stonington," and an arrow pointed east. She passed the hulking Winnebago on the right and turned off One to the side road.

The computer's crapping out this morning had been the last straw. Her patience already pushed to the extreme, her nerves already stretched taut, snapped. She had for one brief moment of insanity considered closing the single glowing green eye permanently with a hammer, but Delores had grabbed the dog and left instead.

Yes, the obstacles seemed to keep coming—one right after another. First her old computer which had to be replaced, then all the other odds and ends that she discovered destroyed—the couch which arrived in pieces, the four-thousand-dollar printer which was gummed up from improper storage. Her insurance claim against the movers scraped five digits. Much she had fixed herself or replaced—an unexpected expense with dwindling finances.

Then there came the electrical problems, so she hired an electrician; the phone problems. Delores knew the damn telephone repairman on a first-name basis, and by the sidelong looks he gave her, Delores knew he was beginning to wonder if the young divorcée had something else on her mind other than the phone.

In some ways, it had been inspiring to discover that she could tear apart a nonfunctional piece of complicated electrical equipment, fix it, put it back together again and have it work. A programmer she was but she had never had much interest in hardware. Today would have been the last day. Tomorrow, everything ready, she could have hung out the proverbial shingle. Then the computer went.

She had stared at the two-week-old computer and part of her died, and the old, familiar tapes began again. The tapes from years growing up with an alcoholic and embittered mother. The tapes which said there was no joy or happiness in life—no success, just a living-dying curse. The tapes that told her that everything she touched she broke.

Here was her new life stillborn. Now all the little failures crept up on her, thirty-three years of them, and she was a little girl all over again, always picked last for the baseball team, excluded from games. Her marriage kaput; her home gone; all her dreams vanished like so much smoke on a windy day. It was a continuous cycle. Build a new dream, a new life, and watch it disappear. All points seemed to lead to the same place, a convoluted maze which eventually led her back to the beginning.

The dog's whining brought her back to the present. Another hill, another curve, another splendiferous view. She began to concentrate on her driving. Where the hell was she? Delores leaned back into the seat, letting the monotonous hum of rubber on concrete soothe her. She glanced at the map, her eyes zeroing in on the red lines along the narrow peninsula of land where thought herself to be.

Distracted from her gloom, she let the sun's deceptive warmth seep into her bones. Outside an icy breeze canceled its heat, but closed in the car it seemed cheery and springlike. She saw a highway sign. *Thirteen.*

One eye on the road and one hand on the steering wheel, she tried to find it on the map—tracing a myriad of little lines with her finger until she ran across the number. She found an Eleven, a Fifteen and a Seventeen, but no Thirteen. *That's odd,* she thought; but if they had an Eleven, a Fifteen and a Seventeen, certainly they had a Thirteen. Perhap's the map was out of date, or the highway number changed.

A horn sounded, and a redneck, in a four-by-four wearing a red L. L. Bean flannel shirt and nylon baseball cap, whizzed past her, gesticulating wildly. She looked down at her speedometer. She had slowed to thirty-five.

"Well, EXCU-U-U-UZE ME!" Delores said to the departing vehicle as it rounded the next bend. She was muttering under her breath about goddamn hicks when she followed him around the curve. The words died on her lips. A green suspension bridge led to an emerald island in a sea of sapphire. She gasped at the sight. A sign which announced Deer Island.

Arf seemed to catch her excitement, jumping around in the backseat. He barked in her ear, and she yelled at him to be quiet. She drove onto the bridge. The heavy railing blocked her view. She got to dry land on the other side and stopped the car at the first available spot. Delores got out of the car, feeling a moment of triumph. She was here.

She laughed at herself; she was so easily pleased you'd think she'd never get angry. After all, what had she accomplished? She answered her own question out loud. "I drove sixty miles without killing myself or my dog, and my car didn't break down. If that's not victory with everything else that's going wrong, I don't know what is."

The dog looked at her quizzically, and she smiled, absently patting his head. "Come on, boy, let's see what there is to see."

She got back into the car and belatedly turned the radio on. Little victories, that was what life was all about, she told herself. You lost, you fought back and sometimes you win a few. Enough small victories accumulated and eventually you succeeded.

She'd overcome everything else, and the computer *was* under warranty. At least she didn't have to pay to get it fixed. She'd get the damned thing repaired, and she'd open for business next week. No big deal, really.

Somewhere in the back of her mind, Delores heard the insistent hiss of her mother's drunken voice. *You can't do it. It'll never work. You're just no good.* She muttered a quiet "Shut up" and the sound receded slightly. A top-forty tune told her to "Come on get happy," and Delores hummed along with the reggae rhythm.

The sun had started its slow descent, and everything was bathed in a golden ethereal light. Clusters of white birches sported flashing yellow leaves which seemed to shine. After a wet August, the grass was the rich, deep color of a well-tended golf course. Devil's paintbrushes splashed the field with brilliant orange. Rose hips blushed a ripe red, telling of the rich, bountiful earth. Everywhere colors caught her eye— the deep magenta of the maples, the kelly green of the pine—and she was dazzled.

It seemed a long time before she reached Stonington. It had been described to her as an artist's colony, and it did exude a picturesque quaintness. The little community hugged the bay. Granite sprinkled its surface like giant stepping stones. She got out to explore the town. Arf dragged her along the road until he found a lamppost where he lifted his leg, letting out a long yellow stream.

"Oh, is that why you were so fussy in the car? Why didn't you tell me?"

He stood on all fours again and yawned. "Okay, okay, I know. You tried." She wandered along the main street. Tourist season ended with Labor Day for all practical purposes. Many of the shops were closed. She paused outside windows and read the many bills and announcements—most of them out-of-date. She and Arf made halting progress up the street—he stopping to nose a bush and she to read a hand-printed card or some other curiosity.

They walked to the pier to watch the bobbing boats. The wind off the water was chill, and soon she was ready to get inside. She took Arf to the car and headed for a small coffee shop she had noticed earlier. Picture windows looked out over the water, and she allowed herself to be mesmerized by the gentle waves which lapped against the pier's supports.

She ordered coffee, and the tape was only so much white noise in her psyche. Things would work out. She knew they would. She, like everyone else, experienced setbacks, but there was a progression there. It seemed an endless cycle, but it was more like a spiral which didn't lead eternally back to the beginning no matter how it appeared.

Delores ignored the waitress's brusque manner. She savored the coffee, refreshed and ready to face the world again. She finished her second cup and decided it was time to leave. A wall map told her that the only highway made a big circle around the Island, following its circumference and leading back to the bridge. She'd see the rest of the island and go home.

She paid the check. A few disoriented and late tourists moved along the street, stopping occasionally to try a door and discover it locked. They, like herself, looked a little lost and confused—dislocated somehow. *Tough luck,* she thought, *the season's over till Memorial Day.*

Arf greeted her with wet kisses and a hero's honors. She hugged the dog. The poor mongrel was so devoted and loyal, she sometimes felt undeserving, and he was her only contact with other living beings besides repairmen. She pushed him gently out of the driver's seat.

"Time to head for home, Arf." He responded with another sloppy kiss. "Yuck!"

Delores pulled away from the curb. At long last, the trip had done what she had hoped it would do. She felt lulled, calm. The sun dipped lower in the sky. The first edges of rose surrounded it with an iridescent halo. She drove on wondering if night would find her before she got off the island. Had she made a wrong turn somewhere?

Alert for a sign, she slowed slightly. There it was again—*Thirteen.* No, no wrong turn. She thought about turning around to go back to town, but surely she would find the bridge soon. Deer Island just wasn't *that* big. She looked at her watch. She had literally been driving for hours. A majority of the time had been spent getting here, yet . . .

The car sped along the highway. Another clump of birches, and she slammed on the brakes. Arf tumbled to the floor. "Sorry, pup." He gave her a dirty look.

Delores stared at the grove—the same configuration as before. Devil's paintbrushes, rose hips, the meadow. The colors were muted in the twilight. The same goddamn place she had seen when she first got onto the island, but that wasn't possible. That would mean she missed the bridge. Day slipped toward evening—the 'tween time, as her grandmother called it.

It couldn't be. She hadn't passed the bridge. The granite-lined road leading to the large suspension bridge was impossible to miss. Besides, there had been no turnoff to speak of, no side street. The main highway led to the bridge. She had checked the map in the café since hers seemed to be out-of-date. All roads led to the one highway, and the highway began and ended with the bridge. There was simply no way to get lost.

She put the car into gear and went on. She must have been mistaken. Even beauty can become monotonous sometimes. The bridge was either somewhere up ahead or she'd misread the map and missed a turn. The only thing she could do was keep going. She'd either stumble across the bridge or the town, and if she found the town, she'd ask for directions.

The sun remained a ruddy ball suspended above the tree line. Delores glanced at the car's clock. It flashed, like her home digitals did when deprived of power, and still read six-fifteen.

"Jesus Christ." The car roared past an eerily familiar cottage. Panic made her press down harder on the gas until everything became a blur —the frozen dusk, the boulders, the grass.

She felt tears threaten, and she bit down hard on her tongue to stave off their flow. The tape began again. *You can't do it. You're no good. You couldn't find your ass with both hands and a road map.*

"No!" She crested a hill. The bay and the town came into focus. "Oh, thank God!" She screamed into a parking place and bolted from the car. The street was deserted. She ran up the street to the café. The door was locked; the restaurant closed. She went to the next shop and the next, stopping each time to look through dirty glass—one building after another. She tried doors, and they were bolted. She tried knocking, and no one came until she exhausted every store, every gas station and every shop in the business district.

Breathless, she scrambled unceremoniously across someone's lawn and banged against the door. Delores waited, rocking from one foot to another, not aware that she had started to cry. A moan escaped her throat, a haunting toneless refrain.

Again, she knocked. Nothing. Delores went next door. She had tried four places, her knuckles bruised from the effort, before she decided the place was as empty as it looked. How could a town full of people just disappear?

Weeping openly, she wound her way back to bay. Arf sat in the driver's seat, watching her expectantly. She got into the car, chasing him to the passenger side.

Now goddamnit, it just couldn't be. She turned the car around in a sloppy U, overshooting the curb, and went back the way she came. The tires' hum no longer soothed, but took on a menacing quality—a sonorous drone which threatened her already collapsing sanity. The flash of the so-called uninterruptable-power-source clock, which had so obviously been interrupted, beat a tattoo in her brain: *6:15, 6:15, 6:15* . . .

The metronome of recrimination increased in crescendo. The dog whined in her ear, hungry, and she had to repress the urge to hit him. Too much like her mother, beat into submission anything that didn't behave.

You're no good. You couldn't find your ass with both hands and a road map, the tires said. *It'll never work. You're cursed*, the engine purred. Delores saw the same grove and wailed.

"This way, it had to be, this way. It had to be." She spoke out loud, her words providing a sharp counterpoint, matching her mother's oft-shrieked message beat for beat, measure for measure.

The sun, now even the dog, seemed suspended—free-floating. The sun should have long since sunk behind the horizon and the night begun, no matter what her clock said. She had indeed been driving around the island for hours. The radio silent. She jabbed at the buttons, trying to find a station. Static.

She had left home so many hours ago just to be in the sun, but now its continued presence scared her. The engine whirred and she looked down at her gas gauge just as the town came back into sight.

"No." Delores slumped over the steering wheel. *It couldn't be, but it was.* She heard someone cough. She looked up. An old man, undoubtedly an old salt judging from his grey beard and boat cap, tottered up the street. She reached for the door handle. It was stuck. She beat against the door, screaming through the closed window. The old man walked toward the café, opened the door and went in.

"No," she heard herself say again. Again she tried the door. It wouldn't budge so she put the car into gear and drove away, screaming into the eternal evening, as the tape played on and on in clocklike regularity—frozen in space and time.

KAREN HABER

The Dark Places
In Between

Seth Davis found religion on a sweltering Friday in February. It had
been a bad day, a very bad day, in a week of bad days, a month of bad
weeks, and a year of nightmares.

He stepped back from his easel that afternoon, sweating, his arms
aching, his fingers stained with umber pigment. He'd been at it since
ten that morning. The late sunlight slanted in through the window of
his rented apartment off Avenida Paolo Frontin and illuminated him in
his corner—a slender man with thinning brown hair, a deep tan, and
deep-set green eyes. Seth looked at the canvas he'd just covered with
acrylic paint, sighed, and put down his brushes.

It was no good.

The colors were wrong. The perspective. The composition. Like a
first-year art student's attempts at expressionism, only more embarrass-

ing. No one who saw it would believe that Seth Davis—the same Seth Davis who'd dominated the Armory Show in '85 and in one week become the art critics' darling—had done it.

Nothing he'd done in months was any good—ever since he'd forced himself to start painting again. And his bank account showed it. He could barely make this month's rent, not to mention Maria's salary. After that, he was busted flat. He could take a job cranking out portraits of the Cristo for the tourists, or hawking ices on Copacabana beach. Or go home. To New York. Bow his head and take a teaching job if he was lucky enough to find one. So are the mighty fallen. The once famous, once successful, once married Seth Davis, reduced to teaching perspective to rebellious high school kids?

No. No. No. No. No.

Maria came bustling in from the kitchen carrying a tray. Her white teeth glinted against her dark skin. "Senhor Seth, the work goes well? You should eat something now. It is bad to go all day with nothing to eat."

"Thanks, Maria." He managed a smile, grateful for the distraction. Gods, he'd been lucky to find such a good maid. She was lucky, too. Lucky to have work at all. *Favelitas* rarely escaped, even to the minor luxury of a tiny room off the kitchen of a starving artist's apartment in an unfashionable district in Rio. He grabbed the bowl of grilled meat and farina she offered and began eating greedily.

Maria peered at the canvas on the paint-splattered easel and smiled brightly. Too brightly. "The painting is going well, yes?"

He froze, tried to nod, to make some insouciant gesture, but when he moved he was pulling back, throwing the bowl at the window, through it. Smash! The glass shattered in a thousand pieces, Maria's mouth formed an O of surprise. The glass splinters glittered in the sunlight like ice needles.

Paint that, he thought, and his blood pounded wildly. Capture that energy, artist! For a moment, he felt giddy, exhilarated. Then he thought of the expense of repairing the broken window and his exultation faded.

"Uh, no," he said quietly. "No, I wouldn't exactly say that it's going well."

Maria stared at him for a moment. Then, silently, she knelt and began picking up fragments of glass and ceramic, cupping them in her apron. Back and forth she trotted, from wastebasket to window, back and forth, now with a broom, methodical, uncomplaining, diligent, until Seth felt ashamed. His left arm stung, and he looked down to see Maria swabbing him with some kind of antiseptic—a splinter of glass must have bounced and cut him.

"You should be more careful." Her eyes rebuked him in stronger terms than her voice.

Meekly, he submitted to her ministrations. Maybe he was losing his mind. Maybe he belonged in Dobbs Ferry, behind the desk of some safe suburban high school classroom.

The memory of past reviews echoed mockingly in his head: "Abstract Expressionism Reinterpreted!" "Seth Davis: One Man with a Singular Vision." He'd been selling everything he painted, had been interviewed by *Time*, by *ARTnews*. Even the curator at the Met sought him out at openings to shake his hand. Rolling right along—right into a wall: Ellen and André.

At first he'd considered their affair to be a passing thing. He'd tried to be open-minded—after all, Ellen and he had been together ten years, married for eight of them, and everybody gets restless sooner or later, don't they? Besides, he'd been spending long hours at the easel— of course Ellen had gotten lonely. So she'd developed an attachment to her French instructor. Well, all right, he told himself. Grin and bear it. So he grinned and grinned. And one day as he was grinning, Ellen put everything she cared about into three large cartons, and moved out.

"Hey, you forgot this!" Seth yelled after her as she drove away in the sleek red BMW he'd bought her. In his hand was the portrait he'd painted of her the first year they were together. Ellen sleek and nude, with her shining blond hair and dancing blue eyes. You forgot me, he thought, and stared at the battered old Mazda—his car—lonely in its right-hand slot in the driveway.

When the lawyers had all gone home, Ellen married André and moved to Nice, leaving only a post office box as her forwarding address. And Seth sold the charming two-story colonial in Bronxville, with the studio that got the good northern light, to pay for the settlement and legal fees, and moved into a small apartment in Rye with a western exposure onto a parking lot.

You should be more careful. Yes.

A samba tune, sad and lovely, snaked into the room through the shattered window accompanied by the percussion of traffic, throbbing up the walls of the building toward him like a persistent, persuasive heartbeat. Horns tooting, motors thrumming, people calling and laughing and fighting and crying. The life of the city was in the sound of its voice.

Seth's toes began to tap to the compelling beat. Why had he come to Rio? For the light. The light and the music. He was aching to be out the door and on the pavement, stepping through the summer sunshine of this February day to the peculiar, seductive rhythms of Rio street life. To lose himself in an all-night samba club, dancing with a pretty carioca until the sun came up. To walk the beach of Leblon at dawn, barely making out the bulk of the Twin Brothers, dark against the only-slightly-lighter violet sky. A yank at his sleeve brought him back to the broken window, the planked wooden floor, to the room and his easel. Maria looked at him thoughtfully.

"I think you come with me tonight," she said. "To Candomble."

"Oh, don't be silly, Maria." He shook his head. "You know I don't go in for that stuff." He started to bob around the room in imitation of the white-garbed priestesses he'd seen. Maria fixed him with a burning stare, stopping him in mid-step as he realized, abashed, he was mocking her religion.

"I'm sorry." He shook his head. "I don't know what's wrong with me."

"Tonight. You come."

He couldn't risk losing Maria. Who would work for a poor artist? She took such good care of him that his friends were jealous. "Mama Maria" they called her, after a night of drinking and arguing about the art market. "Go home to Mama Maria." Well, why not? What harm could it do? There were no parties tonight and he might see something at the ceremony that he'd like to paint. Besides, his luck just might change. He was willing to try anything. Anything.

Wasn't that why he'd come to Rio in the first place? To reconstruct himself, redefine his life. After the breakup, he stopped painting. Had trouble sleeping. Spent his days walking, his nights drinking. When he did sleep, his dreams were haunted by Ellen. She was coming back, she was sorry, she was laughing and dancing into his arms, her blond hair floating behind her on the breeze. He awoke, always to darkness and silence. Alone.

He missed a deadline for a show. And then another. Barry, his agent, lectured him calmly, then less calmly, then pleaded with him, and finally stopped calling. The galleries stopped calling. And *ARTnews*. After six months, Seth took what was left of his savings and ran away to warmth and light and life.

"All right," he said. "I'll come. I'm going for a walk, but I'll meet you after dinner."

At sundown, Maria was waiting for him near the Corcovado tram station. She was dressed in spotless white, her shirt tight and clinging over her thin arms and small breasts. The skirt belled out in thick layers of ruffles to her ankles and bare brown feet. Her dark hair was put up in elaborate braids and woven between the braids were a dozen small white roses.

"I didn't think this was a formal affair," he said, suddenly self-conscious and grubby in his jeans and rumpled blue work shirt.

She gave him a small smile and led him to a private house set back behind a grove of jacaranda trees, bright with purple blooms. Inside, a somber group of celebrants had already assembled. Fascinated, Seth looked around the room and saw gray-haired men in their sixties, children barely steady on their chubby feet, young mothers in aprons, middle-aged businessmen wearing suits stained with sweat, sleek, tanned beach boys in tight pants and sleeveless tank tops. Someone had taken a slice of Rio and set it down in this room where it could vibrate to the steady, hypnotic beat of the *pandeiro*'s drums.

When he first arrived in Rio, Seth had studied the local religions a bit and came away with the sense that they were a colorful mixture of superstition and dance party. The amusing babble of gods' names: Babalawo, Dada, Exu, Iemanja, Legbara, Obaluae. They were just stand-ins for the holy hierarchy imposed on the natives by Christian missionaries, weren't they? He'd always thought so, before. Suddenly, he wasn't so sure.

The *pandeiros* intensified their beat and heads around the room began nodding. Seth watched, fascinated. So this was the secret rite he'd heard so much about. Look at all these people! The smoke-filled room, the serious intensity of the celebrants, and the relentless drumbeat made him wonder if there was something to this religion after all. Maria had spoken of miracles and punishments sent by the gods. Maybe so. Maybe so.

The lights went out, and in their place a hundred candles sprang to fiery life. Seth saw Maria's eyes roll back in her head. The beat of the drums grew louder, faster. Maria's arms went up and her palms inscribed arcs, swaying, reaching toward the ceiling. In a trance, she danced a private prayer, reeling, falling to her knees and bending until the back of her head nearly touched the floor. For him. All for him. He felt humbled and eager. Light-headed and giddy. Gods, he'd like to paint that—to capture the ecstatic look on her face! The drumbeat was intoxicating. *Bumpadabumpadabump.* He began to shuffle his feet. The room grew warm and he rolled up his sleeves, feeling the sweat on his back and arms.

Now a sturdy matron in white turban and dress writhed in the sawdust next to Maria. And a dark-skinned man with a golden earring in his left earlobe dropped to one knee, then the other, as he gyrated across the floor. Sweat glistened on his chest and forehead. A teenaged girl in a white leather miniskirt followed him, and behind her came a stately grandmother in white whose arms glittered from wrist to elbow with golden bracelets. The entire congregation was keening, gibbering, writhing together as the drums beat on and on. The wave of ecstatic worshippers engulfed him, swept him up and along with them.

"Exu," they muttered. "Orisa-Nia." And their faces were contorted with the bliss of private visions somehow shared.

"Aje Shaluga," they sang. "Lemanja. Orisa-Nia."

A pang of doubt stopped Seth in mid-step. What if he was wrong? What if this was far more than a party? What if Exu lived? And Babalawo? The brave hunter Oxossi. The strange, mercurial Orisa-Nia. And he'd been laughing at them.

Was that the beating of the drums or the footsteps of some giant god approaching? He'd be crushed underfoot. He had to beg forgiveness. Quickly. Seth felt the sweat soaking through his clothing, running from him in tiny rivulets. The muttering of the celebrants, the whisper of hands and feet against the sawdust on the floor, the flickering, guttering light from the smoky candles, the smell of warm bodies too close together, the drums, the drums, the drums. The gods were coming. He could hear them.

"Exu," he cried. Was that really his voice? He could scarcely believe it. "Help me, Exu. Orisa-Nia, don't crush me." His voice was swallowed up in the din of fellow worshippers and he shouted louder so the gods could hear him. It was becoming easier. "Please, forgive me. Forgive me. Help me." The drums—and his fear—had full possession of him now. His body was quivering, shaking like a wild thing. He saw only in terms of light and shadow, no color, save for the orange glow of the candles, the white clothing of the celebrants, the dark places in between.

"Ibeji," he sang to the sacred twins. "Orunmila, teach me."

A tall woman to his left began sputtering and jerking. Others came up behind her to support her as she leaned back, back, until the top of her turban was almost touching the floor.

Maria was at Seth's elbow, suddenly, pressing a foil-wrapped bundle into his hand. "It is a visitation—the god Orisa-Nia," she whispered. "Give this to him as tribute and ask for his help."

Seth started toward the woman, then stopped. What was he doing? He'd been caught up in the moment, but did he really think that there was anything to this at all? He tried to pull back, but the crowd surged behind him—he could only go forward. Someone gave him a shove, and he fell to his knees in the sawdust. Could not rise. On his knees, slowly, he approached the woman/god. The sawdust rasped at his jeans. As he neared her, the medium opened her eyes—the pupils were immense, almost swallowing the blue irises, and her gaze was intense, magnetic and unfathomable. Seth began to be afraid.

"Please," he blurted. "Please help me." Shaking, he handed the package to the woman. She took it without glancing at it and continued to stare into his eyes. When she spoke, her voice was deep, blurred, almost that of a man.

"What help do you need?" she asked.

"I'm an artist . . ."

"You are sick in the heart, I think."

He had no answer but nodded.

"Look to the water of life for a cure," she said. "The sacrament—the water of life."

Water of life? Sacrament? The words echoed, distorted, became one with the drums. In her hands there was a goblet, golden and deep, containing a dark, rich liquid. Her eyes held him, transfixed. She was pulling him in, relentlessly. Seth felt weightless, without substance. He was falling now, and he could hear the footsteps of the gods pursuing him. Screaming, Seth fell into darkness.

The next morning, he awoke to the chocolate-velvet scent of brewed coffee. Strange images haunted him—what peculiar dreams he'd had. All that dancing last night has shaken him up. He felt a hundred years old. The sunlight hurt his eyes. It hurt his head, his hands, and every other inch of skin on his body. Aagh. Seth eased himself out of bed and staggered into the main room. Maria was nowhere to be seen. But a fresh pot of coffee was sitting on its heating pad next to his easel. Well, he could take the hint. But first, a shower and some aspirin.

Ten minutes later, vastly improved, he approached the easel. Took a gulp of coffee from his battered blue tin cup. Took another. Placed a clean canvas, newly stretched, upon the worn easel lip. Mixed his colors and dipped his favorite brush, reeking of mineral spirits, into the blue-green paint at the edge of his palette. A fresh start, that's what he needed. Today and right now. He took another sip of coffee.

Two hours later, when Maria returned from the market, he was sitting on the floor resting his forehead against his knees. Without a word, she brought him something to eat, fresh coffee, and put his hardening brushes into the jar filled with paint-clouded paint thinner.

Somehow, he found his way back to the easel. Mixed fresh colors. Reached for his brush—where was it? Did Maria take it away to sand the paint off of it? She was always doing that.

"Maria?"

No answer. Maybe this was the afternoon she went to study English. Well, try this brush instead. He dipped up a bit of umber, of yellow, and turned back to his canvas. The first stroke was good. The second, even better. He didn't stop to question. He didn't dare. The song was strong within him, suddenly, and he couldn't waste time on questions or even on gratitude. He painted until his fingers grew numb, pausing only to warm them on a cup of coffee. By the time Maria returned, he'd finished two canvases and was about to start a third.

She smiled at his glowing face and went into the kitchen without a word. When he'd finished the third painting, she joined him, to view the work.

He'd captured the city he'd always longed to portray: the dark faces and perfect bodies, oiled and glistening on the beach. The brief, sparkling, tragic life of the young Brazilians: they bloomed so quickly, and so quickly were consumed by the poverty, the crime, the demands of family, family, family. Hemmed in between mountains and ocean, squeezed between wealth and poverty. It was the Rio he knew and loved, not the picture-postcard images of Carnival and Cristo sold at every newsstand in the tourist districts.

He painted like a madman. A canvas a day, then two. Three. In a week, he'd produced fifteen paintings and lost five pounds, but he didn't care. He was burning with some cleaner, purer light. Maria moved quietly, almost reverently, around him, bringing food and drink, returning to remove the empty plates.

He sent slides to New York. And when the phone rang, he almost didn't answer, so absorbed was he at the easel. On the sixth ring, he picked up the receiver, and the hiss of the long-distance line made him catch his breath.

"Mr. Davis?" A hearty baritone voice said. "This is Scott Kenneally. How's the weather down there in Rio?"

Seth found his voice. "Beautiful: warm and sunny."

Kenneally sighed. "Wish I could say the same. It's snowing in the Big Apple. Wind chill of minus four."

"That's cold."

"Sure is. Seth, I'll get right to the point. You sent me some slides recently."

Seth's hands began to shake. "Yes. Yes, I did."

"Well, I'm very impressed, Seth. *Very* impressed. I'd been wondering where you went. Didn't you have a big show at the Remington Gallery in '87?"

"Yes. I did." Seth remembered that show: his last good one. "I, uh, had some personal problems after that."

"Went down to Rio to refresh yourself, eh?" Kenneally chortled. "Good idea. I'd say the cure took. But I thought Barry Crockett was representing you."

"He was. I'm looking for a fresh start."

"Just want to make sure there aren't any contractual knots . . ."

"I haven't spoken to Barry in over a year."

"I see. Well, Seth, what you sent me looks fresh and vital—confident without the usual arrogance. I think we can do very, very well with it."

"That's good news. Thank you."

"Tell me, is the work on the slides still available?"

"Yes."

"Could you ship it to me as soon as possible, air freight? Charge it to my account, naturally."

"Yes. Sure." Seth's head swam. This was all happening so quickly.

"I've got several clients on the West Coast who should see your work. And a few in New York. Have you got a fax?"

"Uh, no, not yet."

"Pity. I could fax you our contract to save time. Well, no matter. I'll send it Air Express. And when you return it, use our account number for the charge. We take the standard 30 percent, of course."

"Of course."

He sent the paintings. They sold. Two weeks later, Scott Kenneally was on the phone again.

"Seth, we've got some interest in a show from the Martin Holz Gallery."

"Martin Holz!" It was a name he'd stared at each month in *ARTnews*. Two years ago, he'd dreamed of showcasing his work there. Did he really have a second chance at a Holz show?

Kenneally chuckled. "Yes. They don't usually have an opening this quickly, but Eugene Mabris canceled—he's been doing that lately—and they have a slot open in April. And Sally Carstead—she's a curator at MOMA—saw your slides and went crazy. She's planning a show in '94 called "New Visions" and she wants to see more of your work. I need at least fifteen more paintings, Seth. Can you do it? I realize this is a tremendous burden, but this is your moment. Don't say no."

Could he produce more? Could he?

"Yes," he said. "Yes, yes, yes."

He put the phone down and ran into the kitchen. Grabbed Maria by the shoulders. "More paint, Maria. I've got to get more paint right away."

She smiled triumphantly. "It goes better, yes? The gods guide you now."

"Yes." He grinned back. "Better and better. Maybe your gods *are* taking care of us."

He rented a bigger apartment, with a separate room for the studio. And a better bedroom for Maria. He painted. And painted. Bought more supplies. The better pigments, finely and freshly ground. Only the best. And prestretched canvas of the first quality—that too. A new easel. Sable brushes. A drying rack. He was working so hard, so fast, that time and money meant little, meant nothing. The painting was all, everything. He would let it consume him, have all of him, every last inch from toenails to hair follicles.

Eagerly, he unwrapped the fresh goods, dabbed the sable brush in the new paint. And stopped short.

Nothing. He was empty. He had nothing.

No. Please. No.

Seth felt the tears welling. What was happening?

Maria came in to find him sitting in a corner of his shiny new studio, the half-empty bottle of rum in his hand.

"Dio, what's wrong?" she cried.

"It's all gone," he said. He looked at her blurrily and smiled a sad smile. "All gone, seeped out through my little finger when I wasn't looking." He gestured weakly, his left hand still holding the sable brush.

Maria's eyes narrowed. "Where did you get that?"

"Bought it this morning."

"Where is your old brush?"

He shrugged. "Threw it out. It was practically bald anyway."

But Maria wasn't listening any more. She was digging frantically through the wastebasket, grunting. After a moment, she sat back with a satisfied smile. In her hand was the old brush.

"Seth, you must use this one."

"Why? It's not much good any more. Practically bald."

She placed it in his hand. "*This* one. It has the force of Orisa-Nia. Of the sacrament."

"What?" Seth dropped the brush and pulled back as though it were infected with a virulent disease. "What sacrament? I thought you were kidding."

Maria looked down and nodded. "The sacrament," she said in a tiny voice. "The water of life. It made you strong."

"Christ, don't tell me that!" His voice was high with anger and fear. "I don't believe in it. And I don't want to know about it."

"No? He may not believe, but he sure kneeled before the god he don't believe in." Maria looked at him slyly from the corner of her eye. "If you don't believe, why were you so afraid, that night we go to Candomble? And why did you ask the god for help?"

Seth felt his cheeks burning. "Well, look—I don't want to say that there's nothing to this religion. There must be, for so many people to believe in it. But it's not something I can believe in, Maria. Not me. I don't have any place in the world it comes from. Your world. Not really."

She laughed scornfully and her face was transformed into harsh angles. "*Now* you don't want any? Before, you took the strength the god gives happily. But now you don't want to give the god credit. Be careful, Seth, or He will punish you." She raised her palms upward. "I have taken the sacrament for you before, but next time, Orisa-Nia, He wants *you.*"

Her words chilled him. He started to take a swig from the bottle, but the old paintbrush was in his hand, in his way. He put down the bottle. The paintbrush vibrated with a secret life, a drumbeat of its own—the faint echoes of a god approaching. A dreadful suspicion gripped him.

"Maria." His voice was hoarse. "Maria, what was the sacrament?"

"I cannot tell you."

"Maria, you have to." He was grabbing her hand now, yanking her down toward the floor, terrified and angry, determined to know. He pinned her with his full weight as she writhed desperately, trying to get away. "Tell me!"

"It is made of wine," she said.

"Is that all?"

"No. No, there is more." She closed her eyes.

"What else?" He squeezed her wrists harder and she winced from the pressure.

"It is wine," she said. "Wine. And blood."

"Animal blood?"

"No." It was a whisper. "The blood of innocence. Of children who have died in the night."

"What?" The words hit him like a physical blow. Seth released his hold, pulling back, up and away from her. "Children's blood? I thought Candomble used only animals."

"Not always."

"How did they die?"

"I do not know. Do not ask."

"Don't ask?" Seth flung the brush into a far corner of the room, out of sight. "Jesus! What have I been doing? Blood? The blood of dead kids? Jesus." He stared at her. "Don't tell me anything more. I don't want to know. I don't want this, don't want any part of it. It's evil," he muttered, covering his face with his hands.

She sat up, gave him a reproachful look, and hurried into the kitchen.

Blood of children. He felt the bile rising in his throat and barely made it to the bathroom. He was sick for a long time. How long, he didn't know. When he staggered back into the studio, the sun had vanished behind the mountains. And Maria had gone.

Her room was empty, stripped of her few bits of clothing. The pots on the stove were cold. Maria was gone. But he hadn't intended that she leave. What would he do now?

He didn't paint the next day, or the next. But a call from Kenneally reminded him of the deadline. The Martin Holz show. Reluctantly, he retrieved the brush from the dark corner of his studio and began working.

Strange scenes emerged from under his brush—surreal images of women in white, of huge stone gods striding out of the mountains toward the sea, of guttering candles and strange shadows in dark, ghostly rooms.

Five paintings. Nine. At number ten, the head of the brush disintegrated, leaving a pile of bleached animal hairs in Seth's palm. He stared at them in disbelief. Not now! Please, not now.

Blindly, he reached for a fresh sable brush. It felt like a dead thing in his hand. He dipped it in the paint and dabbed at the canvas. No good. He was ruining it. He peered out the window at the setting sun. Its blood-red rays seemed to mock him. He only had a few days left to finish the work and ship it.

Maria. Find Maria.

He grabbed up a handful of brushes and set out for the Rocinha *favela* near the Tijuca mountains where she had lived. In the blue dusk, he passed groups of children—*favelados*—setting out for their nightly romp through the streets of the city in search of amusement and money. Dark eyes glinted at him, mouths curved in smiles. All the dirty faces, the lilting voices. The charming, graceful, discarded, desperate children that Rio could not feed, could not house. Could not love.

The *favela* spilled down the mountainside, a colorful jumble of tattered packing crates in which people lived. Ramshackle communities of the poor who tapped into water and sewer lines, stole electricity from power lines, poured concrete and built stairs and passageways through the winding alleys that divided the boxes.

In the darkness, Seth slipped on a pile of discarded melon rinds and nearly fell down a narrow concrete stairway. But he caught himself, bruising his elbows and knees. Curious faces, some hostile, peered out of doorways illuminated by candles and, occasionally, by the harsh blue-white light of a gas lantern.

"Maria?" he asked. "Do you know Maria?"

His Portuguese wasn't bad, but even as he asked, he realized that his quest was hopeless. Of course they knew Maria. They knew fifteen, thirty, three hundred Marias. Which one did he want?

Jesus, he thought. I never even bothered to learn her last name.

Some strange fragrance hit him: the thick, cloying perfume of some unknown flower mixed with the reek of rancid cooking oils. The scent hung about him in the humid, dense tropical air.

In desperation, he began to ask about Candomble. "Where can I find a *yalorixa*—a priestess?" he asked a heavyset woman with a pleasant face. She frowned at him and shut the door of her shack.

"Exu? Please, Exu."

The only reply he received was faint, mocking laughter. A group of ragged preteen boys gathered, attracted by his desperate questions.

"Exu," the boys said, and their voices were flat and cold. They were not smiling. "Exu, Americano!" One of the taller, bolder ones gave Seth a push. The others crowded closer. They were no longer picturesque, dirty-faced children with the voices of magpies. They were dangerous and menacing, capable of robbery and murder. Seth began to grow frightened. He'd been warned against entering a *favela* after dark.

They shoved him again, and he wrenched away from their grasping hands and began running, clawing his way through the heavy, fetid air. They chased him downhill, nimble as monkeys, through the winding streets of the *favela*, around corners and through the shadows, into sickly patches of moonlight, hooting, taunting him, throwing rocks. He ran hard, harder than he'd run in years, desperate, blood throbbing in his chest and ears, breath burning in his throat.

The alley broadened into a street and the *favela* receded behind him. Suddenly, cars were whizzing past. Seth was on the Avenida Maracana and the pack of *favelados* was right behind him. Somehow, he flagged down a taxi before the boys could catch him and gratefully collapsed into the back seat, gasping for air. But as the tall white towers of the Leblon district came into view, he realized his wallet was missing. When the taxi slowed at a traffic light, he jumped out and ran, like a thief, until the driver's curses and horn had faded in the distance behind him.

Sweaty and exhausted, he pulled a fresh bottle out of the liquor cabinet and began drinking. Without Maria, he'd never be able to find the original Candomble group, even if he spent all night searching. Bottle in hand, he roamed the apartment.

Everything looked sinister and changed. The shadows were sharper, somehow, and the silence was foreboding. In his studio, the blank canvases stood stacked, waiting. He avoided their silent demands.

The kitchen was dark. The remains of last night's dinner sat, congealed, in the pot where he'd left it. He took another drink and moved on, into Maria's old room.

The gray-striped mattress was stripped, rolled into a cylinder just as she'd left it.

Seth sat on the edge of the wooden bed frame and took another drink. Dust balls littered the floor. His gaze wandered around the room and stopped at a jumble of things in the corner near the window. He knelt and rummaged through it. Red paper shavings, shriveled pieces of green citrus rind, a fragment of fabric, and underneath, a thick, yellow candle and what looked like bits of rusted metal grating. Wait. What the hell was this? Some kind of tiny effigy: a humanoid figure with a pointy head, trident, and jaunty, erect penis.

Hands wobbling, he placed the figure next to the candle and went to find a match. He struck it, lit the candle, inhaled its rich, sweet scent. He watched the flame waver for a moment, casting tall shadows against the walls. He felt mildly foolish.

What do I do now? he wondered. Hop around the room? Smoke a cigar? I can't do this. I don't know how. I need Maria. Without her, I'm just another *extranjero* lost in Brazil. He took another sip from the bottle. And another. He was tired, so tired. He lay down on the cool floorboards before the makeshift altar, remembering the voices of the *favelados* drifting on the wind as they'd chased him, a strange, deadly chorus. He could smell the rancid cooking oil again, and the strange fragrance of the purple flowers.

And in the dark, the answer came to him. Maria had warned him. She'd been right. He must give tribute to Orisa-Nia, the hunter.

He felt the fresh sable brushes in his breast pocket, pressing against him through the thin fabric of his shirt, and pulled them out. Their tips gleamed silky orange-brown in the flickering light of the candle.

"So lovely," he crooned. "Fresh, new, lovely."

He thought of the canvases awaiting him and his pulse pounded like a drumbeat. He could hear the footsteps of the god approaching. Yes.

Seth got to his feet carefully and staggered out of the room, holding onto the walls. A lightweight blue cotton jacket hung in the kitchen on a wall hook and he put it on. Reached into the bowl of green apples near the front door and picked up the slim, graceful paring knife, put it carefully inside his jacket pocket where it clinked against the bottle of wine he'd been drinking. Yes. The sacrament.

He heard the god drawing closer as he shut the door behind him. The brushes had to be dipped in the water of life—in wine and the blood of children who have died in the night. Yes. Yes. He knelt until his forehead touched the ground and that cooled him a bit. Refreshed, he arose. Now he heard the singing, the strange chorus of their high, shrill voices in the dark, windy streets. Yes. Yes. Yes. It grew louder with every step he took.

GUY N. SMITH

I'll See You on Saturday Night

Jerry had been praying fervently for the past three days that Isabel would be at the dance at Cefyn Einon on Saturday night. Nothing else mattered in his own simple life because he was desperately in love with her.

As Floyd, the proprietor of the ramshackle garage where Jerry worked, had once put it, "You was missin' the day the good Lord handed out good looks, boy." Which was, unfortunately, true. Tall and muscular, the girls might have eyed Jerry up from the tip of his working boots but they would have averted their gaze with hopefully disguised repugnance when it reached his face. His features had the appearance of having been squashed into the smallest area possible in order to leave a wide forehead for his shock of straggling, unwashed hair to flop forward onto. When he removed his hands from the pockets of his jeans the length of his arms, in proportion to his body and combined with his humped shoulders, gave him an apelike appearance, and he seemed purposely to shuffle his bowed legs to accentuate this. But he was honest and hardworking and, given the opportunity, would have doted on a female partner. And Isabel Johnson *had* said that she was going to the dance.

On Wednesday, during his lunch hour, Jerry had driven his old van the eight miles over the foothills to Cefyn Einon to purchase a pair of cheap sunglasses from the store where Isabel worked. He could have bought an identical pair in the village shop next to the garage, but the cost of the petrol was well worth the opportunity just to look at her. Petite, with long blond hair, she had taken the job to earn herself some spending money until she went to college in the autumn. Her folks were the richest sheep farmers in the district, but they did not believe in giving away money to be squandered on unnecessary cosmetics by their daughter, who didn't need makeup, anyway.

Isabel had been serving a customer when Jerry had slunk into the shop, tried to make himself as inconspicuous as possible. His stomach had contracted into a hard ball and he was trembling. He licked his lips, wondered if he would be able to speak without stammering. A pair of those sunglasses, please.

"Hallo," she smiled, never used his name, she probably did not even know it.

"A pair of those sunglasses, please," relief because his words came out the way he wanted them to even though his lower lip shook slightly. As she turned away he blurted out, "There's a dance on Saturday night." This time it came out in a rush, sounded silly. He might have said, "It's very hot today," ordinary small talk that would not have seemed out of place.

"Yes," still smiling, popping the purchase into a paper bag. "I know. I'm going."

"Oh!" Surprised because her parents were letting her mix with the local lads, or maybe she was going to defy them over the issue. "So am I." He had not intended to go and become the butt of ribald jokes from the other youths but nothing was going to keep him away from the Cefyn Einon dance now.

"I'll see you on Saturday night, then." She smiled again as she took his money, did not appear to think it strange the way he gulped and dashed from the shop. Before she could change her mind.

And it was all he could do to stop himself shouting across the street to the trickle of shoppers, "Hey, I've gotta date with Isabel Johnson. We're going to the dance on Saturday night!"

Jerry ought not to have told Floyd, that was his big mistake, but there was no way he was going to be able to keep it to himself until Saturday. He would tell Mrs. Eckerson at the grocery shop and she would tell everybody else in the village. That was fine because he wanted them to know; his chest was already beginning to swell with pride and his ungainly shamble had developed an arrogant swagger. What about that then, you guys? You never got yourself a date with Isabel and neither has anybody in Cefyn. Because up until now there was nobody she fancied.

Floyd did not laugh and come out with the off-the-cuff coarse joke which Jerry had braced himself for. The other just grunted, carried on looking for the elusive electrical fault in Mrs. Cade's car which had to be ready by five if he didn't want the sharp edge of her tongue. Maybe he hadn't heard properly.

Jerry hated Floyd, wouldn't have worked for him if there had been anybody else who would have taken him on. The boss was a misshapen giant of a man, all the more grotesque with his dirt-grimed face and those rabbitlike teeth which made him lisp and dribble a string of saliva whenever he spoke. Overweight, ill-tempered and shifty, and becoming even greedier with his overcharging lately. But his one redeeming feature was that he would turn out at any hour of the day or night to help a stranded customer. Which was why the business was as lucrative as it was, because there was no other garage this side of Cefyn Einon.

In spite of his limited schooling Jerry had a way with mechanics, a feel for cars rather than a technical understanding. In his spare time, which was usually only Sundays, he either tinkered with his old van or called up breakers on his CB radio and indulged in silly small talk. It was different talking to people when you didn't have to look at them; so much easier. And if there was nobody willing to chat, then he read comic books, mostly horror comics which were on sale at the newspaper shop in Cefyn. But between now and Saturday night he wasn't going to have time for any of these; he was going to be too busy thinking about Isabel. Yeah, it was a mistake telling Floyd. The boss maybe hadn't laughed because he was scheming, perhaps already thinking up an "urgent" job that he could ask Jerry to work on on Saturday night. Floyd was cunning, you could never trust him, and he was the jealous type, too. He had once passed a dirty remark about Isabel, joking but meant it. If I can't have her, boy, I'll make damned sure *you* don't. Which was slightly disconcerting. But if it came to the crunch, Jerry would tell Floyd where to stuff his garage, because nothing on this earth was going to keep the youth away from that dance.

Jerry always worked Saturday mornings, and often until around two in the afternoon. This morning it was hotter than ever. He had taken off his T-shirt and his torso was grease-stained, though that didn't matter because later he was going to have a bath; usually he didn't bother. He had to finish respraying the wing on Doctor Lewis's Ford; Floyd had already backed the car into the paint shop. And Jerry had a rare favor to ask Floyd.

"Boss," Jerry looked up as the other shuffled across the dusty yard, "is it okay if I do a bit at the old van in the workshop when I've finished? Reckon the engine needs a mite tuning, it's running real rough." Trying not to sound too humble, just humble enough.

"Suppose so." Floyd stroked his stubble with meaty fingers, a habit of his when he wanted to turn something to his own advantage. "But, tell you what, boy . . . I have to go out this afternoon," *and I'm not leaving you the run of the place while I'm gone. "I'll* have a look at your van while you fix the doc's car. That way we'll be through by two-thirty at the latest."

Jerry's mouth dropped open in surprise and he nodded. Probably Floyd would take it out of his wages, but on this very special occasion he wasn't going to argue. He could not risk breaking down on the journey to Cefyn Einon.

Nine o'clock found Jerry changing down a gear to climb the steep hill road that dropped down the other side into Cefyn Einon. The van labored; he thought maybe Floyd had not done a very good job after all. But there was less than two miles to go. If the worst came to the worst, he would walk the rest of the way.

The evening was humid. The sky had been clouding over since mid-afternoon, and now there was a yellowish tinge to the encroaching thunderheads. Dusk had come early; he flicked on the sidelights. The storm would surely break before long. He hated electric storms; they were scary.

On his right the big fir wood looked black and forbidding. He shuddered, thought of that strip story in the comic book he had read the other night, a dark forest that harbored evil. Just like this one; the locals called it Captain's Wood. The legend went back to the last century when an old seafaring man had bought it, retired to live in Cefyn Einon, and when he'd died they'd buried him up there among the trees. Surely that wasn't legal, burying somebody in unconsecrated ground, even Jerry knew that. But they'd got away with it, there was a grave just inside the entrance and somebody tended it, scythed the grass around it. A headstone and a plaque, too; it had become a tourist attraction, was mentioned in a local guidebook so that folks came here in the summer to look at it. Jerry laughed to himself, in all probability there wasn't even a body there, the townspeople had dreamed it all up just to entice visitors so that they would spend their money in the shops.

The van just made it to the brow, and the engine picked up on the downhill slope, coasted all the way down into Cefyn Einon.

It was carnival weekend in Cefyn Einon. Banners and buntings spanned the narrow main street and litter carpeted the pavements. As Jerry found a space to park the van he heard strains of music coming from the open ground where the visiting fair was getting into full swing; marquees, rides, sideshows, a prize if you were fortunate enough to hit the plastic ducks with a doctored air rifle. But none of these interested him tonight.

The atmosphere was heavy with the smell of candy floss and beer, an odor of frying. He was tense, afraid even. A fool's errand. Isabel wasn't going to the dance to date *him;* she was just going along because it was carnival time when everybody went. A sinking feeling that he fought to dispel. She *had* said she would see him there.

He got out of the van, didn't bother to lock it. The town hall was a wooden edifice, needed a coat of paint, its tin roof stood out shabbily amid the row of half-timbered houses. His legs felt as though they would hardly bear the weight of his body as he mounted the steps leading up to it.

"Why, if it isn't our Jerry!" The fat man taking the money at the door grinned, his rotund face shiny with sweat. "What brings you to the dance?"

Jerry just stopped himself from blurting out "Because I've got a date with Isabel Johnson tonight." He just smiled weakly, paid and went inside.

The large rectangular room was crowded, just the stage lights burning so that couples could dance or jive anonymously, smooch if they wanted to. The floor was crowded and there didn't seem to be any vacant chairs either. A full house, everybody here to enjoy themselves, silhouettes that swayed and laughed. Later there would probably be a fight; there usually was on these occasions.

He stood there, his eyes roving the shadowy crowd. Trying to pick out Isabel, afraid that she might be that fair-haired girl with her back to him, dancing with the tall fellow who was stooped so that he could kiss her. When they turned with the music he was relieved to see that it wasn't Isabel Johnson. His eyes smarted in the tobacco smoke, and he could barely see. There were probably three hundred people here, it wasn't going to be easy to find her.

He couldn't dance, he didn't know how to, that was another problem. Suppose when he found her she wanted him to lead her onto the floor. His stomach churned at the thought. Just chatting together then, maybe holding hands toward the end. His mouth was dry, he needed a drink.

There was a queue at the bar in the corner; he joined it. Beer or spirits in plastic cups, the floor was slippery with spilled drink. Jerry ordered a lager, lost some of it when somebody knocked against him. He sipped it as he shuffled his way round the perimeter of the room, peering at those seated on the chairs, squinting as he tried to recognize Isabel. Back at the entrance, his cup was empty so he tossed it amid some scattered litter in the corner. No sign of Isabel, perhaps she had not arrived yet. He decided to stand by the door, scrutinize everybody who came in.

The lights went on at the interval, instantly destroying the pseudo-romantic setting which the shadows had done their best to create. A smoke haze wafted in the draft from the open door as if it were trying to hide Isabel Johnson from his searching gaze. He set off on another tour of the dance floor, checked on everybody while there was still light. And when he had completed the circuit for the second time he knew without any doubt that she was not here.

Still clinging to a vain hope that she would arrive late, stationed by the door again when the lights went off and the local country and western group began playing another number. And when an hour later the fat man closed the door Jerry knew that Isabel would not be coming after all. A bitter disappointment, in some ways a relief because he was spared the embarrassment of trying to dance. But there was no point in remaining here any longer.

He went out through the narrow side exit, paused for one last sweeping glance of the dance floor and the bodies that milled and sweated on it. Then he turned away, dragged his feet all the way back to where the van was parked.

Jerry was just pulling out into the road when it began to rain. A few spots on the windscreen as a warning, and then it was like driving through a waterfall as the torrential downpour hit Cefyn Einon. The wipers struggled to clear a swath, the noise on the van's bodywork was deafening. But Jerry did not care. About anything.

Maybe the engine had been playing up all along, but he was not aware of it until he was almost at the top of the steep hill leading up from the town. A lack of power so that he had to change down into bottom gear, the cylinders missing even then. Laboring, struggling to make it to the top but just managing it. And then dying on him.

As the engine faded the storm outside seemed to realize his helplessness, swept at him with everything it could muster. The wipers faltered under the deluge, the headlights started to dim. Battering at the van, trying to get to him, thunder growling like some carniverous beast of the night that had scented easy prey.

There was just enough momentum left to glide the van off the road. He felt the tires crunching on stony ground, it was impossible to hear them. The lights scintillated on raindrops, just enough for Jerry to recognize his surroundings before the twin beams dimmed still further. He was in the entrance to Captain's Wood, that patch of leveled shale with its crudely painted car-park sign, the wooden gate sagging open on a broken hinge. We're open twenty-four hours a day, come in and view the grave. And there *is* a body buried in it.

Jerry experienced a surge of panic, leaned across and pressed down the lever that locked the passenger door, locked the one on his own side, too. A fearful glance into the back, it was too dark to see, anyway, but he knew that the rear doors were only secured by a length of plastic string because the catch was broken. Flimsy, one swift tug would snap the twine. But there *isn't* anything out there.

There is. There's a body in a grave just inside that gate for a start.

There was a torch on the seat beside him, it had been there since last winter. He flicked the switch; at least it worked even if the battery was low, enough light to see by. He wondered if he could fix the engine. Damn Floyd, he was supposed to have checked it. Jerry hesitated; it was impossible in this storm, he would be drenched within seconds and the engine would be flooded so that it wouldn't start even if he located the original fault. Besides, he did not have any tools with him.

Another thought had him groping in the glove box until his fingers located what he was looking for. His CB radio, he had not used it lately but it was still there. And working!

He found a breaker, some night-riding trucker looking for somebody to talk to. There wasn't any storm five miles south but the transmission was bad.

"Do me a favor, mate," Jerry's voice shook. "I'm broken down on the road to Cefyn Einon at the entrance to . . . Captain's Wood. If you can get to a phone, call up Floyd's garage. Tell him it's Jerry and please could he come out with the breakdown and tow me in."

"Will do. Over and out."

Jerry sighed with momentary relief. The guy sounded genuine, he would call up Floyd. Floyd might or might not come. If he did turn out then there wouldn't be much left in Jerry's wage packet at the end of next week. He sat back, tried not to think about Isabel. Maybe she was ill, there had to be some *reason* why she had not come to the dance. She wouldn't just let him down like that, she wasn't the type. On Monday he would drive back to Cefyn Einon, provided the van was repaired, and find out.

It had almost stopped raining, no more than a light pattering on the tin roof. Even the thunder sounded far away as though the storm had moved on, gone in search of another victim because it could not get to him after all. He might be able to fix the engine after all. No, not now that he had called for Floyd. It was Floyd's fault, let him sort it out. The call-out fee would be the same whoever got the van going.

Outside something howled—a mournful, long drawn-out sound that came from somewhere back in the big wood—and Jerry stiffened. There it went again, vibrated the still atmosphere. He checked again that the doors were locked. They were; except the rear ones. The sweat on his body chilled. He told himself it was probably a sheepdog from one of the farms behind the wood. Or a fox. Foxes barked, vixens screeched, maybe they howled, too. His mind went back to that pile of

comic books he kept under his bed. It couldn't be a *werewolf* because
they only existed in comics. Didn't they?

He continued to listen but whatever it was did not howl again.
Maybe it was creeping up on him stealthily, was crouching outside in
the darkness, knew that the back doors were only tied with string.
Hurry up, Floyd, *please!*

Something struck the windscreen a light thud. He almost cried out,
thought he detected a flutter of tiny wings. A bird that had lost its way
in the stormy night. But birds don't fly in the dark, except owls and
that hadn't been big enough for an owl. A *bat* then. The sudden
implication had him pressing himself back in his seat, remembering
that big double edition of *Spook. Special Vampire Issue!*

Where the hell have you got to, Floyd? What's keeping you?

Floyd wouldn't be coming, not for Jerry. Because he wasn't a rich
customer who would pay over the odds for being rescued on a storm-
lashed night. You can stop where you are, boy, sleep in that old van of
yours, walk back at daylight. And it'll still cost you on Monday to get
towed in.

Outside there was silence which was worse than those noises because
you had the feeling that whatever had made them had found you, was
waiting for you to move.

And suddenly Jerry knew that he had to get out of the van, tensed
rigid with terror at the inevitable prospect. He ought not to have drunk
that lager. He would hang on for another few minutes just in case
Floyd arrived.

Floyd did not come and Jerry could not hold on any longer. He
checked the torch, it was still working. His shaking fingers rested on
the door catch. A minute, no more, and then he would be safe back
inside, waiting out the dawn. He wondered what time it got light.

He eased the door open, the rusty hinges creaked loudly. A quick
flash of the torch all round. There was nothing there. See, it's all right,
and don't get thinking about those comics because they're all rubbish.
He got out, left the door open.

He did not have to walk over toward the gate, he did not know why
he did only that his feet seemed to move in that direction and he was
unable to stop them. Standing there, shining his waning torch inside
the fir wood and realizing that the feeling of discomfort which had
made him leave the van was no longer there.

He wanted to go back, to slam the door and lock it again. Instead he moved further into Captain's Wood until the yellow circle of fading torchlight centered on the neatly tended grave with its scrubbed head-stone standing in the small clearing.

And Jerry screamed loudly when he saw the body lying on the raised grassy mound.

It wasn't the Captain, he realized that even at the height of his terror. It was a girl, wearing a blue summer dress that clung wetly to her slim form, her arms folded across her bosom. Her long fair hair was damp and straggled, her face turned in his direction as if she wasn't really dead and was watching him closely. There was even a trace of a smile on those full red lips.

It was Isabel Johnson!

He did not understand, he did not want to. Isabel had not been at the dance because she was here. Dead. The lure of a legendary grave that drew tourists from far and wide had enticed her here. Like it had drawn himself, an irresistible magnet that had pulled him out of the van. Just come and look, Jerry. And maybe you'll die here, too.

Suddenly he found that he could move again as if the invisible force that held him had released him. He turned away, stumbled and fell, dragged himself up again. Running, holding his torch out in front of him, scared that whatever it was would reach out of the shadows and drag him back.

And as he emerged from the trees he heard Floyd arriving, the breakdown truck swinging into the lay-by where the van was parked. He saw the headlights illuminate the stormy sky then cut out, heard the sound of an engine dying. Then that awful silence was back and Jerry cowered at the entrance to Captain's Wood.

It was Floyd, all right. There was no mistaking that huge ungainly shape that lumbered toward him. *Just as though the other had been expecting to find him over by the wood.*

Jerry heard his rasping breath and then in the wan light of his own dying torch he saw the other's squat features, those protruding teeth wobbling out of the thick lips with a string of spittle hanging from them. He smelled him, too, the sour stench of an unwashed body clothed in greasy, oily overalls.

"She's been getting awful cold waiting for you, boy," Floyd lisped and his deep-sunk eyes seemed to glow briefly in the shadows. "She's been here these past three hours, lying where the dead wait for the dead. I knew you'd come, boy, just like you knew I'd come."

Jerry saw Floyd's arm come up, the heavy spanner clutched in the huge fist, and suddenly he was unable to move again. Floyd was here because the grave had called him to do its bidding, he probably had not even received the trucker's call. It made no difference, anyway.

And somewhere close by he heard Isabel saying, "See you on Saturday night, Jerry."

GRAHAM MASTERTON

Beijing Craps

Like all professional gamblers, whose days are measured only in throws, and rolls, and hands, and spins, it had never seriously occurred to Jack Druce that he would ever die. But that Friday morning at the Golden Lode Casino, at the exact instant when the second hand swept silently past one A.M., he shivered, and lifted his head, and frowned, as if he had been momentarily been touched by the chilly breath of impending extinction.

Alert to the slightest tremor in mood at the craps table, the croupier noticed his hesitation, and said, "Intending to shoot, sir-r-r?" His *r*'s rolled as hard as dice.

Solly Bartholomew noticed Jack's hesitation, too, but didn't lift his eyes from the layout.

Jack nodded, and scooped up the dice, but didn't speak.

He had already stacked up eleven thousand dollars' worth of chips in three hours' play. But for no reason at all he suddenly felt as if the layout had gone cold, the same way that (seventeen years ago) his wife Elaine had grown cold, lying in his arms, asleep first of all, breathing, then not breathing, then dead.

Jack guessed that he and Solly could make two or three thousand more. Solly was the only other professional at the table; a neat man who looked like a small-town realtor, but who threw the dice with all the tight assurance of a practiced arm. Cautiously, showing no outward signs that they knew each other, or that they were working together, he and Jack were carving up the amateurs between them.

There was money around, too. Not yacht money, for sure, but lunch money. They had just been joined by a tall horse-faced overexcited man from Indianapolis in a powder-blue polyester suit who was placing his chips on all the hard-ways bets, and a redhead with her roots showing and a deep withered cleavage who yelped like a chihuahua every time Jack threw a pass. Divorcée, Jack calculated, splashing out with her settlement. She wouldn't stop playing until every last cent of it was totally blown. It was a form of revenge. Jack knew all about women's revenge. Elaine had stopped breathing while he was holding her in his arms, and what revenge could any woman have exacted on any man that was more terrible than that?

Jack blew softly on the ivories, shook them twice, and sent them tumbling off across the soft green felt. "Nine," commented the croupier, and pushed Jack another stack of fifty-dollar chips.

"I'm out," said Jack, and began gathering his winnings in both hands.

Solly hesitated for a moment; then said, "Me too."

"Aw shit," said the tall horse-faced man.

The croupier's eyes flicked sideways toward the pit boss. Jack said, "Something wrong, my friend?" He had spent thirty years of his life dealing with men who communicated whole libraries with the quiver of an eyelid.

"Pit boss'd like a word, sir. And"—turning toward Solly—"you, too, sir. That's if you don't mind."

"I have a plane to catch," Solly complained. Solly always had a plane to catch.

"It's ten after one in the morning," the croupier told him.

"Well, I have to catch some zees before I catch my plane."

"This won't take long, sir, believe me."

Jack and Solly waited with their hands full of chips while the small, neat pit boss approached him. White tuxedo, ruffled pink shirt, smooth Sienese face, eyes like slanted black olives, black hair parted dead-center. The pit boss held out one of his tiny hands, as if to guide them away from the table by the elbow, but he didn't actually touch them. Players were not to be physically touched. It was bad karma.

"Mr. Graf presents his compliments, sir."

"Oh, does he?" asked Jack, sniffing and blinking behind his heavy-rimmed eyeglasses. Beside him, he heard the redhead yelping again.

The pit boss smiled, and went along with the pretense. "Well, sir, Mr. Graf is the joint owner of the Golden Lode, sir. And he would like to see you."

Jack held up his chips. "Listen, my friend, I have my winnings here."

Solly said, "Me too."

"Of course," said the pit boss. His smile slid out of the side of his mouth like the cottonseed oil pouring out of a freshly opened can of sardines. "We'll take care of your winnings, sir. Carlos! Here, take care of these gentlemen's winnings."

"Twelve and a half K," said Jack, pointedly, as if it were more money than he had ever possessed in his life.

"Five," said Solly, without expression.

"Don't worry, sir. Carlos will keep it in the safe for you."

With a great show of reluctance, Jack handed over his chips. "Twelve and a half K," he repeated. "What do you think of that?"

Behind his well-pumiced acne craters, the stone-faced Carlos obviously thought nothing of it at all. One night's winnings for a midwestern mark, that was all. The casino would have it all back tomorrow, or the next night.

"Please . . . this young lady will show you to Mr. Graf," said the pit boss, still smiling. From somewhere behind him, like an assistant in one of those corny Las Vegas lounge magical acts, a Chinese-looking girl appeared, in a skintight dress of cerise silk, with a split all the way up to the top of her thigh.

"Please forrow," she said, and immediately turned and began to walk ahead of them. Jack glanced at Solly and Solly glanced back at Jack. They could cut and run. But Jack had heard of Mr. Graf; and Mr. Graf had a hard, hard reputation; and if they ran away from Mr. Graf, then the chances were that they would have to keep on running, for the rest of their natural-borns.

Whatever had to be faced, had to be faced. Jack and Solly had both been beaten up on before, more than once.

The Chinese-looking girl was already halfway across the casino floor, headed toward the wide violet-carpeted staircase that led down from the restaurant and the offices.

Solly said, "After you, sport," and Jack shambled after her like an obedient mutt, tugging the knot of his necktie, although it was already too tight. During his gambling career, he had deliberately cultivated the dislocated mannerisms of a rube, freshly off the Piedmont redeye from the rural Midwest with a billfold crammed with ready money and no idea of how to play the tables.

In reality he had been born in Providence, Rhode Island, the son of a high school principal, and he was both well educated and extensively traveled. He had lived in Florence, in Aqaba, and Paris; and in the 1950s he had spent nine miserable months in London. But in the late 1960s he had spent six weeks living in Bellflower, Illinois, painstakingly imitating the local mannerisms and the local speech. These days, only a fully bloomed Bellflorian could have detected that his accent wasn't for real. He still said "grass" instead of "grayce."

He had altered his appearance, too. He had cropped his hair short and bought himself a vivid chestnut-brown toupee. He had adopted thick-rimmed eyeglasses and sunbathed in his T-shirt, so that he had acquired that farm-style tan, face and neck and forearms only. Every morning he squeezed lumps of modeling clay in the palms of his hands, to give himself cheesy-looking crescents of dirt under his fingernails.

When he was working, he assumed a crumpled seersucker suit in brown-and-white check, a brown drip-dry shirt, and scuffed tan sneakers. At least, he liked to think that he "assumed" them, and that his "real" clothes were the clothes that hung in the closet of his suite at the Sands hotel. A single gray Armani suit, three handmade shirts, and a pair of polished English shoes.

In reality, however, the "real" clothes had scarcely been worn, because Jack was *always* working. Even the soles of his "real" shoes remained unscratched. He spent all afternoon and most of the night as Jack Druce the Rube. The rest of the time he spent sprawled on his back on his hotel bed with his sheet knotted around his waist like a loincloth, dreaming of Elaine going cold in his arms and whispering numbers to himself. But he needed the "real" clothes to be hanging there waiting for him.

If he ever discarded his "real" clothes, then the "real" Jack Druce would cease to exist; and all that would be left would be Jack Druce the Rube; Jack Druce the Chronic Gambler. The laughing, sophisticated young college graduate would have vanished forever; so would the husband of Elaine; and the father of Roddy, for what that was worth.

On the last day of May, 1961, Jack Druce had been a mathematical whiz kid, the youngest research team-leader that San Fernando Electronics had ever employed. On the last day of May, 1961, San Fernando Electronics had brought 270 employees to Las Vegas, for the company's tenth annual convention. That night, Jack Druce had played dice for the very first time in his life, and doubled his annual salary in four and a half hours.

Jack Druce had woken on the first day of June, 1961, with the certain knowledge that he had been hooked.

Now his house was gone and his car was gone. Not because he couldn't afford them. Most days, technically, he was very rich. The simple fact was that houses and cars didn't figure in his life anymore. He lived in hotels; he walked to work; and he subsisted on free casino snacks and Salem Menthol Lights. His home was the Pass line. He never looked at his watch.

Elaine was gone, too. Elaine and her gradually chilling overdose. And Roddy was gone. Little Roddy, whose memory lived in his billfold, a small Kodak picture of a small boy frowning at the sunshine; the front of his hair shining like gold; a turquoise triangle of swimming pool in the top right-hand corner. Late last year, a glum Puerto Rican police detective had come to Jack's hotel room in Reno and shown him a black-and-white photograph of a wild-eyed young man with cropped hair and an antisocial scowl.

"Who's this?" Jack had asked him, after a long while.

The detective had peered at the photograph more closely, as if he thought that he might have made a mistake.

"That's your son. Wanted for armed robbery. Maybe you know where he is."

"No, no," Jack had told the detective, and produced the small Kodak picture. "You're way off beam. *That's* my son."

"Sir, your son is twenty years old."

But Jack had shaken his head and tapped the small Kodak picture.

"That's my son. Three years old. Armed robbery? You're way off beam."

The Puerto Rican detective had understood then that Jack was living on Casino Time, as opposed to Real Time. People who live on Casino Time are like star travelers who exceed the speed of light, and return to earth to find that twenty years has passed in twenty minutes. He said, without any optimism, "Well . . . if anybody like the guy in the picture shows up . . . you let me know. He's dangerous, you understand? Shot two people already."

"My son's three years old," Jack had repeated, with complete confidence.

"Yes, sir," the detective had replied. "I guess he must be."

Now the Chinese girl led Jack and Solly through thick suffocating velour curtains, and then through double doors of heavy carved Joshua wood.

"I'm not so sure about this," Jack told her; but she turned and half-smiled and said, "Don't be afraid."

Solly said nothing. Solly had an especially sensitive nose for danger. Solly was sniffing the atmosphere, checking it out.

Beyond the double doors, they found themselves in a large gloomy room, ferociously chilly with air-conditioning. In the center of the room stood a gaming table, lit by a single low-hanging lamp of bottle-green glass, a dark secretive lamp that scarcely illuminated the table at all, and gave to the six or seven men and women who were hunched around it a ghastly green look, as if they had been dead for several days.

Jack frowned at them. Two of them looked as if they had one foot in the grave for real. Their white hair shone silvery-green in the reflected light from the lamp; their skin was shrink-wrapped over their skulls, and thick with wriggling veins.

Yet three of the players were almost children—a spotty boy of sixteen or seventeen; a young girl of not much more than twelve; and a blond-headed boy who was so small he could scarcely throw the dice.

All of them, however, shared something in common. They all wore loose Chinese robes, of gleaming black silk, with fire-breathing dragons embroidered on the back, and the name "Nü Kua" in red-silk italics.

"Come," said the Chinese girl, and led Jack and Solly toward the table.

Jack was fascinated to see that the dice appeared to glow fluorescently in the darkness; and that when they were thrown, they left glowing patterns in the air. Solly watched the game over his shoulder for a while, and then murmured, "What the hell kind of craps is *that?*"

Jack looked around the table. "I'm supposed to be talking to Mr. Graf," he said, loudly.

The blond-headed boy left his place and came around the table, smiling and holding out his hand in greeting. He looked no older than five or six.

Jack smiled. "How's tricks, kid?"

"I'm Nevvar Graf," the boy told him, in an unbroken but carefully modulated voice.

"Sure and I'm Tammy Wynette."

The boy continued to hold out his hand. "You don't believe me?" he asked, tilting his head to one side.

"Nevvar Graf has owned the Golden Lode Casino for twenty years, minimum. He's just about old enough to be your grandfather."

The boy smiled. "There are more things on heaven and earth, Horatio."

"Oh, sure," Jack nodded. "Now is Mr. Graf here, because if not, I intend to leave."

"I told you, Mr. Druce, *I'm* Nevvar Graf."

There was something in the tone of the boy's voice that caught Jack's attention. Something far too commanding for a boy of five. And how did he know Jack's name? Jack took off his spectacles and folded them and tucked them slowly into his pocket.

The boy said, "I'm Nevvar Graf, and you're Jack Druce. I've been watching you for years, Mr. Druce. You're good, one of the best arms in the business. Everybody knows Jack Druce. It's always beaten me why you dress so crummy, and talk so dumb, when everybody knows who you are. You saw Carlos downstairs? The minute you leave the Golden Lode, Carlos always gets onto the radio transmitter and warns the doorman at the Diamond Saloon."

Jack said, hoarsely, "Young fellow, I don't know what the hell you think you're playing at, but my name is Keith Kovacs, and I came here from Illinois for the week to gamble a few hundred dollars, just like I've always promised myself; and when my money's all gone, I'll be gone, too.

"Jack Druce?" he added. "I never even heard of anybody called Jack Druce."

The boy popped his knuckles, one by one. "You see that game going on behind me?"

"I see it," said Jack. "Some kind of fancy dice."

"Beijing Craps," the boy told him, with a smile.

Jack shook his head. "Never heard of it."

"Never heard of it, huh?" The boy turned to Solly, and said, "Have *you* heard of it? Beijing Craps?"

Solly nervously sniffed, and lowered his eyes. "Sure. I've heard of it."

The boy circled around Jack and took hold of Solly's hand. "Solly Bartholomew," he said, in that piping voice. "The greatest arm in the east. The onetime scourge of the Atlantic City boardwalk."

Solly didn't attempt to deny it. He stood holding the boy's hand with his eyes on the carpet and said nothing.

"Beijing Craps," the boy repeated. "The legendary magical mystical Beijing Craps. Banned in China since the revolution; banned in Thailand where they don't ban nothing; punishable by flogging in Japan; punishable by death in Vietnam. Illegal in every country in the world, with the exception of Pol Pot's Cambodia, and that's where these dice were smuggled in from."

He tugged Solly's hand. "Come on, Solly, come closer. Take a look."

Solly stayed where he was, his head still lowered. The boy tugged his hand again, then smiled. "You don't want to take a look? You don't have to play."

"You know just what the fuck you're talking about," said Solly, his false teeth clenched together. "If I look, I'll *have* to play."

The boy laughed. "That's up to you, Solly. You're ready for it. You know that you're ready for it. That's why I asked you up here, you and your friend Jack Druce. I've been watching you two lately and you're the crème de la crème. But you're getting bored, too. You're too damned good for your own damned good. What's the fun, when you don't play the game to the limit—*can't* play the game to the limit, because the pit boss is going to suss you out and then you're finished at the Golden Lode; and then you're finished at Caesar's Palace and Glitter Gulch and even Sassy Sally's, and before you know it you're finished in Vegas altogether, then Reno, then Tahoe, then Atlantic City.

"That's when clever men like you start to play Russian roulette, and hoping you'll lose. But Nevvar Graf here has an alternative for you, a different way out, a new life maybe, leave the old life behind, all or nothing. Beijing Craps."

Jack said, dryly, "You're Nevvar Graf, aren't you? You really are."

The boy released Solly's hand and came back to Jack, and looked up at him, his eyes bright with mischief. "I really am. And what you're looking at is proof. Look at me, I'm five years old! And that's the magic of Beijing Craps. You win, you can live your life all over again!"

Solly nodded toward the table, where the white-haired men and women were rasping their breath onto the dice. "What if you lose?"

"You won't lose. You're too good. You *know* you're too good."

Jack stepped up to the table, and inspected the layout. "So what's in it for you?" he wanted to know. "Why'd you want me to play?"

The boy smiled more gently now. "Same as always, Jack. The odds favor the house; and I'm the house."

"Explain it to me," said Jack.

The boy came up and stood beside him. "It's pretty much the same as a regular dice game. You pick up the dice, you make your bet, you shoot; and other players fade your bet. The only difference is that we use special dice, you want to take a look?"

Jack looked across the table at the withered yellow-faced old man who was holding the dice. He had never seen such an expression of dumb panic in anybody's eyes in his whole life; not even on the faces of trust-fund managers who had just gambled away their clients' investments, or husbands who had just lost their houses.

"Mr. Fortunato, will you pass me the dice for just a moment?" asked the boy.

Old Mr. Fortunato hesitated for one moment, the dice held protectively in the cagelike claw of his hand.

"Come on, Mr. Fortunato," the boy coaxed him; and at last he dropped them into the boy's open palm. The boy passed them carefully to Jack.

They were greenish black, these dice, and they tingled and glowed. Holding them in his hand, Jack felt as if the ground were sliding away beneath his feet, like jet lag, or a minor earth tremor. Instead of numbers, they were engraved with tiny demonic figures—figures whose outlines crawled with static electricity.

"There are six Ghosts on each dice," the boy explained. "If you shoot Yo Huang—this one—and Kuan-yin Pusa—this one—that's roughly the same as throwing a seven in craps; and if you shoot Yo Huang and Chung Kuei—here—that's just about the same as throwing eleven. In either case, these are the Beijing equivalent of naturals, okay, and you win.

"Yo Huang was the Lord of the Skies; Kuan-yin Pusa was a good and great sorceress. Chung Kuei was known as the Protector Against Evil Spirits."

Jack slowly rubbed the dice between finger and thumb. "That's three Ghosts. What are the other three?"

"Well," smiled the boy. "They're the bad guys. This one with the hood is Shui-Mu, the Chinese water demon; and this little dwarf guy is Hsu Hao, who changes joy to misery; and this is Yama the judge of hell, who was the first mortal ever to die—and do you know why?"

"I have a feeling you're going to tell me," said Jack.

The boy smiled. "He was the first mortal ever to die because he traveled down the road from whence there is no return."

Solly licked his lips. "The road from whence there is no return? What's that?"

The boy turned and looked at him slyly. "You're traveling down it already, my friend. You should know."

"Let me feel those dice," Solly demanded.

Jack closed his fingers over them. "Solly . . . maybe you shouldn't."

"Oh, yeah? And any particular reason why not? Seeing as how I'm already supposed to be taking the hike with no return?"

There was such a crackling charge of power from the dice that Jack felt as if every nerve in the palm of his hand were wriggling and twitching, centipedes under the skin. He had the irrational but terrible feeling that the dice wanted Solly very badly. The dice knew that Solly was there; and they were hungry for him.

Solly held out his hand, and Jack reluctantly dropped the dice one after the other into his palm. Solly said nothing, but something passed across his eyes like a shadow across a doorway. There was no telling what Solly could feel. Jack suspected that the dice felt different for everybody who held them. It depended on your needs. It depended on your weaknesses.

"So you place your bet," said Jack, without taking his eyes away from Solly. "What do you bet? Your soul, something like that?"

"Oh, no, nothing as melodramatic as that. Anyway, what's a soul worth? Nothing. A soul is like a marker. Once the guy's dead, how's he going to pay?"

"So what's the stake?" Jack persisted.

"Months, that's what you bet," the boy told him. From the other side of the table, Mr. Fortunato hadn't lost sight of the dice for one moment, and when the boy said "months," he shivered, as if the boy had said "millions."

"Months?" asked Solly.

The boy nodded, and then held out his hand for the dice. "The shooter bets as many months as he wants, and the other players collectively put up an equal number of months that he's going to lose. Lunar months, that is, Chinese months. The rest of the players can bet among themselves, too, whether the shooter comes or don't come, except in Beijing Craps we say "dies-a-little" or "lives-a-little"; and there are hard-ways bets, too, just like regular craps, whether the shooter throws two Yo Huangs or two Chung Kueis or whether he digs himself a grave and throws two Yamas."

"But if you win, what?" asked Solly, hoarsely.

"If you win, you win months, that's what. Two, three months; maybe a year; maybe two years, depending what you've bet."

Solly looked around, found himself a chair, dragged it over, and sat down. His breathing was harsh and irregular. "You mean you actually get younger?"

The boy giggled. "Look at me, Solly! Nevvar Graf, five years old!"

Solly rubbed his mouth with his hand, as if he were trying to smear away the taste of greasy hamburger. "Jack," he said. "Jack, we got to give this a shot."

Jack shook his head. "Forget it," he said; although his throat was dry. "I play for money. Months, what's a month? Who wants to play for months?"

The boy shrugged. "What do they say? Time is money. Money is time. It's all the same. You ought to try it, Jack, you'll like it. I mean, let's put it this way. Keeping yourself in toupees and hotel rooms is one thing; but being ten years younger, that's something else. How about fifteen years younger, Jack? How about *twenty* years younger? How about walking away from this table tonight the same age you were when you first started gambling, with your whole life ahead of you, all over again? No more crap tables, no more cards, no more cigar smoke, no more shills? How about a wife and a family, Jack, the way your life was always meant to be?"

"How the hell do *you* know how my life was always meant to be?" Jack retorted.

The boy's eyes gleamed. "I've been working in this business all my life, Jack. You're just one of a million. The International Brotherhood of Optimistic Suckers."

Jack looked at the table; at Solly; at the mean green lamp; at the strange assortment of faces around the layout. He knew with suffocating certainty that he would have to play before he left. Elaine had died in his arms; Roddy had shrunk to a Kodak photograph tucked in his wallet. The chance of starting over burned in the darkness of his present existence like the molten line of the setting sun, burning on the western horizon. To go back! To catch up the sun!

He heard himself saying, "Solly and me, we'll watch for a while."

"Hey, you can watch," Solly told him, abruptly standing up, and sniffing, and clearing his throat. "Me, I'm going to play."

"Solly—" Jack warned; but the boy touched one finger against his lips.

"We're all playing for time here, Jack. We're playing for life. It's your own decision; it's Solly's own decision."

Jack looked at Solly—tried for the first time in a coon's age to look like a friend, somebody who cared; although he didn't find it easy. To the professional craps player, no expression comes easy.

The boy said, "You'll have to change. There's a Chinese screen in the corner, with plenty of robes."

"Change?" Solly wanted to know. "Why?"

"You might *win*, Solly," the boy smiled at him. "You might win *big*. And if you win big, you might find yourself ten years old, all over again. And how would a ten-year-old old boy look, hmh? in a thirty-eight-chest sport coat like yours?"

Solly nodded. "Sure. You're right. I'll change. For sure. If I lose, though—you won't take my suit for collateral?"

"You're a kidder, Solly," the boy grinned at him. "You're a genuine platinum-plated kidder."

Solly disappeared behind the Chinese screen; and while everybody edgily waited for him, the boy whistled "She's My Jeannie with the Light Brown Hair" over and over.

At last Solly emerged in his black silk robe. He looked like an invalid on his way to hydrotherapy. He smiled nervously—first at the rest of the players, then at Nevvar Graf, then at Jack.

Jack hesitated, and then stepped back. He didn't shake Solly's hand. He didn't say a word. He knew that—inside of himself—he was just as much of a victim as Solly.

"All right," said the boy, smacking his hands. "Let's play Beijing Craps!"

From out of the shadows at the back of the room, three Chinese and a Burmese appeared, dressed in the Golden Lode uniform of overtight black tuxedo and frilled shirtfront. The boy said, "Same as regular craps, a boxman, a stickman, and two dealers. In Beijing Craps, though, we call them Tevodas, which means witnesses who can testify to somebody's sins."

It was Mr. Fortunato's turn to roll. Solly stood beside him, watching him with naked eagerness. "Six months," Mr. Fortunato declared, and placed six shimmering gold tokens in front of him; tokens that shone brighter than the bottle-green lamp.

"Two months he dies-a-little," whispered a white-haired old man from the far corner of the table.

"One month he lives-a-little," said the twelve-year-old girl. Jack looked at her closely for the first time and realized that her hair had been permanent-waved in the style of a woman who was old enough to be her mother.

"One month he dies-a-little," said one of the oldest players, a woman whose skull was showing through her skin. Her shriveled hand placed one of her last gold tokens onto the square marked with the face of Yama.

When all the bets had been placed, Mr. Fortunato gasped on the dice, and rolled them. They sparkled and bounced, leaving fluorescent afterimages of Chinese ghosts melting in the air over the tabletop. Yo Huang and Kuan-yin Pusa. Mr. Fortunato had won his six months.

"Mr. Fortunato lives-a-little," intoned the Tevoda, the stickman, and collected the dice and handed them back. Mr. Fortunato breathed a little more easily onto the dice this time; but the old woman who had lost a month betting that he would die-a-little had begun to shudder. Jack swallowed and looked at the blond-haired boy; but the blond-haired boy simply grinned.

Mr. Fortunato bet another six months, and rolled again. He threw Kuan-yin Pusa and Shui-Mu. The blond-haired boy leaned toward Jack and whispered, "He's won again. In Chinese magic, Kuan-yin Pusa trapped Shui-Mu by feeding her with noodles which turned into chains in her stomach and locked her guts up for good. Throwing Kuan-yin Pusa and Shui-Mu is like a point in craps; and what Mr. Fortunato has to do now is to throw them again. But if he throws Yo Huang and Kuan-yin Pusa again, he loses."

Jack watched every roll of the dice intently; and especially the side bets. Some of the players were picking up weeks here and there with easy bets; others lost one month after another with hard-ways bets. Live-a-little, die-a-little. Their lives ebbed and flowed with every roll.

Mr. Fortunato bet a whole year, threw a crap, and lost it. Twelve months of his life, swallowed in an instant. Who knows what age Mr. Fortunato had been when he had started playing this game? Forty? Seventy? Twenty-two? It didn't matter. His age was determined by the dice now; his life depended on Beijing Craps. He coughed and wheezed with stress and badly concealed terror, and passed the dice to Solly with fingers that could scarcely manage to open. Nobody else at the table showed any compassion. The blond boy had aged by three years since Mr. Fortunato had started to play, and was far taller and more composed; although the woman with the skull-like face seemed to have shrunk in her black silk robe almost to nothing, more like a bewildered vivisected monkey than a human.

Jack caught Solly's eyes but he remained impassive. They were professionals, both of them. They helped each other on the tables when the dice were rolling, but they never ventured to give each other criticism, or personal advice, or to warn each other to back off, no matter how cold the table, no matter how vertiginous the bet. You want to fly, you want to die? That's your business. Under the lights, out on the center, there was nobody else but you, and Madame Luck.

"Solly," said Jack; but the adolescent Mr. Graf shot him a glance as hard as a carpet tack, and he said nothing else.

Solly bet six months. He jiggled the dice in the palms of his hands, and breathed on them, and whispered something, and then he rolled. They had once called Solly the Arm of Atlantic City; and his arm didn't fail him now. The dice bounced, glowed, and tumbled, and came up Kuan-yin Pusa and Yo Huang.

Next, he bet a year, and threw another natural. He threw again, and won again. Roll after roll, he played like a genius; played like Jack had never seen him play before. With each win, he gradually began to look younger. His gray hairs wriggled out of sight, his wrinkles unfolded like a played-back film of crumpled wrapping-paper. He stood taller, straighter, and played with even more confidence; and all the other players bet along with him, hard-ways bets, right bets, they shed years and years in front of Jack's eyes. After twenty minutes, he was watching a game played by young, good-looking, vigorous people: attractive young women and smiling young men. Their shriveled skin was plumper and pinker; their hair was thick and shiny; their voices roared with vigor and health.

"How about some champagne?" called Mr. Fortunato.

A twelve-year-old Mr. Graf snapped his fingers stickily to one of the girls. "Bring these people champagne."

Jack didn't bet. Not yet. He was tempted to. But he wanted to bide his time. He wanted to see the losing side of this game, as well as the winning side. He wanted to work out the odds. And although Solly was winning, and consistently winning, it occurred to Jack that the younger he became, the less experienced he became, the more risks he was prepared to take, the wilder his arm.

"Ten years!" grinned a twenty-four-year-old Solly, shaking the dice in his hands. "I'm betting ten years! Fourteen again, and screw the zits!"

He rolled. The dice glowered, shimmered, sparkled. They bounced off the cushion on the opposite side of the layout, but then they seemed almost to *slow down*, as if they were bouncing through transparent glue. The Ghosts glowed malevolently for all to see. Yama and Shui-Mu. Craps. An entire decade was silently sucked from Solly's body and soul; and he visibly shuddered.

After that—as far as Solly was concerned—the table turned as cold as a graveyard. Mr. Graf was shooting, winning a little here and a little there; but Solly was stacking his counters on all the impossible bets, trying to win time, trying to win time, but losing it with every roll. When Mr. Graf finally missed, Solly was white-haired; on the verge of respiratory collapse. He sat hunched over the opposite side of the table, his hands dry like desert thorns, his head bowed.

Jack approached him but didn't touch him. Bad karma to touch him; no matter what affection he felt.

"Solly," he said thickly, "pull out now. You've lost, Solly. Call it quits."

Solly raised his head and stared at Jack with filmy eyes. His neck hung in a brown-measled wattle.

"One more bet," he whispered.

"Solly, for God's sake, you're falling apart. You look about a hundred years old."

Solly wasn't amused. "I'm eighty-seven, two months, and three days exactly, you unctuous bastard, thanks very much. And if I win another thirty on the next roll, I'll be only fifty-seven. And if I bet another thirty after that . . . well, then, I'll be happy to quit. Life was good to me when I was twenty-seven. Twenty-seven is a pretty good age."

Jack said nothing. If Solly bet thirty years and won, then Jack would be happy for him. But if he bet thirty years and *lost* . . .

He looked at Mr. Graf. Mr. Graf had lost six or seven years betting on Solly's last roll, and was looking much older again, and more like the Mr. Graf that Jack had seen hurrying in and out of the Golden Lode, hedged in by minders and shills and hard-faced accountants. Mr. Graf's eyes turned like a lizard's toward Solly. What could he say? Solly had lost and those who had lost were always hooked. Those who had won were hooked, too. So what could he say?

"You're not playing, Mr. Druce? It's your roll, if you're playing."

"If it's all the same to you, I think I'll stay out of it," said Jack, although perspiration was sliding from his armpits and his fingernails were clenched into the palms of his hands.

"Sure thing. It's all the same to me," said Mr. Graf, immediately offering the dice to Mr. Fortunato. With the unashamed greed of the truly fearful, Mr. Fortunato held out his hand.

"Wait, Jack!" wheezed Solly, and took hold of Jack's sleeve, and twisted it. He bent his head close, so that Jack could smell his unexpected age, chalk and cloves and geriatric staleness. "Jack, you're the best arm there ever was. If anybody can win back those years for me, you can. Jack, I'm begging you, Jack. We never did nothing for each other, did we? Never expected nothing, never asked for nothing. You know that. But I'm asking you now, Jack, I'm down on my knees. If you let Fortunato shoot next, I'm dead meat, Jack. I'm gone. You know that."

Jack sniffed, the way that a heroin addict sniffs. He feared this game of Beijing Craps more than any game he had ever come across. It had all the glamour of *punto banco* and all the fascinating horror of standing in front of a speeding express train. He knew that if he rolled those dice just once, he would be caught for good.

Mr. Graf sensed his hesitation, however, and held the glowing dice suspended in the air, just two inches above Mr. Fortunato's open hand.

Jack could almost see the nerves that crawled with anticipation in Mr. Fortunato's palm.

Solly tugged his sleeve even tighter. "Jack, for old time's sake, I'm pleading with you now. I never pled before. I never pled to nobody. But please."

Jack hesitated for one more second. He didn't need to look at his watch. He never did. He knew what time it was. He loosened his necktie, and said, "Give me a minute to change, all right?"

He undressed behind the screen. The black dragon-robe was cold and silky on his skin. He tightened the sash, and then he reemerged, and Mr. Graf was still waiting, still smiling.

Jack approached Nevvar Graf and slowly held out his hand. Mr. Graf smiled secretively, and dropped the dice into Jack's palm. They tumbled and turned as slowly as if they didn't particularly care for gravity. When they touched Jack's palm, they felt like fire and ice and naked voltage.

The players gathered around the table again. The lamp was so dim that all Jack could see of their faces was smudges of paleness in the shadows. He shook the dice and tiny grave-worms of bluish fluorescence wriggled out from between his fingers. He bet six months, and stood back waiting while the side bets were placed.

He threw the dice across the table. They jumped and sparkled with even more brilliance than they had before.

"You see that?" said Mr. Graf, slyly. "Even the *dice* know when an expert is throwing."

Jack had come out with Chung Kuei and Yo Huang. Solly clenched his fists and breathed, "All *right!* You goddamned brilliant son-of-a-bitch!"

Jack threw again, Kuan-yin Pusa and Chung Kuei. He threw them again the next throw, and picked up a whole year. He didn't *feel* any different, but it was stimulating to think that he was a whole year younger.

He continued to win, again and again and again; living-a-little and living-a-little-more, throwing naturals and points as swiftly and confidently as if the dice were loaded—which, in a strange way, they were. The years fell away from him with every win, until he was betting two and three years at a time, and his black silk robe began to hang loosely around his slim twenty-two-year-old frame.

Solly placed numbers to win with almost every throw, and gradually won back the years he had lost before. He played cautiously, however, and didn't risk more than a year at a time, until he reached forty-five.

Then—just as Jack was about to throw again—he placed a hard-ways bet of twenty years.

Jack looked at him sharply, but Solly grinned and winked. "One last throw, my friend, and then I'm going to walk away, and never come back."

But Jack felt something in the dice; as if they had shrunk and tightened in the palm of his hand; as if they had suddenly gone cold. The dice were not going to let Solly go.

Jack said, "Twenty years on one throw, Solly? That's a hell of a bet."

"That's the last bet ever," said Solly. "You just do your bit, and let me take care of myself."

Jack threw the dice. They dropped leadenly onto the layout, scarcely bouncing at all. They came up Shui-Mu and Hsu Hao, a win for Jack; but Solly had bet Shui-Mu and Shui-Mu, and he was immediately aged by twenty years.

Jack was only a little over twenty years old now. He stood straighter and taller, and his hair was thick and wavy and brown. He took off his toupee and crammed it into his pocket. Mr. Graf smiled at him. "Hair today, gone tomorrow, huh, Mr. Druce?"

Jack scooped up the dice and prepared to throw them again. As he did so, Solly put down the gleaming tokens that showed he was staking another twenty years.

"Solly!" called Jack.

Solly looked up. "Don't do it, Solly," Jack warned him, in a clear and youthful voice; although he found that he didn't really care too much whether Solly lost another twenty years or not. Look at the guy, he was practically dead already.

"Just throw, will you?" Solly growled at him.

Jack threw; and won; but Solly lost yet again, and so did two or three of the others at the table. Jack heard from Solly a sharp harsh intake of breath, and then Solly staggered, and gripped the edge of the table to stop himself from falling.

"Solly? You okay?"

Solly's eyes bulged and his face was blue from lack of oxygen. "What do you care?" he gasped. "Will you shoot, for God's sake? Just shoot!"

Mr. Graf was very young again, a small boy peering over the dimly lit center of the table. He said to Solly with utmost calmness, "Do you want an ambulance, sir? Or maybe I should call the house physician?"

"Shoot, that's all," Solly insisted, and placed another twenty years on the table.

Jack slowly juggled the dice. Fire and honey in his hand. "Solly . . . you understand what could happen if you lose?"

"Shoot," hissed Solly, through false teeth that were too large for his shrunken gums.

"Go on," urged Mr. Fortunato; although he too was ancient, with sunken ink-stained eyes and wispy white hair.

Jack shrugged, shook the dice, and threw.

Suddenly, the dice crackled with new vitality. They bounced on the opposite cushion, and tumbled across the table in a cascade of glowing Chinese images. They came to rest right in front of Solly.

Yama and Hsu Hao. Solly had lost.

"I—" he gargled. But traceries of light had already crept out of the dice, trembling and flickering like static electricity. They forked across the baize to the tips of Solly's fingers. Silently, enticingly—right in front of Jack's eyes—the lights crept up Solly's arms, and entwined themselves around him in a brilliant cage.

"*Solly!*" Jack shouted.

But Solly began to shudder uncontrollably. His hair was lifted up on end, and white sparks began to shower out of his nose and his eyes. He looked as if fierce fireworks had been ignited inside his head.

Jack heard a noise that was something like a sob and something like a scream, and then Solly collapsed onto his knees, although his fingers still clung to the edge of the table.

Twitching electricity streamed out of his body, shrinking down his arms and pouring out of his fingertips, back across the craps table and into the dice. They vanished into the Ghosts on the dice like disappearing rats' tails. Solly dropped backward onto the floor, his skull hitting the polished wood with a hollow knock.

The dice remained on the table, softly glowing, as if Solly's life had given them renewed energy.

"Well, Mr. Druce?" asked Nevvar Graf. "We're waiting."

Jack looked down at Solly's crumpled, dried-up body; and then at Nevvar Graf; and then back at the dice. The haunted circle of faces watched him expectantly.

Then—"No," said Jack. "That's it. I'm out."

"You still have five years on the table, Mr. Druce. You'll lose your five years. Rules of the game."

"I'm only twenty-two now. What do five years matter?"

Mr. Graf smiled. "Ask Mr. Fortunato what five years matter. It's an education, Beijing Craps. It teaches you that the time you throw away when you're young, you'll bitterly regret when you're old. Beijing Craps teaches you the value of life, Mr. Druce. What does a month matter, to a bored teenage kid? Nothing: he hopes that month will pass as soon as possible. But tell me what a month matters to a man with only one month left to live."

Jack took a deep, steadying breath. "Whatever, I'm out."

"You'll be back."

"Well, we'll just have to see about that."

"All right," shrugged Mr. Graf. "Carlos—will you escort Mr. Druce out of the casino? And make sure you pay him his winnings. Thank you, Mr. Druce. You have a rare skill with the ivories."

Jack changed back into his loose seersucker suit. Before he left, he nodded to the circle of players. One or two of them nodded back; but most of them seemed to have forgotten him already. Carlos took his arm, the first time that anybody in the casino had touched him, and he was led back out into the bright glittering world of the Golden Lode.

When he had cashed his winnings, he went across to the *punto banco* table. He watched the game for a while, considering a couple of bets. A bleached-blond girl standing next to him was screaming with excitement as she won her first hand. But after Beijing Craps, the idea of playing for money seemed absurdly petty. He glanced back toward the staircase that led up to Mr. Graf's private craps game. Carlos was still standing at the top of the stairs, and he smiled back at Jack with a smile like curdled milk.

Jack knew then that he would never escape. He would be back at that table, no matter how hard he tried to resist it. Maybe not tomorrow; maybe not next week; maybe not for years. But he would be back. No real gambler could resist the temptation of playing for his very life.

He left the Golden Lode and stepped out onto the hot, brilliantly bright sidewalk. He had started playing Beijing Craps at two o'clock in the morning, and now it was well past nine. For the first time in a long time, he felt hungry; and he decided to go back to his hotel room and shower and change, and then treat himself to a meal of prime rib and fried zucchini. He could wear his Armani suit, his *real* suit.

The sidewalk was crowded with shuffling tourists and squalling kids. Las Vegas wasn't what it used to be, back in the days of the mob. Bugsy Siegel would have rolled over in his desert grave to see crèches and stroller parks and family restaurants, and hookers being turned away from casino doors. But Jack didn't care. He had found himself the ultimate game, even in this sanitized Las Vegas, and he was twenty-seven again. He had forgotten how much strength and energy he used to have, at twenty-seven—how light and easy it was to walk.

He went up to his hotel room humming along to the Muzak in the elevator. *Raindrops keep fallin' on my head . . . they keep fallin' . . .* He boogied along the corridor, chafing his feet on the nylon carpet, so that when he reached out for his door handle, there was a sharp crackling spark of static.

To his surprise, however, his door was half-an-inch ajar. He hesitated, then pushed it wide. The room appeared to be empty, but you never knew. There were plenty of scumbags around who followed gamblers back to their hotel rooms, and forcibly relieved them of their winnings.

"Anybody there?" he called, stepping into the room. The bed was made, and there was no utility cart around, so it couldn't have been the maids. Maybe the door had been left open by accident. He went over to the bureau and tugged open the drawers. His gold cufflinks were still there; so was his Gucci ballpen and five hundred dollars in small bills.

He was just about to turn around and close the door, however, when he heard it softly click shut by itself. A voice said, "Freeze, buddy. Stay right where you are."

He stood up straight. In the mirror on top of the bureau, he saw a young man step out from behind the drapes, holding a handgun, .32 by the look of it, although Jack didn't know much about guns.

"Looking for some loose change?" the young man asked him.

"Maybe I should ask you the same question," Jack replied. The young man came around and faced him. He was pale and thin-faced and haggard, and he was dressed in worn-out denims.

"I'm not looking for trouble," he told Jack. "Maybe you should turn around and walk back out of that door and we'll forget the whole thing."

"I'm not going anyplace," Jack retorted. "This is my room."

"Unh-hunh," the young man grinned. "I know whose room this is. This is Mr. Druce's room, and you sure as hell aren't Mr. Druce."

"Of course I'm Mr. Druce. Who do you think I am?"

"Don't kid me," the young man told him, raising his pistol higher. "Mr. Druce just happens to be my father; and there's no way that *you're* my father, buddy."

Jack stared at him. "Mr. Druce is your *father?*"

The young man nodded. "You sound like you know him."

"Know him? I *am* him."

"Are you out of your tree or what?" the young man demanded. "You're not much older than me. How the hell can you be my father?"

"How the hell can you be my son?" Jack retorted. "My son is three years old."

"Oh, yes? Well, that's very interesting. But right now, I think you'd better *vamos,* don't you, before Mr. Druce gets back and finds you here."

Jack said, "Listen, I think we've gotten our lines crossed here. You must be looking for the wrong Mr. Druce. I'm Jack Druce, this is my room, and there's no way in the world that you can be my son, because look—"

Jack reached inside his suit for his wallet, and his Kodak photograph of Roddy by the pool. But the young man instantly cocked his handgun, and tensed up, and said, "Freeze! Freeze! Keep your hands where I can see them!"

"But if I showed you—" Jack began.

The young man screamed *"Freeze!"* at him, and fired. The bullet hit Jack in the right side of his head, and burst out through the back of his skull. Blood and brains were thrown against the yellow flock wallpaper.

Jack thought, *He's killed me. I can't believe it. The punk's gone and killed me.* He opened and closed his mouth, and then his knees folded up under him and he collapsed onto the floor.

The hotel room dwindled away from him like a lighted television picture falling down an endless elevator shaft.

Shaking, the young man hunkered down beside him, and reached into his blood-spattered coat for his wallet. He flicked through it. Over ten thousand dollars in thousand-dollar bills. Jesus. This guy must've made a killing on the tables.

He found a creased Kodak photograph of a small boy next to a swimming pool. He stared at it for a long time. For some inexplicable reason, he found it disturbingly familiar. Must be the guy's son. It was weird, the way that he'd kept on insisting that his name was Jack Druce.

The young man stood up, unsure of what to do next. He couldn't wait here for his father any longer; and he didn't really have to. He'd only come to Las Vegas to ask him for money, and now he had all the money he could possibly want.

He crammed the bills into the pocket of his denim jacket, and stuffed his handgun back into the top of his jeans. He took one last look at the man lying dead on the carpet, and then he left.

He walked along the sidewalk glancing at every middle-aged man who passed him by. He wondered if he would recognize his father if he ever chanced to meet him. He wondered if his father would recognize him.

He passed the Golden Lode Casino, and standing on the steps outside was a young boy, no more than seven years old, wrapped in a black Chinese robe. The young boy was smiling to himself, almost beatifically, as if he were a god.

Roderick Druce smiled at him, and the boy smiled back.

BERNARD TAYLOR

Samhain

Wearing her track suit, Doris stood gasping for breath as the lift took her up to the fifth floor, the top of the apartment building. A minute later at the door of the flat she discovered that she'd come out without her keys and she rang the bell and waited impatiently for Arthur to answer. Then at last, after the fourth ring, the door was opened. She helped it aside with an angry shove and stepped into the hall.

"Arthur," she gasped (she still hadn't got her breath back), "didn't you hear me ringing?"

He shook his head. "No, I'm sorry, dear; I was in the bedroom going through my underwear. You know—I think I need to get some more."

"You need to get a hearing aid, that's what you need." With her words she turned away and strode into the kitchen where she poured herself a glass of water. She would have liked a Coke but there was no sense in half killing yourself to take off a few pounds and then put it all straight back on again. As she stood there slowly sipping the water Arthur came to the open doorway and stood looking at her with the inane smile that always infuriated her so.

"How was the running?" he asked.

Her answer was clipped, cold. "If you mean the jogging, it was fine."

"Yes. Yes, of course—jogging." He nodded. "I have to hand it to you —you've got more energy than I have. If *I* tried a run round the park I'd be dead before I got halfway."

It's a pity you don't try it then, a voice inside her head snapped, *and save me all the trouble you're putting me to.* She kept silent, though, and turned and rinsed the empty glass under the tap.

As she dried the glass and put it away Arthur said solicitously, "I'll bet you're hungry, are you? Would you like me to make you some breakfast?"

"You?" She looked at him with contempt. "You know very well you're useless in the kitchen. You're as incompetent there as you are everywhere else." She paused. "Besides, I'm trying to lose weight, you know that. I've got some pride—even if you haven't."

He looked hurt. "What does that mean?"

"It means it wouldn't hurt *you* to lose a few pounds, either. You do know what this weekend is, don't you?"

He nodded. "Of course. The thirty-first. Halloween."

"*Halloween?*" There was disgust in her tone. "Yes, that's what *they* call it, those idiots out there." She gestured with an impatient hand, taking in the rest of the world. "*I* prefer to call it by its proper name."

"Samhain?"

"Of *course* Samhain."

"All right—Samhain—but so what?"

She made a short, mocking sound of derision. "*So what? he asks. So what?* Maybe it doesn't bother you, the thought of stripping off and dancing around in the nude in front of all our friends. Maybe you don't give it a second thought. Maybe you're happy with your body the way it is. If so, then you've got a lot to be happy about—because there's a lot of it. Personally, if it were me, I'd want to do something about it."

He frowned. "Oh, come on, Doris, what can I do about it? I'm fifty-six years old. I'm not a young man anymore. Besides, there'll be plenty there older than I am. Plenty." He looked hurt and she gave a sigh.

"Oh—forget it, Arthur. I won't say anything else. It doesn't make any difference anyway. You never listen."

She pushed past him and went into the lounge where she flopped down into her easy chair, took off her shoes, put her feet up on the footstool and closed her eyes. After a few moments she heard him come into the room, and then she heard his voice again, irritatingly considerate as always:

"Are you asleep?"

Without opening her eyes she said, "Of course I'm not asleep."

"I just wondered." A pause. "Would you like a cup of coffee?"

She opened her eyes, about to say no, then gave a grudging shrug. "Yes, why not. If you think you can manage it."

"Doris, of course I can manage it." He started off across the room. "You want it black?"

"Of course black. I always have it black."

"Yes, of course."

She turned her head and watched his thick, heavy body move through the doorway, then she sighed, got to her feet and stretched. There was a mirror near the window and she stepped in front of it and looked at herself. She didn't look at all bad for her forty-three years, she thought. And holding herself like this—erect and with her stomach drawn in—she looked *years* younger. Trouble was, it was impossible to sustain the effort. You forgot, and with the forgetting everything sagged again. She must get into the habit of holding herself well; work on her posture as well as everything else. After all, soon she'd be free again . . .

As she looked at her reflection she thought again of the thirty-first. Tomorrow. Everything depended on tomorrow. Tomorrow would see the end to her problems and the beginning of a new life. And the day would bring other bonuses too: at the meeting she'd see that young male witch, the new initiate from Lyddiard, Steve Walker. She hadn't seen him since the initiation ceremony back at the end of April, the Feast of Beltane, but she remembered him well enough: tall, tanned, good-looking and with an obvious taste for older women. Not that she regarded herself as old, Satan forbid, but when he was only in his late twenties one had to acknowledge the age difference. Thinking of him now she remembered how he had smiled at her—and in such a very special way. He'd had his clothes on then, of course, but even so they hadn't been able to disguise the firmness, the clean, muscular lines of his body. Not like Arthur with his pale flab.

She pictured Arthur as he'd be at the dance—as usual making a complete idiot of himself. Some people had no dignity at all. Well, at least *she* knew how to go on. And when *she* danced nobody was going to snigger or look the other way. With the thought she did a couple of steps in front of the mirror. It looked good—and *she* looked pretty good too—a damned sight better than that stupid Shirley Goldberg. Sure Shirley Goldberg's figure was a lot firmer and more up-together these days—but so it should be—she'd spent enough on cosmetic surgery. And it showed, of course. There was no way of disguising those scars. Those scars—good Satan, in the cold weather Shirley Goldberg looked as if she'd been pressed against a wire fence.

Arthur came back into the room then and she sat down and took the cup of coffee he handed her. Looking down at it, she said impatiently, "I said *black*, Arthur. Can't you ever get anything right?"

As he moved back to the kitchen with the offending cup of coffee she reflected on her loathing of him. And it would never change now, she knew that—which was one reason she had decided to get rid of him and look out for a newer model. Well, she had to. They couldn't go on as they were. With him around she had no future at all. Oh, yes, she could leave him, of course— but what good would that do? She'd just be giving up her home in this flat to go and find someplace on her own—and someplace not nearly as comfortable—and almost certainly she'd have to get a job of some kind too. No, she couldn't afford to leave Arthur—and as she couldn't bear the thought of continuing to live with him either, then there was only one thing to be done.

Which she was in the process of taking care of right now. And so much trouble it was, too. She had never dreamed. All those sessions in the coven's library for a start, doing all that research. It was mind-blowingly tedious—but it was the only way to do things, she had no doubt of that.

Thinking of the library, she thought of the books she'd been studying. It hadn't been easy getting access to them. It had surprised her just how closely they were guarded. She had told the coven librarian that she was taking a degree course on the ancient arts. And he had believed her, the fool. She remembered his grave expression as he had brought the old, leather-bound volumes and placed them before her. "Be careful with them, won't you?" he had said. "And do remember that they mustn't be taken out of this room. We wouldn't want them falling into the wrong hands, would we? If that happened, there's no telling where the mischief would stop."

Mischief. *Mischief*—it seemed such a pathetic little word when applied to the act of murder. Not that anyone was going to construe it as murder. It would be put down to heart failure. Simple. She smiled to herself. And now her researches were finished, and she had all the answers she wanted. And now, too, she had the stone and the nail. And this evening she'd have the clay portrait as well.

After a few moments Arthur approached with a fresh cup of coffee —black this time—in his hand. As she took it from him she said, "I'll be out this evening, you haven't forgotten that, have you?"

"Oh, yes, of course." He nodded. "Your art class. I wasn't sure that you'd still be going—what with the feast and everything tomorrow."

Still going? "Of course I'm still going," she said witheringly. Wild horses wouldn't keep her away.

"How are you getting on?" he asked.

"Fine. I'm getting on fine."

"You must really enjoy it, your clay modeling—these past few weeks you've been so keen."

She shrugged. "Yes—I do enjoy it."

"Maybe I could come with you one evening. It might be interesting."

She tried to picture him in the art studio, making a hash of everything. What an embarrassment he would be. "Oh, I don't think it would appeal to you at all," she said.

"Oh . . . What are you making?"

"This and that."

"What, exactly?"

"I've been modeling a figure."

"All this time? Just one? It must be huge."

"No—it's quite small."

"But it's been weeks."

"I've been trying to get it right."

"I see. And are you nearly there, you think?"

"Nearly there. This evening it'll be finished."

"Well, that's nice."

Well, that's nice, the voice in her head mimicked. *You wouldn't think it was so nice if you knew whose figure I was modeling, you old fool.* She wondered for a moment how he would react if she told him that the model was of *him* . . . She frowned momentarily at the thought of her work in the class. Getting his likeness had proved so difficult. It would have been easy if she had some real artistic ability— but she hadn't and that was it. Anyway, after several poor starts she'd been getting on better over the past few sessions and now, this evening, at last, it would be done.

The idea for the clay model was one of the things she'd got from her researches in the library. Not that such means were that secret. On the contrary, she supposed it must be one of the most commonly known methods of disposing of someone. Even so, however, she didn't intend relying on some half-baked old wives' tales handed down; she meant to get it right—which was why she'd gone to the experts.

And that, too, was why she had chosen the thirty-first—that was the day when the spells would be at their most potent. Strange, really, she thought, most people today had no idea what the day really meant— and what it had meant since early times. *Samhain*—that was the real meaning of the thirty-first of October. Samhain, one of the two great witches' festivals of the year—a celebration of fire and the dead and the powers of darkness. In the modern world the thirty-first was generally recognized only as All Hallows' Eve, and celebrated only by children with turnip lanterns, silly masks, games and dressing up. Still, it could be worse, she supposed; in America they made even more nonsense out of the whole thing with their ridiculous trick-or-treating. Huh—if any children came to *her* door carrying bags of flour or whatever and begging for sweets, they'd get something they weren't prepared for, the little monsters. Mind you, that's what came from too much civilization. Thank Satan England hadn't gone *that* far—*yet.* Though it probably would in time. They did say that what America had one day England got the next.

When she was out of the shower and dry again she moved to a chest and opened the bottom drawer. From a small cardboard box she withdrew a long, rusty nail and a large, smooth stone. With these and the clay image she had no doubt of success. They'd be enough to kill Arthur ten times over.

That evening at art class she finished the clay model and carefully placed it in the small box she had brought with her for the purpose. As she did so the instructor, a tall woman with a face like a dispossessed spaniel, came to her, looked over her shoulder and said, "All done, then, Mrs. Armstrong?"

"Yes, all done."

"I'm curious," the instructor said, "as to what you want it for . . ."

Doris turned to her and gave a bleak smile. "Are you?" She put the lid on the box and sealed it with tape. Let the stupid woman be curious; she wasn't going to satisfy her curiosity. What was more, she wouldn't be coming back to the class after this evening; there'd be no need to.

That night as she lay awake in bed thinking of tomorrow and the festival she could hear Arthur's snoring through the wall. That was something else she wouldn't have to put up with for much longer. Just a little while and he'd never snore again.

The thirty-first. It had rained during the night but the morning was clear, bright and promising.

Over the breakfast table Arthur, as usual, was clearly unhappy about his eggs, and she watched, secretly pleased, as he pushed them to one side. "Aren't you going to eat your eggs?" she said.

He frowned. "You know I don't like them like this, Doris," he said. "I tell you every morning and next day they're just the same. Sometimes I think you just don't make the effort."

She looked at him over her coffee cup, hating him. She was glad that his scrambled eggs were like rubber. Glad. If he'd been pleased with them she'd have been disappointed. And he was wrong to say that she didn't make the effort. She *did*. She had to have ways of showing her loathing for him and the eggs were one of those ways. "I worked hard to prepare those eggs for you," she said reproachfully.

After a few moments under her glare he pulled the plate back before him. "I'll try to eat a little," he murmured.

She watched then as he braced himself and dug a fork into the solid yellow mass. Added to his incompetence he had no guts, either. What a wimp. Any other man would have thrown the mess at the wall— which was what it deserved. Not Arthur, though; he put up with it. All the inedible food she had served up to him every morning for the past twenty years, and he accepted it all, ate it all. Her contempt for him grew.

When the evening came she went into her bedroom and took from the box the small clay figure. Then she put on her coat, took her door key and went quietly out of the room. A short ride down in the lift and a few minutes later she was leaving the foyer and stepping out into the late October evening. Moving to the garden behind the apartment block, she stepped over the grass to the ornamental pool where water cascaded into its center from a little waterfall. She had always despised it so, this pathetic little attempt at re-creating nature; now she wouldn't have changed it for anything.

At the side of the pool she looked around, eyes glancing up at the windows of the overlooking flats. She could see no one looking out at her. Then, carefully unwrapping the little clay figure, she stepped closer to the edge of the pool, leaned over and placed the figure on the lip of the waterfall. The water surging over the stone was icy cold. She pressed the figure firmly onto the stone, wedging it in. Then, satisfied that it was secure, she stepped back and looked at it. As she did so she thought of the words she had read in the book in the coven library: *Make ye a picture of clay, like unto the shape of thine enemy, and then, on the night of Samhain or Beltane place it in a running stream till it be worn away.* Well, it was in a running stream now—and it wasn't going to last long by the looks of things; already, even as she watched, the limbs were beginning to crumble . . .

Back upstairs she went straight to her room and began to get ready.

Well before nine o'clock she was dressed and eager to get away. Emerging from her room she came to a stop before the hall mirror and put down her bag—heavier this evening—and made a last survey of her appearance. She had taken great trouble with her makeup, and she had been to the hairdresser just that afternoon. She'd hardly eaten all day, either, and felt about as slim as she had felt in a long while. Under her floor-length deep-blue velvet cloak, her warm ceremonial robe fell to her ankles. Beneath it she wore nothing. She was ready. Now if only Arthur would hurry up, they could get going.

"Arthur?" she shouted in the direction of his bedroom. "Come on, will you? We're going to be late."

When he appeared a few minutes later she shook her head in exasperation. "I thought you were getting ready," she said.

"I *am* ready."

"But—you've got your Burberry on."

"I know."

"You don't mean to say you're going in that, do you?"

"Why not? I shall take it off when we get there."

"You'll take it off *now*. You can't go there looking like that. Where's your cloak? All the others will arrive in cloaks."

"Oh, Doris, for Luci's sake—I can't stand that cloak. Every year I wear it, and I feel like an idiot."

"Well, you'll look like an idiot in *that*. And how d'you think *I'm* going to feel? Of course that doesn't matter to you, does it?—showing me up. And stop blaspheming—I keep telling you!" She continued to glare at him. "Well, I'm not going with you looking like that, so you can just go and put on your cloak."

After a moment's hesitation he went away. When he came back a couple of minutes later Doris still wasn't happy. "What's up with your cloak?" she asked, frowning. "It's not hanging right. You look like a badly tied bag of laundry."

He shrugged. "Well—it's probably my underwear."

"You're wearing *underwear?*"

"Two sets."

"Tell me you're joking."

"What's wrong? I shall be cold. It's not *that* warm, in case you hadn't noticed. I don't want to catch pneumonia."

"You talk as if this were the Dark Ages. Haven't you ever heard of central heating? The Goldbergs' house will be very warm and comfortable. And we shan't be outside for more than a minute or so. For Hell's sake, go and take it off at once."

"Oh, Doris, must I?"

"Of course you must. Oh, my Lord, what a picture! Everybody else dancing around in the total nude and you in your Fruit of the Loom Y-fronts. It makes me shudder to think of it." She shook her head. "You don't take any of this seriously, do you?"

"Satan Almighty, Doris," he sighed, "we go through this every year. If you want the truth, I'd much rather stay home tonight and watch TV."

"Yes, that's all you're fit for. Look at you—a descendent of one of the greatest witches who ever lived and now, tonight of all nights, instead of wanting to go and celebrate our main festival you'd rather stay in and watch TV. And *stop blaspheming.*" She glared at him for a second, then turned, opened the door and strode toward the lift.

The Goldbergs, who were hosting the festival this year, were long-time members of the coven and lived in wide grounds in the heart of the countryside some miles west of Trowbridge. Arthur had wanted to drive but after experiencing a little difficulty getting the car out of the garage Doris had ordered him out of the driver's seat. "My Lord, how can you be so *incompetent!*" she'd snapped as she got behind the wheel. They set off then and got there just after ten, and as Doris steered the Ford Capri along the drive she saw ahead of her a large number of other cars. A rough count gave a number somewhere above forty. She was pleased and her excitement took another surge.

She kept very close to the edge of the driveway as she pulled the car to a stop. A moment later Arthur opened the door, looked down and groaned. "Can't you move it out a little, Doris? It's so muddy here; I'll mess up my shoes."

Doris had known exactly what she was doing and she just shook her head and sighed a long-suffering sigh. "Oh, Arthur, stop being such a damned wimp, will you." She switched off the ignition, got out of the car and started off toward the front of the house. Arthur caught up with her just as she reached the front door where the porch was brightly illuminated by colorful lanterns.

The door was opened by Ralph Goldberg, dressed in a long robe with a gold-colored sash tied loosely at the place where his waist used to be. He greeted them with smiles and words of welcome, at the same time raising his right hand above his head, thumb and pinky extended, in a salute to the devil. Doris repeated the gesture—as did Arthur in a halfhearted way—then they were taking off their outer garments and putting them into Ralph's arms. After that they moved through the hall into the main lounge where the rest of the party revelers were congregated.

"Shall we be sacrificing any chickens?" Steve Walker asked. "I hope so. I've been looking forward to that." He, Shirley Goldberg and Doris were standing together in the center of the crowd of chattering people with glasses of mulled wine in their hands. At his question Shirley shook her head.

"No, I'm afraid not. Ralph got the order in too late and there weren't any available. All they had left were dead ones—fresh or frozen. We could have got some live turkeys but I couldn't face the thought of being faced with eating turkey for days on end afterward. It's bad enough at Christmas when you have to keep up appearances."

The party was well on and Doris was looking forward to the dance and then to being alone with Steve. She hadn't really had a chance to talk to him so far—not with Shirley Goldberg and other people milling around all the time. It wouldn't be long now, though, she thought. For the moment, however, Shirley was holding the reins and, in her customary name-dropping way, was holding the floor too—and was obviously out to impress.

"I got in touch with Joan last night," she was saying.

"Joan?" Doris asked. "Joan who?"

"Joan who? Joan of Arc, of course."

"Oh, that Joan. How was she?"

"Still very bitter."

"Well, it's understandable, isn't it?"

Shirley nodded. "Very bitter. I told her—you ought to get some kind of counseling—or therapy. I mean, it's eating away at her. Though I suppose it's to be expected after what they did to her. Some people—they've got a lot to answer for."

"Right."

"Mind you, in many ways she only had herself to blame—and I as good as told her so. I mean, once you start admitting that you're hearing voices, then people are going to get your number pretty damn quick. Sure to. Still, she had a hard time, there's no denying, and it was rotten luck on her—being set up like that—being made to carry the can for the inefficiency of our armies. Still, she should have kept her mouth shut. If she'd done that, she could be alive today."

"I suppose you're right."

"Of course I'm right. There are procedures that have to be adhered to. You can't go yelling your mouth off and going about things in a half-assed way. You've got to do things *right*. . . ."

Shirley's voice droned on while Doris repeated her words: *You've got to do things right. Right*—and that's how *she* was doing things.

Turning slightly, she saw Arthur sitting near the window in conversation with Thelma Winnecky, a young, blond widow from Purton. Then, glancing above Arthur's head, she saw through the window Ralph Goldberg on the lawn setting light to the bonfire. She looked at her watch. Eleven forty-five. The dancing would start very soon. She hadn't much time.

"Will you excuse me for a moment, please . . . ?" She smiled at Shirley—who was still in full flood—and briefly pressed Steve's hand. Then, turning, she moved from the room.

In the cloakroom near the front door she took from her bag the large, smooth, pale stone she had brought and, with her nail file, carefully scratched Arthur's name upon it. Then she put it back into the bag along with the nail, put on her cloak and went out into the hall, where she opened the front door and slipped out into the night.

Moving swiftly, she walked out onto the drive where the cars were parked. When she got to the Ford she stepped carefully over to the near-side door and, taking a small torch from her purse, shone its beam down at the spot where Arthur had stepped (so complainingly, the wimp!) onto the soft, muddy earth of the verge. And—yes!—very clearly the light picked out the shape of his footprints. Three of them, two right and one left—and as cleanly indented as if he'd worked at it. She smiled, reached back into her bag and took out the nail and the stone.

Holding the nail up against the dull light of the sky, she looked at it. It appeared to be just an ordinary, if rather old-fashioned, nail. It was *not* ordinary, though, and it had cost a bomb—not to mention the difficulty she'd had in getting hold of it. Well, it wasn't something you could get in the local supermarket or even in some fancy ironmonger's shop. What did you do—walk in and say, "I'd like one coffin nail, please?" No, she'd had to go to some old hag of a witch in Frome and pay a fortune—in cash. Cash on the nail, so to speak.

Anyway, she'd got the nail—and it would be worth it, every penny. After a quick glance around she carefully placed the nail's point into the indented heel of Arthur's left footprint, then with the stone she hammered it into the ground. *On the night of Samhain take ye a naile from a coffin that has been buried in the earth,* the book had said, *and put it in the footprint of thy foe. Very soon thereafter thy foe shall sicken and perish.* The nail went in easily; the soil was quite soft. She straightened and looked down. No sign of it. She smiled, turned and moved away.

She didn't reenter the house straightaway but went round to the back where Ralph Goldberg was tending the fire and feeding it with wood. As he did so it crackled and blazed and shot out sparks and made swift moving shadows against the backcloth of the house. He looked around at her and smiled as she approached. "Came out to get a breath of air, did you, Doris?" he asked.

She nodded, returning his smile. "Yes—and to see how it's all going."

"Oh, we'll be ready in a minute." He threw on more wood. "I want to get a good blaze going first. We don't want anyone to catch cold."

"Right." It was funny how things had changed over the years, she thought. Everyone was so comfort-conscious today. In the old days they'd have danced naked round the fire, either till the fire went out or till they dropped. Not now; now the actual dance around the fire was only a token thing—a quick dash naked out into the chill air, link hands and dance around the fire a couple of times and then back indoors to finish the celebrations in the warm.

Ralph glanced at his watch, adjusted a burning log on the fire and gave a nod of satisfaction. "I think we might as well start now." He moved off toward the patio door, then paused briefly and looked back. "Aren't you coming in to disrobe . . . ?"

"Yes, in a minute—I'll be right there." As she spoke she put out her hands toward the heat of the flames and then turned to watch as he went on into the house.

As soon as he had gone she dipped her right hand into her bag and took out the stone. In the flickering light of the fire she looked at it. Arthur's name stood out clearly. *(Choose thy time with care, then take ye a stone, writ with the name of thine adversary . . .)* A quick glance toward the patio window and she took a step forward. (. . . *and place it in fire. . . .)* She muttered a little prayer, took a breath and cast the stone into the heart of the flames.

And it was done. Everything was done. All she had to do now was wait. And she wouldn't have to wait very long. Within twelve hours of the hour of midnight Arthur would be dead.

She sat at the breakfast bar in the Goldbergs' kitchen drinking coffee. She had been there for a long time. There had been no sign of Arthur for a long while and she sat tense and expectant, waiting at any moment for someone to come in and say that he was dead, had been found lying dead in one of the Goldbergs' many spare bedrooms or on some sofa in some other part of the house. It looked as if he'd had a heart attack, they would say, and she would cry and try to look brave in the face of her great tragedy.

The thought should have cheered her more than it did. Oh, yes, she was glad, very glad, when she thought of Arthur getting out of her hair, out of her life at last, but when she thought of Steve Walker it was another matter. She'd seen hardly anything of him after their chat over cocktails and the dance around the fire. He had been close to her then as they'd all circled the crackling flames, and the grasp of his hand in hers had been firm and full of promise. But soon afterward he had just vanished. Then, later, wandering about the huge house alone, she had come upon two people in a room, lying together on a rug, limbs threshing, their movements accompanied by groans and sighs and muttered words. She'd backed out, but not before she had realized who the two were. One was Steve, she was sure. And the other? No mistaking that voice. Shirley Goldberg.

Later, while nursing a coffee, her disappointment and her anger, she'd put her robe back on; there didn't seem much point in doing otherwise. There was no one else around now—the others had all gone off long since to different rooms, either in pairs or groups of three, four, five or six. Now, sitting in the kitchen she turned at the sound of approaching footsteps and braced herself for the news. The door opened.

"*Arthur . . .*" She gaped at him.

He looked a little sheepish. "Ah—there you are. I was wondering."

Then her bitterness at the evening's disappointment flared up. "Where the hell have you been?" she rapped out.

"Been? I haven't been anywhere."

She shook her head in contempt and exasperation. "Well—I want to go home. I've had enough."

"But they'll be serving breakfast soon."

"I don't want any breakfast. I just want to go home." She waited, then when he didn't move she said, "Didn't you hear me? I said I want to go home."

He looked at her, sighed and nodded. "Yes, dear. Whatever you say."

They slipped away without saying their good-byes to anyone, and when they got outside she left Arthur for a moment, went round to the back of the house and looked at the remains of the bonfire. Now it was just a pile of cold ashes. Poking into it with a stick, she uncovered the stone she had put there last night. Bending, she picked it up, blew off the dust and looked at it closely. And suddenly she felt a little touch of pleasure in the midst of her frustration and dissatisfaction. On the stone there was not a sign of Arthur's name. *(If the fire shall destroy the name then so shall the owner of that name be destroyed. . . .)* The name had been burned clean away. With a little smile she dropped the stone back into the ashes and went to join Arthur where he sat waiting in the car.

When they got back to Stratton she put the car away while Arthur went on upstairs. She didn't follow him immediately, but first went toward the communal garden in the center of which lay the ornamental pool and the little waterfall. When she reached the pool she looked at the lip of the stone over which the water ran and saw that there was no trace left of the clay figure. It was gone, without trace. The water had completely worn it away.

And all at once the depression that had hung over her since Steve's betrayal was lifted. What did it matter, anyway? He meant nothing to her. And there were plenty of other men in the world. And soon, very soon, with Arthur gone, she would be free to play the field. She looked at her watch. Just after six. There was very little time to go now. It could happen at any moment. She turned and looked up toward the windows of the flat. "Arthur," she whispered, "your hours are numbered."

Upstairs in the flat she pushed open his bedroom door and found him getting ready for bed. He turned to her and gave a little shrug. "I thought I'd just have a nap for a while . . ."

Hiding the elation that was growing within her, she took in the look of exhaustion on his face and said, "Don't you want any breakfast?" After all, she said to herself, every condemned man was entitled to a good breakfast.

He shook his head. "No, thanks. I'm feeling very tired. I'm too old for all those goings-on. Staying up all night, cavorting around. I think I'll give it a miss next year."

You certainly will, Doris thought, then aloud she said, "Didn't you get any sleep at the Goldbergs'? There were enough beds."

"Oh, I dozed a bit," he said. "But nothing much." He climbed into bed and pulled the covers up over him. "But I think I'll sleep now all right."

She stayed there in the room until he was settled and then crept out into the hall. After a while she began to move around the flat doing odd little chores—for no other reason than simply to keep herself occupied. Then after a while she crept to his bedroom, silently pushed open the door and looked in. The curtains were drawn against the light, but in the gloom she could hear the sound of his breathing. The suspense was unbearable. When was it going to happen?

Later, just before eleven, she quietly went back into his room and in the half-light stood listening to the sound of his breathing. It sounded strange: slow and faint, with touches of harshness as if the breaths came with difficulty. She moved closer to the bed and looked down at him. His flesh had a grayish look about it—a dead look. She called his name but he made no response. Carefully she reached in beneath the bed cover, located his wrist and felt his pulse. Sweet Lord, it was only just discernible—only the faintest little flutter there.

Letting him go, she stepped back from the bed. Now all she had to do was wait. Smiling, she turned and left the room.

Taking the morning paper into the sitting room, she settled in her favorite chair. It was impossible to concentrate, though, and in the end she just gave in to the warm, sparkling thoughts that crowded her mind and, closing her eyes, she laid back her head and let the thoughts take over.

A sudden sound brought her head toward the door, and she realized that she had been sleeping.

Arthur was standing there in his dressing gown. He smiled at her. "You should have gone to bed and had a real nap, like I did," he said. "You look as if you could do with it."

She gaped at him, speechless. When she had found her voice she said, "How do you feel?"

He nodded, smiling. "Oh, much better now after my rest."

"That's good," she murmured. "You look better."

She gazed at him, realizing that her words were true—he *did* look better. So much better. For one thing his color was better than it had been for years—and also he seemed to be holding himself so much straighter—and she saw too an unaccustomed suppleness in his movement as he turned, stepped toward the window, opened it and breathed in the fresh air.

"Now," he said, turning to smile back at her, "I could really eat some breakfast."

She nodded and, almost in a daze, got up and started off toward the kitchen, Arthur walking behind her. "I've already mixed the eggs," he said. "I just have to finish them off."

"No, *I'll* do it," she retorted quickly.

"I really don't mind, Doris. Honestly."

She had reached the kitchen table now and she turned back to face him. She had never hated him so much. Scathingly she said, *"You'll* do it, Arthur? *You?"* She laughed. "Dear Hell, the most inefficient, incompetent man this side of the English Channel. I should let *you* loose in my kitchen? That'll be the day."

Ten minutes later she moved to the breakfast table, where she placed before him a plate of scrambled eggs. Then, setting down in her own place the two lightly boiled eggs she had prepared so perfectly, she sat and began to eat.

As she ate—without looking at him—she waited for him to complain. There was silence, though, and at last she lifted her head and gazed at him. He sat there, very still, just looking down at his plate. And, dear Satan, he looked better than he had for ages. Nothing had worked—not the clay image, nor the coffin nail nor the stone. But how could it be? She had done everything exactly according to the book. Or at least she had tried to. Then what had gone wrong? Was it that the name on the stone hadn't quite disappeared in the fire? Was it that the nail she had bought hadn't come from a coffin? Was it that the clay model hadn't been quite faithful enough in its likeness? Or was it perhaps because there had been no live chickens at the festival and therefore no blood had been spilled . . . ? The questions went on churning through her mind. Whatever had happened, though, it hadn't worked. He was still here.

Thrusting the thoughts, the questions from her mind, she waited for him to speak, to say something about the eggs. Yet still he said nothing. That wasn't like him; and this time she had truly excelled herself; there was no way that anyone could eat the food she had put before him. Every bit of her seething hatred and frustration had gone into its preparation. He had to react soon.

And then, as she watched him he gave a little sigh, pushed the empty plate away from him, got up from the table and moved toward the kitchen. "What's the matter?" she called after him. "You feel sick?"

When he came back a few seconds later she turned to him as he approached. He had a weird, calm look about him that she had never seen before. And suddenly she was afraid. "Arthur," she said, "don't look at me like that."

"I've told you, Doris," he said, shaking his head, "I've told you over and over again—I don't like my eggs like that."

Calmly, he raised the hatchet in his right hand and brought it down.

Very efficiently, more than competently, and without an ounce of wasted effort, he split her skull from crown to jaw with one clean downward blow. Then, aiming the ax from the side, he struck a second time and severed her head from her neck.

Later, when he had cleaned up the mess, he beat up more eggs and scrambled them the way he liked.

TANITH LEE

The Mermaid

(From an original idea by Anne Page)

Michael was a quiet man with never much to say for himself. He worked at his father's ironmongery business, which the old dad was now too frail to see to, and had taken on some new lines in hammer and nails and paint, which pleased the weekenders, who want their cottages all colors, and to hang up their trophy knickknacks, their shells and dried weeds, and other dead hard things from out of the sea. It was the sea was the thing with Michael, too, for though he would never tell you of it, she had bewitched him. As a child he was always on the shores climbing among the steep caves, fishing off the Rock, or just sitting staring away out to where there is nothing, mind you, but what the inner eye and the heart imagine. And it was the sea that gave to Michael the one long speech I ever heard him make.

I had known him since we were children in the village. And when I came back from the city, soul-sore and drinking down a bottle a day, he was the first thing I saw that I knew, as I walked from the train along the street. "Hallo, Michael," I said, "how are you doing?" And Michael nodded and said to me, "I'm going along," as if he had only met me that morning, when it had been three years and more.

I began my writing then, up in the room over the Widow's bakery, and for all I was told *Watch out for the Widow,* she did me no harm except in the pastry way, fattening me up. But it got me off the drink, so maybe it was not so bad a bargain.

And as I sought my path back into the village, and they stopped their jibes about the city and the stranger, I saw Michael here and there, in his father's shop, and in the pub sometimes of an evening, where I drank my two halves slow as cream, or walking along the shore at dusk, by the snow-blue water and under the ashy rose-petal sky, not gray, not pink, clearer than a washed glass, that only the sea knows how to bring.

But Michael, as I say, was no talker. He would stand his round, he would play his game of cards, he would put on the odd bet, he would help you if you needed an item or two and had not the cash, and once, when one of the holiday couples lost a dog, it was Michael went down and found it under the Rock, and brought it in his arms. And when the woman held out a bright leaf of money, Michael turned it gently aside.

But he would neither converse nor confide, not Michael. Nor he never married. And he was a nice-looking man, dark and blue-eyed and not yet much above forty. He could have had three or four but they had given up on him and taken elsewhere. There was never any idea, mind, that Michael had other tastes. He had even courted a girl, when he was a boy, but nothing came of it.

And then, when I had been back a year, there came the storm.

It waked me at three in the morning. I had forgotten how it would sound, the sea, when she was angry.

I stood in the window and looked down the village to the shore, and there were the great waves like spiked combs and the sky tearing at them, and this sound of guns the water makes, and the tall thunder, and the lightning flash like a knife. It filled me with terror and joy, and I put on my clothes and my boots and went out, and in the street I came on others, drawn forth as I had been as if by a powerful cry. We spoke of what boats might be out and if they had got to safety, but there was a primeval thing upon us, that had nothing to do with human sympathy or care. And in the end I went on down the street, past the pub, which had opened itself up again, and through the lane to the Rock.

And when I reached the place, the wind was rending and it was like the edge of chaos, so I stood there drunk as I had not been now in eleven months, with my mouth open, half-blinded, until I saw Michael was there before me, down along the Rock where the spray was coming up and the water ran black as oil. He stood with his feet planted, looking out.

"Come back a way, Michael," I called, "she'll have you off, man, and into all that."

He turned and looked at me, and I saw he had my face, my drunkard's face, and suddenly he grinned and he said, "Had me she already has."

But then a great bomb of water burst against the Rock. I saw him go to his knees and I dashed forward, afraid he would be lugged over and lost. But he was not and he and I pulled away from the edge together.

"You've the right of it," he said, when we stood back drenched on the track. "For she's greedy tonight."

There are moments when you foretell suddenly a man will speak to you, that there is something lodged in his spirit, and now it will be shown. It may be a diamond or a severed head and there is no means to guess, but you must not gainsay him. Not for your own hope, you must not. And so it was with Michael now. For he waited by me, and he said, "I could do with a drink if Alec has the bar open." And then, making no move, he said, "You're a writer, you could write it down maybe."

"Write down what, Michael?"

"The mermaid."

So too when he puts the diamond or the hacked head before you, you do not say to him, *Bloody rot, man.*

"A mermaid is it?" I said. "I always dreamed there were such things."

"I dreamed it," he said, "since I was a boy, and the dad told me stories." His lashes were strung with water so I could not see his eyes to be sure of them. We huddled into a lee of the Rock. It was the pub our flesh wanted, the warmth and the lamplight and the company, if not the liquor. But our souls kept us there in the loud corner of the storm. We could not go away, not yet, till he was done.

"When I was sixteen it was," he said at last, under the scream of the wind. The glass waves smashed upon his voice but could not drown him out. That is how it is when a man must speak to you. Though he whisper in the whirlwind, you will hear, like Job, or Moses on the mountain.

His brain, Michael said, was once full of fantasies, daydreams, and there were night-dreams too, very rich and beautiful, often remembered, all to do with the sea. It had been that way with him since he was a child, and his father told him sea-yarns of his fishing days, and some wonderful lies besides, which to the child were no more than a proper truth, as perhaps in a sort they are. There were cities under the ocean, of coral and crystal and nacre, and great beasts like dragons that could swallow up a ship whole, and there were peoples, whose young girls swung upon the waves, as if upon a garden swing, combing their green-yellow hair the color of canaries, singing, and if you stared you caught a glimpse of their pearl-white breasts and of their silken tails, for they had no legs but were fish from the belly down.

"You know how it is," said Michael, "you're coming to think of girls by then, and you get the strange feelings—between sweetness and sin. And it was those glimmer breasts on the waves, maybe. I'd dream of them after."

"Nor would you be the first," I said. "That dream began long ago." Michael smiled. "With the first fisherman," he said.

We paused in the storm's corner, and the sea cursed us and all mankind. She was the very devil tonight, we said. And then he went on.

It was near the end of the summer of his seventeenth year, and he had been fishing but caught nothing, though it did not greatly trouble him. He was walking back along the shores, with the tide behind him, but he had nothing to fear for he knew its times better than his own body, which was still a surprise to him. It happens now and then at that season, seals stray in and lie along the rocks like tabby cats to sun themselves, and in the afternoon water they play. He had seen them before and liked them, and when first he came around the headland with the old tower, and saw the shape out among the offshore rocks, he reckoned it was a seal, and went carefully.

The sun was westering, and the water gleamed and the objects upon it and in it were dark. But then a big mallow cloud passed over the sun and the light softened, and he saw that on the rocks there sat no seal but a woman, naked as a baby, and with a hank of long hair down her back.

He took her for a holiday-making girl—who else would be so brazen as to swim without covering?—and this was strange, for he had eyed the holiday girls all summer, and they him indeed, and he thought he knew them all, but this one was different. Her hair was very pale for one, and then, although he was too far off to see anything of her well, her skin seemed pale in the same odd fashion, but perhaps this was a trick of the glare upon the ocean. Just at that moment, the sun came out again, and she turned to a silhouette.

Michael stayed, wondering to himself if he had the nerve to go near and take a fair look. He had never seen a woman bare, except in his fancy with the aid of a few pictures picked up round and about. His pulses were beating, and he tingled at the notion. But what if she saw him? Could it be she would not mind? He had heard stories too of the loose girls from the towns. Michael began to tremble at this, as a young man will, and many an older man if it comes to it. He did not know whether to go nearer or to take himself right away. And it was as he was arguing it out that the girl herself decided to be off. Her exit was a simple one. She merely dived from her rock into the sea. He beheld her pale body and hair spring and turn over, and then the upending of something that curved up like a bow against the shining sky, flickering a fan of silvered paper upon its utmost end. Then everything was gone down into the blaze of the water.

Michael stood amazed. And told himself he was seeing things, then that he had seen nothing at all, then that it was a seal, and next a girl, and lastly that he had looked upon that creature of the myth, the innocent, sweet sin of his adolescent lust, the mermaid.

"I never slept that night," said Michael.

"I never thought that you would," said I, softly. "But did you tell a soul?"

"Not one. What could I tell? The dad would have thought me cracked, for all he claimed to have seen them himself in his sea days. No, I was ashamed. I was afraid."

"And then, how long did you hesitate, till back you went?"

"Only the one day," he said.

He returned in the afternoon, to the same spot and better, finding himself a vantage where the cliff comes down to the water and there are the caves. He lay about along a ledge and watched for her and knew she never would come, but as the sun moved over into the west and the sea began to sheen, come she did, up out of the slick mirror of the water, pulling herself, he said, like a live rope. And she sat upon a green rock and he saw her clearly now and near enough, if he had gently thrown a stone, he might have hit her. That was not near enough that he saw her face beyond the form of it that was a woman's, or the details of her body, beyond that she had a narrow back, slim arms, two breasts upon her like little white cups and spangled with wet, and her long hair, and that she combed her hair with a spiny shell, and that below her flat belly she had no legs but a fish's tail, which coiled over into the sea froth, glittering and tensing with muscle, and *alive* and *part* of her.

"She didn't sing," said Michael. "That was all I missed. She made no sound, though once a gull went by, crying, and she raised her head in the way a cat does after a bird. But she was real as my own skin."

And then his lust, for he did lust after her, this made him do a pragmatic, cool thing. It made him look at her in dismay, thinking that if she had no legs, then how might it be possible . . . But there were some markings on her tail, he saw, like the flowering apertures of dolphin. In a boiling rush of embarrassment, he knew what they were, and because of it, not even knowing what he would do, he stood up and shouted at her.

She moved her head, quite slowly, as she had at the passing of the gull. There was nothing shy or timid in the gesture, but something feral there was. Although he could not see her eyes, he saw she stared at and beheld him.

It was a long moment. Every second he expected her to fling herself over back into the sea. But she did not do it until he had taken five or six strides down from the ledge. And then the curving body, the flaunt of the tail, were limpid, nearly flirting.

It was as if she said, *I know your kind, as you know mine. I say no, now. But perhaps not, tomorrow.*

For if the holiday girls were amoral, what must she be, this fey half-being out of ocean?

He had seen her hair was green, too. Pale, pale green like those cream peppermints you can buy in chocolate. Her skin looked only lily-white and her tail like the gray-silver foil that wraps up tobacco and coffee.

Well, he would woo her. He would court her. And he knew how it must be done. For where he would take the mortal girl a carton of talcum or a bunch of flowers, he would bring this one the fish of his catch, raw, as of course she would want them.

He had some pains over it. Going out at dawn the next day, baiting his line for the lovely dainty fish they call along the coast *fairies*, and catching them—because he must; filling up a crock with them, and carrying it down to the offshore rocks where she would come back—because he would accept nothing other.

The water was mild as milk and the beauty of the full-blown summer lay like a kiss upon the sea, the cliffs, the sky. It was a magic time, and anything might happen in it. This he had always truly believed, and now it had been given him to know it for sure.

When he went off he did not go far, only to the shore's edge where the wet sand sank between the claws of the rocks and their emerald gardens, and everything of the land ran out into the water, which looked blue now as the sky was gold.

She came early. He saw her, lifting her effortless, spilling body from the sea. She scented the fish at once, and though she acknowledged Michael with one upraised, untremulous glance, she hurried instantly to the catch and began ravenously to devour it.

Even now he was not near enough to see her sharply, only the suggestion of her features. And that she ate like a wild beast did not alarm or disgust him. She was a creature of the sea, and she was hungry.

When she was finished, she did something exquisite, too, as if to make up for the ravening. She rinsed her face with her hand, in the catlike motion that seemed most ready with her. And having done this, she turned and stared toward him. She seemed to be considering, Michael thought, if he was anything to her or not.

And then his heart jumped up like a hare. For she made a movement, not catlike, not creatural or oceanic. Lifting her left arm, lightly and unmistakably she *beckoned* him to come to her.

Well, he froze. He stopped there like a damned stone and could not make himself try a step. And even as this happened, he swore at himself with the terrible foul words he had gained with his sixteen to seventeen years. But it did no good. And presently, without any sign of displeasure or amusement, the sea girl flipped over and was gone down once more into the water.

At that, he ran. He pelted full tilt at the place she had been, sliding and almost falling, and he was yelling too, pleading that she would stay. But when he reached the spot, there were only the fish bones lying there, some of them cracked by her teeth.

Michael looked out across the empty sea. From this vantage the sun was down behind the headland. A shadow filmed the water, making it transparent and opaque together. Again, before he knew what he did, Michael began to wade out into it, silent now, and he said that tears spurted from his eyes, he could not have said why.

Then from the sea, like a white bird, she darted out. He caught the flash of her—like the lightning it was, so unlooked-for, yet expected. And her arm was raised, and it still beckoned, and he knew that she wished him to follow her, and in that moment he had gone far enough that he could do it.

Unlike half of the village he could swim, could Michael, and he launched himself into the warm sea without another thought.

"There was never," he said, "another hour like that one. It was more, you see, like flying than to swim. And all the doubt left behind on the land."

He had her in sight, for she allowed it, keeping herself above the sea, and he could make her out easily, the glint of her hair and skin, and, every so often, the flare of her fish tail catching the last sun. She went around the cliffs, under the old tower, and he decided she would be going to the bluff beyond, which at low tide is set back from the sea, and crumbling, full of galleries and carious chambers, unsafe and unvisited. It seemed to him she would know this cliff, maybe it had been a land haunt of hers for centuries, for did not her kind live three hundred years at least?

Sure enough she turned toward the bluff, to which the tide was now coming up, and swam in under a deep blind shadow that was falling down into the water from the rocks. She vanished there into some hidden channel, and then reappeared two minutes later above him, before he had got himself frantic, on a high dim overhang. She had ascended so swiftly it was like a challenge. Unable to locate the underwater passage, he dragged himself out and pushed up the bluff-side, slipping and stumbling, on his two legs, to reach her.

Between finally was a sort of tunnel, thickly dark, fishy, and cold, smelling of the core of the ocean, which in its time had been there very much, and when he had thrust himself through this, he found her cave before him.

There could be no doubt it was hers. It was littered with her things, her possessions, what she had borne in to tinker with, for she too was a visitor. She had her trophies of seaweeds, and a hoard of shells, and some keepsakes from the beach, a broken glass in a plastic frame, a scent bottle, a crushed and empty can of beer. Also, scattered about, were the familiar bones of fish, the carapace of a crab.

There was no comfort in the cave. It was stone and rock and slime and impending night. It chilled him right enough, but not sufficiently to send him away. For she was there, somewhere, in the dusk.

"I believe that I spoke to her," said Michael, "some courting phrase."

He trod over the bones and the crab, cautious not to spoil the shells and glass and can, which were her toys, and then he made her out, stretched on the stones before him in the darkness. She glowed, like the phosphorus on the water by night. He gazed down, and she was less than three feet from him, lying there, and he saw her as she was at last.

"If I had thought," he said, "I would always have reckoned it to be like dying. The drowning death. And the door opens, and you see the face of God. All your days you've known you will come to it, and longed for and feared it, but it will be. But then as the door flies wide, you see—it is the *truth* you see. And truth is terrible."

The image that shone up for him on the darkness was the truth of the mermaid.

She was a mammalian female from her head and torso to her lower belly, where she became the fish. But though she was a female, she was not properly a woman. Her face was flat, with little fluttering nostrils set without a nose, and her mouth was wide and lipless and through it he could detect the thin fence of narrow teeth, each of which was pointed. Her eyes were a fish's eyes, round and yellowish, lidless, the soulless eyes that glare from the net. Her hair streamed back and was not hair but a tangle of strange rubbery filaments, and he saw she had no ears but there were the gills there, flaccid as withered pods.

"Even her skin," he said, "for skin she had, to her waist, it was not like skin at all but the hide of a whale, thick and shiny, and here and there algae growing on it and little mosses out of the deep water, feeding on her."

She stank of the ocean floor, of the fish she ate and was. The tail of her was huge and sinuous, gleaming, twitching, and the dark flowers of her ultimate femaleness stared from it. His gorge rose. He choked, but could not move away. He felt the trap, he knew there was no escape for him. She was the sea, which is older than the land, and he had gone to her and was hers.

And then she beckoned again, aimlessly, cruelly. It was like the waving of the sea wrack in the tide, some ancient gesture she had learned, but it drew him closer, near to her, so he leaned and then he kneeled above her, and he could no more have not done it than a man can keep from his last breath.

She put her hand on him then, like his lover. He saw her hand, thin, so he noticed its jelly bones, and the webs between the three fingers which were all she had, and the long greenish curving nails. And in this nightmare instrument, groaning and praying, partly out of his mind, he watched his manhood rise erect for her. But when she drew him in, he shut his eyes.

"She was cold," he said. When he said this to me, the word, the word *cold*, became a new word. Its entire meaning I did not grasp, but in a book you would find it by those other words: *Terror, Hell, Evil* and *Despair*. "My body worked as she made it do. I clung in my mind and prayed and I do not know for what but I think I never called on God. She was *cold*, she was *cold*. She was all the old fish-stinking filth-drowning of the sea. She was the mud and the nothingness. She was the years of the world dying. Ah God. I was fucking death."

He does not remember the end, though he is sure, Michael, that he served her as she required. He came up out of her, as from the bottom of the ocean, and he crawled away and vomited, bringing out the poison, but he could never rid himself of all. And somewhere as he writhed and spewed, he heard a faint silken splash under the bluff, and knew that she was gone, dived down into the deep of the evening tide, vanished, where the night and the horizon touch.

The stars were out when Michael crawled free of the cave and began his long walk homeward.

All the while he walked, in the clean air of the cliffs, he told himself it was done now.

"But it never was done," said Michael. "And never will be done."

We stood together in the lee of the Rock. The storm was quietening and the waves sloping lower and lower. Sometimes with an angry hiss they came up the granite for us, but her rage was turning away toward some other place.

"Hark there," said Michael, "Alec is doing good trade."

And from the village we heard a shouting and banging of the piano in the pub.

As Michael moved out into the slow rain, I nearly put my hand on his arm, to ask him or to tell him something. But I did not know what that would be, for he had said it through and no wise sentence of mine could change it. He had lain with the sea and could lie with no other. He had coupled with death and lived with the memory of that. Each night that he lay down upon his own belly did he feel that under him, that icy twisting and smothering and drawing? And did he dream of them still, the hollow girls swinging on the waves with their round annihilated eyes, their taloned fingers, their silent songs?

"Michael . . ." I said.

"What would you have?" he said.

"I'll buy you a drink," I said.

"Thanks now, but no. It's late. The dad will want me up for the shop bright and early. Good night to you."

He did not say, *Do you not believe me?* or *Never speak of this.* He walked away up the lane as though we had exchanged a few words over the storm. I took note of his progress, and when he had disappeared from sight, I wondered too if he had said any of it to me, that untalking man. But the sea is the thing now, it is she tells you. You have only to listen, to hear.

MIKE CHINN

Rescheduled

He'd forgotten the keys!

Graeme Oaks had traveled all across town and was already dropping his case onto the vinyl-swathed desktop when the thought hit him. Too late, the memory of dropping them carelessly onto the arm of his sofa at home returned. Only last night.

Hoping against all reason, he flipped open the case and rummaged through the tiny assortment of paperback novel, sandwiches anaerobically wrapped in cling-film, bruised apple, a few sulky sheets of paper—but it was a futile exercise. The keys weren't there. He would just have to go back and fetch them.

Sighing in angry resignation, he slid his case under the desk and marched out of the sprawled, open-plan office. Normally he wouldn't have bothered, he'd survived without them before; but he was the only one in the office that the vacationing manager seemed to feel he could trust with the huge bundle of keys—at least until the summer holiday period was over. He laughed harshly, his lips twisting; so much for *that* theory!

As he stepped out into the harsh, metallic daylight, he felt the first knuckling pains of his hangover returning. Or was it the weather? Overhead, misty sunlight was being swallowed by thickening clouds, and the air felt heavy, overbearing.

Thunder soon, he thought, trotting across the road to the local railway station opposite.

A crowd was already waiting on the platform, all their heads turned to face the city-bound line, expectancy drawing their features into stiff, unnatural planes.

There must be one due, Graeme thought gratefully as he weaved around the immobile knots. No one paid him the slightest attention— not even stepping back to let him pass. The imminent arrival absorbed them entirely.

Moments later the twittering hum of the rails announced the train, just before it rounded the curve into sight. Rumbling to a halt, its rusty brakes drove screeching silver wedges into his already throbbing brain. Like a single, many-segmented organism, the crowd surged forward and crammed itself into the grimy carriages, milling briefly until everyone was seated. Lurching like an old drunk, the obsolete three-car unit dragged itself reluctantly away from the steel and concrete station, exhausts growling in suppressed anger at the further abuse it had to endure.

Throughout the journey, Graeme constantly glanced at his wristwatch, cursing as the liquid crystal numbers gleefully raced the sluggish train. Why hadn't his union agreed to let them all on flexi-time? he thought mournfully, then shied away in guilt—since he hadn't even bothered to go to the one meeting that had voted on it. His sense of oppression grew, until he felt the air itself was turning into warm, heavy molasses, dragging at his neck and shoulders.

He'd never been a good riser in the mornings, and these late-night booze-ups with Dave Wallace weren't making things better. He sympathized with Dave—his marriage collapsing in such a messy way, divorce tearing him apart—but getting up late with a whiskey hangover wasn't improving Graeme's occasional absentmindedness.

He rubbed at his brow, trying to massage the pain away. "Nor my damned head!" he murmured, inaudible above the train's rattle. Thank Christ he'd never got trapped into marriage.

A vivid burst of graffiti heralded the long tunnel that led into the central station. Gleaming in primary colors and fake metallic luster that seemed to throb in the failing light, the incomprehensible squiggles looked to Graeme like ancient Hebrew texts, or quotes from the Koran. He found he couldn't look too closely. Combining with his growing headache, they reminded him too much of the bout of migraines he'd suffered five years ago, when hours had been lost in a swirling chaos of fragmenting agony.

Fume-spiked blackness swallowed the train, and the rattling wheels grew louder, filling Graeme's aching head. He tried to close the window in the door next to his seat, but it was jammed. At least we're nearly there, he thought, looking once again at his watch.

Then, predictably, the train began to slow. He almost groaned aloud as it slid to a juddering halt, and stood motionless—simply vibrating loudly into the jet blackness. He looked out of his inky window, but could see only a carriage filled with silent passengers, mirroring his own. There was even a twin to his face staring in at him—a straggly beard which took ten years off his real age, unfashionably long fair hair which was beginning to gray, heavy-lensed glasses that added to his owlish, schoolboy looks.

"Somebody should do something," he heard a voice grumble to the muttering diesel engines. "Privatization can't come too soon, I say. Damn railway's been living off us long enough!"

Something flapped against the window, distracting him from the muted complaint. But it was only a large drop of water, now sliding gracefully down the glass. With the amount of rain they'd suffered this summer, Graeme wasn't surprised some of it was oozing through the brick lining of the tunnel. The ground above must have been saturated. But come summer—and two weeks of sunshine—and there'd be an official drought!

He tried to relax back in his seat, the waiting getting to him, as it always did—and raised blood pressure would really do his pounding head a world of good. That's what they all said, wasn't it: "You're too impatient, Grey. Slow down a bit; watch your blood pressure." Typical attitude in this age of the shrug—no one wanted to get things done anymore. Tomorrow would always do.

Braying loudly, the train began to move again. Graeme bit back his impatience, rubbing the back of his neck to try to relieve the knot of oppressive anxiety which was growing there. Pulling into the station, the train picked its way through the bewildering maze of lines that converged onto the few platforms with the ease of long practice. Once they had pulled up, he had to hold back from hurling abuse at the solid mass of people which pressed against the sides, almost preventing the doors from opening. As it was he had to shoulder his way through the chaos.

"You're all bloody sheep!" he wanted to scream at them. But their blank, frighteningly intent expressions throttled the words. He fled up the escalator to ground level, looking back once to see the milling crowds turned into pillars of flesh, grouped like alien constellations.

Graeme made it across town under a sky the color of old slate, shot through with sooty whorls that spun gracefully. As normal business hours approached, the crowds were thinning appreciably; but the relentless press of time only served to tighten his worries another notch. Yes—he did that too much as well: worry. Or so his last girlfriend had told him. She'd finally had enough of him and left at about the same time as his last migraine attack; he often wondered if there'd been some connection.

The keys were exactly where he'd remembered them: perched brightly on the sofa's arm, next to an empty Scotch bottle that stood precariously upright, cheerfully defying gravity. Snatching them up, he dashed from his first-floor room that always smelled of the laundry below, and headed back for the station. Tension had the atmosphere stretched to the breaking point, and cold needles of apprehension sliced gleefully into his midbrain, slashing through the writhing knot of his intestines. Had he been missed yet? He dreaded the manager imagining that his trust had been betrayed, not doubting some of his dear colleagues would be only too eager to pass on the news.

The station was almost deserted—contrasting sharply with only a few minutes earlier. Graeme found himself alone on his platform; not even a guard or porter busily lounging their day away. A handful of passengers on the platform opposite were gazing blindly about them; to him it almost looked as though they were searching for something other than their connection. Hurriedly, he pulled his eyes away.

A hundred yards from the platform ends was the mouth of the tunnel, yawning vacantly. The rails leading into that black expanse reminded Graeme of a mucus-streaked tongue. Wearily he rubbed at his temples—vaguely disturbed by the imagery conjured by his racing mind—wishing the storm would break.

His train rolled in. He noticed that its faded gray and blue sides were marked with more graffiti—but this was executed crudely with white paint. For a moment, the grotesque curling figures seemed to writhe shapelessly.

He screwed his eyes shut in sudden panic. Of all the stupid times for a recurrence of his migraine trouble! Though hadn't the doctor warned Graeme repeatedly that tension was the main causative agent in his case? He kept his eyes closed while he counted to ten, breathing raggedly. When he opened them again the train was stationary, and the unreadable scribble equally motionless.

He leapt into an empty carriage and sat heavily on a slashed seat, resting his head against the padded back, closing his eyes again. He breathed in deeply and slowly several times, willing the tension out of his nerves, his muscles. By the time he had completed the last exhalation, a peaceful calm had soothed away much of his headache; but a vague anxiety still hung over him, like some adolescent guilt.

Graeme opened his eyes slowly as the train pulled out of the station toward the gaping tunnel. The carriage interior was a disgrace: seats slashed and sprayed with terse, obscene messages. Walls, windows and ceiling were daubed in cryptic black patterns, a vandals' mindless code.

The train's geriatric rattling increased in volume as it plunged into the tunnel, drops from the mouth hitting the windows of Graeme's carriage in loud streaks.

He was surprised to find the train so empty. Even though most workers were now chained to their machines or desks, Graeme had thought shoppers or visiting relatives would be traveling all day long.

More heavy drops thudded against the windows; and he could easily have imagined the desolate three-car unit was really out under a totally lightless sky, suffering a thunderous shower as the storm finally broke. The water rolled languidly down the panes, looking far too viscous for runoff rainwater.

Brakes squealed like daggers through his head, and the train ground to a halt. Alone in his frustration, he shouted loudly and thumped the seat with balled, impotent fists. With a spasm, the engines cut off, and Graeme was left in sudden quiet—punctuated by the occasional tink of cooling metal, and the thick impact of liquid drops.

He pushed down a window and leaned out, trying to see what was causing the delay. No one was moving the entire length of the train; the silence was almost absolute.

He noticed the inky glistening on the wall opposite—but his mind refused to accept the sight of the glutinous fluid running gently across the soot-encrusted bricks. A drop fell on his fingers where they clutched the top of the window, tingling warmly, and he leapt back with a startled scream, wiping the stuff off on the torn upholstery.

From somewhere outside there came a damp rubbing sound, like a moist palm pushed across a cold metal surface. In the tunnel's dark, something rolled itself wetly around the train's sides: Graeme felt the carriage shudder, and the ceiling creak as a weight pressed thoughtfully down.

Pressure thudded behind his eyes, threatening to fragment his vision; his head felt hollow, filled with broken glass. Anxiety had given way to overwhelming, directionless terror.

He found himself glaring at his reflection in a window. He looked more closely at every feature than he had ever done—each whisker, each pore that glimmered with a drop of sour sweat. He challenged the face before him to change, to become unfamiliar—fearing what might instead look in from the darkness.

And then the lights went out.

CRAIG SHAW GARDNER

Going Away

He was lucky to get a place this late in the season, especially a place as nice as this. That's what the rental agent had said at "Joanie's Realty— The Finest Homes on the Florida Keys." Tom figured he was due for some sort of luck, especially after what had happened up North.

He pulled his rental car into the parking lot of the Florida Breeze Condominiums. The condo sign had powder-blue letters on top of that flamingo-pink background that seemed to be everywhere down here. Better than winter-white, Tom thought, as an image came to him of his home, back on the lake.

It had started snowing even earlier than usual that year, all of upstate New York covered by half a foot of white on the day after Halloween. He had stood at the living room window, day after day, staring out at the stillness, the snow-covered ground blending with the ice of the lake and the steel-gray sky beyond, so that it almost looked like the world faded away to nothing on the other side of that living room glass.

With the summer people gone, he was the only living human being for miles. Staring at the never-ending whiteness, it was easy to imagine he was the only person left alive in the whole world. Snow and cold, cold and snow—you couldn't expect anything else where Tom lived, but this was the first time in years he had had to face it alone.

"Tom!" Barbara's voice sounded as if she were next to him in the car. "What's the matter with you? Can't you ever feel *anything?*"

Tom blinked, and pulled the car to a stop in the only open parking spot on this side of the building. He wasn't up North with Barbara—he would never be with Barbara again. He was here, alone, in the winter sun. How many times, even after she was gone, had he heard her accusing voice? He had been hoping that, down here in Florida, it would be different.

Tom got out of the car. The superintendent was expecting him. He moved quickly up the walk toward the three-story white stucco complex.

A thin man, probably in his middle sixties, looked up from where he was watering a cactus garden.

"Mr. Moret?" he called to Tom. "You made good time from Key Largo."

Tom realized the superintendent must have been waiting for him. He pulled the crumpled piece of paper from his pocket. The rental agent had written the super's name in her flowery hand: Mr. Linnehan.

"There wasn't much traffic today, Mr.—" Tom began.

"Call me Bill," the super interrupted. "Nobody uses *Mister* around here. Down here"—he chuckled merrily—"we're all on a permanent vacation."

"That's what I'm looking for," Tom agreed. "A place to sit in the sun and shut off my brain."

Bill nodded as if that was the most natural reaction in the world. "We won't let you do anything else." He sharply twisted the nozzle of the hose to shut off the water. "Around here, that's the law." He tossed the hose down by the edge of the cactus garden and reached for a ring of keys hanging from a loop of his Bermuda shorts. "You're in Unit 103," he called as he turned and walked with surprising speed toward the low stucco building. Tom jogged after him.

"The back patio door leads right onto the beach," Bill continued in the same merry tone as he marched ahead. "Your brain will be shut off in no time at all."

He turned right down a covered walkway and stopped at the corner door, wriggling a key free from the ring. He slid the key in the lock and jiggled it a bit until it turned. The door swung open to a white hallway and what looked like a kitchenette beyond.

Bill pulled the key from the lock and handed it to Tom. "I'm in Unit 112, down at the other end. If you have any questions, I'm generally around." He smiled as he saluted Tom with his index finger. "Have a good time in the sun."

He left Tom alone at the doorway. Tom decided he'd take a look inside before he went to fetch his bags. He walked down the white hall.

White. Nothing but white, outside the window of his lakefront cottage. Still, Tom swore he could see something moving, out there on the shore.

"Tom!" Barbara's voice echoed in his head. "Have you ever once thought about me?"

In a way, he couldn't blame her for her feelings. The snow had come early, and the weather had stayed miserable through December. There was no sun, and, although the Highway Department kept the roads as clear as they could, there was no place to go. At the very least, they had both developed severe cases of cabin fever. And they had started to argue. No, that wasn't quite true. Barbara had started to argue.

The ceaseless snow that winter brought changes to both of them. Barbara raged against it, as if her only escape might be found in anger. She thrust her feelings around the house as if she might burn away the cold and constant gloom with the force of her emotions.

Tom didn't know how to handle her nonstop outbursts. He didn't seem to be capable of arguing. She refused to be comforted, and she wouldn't explain. Tom became increasingly inarticulate as the days and Barbara's emotions went on, as if the ever-falling snow had covered his feelings as completely as the ground outside.

On the day after Christmas, she had told him she was leaving.

Tom blinked. He had somehow managed, in his daydream, to walk down the hall past the kitchenette and into the living room. White curtains had been pulled away from a pair of floor-to-ceiling glass doors. There, giving color to the room around him, were the blue-green ocean and the deep blue sky. He walked across the room and pulled open the door. The warm sea wind hit him full in the face.

Yes, he thought. This was much better than winter.

He closed the glass door and went back out the front way to fetch his suitcase. Bill waved him down as he was coming back up the walk.

"Almost forgot," the superintendent called in his ever-cheerful voice. "This is Friday. We always have a cocktail-hour get-together on Friday. Five P.M., out by the pool." He cackled. "You can meet all the old fogies who live here all the time."

Tom agreed to come. He wouldn't mind meeting some of his neighbors. He had already spent far too long alone this winter.

Alone. Barbara had moved out on New Year's Day, and he had stayed there, all by himself, in the cottage by the snow-covered lake.

And he still couldn't feel anything. He was every bit as numb as Barbara accused him of being. But he had loved Barbara. At least he thought he had. But a man didn't show his feelings. You didn't get angry—you could hurt somebody. You especially couldn't cry—he had probably learned that lesson first of all. Even laughing was wrong if you laughed too loud or too long. Every time some emotion threatened to break through, he felt his parents scolding him, exactly as Barbara had scolded him, not too long ago.

It had been far too quiet. He started turning on the television or the radio every waking moment he was in the house so he could hear more than just himself. Sometimes, on bad days, he would turn on the TV in the living room, the kitchen radio and the bedroom radio, and leave them on all day so there would be noise in every room of the house.

He had survived, somehow, in his cocoon of noise, day after day, almost through all of January. Barbara never called. When he tried to reach her at work, she was never in.

The snow had finally stopped falling on the day Barbara left. On the final Sunday of the month, it came back again, with a fury greater than anything they had seen, all that long winter. A foot an hour, the man on the TV said. Sixty-mile-an-hour winds, the chatty voice on the bedroom radio added. The kitchen radio announcer listed a never-ending litany of closings—schools, churches, social functions, stores—everything bowing to the fury of the storm.

The power had gone in the late afternoon. TV, radios, lights; all flicked off in an instant. But it wasn't quiet. Tom could hear the storm.

There was somebody out there, walking toward him across the frozen lake. And not just anyone. Even through the storm, Tom could tell it was a woman.

The slim figure, the straightforward walk, the way the hair fell away from her face; at first, it had looked like Barbara, out there in the snow. Perhaps, the way Tom felt that day, any woman would have looked like Barbara.

He felt hot tears rolling down his face.

He ran out into the storm, calling to her.

Tom didn't even realize he had been asleep until he opened his eyes. Once he'd brought the suitcase into the room, he'd sat down on the couch, and dreamed about winter.

He stood up and stretched, then took a final look out at the beach. People walked back and forth across the sand in the late afternoon light; an elderly couple, a grossly overweight middle-aged man, a thin blond woman in her early thirties—the sort of woman Tom wouldn't mind getting to meet. Who knew—maybe she, or someone a lot like her, would be staying at the Florida Breeze Condominiums.

Tom wandered into the kitchenette. The digital clock on the microwave informed him it was just after five. Time for that cocktail hour Bill had told him about. Tom decided this would be as good a time as any to get social. He went into the bathroom and washed, then went back out to his suitcase and took out the least wrinkled shirt he could find. He looked at himself in the bathroom mirror as he finished buttoning the light blue shirt. Maybe he wasn't the height of fashion, but if this place was as informal as Bill had said, he would certainly do.

He went out the front door, locking it behind him, and was struck again how different it was here; the heat, the sea breeze, the almost cloudless sky. He wished he could stay here forever, or at least until winter had gone away.

He walked around the corner of the complex to the pool. Bill stood behind a small, portable bar that had been stuck in one corner. There were a couple dozen lawn chairs scattered around the pool, most of them occupied by small, elderly, wrinkled women wearing bright one-piece swimsuits in blues and reds and greens, their skin burnt the color of old furniture. There were a pair of men on the chairs, too—there was nobody swimming in the pool—the men no less wrinkled nor overtanned than the women. Besides himself, Tom realized, Bill was the youngest one there.

Well, if Tom was going to find tropical romance, he'd have to go beyond the Florida Breeze Condominiums. In the meantime, he might as well meet the neighbors. He walked up to Bill and asked him if he had any beer.

"Sure do," Bill replied as he glanced down below the bar. "We try to keep every drink known to man around here. Bud alright?"

Tom felt something dry scrape against his arm. He looked down to see a woman's hand resting there. He glanced over at the woman's face. She smiled at him behind lime-green sunglasses.

"Oh, this must be the young man renting Mabel's place!"

Two more women rose from their chairs to join the first. "It's so nice that someone could enjoy it," one of them added.

The other woman nodded knowingly. "Poor Mabel. It's such a shame that she had to go to the home."

"Now, now," lime-green sunglasses chided. "There's no reason to bother the young man about those things. He's on vacation, after all."

Tom did his best to smile. "It sure is beautiful down here. My name's Tom."

"Tom?" Lime-green sunglasses turned to the first of her companions. "Wasn't your first husband named Tom?"

"What a wonderful memory you have!" the first companion marveled. She smiled, and her face wrinkled up like a mountain range on a surveyor's map. "I've always been partial to the name Tom."

"Got your Bud here," Bill called.

Tom reached for his wallet as he turned back to the bar. "What do I owe you?"

"Not a thing," Bill replied. "Friday night cocktail hour is on the condominium association. Just our way of saying hello."

Tom told Bill he didn't need a glass and took the cold bottle in his hand. He turned around again, and realized the women had gone back to their lawn chairs. He guessed his curiosity value was over.

Bill chuckled behind him.

Tom cleared his throat and looked back at the superintendent.

"Uh," Tom asked, "is there much to do around here?"

"You mean, someplace that isn't filled with old fogies?" Bill replied. "Aren't that many younger people around here. Not that much nightlife, either." Bill paused for a moment, then raised his right eyebrow. "There's a bar down at mile marker sixty-three might have some people your age."

Tom thanked him and finished his beer in silence. He waved as he started to walk back to his condo. Besides Bill, nobody waved back.

Tom shivered, as if he was back up North all over again.

He remembered the storm.

There was a woman out there, out in the snow and raging wind. The storm was too brutal. A person would die out there. Tom had thrown on his coat, hat and gloves, and run out into the fading afternoon light.

As he ran, something changed inside him. Until that moment at the window, he hadn't realized how lonely he was, how empty his life had grown. His thoughts had become as dead as the world outside. But then he had started to cry, and kept on crying, the first time tears would come in all the days with Barbara, and all the days since Barbara had been gone.

He could see the woman by the edge of the lake. She was still walking, and it looked as if she might have waved. He ran as fast as the snow would let him, calling out to her at the top of his voice. The tears had frozen on his face, but he didn't mind. Barbara had accused him of having no feelings, of being barely even there. Well, maybe she had been right, but maybe things could be different, starting now.

He blinked. He couldn't see the woman anymore. He called out again, but there was no answer but the wind. He realized there had never been any answer but the wind. Could she have fallen somewhere? He ran onto the ice at the edge of the lake, but could see nothing but the endless white. There was no sign of the woman anywhere. But she couldn't have vanished that quickly, even in this storm.

Maybe, Tom realized, there hadn't been a woman out here at all. Maybe this whole thing was some sort of hallucination, nothing but the snow, and the wind off the lake, and maybe his feelings, trying to come out any way they could. The feeling of elation, of being able to do something, left him as suddenly as it had arrived, as if it were carried away by the gale, and the numbness returned to his mind and body.

He turned around and she was there. Tom still thought of her as a woman, from the curves of her form and the way her hips had moved when she walked, but now that she stood only a few feet away, he could see she was made of ice.

She held out her arms, as if waiting for Tom's embrace.

"Sometimes," Barbara had said, "I wonder if you're even alive."

He busied himself, putting his clothes away, checking to see what supplies the condominium provided, and what he would have to buy.

He wished he could stop thinking about the snow. Maybe, in a day or two, the memories would start to fade in the Florida heat.

The sun was going down outside, the sky a mix of midnight blue and crimson. Tom decided it was time for his first walk on the beach.

He opened the sliding glass door in his living room, then crossed the small patio and narrow strip of green lawn to step out onto the beach, the sand pure white even in the fading light. He walked down to the ocean, thinking perhaps that he'd take off his shoes and socks and wade out a bit as his introduction to the Keys.

He stopped half a dozen feet from the water. The tide was on its way out, and it had left a row of small pink and blue balloons behind. Men-o'-war, Tom thought. They looked quite beautiful, drying out and dying in the evening sun. He remembered, though, that these things could give you a nasty sting if you got too close. Perhaps tonight was not the best time to go wading.

He turned and saw a woman only a few feet away, walking toward him across the white sand. Maybe she was the same woman he had seen out here before. She was much younger than the women at the cocktail hour.

He smiled at her in surprise. She seemed to smile slightly in return.

"They're beautiful, aren't they?" he asked, pointing down at the living balloons.

She nodded. "The ocean gives up so many things," she said. "Shells, coral, jellyfish."

"They're dying, aren't they?" he asked.

"Sometimes I think life and death happen much faster down here," she replied. "God knows things rot faster in the heat."

He glanced back at her, and they both laughed self-consciously, as if they had disobeyed some unwritten law by starting a conversation without being properly introduced. The woman waved, and continued down the beach.

Tom realized he didn't know her name. At least, he thought, Florida was showing some signs of life.

He decided it was time to go in and take a shower. After that, he'd find something to eat, and maybe even go to that bar Bill had told him about.

He sighed, and marched back across the sand. Maybe things really could be different now.

•   •   •   •

He had run, screaming, from the storm, back to the warmth and safety of his home.

Things had changed, after he had seen the ice queen. But had he even seen her? He had been ignoring his consulting job, spending far too much time alone in the cottage. People had seen stranger things when they were left to themselves for too long.

He had slammed the door behind him, doing his best to force air into his frozen lungs. He waited for some noise, maybe a knock, maybe the crash of icicles as they smashed against the side of the house. There was nothing from outside but the wind. When he regained his courage, he looked back out the window. He couldn't see anything but the storm.

He didn't sleep well that night. The storm was over by morning, and the sun shone with a clarity only possible on cold winter days. The snow had turned all the tree limbs and bushes to a fairy-tale gossamer. Nothing moved in all the expanse of white; nothing living, or dead. The ice queen had to be nothing but his imagination.

He resolved then to leave his brooding behind and return to the world. He threw himself back into his consulting work, checking in with his regular clients, doing his best to gain new ones. And, wherever he found an attractive, single woman, he did his best to talk to her. If that seemed to work, he'd start to flirt a little. He even asked a couple of them to go out and have coffee.

But it wasn't working. Every time a woman touched him, squeezed his shoulder or tapped his hand, he felt the touch of the ice queen. When a couple of the bolder women asked if they might get together some night, all he could see was the ice queen, asking him to dance. Tom had to refuse the women politely and leave, before his feelings, or his fear, got the better of him. And every night, when he went back to his cottage, he felt the ice queen was waiting for him.

Barbara's voice had echoed in his head: "I don't see how anyone can hide his emotions so well." If only she had known.

He had to get away.

So he had come to the tropical Keys, as far away from ice as you could get in February. And now he was going to dinner.

He drove up to mile marker sixty-three, and was pleased that the place Bill had told him about had not only a bar and lounge but a restaurant as well. He pulled his car into the large and crowded lot, and, after a couple minutes' search, found a parking spot in the rear.

He stepped inside the door and saw a crowd of people, waiting to be seated. There, a couple of people into the crowd, was the same woman he had seen on the beach.

She saw him as well. She seemed to blush a bit, but maybe it was only her tan. He tried to think of something to say. She said something instead.

"We meet again. It's no wonder. This is the only decent place to eat around here."

They started talking. After a minute, they left their names with the hostess and went to the bar.

Their conversation went very well. Her name was Alice. She was recently divorced, was down staying at her sister's place. She liked it so much down here, she never wanted to go home. Tom told her something about Barbara. Alice was easy to talk to, blond where Barbara was brunette, blue eyes rather than Barbara's green—really nothing like Barbara at all. There was a forty-five-minute wait for a table, but it seemed like no time at all. Dinner went just as quickly.

As slowly as they sipped their coffee, dinner was over at last. They split the bill, and rose to go, Tom following Alice to the parking lot.

"I'm over here," he said, pointing to the left.

She replied that she was over on the other side. But then she made a shy suggestion.

Things didn't have to end just yet. They were staying virtually next door from each other. Why didn't they take a late-night walk on the beach?

It sounded good to Tom. They agreed to meet in half an hour at the same spot they had first seen each other. Tom walked back to his car and drove home, at peace for the first time in months.

He looked out at the night. The sea was black, the shoreline white, the sky full of stars. In a way, it was a lot like the view from his cottage on the lake. Funny he should think of that now.

He stepped out on the patio and closed the door behind him. He would stroll out to the shore. He didn't want to appear too eager, but he didn't want to be late either.

A moment later, he saw Alice walking toward him on the beach. She had changed. Instead of the sensible blouse and slacks she had worn to the restaurant, she now wore a white dress. She was barefoot.

White dress. White sand. No, he wouldn't let that happen now. He had left the cottage to get away from it.

"Hi," he said.

"Hi," she replied.

Somehow, they were holding hands.

They walked a little, but not very far. They talked more. She was a good talker. They looked out at the dark ocean, and the hazy, tropical stars. He was so far away from winter.

Alice massaged the back of his neck. He felt a sudden chill.

Somehow, they were in each other's arms. He had wanted to kiss a woman like Alice for a very long time.

Alice's arms were very cool against his side.

Tom thought of the ice queen.

No. He would not let that stop him anymore.

They kissed. He felt as if all the breath had left his body. It was such a strange sensation, a tingling unlike any kiss he had ever felt.

"Tom," Alice whispered, "I've been waiting for you all this time."

Somehow, they were lying down on the beach, the white beach that stretched on forever. Alice's arms were around him. Why did he feel so cold?

They kissed again, and he felt ice rather than fire. He couldn't breathe. Alice's arms held him still with a freezing strength. It was as if he were drowning.

He opened his mouth to scream.

"Tom!" Barbara's voice called to him. "What's the matter with you? Can't you feel *anything?*"

His mouth was filled with sand.

CHET WILLIAMSON

A Father's Dream

You have to understand, first of all, that it was a dream. At least I *think* it was. It may have been just *déjà vu*, but I don't really think so. The intensity of the experience, the ease with which I can draw it from my mind, convince me that my memory is correct, that it *must* have been a dream.

These stories are familiar enough. The one I best recall is that about the woman who goes to a friend's country house and sees, or *dreams* she sees, a coach in the drive and a cadaverous coachman who beckons to her. Back in the city, she meets him in the guise of an elevator operator who beckons her into a full car. She leaps back, the doors close, and of course the cable breaks. Thus the premonitory dream. And now mine:

We—that is, my wife, my son, myself—are visiting the summer

house of my brother-in-law in Canada. It is a white frame house, two-storied but small, like a block, square, but taller than its width. It stands by the side of the road under a gray sky. Behind it is a lake, empty of boats. My wife, my son, and I are in the kitchen of the house, having been invited by my brother-in-law to come and vacation there for a few days while he and his wife (they are childless) are elsewhere. They will join us in several days.

The kitchen is a large room with a high ceiling that belies the size of the house as imagined from the outside. It holds a refrigerator, an old, white porcelain sink, webbed with filamented cracks, a white metal table with metal legs, six matching chairs with thinly padded black plastic seats and backs, and green and white wooden cabinets above the sink. Against the outside wall, just under a window, is a couch of worn green corduroy, and next to it an old cabinet that appears to once have been used as a wardrobe. The cabinet is neither green nor white, but a thick, muddy brown, a color whose source I guess to be that of the wood itself rather than paint, for I feel that no one could consciously choose such a color.

The situation, as I relate it now, is fully realized as I come into the consciousness of the dream. No exposition is necessary. Furthermore, I simply know that there is some connection between this cabinet, now used for storing pots, pans, and appliances, and the trundle bed that is in my son's room. This room, next to the one my wife and I occupy, holds a single bed in which my boy sleeps. But beneath that bed is another that rolls out on rusty casters, no more than a bedspring on four short legs with the thinnest of mattresses over it. And I know that this tiny mobile bed and that hulking dark wardrobe have something curiously in common, a property that is in no small way responsible for the pallor and listlessness which has come over the boy ever since our arrival a few days before. There is something in these two pieces of furniture that I find disturbing, even foul. My brother-in-law and his wife arrive, and as we chat I bring up, not very subtly, the bed and the cabinet, and ask them if they have ever connected either piece with "soulsickness"—that is the very word I use. My brother-in-law's wife laughs honestly and without understanding. But his face clouds, and he gives his head one quick shake, like a dog shunting off water, and I know he knows. Then I turn and look for my son, but he is gone, and from out on the road in front of the house comes the sound of raised voices shouting commands. I go outside and see, thirty yards down the

road, a police car and an ambulance, their red lights bright in the gray
day. White-coated men haul canisters, canvas, and poles toward what
lies on the gravel roadside—two children, one with hair the color of
fresh hay under the sun, the other with hair of a flat, lusterless brown—
my son.

I run toward him, thickly, my legs pumping through jelly, I think I
see his chest move (or is it merely the ground as it shifts beneath me?),
and I wake up.

Rather the sensation was one of going to sleep, of *losing* consciousness instead of coming to it, so intensely real were the experiences of
the dream. It was only when I grew aware of the hot flesh of my wife
that I stirred, groaned, realized that I had dreamed. I sat up in amaze-
ment. My wife woke.

"What?" she said.

"A dream."

"Mmm," she said, turning her head on the pillow to face away from
me.

I didn't tell her what the dream had been. If I had, it would ease all
my doubts about the dream being real, for those doubts still exist. Yet I
remember making the conscious choice not to tell her the dream; how
could I otherwise recall negation? It *must* have been true. I *must* have
dreamed it. I remember too getting out of bed and drinking some milk
in the kitchen, thinking that in the story of the dream that the cabinet,
the bed, and the blond boy must fit together this way: the boy slept in
the bed and died in the cabinet (or under it?), and his malign spirit
remained in both items, its presence felt primarily by my son, second-
arily by me, until it manifested itself and lured my son into the path of
a car.

I had to admit that the scenario made a great deal of sense, and put
the lie to what I had always held to be the irrationality of dreams.
Why, it seemed almost plotted. And though it ended with the injury, if
not death, of someone dear to me, I found the novelty of its cohesive-
ness stimulating. I hadn't known I was liable to such flights of fancy. In
my job as a marketing manager for a division of a farm equipment
company, there is little opportunity for creating fantasy worlds. Oh,
every now and then I daydream, perhaps a bit more than my colleagues, but they've always been of the I-wish-I-were variety, not a full-
blown *story*, for God's sake.

The idea flashed through my mind that I should write it down, but I was already sleepy, and the milk only made me more so. If I *had* written it down, or if I had told my wife, then later I might have been able to speak of it without thinking that I would sound like an idiot. But instead I placed it only in my memory, that convoluted realm of doubt, and am now unsure, unsure, unsure as to whether I dreamed it or not.

Enough uncertainties. I know I did.

Three weeks later we drove to my brother-in-law's house in Canada. I'm sure it was the anticipation of that trip that had caused the dream in the first place. We had never been there before, since my brother-in-law had only bought it the previous August. So I was surprised to find myself feeling an easy familiarity with the worn, two-lane road that led unswervingly through a Turner landscape of trees, rocks, and lakes. Now we drove over a wide spit of land that separated two of those lakes, flanked more closely on either side by long rows of cabins and houses.

"It should be one of these," my wife said, craning her neck as though a shift in her head would render her eyes telescopic. My son, in marked contrast, huddled in the back seat, his gaze directed only toward the contents of one of a huge pile of Little Golden Books, his sole voluntary source of literature. Then I saw the house.

I made no premonitory remarks for my wife to later recall. I could not; I think I was partially in shock. For there stood the house of which I had dreamed, white, plain, and square, just off the road and across the gravel shoulder. In the dream I had seen it shadowed by clouds, and now it was awash with sunlight, but that was the only difference.

"It must be that white one," my wife said.

"How do you know?" I asked huskily.

"The picture. Oh yes, that's it."

"What picture?"

"Will sent us a picture. I showed it to you."

"Did you?"

"Sure I did. There's the drive. Pull in."

I recalled no picture. I *did* recall the house, but not from a picture. "I don't think you showed it to me," I said, driving with a crunch across the loose stones of the shoulder. She seldom showed me the photos her brother often sent, and I never read the letters.

"Yes I did," she replied, her eyes still on the house, examining, perhaps estimating. "Bobby, look!"

"Huh?" came the grunt from the back seat. I turned off the ignition.

"We're here," my wife said.

The head came up reluctantly, and the boy squinted at the house. "Is that it? We gonna stay *there?*"

"Yes."

"How long do we hafta?"

At long last I felt that the boy was perhaps more perceptive than I had thought him. "Two weeks," my wife said buoyantly. "You'll love it. We're going to *swim,* and *fish,* and go out in Uncle Will's *boat,* it'll be *great.* Let's go."

Her door opened and she climbed out, then looked back in. *"Hey. Come on,* huh?"

I made myself move. I had been trying to remember if she really *had* shown me a photo, and if that had caused my dream, the whole of which now came back to me more strongly than ever. It made sense. I had seen the picture and dreamed the dream, composing a fantasia upon the flat, bare theme of the house. Inside, there would be no trundle bed, no cabinet that had once been a wardrobe.

But the cabinet was there, along with the trundle bed in the room at the door of which my wife said, "And this will be *perfect* for Bobby."

"Did Will," I asked, "send any pictures of the *inside* of this place?"

She looked at me oddly. "No."

I nodded. Later, while my wife unpacked the clothes in the guest bedroom, I sat on the old couch in the kitchen, and looked across the faded gray and green linoleum floor to where the cabinet sat, heavy, stern, and imposing. In the evening we played Monopoly around the kitchen table. At first my son was sitting across from me with his back to the cabinet, but on the second or third time around the board, he got up and sat in the chair to my left.

"That supposed to change your luck?" my wife asked him. I knew full well it wouldn't. He was a poor Monopoly player, unable even to remember that one needed all of a color group before buying houses.

"I didn't like that seat," he explained, his glance shifting to the cabinet.

"They're all the same," my wife said. The boy did not respond, but rolled and landed on Pennsylvania Avenue, which he bought despite the fact that my wife and I each had one of the other two green properties.

It had been a long drive, and by the game's end (I won, as usual) we were all ready for sleep. Just after midnight I was awakened by a cry from my son's room. My wife did not wake, so I got up and felt my way down the strange, narrow hall to his room, the door of which was ajar, casting out the less dark wedge made by his night-light. I called his name softly, fearing to wake him if he had simply called out in a dream.

"Daddy . . . ," he said, and his voice was shaking. "I'm scared."

"Scared of what?" I asked, sitting on his bed and smoothing his sleep-roughed hair.

"There's something under the bed."

"Sure," I said reassuringly, feeling a ball of cold deep in my throat. "There's another bed under there."

"But somebody's in it," he told me, shivering.

"No there's not."

"*Yes*, I *heard* him." It was *him* he said, not *it*.

"No one's there."

"Yes, *yes* . . ."

I turned on the light. The sheet of his bed hung down over the foot-and-a-half gap between bed and floor, and I hesitated a moment before I lifted it, but lift it I did. "There," I said. "See? Nothing."

He would not hang his head over the side to look.

"Go ahead," I invited. "See for yourself."

He leapt from his bed as though a snake were under it, and scurried to the far wall, where he turned and looked back.

"You see?" I said cheerily.

His face soured. "Pull it out."

I pulled, and the bed rattled out on its rusty rollers. The mattress was bare, of course, but I imagined I could see an indentation, like a thin S, where a small body might have once lain. Suddenly my mouth was full of a bitter taste, and I seemed to sense rather than actually smell an odor of putrefaction, a scent I remembered from the time when I was a boy and had opened the storage cellar door after Trix, our cat, had gotten trapped and died in there. I crouched and sniffed at the mattress, but it only smelled old and slightly damp, and in another second the odor of rot had vanished. "See?" I said, straightening. "Just an old mattress, that's all."

His usually dull eyes were bright with knowledge of my lie. "Somebody was *sleeping* there."

I looked at him for a moment. "You're a big boy. Do you really believe that?"

He sucked his upper lip. "No . . ."

"Well. Let's go back to bed then."

"Take it out of the room. Please."

"Could you sleep then?"

"Yes."

So I did. It was surprisingly light. I put it in the kitchen, stood it up on end next to the cabinet, almost as a challenge. When I passed his room, he was asleep in the soft glow.

I walked into my room at a complete loss as to what to do. The rational man within me said that everything could be explained away— my memory of a dream was really *déjà vu,* my son's fears typical and easily understood. The whole situation was due to imagination, nothing more. But the *gut* feeling, the primal man, said run, take your family and protect them by fleeing this place. There is an evil here you can't understand, one that will hurt you.

But what explanation could I have given my wife? *I had a dream, you see, but nothing I thought important enough to mention. And if we stay here, our son will be run over by a car.*

That would have been wonderful. She thought I was flaky enough as it was, without handing her a story like that. I could not tell her. I chose to be rational, and the choice seemed to be the correct one. We had a pleasant few days until my brother-in-law and his wife returned. My son's interest was piqued by the atmosphere about him that stood in such high contrast to our nearly treeless suburban development back home. Although he would neither bait his own hook with worms or unhook the few small fish he caught (seemingly by accident), he enjoyed the trees, the lake, and let his hand trail in the wake of the canoe as though expecting at any moment to grasp one of the sun diamonds that glimmered on the shifting surface. There was a closet full of games, unfamiliar to him, and in the evenings, besides the Monopoly we had brought from home, we played Clue, Sorry, and Risk. He had trouble, of course, understanding all the rules, but my wife helped him. He tried, as he did at school; but the greater his attempt, the greater his confusion, and the more pronounced became his lack of facility. I must confess to an annoyance beyond what I would have normally felt, for in the back of my mind I was still recalling that enigmatic dream of his dying, or his injury. The first day there I had forbidden him to play outside the front of the house, the side that faced the road. It was no great loss, for the front yard was small, and topped with barren dirt with only a few sparse patches of thin grass with no shade at all. The heavily treed back yard was a paradise compared to it.

I feared the road. At night, after he was in bed, and my wife was dozing in front of the blurred images on the ancient black-and-white TV, I stood at the front window and waited for the infrequent cars to come out of the night, their lights' pale blades followed by the rumble of their approach, the growl of their passing, far too fast for the narrow two-lane road. One night at eleven o'clock, after my wife had gone to bed, I was reading one of the *Cossack Tales* of Gogol I had found on my brother-in-law's shelves. I heard a car approach swiftly, followed by a scream of brakes and a dull thud, like the sound of a full oil drum being struck with a tree limb. At once I went to the front door, expecting to see through the rusty screen the glow of headlights, and perhaps the doleful red blinking of emergency flashers.

But the road was dark, and when I turned on the front porch light that partially illuminated the road, there was no car visible, nor any sign of what the car might have hit. Taking a flashlight, I walked down to the road, nearly expecting, with a low ache of horror, to see a huddled body that would be my son, and perhaps another with sun-blond hair.

I found nothing. There were no tire marks, no puddle of blood. Had I been hypnotized by the late hour and the book, hearing only in my mind what I had thought to someday hear from that house?

Back inside, my son was sleeping in his bed, his right arm hanging over the side, his hand hidden in shadow where another dark hand might have been holding it. I left it there, so as not to wake him. Then I went to the kitchen and looked at the cabinet for a long time. There was no place on it I left unexamined—the underside, tangled with dust and cobwebs; the back, of a wood lighter and thinner than the rest; the top, only an inch from the yellowed paper of the ceiling; and within, where I pushed aside the contents to inspect more closely.

There was nothing of consequence to be found. Aside from the sticking of the doors to the point where it required a solid tug to open them, there was nothing at all remarkable about the piece. Weary, puzzled, disappointed, I went to bed and took a long time to get to sleep.

My brother-in-law and his wife returned the next day, and late in the afternoon he and I went out in the small powerboat and trolled along the lakeshore, staying out far enough to avoid getting snagged in the numerous patches of reeds. We sipped lukewarm Labatt's, flicked away the fat and hungry horseflies, and chatted of nothing in particular.

"Nice little house," I finally said, and he nodded. "Furniture come with it?"

"Uh-huh."

"Who lived there before?"

"Old man down in Toronto used it in the summers. Had to go into a home, so he sold it."

I fished for a while. "Know who owned it before that?"

"No."

"That cabinet," I said after another pause. "The one in the kitchen? Looks like an old wardrobe?"

"Yeah?" He was fiddling with the engine. I couldn't see his face.

"I wonder where it came from."

"Don't know." He turned back toward me, his face expressionless. The engine grew louder. "Let's go up to the end," he said. "My neighbor caught a nice-sized bass up there last week."

I could have asked him more—if he had had any strange feelings about the cabinet or the trundle bed—but he had seemed totally unconcerned when I had mentioned the former, and I'm sure the question would have brought only a look of suspicion, followed by a suggestion that we get in out of the sun. A pang of disappointment went through me as I realized that the conversation had not at all conformed to the other reality of my dream, and I decided that the next day I would meet this neighbor of his and learn if he knew anything of the history of the house.

That evening my brother-in-law and his wife went to bed shortly after sunset. They had had a long drive, and pleaded tiredness. My son went at the same time, and my wife and I read and played gin until eleven o'clock, when we both retired. I fell asleep quickly, and slept soundly until sometime in the early morning, when I was awakened by a dull, thudding sound. I recall thinking it may have been the generator beneath the house, and went back to sleep.

Just after dawn my bladder awoke me, and on the way back from the bathroom I looked into my son's room. His bed was empty. My breath caught sharply in my throat, and, in my underwear, I ran outside, across the sparse front lawn, and onto the stone shoulder of the road, where I looked to both sides and saw nothing. Running down the shoulder, I strained my eyes glaring into the still-dark woods on either side. Still, I saw nothing. Not once during the whole search, I later realized, did I call my son's name. It could have been from a certainty that it would do no good, but I feel it was due more to a fear that he would not answer. The motives seem similar, but there is a subtle difference between the two that makes a far *greater* difference to me.

I walked wearily back to the house. The sun had just crept above the horizon when I pushed open the door, and as it thumped closed I remembered the thudding sound I had heard the night before, like a generator, yes, but also like . . .

Someone pounding on a thick door.

He was inside the cabinet. The door was stuck so tightly that I had to use both hands to open it, and when I did, he toppled out, his head striking the kitchen floor like a ball of hard rubber. I shouted my wife's name, then pulled my son out of the cabinet. His face was a sickly blue-purple, and his eyes, half-open, were yellow rather than white. His jaw hung like a ripe fruit.

Turning him on his back, I pinched his nostrils and blew my breath into his mouth. It was hopeless, for his skin was cold and his arms and legs moved stiffly, rigidly. I would later learn that he had been dead for hours at the time I breathed into his mouth. I kept breathing, harder and faster, in an attempt to make the little chest rise, and stopped only when I became aware of my wife screaming, and my brother-in-law and his wife standing ashen-faced in the doorway.

"The cabinet," I said to them, panting for breath. "He crawled into the cabinet, and . . ." I looked down at him, too exhausted, too empty to weep.

The death was, of course, ruled accidental. The boy had climbed inside (or been *lured* inside, though I mentioned this to no one), pulled the door closed, and had been unable to open it again. The tight fit of the door had allowed no air to enter, and the thickness of the wood held in the boy's screams, screams that must have used up the oxygen within at a terribly fast rate. Only the pounding of his fists had been audible, and I had ignored those, as I had ignored so much else.

It was not rationality that kept me from taking my family away from that place the first time I saw the cabinet and remembered my dream —it was vanity, the vanity of an unsure man who feared being laughed at and ridiculed. And that vanity, that refusal to heed the warnings, that desire to keep that door to wisdom closed, closed the door on my son's life. How could I not feel guilty? I was given a gift of prescience and disregarded it. I might just as well have closed the door on him myself.

My wife—*ex*-wife now—could not understand it, so I am alone with my grief and my guilt.

How fitting, I often think, that the cabinet should have originally been a wardrobe. Where we hang old clothes, outmoded ideas, ancient beliefs. Old rags of the mind. And when we try them on, it's surprising how well they still fit.

We should keep doors open, and I do, all the doors I can. Open doors let truth out. But every night, just before I fall asleep, I hear one close, so clear and sharp a sound that it seems to be in my room. Then I turn on the light and see that the closet door is still open. I walk through my open bedroom door into the other open rooms, and make sure the closets, the cupboards, all the doors are open, all open. Then I go back to my bed again.

But every night that single door closes, drifts shut as I try to drift into sleep, and I can find nothing with which to prop it open.

LYNN S. HIGHTOWER

The Magic House

Her left knee burned, the joint swollen and lumpy. Vicky narrowed her eyes and watched the family. They couldn't tell, just by looking, what an old lady she was turning into. Nobody could tell yet, just by looking.

Everyone else had dressed up. She wore her oldest Levi's—the denim worn to the faded blue of March skies and periwinkle flowers.

The house swarmed with family—aunts, uncles, cousins, grandparents, grandchildren. The bathroom doors opened and closed, and children chased each other through the halls. The big meal was over, and stomachs hung over waistbands. Vicky heard water running, then the heavy *thunk* of pans being washed. The dishwasher would be fagged to death by the end of the day.

Something crashed.

"That's it! You kids get down in the basement."

The grinding boredom of a football game unwound across the color TV. At the last gathering, Vicky had spent the afternoon in the kitchen, washing and drying crystal. Now she was relegated to the den with those too old or too lazy to help. That meant her, Old Grammie, and most of the men.

Grammie dozed in the recliner, inured to the haze of Jack's cigar, and the shattering noise of the children. Vicky saw Mike bearing down on her.

"Honey?"

She ignored him. There were times now, more and more often, when she hated his strength, his understanding, his stiff upper lip. Rheumatoid arthritis can be coped with, we'll take perfect care of you, you can't give in, you have two small children to raise. People sent her articles about victims battling leukemia, cancer, multiple sclerosis, severed limbs, twelfth-degree burns over 130 percent of their body. She always received at least two copies of the *Reader's Digest* disease of the month.

Her own plans involved curling up on the couch and letting her muscles atrophy. Mike could dust her once a week.

Mike touched her shoulder. "Your mom says Sandra moved the baby to their room, so you can rest on your old bed."

Vicky looked up. Her mother stood in the doorway, wiping her red chapped hands on a dish towel. Her bubble hairdo had melted in the heat of the kitchen.

"You shouldn't have moved the baby," Vicky said. She looked at Mike. "Where are the kids?"

"Outside playing."

"Did you make sure their hoods were up?"

"Yeah." Mike drummed his fingers on his belt buckle. "Your knee pretty bad today? You want help up the stairs?"

"Just get me a couple of aspirin."

"You had two aspirin an hour and a half ago. Why don't I bring you a heating pad?"

"Fine, I'll get them myself. Wouldn't want to tear you away from your game."

She stood up, ignoring his outstretched hand. Her mother had moved the aspirin from the high cabinet over the stove to a drawer Vicky could reach—unsafe with small children in the house. She tucked the bottle into her pocket for safekeeping.

The staircase was steep, narrow, and twisted. The carpet had been pulled up recently and the uneven wood tones looked odd. The bannister was loose, and Vicky grimaced. She imagined the family downstairs, listening to her clomping, limping footsteps. She went up swiftly, sweat breaking out on her neck and under her arms.

A diaper bag sat on the dresser in her old room. Vicky sniffed, inhaling the sweet scent of baby powder. The chenille bedspread and tarnished brass bed were familiar, but the room didn't feel like home anymore. She picked threads on the spread. Sharp pain arced through her knuckles and stilled her hands.

The arthritis was invading. Every morning her right hip was stiff, and there were shooting pains in her finger joints. She had seen a picture of advanced arthritis in a woman's hand. The fingers looked like Jack's cigars—stubby, thick, unwieldy. Useless for prying Legos apart, or fastening the buttons on a little girl's jumper.

She closed her eyes, exhausted by midday now every day. Family gatherings had been different when she was a little girl. More formal. For years she had been the only child—lonely, silent, absorbing the conversations of the adults. They would sit for hours over the remains of lunch, talking endlessly, forgetting she was there.

And one afternoon, when it was too cold for wanting to play out, her mind had been drifting along, just like now, when Uncle Stu mentioned the Magic House. What was it he'd said? She couldn't remember the words exactly, just the tension that had come into the room, and her father sending her off to play.

She'd thrown on a jacket and headed for the woods, visions of the Magic House tempting her along. A magic house. She was filled with a buoyant excitement, a tingling curiosity to see such a wonder. What she found was an old log house with no windows, the front door gaping open.

She'd stood and stared for a long time. She was shivering, so she zipped her jacket up. Something about the house bothered her. Maybe somebody lived there, some crazy old man who might get her. The house looked empty. It wouldn't hurt to take a quick peek in the door.

And then she'd heard her mother's voice, insistent, worried.

"Vicky! VicTORia!"

So she'd turned and run home, awash with a strange relief, vowing to go back and find the house another day. She never had.

Vicky's eyes flicked open, and she frowned away the grogginess. She couldn't hear the kids outside, and she wondered if they'd come in. Mike was engrossed in the football game, he might not be checking on them. She started to call his name, then clamped her mouth shut. Did she want to be the invalid wife of the Gothic novel—helpless, useless, demanding? Mike could get her a little silver bell. She sat up stiffly.

The kitchen was clean and empty, still warm from the cooking. She looked out the window over the sink, but saw no sign of Lizzie and Ben. Someone was crying. Vicky heard her mother's soothing voice.

"Now, now, Grammie. There's nothing wrong with the children. No, Mama, they're all okay. It's me, Mama, Susan. I'm right here. Honey, Wendall's home safe in Knoxville. Go on back to sleep now. You're just dreaming."

Vicky had never heard her grandmother cry. The sobs were quiet. They didn't grate on the nerves, like the cries of hungry babies or overtired children. Grammie cried the way Ben did after a nightmare, sobbing softly so the monsters wouldn't hear and come get him.

Vicky stuck her head in the den. Grammie's eyes were shut. Tears had streaked the face powder on her cheeks.

"Mike." Vicky raised her voice. "Mike? Where are the kids?"

"Outside." He yawned and scratched his belly.

They were likely off in the side yard, poking through the woodpile. Vicky snatched her jacket from the overstuffed closet in the hall. She'd be digging splinters out at bath time. She flexed her fingers. Maybe Mike would be doing it.

The children weren't in the side yard, or the backyard, or anywhere in sight. Vicky stood with her weight on her right foot and off her left knee. Her breath crystallized in the sharp chill air. Ben was five and Lizzie was three. They knew better than to go out of the yard. She called their names loudly. They were good, obedient children. They came when they were called.

The forest was hushed, uninviting.

She went quickly, eyes scanning the woods, yelling for the kids every little while. The old instinctive fear was back—the fear that pumped her heart whenever a child tumbled down the stairs or veered into a street, the fear that fed on frowns from the pediatrician and loud crashes at the back of the house.

The underbrush was dry and twisted, caught in the wintry grip of death. Twigs and small branches crunched under her feet and tangled her ankles. She was tiring and her knee radiated heat and pain. She should have asked Mike to go look. She was going to have to turn back and get help.

Vicky ran her tongue across her bottom lip. Fear was healthy; fear didn't get tired. She bent her head and kept going.

She saw something, back a ways, off to the right. She kept walking, shading her eyes and squinting. And there it was, the little wood house, nestled in a thicket of vines and bare brush. It listed to the left, and she imagined it tumbling at the first good poke.

Uncle Stu's words surfaced, sorted somehow from all the old memories. *The children go into the Magic House. Its old bones are hungry, they never come out.*

The hateful rhythm of her limping footsteps was loud on the wooden porch. The planks were spongy in places, cushiony under her feet. The doorknob was rusted through. It spun in useless circles when she twisted it. She pushed, but the door held shut. Could the kids have gotten it open?

Vicky put her shoulder to the door and shoved. A small crack opened at the bottom of the frame, but the door held. Surely Ben and Lizzie hadn't gotten in. She listened carefully, holding her breath. A soft wind rustled the dead gray branches of the trees. She thought of her grandmother, crying in the den.

Somebody else was crying. She heard a sob, quiet and held in. Ben?

Vicky wedged her shoulder against the door, shoving in short hard bursts. Sweat streaked her forehead. Was there a door around back? She stepped off the porch.

The undergrowth, dead and brown, was thickly meshed and snarled with vines. Could she force her way through?

If the children were inside, they had opened the door.

She took a breath and slammed her shoulder into the door. Something snapped and the door swung inward. It was dark inside, moldy smelling.

"Ben? Lizzie?"

The door creaked. Vicky caught it just before it shut.

"Mommy! Mommy, you're here!"

She could barely make them out, huddled at the back of the sagging loft.

"What are you kids doing up there?"

Ben's words spilled one over the other, twanging shrilly. "The door was open and we came in to see. We thought if nobody lived here it could be our playhouse. But the door got stuck. It's dark in here with the door shut, Mommy. Me and Lizzie was scared. But the house didn't want us to leave."

"There's nothing here to be afraid of." Vicky felt her hands shaking.

She looked for something to prop the door open. Nothing. She took off her shoes and wedged them under the crack. The floor was cold and rough through her thick cotton socks. She felt cramped in her jacket, and her breath came hard and ragged. Maybe she could sit down and rest, just long enough to take the edge off the pain.

"Mommie?"

"I'm coming, Lizzie."

A splinter went through her sock, snagging the ball of her foot. She cursed and pulled the fragment out, watching where she walked.

The loft was eight feet high. The ladder had broken through at the top rung. Vicky pursed her lips. She couldn't climb with her knee like it was. It would take a couple of hours to get back with help. Vicky glanced over her shoulder. Sunlight warmed the doorway, leaving the rest of the room in shadows and deep black corners.

"Maybe you should go get Daddy," Ben said.

Vicky looked at her children. They huddled close and quiet, arms around each other. What was it Uncle Stu had been going to say when she was shooed out of the room, all those years ago? She'd asked her father about it later, but he'd said the story was made up, a legend. She hadn't told him about the house she'd found.

"Come down now, Ben. Come on, right now. I'll be here to catch you if you fall."

"I'm not scared." He said it loudly. "Just Lizzie din' want me to leave her." He crawled to the edge and turned, stretching his leg past the broken rung. Vicky put her hands up to steady him. The wood snapped and his foot went through.

Ben shrieked. She caught him and tumbled backward, landing hard. Vicky gritted her teeth and waited. The pain eased. She patted Ben and rocked him, then laughed out loud in a high-pitched shriek that shouldn't fool even a child.

"Gosh, Ben, I didn't know you were going to fly out of the loft."

His tears stopped and his voice was shrill. "Yeah, I didn't tell you I was going to fly out of the loft."

"Sit right here, Ben," Vicky said. "I'll get Lizzie."

She went up slow and steady, testing the rungs. One was soft and she skipped over it, chewing her lip and tasting blood. Vicky stopped on the last rung. Lizzie crouched at the back of the loft, clutching her favorite blanket.

"Come here, honey. Come on, time to go home."

Vicky glanced over her shoulder. There was less light inside. The shoes had slipped and the door was almost shut. A thin wedge of light muscled its way through the door.

"Come here, Lizzie."

Lizzie did not move. Vicky pulled herself into the loft and crawled, dragging her left leg. She grabbed her daughter around the waist and scooted her to the edge of the loft.

"We're going for a piggyback ride, okay, Lizzie? Now climb on my back, that's a good girl. No, I've got your blanket, you just put your arms around my neck and hang on. Now don't let go, okay? There's some pie left at Grandma's, and I hid it at the back of the refrigerator so Uncle Jack won't get it."

Vicky's legs dangled over the side and she kicked her right foot back and forth.

"Ben, look and see, is my foot near the rung?"

"Nope."

She stretched her toes. One step. One more, then pause. The next rung was the soft one.

The door creaked.

"Ben, go open the door all the way."

"You told me to stay put."

"Just do it!"

Vicky stretched her leg, skipping the soft rung. The room filled with light.

Her foot touched the next rung, then slid off. Lizzie screamed and slid down her back. Vicky grabbed wildly and caught Lizzie's arm, the sudden shift in weight making her wobble. The ladder creaked.

"I'm falling, Mommy! Don't let me fall!"

"Lizzie. *Be still.* Your legs are only three feet from the floor. I'm going to let you go on the count of three, then you j ump."

"No, no, don't let me go."

"Ben, come here. Hurry."

He let go of the door. The hinges sighed and the door eased forward.

"Hurry, honey, hurry. Now grab your sister around the legs and help her down."

"Mommy, don't let me go."

Vicky let go. Lizzie shrieked and fell on top of Ben.

"You didn't count to three!"

The door moved silently this time, just a few inches more. The room darkened, and the children fell silent. Vicky's heartbeat was swift and painful.

And then she was down.

Ben pulled on her arm. Lizzie's fingers clamped around her leg. Mike would have swept them both up and carried them home.

"Hold my hand, Lizzie. Hands, Ben."

The door was moving again.

"Come on, kids, *come on.*"

She dragged them across the floor and bent her right knee forward, catching the door before it shut.

A spider swung from a web over the lintel of the door. Vicky jerked back. She yanked free of the kids' hands and swiped at her hair. Her fingertips grazed the soft brown body of the spider, and she smacked it down to the porch.

"Mommy, my acorn!" Lizzie slipped back into the house.

"Damn it, Lizzie, *come here!* Go on out, Ben."

"I got to get my acorn, Mommie. I'm taking it to Daddy."

Vicky followed her daughter back into the gloom. The front door swung shut, leaving them in darkness. Lizzie was rooting in the corner, almost invisible in the shadows.

"Mommy, look. A bear."

Vicky squinted, making out the shape of a quilted teddy bear. It looked tattered and old.

Wood cracked like a pistol shot, and Lizzie slipped and fell.

"It's got my foot!" she shrieked. "It's got my foot!"

The front door thumped. "Mommy?" Ben sounded frantic. "Come out! Mommy?"

Vicky tried to pick Lizzie up, but her daughter's foot had gone through the wood.

"Be still, honey. You're stuck, that's all." Vicky's heartbeat was fast and hard. Just stuck. That was all.

"Somepins got my foot, Mommie. It's squeezing!"

The front door thumped. "Mommy! Let Mommy out!"

Vicky tugged on Lizzie's leg. The harder she pulled, the louder Lizzie cried. Vicky scrabbled at the hole in the floor, pulling out chunk after chunk of the splintery rotten planks. Her fingernails tore, and smears of blood seeped from her hands into the porous hungry wood.

Lizzie's legs looked thin and spindly—little-girl legs that had always seemed sturdy when she pedaled her trike, but looked tiny and fragile now. It was her daughter's legs that mattered, not her own stiff and crippling joints.

Vicky realized that she couldn't hear Ben anymore.

The hole was big enough now. The smell of mold and wet dirt rose on a draft of damp air. Lizzie's foot was tucked under a stud of wood, and Vicky pulled it out gently. Lizzie stopped crying, and Vicky gathered her daughter into her lap.

"Better now?"

Vicky dangled her foot into the hole under the floor, feeling a chill draft of air. There was a cellar under the house, a dirt cellar.

Wood creaked, and the darkness under the floor lightened to thick gray gloom.

"Mommy?"

The voice floated up from under the house.

"Ben?"

"There's a door in the ground. You know by the side of the house? When I opened it I could hear Lizzie cry."

"Ben, where are you right now?"

"There's steps. Kind of a ladder. I'm coming."

"No. No, Ben, stay out, go back up the steps."

"Mommy, I see something. It's white. It looks like . . ."

"Ben?"

Vicky put Lizzie down and stuck her head in the hole. Was that Ben in the corner, standing very still? It was hard to see.

She picked at the wood around the opening. The plank snapped and pain arced through the bones of her fingers to the ball joint of her elbow. But the hole was big enough, and she hung her head down.

It took a minute to make him out, he was so still and silent. She heard the faint rasp of his breath, and was aware, suddenly, of his quiet, hoarse whisper.

"Mommy, Mommy, Mommy . . ."

"Ben?"

"Shhh! They'll hear me. I see a skel'ton, Mommy. A skel'ton head. It's smiling at me, and looking."

"Get out of there, Ben. Go back on the porch."

"Can't, Mommy," he whispered. "Got to stay put."

Vicky leaned further into the hole. She saw dirt, and a heap of rubble in the corner. Skeleton bones? Surely not.

"Ben?"

He turned slowly and saw her.

"Come here. Good boy. Can you reach my hand?"

Ben stretched a chubby, childish arm. His fingertips strained toward hers, hopelessly out of reach.

"Ben," Vicky said. "Sometimes a little boy has to be very brave. You need to go back up the ladder, and go out of the cellar."

Ben shook his head. "It's right by the ladder, Mommy. It *wants* me to come. It's lonesome, I think."

"Don't look at it, honey." Vicky strained her eyes. She didn't see a skull. "Just go up the stairs."

"Okay." But Ben did not move.

"Go on, Ben."

"Okay."

"Ben *do it, do it now!*"

He sobbed softly, deep in his chest. "Come get me. Please, Mommy, I'm scared."

"Okay, Ben. I've got an idea."

Vicky took off her pants. Lizzie sat and sucked her thumb, eyes wide. She clutched the bear, twisting its silk ribbon around her finger.

Amazing the things children took in stride, Vicky thought.

Her legs were cold, covered with chill bumps. They looked white and vulnerable in the gloom. Her knee was thick and swollen. Ugly legs.

Vicky wrapped a pants leg under Lizzie's arms, measuring a loop to fit Ben. She knotted it and slid the pants off Lizzie, lowering them through the hole in the floor.

"Put your head through, Ben. Arms too."

Ben slipped the pants leg over his head.

"Under your arms, honey. Be ready. I'm going to pull you up."

Sure, Mommy, you can do it. Vicky gritted her teeth and pulled.

She had carried her son all his life—in her womb, in her arms, balanced on her hip. It was just the last year or two that she hadn't carried Ben or Lizzie. But, ah, that last year. So much had changed— the muscles, weakened with inactivity, the joints, stiff and painful. Her shoulders ached and her back hurt, but she pulled and felt the weight of him swing free on the other end.

She groaned, and sweat glistened on her forehead and ran down her back. Ben rose another foot.

"Come on, Vicky, you can do it." Her voice sounded strange.

Ben rose another inch, and it was all she could do to hold him. She tried, but couldn't hoist him higher.

"Mommy!"

He kicked and wiggled and the pants slid through Vicky's swollen fingers—stiff fingers, that refused to clamp and hold. Vicky heard the thud of Ben's body hitting the dirt.

"Ben?"

She peered through the hole. Ben stood up and wiped his hands on the back of his legs. He stared up at her, the pants still tied under his arms, trailing to the ground.

"No pants and no kid," Vicky said glumly. She looked at Lizzie, who clutched the bear and sucked her thumb. She looked at Ben, tense and small in the cellar below.

Keep them together, she thought. Keep them in sight.

"Come here, Lizzie. Sit on the edge here, just like that. We're going to the cellar."

Lizzie shook her head.

Vicky took the bear and dropped it down the hole.

Lizzie's thumb popped out of her mouth.

"Bear goes first," Vicky said. "Then me. Then I catch you."

Vicky went feet first and dropped. Pain, hot and cold—knee, shoulder, elbow. Vicky caught her breath, feeling queasy.

"Come on now, Lizzie."

Vicky glanced over her shoulder. White milky light shone down from the doorway. She looked back at the jagged hole she had made. The withered crumbling bodies of dead insects hung under the slats of the floorboards. The dry husk of a spider was wrapped in a brittle web.

She held up the bear to her daughter. "Bear says come. Come for bear."

Lizzie jumped and Vicky caught her, landing in the dirt. Vicky took fast, deep breaths—too fast, too deep.

She crouched against the chill dirt floor, pressed by the walls, the house above her, the dark corners of the room. Vicky's teeth chattered; her chin trembled. The cellar was hushed, a tense dark cavern. She inhaled the dank and moldy smell of dirt, dust, and silence. The cellar

318 Lynn S. Hightower

floor was hard-packed, moist, and icy. It left a film of clammy smudges
on the back of her bare quivering thighs.

Vicky was loath to make a noise. There was a tension here, as if the
cellar held its breath. The children were quiet, unnaturally quiet. Their
silence squeezed her heart, but she was glad for it. Whatever might
crouch in the dark silent corners, she had no mind to disturb it.

"Where's the skel'ton?" Lizzie asked, her voice hushed and awed.

Vicky slipped the loop of pants out from under Ben's arms. The knot
was tight, her joints stiff. She couldn't get the pants untied.

"There's bones," Ben said.

Lizzie froze. "*Really* bones?"

Vicky draped the pants around her neck. This was not a place for her
children. She wanted to get out fast. But her muscles were stiff and
slow, and her bare skin numb and raw.

Vicky grabbed the children's hands. "Come on."

She kept her movements deliberate and soft. Tiptoe, she thought.
Maybe hold your breath. Be careful not to disturb.

She wondered if Ben had really seen bones. She was convinced something bad would happen if she tried to look. Superstition, perhaps. Or
wisdom.

The ladder was nothing more than crumbling planks secured to the
wall. She put Ben on the bottom rung and gave him a push.

"Go, Ben."

He started up the rungs.

"Go, Lizzie."

Lizzie's legs barely reached from one rung to the next. Vicky stayed
behind her, hands on the child's tiny waist.

Ben made it up, and Lizzie was almost there. It was silly not to look
in the corner. There couldn't really be bones, but if there were, someone should be told.

Lizzie scrambled up out of the hole, her small body blocking the
sunlight. Vicky looked at the pile of rubble, making out dirt, and
chunks of white rock.

She was tired now, and achy. It would be good just to rest a minute
—one short minute. Her hand trembled on the ladder. She eased herself down in the dirt. Her left knee was hot and tingly. It would hurt
tonight, she'd never get to sleep; though, oddly enough, she knew she
could sleep right now.

"Vicky! VicTORia!"

Vicky opened her eyes, her mother's voice ringing in her ears. She heard Ben and Lizzie calling. Ben sounded tearful, and Vicky felt sad. A sweet boy, her Ben. She would miss him.

She was very like the house, she knew it. Old, and sagging, the supports rotting out from under her. Just a husk, like the spider she'd seen.

She thought of her children, huddled close by the house, while the woods darkened and chilled around them.

Vicky took a deep breath and used one of the ladder rungs to pull herself up. Her left knee was too stiff to bend. She remembered the aspirin bottle in her pocket. Her swollen fingers were clumsy and the cap wouldn't come off. The bottle slipped out of her hand, bouncing once, and landing in the pile of rubble next to the ladder. Vicky reached for it, then pulled her hand back.

She took the ladder slowly, pulling herself up with her right leg. Cold bracing air flowed down from the doorway, and she took a breath, then another. Ben and Lizzie peered down at her.

"Hurry, Mommy," Lizzie said.

Vicky moved slowly, carefully, no wasted motion. She pulled herself up the last rung and crawled out of the cellar. The sun was going down and it was colder out. She took a deep breath, and the moisture crystallized in a soft white wisp.

Ben and Lizzy were shivering. Their faces were silent and tearful— old and drawn and wizened. She was getting a glimpse, she realized, of how they would look when they aged. She bent over and drew them close, trying to warm them in her arms.

"Time to go home, my babies."

Lizzie leaned over the cellar, and dropped the bear into the darkness.

"What'd you do that for?" Ben said.

"For the skel'ton," Lizzie said. "It's lonely."

DENNIS ETCHISON

When They Gave Us Memory

Halfway around the bay, before passing through the rock, he stopped and listened.

There was only the creaking of masts as sailboats listed back at the docks, straining their ropes and drubbing the pilings where they were moored. That and a distant hissing as water lapped the shore and deposited another layer of broken shells on the sand.

He saw the beach and the pier through the mist, the teenagers with zinc oxide on their noses, the white-legged tourists in walking shorts. No one else, except for the faded statue of an old-fashioned groom or footman in front of the carousel enclosure. The path along the jetty behind him was clear.

Even so, he could not shake the conviction that he was being followed.

He had sensed eyes on him in the restaurant, and the feeling grew when he went down to the pier. At every stand and gift shop he had paused, pretending interest in the souvenirs as he stole glances over his shoulder, but the boards remained empty. Pearly mobiles spinning in Mother Goose's Mall, cotton candy congealing against glass in the Taffy House, postcards curling outside the Fortune Hunter. Nothing else. He tried to let it go.

I should have called first, he thought.

He had hoped to surprise them in Captain Ahab's, their usual lunchtime spot, but the drive was longer than he remembered and he'd arrived late; by then strangers filled every table. Had his parents come early to avoid the noon rush and then gone for a walk? He couldn't imagine his dad sitting any longer than necessary. . . .

By now he had covered most of the waterfront, including the pier and the beach. All that was left was the jetty, a stone path that curved out over the bay in a half circle before returning to shore. In order to complete his search he would have to pass through the rock, an ancient landmark left untouched by the harbor's developers except for the installation of a railing where the foothold narrowed and became treacherous.

Now the natural arch loomed before him, dark and dripping with moisture.

He hesitated as a sudden wind moaned within the cavern.

Leaning on a coin-operated telescope, he caught his breath. Here the sea was calm, lapping gently at colonies of mollusks that clung to the slippery stones, at skittering crustaceans that sought purchase on the slick, eroded surfaces. Farther out, however, past the breakers, whitecaps were already forming where the currents merged in the gulf.

He watched one of the whitecaps detach from the tip of a wave, lift and begin to drift inland. Then another, another, flecks of spume breaking loose and taking flight.

They were coming this way.

When he saw that they were gulls, he waved. They swooped closer, poised just above the railing, their sleek wings fully extended.

Then they cawed, zeroing in on him.

He held out his arms to show that he had no food, no bread or leftover bait, but they dropped closer, feathers ruffling as they hovered in a holding pattern. The largest gull beat the air and cawed again. He noticed the sharp beak, the arrow tongue, the beady eyes focused on his empty fingers, and nervously stuffed his hands into his pockets.

The bird cocked its head, opened its beak wider, and shrieked.

What did it see?

He turned.

There was no one else on the jetty. A quarter mile away, the teenagers and tourists were still on the beach. The concession stands on the pier were boarded up now. It appeared that even the carousel was closed; the statue of the groom was no longer there.

When he turned back, the gulls were gone. He caught a last glimpse of their crescent wings pumping away on the horizon.

Ahead, a wave boomed in the cave.

The tide was rising. As plumes of spray settled over him he imagined the jetty awash, the rock path submerged, cutting off his return to land.

There was nothing left to do but go through before the waters rose any higher.

In the center of the arch a circle of diffused light shone through salt spray. The jetty beyond curved landward again so that there seemed to be nothing but endless sea on the other side. The walls of the cave swam with condensation, winking at him as though encrusted with tiny eyes.

He let go of the railing, hunched his shoulders, and walked forward.

Inside, the pounding of the surf was magnified until the pressure against his eardrums reached an all but unbearable level. He reconsidered, but there was no way around the rock. The jetty leading out from shore was less than a yard wide here, with only jagged boulders and the ocean beyond the railing. And the tide was swelling dangerously. Wasn't that a splash of white foam already bobbing above the path behind him?

Between the ebb and flow he heard water draining away, every drop resonating with the force of a pistol shot. He covered his ears but the throbbing was in the bones of his skull. He took his hands away, and almost lost his footing as a deep, bellowing roar sounded directly in front of him.

The cave wall shimmered and expanded, and something huge and formless spilled out over the rail into the circle of light, blocking his way.

A sea lion.

The massive creature reared its head, settled heavily on its haunches, and bellowed again.

He held the rail tightly and stood stock-still.

After a few seconds the animal twitched its glistening gray whiskers and waddled aside to allow passage. Another, smaller shape wriggled wetly in the shadows. It slapped its flippers and cried out hoarsely, as if welcoming him.

He took a breath, measuring his next step.

"Hi," said a voice.

He froze as something cold touched the middle of his back, then came to rest on his shoulder.

"I hope you don't mind," said the voice, barely audible above the pounding.

He spun around too fast. This time he lost his foothold and went sprawling.

A statue looked down at him. It was the groom from the pier. The cutaway jacket now hung in sodden folds. The figure extended a clammy, gloved hand and helped him to his feet.

"I hope you don't mind, but I recognized you right off."

It was not a statue. It was a young man in costume. A mime, he realized, one whose job it must be to stand in front of the carousel for hours at a time without moving a muscle, attracting customers.

He stared incredulously at the young mime. "You've been following me."

"You're Madsen, aren't you?"

"What?"

"Sure you are. From "As the World Ends"? It's my favorite show! I've been watching it since I was a little boy."

The mime reached under his jacket and brought out a damp piece of paper and a ballpoint pen.

"Would you mind?"

"You've got to be kidding."

The young man blinked through running makeup. The smile faded.

"What's the matter? Too stuck-up to sign autographs for your fans?"

They stood there in the cave, daring each other to back off, as the sea lions barked from the sidelines.

When he finally managed to call from a pay phone, a computerized voice told him that the number he had dialed was no longer in service.

That was impossible. Had it been so long? Only last Christmas he had spoken to them, or was it New Year's? And he had sent his mother something on her birthday, and his father, after the operation. Surely he had done that.

Directory Assistance was unable to help.

Had they taken an unlisted number? That was reasonable, he supposed. Reporters had a way of tracking down relatives for gossipy feature stories; he had learned that the hard way during his first marriage.

He drove out along back streets to the house where he had grown up. The plain stucco one-story had still been his address when he began reading for little theater parts in high school. It was where he had sat up nights memorizing lines in his room, where he had lost his virginity to Carol Moreland while his parents were gone on vacation. After that he had seen them less often as rehearsals kept him away from home except to eat and sleep, until he could afford his own apartment. By his mid-twenties his lifestyle had become something his parents could no longer share or understand.

As he turned the corner he slowed, wondering if this was the right street, after all. The trees were denser and older, their split limbs hanging low over a buckled sidewalk. The houses seemed small and dingy, with cracked driveways and peeling facades. But then he reached the end of the block and recognized the sagging mailbox, the one he had repaired for his dad before moving out.

While maneuvering for a place to park between unfamiliar automobiles, he noticed a sign stuck into the ground at the edge of the property, next to the weathered fence and the oleander bush:

For Sale.

It couldn't be true. But the lawn was parched and overrun with weeds, the screen door rusting, the bare windows clotted with grime. One of the panes had been broken out and left unreplaced. That was not like his dad. It was not like him at all.

He got out of the car and went to the shattered window.

Squinting between the dust and harsh shadows, he saw a torn curtain hanging from a twisted rod, an emptied bookcase. The floor he knew so well was bare, the boards scuffed and warped. Through the kitchen doorway he could make out denuded cupboards and the misaligned geometry of water-damaged linoleum.

He rang the bell at the next house. No one answered there, though when he walked away a pale face withdrew from the front window, as if someone were hiding inside, too frightened of him to open the door.

The post office had no forwarding address.

He was about to give up, when he remembered the real estate company on the sign.

"We don't give out that kind of information," a suspicious woman told him over a cluttered desk.

Don't you recognize me? he thought. Monday through Friday at two o'clock, the most popular show in its time slot? But judging by the mound of papers in front of her, the realtor did not have time to watch afternoon television. Or perhaps she did and mistook him for Madsen, the despicable character he portrayed. Could that be it?

"I'm their son," he explained.

The way he delivered the line he had trouble believing it himself. Even his driver's license would not prove it. He had changed his name years ago.

"Please," he said, allowing his voice to break with a hint of desperation.

"Well," she said, "there *is* a box number. So we can send them the escrow papers. That's all I have. It's the way they wanted it. I'm sorry . . ."

The box number turned out to be a mail drop in Santa Maria that shared space with a parcel delivery service and an instant-printing franchise.

The clerk there was no help. The man refused even to admit that he had a list of names and addresses for those who rented his postal boxes. It was not hard to understand. The one thing such a business had to sell its customers was anonymity.

What else was there to do? He was not ready to quit. It was Saturday and he did not have to be at the studio. He had told Claire he would meet her after the engagement shower tonight, but that was still hours away.

If he did not find them today, what then? A letter? He had come out to tell them the good news in person. They would want to meet his fiancée and her family. There were details to be worked out—the reception, the guest list. He could have his secretary do it all. But his parents deserved to be involved. He owed them that much. He had waited too long already, and the wedding date was closing fast.

"Excuse me," he said again to the man at the counter.

The clerk finished loading a ream of bond paper into the photocopy machine.

"Something else I can do for you?"

"Listen." He felt like a spy attempting to buy secrets behind enemy lines. He took another look at the clerk, the distracted eyes that bulged from the sharp scent of solvent, the ink-stained fingers. "I'll make you an offer. You don't have to tell me anything."

"Right," said the clerk, "I don't."

"All you have to do is take a break." He reached for his wallet. "While you're away, let's say somebody slips behind the counter and gets a peek at your files. By the time you come back I'm gone. You didn't see a thing. How does that sound?"

He took out a twenty and held it casually between two fingers.

"Sounds like you're a cop."

"I'm not."

"Bill collector, then." The clerk's eyes fixed on him. "Are you skip tracing?"

"That's right." He lowered his voice as an old man from the laundromat next door entered and headed for the locked mail compartments, key in hand. He fished out another twenty. "I'm skip tracing. Now can you help me? Or do I get a court order? That would be a lot of trouble. For both of us."

"Then I guess you'll have to get your court order," said the clerk, his back straight, his face steely. "It's hard enough to make a decent living without your kind."

Frustrated, he leaned across the counter. "Okay, I'm not a bill collector. I already told you—I'm looking for my folks. I don't know where they live."

"How come you don't know a thing like that?"

"They moved."

"Sure."

It was no use. He put the money away, defeated.

As he made for the door he passed the old man with the laundry bag, who was fumbling with his letters and relocking his box, one of hundreds of numbered metal compartments set into the wall.

He stopped and faced the clerk again.

"I'll wait, then," he said defiantly. "They have to come in to pick up their mail sooner or later."

The clerk lumbered out from behind the counter. "I don't want you in here. I've seen you before, hanging around."

"You've never seen me in here." You're confused, he thought, like everybody else. I'm not Madsen. "I'm an actor, for God's sake. It's only a part."

"My son was an actor," said the old man.

He was startled by the voice. He looked at the balding head, the stooped posture, the gray skin. It was difficult to believe that anyone could have changed so much.

"*Dad?*" he said.

"I wouldn't have recognized you, son."

"Never in a million years," said his mother.

"No?" He forced a laugh. He had grown the beard three or four years ago, for the show. Didn't they remember?

"Does it itch?" asked his father.

"A little. I guess I don't notice it anymore." He cracked his knuckles and sat back in the Winnebago, then leaned forward again. At his spine was his dad's laundry bag, a pillowcase spilling clothes yet to be folded, socks and underwear and shirts.

"Let me move that for you," said his mother.

"It's all right," he said.

"I used to hang everything up before it wrinkled," she explained. "But we can't do that now. The laundromat is seven blocks, and there's never a place for the RV. . . ."

"Don't they let you use the washer and dryer?" He parted the curtains at the back of the motor home's kitchenette, pointing at the apartment complex adjoining the lot where they were parked. "After all, you're paying for this space."

"Oh, we're not renting," said his mother. "You see, the nice couple who manage the building are friends of ours. We don't even have a proper address."

"Retired folks," added his father with a wink. "Like us."

"And there are families with children who need clean clothes every day . . ."

"They can't be that nice," he said. "Jesus, it would be the least they could do."

He saw his mother avert her eyes. I shouldn't have taken the Lord's name in vain, he thought. *Language, young man,* he remembered her saying. He had said much worse when he was a teenager, but those three words from her were always enough; the words, and the catch in her voice, the disappointment. He was filled with regret. He wanted to reach out and take her hands.

He cleared his throat.

"You must be hungry," she said.

"Not really." How ungrateful that must sound. "Unless you are." Then he remembered Claire. "What time's it getting to be?"

"You'll stay?" said his mother.

He checked his watch.

"Let me take you out to dinner," he said.

"Oh, no. The decent places are all so expensive . . ."

"Even with our seniors' discount," his father said.

"Don't worry about it. It's my treat."

"We couldn't let you do that," said his mother. "We know how hard it's been."

"What do you mean? I can afford it."

His mother smiled indulgently.

"Don't you believe me?" he said. "Do you know how much they're paying me every week?"

"You have a regular job, then?"

He almost laughed. "Well, I don't know if you can call it that, but—"

"It's all right," said his father.

"What is?"

He did not understand. Unless they, too, had him confused with the character he played on "As the World Ends." It was not possible. Was it?

"You don't believe that soap opera, do you?"

Then he saw the portable television set, its antenna poking out between the cardboard cartons above the trundle bed. It was dusty with disuse. He was relieved, until he realized that they did not even know about the show.

"It must have been hard," his father said, "after you and Carol broke up."

His mother leaned closer. "She was never really one of us, you know."

He blinked. "Carol?" The girl he had gone with in high school. "That was—a long time ago."

"You had to find out for yourself," said his father. "I know how it is."

"I could fix something to eat," said his mother.

"Later." I'll go out and pick up some food, he thought. Soon. Time was running out. Like irregular rows of stones, the tops of parked cars cast lengthening shadows across the apartment complex lot; the motor home's shadow was the longest, extending to the side of the building itself, like the adumbration of something long forgotten whose presence remained inescapable. "Just some coffee for now," he said. "If it's not too much trouble."

His mother busied herself with plastic cups and spoons, heating water on the mini-stove. Above the hissing of a propane flame he heard children roaming free in the hallways between the nearby apartments, finding their own reckless way, making choices the consequences of which would not be felt for years to come. When she sat down with the coffee, she had a book under her arm.

"I'll bet you don't remember this," she said.

"What?"

Then he recognized the slender volume as his junior high school yearbook.

"Mama, please," he said.

"Just you wait, now . . ."

He braced himself for yet another look at his infamous full-page portrait as class president, the one with his hair slicked back in the geeky style of the times, his fly partially unzipped for all the world and posterity to see.

Instead she flipped to the back of the book and the group photos. "Here."

Each side of the two-page spread contained a pair of homeroom classes. She tapped one of the wide-angle photographs.

"This one."

His mother beamed.

He scanned the back row of the panorama for his own scrubbed features, centered as always among the tallest in his age group. He did not find it. He checked the caption. Yes, it was his old homeroom, the 7-15's. Had he been absent that day?

"Where?"

She laid a finger near the bottom of the page.

Next to her fingernail was the front row, made up of the shortest

students, mostly boys. The heads of the thirteen-year-olds were no
larger than buckshot. How ridiculously young they looked, dressed in
jeans with rolled cuffs and shirts picked out for them by their mothers,
grinning toothlessly as though it all mattered.

"I don't—"

She tapped her finger.

There, at the edge of the first row, one little boy stood apart from
the rest. He posed with his thumbs hooked in the pockets of his rumpled, ill-fitting denims, his chin stuck out pugnaciously.

Somehow, in that part of his mind where such things were recorded
forever, he seemed to recall a similar T-shirt with faded stripes, the
short sleeves too tight . . .

But he had never looked like this. His clothes were always pressed.
And by then he had already grown to most of his adult height. That
was why he had been chosen for the Drama Club, so that he could play
older characters.

"Let me see this," he said.

He riffled to the portraits of class officers, found the right page and
pressed it flat.

"There. Remember now, Mom?"

"What is it you want to . . . ? Oh, yes! Wasn't he the nicest young
man? I often wonder what became of him. Maybe if you'd had friends
like that . . ."

He took the book away from her.

There was the seventh-grade class president, wearing a letterman's
sweater and a world-weary smirk. If you looked closely you could detect
the unforgettable half-opened zipper.

Only it was not his face.

It was another boy's.

"And this one . . ." his mother said.

She brought out more yearbooks. He recognized the colors of his
school, the dates. And yet each told a different story from the one he
remembered. A very different story.

"These books," he said. "Where did you get them?"

"I've saved them all," she said. "They're the only record of the past
now."

Whose past? According to these he had never been elected class
president, had never served on the student council or edited the school

newspaper or starred in the senior play. He had never earned the grade point average that kept him at the top of his class.

"How could you be proud of someone like that?"

"We are," said his father.

"But—"

"You're our only son," his mother said softly. "You're all we have."

He paced the short distance of the Winnebago's interior.

"Let me get this straight," he said. "You don't remember the acting scholarship, the trip to New York, the auditions, the jobs? The reviews?" He had sent them copies, hadn't he? "Then Hollywood and the series, the daytime TV?"

"That was always your dream, I know," said his mother. "You would have done those things if you'd had the opportunity. I'm sure of it. I only wish we could have helped you more."

"Then what *do* you remember? When was the last time I came out to see you, for example?"

"At the old house?" His mother's hands fidgeted. "Let's see. It would be just after you and Carol—had that trouble. And you went away. Not that we blame you. She was a worthless piece of fluff."

"What else? What about *your* lives?"

"Well, after your father's operation there wasn't anything left, of course, even with the Medicare, so . . ."

"So we made the best of it," said his dad. "The same as you. That's life."

"You didn't get the checks?" he said. "I told my secretary to mail them out." I did, he thought, I swear.

"You would have if you could," said his mother. "We know that. But now you're here, and that's all that matters. We always knew you'd come back."

"Do you need a place to stay, son? Just till you get on your feet. There's always room for one more."

"A family has to take care of its own," said his mother.

"Or we're no better than animals," said his father.

His legs began to fail him. His head reeled under the low ceiling and his eyes lost focus in the dimness. He groped for the door at his back.

"Excuse me," was all he could say before he staggered outside.

· · · ·

After six rings he gave up. He lowered the phone.

Just before he let go of the receiver there was a faint click on the other end.

"Post-Production."

He fumbled it back up to his ear. "Marty?"

"Talk to me."

He felt a surge of relief. "Marty, thank God."

"Who's this?"

A tingle in the pit of his stomach, like the feeling in the middle of the night that wakes you up before you know why.

"Who do you think?"

A shuffling on the other end, Marty's voice fading in and out. "Listen, we're up to our assholes here, so—"

"Put me through to Jack."

"Jack's not here. Who am I speaking to?"

He was afraid to say his name. What if Marty did not recognize it?

"Debbie, then. She's there, isn't she?"

"Who?"

"Debbie Conner." My assistant, he thought. Or at least that's the way I remember it.

"You got the wrong extension. Dial again and—"

"Who's in the booth?"

"Nobody."

"Somebody has to be in the booth! Who's directing?"

"There *is* no director," said Marty. "We don't *need* a director. It's Saturday—we're doing sound cues. Bye."

The phone went dead.

He stood by the pay phone, between Beach Boy's Chinese Food and Sinbad's. To the east, new signs broke the skyline like alien coral. American Diner, Chiporama, Frostie . . . all unrecognizable. When had it happened?

Shaking, he took out another coin.

He could call his agent. Or his accountant. Or his secretary.

But not till Monday morning.

And he could not wait that long.

There was still Claire . . .

But what if she did not know him, either? Was he ready to face that?

Instead he let the receiver slip from his grasp and leafed through the directory.

Marcos, Morehead, Morel . . .

Moreland, Carol.

She was in the book, his old girlfriend. And the address was the same. She was still here. She had never moved.

He could call her . . .

When she answered, what would she say? And what would he say to her? That he had come back to make things right? Was that even possible now? What if she remembered a different past, too—what if it really was too late?

His fingers closed and tore the page out.

He walked on, feeling the boards creak and begin to give way beneath his feet.

HELP KEEP YOUR PIER BEAUTIFUL, warned a sign. PLEASE USE RECEPTACLES.

Without breaking stride he dropped the page into the trash can.

My first love, he thought. So many years ago. And all this time I've told myself I was right to end it. That it was good for both of us to move on, following separate paths. I rationalized that there was more. For me. And for her. I thought she left for the city when I did. I told myself that.

But she didn't have the strength.

Or the recklessness.

People should look after each other. Or we're no better than animals. I did that, didn't I?

No. I went off to find a way, *my* way. Everyone else be damned.

And now the score is evening up. . . .

He raised his collar and continued walking.

The Playland Arcade was still open. Bright lights, people of every age hunkered over the games: Genesis, Big Choice, Party Animal, Battle Zone, Bad Dudes, Banzai Run, Millionaire, Eight Ball, Forgotten Worlds, The Real Ghostbusters.

He stopped to watch them. They were so intent on the play, as balls were lost in the machinery and points accumulated, to be added up or subtracted at the end, depending upon one's control. He considered going inside. Then he noticed a sign at the entrance:

FAMILY FUN ZONE

BAD LANGUAGE

NO   VIOLENCE

LOITERING

He moved on.

Ahead was the old carousel, closed for the night, and opposite it a large unfinished building: FUTURE HOME OF THE MUSEUM OF MARINE MAMMALS. Farther along, at the tip of the pier, only a bait and tackle shop, and beyond that darkness.

Behind him, the waterfront restaurants and shops and street signs pointing the way into a strange town.

I could go back, he thought. But what's left?

What have I done?

I identified with my role, ignoring everything else; that was my mistake. If you do that sort of thing, you become that sort of animal. I was too lost in the game to realize. And now it has come due at last, an empty sum with nothing to draw on. The good eroded by the bad, as if it never existed.

Only this moment.

That was why they gave us memory. Without it everything else falls away, the legacy of the past is trashed and we are left stranded.

The logic is perfect. The future created by the present, the present by the past . . .

But there is one part they don't tell you.

It works retroactively—in both directions.

Now a rumbling sounded directly beneath him, as if the earth were about to open.

It was the tide rolling in, clacking the stones, pounding the boulders and resounding through each fractional inch of the shoreline.

He held the rail.

Out there, he knew, was the rock where something lived, something old, a species out of touch with the mainland and all but forgotten. Were they trapped? Unless someone came to show the way, they would remain there, cut off, until they were finally dragged to shore and installed as curiosities in the marine museum to die.

He wanted to go out there, to be there with them. But the sea was dark, and even the jetty was lost to him now.

A sudden breeze stirred.

He thought he heard a cry drifting in on the waves.

He listened intently, until the cry was no longer distinguishable from any other sound in the night.

Then he shivered as the breeze strafed the pier, swept the boards and returned to the open sea.

The white form of a pelican rose above the breakers and began to circle slowly, its pale wings extended as if anticipating an embrace. As the circle widened to include the pier, it came to rest atop the carousel enclosure.

His eyes followed the line of the roof down to the boardwalk.

Incredibly, the mime was still there. So taken with his role, perhaps, that he was not aware of the hour, unwilling or unable to leave.

You may as well go home now, he thought. It's over.

He walked past, turned and came back, studying the face that was frozen behind a mask of greasepaint.

The mime stared straight ahead, at a spot on the horizon where the sun had gone down.

"Hi."

The mime did not move a muscle.

He cleared his throat and tried again. "Remember? This afternoon. You called me—something. A name. What was it?"

He moved in, closing the distance between them until their faces were inches apart.

"What did you call me?" he said. "I can't remember."

The mime refused to answer.

"Please. I need to know."

They stood there facing each other. Time passed, each second slipping into the next and lost forever. He waited, but there was no response.

JACK CADY

A Sailor's Pay

Only the sea remains the same. The city of Portland grasps its way toward the surrounding hills of Maine where once stood the cold green of conifers. The port hums with off-loading of goods from container ships where once floated only trawlers and lobster boats. I return to a place where darkness is old, if not ancient. I carry an old clasp knife, one blade broken, but with a small marlinespike that is still intact.

The past compels me to deal with shades. Curious matters are reported in the press. I am the last man alive who understands them.

And, the coast of Maine is no wrong place to look for specters. Ships have passed the Portland Head for three hundred and fifty years. This harbor has recorded a thousand wrecks, and it has not recorded wrecks that happened in darkness when the sea swallowed hulls in one enormous gulp. At Portland Head the sea builds during northeast storms. Waves vacuum the bottom.

Expiation is being played out here in hideous resurrection. A Coastguardsman named Tommy pilots a steel-hulled forty-footer, twin diesels screaming wide at twenty-two hundred RPM. An engineman named Case dies horribly. A seaman named Alley fails a task, and an engineman named Wert turns coward; while a madman howls.

The newspaper reports that fishermen report ghosts. It does so tongue in cheek, inferring that the fishermen are drunk. I'll allow they may be drunk, but that doesn't mean their vision is unclear.

My name is Victor Alley. Immediately after WWII I was stationed here, doing harbor patrols from the Coast Guard base in South Portland. I was a very young man, and this is a young man's story.

When you are young, and when the world asks you to go into action, mistakes happen. Unseasoned men ride the great urgency of action and emotion, responding to feelings of duty and feelings of guilt. They do not have words or balance in emergencies. Sometimes people die in order for young men to learn how to handle themselves. Two days after my nineteenth birthday our story went like this:

Winter darkness shrouded the inshore islands, and enclosed the harbor and channel and buoy yard at the Coast Guard base in South Portland. I shot pool in the barracks and hoped my girlfriend would phone. We had already made our evening harbor patrol. The boats were secured. When the call came over the PA to proceed with our boat I did not even rack my cue. Just laid it on the table and ran. Our Cap got fussy when those boats didn't move quick.

As I grabbed foul-weather gear, Wert still searched for his. Then he followed, trotting, not running. His rating called him a third-class engineman, but nobody ever saw him get his hands dirty. He was football-player big, with a moon face.

Case, our first-class engineman, had the engines cracking and stuttering as I made it to the boat basin. Beneath the floodlights the forty-footer seemed more like a tiny ship than a big boat. It was painted white as snow on mountains, and it carried a high bow, a real wave buster. It sported low rails and plenty of working room aft. When we jumped aboard, and I cast off, our bosun mate, Tommy, sapped it hard.

Those engines could scream like animals. The stern grabbed deep, digging in with the twin roar of diesels as the boat moved out. Those engines were still cold. Tommy knew better. He cleared the end of the pier and cut through shallow water, crosscutting flooded tideflats to the channel. Spray rose luminescent in the darkness. I climbed up beside Tom. He was hitting it just way too hard.

"You'll drag the bottom out," I yelled. I could feel fingers of rock reaching toward the hull. Tommy looked kind of crazy. Tall and skinny with thick black hair like a Portuguese. Just crazy. He muttered a name. He stood at the helm totally concentrated, and motioned me away.

I stepped aft. The engine ran at least two-thirds. Tom pushed it that way until we made the channel, and then he ran the engines full. They screamed in overspeed, the bow high and rock-steady in the hard hand of the water. Case tapped my shoulder, and we both moved forward to be away from the scream of engines. We did not know that Wert tagged along behind us.

"The Portland cops called. We're after a boat," Case told me. "Guy who stole it killed his old lady with a knife. He's got their kid in the boat with him. They think."

"Who thinks?"

"The cops didn't find a kid's body. The kid and all of her clothes are missing."

Tommy did not let up. He held it wide open in the middle of the channel, heading seaward. Distant lights of Portland and South Portland started looking fuzzy, the way they do just before winter fog arrives.

Wert interrupted us. The All-American Boy. His voice practically bubbled with excitement. "This beats towing in broken-down fishing boats. A murderer."

"Get back to those engines," Case told him. "Don't take your eyes off that oil pressure for a second."

"If we're going to have a murderer, we'd ought to have a gun." Wert acted conversational.

"You want a gun, join the Army," I told him.

Wert just asked for it, leaving those engines at those RPMs, and then refusing to hurry when Case gave an order.

"You done it this time," Case told Wert. He literally turned Wert around and gave him a shove aft. Then he turned back to me. "He lies better than I tell the truth. Waste of ink to put him on report." Case was tense, and that was unusual. He was mostly easygoing, a guy without enemies. Wert even liked him. He was the kindest man I ever knew. I'd learned a lot from him. Case had broad shoulders, broad face, a nice smile and not much of a beer belly.

"I gotta talk to him." Case motioned at Tommy.

"The engines?"

"Sure," Case said, "and some other stuff."

I figured the engines were either okay, or wrecked by now. "What are we doing?" I asked Case.

"We're hurrying to put the cork in the bottle. There's a cutter checking the channel. We're blocking the seaward side. The killer can't escape through the harbor mouth. At least that's part of it."

"What's the other part?"

Case looked like he wondered if I would understand. "Tommy's acting weird," Case said. "He sorta gets his beanie unscrewed in emergencies. This ain't just about some nut and a stole boat."

I almost understood. I knew the story. During the war Tommy served on a cutter escorting convoys. On a dark night a freighter was torpedoed. There were survivors in the water. Tommy had the deck on the fantail because the gunnery officer was forward.

It was an awful story. Tommy spotted the survivors, and sonar picked up the German sub at the same time. The sub hovered a hundred feet down, directly below the freighter's surviving crew. The captain of the cutter made a command decision. He depth-charged the sub. Men struggling in the water turned to bloody pulp. A few survivors on the outskirts of the explosions did not die. The captain made the decision, but Tommy gave the order to drop the charges. It was one of those things that nobody talks about, and everybody seems to know.

"Tell him not to get too weird." I didn't know what else to say.

"C'mon," Case said. "Let's talk that poor fella out of wrecking those engines."

I followed Case, and he climbed up beside Tommy, who leaned way out around the spray shield. The engines screamed, and the bow rode so high at this speed that he could not see a thing. Case put one hand on Tommy's shoulder, grinned at Tom like Tom had just told a pretty good joke, and then Case eased the controls. Speed came off, the bow dropped, and the boat skidded a little sideways. We'd come far enough that we could see the lighthouse at Portland Head.

"Take a strain," Case said. "Guy with a wild hair crossways can't figure anything out."

"The police boat is out checking the islands," Tommy said. "If he gets in behind the islands, we've lost him." He did not even hear Case.

"Get it figured," Case said. "What you're doing ain't working." He paused as he figured the next move. He looked toward the misty lights that told of fog. "At best we've got an hour. Go up to the Head along the edge of the channel, then double back along the other side. He won't be riding the middle of the channel."

"I want a piece of that clown." Tommy's voice sounded in control, but it still sounded a little crazy.

It came to me, watching him, that Tommy had been quiet for too long. Been holding everything in. I figure he didn't care about the murderer. He just wanted to hit something that needed hitting.

"Cruise it slow," Case said. "Use the searchlight, because he'll be running without lights."

It's a big harbor, nearly as big as Boston. You could hide two hundred lobster boats in this harbor, and the odds on finding even a dozen of them would be pretty long.

"Because the guy's crazy," Case said. "He's runnin', but I doubt he's going to hide. If he hides, we won't find him."

We cruised the starboard side of the channel as far as Portland Head, then turned around and cruised the other side coming back. Fog gathered. An occasional horn or whistle sounded. Fog settled from above until it finally pressed against the water. It was thick above, thinner at the waterline.

A thousand-to-one shot, but there seemed nothing else to do except search the islands. Dull, freezing work. As the ice fog gathered the searchlight became useless. The fog did not lift after nearly five hours. It looked like it was going to be another one of those cold and futile nights.

Wert's teeth chattered. "It's cold."

"It's November."

"Take us home, Tommy."

"Go sit on an engine."

We traded off watching-standing in the bow. Tommy kept the engines barely turning. He searched along the beaches of the dark islands. Didn't use the searchlight. We just stood in the bow and listened, hoping to hear the sound of a lobster boat's engine. It was about 0330 when the cutter in the channel radioed, reporting a target on its radar. A small boat moved along the South Portland side of the channel.

"Got him," Tommy said. "Let's get him good." Tommy had sort of settled down, but now he started to get all ruffled again.

We were all tired, cold, and we had taken some spray five hours back. Nobody was wet, but nobody was exactly dry. Tommy shoved the RPMs ahead, then lowered them a little as he realized he was being stupid. That boat was forty feet of steel hull. Not something to shove through fog at high speed.

The cutter talked us across the harbor and through the fog. We moved too quick, taking radar readings from the cutter. I don't trust radar, and I sure don't trust a set I'm not looking at. I always trusted Tommy.

As we overhauled the cutter we could see its searchlights swallowed by fog. Just beyond the lights, right on the edge of the lights, the lobster boat looked like a little ghost. It was weaving in and out past the rocks.

It's a cliff along there. High-walled and granite and straight up. The lobster boat made its way toward a notch not big enough to be a tiny cove. It was just a place where the rock broke away and guys moored sometimes. We ran past the cutter, taking off speed, and coasted alongside the lobster boat. We were maybe twenty feet away.

The guy was hard to see in the dark and fog lying beneath that rock face. This close in, our searchlight helped. I ran it over the boat and the numbers checked. This was the man.

The guy stood behind the wheel. He turned when our light hit him. He shook his fist and yelled, maybe daring us to come in. The lobster boat edged nearer the rock. I did not believe the guy was insane. He ran the boat too well, discounting the fact that he was where you shouldn't run a boat.

Then he turned his face full to mine, and I believed it. He was like an abandoned beast, like a dog that's been run over and is not yet numb in its dying. The guy's eyes didn't seem like eyes; just sockets; deep, empty, vacant.

Tommy moved in closer, maybe six or eight feet away. The old lobster boat kept chugging. We were so close I could see blistered paint in the glow of our running lights. The madman started howling.

"Can't head him off," Tommy said. "He'll beach that thing. There's nothing but rock in there."

"Beach him," Wert said. "That kid ain't on that boat."

"Get back to those engines."

"If he'd swiped the kid in that kind of hurry, you think he'd have time to pack her clothes?"

"Move it aft," Case told Wert. "Get back to those engines." He paused, like he was thinking about what Wert had said. I couldn't figure if Wert was right or not. He sort of seemed right. "When we figure what we're going to do," Case told Wert, "I'll come and let you know."

Wert laid aft.

"We'll use three of us," Case said. He laid it out. Tommy was to bring the boat close alongside. Three of us would jump. I was to go forward and get the kid, who had to be in the wheelhouse. Wert would kill the engine on the lobster boat. Then Wert was supposed to help Case with the madman.

"And Tommy," Case said, "you hold steady. Because man, if he puts that thing on the rocks we're going to need you."

"He's got a knife."

"Yep," Case said, "and I got myself one hell of a big crescent wrench." He turned aft, yelling at Wert, who stood beside the engines looking determined. Wert rubbed a fist into the open palm of his other hand.

When Tommy closed I jumped. The lobster boat ran in the shadow of the rock face. It loomed over me, darker than the rest of the dark. As I hit I felt the lobster boat shudder and rub the rock someplace deep. I lost my balance. We were so close in that I actually shoved back to my feet by pushing on the rock face; while somewhere behind me Tommy yelled, "Left rudder. Left rudder."

I came from the bow, around the starboard side of the dinky wheelhouse. The madman stepped from the wheel to meet me. I was scared. Couldn't think of what to do, but my legs just ran me into him. Hit him like I was a fullback. He stumbled aft against Case, who was on his knees. I think maybe Case sprained or broke an ankle. That lobster boat was just trash, the decks full of junk and gear. Tommy was still yelling, "Left rudder, left rudder." I heard the forty's engines dig in as Tommy cut to port to give us running room. As the forty's stern slid past I looked up and across, into the pale moon face of Wert. He stood motionless. The guy looked frozen with fear, wide eyes staring. He hadn't jumped.

You never know—even after years you can never decide—if what you do is right. Everything happens so fast. If I didn't detest Wert so much, I would have listened to him. Maybe saved Case.

What happened is that I did what I'd been told. I grabbed the helm and threw it hard to port. The boat edged away from the rock. It handled sluggish, already sinking from the lick it took on the rocks. Forward of the wheel a red light burned in the little cabin. I was supposed to get the kid, and so I went down there. Old coats, old blankets, slickers and boots. A gush of water through the ruptured hull. No kid. I must have wasted half a minute. I turned back to the deck just as a searchlight from the cutter swept us, and just as the forty's engines started howling.

It all happened in slow motion, or that's the way it seems. The madman stood above Case, and the madman howled almost like the engines. He had both hands raised high together, holding one of those long, thin stakes that lobstermen use to pin fish in their traps. The forty roared someplace real close. I heard a bow wave, but you never hear a bow wave—not like that—unless it's pointed right at you. Case yelled something, tried to throw something at the madman, but you can't throw much when you're on your knees. I dived over Case, trying to tackle the madman. There was a shock, the lobster boat driven sideways, a crash of timbers; and a fish smell came off the deck as I rolled. Something, a lobster trap maybe, clipped me alongside the head. Then I was in water that is death-dealing cold, struggling to stay up.

The boat crew from the cutter took us aboard, dried us out and gave us clothes. At first I didn't remember much. I sat for a long time on the messdeck shivering and drinking coffee. Didn't see Tommy. Figured they were working on him. Didn't see Case. Saw Wert. He sat at a table facing me, sullen, wearing his own clothes. He'd got his feet wet, and he put them on a bench, rubbing his legs and rolling up the wet part of his dungarees so they came to his calf.

"There wasn't no kid. I told you. They beached what was left of that boat and there wasn't hide nor hair."

"What happened?" I couldn't remember anything. Then I started to remember a little.

"Tom lost his head and rammed you. Dumped you all in the water, then jumped in to pull you out. The forty's back there now, high and dry and cut wide open."

It was coming back now. "Case?"

Wert just plain looked sick. "Guy stabbed him. Tommy rammed you because he was trying to keep the guy from stabbing Case."

"The madman?"

"Jumped back and got himself killed when the bow of the forty pinched him."

And that's when the memory came clear of Wert's white face rising like a pale moon above the rail, the vacant look, the struggle and noise at my back and the roar of engines.

"Where were you?" I was getting cold again.

He had his story down pat. Like a first-grader reciting about Mary and the lamb. "We were about to jump, and the engines went rough. Case said to check it out because we couldn't afford to lose power. I checked, but before I could jump Tommy kicked it ahead." He turned his back to me, swinging away, and propped his leg up to inspect his toes.

They pulled me off of him, somebody did. Then their chief bosun sent me to wait it out on the fantail. Probably because I had shoes on and Wert didn't.

I went to the fantail figuring that things couldn't get any worse, and they got a million times worse right away.

Bodies are always stored on the fantail. I sat beside Case after I found which one he was. Kind of patted the old blanket he was wrapped in. I couldn't figure out why the best man I knew had to be dead. Wasn't thinking very straight.

Then I did start thinking straight, thinking about what I'd seen when I checked to see which one he was. Case was pretty tore up, but mostly just mangled. There was only one wound above the waist, and that was way above the heart, nearly in the left shoulder. That madman had not stabbed Case to death.

I'd always trusted Tommy. Tommy was my friend. He had taught me a lot. But, Tommy was the one who killed Case while trying to save him.

You never know if what you do is right, and that's especially true when you are young. You operate on the basis of what you know.

One thing I knew was that the local coroner was a lazy old drunk. Twice, while on Shore Patrol, we'd taken bodies to that coroner. He dumped them in a stainless steel tub, cut away the clothes, and said something like "This pore old buster drank hisself to death." I knew that coroner would do no autopsy.

If he saw a wound over the heart he would blame the madman. He'd not say a word about Tommy.

I pulled out my clasp knife. It carried a marlinespike, about the same diameter as a stake that runs through lobster traps. Even today I can't believe my courage and ignorance. I stabbed Case, stabbed a dead man, right where the heart would be. It was just a little blue hole that did not bleed, but, what with arterial damage and salt water, none of the other wounds were bleeding.

I remember vaguely wondering how much jail time you could get for stabbing a dead man.

Years pass, but memory is relentless. Such an act wears on a man's soul. Sometimes the memory lies faded and dull among brighter memories of youth. At the same time, the memory never leaves. Maybe I did Tommy a favor, maybe not. The police filed no civil charges, and the court-martial found him innocent. The court concluded that, although unable to save Case, he may well have saved me. The court did not like the destruction of an expensive boat.

Tommy came to a bad end. He started boozing when on liberty. We saw his tall frame and black hair bent over too many glasses of beer in too many sailor dives. He went AWOL for a month, was reclaimed from a drunk tank.

In those days the Coast Guard was a small and personal outfit. Our cap tried to save Tommy by transferring him to a weather cutter. The Cap figured, since the cutter stayed on station for a month at a time, Tommy would have to stay sober in thirty-day stretches. Tommy slipped overboard one night as the cutter passed the Portland Lightship. The investigating board called it an accident.

And Wert came to an even more macabre end. On a night of no wind he wandered among buoys in the buoy yard. The buoys stood silent, the giant whistles, the lighted bells, the racks of nuns. Some were barnacled, waiting to be sand-blasted and red-leaded. For no reason, and against known laws of physics, a lighted bell rolled on flat ground. It weighed maybe a ton, and it crushed Wert against the pavement of the storage area. There was not a breath of wind, but men on cutters swore they heard the bell toll, and clank, and toll.

When my hitch was up I did not reenlist, but fled from salt water. The next few years were dreary; odd jobs and bad jobs through the Middle West. I attended college at night, got married, finally graduated from college, got divorced. Nothing seemed to go exactly right. It came to me—in, of all places, the bus station in Peoria—that this awful incident of youth kept me from my true calling, the sea. I traded my bus ticket to Chicago for a ticket to Seattle. From Seattle I went to Ketchikan, fished salmon, then finally found a permanent berth on a tug hauling barges from Seattle to Anchorage. After many years I rose to master of my own vessel.

A lot of down-east sailors, mostly fishermen, drift into Alaska. On a snowy January afternoon in Sitka, forty years after the event, I heard stories from a couple of Maine men who vowed never again to enter Portland Harbor. There was enough in their drunken talk to convince me it was time to come to terms with the past. I booked a flight to Portland.

Through the years certain questions haunted that incident of youth. I thought about them on the plane. What happened to the child? What did Tommy see as he kicked the forty-footer ahead? What, for that matter, did I see? I am old now, and am well acquainted with the way the mind manufactures illusions. What did Wert see? What caused a puritanical lobsterman to suddenly sink into the depths of insanity?—for the lobstermen of Maine are usually stern and steady fellows.

After checking into a Portland hotel I went to the newspaper office. The report from so many years ago seemed sketchy, but it did contain the names of men and the name of the child. The child, it was reported, had been taken away by her grandmother before the ugly murder.

It was unlikely the grandmother still lived, but I searched the phone book. The grandmother was not listed, but the child's name was. Of course, she would now be a middle-aged woman. I phoned, made clumsy explanations, and she agreed to meet me for lunch.

To an aging man, the woman who met me in the hotel lobby seemed to shine with both dignity and beauty. The coast of Maine is hard on men, but often even harder on women. This slim lady's face was weathered, crow's-feet around bright gray eyes, and her hands showed that she was not afraid of work. Long, dark hair displayed streaks of gray, and her conservative gray dress fell well below the knee.

"It's a jigsaw puzzle," she told me once we were seated for lunch. "You must remember that I was little more than a baby."

"I wonder what is happening in the harbor," I said. "The newspaper just reports ghost stories." Beyond the windows, banks of piled snow lined streets that are asphalt now, but in my day were brick. Sun glistened on patches of ice, and the thermometer stood at zero.

"I know exactly," she told me. "I own a ship chandlery. The story comes together in bits and pieces. Men talk even when they want to keep quiet."

Men heard more than they saw. In winter darkness of early mornings, when ice fog covered the channel, fishermen reported the low sound of diesels. There would be a nearly hysterical cry of "Left rudder. Left rudder." When that happened men became terrified, and minded their own craft. A radar screen may be completely blank, but no sailor trusts the things, and no sailor fails to react when his vision is muffled by fog.

The sound of engines would then rise to a roar, as men blindly threw their helms over to get away. Then would come a great rip and tearing of metal and wood; and then silence. Into the silence a voice would speak: "A sailor's pay. A sailor's pay."

Men reported the voice as unworldly, or as worldly as the voice of the sea. They then heard the diminishing struggle of men overboard.

"I'll tell what my grandmother told," the woman said. She smiled as if distracted. "The people of Maine have a reputation for being taciturn, but among themselves they chatter like jays." She hesitated, and then made a whispered confession. "I never married. Old-fashioned, maybe, and partly superstitious. My father was insane, my mother no better."

"If this is too difficult for you . . ."

"I never really knew them," she reminded me, "but my grandmother was my best friend."

Beyond the windows bright colors of automobiles contrasted with piled snow and sun-glazed streets. Tall buildings rose to cast dark shadows beside the busy docks.

"Maine used to resemble Alaska," the woman said. "In Alaska people still know each other."

She was right about that. There is still, in Alaska, the feeling that "we are all in this together." When Alaskans meet in improbable places, say Indiana or Australia, they either know each other, or find that they have mutual friends. It's a big state with a small population.

"This was an incident of war," she told me. "Or, maybe it was an incident of youth. The sailor named Tommy came to visit my grandmother on two occasions. He knew my father. During the war they both sailed from this port. My father served aboard a freighter. Tommy sought forgiveness for my father's death."

Old memories stirred. At last there seemed to be some sense to all of this.

Her father, it developed, was one of the survivors from the torpedoing when Tommy followed that fateful order to drop depth charges. Her father was concussed, suffering what must have been awful brain damage. Her mother, who had a reputation for being fey, met his changed condition by sinking into a virulent brand of New England religion. She played the role of saint to his role of hapless sinner before an avenging God. It proved the wrong approach.

"I don't forgive my father," she said. "I don't even excuse him. There is no excuse for murder."

She was correct, of course. No one worth a dime resorts to murder, no matter how crazy he gets. Still, most murders come from situations and passions.

"Tommy believed himself doomed," the woman told me. "In a manner of speaking he saved my father's life during that depth-charging, because he was coxswain in the boat that picked up the few survivors. He felt that fate pushed him into a world where he was forced to kill my father. The depth charges failed, and it was terrible for him to think that he was forced to kill a man after failing to kill him the first time." She smiled, but the smile was small and tight. "Don't be fooled. If the roles were reversed, my father might have done the same thing, and reacted in the same way."

The woman prepared to leave, returning to her everyday work and everyday life. "Try to think about the minds of the men," she said. "And think about the sea, because the incident is only that, an incident."

I saw that she did not know more than she told, but that she *thought* more than she would say.

"Darkness tries to kill light," she murmured. "That is the business of darkness." As I helped her into her coat she added: "Remember that all of you were very young. My father was twenty-five, and Tommy could have been little more."

I thought of the immemorial voice of the sea as I sought to rent a boat. The sea speaks with the sounds of thunder, or it is susurrous, or it hisses, or it murmurs. It is nearly as ancient as the earth. The sea has swallowed men who have spoken a thousand different languages: it has taken into its restless maw Persians, Phoenicians, Romans, Spaniards and Englishmen.

And I thought of Maine and of Portland Harbor while checking the engine of a rented workboat, that, like myself, neared the end of a working life. A thousand vessels have died in these harsh waters, while on land people erected crosses facing the sea. Many of the graves of Maine are invested only by memories.

And I thought of youth, and of the great passions and inarticulateness of youth. I did not wonder why Tommy felt the need to strike out. It is clear that he was quiet because he was too young to mobilize words and alter his confusion. Little wonder he felt doomed.

And, as ice fog began to settle over the harbor around midnight, I thought of Wert. If the sea would not forgive Wert, if, in fact, the unforgiving sea had reached ashore for Wert by using a barnacled buoy, I could still understand. He had been a kid confronted by madness, and he had no experience with madness.

Finally, as I got underway, I thought of Case. He still stood in memory as the finest man I've known. I wondered if the memory were true.

The old boat ran smoothly enough. The gasoline engine puttered as I traced the starboard shoreline. Fog lay heavy above me, and tendrils of fog began to reach toward the surface of the restless and flowing water. The tide was running. Along the coast of Maine it will rise or drop seventeen feet during winter. I searched my memories, of Case smiling, teaching a young sailor how to bend lines, and of Case coaxing the roughness from an engine, as if the engine were a living thing.

Fog clustered on the rails and deck of the workboat. It froze in whitely glowing frost. Fog glazed the silent nuns which marked the channel. Small pieces of driftwood bobbed away from my low wake as I eased from the channel and toward the cliffs. After forty years it seemed a man would forget his local knowledge of rocks and current. Yet, I had total recall of the shoreline. I arrived at the scene of my worst memories.

When the small anchor held I cut the engine. Low sounds of moving water served as background for the muffled clank of a bell. In the far distance a ship's horn hooted, and from the shore a police siren wailed faint through the frozen night. Fog covered the water so absolutely that no light from the city penetrated this dark corner. No living man could discover me here. No living man would want to.

Faint and close astern a gasoline engine puttered. It was unmistakably a lobster boat headed toward this anchorage where sheer cliff gave way to broken rock.

Fear is an old friend. I have known fear in a thousand storms. I have heard fear, and felt it, when my vessel's radio picked up the terrified voices of doomed men; men giving last loran positions as their ship took its final dive. Fear always stands near those who go to sea. At first you learn to bear it, then, finding its true nature and depth, you befriend it.

Somewhere in that fog a ghostly forty-footer was even now being directed across the channel by radar from a ghostly cutter, a ship by now mothballed or sold for scrap. Somewhere close astern a spectral lobsterman puttered across the restless face of moving waters.

The sound of Tommy's diesels rose in the fog, as the sound of the lobsterman closed. The sounds converged, and it was then the lobster boat coasted past. It hugged the cliff.

Red light in the cabin, and red from the port running light, made a diabolic mask of the lobsterman's face. The mask blazed as true madness, not insubstantial apparition. Both man and boat seemed solid as the deck beneath my feet. If anything, it was madness that was spectral.

But, then, I have also known madness at sea. I too, have wielded a knife, if only against a corpse.

The madman cut his engine to a low mutter, then turned to face me as the lobster boat slid past. Torment distorted that face, and it was torment I had never seen. I have seen men die, and seen them live when they wished to die. I have seen victims of hideous burns, and men flayed to pieces when lines or cables parted. Yet, this torment went deeper than physical pain. Forty years were as one hour to this man who had just killed his wife. His face twisted with guilt, and I looked at a man doomed to the perpetual retelling of his story. The face rose from the depths of certain, puritan hell.

The man laughed, his voice casting strokes of anguish through muffling fog. He motioned toward me, beckoning me to follow him. His boat began to rock. With the engine running low there was not enough power to keep the boat's head pointed toward the sea.

The bow of the forty-footer appeared, sliding whitely through mist.

It was as insubstantial as the lobster boat was substantial. The forty-footer wavered, more ghostly than the surrounding fog. Were it not for the solid sound of engines, the forty would be vague as a cloud. I watched the drama unfold; watched ghostly forms of men huddling in quick conversation as the forty swept past, made a turn toward the channel, and eased back toward the lobsterman.

The forty made its turn, then pointed toward the cliffs, closing alongside the lobster boat. I could see Tommy clearly. His black hair glowed above a face only slightly less visible than darkness. For moments his face seemed only surreal as he concentrated on laying the forty alongside. Case and Wert—and a vague shape like an echo of me —stood at the rail. Two figures jumped, and to his credit, Wert tried. His shoulders moved forward, but his feet did not follow. He fumbled, fell against the low rail, regained his feet.

I watched us make mistakes, as young men in action almost always make mistakes. The few minutes of action aboard that lobster boat stretched toward timelessness. A slow-motion movie.

Case fell and rolled. My own vague form hesitated, finding its feet, as the madman stepped from the wheelhouse. The madman carried no weapon, and he raised his arms. As the form ran into him, I could see he only tried to shield his face. The madman fell against the wheelhouse, then rose slowly back to his feet. My form disappeared into the wheelhouse where it would port the helm, then search for a child who was not there. Case slowly stood, his left hand holding a wrench, and his right hand clasped to his left shoulder. His wound came from falling against a spike or a tool.

The madman howled and slowly retreated to the bow. He screamed, "Stay back, stay back, stay back." Then he screamed, "Tommy, Tommy, Tommy."

Case followed him as the forty made a tight sweep away and turned back toward us. Case should have waited for help. That madman was no threat. As the madman pulled a stake from a lobster trap, Case stumbled. He was on his knees, trying to throw the wrench, when my shade appeared from the wheelhouse. The two men were so close that my dive at the madman actually carried me over Case's back; and I, watching my own ghost, saw that the madman tried to stab no one but himself. The sound of the forty's engines rose.

How much did Tommy see? He saw it all. How much did Wert see? Practically none. Wert stood in the stern beside the engines.

And so it was that madness covered Tommy's face, and that in this time of torment two madmen sacrificed themselves on the altars of their guilt.

Tommy, who had killed with depth charges, now drove toward the rocks in a last and frantic display that may—or may not—have had the least thing to do with saving Case; a man who did not need saving. The madman stood facing the huge blade that was the forty's bow, and he screamed in exaltation or expiation, waving his arms toward him as if to attract the bow against his chest.

When the forty hit rock it stumbled, then drove its bow onto the beach, the tearing of steel striking showers of sparks as it crumpled against rocks. Wert tumbled against the engine house as water flooded the stern. Tommy cut the engines, ran aft where the lobster boat lay rolled on its side in shallow water. The bow was sheared away, and beneath the hull extended legs in sea boots; legs of the lobsterman, twisted and torn. Case lay against a crumpled rail with blood draining in arterial spurts, while my faint form lay halfway in shallow water, my head resting on a rock like a young boy nestled against a pillow. Tommy did not dive in, he fell in as he hurried first toward Case, then toward me.

I do not know whether it was my voice—although I think it was—or the voice of the sea that called forth: "A sailor's pay. A sailor's pay."

They gathered about me, the spirits of those four men, as I drew up the anchor and began working the boat back toward moorings in the city. The pale moon face of Wert lived faintly in the mist. It silently protested, explained, attempted to find language that would in some way speak inexpressible thoughts.

Case stood beside me at the helm—the wan form of Case, the kind face of Case—a man who had made his own young mistakes. He did not bare his chest, did not display his wounds. If anything he seemed proud that I had raised a knife to help a friend.

These were my comrades. In many ways they were closer to me than the living crew of my Alaskan vessel.

Tommy and the lobsterman seemed no more than tendrils of fog that intermixed, that somehow bonded together for the present, and perhaps for eternity. It came to me that all of us, or parts of us, are doomed to strut our roles on that obscure stage during all nights when ice fog lies across the harbor. The lobsterman will endure his earned portion of hell, and we, the crew of that forty-footer, will inflict our errors on him.

I now understand that Tommy's silence was the silence of madness. When he could not speak he took action, perhaps even trying to do the right thing; but I know now that no one could protect him from the knowledge that he had killed Case. I also know that Tommy protected me, for he had to have figured out my share of our mistakes. From that weather cutter to which our cap transferred him, he slipped overboard in search of silence. He knew that, sooner or later in his drunkenness, the story would get abroad.

Tommy was heroic in his way. Darkness reached for him twice, the first time with depth charges, the second time with the grounding of the forty. He fought against darkness in the only way he could. He sought the eternal silence of death.

Darkness tries to kill light. I pulled the old clasp knife from my pocket. Wert seemed only confused, while Case smiled. The interleaving forms of the lobsterman and Tommy appeared to express only sadness. It was not the knife that was wanted here, only my understanding. Perhaps the knife should have been thrown overboard.

But, it still rests in my pocket, to be carried until death, and perhaps carried to the grave. This knife is all I have of youth, because I know now that the part of me that remains on that cold coast is the ghost of my youth, forever tied to the rising scream of diesels.

The men disappeared into mist as I groped the final approach to moorage. There is little left to say. I will return to Alaska, and will make three more trips from Anchorage, maybe four. Then I will retire and find a small apartment near the docks. Although I will never finish my business with my comrades and the sea, I think perhaps they have finished their business with me. We, who were never really at war, have somehow still discovered peace. I think that between all of us, all has been forgiven.

JULEEN BRANTINGHAM

Something About Camilla

They ducked out of the gathering in the gym so early that few would notice they'd been there. They'd never been much for the official functions in high school either, had skipped prom and graduation to hold their own celebrations here at the Shamrock. Surprised to find it was still standing, unchanged, the light the same watery yellow, the walls a sludgy green, and high over the bar the cobwebs Sherry had once compared to vampire bats still swayed, sucking fumes of beer and melancholy. There was a new bartender, newer bottles on the shelves in front of the mirror, but the old men at the bar, hunched over their beer like gargoyles, they were the same, looked the same anyway.

"Whatever happened to Camilla?"

She was just making noise, an attempt to forestall the accusations she knew so well, the quick over-the-shoulder glance, the edginess on the verge of a shudder, the bitten-off words: God, Sherry, you're so damn quiet. What's wrong with you? Aren't you having fun? As if silence were a crime. As if her friends didn't know about her silences, didn't know she wasn't inwardly sneering, as she'd been accused of doing. Even them. So she had to make conversational noises.

But her question fell into one of those uncanny silences when an angel moved nearby, leaving everyone thought-struck, dangerously close to speaking aloud something usually covered over with a joke or half-truth. Her timing—she'd always been bad about that, too—gave the question an importance she hadn't meant it to have. She felt them draw back.

"Camilla? I don't think I remember a Camilla. You were always picking up such odd people, Sherry. Are you sure she was in our class?"

Gaynelle, frowning into the negative space between Sherry and Red as if it were a thing of deep significance, was fiddling with the clasp of her diamond bracelet. Nothing less than diamonds for Gaynelle, like the glittery chips of personal history she'd been scattering before them tonight.

Sherry examined her thought as Gaynelle must have examined the bracelet on the jeweler's counter before handing over the Senator's credit card. Is it well made? Is it worth what I'll have to pay? Always doing this to herself, describing, shuffling words around, thinking she should wait to fix it in the second draft, knowing she'd never get to the second draft because she'd get bogged down in the first, trying out different ways of saying the same thing. And, while she was mired down in these constructions, letting the first draft of her life slip away.

By the time she'd sorted out Gaynelle's diamond bracelet and pearls before swine, not that Gaynelle treated them like swine, she found the conversation had taken a few turns without her noticing and they'd fallen into another silence.

Phil was lifting her glass in its self-made puddle precisely that fraction of an inch that when she released it, it would skate an inch or two, following the slant of the wobbly table toward the meaty slabs of Red's arms. The puddle smeared and thinned until the glass wouldn't skate any more. Only then did she look up at Sherry, catching up the stitch of her question.

"Camilla. Wasn't she the one got pregnant our junior year and when she tried to get her boyfriend to marry her, he got all his buddies to say they'd been with her too? Seem to remember she took a fistful of sleeping pills."

"No, that was Ellen, Evelyn, something like that. The one everyone was talking about tonight, had a couple hit records a few years back. C and W," John said.

Pleased smiles around the table, a silent toast by the Outcasts to the continuing popularity of he-done-me-wrong songs.

The Senator's wife launched into a description of a party she'd attended where Willie Nelson was guest of honor—"can't see the attraction myself but the Senator likes him"—and from the way everyone was hanging on her words Sherry knew they had put her question out of their minds, to forget Camilla for all time, as if she'd never existed. She hadn't really cared when she asked, scarcely remembered Camilla herself, only the clutch of sweaty hands, her eyes hard and shiny with a desperate, trapped look. But she suddenly found herself caring very much. Why had her hands always been sweaty? Why had she clutched? They'd all felt trapped, misunderstood, unappreciated in high school, which was why they'd banded together, mutual aid and comfort. Camilla's clutch marked her as one of their own. She *had* been part of the group, hadn't she? For a while? How could the others not even try to remember? Pass on to marriages and promotions and other marks of success, as if they weren't already bored with hearing them, saying them.

Sherry weighed the trouble of raising her voice, forcing herself to buck the tide, against her concern for a pathetic waif nobody else wanted to remember and found that for once she didn't care if they were annoyed. She wanted to hear Camilla had, like the rest of them, attained some small triumph. This was the night for bragging, for ignoring the fact that when you win your dreams, when you move into them you find them tawdry, less satisfying than you could have believed. She plunged into the middle of a conversation about something else entirely.

"You *must* remember Camilla. Seventh grade or maybe eighth. She made those pot holder things and sold them door-to-door."

Jenny gave her the look that said she was being rude, talking about things nobody else cared about, being Sherry again. Then covered it over with a smile of saccharine forgiveness.

"No, I made the pot holders," Gaynelle said in a voice no longer diamond-bright, a voice that grated like cinders, the way they crunched under your feet when you walked to her shabby house in that gray row next to the railroad tracks. Then Sherry remembered it had been Gaynelle, calling herself Gay then in a determined effort to avoid the grandmotherish Nellie. Remembered being dragged along a time or two when she tried to sell them. Remembered the future Senator's wife vomiting in the bushes because, she'd confessed, wiping her mouth on the tail of her dress, she hated walking up to perfect strangers and having them look at her as if they could see the holes in her underpants, as if they knew, no question, she'd had nothing to eat the past three days but cold cereal and little of that. Worse still, have them pay for that knowledge, not for the pot holders she'd sat up late making when she should have been studying. Made with an artist's eye for texture and color, knowing they'd wind up in the stranger's wastebasket.

"Maybe it was paper flowers Camilla made," Sherry said faintly, feeling wretched, knowing Camilla hadn't made paper flowers or sold greeting cards or raked leaves for the quarter or fifty cents that would have put a loaf of bread on her family's table. It was Gay she'd been thinking of, Gay she'd pitied. When had Gay transformed herself to Gaynelle, who'd joined the cheerleading squad their senior year, who'd won a scholarship, who'd dropped out of college to marry the future Senator and put him through law school, and who was as far now from needing pity as the earth was from the moon?

The conversation turned back to John's career, vice president of something important. Sherry tried to look interested but a pudgy ghost hovered at her elbow; there were marks like the oily smears left by a clutching hand on the table top; the sound of Camilla's slightly asthmatic breath filled Sherry's head, not loud enough to drown out the whispery plea: Help me. Why are you doing this? Had Camilla, at some time or other, spoken those words? Did we do something to her? The weak turning on the weakest to escape our own sense of worthlessness?

"We got what we wanted, didn't we?"

For once her timing was right. Nods, smiles just short of smug. Then a flicker, almost doubt. Had they? If attaining the goals you set yourself in high school was success, they had it: John's financial wizardry, Jenny's teaching career, Gaynelle's husband, the authority that hovered around Red even when he wasn't wearing his badge. And Phil. Whatever Phil counted as success, she had it; she wore that sleek, catlike look the way Red wore his invisible badge. And Sherry, she couldn't complain. Two novels had been dismal failures but they'd followed one solid success, the one written in a white-hot passion Thanksgiving week, her first year in college. She was making a living, never cared about being rich 'n' famous. Or so she told herself when she came home from her bread and butter to face another dreary evening at the typewriter. More often, not to face it.

Wondering where the excitement had gone. Which failure had finally smothered it.

Why this vague sense of guilt?

"Camilla . . . ," she began.

"I remember who you mean. She was that little rat-faced kid got caught in the showers with the gym teacher," Red said.

"No, that was—" Jenny began, then jerked, first spilling her drink, then knocking the glass to the floor, where it shattered. There was a fuss with napkins and tissues, needless warnings about broken glass, jokes about not being able to hold her liquor, while her face turned maroon.

Phil wasn't embarrassed. She locked gazes with Red—who'd never made a careless mistake in his life—and allowed cigarette smoke to plume from her mouth to her nose, then blew it in his face. Smiling.

"Take you home." It wasn't a question. Someone who didn't know Phil would have said it wasn't even particularly friendly. Just Phil, her way.

"Why can't I remember Camilla? The memories are so vague. I didn't make her up, did I?" Getting into the car, the solid *thunk* of the door telling her this moment, at least, was really happening. Sometimes she wondered, always making up stories for herself, what was real and what wasn't.

"Probably not. I don't remember a Camilla but a lot of things I thought I'd forgotten have been coming back to me since I got back to town. Remember where we used to go before we were old enough for the Shamrock?"

Before they were old enough and sometimes after, when they had something on their minds that could only be spoken of with darkness to veil their faces, in that peculiar atmosphere where the superficial was peeled away. Some places, some memories you don't forget; they're too much a part of what you are. "Gates will be locked."

The car started with a jerk; gravel spattered.

"They always were. Don't tell me you're too old to climb."

Was Camilla the one who vomited at least once a week in biology? The one who'd embarrassed them, entering every talent competition with her clumsy tap dancing? Sherry worried at the problem like a mouse gnawing a crust. All she could find were these wisps of memory that wouldn't connect.

Why the guilt? What had they done?

Headlights worked magic on the leaves, gave them a springlike tint they hadn't had for months as the car arrowed through tunnels that were tree-lined streets. The trees were older. That was the only real change. The town looked the same but for the occasional new house or store but those weren't really changes, more as if the scenery had been shuffled, the lighting changed. The people they'd known in high school, now wearing hand-me-down faces made for much larger people, had stepped into their parents' shoes, put on responsibility like a kingly mantle; some still couldn't give up dress and hair styles that had been fashionable twenty years ago; they used dated slang to say the same things their parents used to say. It was a strange sort of double vision but it wasn't change. Only the trees were different, older, thicker, resigned to the slow pull of gravity and years.

Phil slapped the steering wheel. "Now I remember who you mean. Camilla's father worked for Swan Rubber, got a job in Akron our freshman year." In reflected light her face was a brittle shell like a Mardi Gras mask Sherry had once seen in New Orleans.

Another wisp of memory: standing at her locker, shuffling through books and papers, late for a French Club meeting and impatient with Camilla, who was holding her back. She didn't want to go to Akron, she said, didn't want to leave her friends. Thinking: We don't like you all that much. Telling her . . . telling her she'd soon make new friends, not meaning that at all. Thinking: God, why does it have to be Camilla? If *I* had a chance to get out of this dreary place . . .

Phil's head pivoted, robotlike, one side white with a spot of rose on her cheek, the other side in shadow. "She went away. That's why we had so much trouble remembering. She just wasn't part of the group long enough to make an impression. That's all it is."

Another wisp: leaves crackling beneath their feet, breath puffing white in front of their faces, darkness, giggles, and something shameful, some dirty little secret, something about Camilla.

What had they done?

The car dipped as Phil steered it onto the verge next to the tall spike-tipped rods of the cemetery fence. Sound died. Light died. Silence rushed in, thick and chilling, and with it panic.

"I think I'll—" What? Stay in the car? Her words were cut off by the slam of Phil's door, so loud Sherry almost expected someone to shout at them to keep quiet, people were trying to sleep. Only there weren't any houses out here on cemetery road. Stifling a giggle, picturing one who might rise in indignation, she fumbled for the door handle, her hand slick. Stay here feeling sick, heart pounding? Better the ghosts in the cemetery than the one who made her arms feel clammy, as if just released from the clutch of sweaty hands.

Help me. Please. Let me out.

A whispery plea as if she no longer had the breath for screaming, no longer had the strength to hope.

Not too old to climb, though the spikes of the fence scared her more than they ever had. Last year's leaves formed a sodden strip between fence and inner road. Should be an owl, she thought; should be a moon and high, scudding clouds. But there was only starlight, bright enough, and rustling leaves and a chill that felt like October. She followed the blur of Phil's tan suede jacket across the road to the nearest row of upright slabs, passing the concrete benches in the "Garden of Meditation." Benches were for sissies, they'd agreed twenty years ago; headstones were for sitting, daring the ghosts to object. They'd been brave about ghosts, knowing the real terrors were to be found in daylight, in school corridors, in classrooms.

Stone was damned cold and uncomfortable, something she'd never noticed twenty years ago. Phil lit another cigarette and Sherry sniffed hungrily, wishing she'd never given them up.

"That was some book."

A fist unclenched. She'd been waiting all night, waiting eighteen years to hear what Phil thought of her first novel. She'd put the six of them in it, of course, scarcely disguised. After it came out the others had phoned, pretending to be angry, secretly—not so secretly flattered. But Phil was the one she'd taken for her viewpoint character, the one she'd admired, wished to be all through high school and after, and Phil was the one who hadn't phoned. Because of that love and admiration, Sherry's portrait had not been flattering. Would Phil understand?

Waiting, still waiting to hear what Phil really thought, it came to her that she hadn't written Camilla in, not even as a walk-on. If she'd tried —everyone else was there from the kindergarten teacher to the ticket seller at the bus station—she must have deleted her in an early draft, someone who cluttered the scenes. It was as if the girl had no character traits of her own, merely echoed those of the Outcasts.

"That Tawny now—" Phil's voice trailed away. "You know, I had people come up to me after the book came out. Didn't know where I came from, never heard me talk about you. But they'd say I was Tawny to the life."

Another silence. Was she pleased or not?

"These past few years . . ." Her voice was distant, colorless. "I've sometimes wondered if it's *my* life I'm leading or if I'm just doing things because they're what Tawny would have done. Strangest feeling."

And that, apparently, was all Sherry was going to get, not nearly enough to feed her hunger.

This reunion was turning out to be a disappointment from beginning to end.

They turned at the sound of a car rolling down the hill, the motor off. Of course Red would have keys to the gate and of course he wouldn't risk weight or dignity climbing the fence, not even for old time's sake.

He opened the door and put a foot outside but didn't get out. "Run you two in," he threatened. "Hooligans. How many headstones have you tipped over?"

"Only a couple little ones. Need your muscle to do the job proper," Phil said.

The door on the passenger side opened and Gaynelle stepped out, her perfectly coifed head a cutout against the lighter sky. She didn't move from the far side of the car, didn't speak, only put one hand on the roof, turned to display her profile. There was a scuffle of dried leaves behind Sherry: John and Jenny, picking their way around the headstones. Sherry's panic returned. They were all here now, as if they'd planned it, as if they'd made an appointment twenty years ago. Something to finish. Something to make sure of.

Sherry waited for someone to say something.

An unfelt breeze moved the trees. How else to account for the moving shadows, the feeling there were more than six people here? It was rustling leaves she heard, not raspy breathing. It was rotting leaves that smelled sour, not sweat.

John cleared his throat. "Sherry, that girl you mentioned? I think I remember her. From math class."

It was a friendship offering. John remembered nothing from math class but the numbers that slid around inside his head and would never stay still, numbers that had threatened to drown him, drive him insane. Sherry would have accepted it for what it was but Red spoke, harshly.

"No you don't. None of you remember. You went away. Couldn't get out fast enough. You left me here with it."

What was he talking about?

The sound of breathing was loud.

Gaynelle walked around to face him, the open door a barrier between them. "It was a joke," she snapped. "It didn't mean anything. We didn't actually *do* anything."

"Didn't we? Whose funeral was it we went to, senior year?"

A pit yawned at Sherry's feet; she fell in: senior year. Last chance to change their luck, put all their bad breaks, all their failures behind them, really knuckle down. Six weeks into the school year they couldn't escape knowing nothing was going to change. The poems Sherry had poured her heart into, passed over with "Very sweet, dear." Didn't want sweet: wanted to grab them by the throats, yank them out of somnolence. Gaynelle passed over for the cheerleading squad again, all her hopes pinned on being chosen one of those bright, pretty ones. Red's father arrested again. Phil's troubles and John's and Jenny's. That night in the cemetery Sherry had been sunk so deep in her own misery she was scarcely aware of theirs. Who was it who'd spoken the thought aloud: Might as well stop kidding ourselves. Cut our throats. Jump off the railroad bridge.

They'd never be able to put it behind them. Whatever *it* was. What held each one of them back.

The Outcasts, failures for all time.

Sherry had started it, in that whispery little voice so suitable for the cemetery, that voice she'd hated, not known how to change.

"Do you remember Camilla? From junior high?"

"Fat," Red put in. "Fat and slow."

"Counted on her fingers."

"Left sweaty smears on all her papers."

Each of them adding up Camilla's faults, the things they'd hated about her.

"That voice of hers. Gave me the shudders. So timid. Always afraid of offending people. Couldn't say what she meant," Sherry said.

Maybe it was witchcraft, fueled by despair. With each word Camilla seemed to grow more solid until, there in the darkness among the headstones, she was as real as any of them. Time and distance meant nothing: Camilla was there, whining, clutching, sweating, the focus of all their misery. They were the Outcasts, the losers, but even *they* had someone they could look down on. From focus to scapegoat in one small step.

Who'd started picking at the dirt by the fence? Who'd suggested making it deeper, making it real? Who'd suggested putting Camilla in it? They were all slightly hysterical by then, slightly mad. Giggling. Unable to stop. Staggering and falling as if they were drunk. Grabbing Camilla . . . flinching at the touch. Silence then. No one giggled; no one said what Sherry felt was going to burst from her throat with a scream: She's real. I can feel her. Hear her.

In silence. But hadn't someone grunted at the weight of the nothing in their hands? Hadn't someone gasped aloud at the thud when they threw her in? A clod of dirt. That's what made the sound. A clod of dirt falling from the side.

Covering over emptiness. Sealing it in with showers of earth and whispered curses, incantations.

Help me. Please. Let me out of here. Why are you doing this?

Next morning, shamed but somehow feeling better for their silliness in the cemetery, none of them could look another in the eye. Half-afraid their idiocy was branded on their foreheads. None of them could talk about it but now and then one would let loose with a laugh, shake her head, and the others would know why.

And somehow, life got better that day for each one.

Days later, Sherry was in earth-science class with Phil and Red when the announcement came over the PA system. She'd had to look at her friends to make sure she'd really heard it, hadn't hallucinated the principal's announcement. Even then . . . disbelieving . . . unable to talk about it.

Help me. Please.

They'd attended her funeral. Felt they owed it to her.

"A joke," Gaynelle repeated. "Nothing happened. It didn't mean anything."

"A joke, yeah. But it brought us luck, didn't it?" John's voice.

Sherry shook her head absentmindedly. Except for the numbers that slid around inside his head, John wasn't known for accuracy; he was blind to subtleties.

Red pulled himself out of the car. "Come over here. Want to show you something."

Sherry heard a click and a beam of yellow light led them to the soggy strip of leaves next to the fence. Red kicked at the leaves, moved down to another place, kicked again. Kneeling, he scraped the soggy mat from the dead grass, clearing a space about a foot square. He put the flashlight down, making a bubble of light, then placed his hands flat on the ground.

"Put your hands here."

Sherry knelt, Phil crowding her to the left, Jenny to the right. Six pairs of hands in a bubble of light. The feel of damp, dead grass.

But not the expected chill: the earth was warm, warm as life.

"What is this, Red? You got your deputies hiding behind the graves, ready to jump out and take pictures of us doing something stupid? Nice footnote to the reunion." But there was an edge to John's voice and he didn't pull his hands away.

"Wait."

Warmth . . . and, very faintly, a pulse.

Sherry snatched her hands back, wiped them on her jacket. The others, except for Red, were doing the same with expressions of disgust.

"It's a trick! It's our own heartbeats we're feeling!"

Phil was muttering swearwords; Jenny began to sob. Someone kicked the flashlight and it rolled away.

Red's teeth were gleaming, all Sherry could see of him aside from the black bulk at her feet.

"This probably isn't even the same place. You can't remember a thing like that after all these years. You're just doing this to scare us." Why didn't she believe it?

Why wasn't he laughing at them now, agreeing it was so?

"I come back here three or four times a year. It's always warm. The beat is always strong. I don't think it's strong enough to get out by itself but maybe if we helped . . ."

"Did you guys ever wonder what we really buried here that night? Did you ever want to dig it up and find out?"

Sherry began to back away, her hands clamped tight across her mouth. Whatever was down there, whatever it had already cost, whatever it would cost in the future, she didn't want it back.

NICHOLAS ROYLE

Parallax

The sky was blue, the trees and grass green, and the gravestones that showed through the foliage were gray. The great crosses poking out of the trees were dark brown, and the shadowy figures grouped around them were of a light shade, perhaps off-white. The whole scene was bathed in the soft orange glow of the late afternoon sun, a blur just behind the veil of branches and leaves.

Debbie was looking at the sky.

"It looks as if a cat had scratched it with its claws."

Tom looked up and saw the scratchings of cirrus; white scars in deep blue.

"Yes; but, Debbie, look at this."

She looked down and considered the scene.

"It must be a deserted graveyard." She had only seen the gravestones rising out of the undergrowth to their left.

"But, Debbie, look at those crosses."

She turned her head to the right and saw three huge wooden crosses rising above the treetops. She stared for a moment.

"I haven't got my glasses with me. Are those people underneath them?"

"People or statues," he answered. "Come on; let's go and have a look."

He took her hand and led her down the path, kicking through the leaves, toward the clearing at the bottom.

They stood in front of three crosses which rose out of a large mound, scaled on the right by stone steps. It looked like a stage. The actors neither moved nor spoke. From left to right on stage level were a Roman soldier, a praying woman, another woman clinging to the base of the center cross, and a second man, his arms fixed in a supplicatory gesture. Above these four, nailed to the center cross, was Christ. The sun cast human shadows on their stony faces. The statue-actors were made of stone, and they were, or had been, white.

"Tom," her voice sounded unnaturally loud in the still air, "what is this? It's weird."

Equally puzzled, Tom shook his head slowly, and walked up to the grassy proscenium. There was a black metal plate there at the feet of the statues. It was crisscrossed with erect nails, pointing up to the sky. Around the bases of many of the nails candle wax had formed runnelled patterns. The candles must have been burned years ago, for the wax was black with accumulated forest dirt. Tom scratched at the dirt with his fingernail but none of it came off. Maybe it wasn't dirt . . .

He looked up and felt his attention suddenly drawn by the cross on the left. It had seemed to move.

"What's the matter, Tom?" Debbie asked, sensing that something wasn't quite right.

"Nothing, nothing. It just looked as if a cross moved. But it was just my looking up like that. Made it appear to move against the trees." Now he put his arm around her shoulders and adopted a mock-professorial tone. "Basic law of physics, Miss Young. Parallax. When a body appears to move in relation to a body behind it, resulting from a change in observation point."

Tom knew that Debbie knew less about physics than he did (which

was practically nothing), so he could quote with confidence this definition of parallax, which he drew from very vague memories of boring
lessons in sunny classrooms. For all Tom knew, the definition might
have been quite wrong; but he had to say something to appease Debbie, for he had thought that the cross had moved, and he knew she
would think he was being foolish. And so he was, anyway: crosses don't
move. It was just that Tom needed longer to convince himself of the
rational than did Debbie.

"I'm going to have a look at the graves," he announced. "I don't
suppose you'd like to?"

"You're quite right, I wouldn't like to particularly. I'll sit down on
the bench."

"Yes, you do that. After all, you need a rest. We must have walked,
what, half a mile maybe. Yes, give your poor legs a rest."

"Kilometer, Tom, half a kilometer. Or two thirds or whatever. We're
not in England now, you know." With this she made a playful swipe
for his backside. He loved her when she was like this. In fact, he loved
her all the time. He bent down to whisper in her ear and told her so.
Then he slipped away to go and look at the graves.

There were ten of them, in two rows: six on one side, four on the
other; feet together. The four together were not spaced out to cover
the same area as the six. They faced four of the graves on the other
side, thereby leaving a space of two graves' width at one end. A huge
cross, like the others in size, but apparently hewn out of stone, stood
over the graves at one end. Tom turned his attention to the headstones.
All the names and inscriptions—apart from the ubiquitous R. I. P.—
were Polish. Ks Julian Pawlowski, Wiaterowi, Wszolek, Kedzierski. He
read one of them out loud:

"Ks Jozef Kronkowski. 11.3.1912–3.9.1982."

He stopped before R. I. P. because he suddenly had the unmistakable feeling of having spoken out loud when and where he shouldn't
have. He turned on his heels and spotted Debbie's red scarf through
the trees. She was looking the other way, but waiting patiently for him
all the same. He told himself not to be so silly, and was making to
leave, when one of the graves caught his eye. It was the grave next but
one to the empty space. The stone slab was slightly adrift. There was a
dark triangle down into which he could look if he so desired; but, he
remembered, he'd seen plenty of half-open tombs in the Père Lachaise
cemetery. He'd peered into those, only to see wine bottles, cigarette

ends, and other such urban debris lying on the stone underneath. No gleaming coffin teak, just more stone.

He looked up; Debbie was beckoning to him. He picked his way through the trees to join her.

"Was it good?" she asked.

"Yes. They're all Polish."

"All Polish. Are they all dead?"

He bent down and kissed her, being the only thing he could do in the situation. She would never share his curiosity, and it was best not to get upset about it. After all . . .

Tom's head suddenly turned sharply to the left. He stared at the small lake at the foot of the slope on which they stood.

"What's the matter, Tom? What is it?"

Tom didn't answer; he just stared at the lake, his eyes lost to her.

"Tom!"

He looked at her, with unseeing eyes, pricked with fear. Then the spell broke as abruptly as it had seized him. He gave his head a little shake and smiled at her.

"Tom. What's wrong?"

"Nothing, darling."

He tried to kiss her. She stopped him and pressed instead for an explanation.

"Oh, it was just one of my dizzy spells, you know. It's all right. Gone now."

"Why did you look at the lake like that?"

"Lake? What lake? Oh, that one. I don't know. Pretty, isn't it? The way the trees are reflected in the surface." In the surface, the calm unruffled surface. Like a sheet of glass or ice. Not a ripple in sight. His eyes were playing tricks on him. There wasn't a breath of wind and he guessed there were no big fish. Yet he'd seen a ripple. No, he couldn't have. It had been his imagination. Of course it had.

He made an effort to pull himself together for Debbie's sake. He smiled at her. She looked concerned.

"Come on, love," he said. "It's nothing."

"I don't think . . ."

He silenced her with a finger on her lips. Then he kissed her. She smiled. Even if still worried, it looked like she was going to let it drop. Holding each other's hands, they glanced down the steep path. A dog was skipping up toward them, still some way off, followed at a short distance by a man. Tom and Debbie looked at each other and held one another again. As they kissed, they felt the air around them move as if someone were passing. The man and the dog should still be coming up the hill. They looked down: no one was there. They looked the other way, toward the graves, and saw the man and the dog a good hundred and fifty yards away.

Debbie was becoming agitated. She began asking questions. Tom couldn't explain because there was no explanation.

"See how time flies," he tried, "when I kiss you?"

Debbie didn't say anything. She just looked frightened.

"Come on," he said. "Let's walk a bit. Get away from all these crosses and things."

They were at the bottom of the hill, looking at another statue scene —Christ lying down with another man in attendance—when the dog bounded up to them. Now they saw him more clearly, they could see he only had three good legs. The front left leg was broken and twisted at an awkward angle. Tom was not a dog lover: he left Debbie fussing over the animal and went to inspect a little plaque on the wall near the statues. Apart from three French words it was written in Polish, of which Tom couldn't understand a word. The French words were "La Pologne Chrétienne," Christian Poland. He looked over at Debbie playing with the dog. She'll be thinking I can't be bothered, he thought. Debbie looked up and smiled. Tom smiled back and walked over. He stroked the dog abstractedly for a moment. The path they were on was right by the fence. On the other side of the fence at the bottom of the slope was the lake. Tom stood at the fence, his knuckles white gripping the wire; he stared at the lake. Debbie looked up. Tom had his back to her. She turned her attention back to the dog. If Tom didn't like dogs, he didn't like them, and that was that. She didn't see his face, the way it was changing as he stared into the lake. The way the features, every single one, indicated stark terror. He flicked his gaze upward and there again was the parallax. Something seemed to disturb the surface of the lake when he shifted his gaze. He'd seen parallax before, of course; he saw instances of it every day, as does every sighted person. So why did the lake terrify him? What was there?

"Tom."

What was there in the lake?

"Tom."

What was there in the lake that was terrifying the living daylights out of him?

He felt a hand on his shoulder and spun round. The fear was all over his face; she could read it there.

"Are you going to tell me what it is?"

"It's nothing. That's what's so stupid . . . I don't know. I honestly don't know."

He was frightened. But he couldn't tell her, because there was nothing to tell. Basic law of physics . . . He needed her comfort. He could tell her that, but he didn't need to because she'd seen it in his eyes, and she held him in her arms. They stayed that way until he felt his strength returning, coming from her; he hoped there wouldn't come a day when he would find it all used up.

The dog was yapping excitedly and jumping up at them, pawing them with his one good front leg.

"What is it, eh?" Tom bent down and talked to the dog. "What's the matter? What are you so excited about? Hmm?"

Debbie was looking away. She didn't want Tom to see her crying. He'd think she was upset; she wasn't. It wasn't sad crying, it was happy. It was emotional, but not sad emotional. The dog's eyes; they were so beautiful, so intelligent, so like . . .

Tom's eyes were beginning to hurt, so he let the tears come. With his hand he found Debbie's leg and hugged it tight. She put her hands in his hair and lowered her eyes to him so that he stood up, and they hugged each other again.

"The dog knows."

"Knows what?" Tom asked, still distracted by the lake.

"About us," she whispered in his ear. "He knows all about us. I can feel it. I can see it in his eyes. Such beautiful, beautiful eyes."

"I know," he said, now understanding. He could be confident that Debbie knew that he knew. They had shared the same experience again, almost as if they were the same person. There was something very strong between them; call it love, call it a psychic experience, call it total empathy, they didn't need to give it a name, it was theirs.

"I keep expecting his owner to appear out of nowhere," Tom said.

"Yes, that gray man."

"Gray?"

"Yes, he was sort of gray. Oh, Tom, I wish we could keep the dog."

"Mmm, but we can't."

"No, I know. Come on. We'll have to leave him."

He took her hand and they walked down the path. The dog followed just behind.

"Look! He's following us. We'll have to just keep walking and see if he leaves us. He'll probably get bored if we pretend we don't know he's there."

They continued going downhill. Twice Tom glanced at the lake and saw the disappearing ripples each time. When the ground leveled out they found themselves beside an apparently deserted house. Most of the windows were bricked in, some were just boarded up. The walls showed signs of age and decay.

"I'm going to have a look round the other side," Tom announced.

The dog was jumping up at Debbie's legs. Tom left them and plunged into the long grass at the side of the house. The ground rose; at the back of the house he was on a level with the first floor. The windows were blocked up, the only door padlocked. On the fourth side Tom found a window with its glass intact. He tried to look in but couldn't focus. Then he saw why: the glass was reflecting the lake across the path and down the slope. The reflection showed surfacing ripples in the middle of the lake. He whirled round and gazed upon the still calm water.

"Tom." Debbie was calling him. Thank Goodness! Back to normality; first though, back to the glass . . . He glanced in the window as he turned to go, and thought he saw something inside. He peered in. It was very dark, he couldn't make anything out. He shrugged and began to turn again, his eyes trailing across the angles, and he saw for the second time, only for a split second, the series of white rounded shapes like . . . like . . . something he'd seen, he was sure, but he couldn't think what. The memory he had was like the memory of a dream—it hovered just beyond his grasp.

He rejoined Debbie and they walked around to the other side of the small lake. At one point Tom thought he saw, out of the corner of his eye, something sticking up out of the lake. Of course, when he looked directly at the lake there was nothing there. His anxiety grew. The dog had disappeared now, presumably having gone in search of his master. A small stream flowed out of the lake at one end. A little way down the stream, on the far bank, was a bonfire. It made a very striking picture: the fire bright in the foreground. Above that the trees, dark, concealing the statues, the crosses, and the graves. And above the trees the sky, now a deep luminous blue; the brilliant white moon wanting just a thin sliver to make it complete.

They stood watching for a few minutes.

"Shall we go?"

"I suppose we'd better."

They went back the way they had come. Tom strayed a little to have another look at the graves. There was something plucking at some part of his brain. It was the dates, something to do with the dates, what was it? He looked at them all. They were all fairly recent, but then why shouldn't they be? The dates specified the day and the month as well as the year. That was it; the numbers of the days, they were all close together. Different months, but each death was around the same time each month. In fact, there seemed to be a sequence: a death a month. The sequence had its gaps here and there, but it still struck Tom as having an order to it. Spring tides, full moons, menstruation, all monthly events. Surely the life span of Polish Christians wasn't governed in this way by the calendar. Ridiculous, thought Tom. He was assuming of course that the deaths were natural. He was also assuming that the date referred to the death; why couldn't it be the date of the burial? After all, this was hardly a graveyard to stick to conventions . . .

Something startled Tom out of his thoughts. He was staring at the second-to-most-recent grave—the one he had noticed earlier for its displaced stone. The stone was no longer displaced. It lay exactly where it was supposed to lie. Well, obviously he'd imagined it the first time. He'd only seen it out of the corner of his eye as he was leaving. Just then, a dead leaf fell and landed on the corner of the next grave. The leaf was black. Tom stared at it for a moment. It looked for all the world like the slab was displaced and you could see in. There we are, Tom told himself, puzzle solved. Now I can go. He ran to join Debbie.

Later that night, when they were alone together and close, Debbie asked Tom if he would see what the time was. As he was reaching over to get his watch, his gaze slipped across Debbie's face and onto the pillow. It was as if he had opened a door, a wrong door, and seen inside when he shouldn't have. Just for a split second, from the moving angle, he saw another face. Not the face of another woman. There never had been any that really counted anymore. It was the face of another Debbie, a Debbie who might leave him. There he was, reaching for the time, presented with the only real fear, the fear that she might leave

him, the fear of what he might become, of what he might not be able
to prevent.

"Love."

"Yes?"

"Are you all right?"

Pause.

"Yes."

"What are you thinking?"

"I'm trying to guess the time."

"No, you're not. What are you thinking about? Hmm?"

"I'd say it was 1:41 . . . close; it's 1:53."

"Tom."

"Hmm?"

"Tell me what you were thinking about."

"I can't."

But now he knew he would, because he had told her he couldn't. She
would press him and he would tell her. He was being unfair, he knew;
he should have resisted the temptation to say "I can't," which really
meant "I can't right now, but I'll let you squeeze it out of me in a
minute or two."

"I'm sorry, Debbie."

"What is it?"

"Please don't ever leave me," he said, scared to look her in the eye.

"Tom, I won't leave you. I've told you that. You've got to believe
me."

"Of course I believe you."

Of course he believed her. He knew that if she always felt the same,
she would never leave him. At least, not in that way. But there was
always the other way, over which she didn't have as much control, and
what control she could have was only indirect.

She cut into his thoughts: "Don't worry, Tom. You mustn't worry.
There's nothing to worry about."

But she knew that he would still worry sometimes, and the knowledge upset her. It occasionally gave her troubled dreams; three times
she had walked in her sleep. On the first two occasions she had gone to
the kitchen, opened a cupboard door, closed it again, and woken up
sitting at the kitchen table. The third time she had woken Tom in
climbing out of the bed. He had followed her and carefully guided her

back into bed without waking her. If only he wouldn't worry when he had no cause to do so.

That night Debbie dreamt of a rabbit that was being chased mercilessly by an elephant through a desert landscape. Tom's dream involved a statue of Christ being crucified and burnt to death on the cross. When Tom started to look away, he would see an expression of unbearable agony appear on the statue's face.

The following day, Debbie and Tom both had work to go to. They both had a long hard day, their lunch hours unfortunately not coinciding, and by the evening they were extremely tired, and quite ready to just drop into bed and go straight to sleep.

Tom went to the Polish cemetery again in the night. The moon was full. It made the statues glow with a ghostly luster which excited and frightened. The hooting of owls and screeching of other unidentified birds set the nerves on edge. As he walked through the trees, his very motion quite naturally caused his head to move. Consequently, the limits of his field of vision were constantly changing. Trees, crosses, statues, all seemed to move just as he did. He walked past the graves. They shone silver in the moonlight. There was a gaping black hole in the sand where an eleventh grave had been dug. In the distance through the trees, half-obscured, he saw a statue sway slightly. He slid his eyes through the angles; the statue stepped off its grassy pedestal and was hidden by the trees. Seconds later he felt a rush of air to his left. He glanced back anxiously at the graves to see a white shape—he turned his head slowly away—climb into the open grave. As Tom stood in front of the main crucifixion scene, his frightened eyes were drawn to black candles burning on the nails, dancing flickering flames. He found himself hurrying down the hill. Down toward the boarded-up old house, he was overtaken on the path by a huddled party of men and women. They moved silently past him like a low gray cloud, and entered the house by means of the padlocked door, now flung open. He heard the splashing of water on his left. He turned to the lake and saw concentric circles which disappeared as he stared. Looking back up the path, he saw the shoulder of one of the statues catching its own moonlight. The white rounded shape seemed familiar, evocative. The silent gray group passed him again, going uphill, carrying something large and white. They gathered around the main crucifixion scene, obscuring it from view, then left without their burden. Tom ran up the slope, feeling an irrational compulsion to see the people close to, but when he got to the area beyond the statues, they were nowhere to be seen. He was near the iron gates; he fled toward them and out of the wood. He walked home and found Debbie asleep in bed. Not wishing to disturb her sleep, he climbed in carefully beside her, and allowed his eyelids to close.

Tom was standing above the small lake, moving his head slowly and continuously from side to side. The circles kept breaking on the surface. Breaking and breaking . . . He slid his head further round and the surface of the lake was broken, sending concentric waves to the sides, as up through the pale moonlit water there rose the black and white figure of a nun. Tom slipped through the angles of vision several more times, to see each time the nun rise further out of the water . . .

Tom was wrenched away from the nun in the lake by a persistent scratching at the front door. He got out of bed, went and opened the door. The three-legged dog hopped in off the step. Tom bent down to stroke him but he skipped away, jumping at the large blanketed mound lying in the bed. Tom pulled back the covers. In Debbie's place lay a white statue of Mary, mother of Jesus. A noise in the doorway, Tom spun round. A nun, water dripping from the folds of her habit, stepped into the room. Her hand reached out for Tom's; he pulled away. She lifted up her head so he could see her face. Debbie's face. He whirled round to the bed—it was empty—and back to the nun, now a statue in nun's clothes. He picked up the nun-statue and dashed it to the floor, shattering it into scattering pieces.

Tom awoke on the floor, covered in sweat, shivering, a blanket twisted around him. He was frightened. He called out for Debbie, but she didn't reply. He pulled himself up and turned to the bed. It was empty. He ran to the kitchen, she wasn't there. Then he noticed that the front door was standing open. Grabbing a blanket from the bed, and jamming his feet into a pair of shoes, he ran out of the house.

She's all right, she's all right, he told himself over and over again, as he ran along the rue St. Jean. The full moon made the white houses look like the faces of sick people. Their ghastly white pallor and the black holes of the window-eyes. He careered into the iron gates, hitting his shin sharply against one of the bars, cursed, and was swallowed up by the trees. Branches swung and whipped him cruelly. He tore his fingernails on the bark of a trunk. All around him, whenever he wasn't looking properly, everything seemed to be moving. If he fixed his stare for a second, the statue, the tree, the cross stood quite still according to its nature. He reached the path going downhill and saw her shimmering white through the trees, moving so slowly, but already so close to the lake. He ran, half fell, down the little hill, and heard the splashing before he made the turn into the trees in front of the lake. He raced between the trunks, losing his shoes in the soft boggy ground, reached the water's edge, saw the back of her head go under, her shining hair floating a moment on the surface. He ran, swam, and got to the middle of the lake just as Debbie was floating back up to break the surface . . . Sending concentric waves to the sides, as up through the pale moonlit water there rose a familiar form. Her white nightdress was blackened with mud and sludge, black weed hooded her hair and framed her white face. Her eyes were open. He closed them. As he held her body tightly to his own and she dribbled lake water from the pressure on her lungs, his eyes slid along the shore of the lake, taking in the little group of gray people—there were eleven of them—standing there quietly watching him.

SHARON WEBB

The Door

The tattered shrubbery of autumn fathered the dead leaves of winter. Blowing before cold winds, they littered the seared grass with scraps of fading gold and orange.

Time for snow, thought Allison. Time for waiting. Time to hibernate for a while, to shut down for a while, like the trees.

The house knew it. It knew how to close in upon itself in the winter, knew how to suck in wisps of cold air through wooden crevices and send them scurrying through its halls and its rooms and hearths, breathing them out again from dusty flues.

Its shutters barred the coming winter. Its gables shrugged off the drifting leaves, and later would ignore the snow ridges riding the blackness of its roof.

Though they had bought the place for less than half its value, it had been madness to buy it—an October madness that coated porches and balustrades with a yellow late-afternoon glow reflected by the goldenrods in its unkempt lawn, answered by the mellowing hickories, hinted by the giant oaks. Enchanted, they signed the contract with trembling fingers, exchanging looks of bashful triumph and awe over what they had done. It *was* a bargain. And yet, it was more than they really could afford even with the modest income from Allison's trust fund.

That night, back at the apartment, secure in concrete conformity, they walked through the house again in their mind's eye, lingering for a moment in the front hall, running up the curving stairway, exploring the bedrooms one by one.

"It'll take an awful lot of paint," said Jeffry.

"Gallons," she agreed, "and tons of firewood to heat it. Four fireplaces"—she wondered at it—"not counting the stove in the kitchen."

But it really was a bargain, they told each other. So close to the university they'd save on gas, and firewood wasn't so high. They agreed it would have to be painted and perfect before they moved in—at least for those rooms they'd use at first. And they'd have the long fall break between quarters to get settled before Jeff had to get back to his art students and Allison to her graduate work in music.

Cracked mortar and flaking paint yielded to the persistent scrape of putty knife and wire brush. Paint insinuated itself on the walls: Williamsburg blue for the dining room, where Allison's collection of pewter mugs would line the mantle; bright white above the kitchen's dark wainscoting—blue onion plates would stand on shelves on either side of the cast-iron stove; midnight blue for the big bathroom to hide its pipes and show off its old claw-footed tub. Paint spilled from the wide soft brushes that Jeffry, artist that he was, insisted on using instead of rollers. Not satisfied with discount store colors, he mixed his own, adding gleaming old gold to the plaster touching the dark wood of the study and the master bedroom.

But what for the parlor? Allison wanted a sunny yellow—the parlor *was* on the north side of the house—but Jeffry was holding out for stark white, foil for his dark-framed still lifes.

Unable to decide, they left it for a time and ran together up the broad stairway to the second floor, and up again, single-file, feet scuffing on the narrow steps to the attic room.

"What do you think of oyster?" asked Allison.

Jeffry raised an eyebrow. "For a studio? It's got to be white. I don't want oyster mucking up my north light."

And white it became. It wasn't until they attacked the studio with paint brush and drop cloth that they noticed the regular line against irregular random wall boards.

"Listen." Jeffry's angular fingers tapped a rhythm against the wall. Dull thuds gave way to hollow drummings. "It's a door of some sort."

Allison's paint-stained fingers whispered over the plaster. "There must be a latch—if it's a door. Do you really think it's a door?" She shivered with pleasure. Could it really be a secret room? On her knees, blue jeans pressed against the dark floor, thick brown hair falling against her face, she ran long fingers along the grooves in the wall. "It won't open," she said, wanting it to and yet not wanting the wonder to wear off if it were really true. Like Christmas presents, she thought. They could be anything inside their wrappings, magical things, but when you opened them, the wonder was gone. Childish, she thought, and yet somehow she was relieved when the door, if it was a door, failed to give way to Jeffry's insistent tapping and probing.

"Probably just a space in the roof next to the chimney," he said, losing interest. "Probably just a way to help warm the attic."

But Allison tucked the thought into a corner of her mind reserved for fantasy. There, it *was* a room. A place that once hid runaway slaves, or treasure perhaps, or even a ghost—a Charles Dickens ghost to be sure, with clanking chains.

Though there was still much work left to do, they moved in the next day. They drove their old Mercedes just ahead of the moving van and ran through a drizzly rain that plastered the dying leaves to the wide porch and drove cold winds through the open door into the heart of the house.

Allison carried Budge in his cage, the bars wrapped against the cold with her blue raincoat. Damp and shivering, she took him to a corner of the kitchen and plugged in the small electric heater to warm them both—she, standing, rubbing her hands on opposite arms; he, huddled on his perch, fluffing blue-green feathers until the white down showed through.

Jeffry came behind, the bulge in his jacket giving way to a white woolly muzzle and two solemn round eyes peeping through a mop of woolly hair.

"Ralph, ralph," yapped the peek-a-poo, speaking his name, jumping from the shelter of the jacket to the warmth of the fire, shivering from the cold and small dog nerves.

"Poor little guy." Allison scratched the little head behind the ears, bringing forth doggie smiles and pants of ecstasy. "Poor Ralph. It's all so strange, isn't it?"

The harsh sounds of furniture scuffing across the porch sent Allison running. Fearing for her piano, she pestered the movers, insisting that they double-wrap the instrument with thick quilts. Grunting, they strained with the weight of it and finally rested it in front of the wide bay windows of the parlor. The black piano, stark against the unpainted walls, seemed to fade them to an indeterminate, tentative gray as if the leaden sky had crept in and touched itself to the plaster.

Allison shivered. "It needs yellow paint," she said.

"White." Jeffry set the heavy brass music stand in a niche beside the piano.

"It needs something," she said. Soon. She didn't know if she could practice in that gray room without her fingers stiffening from the chill she felt, a chill that seemed to come from somewhere deep inside the house. It needs to be yellow, she thought, and it cheered her to think of sun-yellow pigment burning from the walls.

Nothing else went into the parlor except a straight chair, and Allison's oboe tucked in its case beside it.

The kitchen was definitely the all-purpose room, she decided. It was nearly as big as their whole apartment had been. She tugged the little settee in place in front of the cast-iron stove and set the bentwood rocker next to it.

When the movers left, they lighted a fire and sat before it, staving off hunger pangs with a beer and a bag of potato chips, while Budge chittered in his cage and Ralph, hoping for a handout, solemnly danced on small hind legs.

Afterward, stretched out in front of the fire, Jeffry said, "We'd better get on with unpacking." But he made no move to get up.

"It's hard to believe, isn't it?" Her hand covered his. "I mean that it's ours."

"It's ours, all right—for better or worse."

"For richer or poorer?"

His smile was tight. "Especially poorer. We may have to do without furniture for a while."

"But we have as much furniture as we ever did. We just have more house."

He kissed her swiftly, and then looking around the room said, "Schofield's folly."

"You're not regretting it are you, Jeff?" she said, not wanting him to.

Dark lashes shaded his eyes. "No. It's just a little overwhelming. That's all."

But a little part of him withdrew and slipped away just beyond her reach. She pressed her hand against his, trying to draw him back, but though he smiled at the touch, he seemed to be somewhere else.

By seven, the essentials were unpacked and the packing crates and boxes stored in the chilly unused bedrooms.

While Jeffry hung curtain rods and towel racks upstairs, Allison, wanting to celebrate, broiled lobster tails with lemon and cheese sauce and made a salad with fresh spinach and mushrooms.

"Soup's on," she called up the stairs.

"Smells good," he said, walking into the room, hammer and screwdriver in hand. He stopped at the doorway.

She had lighted a fire in the dining room. Two candles in pewter holders flickered on the honeyed oak table, their twin lights reflected in the green bottle of wine.

He grinned. "What's this?"

"Ockfener Bockstein," she said, touching the bottle, choosing to misunderstand him. "Spätlese."

"Ah. Gracious living."

"Be glad," she said. "Tomorrow we have Mr. Armour's tube steaks —specialty of the house."

They ate, savoring the lobster, and afterward sat sipping the rest of the wine as the fire flickered and cast long shadows behind them. Allison ran her fingers over his back. She sniffed deeply. "It even smells nice here," she said, trying to identify the faint fragrance that suddenly puffed into the room. Gardenias, she decided. Like an old corsage pressed in a scrapbook.

"A little musty, if you ask me," he said, and she felt his muscles tighten under his sweater. "I think I'll unpack a few things in the studio." He stood, stretched before the fire, rebounded like a coiled wire. Then he was gone up the stairs.

Fighting disappointment, she cleared away the dishes, washing them, drying them carefully, setting them away in the tall oak cabinet. When she finished, she decided against interrupting him in his studio. She needed to practice anyway, she told herself.

She left the parlor door open so that it might catch some warmth from the dining room fire across the hall. Fitting her oboe together, placing its reed, she warmed up and began to play. As the notes slid from the polished black instrument, she lost herself, as she always did, in the Mozart.

She sensed the moth and its movement before she really saw it. She watched it hover and glide on the reedy sounds of the oboe as if it were an extension of the music, now here in the light, now there in the filtering shadows.

Beautiful, she said to herself as she played. A luna moth, pale green, lovely as the finest, thinnest velvet, moving—programmed almost, to the sound of her oboe.

It hovered, wings pulsing for a second, as the dying notes from the Mozart echoed and stopped and then it slid away and settled on the floor, motionless, in the corner by the marble parlor hearth.

Not until after it stopped did Allison wonder about it. A luna moth. This time of year?

Laying the instrument aside, she went to the corner where the moth lay, touched it, picked it up.

It was quite dead. Dead, and rigid in its death, it lay desiccated on her palm, pale green dust on cobweb.

But it flew. Didn't it?

She stared uneasily at the dead moth. Air currents. Just a draft, that was all. Wasn't it?

Holding it lightly, fingers curled, she ran up the steps to the second floor and on to the attic, calling, "Jeffry. Oh, Jeff."

Silhouetted in the single doorway, he stood at the head of the narrow stairs.

"Look, Jeff," she said, feeling foolish, feeling a little frightened. She held out her palm to him, the moth green silk against cool flesh.

He stood, not moving, watching her silently.

"Jeff?"

The odor of gardenias caught her nostrils and clung heavy as dust. And behind the barrier of Jeffry's body, somewhere within the studio came the unmistakable sound of a door closing.

A low growl from behind her startled Allison. Whirling, she teetered on the narrow step, outstretched hand still curled around the luna moth. Ralph, legs stiff, lips curled back over small teeth, stared at the door to the studio, crept as if on knife blades toward the studio. The fur stood up along his back as he crept, growls gurgling deep in his throat, and in his eyes glowed an emotion so awful, so alien, that Allison cried out in shock.

"Jeff, was that the door? The one in the wall? I heard—"

Jeffry, not moving, his voice in counterpoint to the dog's low growls, said, "Door? There is no door."

"I know what I heard." Allison stroked and soothed Ralph, who huddled on his bed beside the kitchen stove. Comforted by warm milk and three drops of peach brandy, his tremblings had subsided to an occasional twitch and soft breathy whimperings. "Poor little guy. He sensed something, too." Her voice was fiercer than she intended.

Jeffry eyed her calmly. "Are you suggesting that the house is haunted?"

Put that way, it seemed ridiculous. Was that really what she was thinking? "I'm not suggesting anything of the kind. I just know what I know," she finished lamely.

"Well, it's pretty silly if you ask me."

"Pretty—" echoed Budge from his cage, using half his vocabulary.

"Pretty bird," said Allison absently. "Pretty bird." She stood up and picked up the cover to slip over the cage. "If you repeat things often enough to them, they'll learn."

Jeffry reached out and caught a lock of her dark hair, tugging gently, making her face him. He kissed her lightly. "I give you credit for as much sense as a parakeet," he said, grinning, "so listen and repeat after me, 'There are no ghosts.' "

"But I didn't say—"

"There are no ghosts."

She felt a smile creep, crooked, onto her face. "Okay. You win. Let's go to bed."

The bedroom seemed homey even without the white eyelet curtains Allison planned to put up. She turned down the thick brown and gold quilt on the cherry spindle bed, and plumped the pillows. Slipping out of her clothes, she shivered into her ivory ruffled granny gown and plunged into the bed. "Tomorrow, we bring up wood for that fireplace," she said. "You know what we need?"

"What?"

"A brass bedwarmer. To hang by the fireplace. You fill it with hot coals and run it between the sheets."

"I already have a bedwarmer," he said, reaching for her.

Later, feeling warm and close and satisfied, Allison sank into a dark sleep. For a time she slept heavily and then the dreaming began—the insistent, jumbled dreaming that lightened her sleep and made her turn and toss and mutter. Half awake, limbs heavy and unresponsive, she felt the dream begin to fade, replaced by something else—something caressing her eyelids and cheek. Trying to waken, unable to waken, she felt tiny spidery movements across her face, felt soft velvet cover her mouth and nostrils, felt tiny feather dusters slither across her lips.

Choking claustrophobia seized her. Struggling, hands clawing at her face, she jumped to her feet, tangling them in the covers, and snapped on the bedside lamp. There on the night table, lovely and delicate in the glow of the lamp, lay the luna moth—quite still and dead.

"Jeff. Look." She reached for him in the shadows, but the mound beside her was only quilt and pillow. He was gone.

Padding across the floor, barefoot, she went after him, her footsteps quickening to the beat of her heart. In the hall she saw the yellow gleam of light from the studio. Running up the stairs, reaching ahead for the banister, she called, "Jeff. Jeff."

He stood in front of his easel, stretched canvas showing dim charcoal lines. He held a palette, mixed a color, as she watched.

"Jeff."

He looked at her for the first time, remotely, without interest.

"Jeff?"

"I'm working, Allison. Go to bed."

She made her voice very calm. "I have to talk to you."

Angular fingers gripped the palette knife, working pigments, swirling them together, until a color Allison had never seen him use appeared. A pale, luminous, shimmering green—sensuous, like the finest, thinnest velvet.

She sucked in her breath.

"Go to bed, Allison." He did not look up.

Rebuffed, not knowing why, she crept down the dark stairs and went back to the bedroom. She looked up along the ceiling with its dark beams to the place where the studio stood just above her, and wondered why she felt so anxious. After all, Jeff had worked at night before when he couldn't sleep.

The luna moth lay on the night table. She picked it up and thrust it into a drawer. She wasn't sure just why.

She crawled into bed, drawing the quilt over her shoulders. It made a faint crackling sound as if it moved over dry leaves. Pushing back the covers, running nervous fingers through the sheets, she touched the paper thrust part way under Jeffry's pillow. It was a letter brittle with age. Where had it come from?

As she opened the folded yellowing sheets, a faint odor of dust and gardenias stung her nostrils. The black ink pigments had faded to a faint browning purple. The script began, "Beloved . . ."

Deciphering the slanting feminine hand, reading slowly through the stilted phrases, she felt a small chill grow, skitter up her spine, and crouch at the nape of her neck.

The letter was smoothly, silkily obscene. It insinuated its sleazy perversions cozily, coquettishly, into Allison's brain; seemed to whisper in her brain its filthy little cruelties and lusts with coiled tongue flicking over loose wet lips. Purring, enticing, coaxing—toward the rotting depths of madness.

Allison felt the sickness grow inside her, a sickness that drained cold sweat from her hands and stained the yellowing paper, a shuddering, clammy sickness that sang one thought over and over in her brain: It's here. It's really here.

She wanted to crush the letter in her hands, wanted to feel its brittle pages crack and crumble between her fingers. She wanted to burn it to an oily ash in the cold fireplace, whisk it away, rid the house of it. But she lay huddled in the bed, the letter on the quilt beside her.

It wanted Jeffry. She knew it as surely as she had ever known anything. She could feel it, waiting, biding its time, showing its hand and then laughing at her discomfort—complacent and very self-assured.

What was it? An essence of the house itself? Something born of organic mortar and board? Or was it a mind-sick soul trapped inside? Or maybe there wasn't any difference now. Maybe the two had merged so completely that they couldn't exist one without the other.

She wanted to crush the letter, but she did not dare. It was proof. The only proof she had. But as soon as the thought entered her head, an unsteady smile came to her lips. Proof. Of what? The ghost of plaster past?

Now there was logic for you. She felt a giggle rise in her throat. What could be more logical than a haunted house? Follows every rule of logic, don'tcha know. Allison can sense presences; Allison senses a presence; therefore, there *is* a presence. Inexorable logic.

Now how would her freshman professor—what was his name?—how would he have attacked that one?

"On what authority do we have it that Allison really senses presences?" she asked herself. "Oh no, my dear, the flaw is in your premise. And when we have a flawed premise, we must throw it out."

Feeling immensely cheered by her flawed premise, warmed by the imagined scorn of Dr. What's-His-Name, Allison snuggled under the quilt and snapped off the lamp. But sleep didn't come—only disquieting thoughts borne on the faint odor of gardenias until dawn faded the night into shades of gray.

Rising, wrapping her robe around her, she stood by the window and watched a flat gray mist silhouette the bare limbs of the poplar. Jeffry was still gone.

She headed for the stairs, soft slippers padding against the floor. What she needed was a cup of coffee.

The hall was dark. Where was the light switch? Fumbling, fingers patting the wall, she inched forward when something soft as silk touched her throat and slithered across it. Her heart contracted and she jerked away, fingers leaping to her throat.

She would not scream. She would not.

Crouching, hugging the wall, she found the light switch and snapped it on.

There was nothing there. Nothing but the head of the stairs plunging below her.

A footstep behind her. Jeff.

She clutched at him. "There *is* something here. There is. It tried to kill me." Her voice came in little gasps as she told him what had happened. There was a look in his eyes that she could not read.

"You've got to calm down." Hands still on her shoulder, he steered her firmly, impersonally, down to the kitchen. "We'll make coffee."

He flicked on the light, and Ralph rose unsteadily from his basket, whimpering softly. Clots of drying blood matted his little forepaws.

"Oh, God!" Allison knelt, gathered him up, touched the damp little paws.

"Look," said Jeffry across the room. "He must have been after

Budge." Deep splintered grooves clawed the paneled wall beneath the parakeet's cage. Drops of blood stained the floor beneath it.

Still holding Ralph, Allison ran to the cage and snatched the cover from it. Budge stirred sleepily on his perch as Allison's hand recoiled. Laced daintily through the bars was a silk scarf of the palest, softest green.

Allison felt her voice grow unnaturally calm. "Now do you believe me? That's what touched me in the hall. It must have been." Fingers digging into the dog's soft white fur, she turned and faced Jeff. "We've got to move away from here. Right away."

"This is our home."

"Home? And what about that?" Her chin flicked toward the cage, toward the silken scarf. "Where did it come from?"

"That's *your* scarf, Allison."

For the third time she said, "I've never owned a scarf like that."

Jeff finished dabbing Ralph's paws with peroxide while Allison held him. Then he took the little dog and placed him in his basket. Straightening, he said, "Come with me."

He led her up the stairs toward the studio. "I want you to see what I've been working on." He opened the door and led her into the room.

An unfinished picture stood on the easel, a still life—a pair of long kid gloves lay tossed across a table as if someone had removed them in haste. They lay next to a dewy gardenia. On its dark glossy leaves perched a delicate luna moth. And next to it, coiled carelessly, lay a pale green silken scarf, and in its folds a letter in slanting Victorian script.

"You see. It's yours. I painted it from memory." He smiled and reached for his palette, touched his brushes. "I think I'll work for a while and then I think I'll paint the parlor for you. Would you like that?"

But she was gone, running down the narrow steps to their bedroom. The drawer to the night table lay open. The luna moth was gone. Plunging cold fingers into the unmade bed, she searched the folds of sheet and quilt, kneaded the pillows, tugged at the blanket.

There was no letter. None at all.

A cold mist seemed to grow around her. Befogged, she walked into the hall and, touching the banister, went down the stairs into the parlor and slipped onto the piano bench, fingers touching the keys. A slow breath and the Grieg concerto echoed in the room.

She played for two hours before Jeffry appeared, paint buckets in hand. Then she slipped away up the stairs.

She soaked for a long time in the old claw-footed tub in the midnight blue bathroom. As she soaked, she felt the cold mist around her thaw and the taut muscles of her body relax. Maybe it was fatigue. She'd just needed a rest and a long hot bath. She toweled dry in front of the old gas heater and slipped on her clothes, pulling warm woolen cloth over her body. Refreshed, almost elated, she went down the stairs to the parlor.

"Jeff?"

But Jeffry didn't hear her as his wide brush whispered across the walls, leaving its track of pale shimmering green.

She watched, silent. With each pass of the brush across the wall, she felt the cold mist grow again and press around her. Stumbling, she turned, went to the kitchen, and curled up on the settee, toes pressed under her. Ralph, limping a little, jumped in her lap. Poor paws, she thought remotely. Poor little feet.

"Pretty," said Budge from his cage. "Pretty."

"Pretty bird," she said mechanically.

"Pretty," answered Budge. "Pretty Jeffry . . . touch me . . . touch me there—"

Somehow she was on her feet, running, Ralph frolicking beside her, running up the stairs to the second floor, then up again to the attic room. Jeffry's painting still stood on the easel, oils wet.

"I won't go," she said aloud to the painting, to the walls.

On the floor beside her came a low growl, the dog's hackles rising on his back as a hidden door along the wall shushed open.

The coldness, the mistiness grew around her, but strangely there was no curiosity. She knew somehow what lay behind the door. Nothing much. Just a withered brown gardenia, a silk scarf, a fragile letter, and a luna moth, quite dead, perched on a pair of yellowed long kid gloves.

"I won't go," she said again.

The thought pushed against her mind. You must.

No. She wasn't going to leave. She was not going to run like a frightened gray mouse, because if she did— If she ran now, she'd never stop. "I won't."

An answering breathy laugh that was not a laugh, but only the specter of one deep inside her head.

Cold tendrils crept down her spine. "It's my house. My husband."

The cold mist grew large. So large—or was it she growing smaller? Distantly, she felt it enter her, pressing, freezing. And with the mist a chilling fear erupted. She tried to run, but her limbs were rigid, her body remote and disobedient.

The dog's lips slid back, baring small sharp teeth.

The flutter of bird wings. Tiny claws, sharp as glass. A voice mocking hers: "Jeffry . . . Jeffry, I'm coming . . . Beloved . . ."

A low growl, and small teeth sank into her ankle, tearing flesh down to the bone.

DAVID SUTTON

Photo-Call

Jeremy Hitching cringed inwardly when he thought about his first letter to the photographer.

In fact, he had to read it again, even though it was a form of mental masochism, just to be sure he'd written all those sickly, hero-worship sorts of things. And, yes, he had, though he wondered now why on earth he had bothered to keep copies of the correspondence. The faded copy-sheets in the thin pink folder were interspersed with polite but fended-off replies, on the thick-textured cream stock, of Norton Evans Bainbridge. Jeremy glanced at Bainbridge's flamboyant signature on each of his letters, an unreadable scrawl of blue ink, the first *N* of his christian name a large dramatic curve that swept up from the typed "Sincerely" over the main text of the letters themselves. He shuffled the papers together to square them, dismissing the youthful exuberance contained within the pages, tossed the file aside and picked up the photographer's coffee-table book, published just that year.

Dreams & Decay, its title, summed up the photographer's obsessions, which had coincidentally been Jeremy's also, and was why he had held Bainbridge's work in such reverence. He flipped the heavy pages back, the white paper crisp and shiny between his thin, bony fingers. Each large page had the sumptuous superfluousness of a wide, one-and-a-half-inch white border framing each of the black-and-white photographs and at the end of the book each of the plates was fully described if you needed to fathom deeper into the photographer's art. Now that Jeremy was at last to meet him, he felt he should at least familiarize himself with Bainbridge's latest published work.

He found himself flicking through the pages quickly and occasionally stopping to pore over one of the pictures. Here was an old-fashioned central-heating radiator, filling the frame, its contours reminiscent now of Giger's *Alien* designs of organic buildings. But the picture gave an awesome, if simple, insight into decay: the radiator's paint job had peeled through heat or weathering over its entire surface, like thick, shiny bits of pallid skin curling off, revealing a darker paint color beneath. Another picture was more atmospheric: a large unsightly room bathed in sunshine from an open doorway and, huddled in a group, two cane chairs and behind them a lurking sofa. On the shadowed floor in the foreground some rags and detritus, possibly fallen plaster from a ceiling out of frame. The soft focus and light quality drew the viewer to query the picture's hidden mysteries. But it was Bainbridge's landscapes of urban decay that had swept the photographer to the forefront of his profession. Working exclusively in black and white, he had managed to capture the very heart of the country's iron-wracked decay.

Even the few portraits he did reflected this preoccupation: a mother with rickety pushchair, its resident's face howling a discord, stood center frame. The rest was all technique—Bainbridge combined that print with a background of a noxious black tank from which some unnameable chemical had spilt. Its blistered surface drooled and dribbled around the figures. Bainbridge rarely used montage, but when he did, it was always with human subjects. His landscapes and captured objects were shot with just their natural light.

The pictures fascinated Jeremy still, even though his own expertise in the art had developed immensely since the first, faltering fan letter. It had been written just after an exhibition of Bainbridge's work in

1978 at the local museum and art gallery. The photographer had taken as his theme the sea, but what a collusion of nature and its unnatural adversary—man! In monochrome, as always, but wind-shivered sands led the eye to the salt-blistered detritus of an abandoned pier; or a broad estuary with a ghostly sunset over the distant ocean revealed a jumble of wrecks in the half-light. Such juxtaposition had sent shivers down Jeremy's spine. And of course, he had soon bought himself an SLR camera, a Canon with both auto and manual mode, to make the learning easier, and a couple of lenses to experiment with.

Mainly though, at that exhibition, he'd hoped to meet the master photographer, the man who would become his unknown mentor. Of course, it was a traveling exhibition and Bainbridge wasn't part of it, so the shining surfaces of Kodak paper were his only contact with the mind and eye of Bainbridge. It was enough for a while and as time passed he no longer felt such desperate need to see the man.

After all, his own photos were improving and he'd sold a few from his portfolio to various magazines and paperback houses (for their "stock" cover files). He'd had to move into color, of course, but his theme of decay was still consistent with that of his invisible tutor. Yes, every photo that Bainbridge produced, Jeremy would study, assessing ways he could emulate him, ways he could improve on him, if that were possible. He believed he'd come close, once or twice, when the nuance of lighting and the careful attention to an f-stop had gelled in the darkroom. It was then he produced an essence of the bizarre and repellent that represented our crumbling society.

All that aside, the greatest, albeit inadvertent, benefit that Bainbridge had bestowed on his distant protégé was to bring him out of his shell. Jeremy had always been shy, acutely so in his teens. This had led to advantages and disadvantages, but which outweighed the other is a matter of conjecture. Indeed, Jeremy pondered long and hard in those lonely years between thirteen and twenty. Loneliness was one of the disadvantages and his reticence with other people extended, naturally, to women. He became, year by year, shy, giggly, clumsy and downright incapable of chatting to girls, let alone moving further into a relationship with one or more of them. And an advantage? He often cited to himself his unique outlook, which he regarded as supremely important to his later interest in taking pictures and the unusual slant on the world that came out of it. Forget for a moment that he had plagiarized the work of another!

Jeremy was also pretty unique looking, a circumstance he supposed had led him to his general awkwardness. He was thin, very thin and bony, but not particularly tall to compensate for it. His face, a pale oval with extremely abundant freckles, was surmounted by a crop of bright ginger hair. He looked and felt like a Day-Glo mop. Once seen, you'd imagine, never forgotten, but Jeremy's pale and liquid blue eyes and rather unusual bloated lips did not help at all really, because he had never made enough impression on people for them to remember him anyway. He hardly ever spoke, unless spoken to, keeping his larynx for answering queries in as curt a manner possible. Standoffish would be a term people applied to Jeremy, if they thought about it, but really it was merely his oppressive timidity. To cap it all, his suits never fitted his thin shoulders and the sleeves invariably hung down ridiculously over his hands. Trousers somehow bagged around his pinched buttocks. Made-to-measure may have cured some of the gawkiness he suffered due to his apparel, but he'd never had the courage to get properly fitted up.

All that had changed of course. Photography, via Bainbridge, had led him to take the unparalleled step of joining the local photo society and he had begun to attend their regular meetings. He was twenty-one years old and bashful to a fault, but lo and behold, he found some of the other members crazier than he secretly imagined himself to be. (He'd read *Psycho* when he was seventeen and had horrified himself by so readily relating to Norman Bates.) They'd have described themselves as extrovert, but in fact some of the group's members were just plain crazy. They had wonderfully warped notions about life and how they fitted into the scheme of things, but most of all how good they were with a camera. One or two of them were fundamentally porno freaks as far as Jeremy was concerned and generally stuck to "glamour" work, occasionally taking up the society's offer of cheap weekend studio work-shops with free models provided. Others couldn't see Jeremy's compulsion for what he believed it was: genius in the making. And a couple, at least, he found companionship with, bringing him to their collective bosom as it were, understanding the fire that possessed him and in the meantime helping the butterfly finally escape from the cocoon he'd been imprisoned in for so long. Meeting followed meeting, followed by weekend photo courses; nature photography; studio techniques; and so on. The carapace of isolation was shed and Jeremy emerged a genuine Human Being. It little mattered that he ended up as screwy as the rest of the society's members when photo jargon vomited out with every sentence they uttered. Jeremy even began doing some glamour work, feeling casual and relaxed with the chesty ladies hired for such occasions; but they really didn't fulfill his desire for decay, the tonal quality and feeling that Bainbridge captured with every frame.

Everyone had their own ideas and opinions as to what made a good picture and local exhibitions allowed the club members to grasp the mettle and criticize one another's prints. It was during this time that Jeremy became involved in his own darkroom work, courtesy of the society, and could take control of the process and thus the quality that had eluded him with commercial developing and printing agencies. Other group members had to admire his technical ability, if not his subject matter. One of his found objects, a crushed doll spattered with blood—he didn't know how the blood got there—lying in an oily trench on an abandoned factory site, was used on the cover of a horror novel by Jack Martin. He'd taken it using a twenty-eight millimeter, close up, so that the pool of vile liquid in which the doll lay half-submerged was displayed fully; and reflected in the pool was a tall piece of rubble from the derelict site, in silhouette, and which looked like a hovering, hooded human figure. Just the correct choice of angle had seen to that, plus the embryonic light of dawn. The darkroom work had done the rest.

"Well done, old chap," one of the porno freaks had said to him when he produced the paperback cover proofs at one of the meetings. "Not quite the Bainbridge style, though, eh?" A dig.

"Commercially, Bainbridge is out of it," Jeremy remembered replying. "He's just been in the right place at the right time for art photography. He wouldn't," Jeremy added, "be caught dead doing commercial stuff like this." He hadn't felt the need to defend himself to the oaf —at least he was doing creative work of some sort.

"Mind you," the porno merchant persisted, his horrible mouth with its ever-hung lower jaw closing around the words, "you'll find it hard to make a living with that kind of stuff." He pointed a warty finger at the cover proofs.

Jeremy felt his face go red in anger. "I'm not interested in fame!" he rebuked, lying to himself at the same time. What a snob, he thought, the book covers quivering in his hands.

"Marvelous," a more amenable member, Carl Medley, interrupted the conversation with a sincere remark. At least he was a genuine friend who supported Jeremy's work and style preferences. All in all he had been well pleased with the small success he had been having and his confidence grew accordingly.

Not long after that, more of Jeremy's portfolio began to sell. His color work had drifted away from his preceptor's style and toward more salable products, but whenever he could, he would load some raw black-and-white stock into the Canon, absorb some Bainbridge aura and take himself off to weed-choked, derelict housing estates, to empty, water-corroded factories, abandoned gasworks, rubbish-choked canals.

As his ability grew, so did his gushing letters to Bainbridge dry up, but not before he had sent him a few copies of his own, derivative work. And with them a letter that reveled in his love and desire to emulate the great photographer's work. Unkindly, it must have driven home to Bainbridge Jeremy's thoughtless imitation of style *and* content.

The last reply he had had from Bainbridge came, of course, with the heavy coffee-table book of the artist's work. He was delighted that the photographer felt him worthy of a free copy (it cost after all a penny off twenty-six quid), even though his last correspondence, with those prints of his, had been some time ago and he hadn't really expected, or cared for, a reply. Recent work had found Jeremy thinking that he'd finally cracked Bainbridge's method. No longer did he find it necessary to bracket so many of his shots, an economy brought about by more judicious attention to exposure, lighting and speed. His special folio of decay was a testament to hard work, but also an insincere attitude to his own originality which was now in any case just a matter of conjecture: Jeremy had devoted himself so fully to exploring where Bainbridge was at that any of his own original thinking was long gone.

He put down the book at last and flipped the letter from where it was tucked in behind the dust jacket.

"My dear Mr. Hitching," it began, still on that gorgeous parchment, which a typewriter reduced to mere pulp stock. Such paper deserved a calligrapher's hand, Jeremy thought. He continued to reread the text, annoyed at a renegade *e* that refused to sit in alignment with the rest of the typewritten text. It irritated him slightly that Bainbridge should use a clapped-out typewriter with his money and prestige. "Delighted to see some of your recent work," the letter droned, ". . . improving immensely . . . hope you enjoy my latest book . . . how about meeting soon, you are, judging by your letters, my biggest fan!" Jeremy scowled at that one, even though he'd brought it upon himself really. "What say you we meet up for a photo session? . . . the ideal place for some creative new work. . . ."

The letter suggested a date and gave an anonymous address in the Midlands, not too far to travel. Bainbridge's *N* flourished irksomely across the body of the letter as usual. Jeremy was peeved by the letter's tone, that of a great teacher to a beginner in his subject. The fact was Jeremy now thought of himself as a rival in many ways. That's why his effusive letters had virtually dried up. They'd become less frequent and more adept at pointing out how Bainbridge's technique had been analyzed, dissected and finally displayed in his own photos. One thing, however, he had to admit to a strong desire to meet the man at long last and see what he looked like (the photographer's portrait had never been published so far as he knew, not even in his own enigmatic books). There might be rewards as well—Bainbridge knew the publishers, agents, people who might be persuaded to give his work a more appreciative public than on forgettable paperback covers.

A chilly March morning saw Jeremy stowing his aluminium camera case and tripod on the back seat of his Nissan hatchback. He tossed *Dreams & Decay* on the passenger seat as well and headed for the outskirts of Birmingham. It was a Saturday and traffic was light at this time of day on the M6, the monotonous gray tarmac slipping beneath his wheels in an endless hissing roar. That was something else the shy beanpole had become: a road hog. He liked to travel at speed, his driving confident and assured; other motorists were not so sure. He stopped briefly for breakfast at a Little Chef, its car park mainly littered with container trucks. An early dawn sun attacked the glass of the cabs and the windows of the restaurant with red light. "Red sky in morning, shepherd's warning," he reminded himself, wondering why such pointless sayings ever got into common usage. The fast-food unit was hot after the cold air outside and smelled of bacon and eggs, which is what he ordered, washed down with coffee out of the ubiquitous plastic cup. He watched the sun rise, burning off the haze in distant fields. Recumbent cows appeared like apports where they rested as the fog lifted. Sunlight jeweled the dew on the meadows. Air brakes hissed outside and trucks sped away; it was all soft and pleasant. Muzak thrummed around him. Yes, it was going to be a good day. He felt self-reliant, ready to point his camera like a magic paintbrush and tint the world gray, blotched and crumbling.

He hiked the car up to eighty and slipped a cassette into the waiting slot. ZZ Top were asking some girl to slip inside their sleeping bag while delivering a thundering rhythm to the car's upholstery. After a while he felt warm, amaranthine, suffused with immortality, and his head rocked to the rhythm. Distant high-rises indicated his nearness to Birmingham and with them in the glow of light, the vomited refuse of the city; run-down factories, scrap yards, oily gas and chemical pumping stations, dwellings with tawdry backyards, all heaped outside the glitter of the compact shopping center. Jeremy didn't need to go right into the city, but nevertheless decided to consult a map and Bainbridge's instructions to find the location, so he pulled into the one-way system and drove around until he found a quiet parking space in the business district. It was nine o'clock and the place was warming up with people drifting toward the shops. Buses trundled past in long lines, queuing to load in front of banks and solicitors' offices.

Having memorized the route, Jeremy got out and crossed the road to a kiosk where he bought twenty cigarettes. He lit one straight away, breathing deeply, and looked at the now harsh sunlight forcing bold shadows from the buildings. Smoking was something else reasonably new. In his teens, he wouldn't have dreamed of the habit. Now it was a nonchalance that he had acquired, along with his forthright manner. It looked good in the studio when he was working with models, if nothing else.

As he drove the final stretch of the journey, Jeremy began to feel queasy. He rammed another cassette in and lit a second cigarette, opening the ashtray to a profusion of stinking nub-ends. This time the speakers roared out Jim Morrison, asking him to break on through (to the other side). The pukishness didn't end with the nicotine as he hoped it would and his nerves jangled. He started to feel the way he used to when he was younger and meeting people for the first time, or going to job interviews. His mouth was dry. He yawned without feeling the least bit tired. The road ahead became largely a blur, his hands tingled on the steering wheel; his pace slowed considerably as his normally unhesitant driving was sapped by the churning in his abdomen. At one point he really thought he was going to throw up his breakfast and was forced to stop on a quiet side-road with the window open. Cool air blew in, touching his red-hot face and neck. His skin felt sunburnt and oozed perspiration.

Jeremy shouted at himself mentally. These sensations, familiar though they were, were old enemies from his teens and he thought they'd been dispatched to oblivion over the years of confidence building. Sullenly he realized that his subconscious had simply kept them stored up in order to wreak vengeance at some future time. He cursed himself, watched people moving about nearby and tried to quell the feelings by filling his mind with the insignificant details of his surroundings. He must press on, he realized, and started the engine. Jeremy reckoned the whole of the last fifteen minutes to have been an almost supernatural aberration, as though someone were willing him to feel ill. Well, he'd use his own willpower to defend himself. The Nissan roared off, angry under his command. Tires squealed briefly as he cornered. Eyes turned toward him, but all they received back for their disdain was The Doors churning out their message very loudly.

When Jeremy arrived on Saltash Road, he realized through his nausea why Bainbridge had suggested the location, for it was a crumbling street of terraced dwellings, all unoccupied. The road had become so underused that weeds had sprouted in clumps through the ashphalt and wind-strewn litter choked the narrow, overgrown gardens. A lamppost tilted out over the thin street, heaving up paving slabs at its base. Green slime patterned walls where drainpipes had cracked and allowed water to escape unchecked. A wisp of old curtain fluttered against the jagged glass of a broken window, shredded by its wind-induced fidgeting.

Jeremy cruised along until he reached number twenty-three. He stopped the engine and stepped out quickly. The silence was impressive and so was the property. Some occupier, in his wisdom, had painted the bricks a bolder red than their natural color. Over the years, or possibly even months, this had flaked off in parts and it all looked like a mottling of dried and wet blood. He glanced at the time on his digital and noticed he was a few minutes late, but there was no sign of another car in the road. A flicker of annoyance crossed his face as he slid the camera case from the rear seat and slammed the car's door shut. The engine clicked at him, cooling in the strange quiet. Putting the case down, he lit a cigarette before moving over broken slates which crunched like old glass beneath his tennis shoes. The front door was wedged open by the lifting quarry tiles of the hall and bright sunlight shimmered in.

He stepped inside.

A shiver of excitement ran across his scalp like a thousand ants, which then crawled quickly down his spine. *This* was it. An evocation of unsurpassable decay and desolation. He fingered his camera case, itching to do the business; but where was Bainbridge? Never mind, he thought, take stock, explore and pick the viewpoints, plenty of time, yet in his mind as he walked along, a hundred frames of film clicked off. He put down the case and extracted the Canon, its autowind in place from a previous field trip.

A long hall stretched to, it seemed, an impossible length of the house, the light a soft gray ambience. Strips of skinned wallpaper hung limply, like the shredded skin of a diseased throat, and pools of rancid water and detritus splashed under his marching shoes. Jeremy couldn't understand what was making him walk so fast along the impossible hallway; the passage that was so long. By the time he had approached the far door—and noticed within its shadow the shattered water pipe that had been responsible for the water all over the floor and the effect it had had upon the walls: the plaster blistered into bubbles like a multitude of pale, threatening breasts—he saw that the door was drifting open like a soft whisper in a dream. As the light from the room on the other side slid across the door he noticed for the first time the bloated fungi that clasped to the lower, sodden timbers, a livid white color under a wet black capping of slimy flesh. His intestines roiled like tubifex, the sick feeling coming on heavy again. His cool, thin-veined hands began to slick with sweat and he wiped them on his cords one at a time. Adrenaline pumped electricity into his nerves and his skin bubbled into pimples of gooseflesh. Jeremy raised the camera in a suddenly fearful expectation—though the shaking of his hands would have devastated any exposures he might have hoped to make—when the figure revealed itself in the distant room.

A sudden gunshot of automatic fire made him let go the shutter release, but not before he'd burst off half the film cartridge with his nerve-struck index finger. The Canon's noisy mirror clacked like a demented clown. Jeremy then looked at the short, shadowed figure in the far room, a room that resembled his own pictures, and saw for the first time Norton Evans Bainbridge. The photographer was tiny, almost a midget, Jeremy observed, and he wanted to laugh, as much for his own

nervousness as at the sight he beheld. However, the resonance of the
scene was so much like one of Bainbridge's prints that he was rendered
speechless.

"Mr. Hitching, the copycat," the squealing, high-pitched voice of
the midget said. It was almost a female voice, Jeremy noticed, adding
to his terror. He felt disorientated. "Mr. Jeremy Hitching, the *vile*
copycat," the screeching continued, holding back a passion only a
whisper away from sudden violence.

Jeremy saw the man move forward into more light, revealing atop
the diminutive black-clad body a head of swollen yellow flesh, like a
small wrinkled pumpkin left too long on the shelf. His dark eyes darted
from side to side like a photographer's, as though checking the perspective. Jeremy saw pudgy hands glued to a camera, its lens twinkling like
an extreme orifice near the midget's midriff. Bainbridge's lips quivered,
two prosthetic pieces of red flesh stuck appallingly to the vegetable
head. Jeremy began to stammer, slipping back ten years, eclipsed once
again by his teenage shyness, his bold hands suddenly cold as ice, the
camera an icy brick within them.

"The *photographer*," the word came out like an insult, "who thinks
he can duplicate my creations, my babies. The sniveling *amateur*
whose ability ranks with that of a queasy chimpanzee!" Bainbridge's
sibilant falsetto screamed along the hall; trapped, it echoed back. The
monstrous dwarf continued its androgynous tirade while Jeremy sank
like a castrated marionette into a stuttering, incomprehensible child.
His nose ran like a boy's, while the matriarchal whining lashed on.
"This little prick, this ineffectual masturbator who thinks his masculin-
ity can reveal some artistic integrity by sucking his master's nipples!" A
hand slapped his face like a flying piece of concrete and for seconds he
dreamed of his mother slapping him, slapping and slapping and shouting at his shivering naked little body. Finally he sprawled to the floor,
falling into a pool of water which wet his pants like an incontinent
child. He began to cry, his camera rolling toward the crumbling skirt-
ing board, its shattered lens winking coyly at him.

Jeremy lifted himself and ran finally as the diminutive physique of
Bainbridge dwelt over him, vilifying him for his tears, its heaving chest
covered by a mold-smeared shirt, and on his way his hand burst one of
the wall's white breasts, releasing the glutinous fluid it had held in
check. The midget screamed hysterically at his retreating back. "Ha.
Haaa! The boy, the *little* snotty boy." Dreams and decay smothered

him like a shroud of diabolic supernal knowledge: Jeremy was reduced to sobbing uncontrollably as he struggled to his car. He grabbed Bainbridge's book from the seat where it lay like an invective and meant to tear it in his childish rage. The slippery pages resisted and his shaking hands lashed at it again and again hopelessly. It fell open finally to reveal a dedication he hadn't noticed before, which he read through eyes rimmed red with hate and terror. ". . . in memory of my brother, who didn't survive to see this, his finest work recorded in book form."

"P . . . p . . . po . . . posthumously!" Jeremy stammered. "Posthumously," he bawled, completing his journey back to youthful terror.

MARK MORRIS

Against the Skin

The rabbit jerked once more, but Lee knew there was no way it could escape, not with its leg almost chopped through. He wrestled the great iron jaws of the trap apart, then picked up the rabbit and deftly broke its neck. Hooking the carcass to his belt, he continued on his way.

Of course, fox was what he was really after. He could get a lot more for fox fur than he could for rabbit meat, but he was lucky if he caught more than one or two foxes a week. Sometimes it was hard enough just catching the rabbits. Quite often he would come around and find his traps clogged with weasels, stoats, birds, stuff like that: once, he remembered, he had caught a rat as big as an alley cat, and which had hissed and snarled and bared its teeth like one too. That had shaken Lee so much that he hadn't dared get too close, had had to go fetch his air rifle to shoot the damn thing.

Today, though, had been a good day. He had got three rabbits in his traps and a pigeon in one of his snares—they were always good for a few bob. Now he was tramping through the woods to check on his final trap, the corpses swinging at his waist like war trophies.

It was a warm September morning, fresh dew on the grass, the leaves just about on the turn. Flies congregated in clouds, buzzing lazily; birds twittered in the trees. The stream, due to the heavy rainfall over the last two weeks, was rushing along as though late for an appointment.

Lee's final trap had been sprung, but whatever had been in there had got away. From the tuft of bloodied fur the creature had left behind, it had obviously been something of a struggle. Lee wondered whether he ought to cast about a bit, see if the animal was still around. The fur suggested another rabbit, and from the looks of things it was badly wounded. It had probably crawled off to die in a bush somewhere.

He picked up a stick and thrashed halfheartedly at the surrounding undergrowth, but after a few minutes he gave up. Flies were droning round his head and he was desperate for a pint. Besides, today's was a good haul as it stood. Might as well let the poor little bugger die in peace.

He took a sack from his jacket and stuffed his catch inside, then carefully reset the trap. That done, he heaved the sack onto his shoulder. Next stop the market to earn himself a little money, and then it was off to the pub for his lunch.

As he entered the main bar of The Vine he was met by a chorus of greetings. He raised a hand, then went to the bar and ordered sausage, beans, chips and a pint of bitter. At this hour the pub was a sociable place: sunshine slanted in through the windows, gleaming on the horse brasses that adorned the walls; the greasy smell of food and the scraping of cutlery on plates made him hungry; the click of pool balls and the bleeps from the fruit machine provided a soothing backdrop to the buzz of conversation. Lee moved from the bar to where his mates were seated, already sucking at the froth in his glass. When he got to the table, the beer was half-gone.

"Thirsty work, killing things," Reg Trenshaw said. His words were greeted with laughter.

"Aye, it is that," Lee replied. He sat down. "Better than sitting on your arse all day, though."

Reg stuck his nose in the air. "I'll have you know, I'm what is known as a casual laborer."

"Aye, very casual," said Lee. Laughter exploded around him once more. Reg grinned too, and companionably punched his arm.

"How many d'you get today, then?" Peter Raven asked. He was the youngest of the group, only twenty-two. The others were in their late twenties or early thirties; Lee himself was twenty-eight.

"Three rabbits and a pigeon," Lee replied. "I've already flogged 'em down the market."

Darren Buckle, hunched over his pint, said solemnly, "Not much meat on a pigeon."

Lee looked at him, unsure whether he was joking or not. You could never tell with Darren. In the end he shook his head. "No, not much," he agreed.

"Sausage, beans and chips," a voice said shyly beside him. Lee turned to see a dark-haired girl in her late teens holding a plate of steaming food.

"Aye, that's me, love. Just put it down there." She did so and Lee tucked in.

As he ate, the conversation ebbed and flowed around him. Football, pigeon racing, women, cars and work were discussed. Occasionally, when he felt the tide of conversation flowing his way, Lee would toss in the odd comment, but on the whole he was content just to sit and eat and listen.

Around twenty past one the gathering began to break up. Darren Buckle and Peter Raven, who both worked at a nearby garage, got up to go. Peter drained the last of his pint.

"Well, I'll see you all tonight, then," he said.

"Tonight?" Lee asked, confused.

"Aye. Bloody hell, Lee, you've got a mind like a sieve. It's Michelle Pattison's party at the Bar Bados. Don't tell us you've forgotten already."

Lee had forgotten, but he shook his head. "Course not," he said, "I'll be there."

The Bar Bados was sleazy and run-down. Somehow it looked even more depressing now than it had done as a carpet showroom. Lee knew it was a favorite haunt of drug pushers, prostitutes and pickpockets, but that didn't bother him. If the price was right, he was not averse to anything that the first two had to offer, and as for the latter, well, his trousers were so tight that even he had trouble getting his hands into the pockets.

Outside the door were two gorillas in dinner suits. As Lee walked up, one of them stepped forward and planted a large, hairy hand in the middle of his chest.

"I've come for the party," Lee said, showing his invitation, "Michelle Pattison's."

Grudgingly the bouncers let him through, disappointed that he hadn't wanted to cause trouble. Lee thought it a joke that they bothered having bouncers on the door at all. The only people they refused to let in were the police.

He made his way to the bar, through an almost tangible cloud of sweat and marijuana smoke. The barmaid was a large-breasted bottle-blonde with an expression that hovered somewhere between stupid hostility and boredom. Lee asked her for a pint of bitter. She gave him lager in an unwashed glass, then moved on before he could complain.

He sighed and looked around for his mates. The dance floor was a smoke-covered arena of writhing, sweaty bodies trapped by colored lights. The music that throbbed from the speakers was muffled and distorted. Lee spotted his mates sitting at a table to the right of the stage, and skirted toward them round the edge of the dance floor. He held his beer above his head to avoid being jogged; his feet slid on crushed cigarette butts and patches of wet. As he got near the table, Peter Raven spotted him and raised a hand in greeting.

"Lee, over here," he shouted unnecessarily. Lee acknowledged the gesture and struggled his way through.

"We were beginning to think you weren't gonna come," Peter said, pulling out a chair with a slashed seat for him.

"I never like to get to these dos too early," Lee replied, sitting down, "otherwise I'm always blind drunk by the time the birds start to arrive."

"Aye, and there's some nice ones here tonight," Peter said. "Look at that lot." He pointed at a group of four girls who were dancing around a pile of shoes and handbags. One of them was Michelle Pattison. Their intent expressions and heavy makeup made the scene appear somehow primitive, like a rain dance or a mating ritual.

"Yeah, they're all right," Lee said, nodding, though the prospect of breaking into the hallowed circle was a daunting one. He looked around, trying to pick out a girl who looked as though she might be on her own. "Mind you, she's more my type," he said, pointing across at a petite, darkly attractive girl with short black hair, who was sitting alone on the other side of the room.

"Why don't you go and chat her up, then?" Peter said. "Quick, before someone else does."

Lee nodded. "Yeah," he said, "I think I will. I'll see you in a bit." He stood up, still clutching his pint, and maneuvered his way through the forest of flailing limbs on the dance floor. As he approached her table, Lee saw the girl look up and smile as though she'd been expecting him.

"Hello," she said. She hadn't raised her voice, but Lee could hear her clearly over the music. "Who are you?"

"My name's Lee, Lee Mitchell. I saw you sitting on your own and thought you might like some company."

"That's very kind of you," she said, and smiled at him again.

She was wan and frail looking, she wore no makeup, and her clothes were drab, but in that instant Lee decided she was beautiful. He leaned forward, staring into her eyes, which were large and, in this light, seemed black as ebony. "W-Would you like to dance?" he asked.

The girl glanced at the dance floor, then gave the tiniest shake of her head. "No, thank you. I'd rather just sit here and talk."

Lee nodded, trying to look enthusiastic, though conversation was not one of his strong points. Most of the girls he had known had shared his bed in exchange for a few drinks and a dancing partner for the evening. Looking down at his empty glass, he said, "Can I buy you a drink, then?"

The girl gave a little half-smile as though she had a secret joke she was unwilling to share. "That would be nice," she said. "I'll just have a Perrier water, please."

"A what?" Lee said. The girl repeated her order. "Do they do that here?" Lee wanted to know. The girl assured him they did, and Lee went to the bar, clutching his empty pint glass in one hand and a crumpled five-pound note in the other.

The area in front of the bar was crammed with people and hot as an oven. As Lee queued, he glanced back at the girl to make sure she was still there. She was—a tiny, dark-haired figure who from this distance looked no more than twelve or thirteen years old. Looking at her, Lee felt nervous. He had never actually sat down and talked to a girl before, not properly anyway. What could they talk about? She was obviously much brainier than most of the slags he went off with. Did that mean she would be harder to coax into bed? Lee hoped not, because he wanted her badly; his hard-on was almost embarrassing.

As he watched the girl, his heart suddenly jumped. A blond-haired, bearded man had approached her and was asking her something. Lee held his breath, and was relieved when he saw the girl shake her head. The bearded man walked away, looking disappointed.

"Yes?" The barmaid's harsh voice jolted him out of his reverie. Without realizing it he had shuffled to the front of the queue.

"Er . . . a pint of bitter and a . . . a Perry water, please," he said. Had he got that right? Obviously he had, for the barmaid went straight to a bottle with a green label and poured the contents into a glass. Drinks in hand, Lee swayed back to the table.

"Here we are," he said, setting the glasses down. "Sorry I was so long. It's packed up there."

The girl flashed her little half-smile again. "Thank you."

Lee took a long swig of beer, then hastily wiped away the mustache it made. "Do you know," he said suddenly, "you haven't told me your name."

The girl hesitated, and Lee frowned. Why was she so nervous about giving her name? Then she said decisively, "Joanna. My name's Joanna."

Lee nodded. "That's a nice name. Tell me, Joanna, what do you do?"

This time the reply was more confident. "I'm a secretary at Smith's in town. Why, what do you do?"

Surely it was Lee's imagination that the question had sounded like a challenge? "I'm the one in eight," he said. When the girl looked puzzled, he added, "Unemployed."

"Oh, I see." Joanna sipped her Perrier water, then abruptly leaned forward and gazed at him intently. "But what would you really *like* to do?" she asked.

Lee thought this over. In truth he had been on the dole so long that *any* job would seem a godsend. With his poaching and his supplementary and his rent money from the council, he reckoned he earned about the same as many of his mates, but that wasn't the point. A proper job was much more than just a wage packet—it was self-respect; it was an end to breaking the law in order to survive; it was a chance to *do* something with his life. Poaching kept him above the breadline, but all the same Lee didn't particularly *enjoy* killing animals, and he enjoyed the human reactions to it even less: the way people looked at him as though he was a child-murderer, the way they assumed he was a sicko who liked inflicting pain on innocent creatures. After his trial, when his picture had appeared in the paper, the animal-rights lot had broken his windows and daubed his walls. They didn't seem to care that he had bills to pay, food to buy. And they even seemed to have overlooked the fact that he had a dog—Sabre—who he could ill afford, but who was always sleek and well cared for. Lee was certainly no saint, and had never claimed to be, but by the same token he was no ogre either.

All these thoughts passed through his head in just a few seconds. When he looked up, Joanna was still staring at him.

"What would I really like to do? Oh, I dunno—brain surgery or something. Only I don't think they'd accept me; I couldn't even get biology CSE at school."

Joanna smiled stiffly, though Lee could see that his joke hadn't gone down too well. Maybe she thought he was a layabout, maybe she thought if he was on the dole he wouldn't be able to afford to keep buying her drinks. He couldn't give her that impression, could he? Draining his glass for the second time, and trying to hold down a burp, he said, "Another drink?"

"I've hardly started this one," Joanna replied, "though you go ahead. Would you like me to . . . ?" She reached for a small black handbag at her side. Lee, recognizing her intention, stood up hastily, holding up his hand like a traffic policeman halting a line of cars.

"No, no, that's all right, love, you put your money away. I've got plenty, don't you worry about that." Hell, that sounded awful, as though he were trying to buy her. Lee knew you had to be careful what you said to birds; they took offense so easily. He turned and stumbled away toward the bar, the flashing lights and the speed with which he had consumed his two pints making him feel a little unsteady on his feet.

An hour and four pints later Lee was confident he had won Joanna over. The beer had given him the confidence to maintain a steady and, in his opinion, interesting flood of chatter. Joanna had smiled a great deal, but she had not said too much herself. Well, that was okay by Lee; most women talked too much anyway. On his seventh trip to the bar he encountered Peter Raven.

"How y'gettin' on with that bird?" Raven asked; his face was slack and stupid with drink. Lee, who was in much the same condition, winked and gave the thumbs-up.

"Great. Got her eatin' out o' my hand."

For some reason this struck Raven as excruciatingly funny, and he went off into a fit of drunken giggles. "Reckon you'll get her into bed?" he snorted.

Lee nodded confidently. "No problem."

By the end of the evening Lee was so drunk he could barely stand up. For the last couple of hours he had been spouting bullshit, too pissed to do anything else, but frightened of the silences between himself and Joanna. She, however, had sat through his slurred spiel, smiling and nodding as though it were the most enthralling thing she had ever heard. Lee reckoned he could have told her his shoe size or counted up to a thousand and she would have found it interesting. This discovery cheered him, gave him confidence. This bird was just like all the rest, he thought; she wasn't at all brainy. He patted his hip pocket, happily convinced that the condoms in there had not been bought in vain after all.

The lights came on, and Lee looked around in surprise. The club was only about a quarter full now. People were standing by the exits, waiting for taxis or struggling into coats. The bouncers were looking for drunks they could take round the back and beat up. The deejay, a tired, pasty, balding man in his late thirties, was glumly winding up a length of cable. "C'mon," Lee said with what he hoped was an enticing grin, "time t'go home." He stood up, but somehow the chair got tangled in his legs. He fell backward into a pool of beer, hearing wood splinter.

For a moment the room whirled and spun, then shadows fell over him and giant, hairy paws groped for his throat. "It's all right," he heard the girl say, "he's with me. I'll see he gets home."

Hands reached under his armpits and dragged him up. Lee came face-to-face with Joanna. God, she's strong, his befuddled mind thought. "Shtupid chair," he told her, sniggering.

"Come on," Joanna said, and hauled him out into the night.

It was cold. Lee shivered and wished he'd brought a jacket. It took him a moment to realize it was fog, and not his drunkenness, that blurred the street. "Taxi," he shouted, and went staggering off, searching for transport. Joanna ran after him and caught hold of his arm.

"No, come on," she said, "this way. If we're quick, we can catch the night bus."

Lee allowed himself to be led, gaping blearily about. Fog sat on the world like a hangover: Lee was sure it was this, and not the beer in his stomach, that made him feel sick. He shivered again and put his arm around Joanna as the fog closed about them like a cold womb.

Suddenly he jumped back; a long, serpentine neck supporting a flat, glowing head loomed from the greyness. "Silly," Joanna hissed in his ear, "it's only a lamppost."

Lee smiled nervously. "Can we stop a minute? I'm not feeling too good."

"We're there now," Joanna said, pointing, "just a few more steps."

Lee looked up. The bus stop seemed incongruous, something solid and ordinary jutting from the grey void. He shook his arm free from Joanna's grip and staggered to it gratefully. Then he sank to his knees and closed his eyes, his head resting against the cool concrete.

He was woken by the metallic hiss of pneumatic doors opening. He scrambled to his feet, dazed, trying to make sense of the green wall, the squares of light, the staring faces. A man in a green uniform leaned toward him from behind a steering wheel.

"You gettin' on or what?"

Lee gazed blearily about him. "Where's Joanna?"

The bus driver was obviously in no mood for games. "Who?" he asked dangerously.

"Joanna . . . the girl . . . there was a girl with me."

The bus driver shook his head. "No girl, mate, only you."

Lee looked around, confused, then shrugged. "Stupid cow," he muttered, and boarded the bus.

He paid his fare and swayed toward the back seats. The sickness had climbed from his stomach to his head where it sat, pounding. He sank into a corner, immediately feeling warm and snug despite the pain. He was only dimly aware of the hiss of the doors closing before the chugging of the engine lulled him to sleep.

He woke later. How much later he wasn't sure. Blearily he looked around him. He had a feeling he had been asleep for hours, but the bus was still as full now as when he had got on. He sat for a moment, trying to draw his muddled thoughts together. His head still throbbed thickly, but he must have slept through the worst of it. Around him conversation droned, merging with the engine. Lee could not make out any of the words. He stretched himself from his cramped position and looked out of the window. It gave him no clue. The bus was cocooned in fog; Lee couldn't even see any streetlights now.

He leaned forward and tapped an old man on the shoulder. " 'Scuse me."

The man turned to look at him. He wore a brown overcoat and a cloth cap. Hair jabbed from beneath the cap like grey straw.

" 'Scuse me," Lee repeated, "but are we anywhere near Headingley?"

The man smiled widely without opening his mouth. "Soon," he said; his voice sounded thick and wet as though his false teeth didn't fit properly. "Very soon."

"Thanks," Lee said and sat back, relieved. The man nodded and smiled.

Lee looked around the bus, and it struck him for the first time how clean it was. There were no ripped seats, no graffiti, no advertisements for cheap fares or late-night services. It looked, in fact, like a bus that had just rolled straight off the production line.

He leaned back. The drone of conversation went on and on, and after a while he found himself nodding off again. Just before sleep claimed him, he thought how strange it was that they had neither stopped at any other bus stops nor turned any corners.

Lee could see countryside, and wondered vaguely where Leeds and the fog had gone. "It's a real pea-souper," the old man said, though now he was wearing a track suit and carrying a tennis racket.

"Well, it was," said Lee. "It's gone now."

The old man nodded sadly. "It's like that," he said, "it comes and goes."

Lee was almost jerked out of his seat as the bus suddenly pulled violently into the curb. He watched as the driver stood up and addressed the passengers.

"Which one of you came on drunk?" he demanded. Lee shrank lower into his seat, but the driver had seen him.

"It was you, wasn't it?" he said. Lee opened his mouth, but found he couldn't answer. Suddenly the driver had a whirring drill in his hand.

"People like you need to be taught a lesson," he purred, and advanced slowly.

"Stop him!" Lee screamed to the passengers. "Stop him, *he's the driller killer!*"

One by one, the passengers turned to look at Lee. He gasped as he saw the front of their heads for the first time. They had no faces . . .

Lee jerked awake. Despite his chattering teeth he was bathed in sweat. Where was he? In bed? He looked around, confused. He seemed to be in a sort of dark corridor: he could just make out an aisle flanked by dim rows of rectangular shapes. Suddenly it came back to him. The bus—he was on a bus. He groaned. He must have missed his stop and gone right through. The driver must have taken the bus back to the depot, locked up and gone home without realizing he was still aboard.

It was silent now, but this time Lee didn't feel like sleeping. He had to get out and make his way home before someone found him. He didn't think he'd actually done anything wrong, but his presence might take an awful lot of explaining.

He got up and made his way to the front of the bus, gripping the solid backs of the seats as though he were on a tightrope. His legs still felt a little unsteady, though his shock on waking had sobered him somewhat. He let himself into the driver's cab, and was about to switch on the lights when he realized how stupid the action would be; after all, he didn't want to draw attention to himself. He groped on the panel, looking for a switch or lever that would open the doors, but couldn't find one. For a moment, panic surged through him. How was he going to get out? Then he found the button he was looking for and pressed it.

Immediately a babble of conversation filled the bus, and Lee looked round wildly, half expecting the empty seats to be suddenly full of people again. Realizing what he had done, he pressed the button and abruptly the drone of conversation ceased.

Lee felt disturbed. Why did the bus company need to record conversation? What possible purpose could it serve? Curiously he pressed the button again. Conversation babbled. Suddenly scared, Lee jabbed at the button, shutting it off. In the dark, silent, empty bus the voices had been eerie and unnatural.

"Pillock," Lee said to himself, as all at once he realized there would be an emergency exit at the back of the bus. He picked his way down the aisle again, pulling himself along by the jutting seats as though trying to locate his place in a dark cinema. He reached the back and groped for a catch, and sure enough there it was. He released it and the long window at the back came open with a quiet clunk.

Lee lowered himself out of the window and onto the concrete floor below. He was happy to get off the bus, but now where was he? He looked around, his eyes gradually adapting to the darkness.

He appeared to be in a huge, square room, like an aircraft hangar, empty of everything but the bus he had arrived in. He felt uneasy, apprehensive: where were all the other buses? And why was this depot so featureless? Slowly he pivoted on his heels, looking for a way out. It was a few minutes before he noticed the door.

Lee walked over to it, the echo of his footsteps lost in the vastness of the depot. He felt increasingly nervous, certain now that something was wrong. This wasn't a bus depot at all; no stretch of the imagination could believe it so. Then what was it? And what was the bus doing here? Was it in for repair? Had it been stolen? Questions kept his headache company. Lee would have been happy to leave them all unanswered if only this door led outside.

But it didn't. Even before he had opened it fully, Lee knew he wasn't going to be in luck. The first thing he was aware of was a pale green glow, like something out of a science fiction film. He opened the door fully to find himself looking down a long, narrow corridor. He began to feel sick again; this was like nothing he had ever seen before. The walls, floor and ceiling of the corridor seemed to be made from beaten copper, lit from above by pale green strip lighting.

Lee took a cautious step into the corridor: the gleaming, dimpled walls distorted his reflections, transforming them into writhing, sickly green phantoms. The phantoms, one on either side, accompanied him as he started down.

Up ahead the corridor branched off at a right angle. Please let it lead outside, Lee breathed to himself, please, please, *please.*

He came to the bend in the corridor. Another corridor, identical to the first, stretched ahead. For a moment Lee felt like going back to the familiar territory of the bus, but the urge to get out of this place, to see the outside world again, was too strong. Taking a deep breath, he started forward.

This corridor was longer than the first, and, Lee felt sure, darker too. The green light seemed dense, murky, giving Lee the impression that he was heading downward into the earth.

Nervousness and alcohol made him queasy. He forced himself to keep moving, his footsteps clanging softly on the metal floor.

Up ahead the corridor branched off to the left. Lee approached, hope and fear increasing with each step. As he got closer, the slight buzzing that came from the lights overhead seemed to grow steadily louder.

Lee reached the bend in the corridor and looked down it. Yet another corridor stretched ahead of him. For a moment he was swamped by a wave of terror and despair. He imagined himself wandering for days through corridor after corridor, eventually becoming hopelessly lost and hopelessly mad. He stood, undecided. What should he do? Go on or go back?

Two things decided him. The first was that Lee suddenly noticed the corridor ahead had doors set into the walls at regular intervals. They were made of the same beaten coppery metal as the walls, and at first glance had been unnoticeable. The second was far more sinister. From somewhere behind him came a snuffling and a snorting as though some animal were tracking him. He looked over his shoulder, and thought he could detect something way back in the murk of the corridor; a looming shadow on the walls and a pale, bloated shape. Fear overcame his curiosity and he plunged into the corridor.

The light here was even more dingy. Lee groped his way to the nearest door and grasped the handle. Should he enter? A sudden thought, sharp and clear, crystallized in his mind: was he *meant* to enter? His hand, limp and sweaty, hovered over the handle. A further outbreak of snorting and snuffling, closer now, reverberated from the walls of the corridor behind him. Bracing himself, he yanked down the door handle and entered.

Immediately light blinded him. Lee threw up his hands, terrified at his sudden inability to see where he was. He felt vulnerable as a rabbit caught in the glare of headlights. Scrabbling behind him, he found the door handle and pushed, closing out the piglike snorting from the corridor. He stayed in that position for a moment, crouched with his weight against the door, until his eyes adjusted to the light.

Little by little the glare subsided, and Lee was able to make out vague shapes. His first thought was that he was in an operating theater, his second in an abattoir. The brightly lit room was dominated by a white man-sized slab which was streaked with blood and scraps of offal. The smell that hung in the air was rich and hot and sickly. Lee moved away from the door and began a cautious examination of the room, taking care not to step in the blood that lay in small pools about the floor.

Mark Morris

The room was white-tiled, square and functional, lit from above by the same strip lighting as in the corridors, except this was white instead of green. Along one wall was a runnel supporting a row of butcher's hooks, while along another wall hung an assortment of oddly shaped implements. Lee examined them, feeling uncomfortable and afraid. There was an assortment of knives of various sizes, the blades peculiarly curved, and many tools that he couldn't put a name to. He lifted one down from its hook, a small, sickle-shaped implement with a fine, serrated blade. Lee was surprised at how heavy the thing was, then noticed what appeared to be a small motor inside the handle. Intrigued, he looked for a switch, found one, and turned the tool on. With a high-pitched whir the blade began to spin, the teeth blurring together as it picked up speed. He turned the tool off, shuddering. The whirring noise reminded him of the dream he had had on the bus.

He put the tool back on its hook. Then it struck him that it might come in useful if he had to defend himself against the snorting thing outside. He reached for the blade again, then hesitated and drew his hand away. For some reason, just holding the tool gave him the creeps.

Lee tried to make sense of the situation. Maybe the bus depot backed onto a slaughterhouse, and those metal corridors that he had come through were where the animals were kept, prior to being slaughtered. It wasn't a very plausible explanation, but it was the best Lee could manage. He needed some shred of rationality to cling to.

He jumped as something soft and heavy thumped against the door. He stood still and listened. After a moment the noise came again, followed by a grunting and sniffing. The thing outside must have picked up his scent. Lee looked round wildly as the handle of the door began to turn.

He noticed what appeared to be a cupboard set into the wall beneath the butcher's hooks. He hurried across to it, praying that it wouldn't be locked. It wasn't. Lee tugged it open and dived inside, aware that behind him the snorting was growing louder as whatever-it-was entered the room.

He found himself in a space about the size of a bathroom. It was dim, but he could make out a rack of clothes along the wall behind him. Despite his terror, he found the clothes strange and intriguing. Although in different sizes, they were all identical—pale pink body stockings, each with a dark, furry hood. Lee examined them curiously.

The material was odd; pliable, almost rubbery in texture, smooth in parts, rough in others.

Lee turned his attention to the door as something plopped against it from outside. He held his breath as he heard the familiar terrifying sniffing and snorting, and he shrank back against the rack of clothes. Go away, he prayed silently, go away, *go away*. His prayers were not answered. The door handle turned and the door slowly opened inward.

Light flooded into the room, bringing with it a whirring sound—and a nightmare. Shapes filled the doorway: grey, bloated creatures, their skin as soft as dough. They had vaguely human features, though with snouts instead of noses, and stodgy, three-fingered hands. Lee crammed himself back against the far wall, too frightened even to scream. The creatures parted to form a tunnel, and a petite dark-haired girl appeared, holding the whirring sickle-shaped blade that Lee had examined earlier. It was Joanna.

"Hello, Lee," she said brightly. She smiled, hugely now, and came toward him. Lee began to whimper.

And as the creatures held him down, he suddenly realized what those pale pink things on the rack really were.

ASHLEY McCONNELL

Of Natural
Causes

The body in the coffin didn't look like my mother.

I leaned over to look at it more closely, my breath ruffling the snow-white hair brushed straight back off the forehead; that was the way we'd told the funeral director my mother wore her hair, brushed back straight as a line. Untrimmed. That was because she hadn't been to a hairdresser in months. Maybe years. Hadn't worn makeup either, but this corpse had a discreet veil of face powder, a trace of pinkish lipstick smudged at the corner of its upper lip. No one had tried to mascara the stubby eyelashes. My mother wore mascara.

My mother used to wear mascara, years ago, before she died. Before she lived only to shuffle bent-backed from the tall four-poster bed to the tilt-back chair in the tiny, stygian den, back and forth day after day, while my father sat in the light from the window in the kitchen, playing endless games of solitaire, waiting for her to finish her dying so he could bury her and sell the house and all the memories and be done with it. My mother taught me how to roll up my brown hair, taking advantage of the curl she never had, how to do my eyes. My lashes are longer than my mother's.

I reached out to touch the corpse's hands, twined about with a rosary. They had a cool, slightly waxy feel, as if this were really a mannequin that someone had stored overnight in a refrigerator for some reason, pulling it out to dress it in the dress I had chosen, green leafy patterns against blue silk, my mother's dress. It didn't look like my mother. I had no feeling my mother was dead.

I stepped away, reluctant to turn my back on the coffin. My father and my sister and my aunts and uncle glanced at me as I passed them by, and my sister jerked her head to the empty seat beside her. I ignored them and took the seat I had chosen in the fourth row, leaning against the wall, staring at their backs, listening for someone else to come in. There were seats for forty-nine people, seven rows of seven seats, and there were only six of us. Plus my nephews, ages ten and eight, playing Metal Creatures Who Save the Universe up and down the halls of the funeral home.

If my mother was really dead, she should be lying in state in an Irish wake in her hometown in Oklahoma, or at least in Albuquerque where she'd lived for fifteen years, and her rosary should be packed with people who knew her and cared about her and would pray her on her way to heaven. Members of the Altar Society should have been coming by all afternoon to leave condolences and casseroles.

Instead my father popped next door to let the neighbors know, and they shrugged and went on a family picnic. My parents had lived there five years and the neighbors had never seen my mother. And we went out the night my mother died and had dinner at Furr's.

My uncle came up beside me and put his arm around my shoulder, squeezing it tightly. "It's all over now," he half shouted. My uncle was going deaf. "She isn't suffering any more. You can thank God for that."

I pulled away. I didn't want comfort from an uncle I had seen twice in thirty years. I didn't need comfort. That wasn't my mother. My mother wasn't dead. I wasn't even sure that was a person lying in that bronze box. Certainly not my mother. My mother was a large, hearty, buxom woman who laughed easily and cried easily—more and more easily—and somehow had shrunk, dissolved away to a fragile, wasted

woman leaning on a walker, clicking back and forth from bed to recliner, recliner to bed, all alone, refusing to eat, taking her pills and
medications when she was reminded, sometimes taking them twice
because my father never believed she would take them on her own—
and I had been planning to come out and visit her for Easter, just
yesterday.

My mother would have had roomfuls of flowers for her viewing, not
three small bouquets and a red-and-white chrysanthemum casket
wreath, size small. We had looked at pictures of casket wreaths in a
book in the funeral director's office yesterday. Flowers were terribly
expensive, and they didn't have irises. My mother won a prize once for
her blue irises. We found the ribbons this morning, carefully packed
away, and showed them to my father. He didn't remember her ever
having done that. He wanted to throw the ribbons away, and I stopped
him. Mom wouldn't want her prizes thrown away.

The deacon stumped to the prie-dieu and sank down for a brief
prayer. A deacon, not even a priest. The parish priest here didn't know
my mother, couldn't spare the time. The recorded organ music muted,
shut off with an audible click.

My father tilted his head to my sister. He was trying to whisper, and
his voice echoed. "Any idea why Sherry won't come join the family?"

My name is Cheryln. Only Mom called me that.

Patsy shook her head and shot me a glare. The boys came in, settling
down beside their mother. I shook my head again, and then we all went
to our knees and started the First Glorious Mystery.

Afterward the deacon murmured a few words to my father and
slipped away. I stayed, leaning against the wall, watching the corpse,
watching my family, wondering where my mother had gotten to. Aunt
Elaine and Aunt Margery stepped out into the hallway to sneak cigarettes and talk about a friend of Margery's who was in a coma in an
Amarillo hospice. Elaine had timed the rosary, glancing at her dia-
mond-crusted watch at the end of every decade. She'd mentioned that
a golf tournament at her Denver country club started tomorrow. Their
voices carried from the hallway to the viewing room, punctuated with
cancers and par fives indiscriminately.

My father went up to the prie-dieu and knelt, staring at the body in
the coffin. After a while he struggled to his feet, puffing slightly, and
moved out of my line of vision. A while after that, my sister's hand
clamped on my shoulder.

"Come on. We're going back to the house."

"I want to stay here."

"You can't spend your life sitting here. Come on, they're already in the car. We almost left you."

I twisted out of her grip. "In a minute."

She made a sharp, exasperated sound and left. I rose to my feet, fumbling for my purse, and went back to the coffin. The corpse's hair was soft. As soft as my own, white instead of brown. It still didn't look like my mother.

I paused at the door and looked back once more. The organ music had come back on almost as soon as the deacon had finished the final blessings, and there was a hint of incense in the air. A spotlight illuminated the body, the slightly disarrayed hair. Nobody else was in the room. I wished she would open her eyes and talk to me.

They gathered around the den table that night for the wake, faces flickering in and out of my focus in the light from the fake-Tiffany Coca-Cola lamp, talking about Florida weather, about Aunt Margery's friend, about blood pressure. My sister, who is not a doctor and not a nurse, produced a blood-pressure cuff. She runs a business selling home medical supplies. We all go to her for second opinions; it's cheaper.

"Frances never did have high blood pressure," my father said, watching as Patsy slipped the Velcro around his arm. "I was always the one with high blood pressure."

"I thought she had a stroke," Uncle Mike said. "Did she, er . . ."

"Did she have another stroke, Dave?" Elaine said.

"Well, I'll tell you," Daddy said, still absorbed in the process of inflating the cuff. "I woke up around two A.M., and I heard her get up to go to the bathroom. And I heard her get back into bed beside me, and I fell asleep.

"I got up at seven, just like I always do, and she was just lying there, with her one hand curled up under her chin the way she did, in a normal sleeping posture. Didn't look any different from the way she usually does—did. One foot out from under the covers, like she didn't pull it in.

"And I came in around ten, ten-thirty to tell her to get up and eat some brunch, and she was still lying there. And I called her name a couple of times, and then I thought, Oh, Lord, and I called the police."

"One-twenty over eighty," my sister announced.

"They asked me if I wanted to take her to the hospital, but hell, she was dead, wasn't she? So I told them to take her straight to the funeral home. They called the ambulance."

"Hey, try that thing on me next," Uncle Mike said. "I've been worried about my blood pressure."

I got up quietly and slipped out, back to the back bedroom. The old rocking chair moved gently back and forth as I studied the bed. That was where she died, lying there who knows how long, alone, without anybody even to touch her to find out if her body was cold. One hand curled up under her chin, and one foot stuck out from under the covers. The bed was neatly made now. Patsy had been in here, neatening things. She hadn't wanted Mike and Margery and Elaine to think their sister had died in an unmade bed.

Beside the bed, on the nightstand, a green Princess telephone rested askew on a telephone book. Propped against it was a box of pink tissues, the kind she would hold in her hand and tuck up her sleeves. There was some connection, some mysterious comfort tissues must give old women, I thought; they all squirreled them away against a supermarket famine. Beside the tissues, a bottle of hand lotion, a vial of medicine that would have to be thrown away now. A worn rosary, polished with constant use, was draped over the bedpost. I could not remember ever having seen that bedpost without a rosary available on it, smooth, dark brown beads against a carved dark brown headboard. My sister would be getting the bedroom set; after all, she was married, and a single woman didn't need a queen-size bed.

A papal blessing hung on the wall over the bed. Dusty bottles of holy water were jumbled in with cosmetics, perfume, and at least sixteen emery boards scattered on the dresser. A series of pictures on the wall showed my sister, her children, my father, his mother, my mother's mother; my high school graduation picture was stuck in a corner of my sister's family portrait. My mother was Irish, aggressively Irish, and her family and her religion were the most important things in the world. Neither one seemed very interested in her now.

The closets were full of clothes and shoes. "You may as well go through them," Patsy had said, "they're your size." Not hers, of course, heavens no, Patsy was a perfect size eight and always would be, but my mother's weight had fluctuated up and down in a way I had charted on my own bathroom scales for ten years. Tomorrow, after the funeral, I would sort clothes. Tonight I should put away that bottle of nitroglycerin pills on the nightstand, before Patsy came back in, cleaning again. Faint laughter echoed from the den.

Rocking back and forth, I thought about it, looked over to the walker propped in the corner. Patsy would be taking that back to the office with her day after tomorrow. Patsy was very efficient.

I left the vial undisturbed and went to bed.

She came to me in my dreams, expected almost, feared. But it was only my mother, my mother as she had looked ten years before, as she had looked the day I went to buy my first car, and she had insisted on finishing up the salad before we went. And the dealership was going to close, so my father and I got into the car to go, not waiting for her. She came outside still wearing her apron and called to us to wait, but there was no time, and we left her standing in the driveway.

She was still taller than me then, a solid, heavy woman with short gray hair tinted purple. I had never known my mother with dark hair, though of course there were pictures; I rather liked her purple hair. In my dream she was wearing orange polyester slacks, and an orange and green polyester blouse, and she was cutting up celery for a salad, and she was talking to me. I couldn't hear her; it was as if I were separated from her by a glass wall of which she was not aware, and she couldn't see my frustration, couldn't hear me telling her I couldn't hear her.

She started stripping a bunch of carrots, and I leaned up against the glass wall and cried because I couldn't hear, and I so wanted to hear my mother's voice again. She didn't notice, even when she looked up and straight at me, still talking, waving the peeler for emphasis, jabbing it at me.

The dream changed, and she was kneeling in the garden, jabbing now at the earth with a trowel. Once again, she was talking to me and I couldn't hear her. This time, though, she seemed to realize something was wrong, and she sat back wearily with a puzzled look on her face, put the trowel aside, and held out her hand. I thought there might be something in it, but I couldn't tell what; I was reaching for it when Patsy knocked on the door.

Given the scarcity of priests in the parish, we had been informed, there would be no special Mass for my mother. They would say the Mass for the Dead at the regular eight-thirty service.

It was a huge parish, and the church was a six-sided box, with three aisles leading to the altar instead of a single nave. The bronze box waited in the rightmost aisle, and we filed into the pew beside it.

Eternal rest grant unto them O Lord

As the deacon had been a stranger, so was the priest celebrating the Mass. There was a priest my mother knew in town—a priest who was Irish, who had grown up in a house two blocks away from hers in Okmulgee. But Father McCormick's Provincial Superior was in town that day and had informed him that he would place himself at the Provincial's disposal, and Father had taken a vow of obedience, and a stranger said my mother's last Mass. The good Catholics who attended a Lenten Friday morning mass must have wondered who we were.

We had gone to see Father McCormick the day before, early in the morning before the Provincial arrived, and he took one look at me and said, "Now there's a Dinnevan. Just exactly like her mother—"

and let perpetual light shine upon them

The funeral home had supplied two of the four pallbearers. My mother had told me once that when her grandmother, the best midwife in all of County Clare, had died, she was followed to her grave by the whole town of Quilty. Quite an honor, that was, to have been at Mary Margaret Dinnevan's burying and lifted a glass to her memory. My mother told the story with her eyes shining, almost as if she had been there.

Be merciful we beseech you, Lord, to the soul of your handmaid Frances

We filed out of church and into the limousines, the boys quiet and respectful for once, and had to wait a few minutes for the parking lot to clear out before we could go. The drivers' breath hung in the air as they stood outside and watched. Aunt Elaine checked her watch again. I huddled deeper into the coat I'd borrowed at the last minute from the coat closet; coming from a hot climate, I wasn't prepared for late winter snow. It was Mom's old gray artificial fur; I remembered her wearing it years ago to a school play, bundled up and beaming at me. I remembered her laughing, wearing this coat.

My hands fumbled in the pockets, and pulled out a pair of white gloves and a wad of Kleenex. I pulled the gloves on gratefully; they fit, for a change. The Kleenex I put back. One never knew when one might need it.

May her soul and all the souls of the faithful departed

The priest, whose name I didn't know, followed us out to the cemetery. It was a new cemetery, with small white modern headstones almost invisible against the snow. We saw grave diggers sizing a hole as we followed the roadway, shouting at each other as if they weren't only six feet apart sticking shovels in the earth.

Two rows of metal chairs, thoughtfully covered with fake-fur sheaths, faced a low platform set by the side of the road. The snow around it was unmarked. We pulled up, and the boys burst out of the limousine and ran up to the hearse, clamoring to have their pictures taken; Patsy yanked them back with a look, and my father conferred with the funeral director. The director was calling my father David, and it annoyed him. Nobody called my father David except my mother. I moved up behind him to hear what he said to my sister. Neither of them looked at me.

"They don't do the actual interment now," he said. "They'll do that later on this afternoon when there aren't any people around. They do it that way for all of them now." Patsy nodded and herded the boys into the first row of seats beside my father. Uncle Mike and Margery and Elaine clustered around, trying not to be the first one into the second row, and the priest from St. Raphael's looked the scene over, his brow slightly furrowed. I followed Elaine into the last available chair, and the priest turned to the bronze coffin and began the prayers for Christian burial.

through the mercy of God

The holy water the priest sprinkled on us was cold. I watched a trickle of it move across the top of the coffin and chill into immobility. The murmur of familiar prayers kept my lips moving, stiffly, determinedly.

I am the Resurrection and the Life; he who believes in Me, even if he die, shall live; and whoever lives and believes in Me, shall never die

"Amen," we chorused. The priest stepped back and closed his missal, and we held our breaths, uncertainly. The funeral director moved up and tapped my father on the shoulder, and at the signal we all stood and moved slowly away toward the limousines that would take us home.

I craned my neck to watch the bronze coffin shrink out of sight, sitting alone on the platform in the snow, with two rows of empty cloth-covered metal chairs as honor guard before it, as the limousines pulled away.

rest in peace

Mike and Margery and Elaine had to leave immediately for the airport. Patsy set my father to going through old files and told me to start sorting clothes while she played chauffeur; she bustled out the door, leaving me and my father looking at one another.

"Well," my father said. He looked around. "First thing I'm going to do is get rid of the damned piano." He turned back to the file cabinets set in a small nook in the back of the huge den. "Got that for her three years ago so she could exercise her hand after that stroke, and you know how many times she played it?"

I shook my head, having heard this story every time I came to visit my parents, knowing too that my father had to tell it again, knowing too the part he always left out.

"Twice! Maybe three times, is all. That's all she played it. A baby grand piano. I paid more than four thousand dollars for the damned thing, and she only played it three times. Or twice."

My mother had never sat down to the piano without my father making some remark about "noise." My father, who had taken lessons longer as a boy, never sat down to it at all.

I stripped off the heavy coat and carried it back to the back bedroom, laying it on mother's side of the bed. I should change out of my good dress, too, but that could wait. I kicked off my shoes instead.

rest in peace

I could remember my mother wearing some of these clothes; she never threw anything away. Most of them came from a mail-order house, and more of them were orange than I remembered. I paged through the hangers of blouses and slacks and dresses lining the walk-in closet and decided that it would be easier to go through the shoes first. She had golf shoes from before I was born, a white pair and a brown pair, surprisingly heavy, with metal spikes. I hefted them in my hands and tried to recall when Mom had played golf.

"She always said she wanted to learn," my father said behind me, answering my thoughts. "Then I went out and bought her a set of golf clubs, and she never touched them. I gave her one lesson and she just lost interest."

I looked down at the shoes in my hand and smiled to myself. I'd taken driving lessons from my father once.

Daddy dropped an armful of coats from the front closet on the bed. "Patsy says you'll want to try these on."

I nodded, unable to speak suddenly, my throat constricting. I stretched my neck, looking up to the ceiling, and swallowed hard three times. "Daddy, what was the doctor's name?"

"What?"

"What was the name of the doctor you said Mom saw last Friday?" My voice wasn't very shaky. I swallowed once more to be sure, and had to clamp my teeth against a sudden silent wail. My father looked at me, bewildered.

"Dr. Brown, why?"

"What department is he in?"

"It was a she, and I don't know. Mom went in for blood tests. May I ask why?" "May I" was run together into one word, and he leaned on the word "why."

"I just want to know what my mother died of!" I gasped, and tears started flooding down my face. I've never been a "pretty" crier, with crystal tears rolling limpid down my cheeks. Hell, no. My face goes red and my lips strain back, and I can't breathe except in choking sobs. I remember my mother crying that way once, sitting in her yellow recliner chair alone in the living room, quiet gasping sobs from a red face, weeping because she was lonely, because her husband and her daughters were impatient with her, because her family had no time for her, because she was alone, and because she didn't know how to be whatever it was they wanted her to be. I had crept by unnoticed. I hadn't known what to say to my mother then, and besides, I wanted to get out of the house to go to a movie. I left her behind me, crying. Now I was crying too, and I didn't know why. I had only asked a reasonable question.

"Well, Sherry, I don't know. They took her directly to the funeral home."

"Didn't anybody *ask?*" It seemed insane to me to find a body lying beside where you had slept all night and never ask why it had died. Much less your wife, whom you loved.

"You know the shape she was in," he replied defensively. "We'd all been expecting it." That was my father. Pragmatic. He had, after all, been expecting it for years, planning the situation. How he would react, what he would do, how he would pay for the funeral, what knickknacks he could get rid of immediately, what would have to wait until the estate was probated. Who would get the crystal. Where he would travel, sightseeing, once my mother was buried.

"I want to call the doctor, okay?" Damn it, Daddy, is that all right with you?

"Okay. Okay, fine. I have no objection . . ." He did, probably, but he wouldn't state it to me. My father was seventy-two, and he had never justified himself in his life; but his shoulders were a bit more bowed as he closed the bedroom door behind him. My father could never handle tears.

Once I had gotten into an argument at the kitchen table, trying to explain to my father why something had happened at school—it couldn't have been important, I can't remember what it was—and I had started crying in frustration. My father, reverting to old military days, had ordered me to stop crying and straighten up. My mother had protested. My father, taken aback that his authority would be questioned, had grumbled, "Oh, very well, cry at will."

I cried at will now, sweeping the coats off the bed onto the floor, then picking up the fur in my arms and folding over it, stroking the gray fur as if it were gray hair, sitting in the rocking chair and rocking back and forth and weeping, splashing hot tears onto my arms, reaching blindly for the Kleenex and blowing my nose and crying with my face stretched tight and my throat constricted, muffling the sound with the coat in my arms because that was the closest I could come to hugging my mother and she was gone in a box and I couldn't hug her anymore and tell her I was sorry, so sorry for creeping away that day.

rest in peace

I couldn't bring myself to pick up the phone that day. I cried until it was almost dark, and took the excuse to go to bed early. If I was in bed, Patsy wouldn't come in to tell me to face reality.

And after a long while, when the house was quiet, I fell asleep again, and I dreamed again about my mother.

We were sitting at the kitchen table, and she was reading to me. A poem, I think. My mother used to read to me, and it irritated me, because she read the way the nuns had taught her sixty-five years before, when Speaking was as much a required course as Reading—with artificial emphases and precise enunciation and flourishing gestures carefully matched to the text. I didn't want to listen. I couldn't listen. I couldn't hear.

Then she shut the book and looked up at me, straight into my eyes, and said something very important.

And I still couldn't hear.

Her hand clenched my arm, and in my dream I twisted my head back and forth, trying to hear, trying to read her lips, asking her to speak louder. It was very important, whatever it was; and her hand squeezed even tighter. I almost heard her. I almost had it—

Until I woke up, despairing, bewildered, to find Patsy standing over me.

"Sherry! Sherry, wake up! Wake up! You're going to wake the whole house! Sherry, shut up!"

And my mother was not there anywhere.

"Yes, I heard about it," Dr. Brown said. "I was a little surprised, of course, but it wasn't unusual."

"I don't understand. Do people just—die like that? From nothing?"

"Well, your mother was seventy-five. And it could have been a number of things. She could have had another stroke, or a heart attack, or a blood clot from the medication she was taking. The normal life expectancy for women is only seventy-two, you know."

It isn't what *I* expected, I wanted to say. My grandmother died at ninety-three, and what does *that* say about normal life expectancy? But the doctor was trying to be helpful. She'd gotten out the records and told me all about the last visit, one week to the day before my mother died, and there was nothing to explain it. Without an autopsy, there would never be anything to explain it. She sounded professional and sympathetic and compassionate and she could not keep my mother from sitting alone in her recliner and crying and dying of loneliness. My mother died for no reason.

Except my mother didn't die at all. I had dreamed about her, and she was alive. She was trying to tell me so. She was trying to tell me something.

rest in peace

I thanked the doctor for her time and replaced the phone in its cradle. I stared at it a long time, and then got up slowly, my bones creaking from sitting so long, and shuffled into the bedroom.

rest in peace

The clothes still had to be sorted. Patsy wanted to take the discards to the church tomorrow before she left. I shivered, looked around for an open window, and couldn't find one; I shrugged the coat around my shoulders and went into the closet. So many, many dresses. Blouses.

Slacks. Such pretty, bright colors. And so many shoes, shoes to go with them all.

Patsy had come back. I could hear her yelling at the boys, rattling pans in the kitchen. I kept going, pulling blouses off hangers, holding them against myself, discarding one or two with ripped hems and missing buttons, carefully folding the red ones, the blue ones, the orange ones into neat stacks on the bed.

The door opened. It was Patsy.

"Are you coming to lunch?"

I shook my head, folded another blouse, black with bright blue flowers, and placed it on the bed. She picked it up, tossed it back down again.

"You don't have to fold the ones going to the church. They'll take care of that."

"I'm keeping those. They're good clothes."

She looked at the three or four garments on the floor, nudged them with her toe, and then picked up a stack from the bed, shuffling through them quickly. "They're old, and they've got no style. For God's sake, throw them away. You can't keep everything. And you've got to eat. You can't spend the rest of your life sitting in here, it's not healthy. Come on out and join the rest of us."

"No!" I snatched the blouses away from her. Patsy had never understood about good clothes. And I was getting terribly tired of the way she ordered me to come out. She didn't really want me out there in the kitchen with all of them, I could tell by her voice. She was too impatient. And I was too tired. "They're mine! You can't give these away, I want them, they're *mine.*"

"Come out and eat, then."

"Just leave me alone, will you? I'm not hungry!"

"Okay, damn it. You want to be left alone, I'll leave you alone. Let me know when you want to join us in the real world!" Throwing up her hands in defeat, she slammed the door behind her, and I went on sorting and stacking.

Sorting good clothes is hard work, choosing what to keep and what to give away. I could still hear sounds from the other part of the house, vague sounds. It didn't matter. Just David, no doubt, talking to Patsy at the kitchen table, the way he always did. The chill hadn't gone away, but I refused to think about it, refused to look at myself in the mirror when it reflected the dresses, the blouses, the coats. I know what I look like. My hair is ragged and white, and I am bent and tired and alone.

I kept going through the clothes, until it was time to take my pills. There were quite a lot of them, more than I remembered, but then David always had to remind me. But not this time, I thought proudly. I could remember for myself, if they'd just let me. If they'd just love me.

And now it's time to lie down, and pull my coat up over me, my lovely happy warm coat will make the chill go away. I can't seem to get my one foot under the cover, but that doesn't matter, it will be warm enough. And curl my hand under my chin—

BRIAN MOONEY
and
STEPHEN JONES

Mulberry's Crystal

It might seem irrational, but over the past two weeks I have come to detest sunsets.

If it hadn't been for an exceptionally beautiful sunset, I would not have lingered that evening on London's Westminster Bridge and I would not have renewed my acquaintance with Silas Mulberry.

And I would not now be praying as I have never prayed before, praying fervently for my life. Not that Mulberry himself is any threat to me. Mulberry is dead . . . Or, at least, I think he's dead . . . No, it's his legacy to me that has me running scared.

I had been south of the River Thames on business and had decided to walk back to my lodgings in Pimlico. The day was fading slowly when I reached Westminster Bridge and I was instantly attracted by the streaks of crimson dying in the blue-green evening sky.

Halfway across the bridge I stopped to immerse myself in the sight and stayed there until the fast-flowing waters below me were no more than a dark swirl framed by the lights of the city.

As I was leaving the bridge, a voice hailed me hesitantly, "Er . . . it's Wilcox, isn't it?" And when I answered yes, said, "You remember me? Mulberry . . . Silas Mulberry?"

I remembered Mulberry. We had been to university together some ten years earlier. The gaunt figure did not appear to have changed much, although because of his broad-brimmed hat I could see little of his features other than the long tapering nose and the tight thin lips. "Hello, Mulberry," I said curtly, and then realizing how rude I sounded, went on a little more courteously, "How are you? It's been a long time."

I will not pretend that I was glad to see the man. I was probably the nearest to a friend that he had ever had, but we had finally parted under rather unpleasant circumstances.

Mulberry had mixed but little with the other students, preferring instead to spend his leisure hours in the college library poring over certain ancient and musty tomes, delving into the secrets of occult lore. I had, in those days, a passing interest in the supernatural and it was this which had brought us together. I quickly discovered that compared with Mulberry I was something of an innocent, and I am sure that he tolerated me only because he occasionally needed an audience, someone to whom he could display his startling—and at times frightening—knowledge. The break between us had occurred when Mulberry suggested we attempt to invoke one of the darker powers.

The ritual would have involved a blood sacrifice, and I demurred. We parted in mutual antipathy.

I don't know if he ever carried out his experiment. I doubt it, for he had no contact with any other person who would have had the interest, the knowledge or the stomach for such a thing.

But that had been a decade ago, and now Mulberry's voice betrayed eagerness as he responded to my greeting. We talked inconsequentially for several minutes before he said, "Look here, Wilcox, why don't we go back to my place for a drink? I only lodge a few minutes away, and I can offer you a rather good brandy. And I have something I'd like you to see."

The invitation sounded almost pathetic in its intensity. My impulse was to refuse, but then I decided that it wouldn't hurt to have a drink with the man and I had nothing better to do anyway. Besides, knowing of Mulberry's former interests, it was just possible that the "something" he wished to show me might be interesting, not to mention advantageous . . . I have neglected to mention that I am in antiques, not as a dealer in my own right, but as an agent for those collectors who are none too scrupulous about where their prized possessions come from.

Silas Mulberry's rooms were very near to Lambeth North tube station. He lived in a seedy house which fifty years ago might have been described as "a desirable residence." We had to climb four flights of grubby, dimly lit stairs before we reached the two rooms which comprised Mulberry's apartments. He didn't bother to use the main light, going instead to a lamp on a low table at one side of his living room.

I glanced around and realized that I could almost have been back in his quarters at college. The room was sparsely furnished, and what furniture there was was covered with books and papers which spilled over onto the floor. The walls were lined with shelves, obviously homemade, and filled with tattered volumes.

While my host excused himself so that he could prepare refreshments, I walked about the room glancing at the bookshelves, sometimes selecting a volume and thumbing through it. Mulberry's tastes had not changed over the years. He still had a considerable predilection for the macabre and the outré.

Mulberry was right. The brandy was good, and he had even managed to put together an acceptable snack. For a while we made small talk, of the "whatever happened to old so-and-so" variety, and then I reminded him that he had "something" in particular to show me. "Yes, indeed . . ." he gabbled. "It's in the bedroom . . . I'll go and get it."

He returned with a heavy-looking bundle, wrapped in cloth, which he set down beside me. Delicately moving aside the wrappings, he revealed a beautifully carved box of black onyx. My professional instincts were at once alerted: I had seen something similar change hands for nearly nine thousand pounds.

I noticed that Mulberry's fingers trembled as they brushed the artifact and I glanced sharply at his face. For the first time, I paid some attention to my companion's eyes. They were as they had been when I first met him, deep-set and inky black, but as I remembered them they had always mirrored contempt for those around him: Now they reflected a fear which had not been apparent in his manner.

Hardly taking his gaze from the onyx box, Mulberry fumbled for the brandy bottle and helped us both to generous measures. The bottle rattled almost imperceptibly against the glasses when he poured. Then he began to talk softly, almost as if he was whispering to himself . . .

"There's a story to that thing, Wilcox; or rather to its contents. But before I tell you I had better mention that I haven't got very long to live."

What the hell does one say when told a thing like that? I believe I made some sort of sympathetic murmurings, and then, "What's the trouble?" I asked. "Cancer? Heart?"

He smiled ruefully. "If it was only as simple as that . . . No, I am going to be killed, murdered you might say: Slain deliberately and with malice aforethought."

I looked closely at him to see if he was pulling my leg, but no . . . he was quite serious. I should have realized that Silas Mulberry would not make a joke like that, nor indeed a joke of any kind. As I recalled our university days, he had never displayed a sense of humor. I don't think that he even knew what a joke was.

"Then go to the police," I told him firmly. "If you know that someone intends to murder you, then you must have a good idea who it is. Report them to the police, who will give you protection."

"Believe me, Wilcox, the police would be completely helpless against what is going to kill me. In fact, if I told them about it they'd probably dismiss me as a crank! Anyway, even if they did believe me, even if they would give me protection, there would be nothing that they could do . . . Nothing . . ." He gulped down his brandy and refilled the glass.

"Do you want to tell me about it?" I asked, knowing full well that he did.

"Yes, please . . . That's why I asked you to come here. Despite your squeamishness, I always thought that you were a promising student of the occult and with proper training you could have become adept. Therefore, I don't think you will scoff at my story."

I served myself some more of the excellent cognac. "Why not try me?" I invited. I was already counting the profits mentally—an antique piece with a sordid or macabre history could always command a high price.

• • • •

"You may or may not have heard of Cardinal Yves D'Acard," Mulberry began. "D'Acard was a famous—or perhaps 'infamous' is a better word—yes, he was an infamous satanist in fifteenth-century France. His origins were humble enough—he was the son of a peasant—but he was fortunate in that his father's lord saw more than an ordinary clod in him and had the boy educated for the priesthood.

"When D'Acard was ordained, his master took him into his household as cleric, secretary and tutor. We know little more about that phase of his life than that he was a member of the household for a number of years. But when he reappeared into history he was already a bishop, so we can safely assume that somehow he had already received his power from the Dark One and was using it to advance himself.

"Of course, for many years only his acolytes were aware of D'Acard's secret life, for the prelate played his dual role of churchman and satanist well. Before long he became a very powerful man, able to command the services of every Inquisition in Europe and able to manipulate almost every statesman that he chose to.

"Certainly he used his ecclesiastical and temporal powers to further the will and work of his evil Master, and there can be little doubt that his was the genius behind some of the bloodiest and most far-reaching acts of his time. I think that he might have become the most powerful man in the world of his day if he had not become trapped in the mire of his own depravity.

"As you know, Wilcox, successful enactments of the Black Mass require deeds of the most appalling nature and beastliness. D'Acard became drunk with his own hideous lusts and as a result became careless for his own safety.

"Eventually, in one of the witch-hunts, a number of D'Acard's disciples were seized and put to the question. Of course, under torture they betrayed him and D'Acard was arrested. He was sentenced to be burned at the stake and all of his personal belongings would be forfeit to the State.

"However, among the Cardinal's treasures was a certain crystal ball, rather like those used by fairground fortune-tellers. It was rumored that the crystal was a gift from Satan and that in fact it was an extension of D'Acard's own personality. Nobody quite knew what the function of the crystal was, but they were certain that those who came into contact with it suffered some terrifying fate.

"On the morning set for the execution, the guards went to take Cardinal D'Acard from his dungeon only to find that he had disappeared. At much the same time, it was discovered that the crystal ball had vanished from among the other treasures. After considerable investigation, the authorities concluded that in both cases the Devil had claimed his own.

"Anyway, thereafter little was heard of the crystal except that every once in a long while there would be a rumor that it had surfaced again. Each time that it allegedly did so, terrible stories were attributed to it. And now . . . and now, I have the crystal, and Wilcox . . . I am terrified, terrified beyond my powers of explanation."

I nodded casually at the onyx box on the table. "Is the crystal in there?" I asked.

"Yes." His answer was barely audible. "Yes, that's it . . . and I curse the day it fell into my hands. Wilcox, you have no conception of the evil which pervades it . . ." His voice lapsed into inarticulate mutterings and I noticed that his lips were livid. He rubbed ineffectually at his face with pale hands that twitched.

I rather callously hoped that he would postpone his nervous breakdown until after I had left him. But I was very interested in acquiring the crystal.

Contrary to Mulberry's apparent belief, I had lost all fascination for the occult years ago, but I had become strongly attracted to the material things of life. I had a good idea where I would be able to sell the crystal for a great deal of money.

"I take it that D'Acard's crystal is to be the agent of your death?" I inquired, striving to make my voice awed and sympathetic, and when he nodded I went on: "May I see it? If it's not too disturbing for you, of course . . ."

He hesitated, then nodded. Gingerly he lifted the lid of the box to reveal a crystal globe, gleaming icily, reposing on a small cushion of red satin. It was quite beautiful, and I had a sudden impulse to touch it, to caress it. I reached forward to lift it from the box.

"Don't do that, you fool!" screeched Mulberry, slamming down the lid upon the crystal. He seemed so overwrought that for a brief moment I thought he was going to attack me. Then he subsided into his chair. "I'm sorry . . ." he apologized weakly, "I think that it's the touching of the thing which gives it power over a person. I don't want

you to go through the same terrors that I am. If you promise me that you will not attempt to touch the crystal, I'll let you see it again."

I assented, so he reopened the carved box and almost tenderly lifted out the globe and its satin cushion. Despite his apparently genuine terror, he acted as tenderly with the crystal as if he were a lover touching a woman's body.

"How did you acquire the crystal?" I asked.

"What? Oh . . . I discovered it in an antique shop, one of those down New King's Road. I knew it for what it was the moment I saw it. No one who has studied the occult as extensively as I have could have mistaken the thing. I am not sure if the dealer knew what it was, or if he just recognized it as a genuinely unique piece, but the price that he asked was too high for me to pay. However, damned fool that I am, I just had to have it.

"I returned to the shop late the same evening, intending to break in. To my surprise, the shop door was still open but the proprietor wasn't anywhere to be seen. I poked around the shop for a while but couldn't find the onyx box. Then, just as I was about to give up and leave, I heard a cry from above me. It was just a low cry, but there was something peculiarly horrible about it. No matter how I appear to you at the moment, Wilcox, I am not a physical coward—no man who chooses to make his life's work the occult can afford to be a coward.

"I remembered noticing some stairs behind the tiny counter at the back of the shop, and I ascended these to find myself in the living room of a small flat. The owner of the antique shop was not there, nor was he in any of the other rooms. But in the living room, unguarded on a table, was the crystal in its box. I snatched it up and made good my escape. A couple of days later I knew that I was doomed."

"And how did you know that?" I inquired.

"The dreams, Wilcox, the dreams that came to me and have come nightly ever since. I have tried to stay awake to avoid those dreams, Wilcox, but each night some force seems to overcome me, as if I were drugged."

"Tell me, Mulberry, why have you given me this story?"

"When I'm dead, Wilcox, I want you to have the crystal. I'm sure that fate deliberately flung us together again after all these years, so that between us we can make an end of this dreadful thing.

"I want you to promise me that you will take the crystal, in its box, and somehow destroy the unholy thing. See that nobody else ever falls victim to it."

"Mulberry, my business is antiques," I quickly replied. "I would no more destroy that crystal than I would the *Mona Lisa*. But I'll tell you what I will do. I'll relieve you of it, and perhaps when it's gone this delusion of yours will go too. I'll give you two thousand pounds—take it or leave it."

He sprang to his feet. For a moment his fists clenched and his eyes blazed, then as quickly he collapsed back into his chair. He shook his head in despair. "Oh, Wilcox . . . I thought that if anyone would understand it would be you. But all you can see is a quick profit.

"Oh, I'm not condemning you. Although our motives were different, my greed was as great as yours. I wanted the power I thought D'Acard's crystal would bring me, you want the wealth. No, Wilcox, I will not sell you the crystal. Please go now, there's a good fellow. Just get out and leave me alone."

I shrugged, picked up my coat. Before leaving, I threw my card on the table. "If you change your mind, call me," I told him.

I was through the door, indeed had almost closed it, when a dreadful shriek shocked me to stillness. Steeling myself, I slammed back through the doorway. Silas Mulberry was not there anymore.

I checked the bedroom. He was not there either. All the windows were securely fastened. Then I noticed that the crystal was glowing and I went to it, almost unwillingly. As I bent over the pulsating orb, I thought that I could see a falling speck, oddly manlike, in the heart of the globe. But when I peered more closely there was nothing.

I picked up the crystal to place it into the onyx box and found it to be cold, cold with a bitterness which seemed to permeate to my very bones. Hastily I thrust the crystal into its container and left the room clutching it beneath my coat.

Already inquisitive neighbors had begun to cluster around the open door, no doubt drawn by the shriek. No one tried to stop me as I pushed my way through, contenting themselves with gaping foolishly.

That night I had the first dream. At first I was sitting quietly in my lounge, staring intently at the crystal. The globe shone and pulsed fiercely as with a dreadful life.

Then it seemed to grow larger, expanding momentarily until it filled the whole room and engulfed me. As I was drawn through the glassy surface of the crystal a scalding cold, a burning, freezing agony, flayed me. I screamed aloud and then I found myself falling, tumbling and swirling down and around until at last I was caught by something which tossed me high into the air once more.

Unspeakable agonies slashed at my mutilated body and I continued to scream. But I did not scream alone. My ears were assailed by incessant wails of torment. I became aware that others, countless others, were falling with me and that the hideous noise was the collective cry of many souls in pain. One of the other figures tumbled close by me, and I am sure that I recognized Silas Mulberry, his mouth wide and twisted in an eternal howl.

Then a vision came to me as the dream changed. I was no longer tumbling with the others, but seemed to be suspended in the void far away. In the depths below me was an indistinct shape and it took many long moments for my eyes to focus properly upon it. I was looking upon a man, clothed in the red robes and biretta of a cardinal.

His face was handsome, yet corrupt and evil, and his thick lips rippled with insane laughter. His gloved hands sifted and teased and tumbled innumerable dark motes, tiny, shaped specks which soared and fell and shrieked unceasingly.

Suddenly the dream ended, and as I awoke I realized how it was that Satan had rewarded his faithful servant, Cardinal Yves D'Acard.

Every night the dreams come, and they grow worse. Every day I pray, although—I am sure—to no avail. I don't think that I have much time left.

DAVID S. GARNETT

Together

The house looked quite good in the twilight, thought Adam as he locked the garage. The peeling paintwork could hardly be seen.

Tomorrow was Friday, but he wasn't looking forward to the weekend because he'd have to spend most of Saturday and Sunday decorating. All the neighbors hired painters, but Adam couldn't afford such luxuries; he had to pretend that he preferred to do the job himself.

Within a year of moving into the house, part of the foundations had given way and had to be underpinned; there was still a jagged crack across the side wall which no amount of repair could disguise. The wood around the window frames had already begun to rot, the guttering leaked, and the drains regularly overflowed. None of the other houses in the road seemed to have the same sort of problems.

Things had been just as bad inside, with the plaster flaking in various places and the paper peeling from the damp patches in the corners. There were drafts even when no doors or windows were open. Kitchen drawers refused to shut properly, taps dripped, there was something wrong with the wiring and light bulbs kept blowing.

But since Janet had been at home, things had definitely improved. Maybe because the heating was on all day during last winter, the house had dried out and was no longer so cold. Janet had also done quite a bit of interior decoration, and it was surprising how many defects could be masked by a coat of paint.

Adam went inside the house and into the front room. Janet was lying on the sofa, staring at the television and watching a comedy show. She hadn't noticed Adam, and she gazed as though hypnotized at the screen.

Suddenly she became aware of him, and her expression changed as she turned her head. It was for only a moment, but Adam thought she looked scared. Then she smiled in recognition, before focusing her attention back on the television.

"Hello," he said.

"Hello," Janet replied, after a few seconds. "Back already?"

"It's eight o'clock, Janet. I've been gone nearly twelve hours."

"Eight o'clock?" She picked up the remote control and changed stations.

Adam took off his coat and threw it over the back of the armchair by the window. Janet rose, picked up the coat and went out into the hall. Adam heard the cupboard open and close as she put his coat away, then she resumed her seat and watched the screen again.

After a moment, she glanced up at him and repeated her welcoming smile, as though he'd only just come in. Adam leaned over to kiss her cheek. She patted the sofa next to her, and he sat down by her side.

"Busy day?"

Adam nodded, then said, "Yeah." He gazed at the television, watching the adverts. "What about you?"

Janet didn't reply. She flicked over to another station.

"Shall I put the kettle on?" Adam asked. "Would you like a cup of tea?"

"I'll do it," Janet said, and she stood up again.

Adam glanced around the room, comparing it with the outside of the house. There wasn't a thing out of place, and there wasn't a speck of dust or dirt anywhere. Janet seemed to clean the whole house every day, but then he supposed she didn't have much else to do with her time.

No, no. That wasn't fair.

He envied Janet. He wished that he didn't have to work, and he didn't begrudge the fact that she no longer had a job. Not really. After all, work took up so much of one's life and they'd both spent far too long away from each other. The ironic thing was that now Janet had so much free time, they still weren't together enough. He was having to put in more hours than ever, partly to try to make up for the drop in income since his wife had been at home.

He went into the kitchen. Janet was mopping up some drops of water which had splashed into the sink when she'd filled the kettle.

"Busy day?" she asked again. But at least this time she turned to look at him, and all Adam needed to do was nod, then she began wiping at the draining board.

Adam looked around the kitchen. There wasn't a single cup or dish or spoon or pan or jar or packet or can in sight. Everything was in its proper place and out of sight.

"Any plans for something to eat?" he asked, although he could guess the answer.

Janet stared at him as though she hadn't understood the question, then she shook her head.

It wasn't as though she'd forgotten to cook anything, just that it had never occurred to her. This was happening more and more frequently. With nothing to fill her day, Janet did less and less—apart from endlessly clean and tidy up.

When they'd both worked, Adam had done his fair share of the household chores. But it was too late to start cooking now, and anyway Janet no longer liked him to—she'd moan about the mess he made, or complain that he'd put things back in the wrong places.

"How about a take-away?" Adam suggested.

"What?"

"What about a take-away meal?"

"Oh, well, er, sure, good idea."

"Chinese? Indian?"

"Whatever you want," said Janet.

"Indian?"

"If you like. I'll have the usual."

Adam went to phone in the order. Then he drank his tea, put on his coat again and went outside. Janet didn't seem to notice him leave.

He opened the garage and started the car. The roar from the exhaust reminded him that he had to buy a new silencer.

Money, money, money—and now he was about to spend even more. Adam knew it was absurd, but he couldn't really even afford to buy a couple of take-away curries. He'd never have been able to survive if it wasn't for his overdraft and credit cards.

Things had been different when there had been two salaries coming in, but now financial survival seemed almost impossible. And there was only one reason.

The house.

It was too big—and too expensive.

Three years ago, when they were about to marry, it had all seemed so different.

Janet was American, and the year before Adam met her she had come to work in the British branch of the market research company where she was employed. When they first started going out there was nothing she liked better than visiting stately homes . . . castles or simply just stopping to look at old houses they happened to drive past. According to her, there were no really old buildings in the States. Adam didn't know, he'd never been there—and the way things were going, it seemed he never would.

No matter how much she liked old houses, Janet insisted she didn't want to buy one. She hated the idea of living in a place which had once belonged to other people.

Where they lived hadn't bothered Adam too much, and he was happy to let Janet have her own way. The new house which she chose did seem overpriced, he argued at first. But they were both working, Janet reasoned, so what difference did a few thousand pounds make? And anyway, wasn't she earning more than he was . . . ?

But did they really need two bathrooms, three reception rooms, four bedrooms? They would when they started a family, Janet had explained.

They hadn't wanted children immediately. They were both in their mid-twenties, and they had their careers to think about. And it was an expensive business to have kids. They had discussed how the best time for people to have children was in their teens, or else as late as possible.

It wasn't late now, not yet, but they never discussed it anymore. There was very little they did discuss.

Last year Janet's company had transferred its European headquarters to Brussels, and she'd been offered the chance to go and work in Belgium. Instead she had given up her job.

"I can't go and leave the house," she'd said—as though that were more important than not leaving her husband.

Adam had grown to hate the house. It wasn't just the mortgage repayments, although that was a major factor. Each penny he earned seemed to go on the house, and they simply couldn't afford to live here much longer. Every week he was going deeper into debt. They would have to sell up and move to a cheaper place.

This wasn't something he'd spoken to Janet about, not yet. He was letting things go until the only available option would be to move.

There was no reason why Janet had to lose her job. She could have stayed on with the company in England, but instead she had quit. Adam had been amazed at her decision; he knew how much she enjoyed what she did. He assumed that after working for so many years, she just wanted an extended holiday. But in the nine months since, she had never looked for more work, and she seldom went out at all these days.

Adam glanced at Janet, lying by his side. She was fast asleep, turned away from him, wearing a cotton nightgown. At one time she used to go to bed naked, her nudity a constant invitation. Not anymore.

Adam couldn't remember when they had last made love—two or three weeks at least. But he was still in love with her.

Pity that she seemed to love the house more than she did him.

He smiled at the thought and switched off the lamp. He was still awake when Janet said something.

"What?" he asked, glancing toward her in the gloom.

She was breathing slowly and deeply; she was still asleep, just dreaming.

Janet muttered something else and rolled over onto her back. Her knee touched his thigh as she opened her legs, and her breathing began to grow heavier, faster.

"Janet?" said Adam. "Janet?" He reached for the lamp switch, thinking she was having a nightmare.

He stared at his wife, recognizing her expression, her movements.

Her eyes were shut, but her mouth was half-open, her face and neck damp with sweat. She writhed in ecstasy, moaning with pleasure. It was as if she were making love—but with a passion that Adam had never known, not even in the early days.

"Yes," she sighed. "Oh, yes, yes, yes . . ."

And that was when Adam realized his wife had a lover.

The fact that Janet had a lover would explain so much. Adam had thought she would soon become restless and bored at home on her own. But she wasn't on her own, he had discovered, not all the time.

Was that why she seemed so much more content and happier than when she'd been working? Adam had originally supposed it was because after so many years of constant work, she was no longer under any pressure.

Janet had a past, a life before she had met Adam. Whatever Janet had done before she knew him had made her into the woman she was, the woman he loved. One of the things which first attracted Adam to her was that because she was an American she had a background which was so unlike his own.

Much of what he knew of his wife's previous life he'd learned from her sister, Ruby. Ruby had suddenly appeared last year, and until then he didn't even know that Janet had a sister. She'd claimed to be an only child, and that her parents were dead. Only the latter was true.

Ruby was one year younger than Janet, and she had tracked down her sister in order to heal the rift between them. Adam heard the full story on her last evening, when they went out to a restaurant and Ruby drank too much. In the two minutes while Janet was in the Ladies', Ruby told Adam more than he ever wanted to know, more than he could ever forget.

Up until then, she had been very reserved and not said much to Adam, but whenever he came home from work he would find the two sisters sitting together in intimate silence—obviously having just stopped talking because he had arrived.

He had begun to feel like an intruder in his own home.

Adam wasn't sure what it was, but there was something about Ruby that he didn't like, and he was glad she was leaving.

"It's odd the way things work out," Ruby had remarked, as she watched Janet vanish through the door at the far end of the restaurant.

"If it hadn't been for me, Janet would never have come to England and you two would never have met."

Adam raised his glass in a toast. "Thanks."

Ruby nodded slowly. "I'm glad Janet and I have gotten things settled between us. We've been sisters too long to stay enemies forever."

Without speaking, Adam topped up her glass.

"She's never said anything to you?" Ruby asked.

"I told you," said Adam. "Until the other day, I didn't know you existed."

"But I knew about you. The last time I heard from Janet was when she wrote to say she was getting married—and that I wasn't invited." She took a mouthful of her wine.

"What was it all about?" Adam realized he had to prompt her, or else Ruby would never get around to telling him. And once Janet returned, he'd never find out.

"It all seems so strange, looking back on it." Ruby's eyes were focused far away, as if gazing back over the years. "But it's the old story of the boy next door. We were both in love with the same guy." She smiled wistfully, then looked at Adam. "You sure you don't mind hearing this?"

"Go on." From the way Ruby watched him, Adam guessed he wasn't going to like this. He didn't want to know; but he didn't want not to know.

"There isn't much to tell. Michael used to date both Janet and me, and he hated it if either of us went out with someone else. Sometimes all three of us would go out together, even when we were at college." Ruby laughed at the memory.

"In the end, we gave him an ultimatum, said he had to choose between us. He chose Janet." Ruby twisted her wineglass between her fingers. "They started living together, but Mike grew more and more jealous and possessive. He'd hardly allow her out of his sight—except when he was with me. Janet found out we were still seeing each other and she walked out. But he kept on telephoning and following her around, even when I moved in to live with him. Janet took a job overseas to get away from him—and me." She leaned back as though that was the end of the story.

"Then what?" said Adam, knowing there was more.

Ruby took another sip of her drink, and she shrugged. "Janet was still his favorite, he was obsessed with her. I was only second-best, and I knew it. But I told him I was all he had because Janet was getting married. And on the day of your wedding, Michael slit his throat. I found him when I came home. The last thing he must have done was write Janet's name on a mirror. In his own blood." Her knuckles were white as she gripped the stem of her glass.

"He'd bought both of us identical mirrors one Christmas. I notice Janet's still got hers, on your upstairs landing. I didn't keep mine, not after what happened. I smashed it and threw it away." Ruby finished her drink in a single gulp, and a few seconds later Janet had returned.

Adam's instinctive dislike of Ruby had proved correct. Drunk or not, there had been no need for her to tell him. It was pure vindictiveness. Ruby blamed Janet for what had happened, and she was avenging herself against her sister through Adam. He wondered how long Janet had known about the suicide, but he never asked, never told her that he knew.

Perhaps it was because of Michael that Janet didn't want to go back to America; it would revive too many bad memories. But when they saw Ruby off at Heathrow and Adam again mentioned the possibility of them visiting the States, Janet had said; "I don't have to go back. Not now."

He still didn't know what she meant by that, and the following day Janet announced that she was giving up her job.

Janet had met many men in her line of work—and now that she had so much free time, there was plenty of opportunity for infidelity.

It had never occurred to Adam until now that she might have been unfaithful. He had kept to his marriage vows, and he'd assumed that Janet had done likewise, even though they were growing away from each other.

He'd attributed this to his longer hours at the office, which caused him to spend less time with Janet. Had she taken a lover because they were drifting apart—or was this man the reason that she had grown so indifferent?

Now that he knew, other things began to make sense.

There were the records which had been put back in the wrong order. He'd thought that Janet's tastes must have been changing, that she'd been going through his albums in her free time—but it must have been her lover. The same with books. That couldn't have been Janet—she wouldn't read his kind of books any more than she'd play his type of music.

It wasn't only records and books which had been touched. There were the clothes in Adam's drawers which had been disturbed, and the things in the wardrobe which no longer hung straight.

He'd noticed these clues before, but never connected them until now.

The question was: what should he do about it?

He couldn't come out and confront Janet with what he suspected. She'd only deny it and would be far more careful in future. That way Adam would never know the truth, or discover who the new man in her life was.

And he wasn't at all sure that he wanted to find out.

What if he was someone he already knew?

Perhaps if he faced Janet, it would make her give him up. Maybe it was his own fault for not providing everything she wanted. It wasn't just sex. There was far more to it than that. If only he had more money and more time, that was what Janet needed.

The last thing Adam wanted was to split up with his wife. They had to make a new start together.

Which meant getting rid of the house.

Adam sat at his desk, staring at the file in front of him. It was the final draft for the tender his company was submitting to the hospital board, the full specifications and details for equipping the new X-ray unit. He'd had the documents for most of the morning, and he still couldn't make much sense of them. His eyes kept reading and rereading, but his brain simply wasn't paying any attention.

After what he'd discovered last night, he found it hard to concentrate on anything except his wife and her lover.

Janet had still been asleep when he left for work. That wasn't unusual, she spent more and more of her life in bed these days.

In bed with her lover.

Adam's mind was immediately filled with the image of his wife making love to someone else, and he let the file drop onto his desk. He stood up quickly.

Margaret was working at the office computer in the corner, and she glanced up at him. "Are you alright?"

He nodded impatiently. "Yes, yes."

His secretary stared at him for a few seconds, then looked back at the VDU screen.

Adam reached for the telephone, then paused. The picture of Janet had been in his head for only an instant, and he told himself that it must have been there because he had just been thinking of her.

He only believed what his own senses told him, or what could be deduced through the process of logical thought. He certainly didn't believe in telepathy—but for a moment he was convinced that he'd picked up a direct mental image of what Janet had been doing.

And what she was still doing.

At this very moment she was making love—in Adam's home, Adam's bed. With someone else.

No, he told himself, he was just guessing, wildly imagining what was going on. But he knew this was no mere suspicion, and it was more than just intuition. He felt absolutely certain of what was happening eight miles away at this very minute.

He was angry and confused, felt both betrayed and worried. He could simply stay here and wonder, but unless he did something now he would never know the truth.

Adam made up his mind; he was going home.

"I've got to go out, Margaret," he said, as he walked to the door. "I'll . . . I'll be back later."

"But—"

His secretary's protest was silenced by the door closing behind him.

At this time of day, he could be back home in fifteen minutes. Now he was outside, his decision to leave seemed rather foolish. There was nothing to it, he rationalized. Nothing could be happening, although there was no harm in setting his mind to rest.

But if Janet was there with her lover—what then?

He wasn't sure.

It would be best to bring things into the open. Even if the man wasn't there now, it made no real difference. In fact, it would be much better if he wasn't. Adam and Janet had to talk this through.

Perhaps that was the biggest problem of all; they simply didn't talk together anymore.

There were no unfamiliar cars nearby, and Adam stopped his own car outside the house. He'd considered parking further down the road, but that would have been too melodramatic. No one could leave the house without him seeing.

He went inside quietly, softly closing the door behind him. He paused in the hallway, listening. There was no sound, no sign of anyone. He glanced into the front room, to see if Janet was there.

Then he heard a noise from upstairs. It was a voice.

A man's voice, followed a moment later by a woman laughing.

Adam sprinted up the stairs.

"Adam!" said Janet. "What are you doing here?" She was on the landing, holding a bath towel around herself.

He brushed past her and went into the bedroom.

There was no one there.

Janet followed him inside. "What's going on?" she said. "Is something the matter?"

"Where is he?" Adam demanded.

"Who? Where's who?"

"Your lover."

Janet stared at him, and she seemed to hesitate a moment before she said: "My lover?"

"Don't pretend you don't know."

"But . . ." She shook her head.

"Don't deny it."

"There's nothing to deny. You're crazy!" Janet forced a laugh.

The duvet had been pulled back, but when Adam felt the bed it was still warm. He must have interrupted them, so he couldn't be far away.

Adam looked under the bed, then opened the wardrobes; but the intruder wasn't in the bedroom.

"Where is he?" Adam repeated.

Janet said nothing. She was a little flushed, although she seemed quite calm.

"Why aren't you dressed?" Adam asked.

"Because I was getting up. I wasn't feeling too good this morning."

"But you're not wearing anything."

"I was in the bathroom, going to have a shower. I thought I heard a noise downstairs, then I saw you."

"I heard a man's voice," Adam told her.

"What?" Janet laughed again. "It was the radio, it must have been. I switched it off when I heard someone downstairs."

"Got an answer for everything, haven't you?"

Adam guessed what she was doing—deliberately delaying him so that her lover could make his escape. He hurried from the bedroom and dashed downstairs. He checked all the rooms quickly, but there was no trace of anyone. He opened the front door and looked down the road, then went out the back.

The man couldn't have got away in such a short time, he must still have been in the house.

Adam rushed back upstairs.

He noticed Janet dressing as he went by to search the other rooms, and she followed him, buttoning her blouse.

"Is this some kind of game, Adam?"

He stared at her, but said nothing.

"You're serious," she said, no longer half-amused. "If you think that I, that I . . ." She shook her head angrily, searching for the words. "I'm going out. And I hope you'll have recovered by the time I get back."

Janet went downstairs as Adam entered the smallest bedroom, and when he came out again he heard the front door slam.

There was nobody in the house, not even in the attic or the garage. Not anymore.

He tried to relax, making himself a cup of instant coffee.

They'd fooled him this time, that was all. Janet's denial was so transparent. He knew what was happening, and it wasn't going to occur again.

As soon as he finished his coffee, he'd go to the estate agent and put the house on the market.

He stared out of the window, wondering where Janet had gone. At least this had got her out of the house, he thought, and he smiled for a moment.

Then he heard a door close in the room directly above him—his and Janet's bedroom.

There was someone!

He raced back upstairs, then halted outside the bedroom, his hand on the handle, his ear to the door. His heart was thumping and he was breathing heavily. Slowly, he twisted the handle—then threw the door wide open.

Empty, or so it seemed.

But there was someone inside, he was convinced. He could neither see nor hear anyone, but he had the evidence of the least used of his senses. He could smell someone.

There was a hint of tobacco in the room, although neither Adam or Janet smoked, and also the odor of an after-shave which wasn't his. It could have been there when he examined the room before, but he hadn't noticed.

He stepped slowly inside and went through the same search as before —under the bed, behind the dressing table, in the wardrobes. He even opened the window and looked out.

Nobody. Nobody at all.

He couldn't smell anything now; but maybe he'd become used to it.

Angrily, he punched his right fist into the palm of his left hand. He sat on the bed, trying to calm down again.

There was no one here; perhaps there never had been.

It was only the house getting to him. It was full of strange noises and odd smells. Doors were always seeming to close for no reason. That was all he'd heard, all there was.

Adam walked along the landing and turned to go downstairs. Sensing a movement behind him, he spun around swiftly.

He saw himself, his own image in the big mirror on the wall at the top of the stairs.

He laughed aloud in both relief and amusement as he started to go down the steps, watching as his reflection did the same. Still smiling, he winked at himself—then missed his footing and slipped, frantically reaching out for support.

He grabbed hold of the bottom edge of the mirror and almost regained his balance, but then the mountings were suddenly wrenched from the wall and he toppled over backward. Still holding the mirror, Adam thumped into the banister before tumbling all the way down the stairs and crashing to the floor.

Consciousness returned very slowly, but he could feel nothing of his body. He tried to move; his limbs refused to obey. He couldn't even open his eyes. It was as though his mind had no control over his muscles, and his immediate thought was that he was totally paralyzed.

He had no idea how long lay there, although it seemed an eternity. Where was Janet?

Gradually, his senses came back to him. But it was more of an awareness of his surroundings than a return to normality. He lay sprawled at the bottom of the stairs, and all around him were pieces of shattered glass from the broken mirror.

He wasn't sure how he knew this, because how could he see himself on the ground?

It was as if he were above himself, staring sightlessly down, watching without eyes—and observing his own corpse.

Adam was dead.

His body lay cold and twisted, his clothes and the carpet soaked with dark congealing blood from the ugly wound in his neck, where a shard of glass was embedded like a knife in his throat.

His physical being was dead, yet a part of him survived—a part not limited by mortal constraints.

Realization of death came as no shock or surprise; he was beyond such reactions and emotions. In some way, however, it was reassuring to know that everything had not come to an abrupt halt merely because his frail human figure had ceased to function.

He had no single substance, nothing which he could identify as himself. Instead he was everywhere in the house at once. He had become a part of the timbers and bricks, of all the furniture and each object in every room.

His body twitched.

No, not his body. It wasn't his body anymore. It was a shell called Adam, and its lifeless mass began to move, arms and legs slowly writhing. Another identity was taking over his material shape, reanimating it.

Then he heard Janet outside, putting her key into the front door lock.

Yet it wasn't exactly hearing, no more than his knowledge of what had previously been his body struggling to rise to its feet was seeing; it was instead an absolute comprehension of what went on within the house.

He could feel the door opening, sense the pressure of Janet's feet on the hall floor.

What was once Adam's human form staggered upright, and the broken dagger of glass fell from its neck to the ground.

He wanted to cry out, to warn Janet, to save her. To do something. Anything.

But there was nothing he could do, nothing at all, and there would be nothing ever again.

His future was eternally restricted to total perception of whatever went on inside the house.

Inside himself.

Janet turned and saw the corpse lurching unsteadily toward her, trailing sticky footprints of blood.

She froze, unable to move.

The dead man's arms went around her, drawing her close.

Janet shivered.

"You're cold, Michael," she whispered, and they kissed.

DAVID MORRELL

The Beautiful Uncut Hair of Graves

Despite the rain, you've been to the cemetery yet again, ignoring the cold autumn gusts slanting under your bowed umbrella, the drenched drab leaves blowing against your soaked pant legs and shoes.

Two graves. You shiver, blinking through tears toward the freshly laid sod. There aren't any tombstones. There won't be for a year. But you imagine what the markers will look like, each birth date different, the death dates—God help you—the same. Simon and Esther Weinberg. Your parents. You silently mouth the kaddish prayers that Rabbi Goldstein recited at the funeral. Losing strength, you turn to trudge back to your rain-beaded car, to throw your umbrella on the passenger seat and jab the button marked Defroster, to try to control your trembling hands and somehow suppress your chest-swelling rage, your heart-numbing grief.

Eyes swollen from tears, you manage to drive back to your parents' home. An estate on Lake Michigan, north of Chicago, the mansion feels ghostly, hollow without its proper occupants. You cross the enormous vestibule and enter the oak-paneled study. One wall is lined with books, another with photographs of your precious father shaking hands with local and national dignitaries, even a president. As you sit at the massive desk to resume sorting through your father's papers, the last of them, the documents unsealed from your parents' safe-deposit box, your wife appears in the study's doorway, a coffee cup in her hand. She slumps against the wall and frowns as she did when you obeyed your repeated, so intense compulsion to go back—yet *again*—to the cemetery.

"Why?" she asks.

You squint up from the documents. "Isn't it obvious? I feel the need to be with them."

"That's not what I meant." Rebecca says. She's forty-nine, tall, with a narrow face and pensive eyes. "All the work you've been doing. All the documents and the meetings. All the phone calls. Can't you let yourself relax? You look terrible."

"How the hell should I look? My father's chest was crushed. My mother's head was . . . The asshole drunk who hit their car got away with just a few stitches."

"Not what I meant," Rebecca repeats. Using two hands, both of them shaky, she raises the coffee cup to her lips. "Don't make sympathy sound like an accusation. You've got *every* right to look terrible. It's bad enough to lose *one* parent, let alone *two at once*, and the way they died was"—she shakes her head—"obscene. But what you're doing, your compulsion to . . . I'm afraid you'll push yourself until you collapse. Don't torture yourself. Your father assigned an executor for his estate, a perfectly competent lawyer from his firm. Let the man do his job. I grant, you're a wonderful attorney, but right now it's time to let someone else take charge. For God's sake, Jacob—and if not for God, then for me—get some rest."

You sigh, knowing she means well and wants only what's best for you. But she doesn't understand: you *need* to keep busy, you *need* to distract yourself with minutiae so that your mind doesn't snap from confronting the full horror of losing your parents.

"I'm almost finished," you say. "Just a few more documents from the safe-deposit box. Then I promise I'll try to rest. A bath sounds . . .

Lord, I still can't believe . . . How much I miss . . . Pour me a scotch. I think my nerves need numbing."

"I'll have one with you."

As Rebecca crosses the study toward the liquor cabinet, you glance down toward the next document: a faded copy of your birth certificate. You shake your head. "Dad kept *everything*. What a pack rat." Your tone is bittersweet, your throat tight with affection. "That's why his estate's so hard to sort through. It's so difficult to tell what's important, what's sentimental, and what's just . . ."

You glance at the next document, almost set it aside, take another look, frown, feel what seems to be a frozen fishhook in your stomach, and murmur, "God." Your breathing fails.

"Jacob?" Your wife turns from pouring the scotch and hurriedly puts the bottle down, rushing toward you. "What's wrong? Your face. You're as gray as—!"

You keep staring toward the document, feeling as if you've been punched in the ribs, the wind knocked out of you. Rebecca crouches beside you, touching your face. You swallow and manage to breathe. "I . . ."

"*What?* Jacob, tell me. What's the matter?"

"There has to be some mistake." You point toward the document.

Rebecca hurriedly reads it. "I don't understand. It's crammed with legal jargon. A woman's promising to give up two children for adoption, is that what this means?"

"Yes." You have trouble speaking. "Look at the date."

"August fifteen, nineteen thirty-eight."

"A week before my birthday. Same year." You sound hoarse.

"So what? That's just a coincidence. Your father did all kinds of legal work, probably including adoptions."

"But he wouldn't have kept a business affidavit with his personal papers in his private safe-deposit box. Here, at the bottom, look at the place where this was notarized."

"Redwood Point, California."

"Right," you say. "Now check this copy of my birth certificate. The place of birth is . . ."

"Redwood Point, California." Rebecca's voice drops.

"Still think it's just a coincidence?"

"It has to be. Jacob, you've been under a lot of strain, but this is *one* strain you don't have to deal with. You know you're not adopted."

"Do I? *How?*"

"Well, it's . . ."

You gesture impatiently.

"I mean, it's something a person takes for granted," Rebecca says.

"Why?"

"Because your parents would have told you."

"*Why?* If they didn't need to, why would they have taken the chance of shocking me? Wasn't it better for my parents to leave well enough alone?"

"Listen to me, Jacob. You're letting your imagination get control of you."

"Maybe." You stand, your legs unsteady, cross to the liquor cabinet, and finish pouring the drinks that Rebecca had started preparing. "*Maybe.*" You swallow an inch of the drink: made deliberately strong, it burns your throat. "But I won't know for sure, will I? Unless I find out why my father kept that woman's adoption agreement with his private papers, and how it happened that I was born one week later and in the same place that the woman signed and dated her consent form."

"So what?" Rebecca rubs her forehead. "Don't you see? It doesn't make a difference! Your parents loved you! *You* loved *them.* Suppose, despite Lord knows how many odds, suppose your suspicion turns out to be correct. What will it change? It won't make your grief any less. It won't affect a lifetime of love."

"It might affect a lot of things."

"Look, finish your drink. It's Friday. We still have time to go to temple. If ever you needed to focus your spirit, it's now."

In anguish, you swallow a third of your drink. "Take another look at that adoption consent. The woman agrees to give up *two* babies. If I *was* adopted, that means somewhere out there I've got a brother or a sister. A *twin.*"

"A stranger to you. Jacob, there's more to being a brother or a sister than just the biological connection."

Your stomach recoils as you gulp the last of the scotch. "Keep looking at the consent form. At the bottom. The woman's name."

"Mary Reilly."

"Irish."

"So?" Rebecca asks.

"Go to temple? Think about it. Have you ever heard of any Irish who . . . ? It could be I wasn't born Jewish."

• • • •

Your uncle's normally slack-jowled features tighten in confusion. "Adopted? What on earth would make you think—?"

You sit beside him on the sofa in his living room and explain as you show him the documents.

His age-wrinkled brow contorts. He shakes his bald head. "Coincidence."

"That's what my wife claims."

"Then listen to her. And listen to *me.* Jacob, your father and I were as close as two brothers can possibly be. We kept no secrets from each other. Neither of us ever did anything important without first asking the other's opinion. When Simon—may he rest in peace—decided to marry your mother, he discussed it with *me* long before he talked to our parents. Believe me, trust me, if he and Esther had planned to adopt a child, *I'd have been told.*"

You exhale, wanting to believe but tortured by doubts. "Then why . . . ?" Your skull throbs.

"Tell me, Jacob."

"All right, let's pretend it *is* a coincidence that these documents were together in my parents' safe-deposit box. Let's pretend that they're unrelated matters. But why . . . ? As far as I know, Dad always lived here in Chicago. I never thought about it before, but why wasn't I born here instead of in California?"

Your uncle strains to concentrate. Weary, he shrugs. "That was so long ago. Nineteen"—he peers through his glasses toward your birth certificate—"thirty-eight. So many years. It's hard to remember." He pauses. "Your mother and father wanted children very much. *That* I remember. But no matter how hard they tried . . . Well, your father and mother were terribly discouraged. Then one afternoon, he came to my office, beaming. He told me to take the rest of the day off. We had something to celebrate. Your mother was pregnant."

Thinking of your parents and how much you miss them, you wince with grief. But restraining tears, you can't help saying, "That still doesn't explain why I was born in California."

"I'm coming to that." Your uncle rubs his wizened chin. "Yes, I'm starting to . . . Nineteen thirty-eight. The worst of the Depression was over, but times still weren't good. Your father said that with the baby coming, he needed to earn more money. He felt that California— Los Angeles—offered better opportunities. I tried to talk him out of it.

In another year, I said, Chicago will have turned the corner. Besides, he'd have to go through the trouble of being certified to practice law in California. But he insisted. And of course, I was right. Chicago did soon turn the corner. What's more, as it happened, your father and mother didn't care for Los Angeles, so after six or seven months, they came back, right after you were born."

"That still doesn't . . ."

"What?"

"Los Angeles isn't Redwood Point. I never heard of the place. What were my parents doing there?"

"Oh, that." Your uncle raises his thin white eyebrows. "No mystery. Redwood Point was a resort up the coast. In August, L.A. was brutally hot. As your mother came close to giving birth, your father decided she ought to be someplace where she'd wouldn't feel the heat, close to the sea, where the breeze would make her comfortable. So they took a sort of vacation, and you were born there."

"Yes," you say. "Perfectly logical. Nothing mysterious. Except . . ." You gesture toward the coffee table. "Why did my father keep this woman's adoption agreement?"

Your uncle lifts his liver-spotted hands in exasperation. "*Oy vay.* For all we know, he found a chance to do some legal work while he was in Redwood Point. To help pay your mother's hospital and doctor bills. When he moved back to Chicago, it might be some business papers got mixed in with his personal ones. By accident, everything to do with Redwood Point got grouped together."

"And my father never noticed the mistake no matter how many times he must have gone to his safe-deposit box? I have trouble believing . . ."

"Jacob, Jacob. Last month, I went to my safe-deposit box and found a treasury bond that I didn't remember even buying, let alone putting in the box. Oversights happen."

"My father was the most organized person I ever knew."

"God knows I love him, and God knows I miss him." Your uncle bites his pale lower lip, then breathes with effort, seized with emotion. "But he wasn't perfect, and life isn't tidy. We'll probably never know for sure how this document came to be with his private papers. But this much I do know. You can count on it. You're Simon and Esther's natural child. You weren't adopted."

You stare at the floor and nod. "Thank you."

"No need to thank me. Just go home, get some rest, and stop thinking so much. What happened to Simon and Esther has been a shock to all of us. We'll be a long time missing them."

"Yes," you say, "a long time."

"Rebecca? How is . . . ?"

"The same as me. She still can't believe they're dead."

Your uncle's bony fingers clutch your hand. "I haven't seen either of you since the funeral. It's important for family to stick together. Why don't both of you come over for honey cake on Rosh Hashanah?"

"I'd like to, Uncle. But I'm sorry, I'll be out of town."

"Where are . . . ?"

"Redwood Point."

The major airport nearest your destination is at Salinas. There you rent a car and drive west to the coast, then south past Carmel and Big Sur. Preoccupied, you barely notice the dramatic scenery: the windblown cypresses, the rugged cliffs, the whitecaps hitting the shore. You ask yourself why you didn't merely phone the authorities at Redwood Point, explain that you were a lawyer in Chicago, and ask for information that you needed to settle an estate. Why did you feel compelled to come all this way to a town so small that it isn't listed in your Hammond atlas and could only be located in the Chicago library on its large map of California? For that matter, why do you feel compelled at all? Both your wife and your uncle have urged you to leave the matter alone. You're not adopted, you've been assured, and even if you were, what difference would it make?

The answers trouble you. One, you might have a brother or a sister, a twin, and now that you've lost your parents, you feel an anxious need to fill the vacuum of their loss by finding an unsuspected member of your family. Two, you suffer a form of midlife crisis, but not in the common sense of the term. To have lived these many years and possibly never have known your birth parents makes you uncertain of your identity. Yes, you loved the parents you knew, but your present limbo state of insecure uncertainty makes you desperate to discover the truth, one way or the other, so you can dismiss the possibility of your having been adopted or else adjust to the fact that you were. But this way, not being certain, is maddening, given the stress of double grief. And three, the most insistent reason, an identity crisis of frantic concern, you want to learn if after a lifetime—of having been circumcised, of Hebrew lessons, of your bar mitzvah, of Friday nights at temple, of scrupulous observance of sacred holidays—of being a Jew . . . if after all that, you might have been born a gentile. You tell yourself that being a Jew has nothing to do with race and genes, that it's a matter of culture and religion. But deep in your heart, you've always thought of yourself proudly as being *completely* a Jew, and your sense of self feels threatened. Who *am* I? you think.

You increase speed toward your destination and brood about your irrational stubborn refusal to let Rebecca travel here with you. Why did you insist on coming alone?

Because, you decide with grim determination.

Because I don't want anybody holding me back.

The Pacific Coast Highway pivots above a granite cliff. In crevasses, stunted misshapen fir trees cling to shallow soil and fight for survival. A weather-beaten sign abruptly says REDWOOD POINT. With equal abruptness, you see a town below you on the right, its buildings dismal even from a distance, their unpainted listing structures spread along an inwardly curving bay at the center of which a half-destroyed pier projects toward the ocean. The only beauty is the glint of the afternoon sun on the whitecapped waves.

Your stomach sinks. Redwood Point. A resort? Or at least that's what your uncle said. Maybe in 1938, you think. But not anymore. And as you steer off the highway, tapping your brakes, weaving down the bumpy narrow road past shorter, more twisted cypresses toward the dingy town where your birth certificate says you entered the world, you feel hollow. You pass a ramshackle boarded-up hotel. On a ridge that looks over the town, you notice the charred collapsed remnant of what seems to have been another hotel and decide, discouraged, that your wife and your uncle were right. This lengthy, fatiguing journey was needless. So many years. A ghost of a town that might have been famous once. You'll never find answers here.

The dusty road levels off and leads past dilapidated buildings toward the skeleton of the pier. You stop beside a shack, get out, and inhale the salty breeze from the ocean. An old man sits slumped on a chair on the few safe boards at the front of the pier. Obeying an impulse, you approach, your footsteps crunching on seashells and gravel.

"Excuse me," you say.

The old man has his back turned, staring toward the ocean.
The odor of decay—dead fish along the shore—pinches your nostrils.
"Excuse me," you repeat.
Slowly the old man turns. He cocks his shriveled head, either in curiosity or antagonism.
You ask the question that occurred to you driving down the slope. "Why is this town called Redwood Point? This far south, there *aren't* any redwoods."
"You're looking at it."
"I'm not sure what . . ."
The old man gestures toward the ruin of the pier. "The planks are made of redwood. In its heyday"—he sips from a beer can—"used to be lovely. The way it stuck out toward the bay, so proud." He sighs, nostalgic. "Redwood Point."
"Is there a hospital?"
"You sick?"
"Just curious."
The old man squints. "The nearest hospital's forty miles up the coast."
"What about a doctor?"
"Used to be. Say, how come you ask so many questions?"
"I told you I'm just curious. Is there a courthouse?"
"Does this look like a county seat? We used to be something. Now we're . . ." The old man tosses his beer can toward a trash container. He misses. "Shit."
"Well, what about . . . Have you got a police force?"
"Sure. Chief Kitrick." The old man coughs. "For all the good he does. Not that we need him. Nothing happens here. That's why he doesn't have deputies."
"So where can I find him?"
"Easy. This time of day, the Redwood Bar."
"Can you tell me where . . . ?"
"Behind you." The old man opens another beer. "Take a left. It's the only place that looks decent."

The Redwood Bar, on a cracked concrete road above the beach, has fresh redwood siding that makes the adjacent buildings look even more dingy. You pass through a door that has an anchor painted on it and feel as if you've entered a tackle shop or boarded a trawler. Fishing poles stand in a corner. A net rimmed with buoys hangs on one wall. Various nautical instruments, a sextant, a compass, others you can't identify, all looking ancient despite their gleaming metal, sit on a shelf beside a polished weathered navigation wheel that hangs behind the bar. The sturdy rectangular tables all have captain's chairs.

Voices in the far right corner attract your attention. Five men sit playing cards. A haze of cigarette smoke dims the light above their table. One of the men—in his fifties, large chested, with short sandy hair and a ruddy complexion—wears a policeman's uniform. He studies his cards.

A companion calls to the bartender, "Ray, another beer, huh? How about you, Hank?"

"It's only ten to five. I'm not off duty yet," the policeman says and sets down his cards. "Full house."

"Damn. Beats me."

"It's sure as hell better than a straight."

The men throw in their cards.

The policeman scoops up quarters. "My deal. Seven-card stud." As he shuffles the cards, he squints in your direction.

The bartender sets a beer on the table and approaches you. "What'll it be?"

"Uh, club soda," you say. "What I . . . Actually I wanted to talk to Chief Kitrick."

Overhearing, the policeman squints even harder. "Something urgent?"

"No. Not exactly." You shrug, self-conscious. "This happened many years ago. I guess it can wait a little longer."

The policeman frowns. "Then we'll finish this hand if that's okay."

"Go right ahead."

At the bar, you pay for and sip your club soda. Turning toward the wall across from you, you notice photographs, dozens of them, the images yellowed, wrinkled, and faded. But even at a distance, you know what the photographs represent, and compelled, repressing a shiver, you walk toward them.

Redwood Point. The photographs depict the resort in its prime, fifty, sixty years ago. Vintage automobiles gleam with newness on what was once a smoothly paved, busy street outside. The beach is crowded with vacationers in old-fashioned bathing suits. The impressive long pier is lined with fishermen. Boats dot the bay. Pedestrians stroll the sidewalks, glancing at shops or pointing toward the ocean. Some eat hot dogs and cotton candy. All are well dressed, and the buildings look clean, their windows shiny. The Depression, you think. But not everyone was out of work, and here the financially advantaged sought refuge from the summer heat and the city squalor. A splendid hotel—guests holding frosted glasses or fanning themselves on the spacious porch—is unmistakably the ramshackle ruin you saw as you drove in. Another building, expansive, with peaks and gables of Victorian design, sits on a ridge above the town, presumably the charred wreckage you noticed earlier. Ghosts. You shake your head. Most of the people in these photographs have long since died, and the buildings have died as well but just haven't fallen down. What a waste, you think. What *happened* here? How could time have been so cruel to this place?

"It sure was pretty once," a husky voice says behind you.

You turn toward Chief Kitrick and notice he holds a glass of beer.

"After five. Off duty now," he says. "Thanks for letting me finish the game. What can I do for you? Something about years ago, you said?"

"Yes. About the time that these photographs were taken."

The chief's eyes change focus. "Oh?"

"Can we find a place to talk? It's kind of personal."

Chief Kitrick gestures. "My office is just next door."

It smells musty. A cobweb dangles from a corner of the ceiling. You pass a bench in the waiting area, go through a squeaky gate, and face three desks, two of which are dusty and bare, in a spacious administration area. A phone, but no two-way radio. A file cabinet. A calendar on one wall. An office this size—obviously at one time, several policemen had worked here. You sense a vacuum, the absence of the bustle of former years. You can almost hear the echoes of decades-old conversations.

Chief Kitrick points toward a wooden chair. "Years ago?"

You sit. "Nineteen thirty-eight."

"That *is* years ago."

"I was born here." You hesitate. "My parents both died three weeks ago, and . . ."

"I lost my own dad just a year ago. You have my sympathy."

You nod, exhale, and try to order your thoughts. "When I went through my father's papers, I found . . . There's a possibility I may have been adopted."

As in the bar, the chief's eyes change focus.

"And then again maybe not," you continue. "But if I *was* adopted, I think my mother's name was Mary Reilly. I came here because . . . Well, I thought there might be records I could check."

"What kind of records?"

"The birth certificate my father was sent lists the time and place where I was born, and my parents' names, Simon and Esther Weinberg."

"Jewish."

You tense. "Does that matter?"

"Just making a comment. Responding to what you said."

You debate, then resume. "But the type of birth certificate parents receive is a shortened version of the one that's filed at the county courthouse."

"Which in this case is forty miles north. Cape Verde."

"I didn't know that before I came here. But I did think there'd be a hospital. *It* would have a detailed record about my birth."

"No hospital. Never was," the chief says.

"So I learned. But a resort as popular as Redwood Point was in the thirties would have needed *some* kind of medical facility."

"A clinic," the chief says. "I once heard my father mention it. But it closed back in the forties."

"Do you know what happened to its records?"

Chief Kitrick raises his shoulders. "Packed up. Shipped somewhere. Put in storage. Not here, though. I know every speck of this town, and there aren't any medical records from the old days. I don't see how those records would help."

"My file would mention who my mother was. See, I'm a lawyer, and—"

The chief frowns.

"—the standard practice with adoptions is to amend the birth certificate at the courthouse so it lists the adopting parents as the birth parents. But the *original* birth certificate, naming the birth parents, isn't destroyed. It's sealed in a file and put in a separate section of the records."

"Then it seems to me you ought to go to the county courthouse and look for that file," Chief Kitrick says.

"The trouble is, even with whatever influence I have as a lawyer, it would take me months of petitions to get that sealed file opened—and maybe never. But hospital records are easier. All I need is a sympathetic doctor who . . ." A thought makes your heart beat faster. "Would you know the names of any doctors who used to practice here? Maybe *they'd* know who . . ."

"Nope, hasn't been a doctor here in quite a while. When we get sick, we have to drive up the coast. I don't want to sound discouraging, Mr. . . . ?"

"Weinberg."

"Yeah. Weinberg. Nineteen thirty-eight. We're talking ancient history. I suspect you're wasting your time. Who remembers that far back? If they're even still alive, that is. And God knows where the clinic's records are."

"Then I guess I'll have to do this the hard way." You stand. "The county courthouse. Thanks for your help."

"I don't think I helped at all. But Mr. Weinberg . . . ?"

"Yes?" You pause at the gate.

"Sometimes it's best to leave the past alone."

"How I wish I could," you tell him, leaving.

Cape Verde turns out to be a pleasant attractive town of twenty thousand people, its architecture predominantly Spanish: red-tiled roofs and clean bright adobe walls. After the blight of Redwood Point, you feel less depressed, but only until you hear a baby crying in the motel room next to yours. After a half-sleepless night during which you phone Rebecca to assure her that you're all right but ignore her pleas for you to come home, you ask directions from the desk clerk and drive to the courthouse, which looks like a hacienda, arriving there shortly after nine o'clock.

The office of the county recorder is on the second floor, at the rear, and the red-haired young man behind the counter doesn't think twice about your request. "Birth records? Nineteen thirty-eight? Sure." After all, those records are open to the public. You don't need to give a reason.

Ten minutes later, the clerk returns with a large dusty ledger. There isn't a desk, so you need to stand at the end of the counter. While the young man goes back to work, you flip the ledger's pages to August and study them.

The records are grouped according to districts in the county. When you get to the section for Redwood Point, you read carefully. What you're looking for is not just a record of *your* birth but a reference to Mary Reilly. Twenty children were born that August. For a moment that strikes you as unusual—so many for so small a community. But then you remember that in August the resort would have been at its busiest, and maybe other expecting parents had gone there to escape the summer's heat, to allow the mother a comfortable delivery, just as your own parents had, according to your uncle.

You note the names of various mothers and fathers. Miriam and David Meyer. Ruth and Henry Begelman. Gail and Jeffrey Markowitz. With a shock of recognition, you come upon your own birth record— parents, Esther and Simon Weinberg. But that proves nothing, you remind yourself. You glance toward the bottom of the form. Medical facility: Redwood Point Clinic. Certifier: Jonathan Adams, M.D. Attendant: June Engle, R.N. Adams was presumably the doctor who took care of your mother, you conclude. A quick glance through the other Redwood Point certificates shows that Adams and Engle signed every document.

But nowhere do you find a reference to Mary Reilly. You search ahead to September in case Mary Reilly was late giving birth. No mention of her. Still, you think, maybe she signed the adoption consent forms *early* in her pregnancy, so you check the records for the remaining months of 1938. Nothing.

You ask the clerk for the 1939 birth certificates. Again he complies. But after you reach the April records and go so far as to check those in May and still find no mention of Mary Reilly, you frown. Even if she impossibly knew during her first month that she was pregnant and even if her pregnancy lasted ten months instead of nine, she still ought to be in these records. *What happened?* Did she change her mind and leave town to hide somewhere and deliver the two children she'd promised to let others adopt? Might be, you think, and a competent lawyer could have told her that her consent form, no matter how official and complex it looked, wasn't legally binding. Or did she—?

"Death records, please," you ask the clerk, "for nineteen thirty-eight and 'thirty-nine."

This time, the young man looks somewhat annoyed as he trudges off to find those records. But when he returns and you tensely inspect the ledgers, you find no indication that Mary Reilly died during childbirth.

"Thanks," you tell the clerk as you put away your notes. "You've been very helpful."

The young man, grateful not to bring more ledgers, grins.

"There's just one other thing."

The young man's shoulders sag.

"This birth certificate for Jacob Weinberg." You point toward an open ledger.

"What about it?"

"It lists Esther and Simon Weinberg as his parents. But it may be Jacob was adopted. If so, there'll be an alternative birth certificate that indicates the biological mother's name. I'd like to have a look at—"

"Original birth certificates in the case of adoptions aren't available to the public."

"But I'm an attorney, and—"

"They're not available to attorneys either, and if you're a lawyer, you should know that."

"Well, yes, I do, but—"

"See a judge. Bring a court order. I'll be glad to oblige. Otherwise, man, the rule is strict. Those records are sealed. I'd lose my job."

"Sure." Your voice cracks. "I understand."

The county's Department of Human Services is also in the Cape Verde courthouse. On the third floor, you wait in a lobby until the official in charge of adoptions returns from an appointment. Her name, you've learned, is Becky Hughes. She shakes your hand and escorts you into her office. She's in her thirties, blond, well dressed, but slightly overweight. Her intelligence and commitment to her work are evident.

"The clerk downstairs did exactly what he should have," Becky says.

But apparently you don't look convinced.

"The sealed-file rule on original birth certificates in the case of adoptions is a good one, Counselor."

"And when it's important, so is another rule: Nothing ventured, nothing gained."

"Important?" Becky taps her fingers on her desk. "In the case of adoptions, nothing's more important than preserving the anonymity of the biological mother." She glances toward a coffee pot on a counter. "You want some?"

You shake your head. "My nerves are on edge already."

"Decaffeinated."

"All right, then, sure, why not?"

She pours two cups, sets yours on the desk, and sits across from you.

"When a woman gives her baby up, she often feels so guilty about it
. . . Maybe she isn't married and comes from a strict religious background that makes her feel ashamed, or maybe she's seventeen and
realizes she doesn't have the resources to take proper care of the child,
or maybe she's got too many children already, or . . . For whatever
reason, if a woman chooses to have a child instead of abort it and gives
it up for adoption . . . she usually has such strong emotions that her
mental health demands an absolute break from the past. She trains
herself to believe that the child is on another planet. She struggles to go
on with her life. And it's cruel for a lawyer or a son or a daughter to
track her down many years later and remind her of . . ."

"I understand," you say. "But in *this* case, the mother is probably
dead."

Becky's fingers stop tapping. "Keep talking, Counselor."

"I don't have a client. Or to put it another way, I do, but the client
is . . ." You point toward your chest.

"*You?*"

"I think I . . ." You explain about the drunk driver, about the
deaths of the man and woman that you lovingly thought of as your
parents.

"And you want to know if they *were* your parents?" Becky asks.

"Yes, and if I've got a twin—a brother or a sister that I never knew
about—and . . ." You almost add, if I was born a Jew.

"Counselor, I apologize, but you're a fool."

"That's what my wife and uncle say, not to mention a cop in Redwood Point."

"Redwood Point?"

"A small town forty miles south."

"Forty or four thousand miles. What difference does . . . ? Did
Esther and Simon love you?"

"They *worshiped* me." Your eyes sting with grief.

"Then they *are* your parents. Counselor, I was adopted. And the
man and woman who adopted me *abused* me. And that's why I'm in
this office—to make sure that other adopted children don't go into
homes where they suffer what I did. At the same time, I don't want to
see a *mother* abused. If a woman's wise enough to know she can't
properly raise a child, if she gives it up for adoption . . . in *my* opinion she deserves a medal . . . and *deserves* to be protected."

"I understand," you say. "But I don't want to meet my mother.

She's probably dead. All I want is . . . I need to know if . . . The fact. *Was* I adopted?"

Becky studies you, nods, picks up the phone, and taps three numbers. "Records? Charley? How you doing, kid? Great. Listen, an attorney was down there a while ago, wanted a sealed adoption file. Yeah, you did the right thing. But here's what I want. It won't break the rules if you check to see if there *is* a sealed file." Becky tells him the date, place, and names that you earlier gave her. "I'll hold." Minutes seem like hours. She straightens. "Yeah, Charley, what have you got?" Becky sets down the phone. "Counselor, there's no sealed file. Relax. You're not adopted. Go back to your wife."

"Unless," you say.

"Unless?"

"The adoption wasn't arranged through an agency but instead was a private arrangement between the birth mother and the couple who wanted to adopt. The gray market."

"Yes, but even then, local officials have to sanction the adoption. There has to be a legal record of the transfer. In your case, there isn't." Becky looks uncomfortable. "Let me explain. These days, babies available for adoption are scarce. Because of birth control and legalized abortions. But even *today*, the babies in demand are WASPs. A black? A Hispanic? An Oriental? Forget it. Very few parents in those groups want to adopt, and even fewer Anglos want children from those groups. Fifty years ago, the situation was worse. There were so many WASPs who got pregnant by mistake and wanted to surrender their babies . . . Counselor, this might offend you, but I have to say it."

"I don't offend easily."

"Your last name is Weinberg," Becky says. "Jewish. Back in the thirties, the same as now, the majority of parents wanting to adopt were Protestants, and they wanted a child from a Protestant mother. If *you* were put up for adoption, even on the gray market, almost every couple looking to adopt would not have wanted a Jewish baby. The prospects would have been so slim that your mother's *final* option would have been . . ."

"The *black* market?" Your cheek muscles twitch.

"Baby selling. It's a violation of the antislavery law, paying money for a human being. But it happens, and lawyers and doctors who *arrange* for it to happen make a fortune from desperate couples who can't get a child any other way."

"But what if my mother was *Irish?*"

Becky blinks. "You're suggesting . . . ?"

"Jewish couples." You cringe, remembering the last names of parents you read in the ledgers. "Meyer. Begelman. Markowitz. Weinberg. Jews."

"So desperate for a baby that after looking everywhere for a Jewish mother willing to give up her child, they adopted . . . ?"

"WASPs. And arranged it so none of their relatives would know."

All speculation, you strain to remind yourself. There's no way to link Mary Reilly with you, except that you were born in the town where she signed the agreement and the agreement is dated a week before your birthday. Tenuous evidence, to say the least. Your legal training warns you that you'd never allow it to be used in court. Even the uniform presence of Jewish names on the birth certificates from Redwood Point that August so long ago has a possible, benign, and logical explanation: the resort might have catered to a Jewish clientele, providing kosher meals, for example. Perhaps there'd been a synagogue.

But logic is no match for your deepening unease. You can't account for the chill in the pit of your stomach, but you feel that something's terribly wrong. Back in your motel room, you pace, struggling to decide what to do next. Go back to Redwood Point and ask Chief Kitrick more questions? *What* questions? He'd react the same as Becky Hughes had. Assumptions, Mr. Weinberg. Inconclusive.

Then it strikes you. The name you found in the records. Dr. Jonathan Adams. The physician who certified not only *your* birth but *all* the births in Redwood Point. Your excitement abruptly falters. So long ago. The doctor would probably be dead by now. At once your pulse quickens. Dead? Not necessarily. Simon and Esther were still alive until three weeks ago. Grief squeezing your throat, you concentrate. Dr. Adams might have been as young as Simon and Esther. There's a chance he . . .

But how to find him? The Redwood Point Clinic went out of business in the forties. Dr. Adams might have gone anywhere. You reach for the phone. A year ago, you were hired to litigate a malpractice suit against a drug-addicted ophthalmologist whose carelessness blinded a patient. You spent many hours talking to the American Medical Association. Opening the phone-number booklet that you always keep in your briefcase, you call the AMA's national headquarters in Chicago. Dr.

Jonathan Adams? The deep male voice on the end of the line sounds eager to show his efficiency. Even through the static of a long-distance line, you hear fingers tap a computer keyboard.

"Dr. Jonathan Adams? Sorry. There isn't a . . . Wait, there *is* a Jonathan Adams *Junior.* An obstetrician. In San Francisco. His office number is . . ."

You hurriedly write it down and with equal speed press the numbers on your phone. Just as lawyers often want their sons and daughters to be lawyers, so doctors encourage their children to be doctors, and on occasion they give a son their first name. This doctor might not be the son of the man who signed your birth certificate, but you have to find out. *Obstetrician?* Another common denominator. Like father, like . . . ?

A secretary answers.

"Dr. Adams, please," you say.

"The doctor is with a patient at the moment. May he call you back?"

"By all means, and this is my number. But I think he'll want to talk to me now. Just tell him it's about his father. Tell him it's about the clinic at Redwood Point."

The secretary sounds confused. "But I can't interrupt when the doctor's with . . ."

"Do it," you say. "I guarantee the doctor will understand the emergency."

"Well . . . If you're . . ."

"Certain? Yes. Absolutely."

"Just a moment, please."

Thirty seconds later, a tense male voice says, "Dr. Adams here. What's this all about?"

"I told your secretary. I assumed she told *you.* It's about your father. It's about nineteen thirty-eight. It's about the Redwood Point Clinic."

"I had nothing to do with . . . Oh, dear Jesus."

You hear a forceful click, then static. You set down the phone. And nod.

Throughout the stressful afternoon, you investigate your only other lead, trying to discover what happened to June Engle, the nurse whose name appears on the Redwood Point birth certificates. If not dead, she'd certainly have retired by now. Even so, many ex-nurses maintain ties with their former profession, continuing to belong to professional organizations and subscribing to journals devoted to nursing. But no matter how many calls you make to various associations, you can't find a trace of June Engle.

By then, it's evening. Between calls, you've ordered room service, but the poached salmon goes untasted, the bile in your mouth having taken away your appetite. You get the home phone number for Dr. Adams from San Francisco information.

A woman answers, weary. "He's still at . . . No, just a minute. I think I hear him coming in the door."

Your fingers cramp on the phone.

The now familiar taut male voice, slightly out of breath, says, "Yes, Dr. Adams speaking."

"It's me again. I called you at your office today. About the Redwood Point Clinic? About nineteen thirty-eight?"

"You son of a—!"

"Don't hang up this time, Doctor. All you have to do is answer my questions, and I'll leave you alone."

"There are laws against harassment."

"Believe me, I know all about the law. I practice it in Chicago. Doctor, why are you so defensive? Why would questions about that clinic make you nervous?"

"I don't have to talk to you."

"But you make it seem that you're hiding something if you don't."

You hear the doctor swallow. "Why do you . . . ? I had nothing to do with that clinic. My father died ten years ago. Can't you leave the past alone?"

"Not *my* past, I can't," you insist. "Your father signed my birth certificate at Redwood Point in nineteen thirty-eight. There are things I need to know."

The doctor hesitates. "All right. Such as?"

"Black market adoptions." Hearing the doctor inhale, you continue. "I think your father put the wrong information on my birth certificate. I think he never recorded my biological mother's name and instead put down the names of the couple who adopted me. That's why there isn't a sealed birth certificate listing my actual mother's name. The adoption was never legally sanctioned, so there wasn't any need to amend the erroneous birth certificate on file at the courthouse."

"Jesus," the doctor says.

"Am I right?"

"How the hell would *I* know? I was just a kid when my father closed the clinic and left Redwood Point in the early forties. If you *were* illegally adopted, it wouldn't have anything to do with *me.*"

"Exactly. And your father's dead, so he can't be prosecuted. And anyway it happened so long ago, who would care? Except *me.* But, Doctor, you're nervous about my questions. That makes it obvious you know *something.* Certainly *you* can't be charged for something your father did. So what would it hurt if you tell me what you know?"

The doctor's throat sounds dry. "My father's memory."

"Ah," you say. "Yes, his reputation. Look, I'm not interested in spreading scandal and ruining anybody, dead or alive. All I want is the truth. *About me. Who* was my mother? *Do I have a brother or a sister somewhere?* Was I *adopted?*"

"So much money."

"What?" You clutch the phone harder.

"When my father closed the clinic and left Redwood Point, he had so much money. I was just a kid, but even *I* knew that he couldn't have earned a small fortune merely delivering babies at a resort. And there were always *so* many babies. I remember him walking up to the nursery every morning. And then it burned down. And the next thing, he closed the clinic and bought a mansion in San Francisco and never worked again."

"The nursery? You mean like a *plant* nursery?"

"No. The building on the ridge above town. Big, with all kinds of chimneys and gables."

"Victorian?"

"Yes. And that's where the pregnant women lived."

You shiver. Your chest feels encased with ice.

"My father always called it the nursery. I remember him smiling when he said it. *Why pick on him?*" the doctor asks. "All he did was deliver babies! And he did it well! And if someone paid him lots of money to put false information on birth certificates, which I don't even know if he did . . ."

"But you suspect."

"Yes. God damn it, that's what I suspect," Dr. Adams admits. "But I can't prove it, and I never asked. It's the Gunthers you should blame! *They* ran the nursery! Anyway if the babies got loving parents, and if the adopting couples finally got the children they desperately wanted, what's the harm? Who got hurt? Leave the past alone!"

For a moment, you have trouble speaking. "Thank you, Doctor. I appreciate your honesty. I have only one more question."

"Get on with it. I want to finish this."

"The Gunthers. The people who ran the nursery."

"A husband and wife. I don't recall their first names."

"Have you any idea what happened to them?"

"After the nursery burned down? God only knows," Dr. Adams says.

"And what about June Engle, the nurse who assisted your father?"

"You said you had only *one* more question." The doctor breathes sharply. "Never mind, I'll answer if you promise to leave me alone. June Engle was born and raised in Redwood Point. When we moved away, she said she was staying behind. It could be she's still there."

"Could be. If she's still alive." Chilled again, you set down the phone.

The same as last night, a baby cries in the room next to yours. You pace and phone Rebecca. You're as good as can be expected, you say. You don't yet know when you'll be home. You try to sleep. Apprehension jerks you awake.

The morning is overcast, as gray as your thoughts. After checking out of the motel, you follow the desk clerk's directions to Cape Verde's public library. A disturbing hour later, under a thickening gloomy sky, you drive back to Redwood Point.

From the highway along the cliff, the town looks even bleaker. You steer down the bumpy road, reach the ramshackle boarded-up hotel, and park your rented car. Through weeds that cling to your pant legs, you walk beyond the hotel's once splendid porch, find eroded stone steps that angle up a slope, and climb to the barren ridge above the town.

Barren with one exception: the charred timbers and flame-scorched toppled walls of the peaked, gabled, Victorian structure that Dr. Adams Jr. had called the nursery. That word makes you feel as if an icy needle has pierced your heart. The clouds hang deeper, darker. A chill wind makes you hug your chest. The nursery. And in 1941 . . . you learned from old newspapers on microfilm at the Cape Verde library . . . thirteen women died here, burned to death, incinerated—their corpses grotesquely blackened and crisped—in a massive blaze, the cause of which the authorities were never able to determine.

Thirteen women. *Exclusively* women. You want to shout in outrage. And were they pregnant? *And were there also . . . ?* Sickened, imagining their screams of fright, their wails for help, their shrieks of indescribable agony, you sense so repressive an atmosphere about this ruin that you stumble back as if shoved. With wavering legs that you barely control, you manage your way down the unsteady stone slabs. Lurching through the clinging weeds below the slope, you stumble past the repulsive listing hotel to reach your car, where you lean against its hood and try not to vomit, sweating despite the increasingly bitter wind.

The nursery, you think.

Dear God.

The Redwood Bar is no different than when you left it. Chief Kitrick and his friends again play cards at the far right corner table. The haze of cigarette smoke again dims the light above them. The waiter stands behind the bar on your left, the antique nautical instruments gleaming on a shelf behind him. But your compulsion directs you toward the wrinkled, faded photographs on the wall to your right.

This time, you study them without innocence. You see a yellowed image of the peaked, gabled nursery. You narrow your gaze toward small details that you failed to give importance to the first time you saw these photographs. Several woman, diminished because the cameraman took a long shot of the large Victorian building, sit on a lawn that's bordered by flower gardens, their backs to a windowed brick wall of the . . . your mind balks . . . the nursery.

Each of the women—young! so young!—holds an infant in her lap. The women smile so sweetly. Are they acting? Were they forced to smile?

Was one of those women your mother? Is one of those infants you? Mary Reilly, what desperation made you smile like that?

Behind you, Chief Kitrick's husky voice says, "These days, not many tourists pay us a second visit."

"Yeah, I can't get enough of Redwood Point." Turning, you notice that Chief Kitrick—it isn't yet five o'clock—holds a glass of beer. "You might say it haunts me."

Chief Kitrick sips his beer. "I gather you didn't find what you wanted at the courthouse."

"Actually I learned more than I expected." Your voice shakes. "Do you want to talk here or in your office?"

"It depends on what you want to talk about."

"The Gunthers."

You pass through the squeaky gate in the office. Chief Kitrick sits behind his desk. His face looks more flushed than it did two days ago. "The Gunthers? My, my. I haven't heard that name in years. What about them?"

"That's the question, isn't it? What about them? Tell me."

Chief Kitrick shrugs. "There isn't much *to* tell. I don't remember them. I was just a toddler when they . . . All I know is what I heard when I was growing up, and that's not a lot. A husband and wife, they ran a boarding house."

"The nursery."

Chief Kitrick frowns. "I don't believe I ever heard it called the nursery. What's *that* supposed to mean?"

"The Gunthers took in young women. *Pregnant* women. And after the babies were born, the Gunthers arranged to sell them to desperate Jewish couples who couldn't have children of their own. Black market adoptions."

Chief Kitrick slowly straightens. "Black market . . . ? Where on earth did you get such a crazy . . . ?"

You press your hands on the desk and lean forward. "See, back then, adoption agencies didn't want to give babies to Jews instead of WASPs. So the Gunthers provided the service. They and the doctor who delivered the babies earned a fortune. But I don't think that's the whole story. I've got a terrible feeling that there's something more, something worse, though I'm not sure what it is. All I do know is that thirteen women—they were probably pregnant—died in the fire that destroyed the nursery in nineteen forty-one."

"Oh, sure, the fire," Chief Kitrick says. "I heard about *that*. Fact is, I even vaguely remember seeing the flames up there on the bluff that night, despite how little I was. The whole town was lit like day. A terrible thing, all those women dying like that."

"Yes." You swallow. "Terrible. And then the Gunthers left, and so did the doctor. *Why?*"

Chief Kitrick shrugs. "Your guess is as good as . . . Maybe the

Gunthers didn't want to rebuild. Maybe they thought it was time for a change."

"No, I think they left because the fire happened in November and the authorities started asking questions about why all those women, and *only* women, were in that boarding house after the tourist season was over. I think the Gunthers and the doctor became so afraid that they left town to make it hard for the authorities to question them, to discourage an investigation that might have led to charges being filed."

"Think all you want. There's no way to prove it. But I *can* tell you *this*. As I grew up, I'd sometimes hear people talking about the Gunthers, and everything the townsfolk said was always about how nice the Gunthers were, how generous. Sure, Redwood Point was once a popular resort, but that was just during the tourist season. The rest of the year, the thirties, the Depression, this town would have starved if not for that boarding house. That place was always busy, year round, and the Gunthers always spent plenty of money here. So many guests. They ate a lot of food, and the Gunthers bought it locally, and they always hired local help. Cooks. Maids. Ladies in town to do washing and ironing. Caretakers to manage the grounds and make sure everything was repaired and looked good. This town owed a lot to the Gunthers, and after they left, well, that's when things started going to hell. Redwood Point couldn't support itself on the tourists alone. The merchants couldn't afford to maintain their shops as nice as before. The town began looking dingy. Not as many tourists came. Fewer and . . . Well, you can see where we ended. At *one* time, though, this town depended on the Gunthers, and you won't find anyone speaking ill about them."

"Exactly. That's what bothers me."

"I don't understand."

"All those pregnant women coming to that boarding house," you say. "All year round. All through the thirties into the early forties. Even if the Gunthers hadn't hired local servants, the town couldn't have helped but notice that something was wrong about that boarding house. The people here *knew* what was going on. Couples arriving childless but leaving with a baby. The whole town—even the chief of police—*had* to be aware that the Gunthers were selling babies."

"Now stop right there." Chief Kitrick stands, eyes glinting with fury. "The chief of police back then was my father, and I won't let you talk about him like that."

You raise your hands in disgust. "The scheme couldn't have worked unless the chief of police turned his back. The Gunthers probably bribed him. But then the fire ruined everything. Because it attracted outsiders. Fire investigators. The county coroner. Maybe the state police. And when they started asking questions about the nursery, the Gunthers and the doctor got out of town."

"I told you I won't listen to you insult my father! Bribes? Why, my father never—"

"Sure," you say. "A pillar of the community. Just like everybody else."

"Get out!"

"Right. As soon as you tell me one more thing. June Engle. Is she still alive? Is she still here in town?"

"I never heard of her," Chief Kitrick growls.

"Right."

Chief Kitrick glares from the open door to his office. You get in your car, drive up the bumpy street, turn, go into reverse, shift forward, and pass him. The chief glares harder. In your rearview mirror, you see his diminishing angry profile. You reduce speed and steer toward the left as if taking the upward jolting road out of town. But with a cautious glance toward the chief, you see him stride in nervous victory along the sidewalk. You see him open the door to the bar, and the moment you're out of sight around the corner, you stop.

The clouds are darker, thicker, lower. The wind increases, keening. Sporadic raindrops speckle your windshield. You step from the car, button your jacket, and squint through the biting wind toward the broken skeleton of the pier. The old man you met two days ago no longer slumps on his rickety chair, but just before you turned the corner, movement on your right—through a dusty window in a shack near the pier—attracted your attention. You approach the shack, the door to which faces the seething ocean, but you don't have a chance to knock before the wobbly door creaks open. The old man, wearing a frayed rumpled sweater, cocks his head, frowning, a homemade cigarette dangling from his lips.

You reach for your wallet. "I spoke to you the other day, remember?"

"Yep."

You take a hundred-dollar bill from your wallet. The old man's blood-

shot eyes widen. Beyond him, on a table in the shack, you notice a half-
dozen empty beer bottles. "Want to earn some quick easy money?"
  "Depends."
  "June Engle."
  "So?"
  "Ever heard of her?"
  "Yep."
  "Is she still alive?"
  "Yep."
  "Here in town?"
  "Yep."
  "Where can I find her?"
  "This time of day?"
  What the old man tells you makes your hand shake when you hand
him the money. Shivering but not from the wind, you return to your
car. You make sure to take an indirect route to where the old man sent
you, lest the chief glance out the tavern window and see you driving
past.
  "At the synagogue," the old man told you. "Or what used to be the
. . . Ain't that what they call it? A synagogue?"
  The sporadic raindrops become a drizzle. A chilling dampness per-
meates the car, despite its blasting heater. At the far end of town,
above the beach, you come to a dismal, single-story, flat-roofed structure. The redwood walls are cracked and warped. The windows are
covered with peeling plywood. Waist-high weeds surround it. Heart
pounding, you step from the car, ignore the wind that whips drizzle
against you, and frown at a narrow path through the weeds that takes
you to the front door. A slab of plywood, the door hangs by one hinge
and almost falls as you enter.
  You face a small vestibule. Sand has drifted in. An animal has made a
nest in one corner. Cobwebs hang from the ceiling. The pungent odor
of mold attacks your nostrils. Hebraic letters on a wall are so faded that
you can't read them. But mostly what you notice is the path through
the sand and dust on the floor toward the entrance to the temple.
  The peak of your skull feels naked. Instinctively you look around in
search of a yarmulke. But after so many years, there aren't any. Remov-
ing a handkerchief from your pocket, you place it on your head, open
the door to the temple, and find yourself paralyzed, astonished by what
you see.

The temple—or what used to be the temple—is barren of furniture. The back wall has an alcove where a curtain once concealed the torah. Before the alcove, an old woman kneels on bony knees, her hips withered, a handkerchief tied around her head. She murmurs, hands fidgeting as if she holds something before her.

At last you're able to move. Inching forward, pausing beside her, you see what she clutches: a rosary. Tears trickle down her cheeks. As close as you are, you still have to strain to distinguish what she murmurs.

". . . deliver us from evil. Amen."

"June Engle?"

She doesn't respond, just keeps fingering the beads and praying. "Hail, Mary . . . blessed is the fruit of thy womb . . ."

"June, my name is Jacob Weinberg."

"Pray for us sinners now and at the hour of our death . . ."

"June, I want to talk to you about Dr. Adams. About the clinic."

The old woman's fingers tighten on the rosary. Slowly she turns and blinks up through tear-brimmed eyes. "The clinic?"

"Yes. And about the Gunthers. About the nursery."

"God help me. God help *them.*" She wavers, her face pale.

"Come on, June, you'll faint if you kneel much longer. I'll help you up." You touch her appallingly fleshless arms and gently raise her to her feet. She wobbles. You hold her husk of a body against you. "The nursery. Is that why you're here, June? You're doing penance?"

"Thirty pieces of silver."

"Yes." Your voice echoes eerily. "I think I understand. Dr. Adams and the Gunthers made a lot of money. Did *you* make a lot of money, June? Did they pay you well?"

"Thirty pieces of silver."

"Tell me about the nursery, June. I promise you'll feel better."

"Ivy, rose, heather, iris."

You cringe, suspecting that she's gone insane. Just as you first thought that the expression "the nursery" referred to a *plant* nursery, so June Engle has made that same connection. But she knows better. She *knows* that the nursery had nothing to do with plants but instead with babies from unmarried pregnant women. Or at least she *ought* to know unless the consequence of age and what seems to be guilt has affected her mind and her memory. She appears to be free-associating.

"Violet, lily, daisy, fern," she babbles.

Your chest cramps as you realize that those words make perfect sense in the context of . . . They might be . . . "Are those names, June? You're telling me that the women in the nursery called themselves after plants and flowers?"

"Orval Gunther chose them. Anonymous." June weeps. "Nobody would know who they really were. They could hide their shame, protect their identities."

"But how did they learn about the nursery?"

"Advertisements." June's shriveled knuckles paw at her eyes. "In big-city papers. The personal columns."

"*Advertisements?* But that was taking an awful risk. The police might have . . ."

"No. Not Orval. He never took risks. He was clever. So clever. All he promised was a rest home for pregnant women. 'Feel alone?' the ad read. 'Need a caring trained staff to help you give birth in strictest privacy? No questions asked. We guarantee to relieve your insecurity. Let us help you with your burden.' Sweet Lord, those women came here by the *hundreds.*"

June trembles against you. Her tears soak through your jacket, as chilling as the wind-driven rain that trickles through the roof.

"Did those women get any money for the babies they gave to strangers?"

"*Get?* No, they paid!" June stiffens, her feeble arms gaining amazing strength as she pushes from your grasp. "Orval, that son of a . . . ! He charged them room and board! Five hundred dollars!"

Her knees sag.

You grasp her. *"Five hundred . . . ?* And the couples who took the babies? How much did the Gunthers get from *them?*"

"Sometimes as high as ten thousand dollars."

The arms with which you hold her shake. Ten thousand dollars? During the Depression? Hundreds of pregnant women? Dr. Adams Jr. hadn't exaggerated. The Gunthers had earned a fortune.

"And Orval's wife was worse than he was. Eve! She was a monster! All she cared about was . . . *Pregnant women* didn't matter! *Babies* didn't matter. *Money* mattered."

"But if you thought they were monsters . . . ? June, why did you help them?"

She clutches her rosary. "Thirty pieces of silver. Holy Mary, mother of . . . Ivy, Rose, Heather, Iris. Violet, Lily, Daisy, Fern."

You force her to look at you. "I told you my name was Jacob Wein-

berg. But I might not be . . . I think my mother's name was Mary
Reilly. I think I was born here. In nineteen thirty-eight. Did you ever
know a woman who . . . ?"

June sobs. "Mary Reilly? If she stayed with the Gunthers, she
wouldn't have used her real name. So many women! She might have
been Orchid or Pansy. There's no way to tell who . . ."

"She was pregnant with twins. She promised to give up both children. Do you remember a woman who . . . ?"

"Twins? *Several* women had twins. The Gunthers, damn them, were
ecstatic. Two for the price of one, they said."

"But my parents"—the word sticks in your mouth—"took only *me.*
Was it common for childless parents to separate twins?"

"Money!" June cringes. "It all depended on how much *money* the
couples could afford. Sometimes twins were separated. There's no way
to tell where the other child went."

"But weren't there records?"

"The Gunthers were smart. They *never* kept records. In case the
police . . . And then the fire . . . Even if there *had* been records,
secret records, the fire would have . . ."

Your stomach plummets. Despite your urgent need for answers, you
realized you've reached a dead end.

Then June murmurs something that you barely hear, but the little
you do hear chokes you. "What? I didn't . . . June, please say that
again."

"Thirty pieces of silver. For that, I . . . Oh, how I paid. Seven
stillborn children."

"*Yours?*"

"I thought, with the money the Gunthers paid me, my husband and
I could raise our children in luxury, give them every advantage, send
them to medical school or . . . God help me, what I did for the
Gunthers cursed my womb. It made me worse than barren. It doomed
me to carry lifeless children. My penance! It forced me to suffer! Just
like . . . !"

"The mothers who gave up their children and possibly later regret-
ted it?"

"No! Like the . . . !"

What you hear next makes you retch. *Black market adoptions,* you
told Chief Kitrick. *But I don't think that's the whole story. I've got the*

terrible feeling that there's something more, something worse, though I'm not sure what it is.

Now you *are* sure what that something worse is, and the revelation makes you weep in outrage. "Show me, June," you manage to say. "Take me. I promise it'll be your salvation." You try to remember what you know about Catholicism. "You need to confess, and after that, your conscience will be at peace."

"I'll *never* be at peace."

"You're wrong, June. You *will.* You've kept your secret too long. It festers inside you. You *have* to let out the poison. After all these years, your prayers here in the synagogue have been sufficient. You've suffered enough. What you need now is absolution."

"You think if I go there . . . ?" June shudders.

"And pray one last time. *Yes.* I beg you. Show me. Your torment will finally end."

"So long! I haven't been there since . . ."

"Nineteen forty-one? That's what I mean, June. It's time. It's finally time."

Through biting wind and chilling rain, you escort June from the ghost of the synagogue into the sheltering warmth of your car. You're so angry that you don't bother taking an indirect route. You don't care if . . . in fact, you almost *want* . . . Chief Kitrick to see you driving past the tavern. You steer left up the bumpy road out of town, its jolts diminished by the storm-soaked earth. When you reach the coastal highway, you assure June yet again and prompt her for further directions.

"It's been so long. I don't . . . Yes. Turn to the right," she says. A half mile later, she trembles, adding, "Now left here. Up that muddy road. Do you think you can . . . ?"

"Force this car through the mud to the top? If I have to, I'll get out and push. And if *that* doesn't work, we'll walk. God help me, I'll carry you. I'll sink to my knees and *crawl.*"

But the car's front-wheel drive defeats the mud. At once you gain traction, thrust over a hill, swivel to a stop, and scowl through the rain toward an unexpected meadow. Even in early October, the grass is lush. Amazingly, *horribly* so. Knowing its secret, you suddenly recall— from your innocent youth—lines from a poem you studied in college. Walt Whitman's "Song of Myself."

A child said What is the grass? *fetching it to me with full
hands.
How could I answer the child? I do not know what it is any more
than he.
I guess it must be the flag of my disposition.*

You force your way out of the car. You struggle around its hood,
ignore the mud, confront the stinging wind and rain, and help June
waver from the passenger seat. The bullet-dark clouds roil above the
meadow.

"Was it here?" you demand. "Tell me! Is *this* where . . . ?"

"Yes! Can't you hear them wail? Can't you hear them *suffer?*"

*. . . the flag of my disposition, out of hopeful green stuff woven.
Or I guess it is the handkerchief of the Lord.
Or I guess the grass is itself a child, the produced babe of the
vegetation.*

"June! In the name of God"—rain stings your face—"tell me!"

*. . . a uniform hieroglyphic . . .
Sprouting alike in broad zones and narrow zones,
Growing among black folks as among white.*

"Tell me, June!"

"Can't you *sense?* Can't you feel the horror?"

"Yes, June." You sink to your knees. You caress the grass. "I can."

And now it seems to me the beautiful uncut hair of graves.

"How many, June?" You lean forward, your face almost touching the
grass.

"Two hundred. Maybe more. All those years. So many babies." June
weeps behind you. "I finally couldn't count anymore."

"But *why?*" You raise your head toward the angry rain. "Why did
they have to die?"

"Some were sickly. Some were deformed. If the Gunthers decided
they couldn't sell them . . ."

"They murdered them? Smothered them? Strangled them?"

"Let them starve to death. The wails." June cringes. "Those poor,
hungry, suffering babies. Some took as long as *three days* to die. In my
nightmares, I heard them wailing. I *still* hear them wailing." June

hobbles toward you. "At first, the Gunthers took the bodies in a boat and dumped them at sea. But one of the corpses washed up on the beach, and if it hadn't been for the chief of police they bribed . . ." June's voice breaks. "So the Gunthers decided they needed a safer way to dispose of the bodies. They brought them here and buried them in paper bags or potato sacks or butter boxes."

"Butter boxes?"

"Some of the babies were born prematurely." June sinks beside you, weeping. "They were small, so terribly small."

"Two hundred?" The frenzied wind thrusts your words down your throat. With a shudder, you realize that if your mother *was* Mary Reilly, *Irish*, there'd have been a chance of your having been born with red hair. The Gunthers might have decided that you looked too obviously gentile. They might have buried you here with . . .

Your brother or your sister? Your twin? Is your counterpart under the grass you clutch? You shriek. "Two hundred!"

Despite the howl of the storm, you hear a car, its engine roaring, its tires spinning, fighting for traction in the mud. You see a police car crest the rain-shrouded hill and skid to a stop.

Chief Kitrick shoves his door open, stalking toward you through the raging gloom. "God damn it, I told you to leave the past alone."

You stand, draw back a fist, and strike his mouth so hard he drops to the mushy ground. "You knew! You son of a bitch, you knew all along!"

The chief wipes blood from his mangled lips. In fury, he fumbles to draw his gun.

"That's right! Go ahead, kill me!" You spread out your arms, lashed by the rain. "But June'll be a witness, and you'll have to kill her as well! So what, though, huh? Two murders won't matter, will they? Not compared to a couple of hundred children!"

"I had nothing to do with—"

"Killing these babies? No, but your *father* did!"

"He wasn't involved!"

"He let it happen! He took the Gunthers' money and turned his back! That *makes* him involved! He's as much to blame as the Gunthers! The whole fucking town was involved!" You pivot toward the ridge, buffeted by the full strength of the storm. In the blinding gale, you can't see the town, but you shriek at it nonetheless. "You bastards! You sons of bitches! You knew! You all let it happen! You did nothing to stop it! You're responsible, as much as the Gunthers, for killing all these babies! That's why your town fell apart! God cursed you! Bastards! Sons of—!"

Abruptly you realize the terrible irony of your words. Bastards? *All* of these murdered children were bastards. You spin toward the grass, the beautiful uncut hair of graves, and lose control. Falling, you hug the rain-soaked earth, the drenched lush leaves of grass. "Poor babies! Poor sweet babies!"

"You can't prove anything, Weinberg," Chief Kitrick growls. "All you've got are suppositions. After fifty years, there won't be anything left of those babies. They've long since rotted and turned into—"

"Grass," you moan, tears scalding your face. "The beautiful grass."

"The doctor who delivered the babies is dead. The Gunthers—my father kept track of them—died as well. In agony, if that satisfies your need for justice. Orval got stomach cancer. Eve died from alcoholism."

"And now they burn in hell," June murmurs.

"I was raised to be . . . I'm a *Jew,*" you moan and suddenly understand the significance of your pronouncement. No matter the circumstances of your birth, you *are* a Jew, totally, completely. "I don't believe in hell. But I wish . . . Oh God, how I wish . . ."

"The only proof you have," Chief Kitrick says, "is this old woman, a Catholic who goes every afternoon to pray in a ruined synagogue. She's nuts. You're a lawyer. You know her testimony wouldn't be accepted in court. It's over, Weinberg. It ended fifty years ago."

"No! It never ended! The grass keeps growing!" You sprawl on your stomach, feeling the chill wet earth, hugging the fertile grass. You try to embrace your brother or your sister and quiver with the understanding that *all* of these children are your brothers and sisters. "God help them! God have mercy!"

What do you think has become of the children?
They are alive and well somewhere,
The smallest sprout shows there is really no death,
And if ever there was it led forward life, and does not wait at
the end to arrest it.
All goes onward and outward, nothing collapses,
And to die is different from what any one supposed, and luckier.

"Luckier?" You embrace the grass, rubbing your face against it, wiping your tears. "*Luckier?* Whitman, you stupid—! The horror!" Through the rain-soaked earth, you think you hear babies crying and raise your face toward the furious storm. Swallowing rain, tasting the salt of your tears, you recite the kaddish prayers. You mourn Mary Reilly, Simon and Esther Weinberg, your brother or your sister, all these children.

And yourself.

"Deliver us from evil," June Engle murmurs. "Pray for us sinners. Now and at the hour of our death."